O F
L O V E
A N D
L I F E

O F
L O V E
A N D
L I F E

Three novels selected and condensed
by Reader's Digest

The Reader's Digest Association Limited, London

With the exception of actual personages identified as such, the
characters and incidents in the fictional selections in this volume
are entirely the product of the authors' imaginations and have no
relation to any person or event in real life.

The Reader's Digest Association Limited
11 Westferry Circus, Canary Wharf, London E14 4HE

www.readersdigest.co.uk

ISBN 0-276-42996-6

For information as to ownership of copyright in the material of
this book, and acknowledgments, see last page.

CONTENTS

Love and Devotion

ERICA JAMES

%

'I want you to make a promise,
Harriet. If anything happens to Jeff
and me, I want you to look after
our children.'
As Harriet agrees to her sister
Felicity's plea, she does so thinking
that she'll probably never be called
upon to keep this promise.
But four years later, it dominates
her every waking moment.

%

PROLOGUE

CHRISTMAS EVE. The night sky was patchy with clouds racing across the moon and stars, and the wind was gusting. Harriet and her sister were in the Wendy house. It was quite a squash; they were no longer the size they'd been when their father had made it for them more than twenty years ago. Felicity, six months pregnant with her second child, was having trouble getting comfortable on the small wooden chair.

It had been Felicity's idea for them to sneak out here in the freezing cold and the dark. But she was known for her impetuosity. It was what everyone loved about Felicity—her spontaneity and sense of fun. Harriet watched her sister light the candles they'd brought with them and asked, 'So why are we here when we could be in the warm, wrapping presents and binging on Mum's mince pies and marzipan dates?'

In the flickering candlelight, Felicity's face was suddenly solemn, her eyes large and luminous. 'I have something I want to ask you,' she said. 'I want you to make me a promise, Harriet. If anything happens to Jeff and me, I want you to look after our children.'

The wind gusted outside. A shiver went through Harriet. 'Nothing's going to happen to you, Felicity,' she said. 'I'm always going to be the eccentric aunt who makes it her business to turn up with embarrassingly inappropriate presents for your children.'

'I'm being serious, Harriet. You have to promise that if anything happens to me, you'll take care of them. I wouldn't trust anyone but you. I need you to say yes for my peace of mind.'

Putting her sister's irrational insistence down to cranked-up hormone levels—that and Felicity's famously temperamental nature—Harriet said, 'Of course I will. Providing you don't have more than two. Two

I think I could handle. Any more and I'd turn into the Child Catcher from *Chitty Chitty Bang Bang*.'

'You promise? Hand on heart?'

'I promise.'

Smiling once more, Felicity said, 'Good. That's settled then. Now I have nothing to worry about.'

The promise was never referred to again. Not until four years later, when it dominated Harriet's every waking thought.

AUGUST

When I am dead, my dearest,
Sing no sad songs for me;
Plant thou no roses at my head,
Nor shady cypress tree:
Be the green grass above me
With showers and dewdrops wet;
And if thou wilt, remember,
And if thou wilt, forget.

I shall not see the shadows,
I shall not feel the rain;
I shall not hear the nightingale
Sing on, as if in pain;
And dreaming through the twilight
That doth not rise nor set,
Haply I may remember,
And haply may forget.

'Song', CHRISTINA ROSSETTI

SWIFT BY NAME and swift by nature, Harriet shut the door after her and marched quickly down the drive, her arms swinging, her shoes tappety-tap-tapping in the still August air. Hand in hand, the children trailed silently behind her. She was often told that for someone so small, she walked remarkably fast. Those who knew her well knew that it was a side effect of a restless mind, of a mind on the run.

For what felt like for ever, Harriet had been plagued with a sense of permanently running on the spot, of getting nowhere fast. There had been so much to do, and far too much to come to terms with. She doubted the latter was ever going to happen. But that was something she kept to herself. It was better to let people think that she had it all under control, that she believed them when they said time would heal, and apparently we are never given more than we can handle. What was that supposed to mean? That this was deliberate? That she and her family had been picked out especially for this particular assignment? Oh, the Swifts—they'll handle this one; they'll cope just fine with the death of their eldest daughter and son-in-law.

Anyone observing them would think that Harriet and her parents were coping admirably, but Harriet knew all too well that Bob and Eileen Swift had their brave public faces for neighbours and friends. Once the front door was closed, the masks would drop. But only so far. There were the children, Carrie and Joel, to think of. 'Oh, those poor little ones!' had been the cry when news of the accident had spread.

Tappety-tap-tap went Harriet's shoes as she walked faster, her head lowered, her gaze to the ground so there would be no risk of catching the eye of a neighbour who, given the chance, would seize the opportunity to console or advise and smother her with sympathy. She wanted none of it. All she wanted was for their lives to be the way they were four months ago, before a joy-riding kid high on God knew what smashed into her brother-in-law's car killing him and Felicity instantly.

Harriet had been called many things in her life—aloof, pig-headed, obsessively independent, opinionated, analytical, quick to judge, reliable, insular, logical, quick-tempered, cynical, pragmatic, even too loyal for her own good—but not once had she been described as motherly. And yet here she was, at the age of thirty-two, the legal guardian to her sister's orphaned children. Some days she wanted to scream and kick against the unfairness of it all. Some days she woke up terrified she didn't have the strength to do what was expected of her. Other days she had to fight the urge to walk away.

'Auntie Harriet, please can we slow down?'

Harriet stopped abruptly. 'Carrie, I've told you before, it's just plain old Harriet.' She was convinced her niece was doing it deliberately. Carrie had never called her 'auntie' when her mother had been alive.

The girl stared back at her, a frown just forming around her blue-grey eyes. Harriet didn't find it easy looking at her niece; it was too much like looking in a mirror. They had the same pale complexion that tended to freckle across the bridge of the nose, the same cool, wide-set eyes and neat chin (the Swift Chin as it was called), and the same dark brown, almost black hair—the only difference being that Harriet's was shoulder-length and loose today, and Carrie's was plaited in a single rope that hung down to her waist. At nine years old, as if possessed of some kind of superior X-ray vision, Carrie had already perfected the art of being able to see right through a half-truth. Harriet knew she would have to play it straight with her niece; she was one smart cookie.

'You always walk too fast,' Carrie said. 'It's not fair to Joel. He can't keep up; he's only little.'

Joel, four years old, vulnerably sweet-natured and unbearably anxious, was the spitting image of Felicity, with the same mousy hair streaked through with sun-lightened gold. Sometimes, when Harriet's heart was heavy with the rawness of grief, she couldn't trust herself to look at him. 'If he can't keep up, then we're going to have to stretch his legs,' she said matter-of-factly.

The little boy bent his head and peered doubtfully at his trousers, which were several inches too long. 'Will I be as tall as Carrie then?'

Harriet eyed him thoughtfully. 'Maybe.' She straightened his hair—she must have forgotten to brush it before leaving the house. At what age did they start doing it for themselves? Taking his hand, she moved on, trying not to react to the soft warmth of his fingers wrapped in hers.

Harriet doubted there was anyone less suited or more ill-equipped to take care of her sister's children, but she'd loved Felicity and a promise was a promise. Even if that promise had been made in the sure knowledge that she would never have to keep it. After all, sisters didn't die, did they? Especially not when they were only thirty-three.

When her father had telephoned Harriet to break the awful news to her, his voice had been so choked with tears it was scarcely recognisable. Harriet had heard his words all too clearly, but a part of her had refused to take them in. She and Felicity had been talking on the phone earlier that week; Harriet had been trying to encourage her to come and stay in Oxford but Felicity had cried off, saying she was too busy sorting out the house she and Jeff had recently moved into in Newcastle.

The days that followed were a blur of confusion and shock, and it was a while before the full extent of what lay ahead hit Harriet. Her brain was conveniently numbed; it fooled her into thinking that the upheaval they were facing was only temporary. That just as soon as they had all recovered from the worst of their grief, they would pick up the broken pieces of their lives and carry on. Carrie and Joel would now live with their grandparents, while Harriet would spend Monday to Friday working in Oxford and the weekends in Cheshire looking after the children so that her parents could have a break.

For more than three months this was the structure of their lives, but Harriet had known that it could only ever be a short-term measure. Every Friday night she would battle through the traffic on the M6 up to Cheshire and arrive in Kings Melford to find that her mother looked more tired than she had the week before. The strain of taking care of the children was clearly taking its toll, and not just because Bob and Eileen weren't young any more. Five years ago Eileen had been diagnosed as suffering from ME and while she never uttered a word of complaint, there was a limit to what she could do. And always in the back of Harriet's mind was the promise she had made: *You have to promise that if anything happens to me, you'll take care of them. I wouldn't trust anyone but you.* Another person might have conveniently forgotten those words, but not Harriet. They kept her awake night after night. In the end she knew she had only one realistic option. But it was such a costly sacrifice and she tried every which way to avoid it. For a while she managed to convince herself that the children should move down to Oxford and live with her. But her one-bedroomed flat was far too small for them all. And even if she found a larger place and paid for child care, the thought of being solely responsible for Carrie and Joel, without her parents on hand, panicked her. She needed Bob and Eileen there as a permanent safety net. The answer, then, was to resign from her job as a computer programmer, sell her flat and return to Cheshire.

This she had done and she'd been living back in Maple Drive, her childhood home, for a fortnight now. Just as soon as she'd found a new job and could afford to buy or maybe rent a house near her parents she wouldn't feel as if her sacrifice had sucked the life out of her. But it was proving harder than she'd imagined. She missed her old life, her job and of course her boyfriend, Spencer.

At the end of Maple Drive they turned right and continued along the busy street that was the main road into Kings Melford. Rush-hour traffic had petered out, but the centre of town, less than a mile away, wasn't their destination.

Edna Gannet's corner shop was not for the faint-hearted. The caustic old woman who had run Gannet Stores for more than thirty years had terrorised generations of children with her meanness and breathtaking rudeness; grown men had been known to quake in her presence. With a hand on Joel's shoulder, Harriet approached the counter. 'Mrs Gannet,' she said, 'I wonder if you have any large blocks of salt like my mother used to buy when . . .' Her voice trailed off. She was about to say, 'when Felicity and I were little'.

Not missing a beat, Edna said, 'And what would you be wanting with blocks of salt?'

'Sculpture classes for the children. Do you have any?'

'I've not sold blocks of salt for many a year. Not much call for it these days.' The old woman shrugged.

Standing by the comics now, Carrie said, 'Could I have this, please?'

With the scent of a sale in her nostrils, Edna whipped round. Harriet said, 'Whoa there, little miss. I bought you one the other day. Do you think I'm made of money?' She saw a determined expression settle on Carrie's face, and knew that the girl was too much like herself to beg.

'Surely you wouldn't deprive the girl of a bit of reading matter?' chipped in Edna. 'They're educational these days. Not like the rubbish you used to read.'

Harriet shot her a sharp look. She wasn't going to be emotionally blackmailed by anyone. Especially not by Edna Gannet. She felt a tug at her sleeve.

'Can I have one too? *Please?*' asked Joel.

Heaven help her, but Harriet gave in. She handed her money over to Edna, who was openly smirking, and the children thanked her. Then the wretched woman slid two small paper bags over the counter. Carrie and Joel looked inside the bags and, suddenly shy, they smiled awkwardly at the old woman. Not quite meeting Harriet's gaze, Edna said, 'Just something to keep them from dwelling on . . .'

With unspoken sympathy quivering in the air, Harriet hustled her niece and nephew outside. In all the years she had known Edna Gannet, she had never seen her act so out of character. She took a deep, steadying breath to fight back a wave of tearful panic. With Joel on her hip and Carrie running to keep up, she headed for home. Only when they'd turned the corner into Maple Drive did she slow down.

Maple Drive was the archetypal suburban cul-de-sac, flanked either side with tidy gardens and rows of fascia-boarded houses. Harriet's parents had bought number 20 in 1969 when they had been expecting Felicity—Harriet had followed on only a year later.

The only people who had lived in the neighbourhood as long as the Swifts were the McKendricks: Dr Harvey McKendrick and his wife, Freda. They lived at number 14. Harriet and her sister had been more or less the same age as the McKendrick boys, Dominic and Miles, and they had all grown up together. Passing the recently decorated house, she kept her gaze firmly on the pavement. Freda never went out but she was sure to be watching the world go by. Freda was agoraphobic, but everyone pretended she wasn't. It maddened Harriet.

Several years ago, at the McKendricks' New Year's Day drinks party, after one too many glasses of mulled wine, Harriet had said as much to Dominic and Miles. Dominic, who lived in Cambridge and rarely honoured his parents with his presence, had agreed with her. But Miles, who lived in nearby Maywood, had disagreed and suggested his brother spent more time with their mother before he offered an opinion.

Both Miles and his father had attended Felicity and Jeff's funeral; Freda, not surprisingly, had made her apologies. Dominic hadn't even bothered to send flowers or a card. Harriet didn't think she would ever forgive him for that.

Walking up the drive of number 20, Harriet could hear her father mowing the lawn in the back garden. The sound of a normal family going about its normal everyday business. If only.

Bob Swift switched off the mower and carried the grass box down to the compost heap. The garden had always been a place of refuge for him, somewhere he could be alone to work through whatever was troubling him. But he knew he could potter about here for the rest of his days and never work through the pain of losing Felicity.

For the first ten years of their marriage, he and Eileen had been desperate for a baby, but they'd had to endure a string of heartbreaking miscarriages before Felicity had finally arrived. He could still remember that moment when he'd first held her, and had been overwhelmed at the fragility of the life for which he was now responsible. It had been love at first sight, for both him and Eileen. And miraculously, a year later—sooner than they might have liked—he was standing in the same hospital cradling a second daughter: Harriet. 'Look, Felicity,' he'd said, 'what do you think of your little sister?'

She'd smiled and stroked one of Harriet's tiny hands, then reached out to hold her as though she were a doll. Friends had warned them that they would have terrible sibling rivalry to cope with, that Felicity would inevitably be jealous. How wrong those doom-mongers had been. Felicity, an easy-going, good-natured child, never showed any jealousy.

And if Felicity was always there to look out for Harriet, Harriet in turn worshipped her older sister and hated to be separated from her. The years passed, and their close relationship survived the strains of puberty and adolescence.

'We're such a lucky family,' Eileen used to say. She said it the last time they saw Felicity alive. They were driving home after spending a couple of days with her and Jeff and the grandchildren in their new home in Newcastle. It was the third move in as many years for the young family and Bob suspected that Felicity longed for a time when Jeff would be happy to settle and put down roots, if only for the children's sake. That was something Bob had always been proud of—that he'd never uprooted his daughters while they were growing up. He'd always put their happiness before his own, always wanted to keep them safe.

But he hadn't, had he? He'd failed to keep Felicity safe.

Suddenly fearful that his legs would give way, Bob dropped the grass box and reached out to one of the wooden sides of the compost heap. He put a hand to his face and felt wetness on his cheeks. He hunted through his trouser pockets for a tissue, scoured his eyes with it and blew his nose. It was always the same when he thought of his darling girl. On an irrational impulse, he crossed the lawn to the Wendy house and slipped inside. He pulled out one of the red plastic chairs and sat down. Stuffing the tissue back into his pocket, he told himself there would be no more tears. He had to be strong, for Eileen and for the children. Whatever else, he mustn't let Carrie and Joel see him cry. Or Harriet. He didn't want her to think he couldn't cope. But thank God for Harriet. Thank God she had accepted that he and Eileen couldn't do this alone. There were no relatives on Jeff's side of the family who could take on the children so it was down to them. It seemed as if Harriet was the one making all the decisions. But it couldn't go on. He had days when he alternated between relief that Harriet was so capable and shame that he wasn't doing more. Other times it seemed his grief was like a volcano, that one day soon it would erupt and spew out molten anger that would destroy him and anyone around him.

A week later Bob was cutting the grass again. Eileen stood at the open window in their bedroom and watched him. Grief changes a person for ever, she thought. And no one knew this better than she did. With each baby she had lost and grieved for, a little bit of her had changed and slowly died. Before Felicity's birth she had lived in constant dread that if she and Bob had to resign themselves to being a childless couple, then the darkness that had been edging in would eventually eclipse their love for each other.

Eileen always thought of that period in their lives as the Wilderness Years. But then Felicity had been born, a miracle baby in all ways. At once the world was a brighter place. No more worries that Bob would stop loving her and seek permanent solace in the arms of another. To this day Eileen had kept to herself her knowledge about his two affairs during the Wilderness Years. She had never wanted to confront Bob because as hurtful as it was, she'd understood why he'd done it. It was nothing more than an antidote to the anguish.

Still staring down at her husband, Eileen tried to shake off the fear that the shadowy darkness might return. Felicity had meant the world to Bob. He loved Harriet too, of course, but from the moment she was born, Felicity had been the centre of his universe. Tears filled Eileen's eyes. She turned away from the window, blinking. She had work to do. She was supposed to be helping Harriet pack up the last of Felicity's clothes for the charity shop. When Bob had realised what she and Harriet would be doing today he had told them that he'd cut the grass and then take the children out. 'It's not right for them to see their mother's things being shoved into bin liners.'

She could hear Bob in the kitchen washing his hands. Minutes later, the back door shut and then the car engine started up. Moving round the bed that was covered with neatly folded clothes, Eileen looked out onto the landing, where Harriet was sorting through her sister's shoe collection. Of the two daughters, Harriet had always been the more conservative and guarded. Whereas Felicity had been a powder keg of enthusiasm, Harriet had played her cards much closer to her chest. To Eileen's knowledge Harriet had only ever confided in Felicity. Without her sister around, who would Harriet turn to now? It seemed unlikely that the boyfriend in Oxford—a young man they'd heard little about—would fill the space Felicity had left.

Neither Eileen nor Bob was surprised that Harriet still wasn't married. 'I'm never going to marry,' she'd announced when she was twelve years old. 'I'm going to live alone in a huge mansion and I'll be my own boss with my own company. I don't want anyone ever to tell me what to do.'

The mansion hadn't materialised, nor had her own business, but Eileen knew her daughter relished living alone. How different it was for Harriet now, thought Eileen sadly, squeezed into Felicity's old bedroom.

With enormous effort, Eileen tried once more to concentrate on what she was supposed to be doing, but overcome by a sudden wave of sadness, she buried her face in a brightly coloured woollen sweater. It smelt so evocatively of her daughter, it caused a sob to catch in her throat. She let out a stifled cry. At once Harriet was by her side. 'Are you OK, Mum?'

'It's all right, I'm just being silly.' But despite her brave words, she couldn't fight the misery that had crept up on her as it so often did. Clearing a space on the bed for her mother to sit down, Harriet heard the sound of knocking, followed by a familiar 'Yoo-hoo!'

Without checking with her mother, Harriet leaned over the banister. 'Come on up, Dora.' If anyone could lift her mother's spirits, it was Dora Gold. She lived across the road and was her mother's closest friend. She'd been divorced and widowed, in that order, and was prepared to kiss as many ageing frogs as it took to find husband number three. She was always telling them some tale or other about a date she'd just been on. Harriet hoped Dora had an interesting tale to distract Eileen and take her mind off Felicity.

Dora did better than that. She took one look at the piles of clothes on the bed and said, 'I'm giving us exactly one hour to sort through everything and then the three of us are going for lunch.'

But in the end it was only Dora and Eileen who went for lunch. Harriet excused herself by saying she had a phone call to make. She hadn't seen or spoken to Spencer in three weeks because he'd been away

17

in South Africa visiting distant cousins. It was a trip he'd arranged just days before they'd started seeing each other. Today was his first day back in the office.

Spencer had asked her out three months before Felicity's death (everything was now measured in terms of pre or post Felicity's death) and initially they'd kept their relationship from everyone at work—an office romance was such a cliché.

Spencer had only been at C.K. Support Services for five months, whereas Harriet had been there for five years. It was her second job since leaving university, but despite the lack of career opportunities within the small software house, the work, and the level she was at— Senior Analyst—suited her perfectly. She was good at her job, could run rings round most of her colleagues. Some would say that she did nothing but sit with her feet up on the desk staring at a blank computer screen for most of the day. And they'd be right. But that was when she was at her most creative. Computer programming involved a lot of thinking. In fact, the bulk of what she did was in her head.

The first time she'd met Spencer, she'd recognised a kindred spirit and wondered if this would be the meeting of minds she'd always craved. It was no secret among her friends that she didn't suffer fools gladly. 'Your bog-standard lager-loving footie fanatic stands no chance with you, does he?' Erin had once remarked. Erin was the same age as Harriet and lived in the flat above hers; she had no qualms about who she came home with after a drunken night out.

As she got to know Spencer, Harriet realised he ticked a good number of boxes. She liked his clear-cut way of thinking, his steadiness, his understanding and appreciation that she needed her own space.

But then Felicity died and everything changed.

Spencer was the first person she told about her decision to hand in her notice and move back to Cheshire. 'Aren't you surprised?' she'd said when he hardly reacted.

'Sorry, Harriet, but I saw it coming. It was obvious.'

Never afraid to confront an issue, she said, 'It's going to change things between us, isn't it?'

He'd put a hand on her shoulder. 'For now, you've got more than enough on your plate without worrying about us. We'll find a way.'

But she did worry. And it annoyed her that she did. Being needy had never been on her personal agenda.

It was ages before Spencer answered his mobile. Time enough for paranoia to set in. Was he trying to avoid her?

'Hi there, Harriet. How's it going?' The sound of his voice, so easy, so assured, chased away the doubts.

'Not bad,' she said, 'all things considered.' She wanted to explain what she'd spent the morning doing, but couldn't be bothered. Other people's problems were exactly that. Other people's. Given the choice, wouldn't she rather cross the road than risk being contaminated by grief? 'Tell me how South Africa was. Did you send me a postcard?'

They discussed his trip, but then they seemed to run out of things to say. 'Look,' he said, 'I can't chat for long, but are you still coming down tomorrow?'

'Of course. Why do you ask?' When he didn't answer her question, she said, 'It shouldn't take too long to pack up the last of my things at the flat. The agent says the buyer is all set to go.' She couldn't bring herself to ask if he was still on for lending a hand as he had promised. Instead she said, 'Spencer, if you've got something to say, just say it.'

A pause. And then: 'This isn't the time, Harriet. Why don't we speak tomorrow? I'll meet you at your flat as we agreed. Around twelve.'

After a brisk goodbye she rang off. Without the aid of a crystal ball she knew exactly what the future held. It was adios time, inevitably. Why would Spencer want to stay involved with her now that she lived so far away and had two children to bring up?

Smarting with hurt pride, she flipped open her mobile again and scrolled through for the number she always tapped in when she needed a good rant. She'd got as far as putting the phone to her ear when she realised what she was doing. Very slowly, she closed the mobile. It was one of the things she found almost impossible to come to terms with: accepting that Felicity was no longer around to talk to.

She decided she needed some fresh air to clear her head and improve her mood. But when she stepped outside she discovered that fresh air was in short supply. August, with its unbreathable, muggy air that was thick with pollen, was her least favourite month of the year. It was when her asthma was at its worst and she always had to be sure she was never too far from her inhaler.

She looked across the road and saw a large white van. Its tailgate was lowered and furniture, piled higgledy-piggledy, was clearly in the process of being removed and carried up the drive. Just then, a stockily built man in baggy shorts appeared in the open doorway. Annoyed she'd been caught gawping, Harriet walked on down the road.

'Where do you want this?'

Will bobbed up from behind the sofa, where he was plugging in the CD player, and checked out the large box Marty was holding. 'Bung it on top of the other box over there in the corner,' he said.

'I will, but on condition that we stop for some lunch. If not, I'll have

19

you in an industrial tribunal faster than you can say, "Put the kettle on."'

'Would that be before or after I've had you arrested for a breach of the Public Order Act? Who'd you borrow those shorts from? Johnny Vegas?'

'Ha-ha. And here's me doing the best-friend routine only to be on the receiving end of fattist jokes. I'm starving.'

'If you stop whinging long enough, lunch will be brought out to you in the garden in about quarter of an hour.'

Minutes later, with Marty taking a break outside, Will set to work on throwing some lunch together. They'd been friends long enough to know each other's likes and dislikes perfectly. Not dissimilar from a marriage, really. Except Will's friendship with Marty had never turned sour, unlike his marriage. It was eight years since he and Maxine had divorced but it still felt as if it were yesterday, probably because Maxine never let him forget what a bastard he'd been. Oh, and a loser, too. That was a constant favourite of hers. 'The trouble with you, William Hart,' she'd said only last week when she was in his office, interrogating him about his reasons for moving, 'is that you refuse to grow up. What's wrong with where you are?'

'Well, honey,' he'd replied, all silky-smooth and knowing it would annoy the hell out of her, 'I'd tell you if it was any of your business. But seeing as it isn't, you'll have to reach your own conclusion.'

Fortunately she hadn't stuck around and after she'd swept off in one of her up-yours-see-you-around-sucker flounces, and after he'd said, 'Be sure to give my best wishes to PC Plod, won't you?' he'd closed the door of his ramshackle office and, tuning to Radio Four, he'd rolled up his sleeves for his afternoon fix of *The Archers*. It didn't take much to please him these days.

He supposed that in Maxine's eyes he would always be the bad guy. The big girl's blouse of a husband who dared to have an early midlife crisis. The lousy husband who played around. The brute of a husband who broke her heart. It wasn't easy playing the villain every day of his life. Just occasionally he'd like to think he was a cut above your average no-good ex-husband. He'd never once raised his hand to a woman. He'd never drunk to excess. He'd never picked his nose in public. And if he'd been such a bad lot, why had she stuck around as long as she had? The answer to that, as she'd repeatedly flung at him, was the only good things to come out of their relationship: Gemma and Suzie. Their gorgeous daughters—Gemma, seventeen and Suzie, nineteen—were the crowning glory of his life.

In many ways, marrying Maxine had been the best thing he'd ever done. But he'd withhold that fact from her to his dying day. A man was entitled to his pride.

'Hey, you in there!' called Marty from the garden. 'Any chance of something to eat?'

They took their lunch down to the end of the garden, unlocked the wooden gate and went and sat on the bench that overlooked the canal. It was a most perfect spot, the main reason Will had bought the house.

As if picking up on his thoughts, Marty said, 'Here's to you and your new home.' They tapped their cans of beer together. 'Cheers. So how do you think you'll like living here?'

'It'll do. Though it's tempting to nuke the house and start over. Those hideous carpets and curtains can't have slipped your notice, surely?'

Marty laughed. 'I thought retro was all the rage?'

'I'm a purist. Give me a fine pair of Queen Anne legs any day.'

'You antique dealers are all the same; just a bunch of screaming snobs. I caught sight of one of your neighbours earlier. As natives go, she didn't look the sort to welcome you with open arms.'

'I expect she was in shock at the sight of you in those shorts. You look like that short fat guy from *It Ain't Half Hot Mum*. If you're not careful, you'll turn into your dad.'

'Gravity and nasal hair come to us all. Even you, Will. It's time to give in. It's time to grow up. We're forty-six, heading fast towards our pensions, arthritic joints and overactive bladders.'

'Speak for yourself. I'm only forty-five.'

'Bullshit! You're forty-six next month.'

'So what's brought this on? Why the mood?'

Marty looked glum and drank some more of his beer. 'Perhaps it's my turn now for the midlife crisis.'

'Ah, well, there's your mistake. You should have got it over and done with in your thirties, as I did. With all that behind me, the world looks pretty rosy from where I'm sitting.' Will laughed.

'You've never regretted it, then? Never thought what it might have been like if you'd kept your nerve and played the game?'

'Not once. If I'd stayed, the stress would have had me going on the rampage with a machete and wiping out the entire firm. I know I made the right decision. Life's been bloody good to me since I opted out.'

'That's what I hate about you, Will; you're perpetually upbeat. You've no idea how sickening it is.'

Marty left after he'd helped Will heave the beds upstairs. There was a double in the main bedroom and two singles: one in the room that would be Gemma's and another in the room that would be Suzie's. These days the girls rarely stayed with him—Suzie was away at university and only home for the holidays—but it was important to Will that they knew they could stop over with him whenever they wanted to.

He liked to think that despite their differences, he and Maxine had done their best by the girls, that their divorce hadn't harmed them too much. It was possible, though, that he'd got it completely wrong. Beneath the apparent acceptance, they might despise him as much as Maxine did. And as Maxine would have it, they had every reason to.

The affairs, none of which were of any real consequence, had been the final straw for Maxine. He wasn't proud of what he'd done and still cringed at the memory of the lies and skulking about he'd got up to. It was pretty pathetic. It was also madness. He'd been out of his tiny mind. Which wasn't far off the literal truth. Officially, he'd had some kind of nervous breakdown. Unofficially, he'd just been a bloody idiot and had wrecked his promising career and his marriage.

It was not the future he'd planned for himself, when, fresh out of law school with Marty, he had landed a plum of a training contract with Carlton Webb Davis, a top Manchester law firm. They'd both opted to work in Manchester rather than London, figuring that they'd soon become a pair of big fish in the small pond. But Will had another compelling reason to move back to the Northwest where he'd grown up; he'd just met the most stunning girl. She lived in Cheshire and worked for her father, who ran an auction house in Maywood. They'd met during his last term at law school. He was home for the weekend, a few months after his dad had died and his mother was having a clearout. She wanted to sell some of the furniture. Will had arranged for a valuer to come to the house when he'd be around, just to ensure that his mother wouldn't be shafted by some smart-talking smoothie. In Will's opinion, antique dealers were right at the bottom of the food chain, along with politicians and secondhand car dealers. Coming from a lawyer, as was later pointed out to him, this was rich indeed.

Bang on ten o'clock, he'd opened the front door and got the surprise of his life. The attractive girl produced a business card: *Maxine Stone, of Christopher Stone, Auctioneers and Valuers of Fine Art, Antique and Contemporary Items, Maywood, Cheshire.* Miss Maxine Stone was gorgeous. Almost as tall as him, and dressed in an impeccable black suit, her hair was tied back in a prim little bun, which he found wildly sexy. She was looking him straight in the eye (hers were green) and smiling confidently.

His mother, always the perfect hostess, bustled around making tea. It was some time before they got down to the meat of the matter—the fate of an ugly set of bedroom furniture—but Will didn't care. He was mesmerised. He wanted her! He watched her face intently as she chatted amiably with his mother. 'Well, I find that hard to believe,' he suddenly heard his mother say. 'Don't you, Will?'

22

'Sorry,' he said, 'I was miles away.' He was mentally unpinning all that ash-blonde hair and running his fingers through it. 'What don't you believe, Mum?'

'That Maxine hasn't been snapped up by a handsome young man.' Only his mother could have been on first-name terms so soon with a complete stranger, openly enquiring about her marital status.

His eyes locked with Maxine's. 'Perhaps she's waiting for the right man,' he said as his mother went out to the kitchen to refill the teapot.

'Perhaps you're right,' Maxine said.

Two weeks later, when he'd come home for another weekend and was lying in bed with Maxine, he said, 'I think we should do this more often.'

They were married two years later, after he'd finished his training contract and was fully qualified. Carlton Webb Davis made him an attractive offer and Maxine continued to work for her father, Christopher Stone. They were perfectly matched: both ambitious, both in a hurry to make a name for themselves. For Maxine it was a foregone conclusion that she would take over her father's auction room when he retired and Will was climbing the greasy pole with chest-beating aplomb. It meant that he was rarely at home, but the more clients who kept him out till all hours, the more supportive Maxine was. Even when Suzie and Gemma came along, she never once complained that he wasn't there to change the nappies or read the bedtime stories. Not that she did a lot of that herself: they had help—a series of nannies. His plan was to be the youngest ever senior partner at Carlton Webb Davis and if anything was guaranteed to turn Maxine on, it was the thought of her man being the Big Cheese.

But when it all started to go wrong, when he began to morph from Superman into a snivelling burnt-out wreck, Maxine was not amused.

The day he realised he couldn't go on this way was one of the scariest moments of his life. For a while now he'd grown tired of sitting through sixteen-hour meetings just so that a roomful of tossers could flex their egos. Then late one night, after he'd sat through hours of client argy-bargy, he had suddenly banged his fist on the table and said, 'Will you just sign the sodding contract and have done with it? Some of us have better things to do with our lives than jerk others about.'

The following morning he was called to the fifth floor to explain himself. 'Trouble at home,' he'd lied.

'Then sort it, William. And sooner rather than later.'

For a few weeks he continued to play the game, keeping a tight lid on his cynicism and temper, but before long, he realised he couldn't go on. The price was too high. He wanted his life back. He wanted to spend time with his daughters, to sit on their beds at night and read to them, or in Suzie's case, sing her her favourite lullaby, 'Scarlet Ribbons'. But more than anything, he wanted to stop feeling so knackered he couldn't make it in bed any more.

However, Maxine saw things differently. 'It's just a bad patch,' she said. 'Why don't we go on holiday without the children?'

They went away together to a relaxing hotel in southern Italy, but all it did was give him some courage on his return to the office: without telling Maxine, he handed in his notice. He was immediately put on 'gardening leave' and for a full month he managed to keep Maxine in ignorance of this. He'd get up in the morning as usual, drive off in his BMW and then spend the day anywhere but in Manchester. He'd go across to North Wales, the Peak District, or up to the Lakes. He'd browse round bookstores and stately homes. He also visited antique shops and attended a couple of auctions; to his surprise, he began to understand how addictive they were. No wonder Maxine got a thrill out of her work.

He grew fond of playing truant and would return home with a faint spring in his step. Maxine was delighted to see the improvement in him; as far as she was concerned they were now back on track. There was even some bedroom action again.

But inevitably she found out—he was spotted at an auction by one of her colleagues—and she went ballistic. 'What's happened to you?' she screamed. 'You're not the man I married.'

He tried to explain how he felt, how ill he'd begun to feel. He couldn't bring himself to admit to his panic attacks. But all she was interested in was how they were going to manage financially.

It was a real enough concern. And while Maxine was prepared to ride out the storm sheltering in the safety of her father's cavernous wallet, Will was not. They sold their expensive house and made drastic economy measures. The nanny was sent packing and he became a house-husband. Temporarily, he assured Maxine. Secretly, though, he enjoyed doing the school run, taking the girls swimming, and cooking the tea. But it was no job for a real man, as Maxine would imply with one of her steely power-suited looks when she came home after a hard day's graft at the saleroom. She was all for him getting off his backside and submitting his CV to whichever law firm would be desperate enough to have him. She missed the perks of having a husband who spent his every waking moment killing himself through stress.

That was when the affairs started. If he had to defend himself, and he had tried to do so many times, his actions were those of a man trying to gain a modicum of self-respect: if his wife could no longer bear to look at him or regard him as attractive then he was sure as hell going to find the affirmation he needed elsewhere. It was a mistake, of course. His self-respect had no intention of showing up while he was cheating on his wife. Even without knowing about the affairs, Maxine's loathing for him was growing on a daily basis. When he announced that he was going into business, and confessed exactly what line of business he was considering, she threw hot, scathing scorn at him. 'You, an antique dealer!' she crowed. 'You don't know the first thing about it.'

'Actually,' he said, 'I do. You've taught me all you know.'

When their divorce was finalised and the money shared out, he took a gamble and opened an antiques shop, rapidly discovering that only throwing his gelt at a three-legged horse in the 2.30 at Uttoxeter would have been riskier. Nonetheless, he read up, did his homework and got lucky when he stumbled across an expert willing to share his knowledge. His name was Jarvis and he took a liking to Will, becoming his self-appointed mentor. He still was.

All these years on, his life could not be more different. Nothing would make him go back to those days in the soulless air-conditioned offices of Carlton Webb Davis. Not unless he was armed with a machete.

He was sprawled comfortably on the sofa that evening, having decided to take a break from unpacking, when his mobile rang. It was his eldest daughter, Suzie. 'Hi, Dad. How did the move go? How's the new house? And can you lend me some money? *Pleee-ase.*'

'The move went well,' he said. 'Marty helped. The house is horrible. And how much do you want?'

'How much can you spare?'

'For you, my very last shirt button. What do you need it for?'

'My coke dealer's raised his prices.'

He laughed. 'Why do you really want the money?'

'Promise you won't hit the roof?'

'Have I ever been that sort of father?'

'I've bumped the car and want to get it fixed before Mum sees it.'

'Mm . . . why don't you do what the rest of us do? Get it sorted on your insurance. If I'm not mistaken, I already pay for that anyway.'

'Um . . . thing is, it . . . it wasn't my car. It was Steve's.'

'Steve's?' Will sat up. 'Hang on, let me get this straight. You mean you were driving PC Plod's brand-new Jag? The *Shaguar*?' His laughter bouncing off the sitting-room walls drowned out her answer.

'Dad, it isn't funny. They're back from Paris next week with Gemma and I need to get it fixed before Steve sees it.' Will was still laughing when he ended the call. He was picturing the expression on the face of his ex-wife's second husband when he saw what had happened to his precious new car. Steve Dodd, aka PC Plod because he used to be something big in the police force, had tried hard to be a model step-father to Suzie and Gemma, but he suspected that Steve was going to have his work cut out keeping his cool over this. Unless, of course, for Suzie's sake, Will could get it sorted before anyone was the wiser.

Ten minutes later, when he was hunting through the Yellow Pages for a suitable body shop, his mobile chirruped with a text message from Sandra. Sandra was a fellow dealer and had one of those open marriages that he thought only ever existed in people's heads. Seemingly her husband would be around for the foreseeable future, so any nocturnal visits from Will would be inappropriate. To be honest he was relieved. He was too tired for one of Sandra's sexual marathons.

Putting his mobile aside, he returned his attention to more important matters: finding a body shop for PC Plod's pranged car.

It was raining when Harriet arrived in Oxford. Her flat felt cold and empty, as if it had fallen asleep in her absence. Or . . . as if it had died. She briskly chased the thought away and went round checking there was nothing amiss. Constant activity was the only answer.

She'd set off early that morning. Her father had offered to come with her, but Harriet had suggested he ought to take the children out for the day to give Mum a break. It was obvious to them all that Eileen wasn't getting enough rest, and if that went on for too long, Harriet knew her mother would be stuck in bed for days.

The first room she tackled was the bedroom. It didn't take her long. Most of her clothes were already up in Cheshire; what little furniture she had was being put into storage. From her bedroom she moved to the bathroom, then the sitting room, and with the first shelf of her books packed, the buzzer for the intercom sounded. Spencer.

She buzzed him up and, fixing a smile to her face, opened the door. 'Hi,' she said. If nothing else, he was going to remember her for being positive and upbeat. But the moment he leaned in for a kiss a flood of happy memories came back and hope surfaced, too. Maybe he would stand by her after all.

'You've been busy,' he said, taking off his wet coat and eyeing the narrow hall that was crowded with boxes and bin liners.

'You know me. If a job's got to be done, best to get it over and done with.' Like ending their doomed relationship, she thought. Noticing the carrier bag he was holding, she said, 'What's that?'

'Lunch. I knew you'd be too busy to go out, so I called in at the deli.'

They sat opposite each other at the circular table and ate in silence, like an ancient married couple. When she couldn't take the awkward-ness any longer, Harriet put down her baguette and said, 'I think we need to talk. You said on the phone yesterday that there was something you wanted to say to me.' She was throwing him a line.

He slowly finished what was in his mouth. 'It'll keep,' he murmured. 'Any luck on the job front yet?'

She would never have thought he was the cowardly type. But, prepared to give him some slack, she said, 'I haven't had time to approach a job agency. My niece and nephew are incredibly time-consuming.'

'How are they coming to terms with everything?'

'They seem OK,' she said, 'but how do we really know what's going on inside their heads?'

'Have you thought about counselling?'

'They've been seeing a woman for a couple of weeks. I've no idea if it's helping them.'

'What about for you and your parents?'

She shrugged. 'Not really our thing.'

He hesitated. 'Have you thought of keeping a journal?'

Harriet couldn't think of anything worse. She'd feel too exposed and vulnerable putting down any of the thoughts she'd had since Felicity had died. She also felt that if Spencer knew the first thing about her, he wouldn't have made such a suggestion. Looking at him across the table, she felt like she was having lunch with a stranger. It hit her then, that that was the reality. They scarcely knew each other.

Seizing the moment, she said, 'Spencer, I think we should get this over with. I can't think of a single reason why you would want to carry on seeing me now that my circumstances have changed so dramatically.'

He stopped eating, looking a picture of awkwardness. 'You knew, then, what it was I wanted to say? But you do see, don't you? It's the children. I've never wanted any, and . . . well, if we're to continue seeing each other, if we were to get seriously involved, the children would be a factor. And I'm not convinced—'

'Please,' she interrupted him, 'you don't have to explain. Believe me, I know *exactly* how you feel.'

Driving home later that evening, Harriet realised she was more hurt and disappointed than she'd expected. But what hurt the most was the look of pure relief on Spencer's face when they'd said goodbye. Rejection was an ugly thing. By the time she reached Keele Services on the M6 she had to stop and be sick. Spencer had been the only thing left that symbolised the woman she had been before Felicity's death—the woman she still wanted to be. Losing him meant she had to submit to the only certainty in her new life: she was now a parent. A parent whose will had to be subjugated to the needs of the children in her care.

Feeling pathetically sorry for herself she thought of everything she'd lost—her sister, her home, her job, her identity, and now her boyfriend. What next? Her mind?

Carrie closed the door of the Wendy house, looked at Joel and frowned. He was sucking his thumb and rubbing his cheek with his silky. His silky was a pale pink scarf Mum had worn when he'd been a baby; he always carried it. He was acting like a baby now, making that humming noise he made when he was tired or upset. None of the grown-ups seemed to notice that he was doing it more and more, but Carrie knew he had to stop. If he did it when he went to school, he'd be laughed at. 'Joel,' she said, 'do you remember Daddy saying that big boys don't suck their thumbs?'

Joel unplugged his thumb. 'Mummy said I could do it.'

'Yes, but that was when you were very little. Now you're a big boy. When you go to big school in a few weeks' time, you'll get laughed at if you don't act like all the other children.'

He shook his head and put his thumb back in his mouth. Carrie tried to look stern. 'If you don't do as I say, I won't let you sleep in my bed.'

The thumb was out again. 'But I don't like sleeping on my own.'

'Then you have to do as I say.'

He looked thoughtful. 'Can I take silky to school with me?'

'No. You wouldn't want to lose it, would you? And someone might take it. You see, Joel, not everyone's as nice as us.'

'Grandma and Granddad are nice.'

'That's true.'

'And Harriet. She's nice.'

Carrie wasn't so sure about this. For the last few days, since Harriet had come back from wherever it was she'd been, she hadn't seemed at all nice. She'd told Carrie off for not eating enough of her cereal yesterday and then had snapped at her because she hadn't tidied her room.

Carrie often wished that Harriet could be more like their mother. Mum had been kind and patient, and her voice had always been gentle and full of happiness, like she was about to burst out laughing. Carrie used to love it when Mum read to her; she did all the voices, even the funny deep ones. Harriet never did that. She always rushed it as if she was in a hurry to do something else. She could look pretty sometimes, like Mum, but not when she was cross. Carrie knew for a fact that Harriet didn't like children. If she did like them, she'd be married with some of her own. Maybe then it wouldn't be so bad. If they had some cousins to play with, there wouldn't be time to think about . . .

Carrie stopped quickly. She'd promised herself not to let her mind get confused with sad thoughts about Mum and Dad. She had to remember what Grandma had told her, that they were happy where they were in heaven. Carrie often wished she and Joel could be there too. But if that happened then she'd miss Grandma and Granddad, who were always nice and hardly ever told them off.

Deciding it was too hot in the Wendy house, Carrie got up and opened the two windows either side of the door. She lifted the lid of the toy box and looked inside. There was the plastic tea set Joel loved playing with. 'Let's have a tea party,' she said, knowing it would please him.

Joel sprang into life. 'Can we have real water like we did last time? Not pretend water.'

She passed him a matching teapot and milk jug. 'Yes. But only if you promise not to spill it everywhere. We mustn't make extra work for Grandma and Granddad.' And quoting her aunt, she added, 'Grandma isn't very well, so we have to be extra good.'

'Is Grandma going to die like Mummy and Daddy?' he asked.

'Don't be stupid. No one is going to die, Joel.' Carrie didn't know if this was true. She and Joel weren't supposed to know that their grandmother had anything wrong with her. But Carrie often listened at the top of the stairs when everyone thought she was asleep in bed and one night she had heard Harriet telling Grandma that she should rest more, that if she didn't, she'd make herself more ill than she already was.

'Mummy and Daddy died,' Joel said, his voice shrill and persistent.

'Oh, stop going on about it, will you?' Carrie snapped. 'You're just a silly little boy who doesn't know anything.' She grabbed the teapot and the milk jug. 'Now stay here while I go and fill these.'

She didn't know why but her legs were shaking when she stepped out into the sunshine. She walked uncertainly across the lawn to the tap on the end of the garage. Her heart was racing and her throat felt tight. It was an effort to swallow. Maybe she had what was making Grandma ill. Maybe she was dying. She suddenly thought of Joel and how lonely and frightened he'd be without her.

At night, when her brother was sleeping next to her, his silky wrapped around his thumb-sucking hand, she often worried about who would look after them if anything happened to their grandparents. Or Harriet. What if she and Joel were left on their own? Would they be made to stay in an orphanage?

Suddenly Carrie's throat was so tight she was struggling to breathe. It only loosened when hot tears splashed onto her cheeks. She drew her forearm across her face and wiped them away. Just as Joel had to stop sucking his thumb, she had to learn not to cry. She had to be good, too. Because if Grandma wasn't well and they annoyed Harriet, their aunt might decide not to look after them any more and they'd end up in an orphanage wearing clothes that didn't fit and shoes with holes in them.

She filled the plastic teapot and jug and went back to the Wendy house. When she pushed the door open, she found Joel lying on the floor crying. She dropped to her knees and pulled her brother onto her lap. 'What's the matter, Joel? Have you hurt yourself?'

He lifted his head from her shoulder. 'You . . . you shouted at me. You called me silly. And I'm not. Mummy said I was clever.'

'Oh, Joel, I'm sorry. Of course you're not silly. Please don't cry.'

But the more she tried to calm him the more he cried, shuddering and gulping in her arms. She tried to think what their mother would have done if she were here. Then it came to her: Mum would have given him a drink. She poured Joel a cup of water from the teapot. 'Look, Joel,' she said, 'I've got you a drink. Sit up straight and you can have it.' Within seconds he was calm and drinking thirstily. Still holding him, she said, 'Don't worry, Joel, I'll take care of you. I'll always look after you.'

It was probably a first, but for once the commotion going on downstairs had nothing to do with Gemma. The way Steve was carrying on, anyone would think Suzie had done it deliberately. What a twat! Kicking up such a fuss just because his stupid car had been damaged. Unluckily for Suzie, the garage had cocked up big-time by bodging the respray. They'd only been in the house ten minutes when he'd looked out of the sitting-room window and nearly had a fit. Mum had immediately taken Steve's side, as she always did these days. 'What the hell did you think you were doing, driving Steve's car, anyway?' she'd shouted.

'I'd run out of petrol in mine,' Suzie replied.

'And you thought that gave you the right to help yourself to mine?' Steve had blustered, his nostrils flaring. 'Well, I'll tell you this for nothing; I'm going to get it fixed properly and you're going to pay for it. What's more, we'll stop your allowance.'

That was when Gemma had decided she'd had enough and had gone to lie on her bed. She was knackered. The last two weeks had been exhausting. As part of the student exchange system the school ran, she'd been staying with the Léon family in Paris. Véronique Léon had been way too serious but her nineteen-year-old brother, Marcel, had more than made up for any inadequacy on his sister's behalf. Home from university, Marcel had offered to take her out. They'd gone to the cinemas, they'd sat around in smoky bars and one night they'd gone to a party and didn't come home until seven in the morning. Marcel had made it pretty obvious that he wanted to go to bed with her, and deciding that she quite fancied him, and that she might just as well get the whole virginity thing over and done with, she'd gone along with it. The first time had been the letdown she'd expected. It hadn't hurt, but then it hadn't been all that great either. But the second time had been OK. The third and fourth time she began to see what all the fuss was about. When Mum and Steve had met her at the airport she'd been convinced that they would take one look at her and guess.

For some reason she thought of her father and, not having spoken to him for some time, she dug around in her rucksack for her mobile.

Within seconds he answered. 'Hi, Bobtail,' he said, 'how was France? Have you come back stinking of Gauloises and with a liking for incomprehensible black and white films shot from arty angles?'

'Easy there, Dad. You've got to handle those stereotypes with care. How about I come round and see the new house and tell you all about it?'

'When do you want to come?'

'Now would be great but I don't think Mum would appreciate driving me anywhere.' She started to tell her father about Suzie and Steve's car.

'Damn!' he interrupted her. 'I knew we wouldn't get away with it. Suzie asked me for help and I organised for it to be fixed. Trouble was, the only garage that could do the job at such short notice wasn't exactly the best. On a scale of one to ten, how mad is Steve?'

'How would you rate six inches off the ground with incandescent rage?'

'Sounds like Suzie needs a good defence lawyer. Shall I just happen to be passing and call in?'

Maxine was staring into the freezer hoping for inspiration. More often than not Steve cooked, but he was currently upstairs in the shower, trying to calm down. Maxine had never seen him so furious, and frankly, she didn't blame him. If Suzie had bumped *her* new car she'd be hopping mad. The shame of it was, she and Steve hadn't managed to get away together, just the two of them, in ages, and when they did manage it, it was ruined.

Paris had been Steve's idea. He'd wanted to celebrate their fifth wedding anniversary by doing something special. 'We could treat ourselves to a decent hotel. It could be a second honeymoon for us,' he'd said.

'But I've already had a second one,' she'd said, 'when I married you.'

'Yes, but did the first one really count?'

Steve didn't often badmouth Will—that was her job—but she supposed that occasionally it was natural that Husband Number Two would feel the need to check his stock against that of Husband Number One. Not that he needed to worry. Will didn't compare at all. Steve was everything that Will could never be. He was dependable, hard-working, solid, ambitious, organised and, most importantly, all grown up.

It transpired that the only week she and Steve could both get away from work coincided with Gemma's trip to Paris. 'I might know you'd find some way to keep an eye on me,' Gemma had said.

'Paris is a big city,' Maxine had mollified her, 'quite large enough for us to avoid bumping into each other.'

Maxine sighed, and deciding on chicken Kiev for supper. After putting them on a dish and shoving them into the oven, she went over to the wine rack. A large glass of wine was just what was needed. She had the cork almost out when the doorbell rang. If it was one of the girls' friends— 'Oh, it's you.'

'*Bonjour, ma chérie!* Is that the pungent smell of a ripe Brie fresh from its travels across the Channel? Or is it the smell of a daughter being roasted on the spit?'

Maxine frowned. 'It's really not a good time for one of your tiresome stand-up routines, Will. I'm tired and likely to attack.'

From behind Maxine came the thundering of feet. 'Hey, Dad!'

'Wow! Look at you, Gemma, you're positively glowing.'

Maxine's head was beginning to ache. 'OK, Will,' she conceded. 'You've got twenty minutes, then our supper's ready.'

Will followed Maxine and Gemma through to the kitchen, glancing left and right, an imaginary rifle cocked. *Come on, you bastard! Where're you hiding? I'll teach you to pick on one of my daughters!*

'Hello, Will, what are you doing here?'

Will spun round. He fired and blew a hole clean through Steve's head. *Boom! Job done.* As far as Will was concerned, what Maxine saw in Steve was another of life's great mysteries. Steve was too short, too ugly, too old, too hairy and much too successful. Five years ago, Steve had taken early retirement from the police force and had started his own security firm, installing burglar alarms and CCTV systems. Will didn't need to be a genius to work out that business was booming—the prestigious Victorian house opposite the park and the top-of-the-range Jag (slightly damaged) told its own story. Combine that with Maxine's earnings from Stone's Auctioneers, which she now ran, and they were fairly rolling in it.

Will turned up the charm. 'Hi, Steve. Good holiday?'

'Yes, but I have to tell you I'm not at all pleased with Suzie, she's—'

He was interrupted by the girl herself coming into the kitchen. 'Hey, Dad, I didn't know you were here.' She came over and planted a kiss on his cheek. He put his arm round her.

'Steve,' he said, 'I've got something to say. You won't like it, and I'm ashamed of myself for being such a coward, but'—he lowered his gaze — 'well, the thing is, I reversed into your car when you were away and—'

'But, Dad—'

He tightened his hold on Suzie. 'It's OK, you don't need to cover for me any more, Suzie. I don't know what I was thinking of. I'm really sorry, Steve. I tried my best to get it fixed before you came home, but if you want to get it done properly, just send me the bill.'

It was anyone's guess how much he'd be down on the deal by the time Steve had shopped around to find the most expensive garage to exact his revenge, but Will didn't care. He'd be damned before he'd stand back and let Steve punish Suzie. End of story.

Twenty minutes later he left, but instead of taking the road away from the centre of town, he drove into Kings Melford. A fraction smaller than Maywood, but definitely more attractive, it had an abundance of black and white half-timbered buildings, and a quaint cobbled square that had been the original marketplace, going back to the time of Henry VIII.

The Shropshire Union Canal skirted the top of the town and when it was built it became an important part of the system for transporting salt out of Cheshire. Nowadays it wasn't the canal workers who stopped off in Kings Melford to stock up on provisions and fuel; it was the people cruising the waterways in their pleasure crafts. There was a purpose-built marina a short walk along the towpath to The Navigation—the best pub in the town, and Will's current destination—and a couple of boat firms.

He passed Hart's Antique Emporium, and gave his most recent business venture a salute. Strictly speaking, it wasn't just *his* business: Jarvis owned the building—originally called The Tavern, it had started life as an inn—and rented it out to Will for a nominal amount, on the basis that he took a percentage of the profits.

Just as Will expected, he found Jarvis in his usual chair in the snug of The Navigation. He was alone and doing the crossword. Now in his seventies, and regarded as one of the town's last great characters, this evening he was dressed to kill in olive-green corduroy trousers, a plaid shirt and purple waistcoat and a red silk cravat. But it was the burgundy monogrammed carpet slippers that really pulled the ensemble together.

'Another of what you're drinking?' Will asked.

Jarvis looked up from his near-empty glass. 'As ever, laddie, your timing is perfect. I'll have a double of my usual malt.'

When they were both settled with their drinks, Will said, 'It's been a good week. Your cut should be up nicely this month.'

Jarvis waved his comment aside, as only a man could who didn't have to worry where his next guinea was coming from. The first time Will set eyes on him was when he'd been going through his breakdown phase. Will had been playing truant at an auction and had noticed a dapper man in a fedora. His manner had such an air of authority that Will couldn't take his eyes off him. He saw him again at another saleroom in Shropshire, and then in The Navigation, not long before he and Maxine split up. Will had introduced himself and discovered that the man was Jarvis Cooper, a local dealer. After buying him a drink, Will mentioned that he was thinking of getting into the business himself.

'Don't do it, laddie,' Jarvis had said in the kind of voice Noël Coward had used to tell Mrs Worthington not to put her daughter on the stage. 'Buying and selling is like trying to satisfy an insatiable nymphomaniac; the more you give her, the more she'll take from you.'

'I rather like the sound of that. Where do I sign up?'

Jarvis had laughed and asked if he'd like to have a look at The Tavern. Thinking this was an invitation to join him on a pub crawl, he'd agreed. The Tavern turned out to be a rambling, three-storey Aladdin's cave. It was chock-full of goodies that ranged from fifties tat to exquisite pieces of porcelain. Jarvis had a particular weakness for Royal Worcester and there were cabinets of the stuff. 'Your first lesson,' he said, unlocking one of the cabinets and selecting a fragile cup and saucer. 'If you're to make your way in this business you have to *feel* it. You have to breathe in the workmanship. Picture the artist bent over his bench as he laboured.'

Watching Jarvis cradle the porcelain, clucking and cooing over it, Will began to see a whole new world open up. He wanted to feel what Jarvis felt. He wanted that buzz that clearly brought this old-timer to life.

Under Jarvis's tutelage, Will learned fast. His days revolved around researching, collecting, buying and selling, and he soon realised that being in the antique trade wasn't about money. It was the thrill of the chase.

After finishing his drink, Will left Jarvis to his crossword and drove on to his next port of call. Sandra had texted him earlier to say that the coast would be clear that evening, after all. Fresh out of the bath, she was in frisky mood. Exchanging a few pleasantries—jacket and shoes off—she led the way upstairs.

Later, when Sandra went back downstairs to make a postcoital cup of tea, Will stared up at the ceiling and thought of Sandra's husband. No guilt, he told himself. Sandra and her husband have an open marriage. But deep down, Will knew it was wrong. Even in the most open of relationships people could get hurt. He suddenly didn't want to hang around.

He drove home, bone-tired. As he turned into Maple Drive, he saw a figure in a baseball cap crossing the road. A lad out for a night of petty thieving? Will slowed his speed and drew alongside the boy. Deciding to be a good neighbour and challenge him, Will leaned across the passenger seat to the open window. 'You're out late, sonny.'

The boy turned and gave him a look that could have cut through graphite. It wasn't a boy. It was the daughter of the couple who lived opposite him. That and the mother of those two young children he saw occasionally. 'I'm sorry,' he called out of the window, 'it was the cap. It makes you look like a boy.'

As he got ready for bed he wondered what she'd been doing out so late. He knew next to nothing about his neighbours. Perhaps now, after his monumental gaffe, he ought to make more of an effort to be sociable.

It was the last week of August and with only six days to go until the start of term, Harriet and her parents, plus Carrie and Joel, were meeting the headmistress of Kings Melford Junior School. Privately Harriet was counting the days until the children would go to school so she could make a start on finding a job. The school was just as Harriet remembered it: an expanse of depressing dark brickwork and slate rooftops. But despite its daunting appearance, both she and Felicity had enjoyed their time there.

Impatient to get on, Harriet took hold of the children's hands. 'OK, kiddos, let's get this over and done with.' She dragged them through the doors, ignoring the dead-weight reluctance in their bodies.

The headmistress, all bustling efficiency, greeted them with a handshake. Her name was Mrs Thompson. 'And you two must be Carrie and Joel,' she said with excruciating cheerfulness, pushing her shaggy head into their faces. 'We're all looking forward to having you here with us.'

Carrie gave the woman a cool stare. Joel edged away.

'And now that you're such a big boy starting school,' she laughed, giving Joel's grubby silky a disapproving look, 'you'll be able to leave that at home, won't you? Now then,' she continued to the adults, still using the same patronising tone, 'I thought we'd have a little look around the school, and then stop for a little chat in my office.'

Where I might give you a *little* slap, you irritating woman, thought Harriet as they fell in behind her. Mrs Thompson pushed open a door and suddenly turned on Carrie. 'This will be your classroom.'

They dutifully trooped in. Harriet didn't know exactly how old she'd been, but this had been her classroom at some stage. She could remember being told off for talking to Miles McKendrick. He now ran Novel Ways, the bookshop over in Maywood. She really should give him a ring. An old friend would go a long way to cheering her up.

When they were back out in the corridor, she felt a hand slip through hers. It was Joel, his eyes brimming with tearful misery. Her heart sank. What now?

'You OK, Joel?' It was a stupid question, but what else could she say? But then he did something that inexplicably made her throat constrict. He leaned against her, his head resting on her side, his face hidden. She knew he was trying hard not to cry. Leaving the others to go on without them, she prised him away from her and bent down to him. 'What is it?'

He raised his head. 'I want to go home,' he whispered, his lip trembling.

'Any particular reason why?'

His eyes flickered to the far end of the corridor where the head-mistress stood.

'You don't like Mrs Thompson?'

Joel shook his head. Tears spilled down his cheeks.

Harriet had to steel herself. She hated it when he cried. It made her want to cry too. 'That's OK,' she said quietly. 'Promise you won't tell anyone, but I don't like Mrs Thompson either. The good news is that you'll hardly see anything of her. She's a headmistress, which means she has to sit behind a big desk every day.'

He peered over the top of his silky. 'Really?'

'For sure. Come on, we'd better catch up with the others.'

She should have felt relieved that yet another crisis had been averted, but all she felt was exhaustion. Was that how it was going to be for the next thirteen and a half years long years until Joel was eighteen and legally no longer her responsibility? She'd get less for murder.

That evening, while her mother was upstairs supervising the children's bedtime, Harriet helped her father clear away the supper things. When they had finished, Bob said, 'Harriet, I need to talk to you.'

It sounded ominous and at once Harriet was worried that it was about her mother. Was Mum's ME getting worse? 'What is it, Dad?'

'Don't look so worried. I don't want you to take this the wrong way, and your mother and I certainly aren't criticising you, but—'

The 'but' hung in the air. 'But what?'

He took a fortifying breath. 'Your mother and I are worried. We think that you're a little too hard on the children.'

Harriet sat back in her chair. What the hell did that mean?

'It's your manner. You're so short with them. So brusque. We're worried that you're scaring them. Adding to their problems.'

Just then the telephone rang. With a look of relief, Bob went to answer it. Left on her own, Harriet stared at the table. The injustice of her father's remarks made her head throb, and claustrophobia crushed in on her. Within seconds, she was hurtling down the drive and across the road, heading for the footpath and the canal. As a teenager it was where she had always gone when she was annoyed or upset. Boiling over with fury, she could hardly breathe at the unfairness of it. After all the sacrifices she had made, her parents had the nerve to criticise her. How could they turn on her? Was it her fault that she wasn't the mater-nal type? Not for the first time she wondered why the hell her sister had thought she would be any good at raising her children. Perhaps her parents wished it had been her who'd died. She'd always known that Felicity had been the special daughter for her father. It had never bothered Harriet before, this preference, but it hurt now, knowing that her death would have had dramatically less impact.

She was so deep in thought that she didn't notice the man sitting on the bench until she was almost upon him. It was their new neighbour, drinking from a bottle of beer. He smiled at her. 'You look different without the cap,' he said.

A week had passed since he'd mistaken her for a boy late at night. She had been too upset at the time to stop and put him right; she'd learned that afternoon that completion had taken place on her flat. The finality of it had left her feeling trapped and isolated. She now had no reason to return to Oxford. And there hadn't been so much as an email or text message from Spencer.

Even if Harriet had had the nerve to blank their new neighbour and walk on by, she wouldn't have been able to. He was now on his feet, effectively blocking her path. 'Hi,' he said. 'I'm Will Hart. I don't suppose you'd like to join me in a drink'—he held up his bottle of beer as though indicating what sort of drink—'so that I can pick your brains about the neighbourhood?'

Small talk over a beer? No. With her parents' criticism still ringing in her ears, she needed to be alone.

'It would also give me the opportunity to apologise properly for the other night,' he added.

Imagining herself gulping down a cold beer, she wavered.

'I have wine if you'd prefer. Or maybe a soft drink.'

All resolve gone, she said, 'Thank you, a beer would be nice.'

Will snapped the lids off his last two bottles in the fridge and put them on a tray, and went back outside to the garden. He hoped she was feeling a bit less spiky now. When she'd appeared on the towpath she'd had a face like thunder. He wondered what she was so angry about. There was no mistaking her for a boy today. Her hair, which must have been tied up under her baseball cap that night last week, was shoulder-length and framed a small, pensive face with wide cheekbones.

'Here we go, then,' he said, pushing open the gate and joining her on the bench.

He guessed that she was in her late twenties and he'd put money on a smile from her being rarer than an eclipse. She was small and delicately built; her foot was tapping the ground and he suspected she was one of those high-energy people who are always on the move.

Watching her take a long, thirsty swig of her beer, he said, 'May I ask the name of the person with whom I'm drinking?'

Without looking at him, she said, 'Harriet. Harriet Swift.'

'Well, Harriet Swift, it's good to meet you. Am I right in thinking that you and your children live with your parents opposite me?'

She turned round sharply. Blue-grey eyes stared back at him with laser strength. 'They're not my children. They're my niece and nephew.'

'So where are their parents? Whooping it up on holiday somewhere hot and exotic?' From the way her eyes narrowed, he knew at once he'd said something wrong. The foot had stopped tapping.

When she answered him, her voice was eerily flat. 'They were killed in a car crash in April. The children's mother was my only sister.'

Horrified by his blunder, he said, 'I . . . I'm sorry. I had no idea.'

'Please don't say you're sorry. You don't know me and you didn't know Felicity. So no platitudes. However well-meant.'

All he could think to say was, 'How old are the children?'

'Nine and four and a half.'

'Nice ages. I remember them well. I have children,' he said, 'but older than that. They live with their mother in Maywood. What are their names, your nephew and niece?'

'Carrie and Joel.'

She reminded him of a hedgehog curling itself up into a ball when under attack. Her clipped answers told him she didn't want to discuss the matter any further; time to change tack to a safer line of questioning. 'I'm in the antique trade,' he said. 'What kind of work do you do?'

'I'm a computer programmer. And if you really want to know, I've given up a bloody good job to take care of Carrie and Joel, only to have my parents now accuse me of scaring the children. How's that for gratitude! I've given up my flat, my career, my boyfriend, for what?'

Was there nothing he could get right with this woman? He wasn't surprised she scared the kids; she scared the hell out of him.

For days afterwards, Harriet felt the embarrassment of losing her composure in front of a virtual stranger. She'd hastily mumbled some kind of goodbye and gone back home. Naturally, her parents told her she'd overreacted. 'All you need to do is be more patient with the children,' her mother had said. 'Particularly with Joel. Miss Fryer says he misses the—'

'Oh, so now you're throwing Miss Fryer at me?' she'd retaliated. 'As if it isn't obvious what the children miss!'

Miss Fryer was the children's counsellor. For the last two months, every week Harriet had driven the children to her office, where they were encouraged to share their feelings with a woman they hardly knew.

'For goodness' sake, just try to be a little less stern with them,' her father had joined in, his voice sharper than she was used to hearing. 'We know it's not easy for you, Harriet. And we do appreciate all that you're doing, but snapping at Carrie for leaving her socks on the sofa won't help.'

Then why are you snapping at me? she'd thought indignantly.

That had been three days ago, and since then Harriet had tried hard to do what her parents had suggested. But it wasn't easy. If she called up the stairs, as she was about to, to tell them to get a move on, would that be tantamount to child abuse? 'Come on, you two, I haven't got all day!'

Seconds later, the sound of the toilet flushing could be heard, followed by scuffling footsteps across the landing. Carrie led the way with Joel close behind. 'Did you wash your hands?' Harriet asked them.

Joel held his out for inspection. 'We used Grandma's squirty soap.'

'Yes, I can smell it from here. Is there any left? Or have you splattered it—' She stopped herself short, remembering she was supposed to be St Harriet, the Patron Saint of the Meek and bloody Mild. 'Mm . . . well done, you two,' she added. 'Right then, let's say goodbye to Grandma and get going. We've got a lot to do.' In her jeans pocket was a lengthy list of items they needed for the start of term.

Harriet's mother was in the sitting room with Dora. The coffee table and the floor were covered with items of school uniform waiting to have name tags sewn onto them.

'We're off now, Mum. You're sure there's nothing we can get you?'

Eileen shook her head. 'I can't think of anything, darling. How about you, Dora?'

'No, but I have something here for the children. Here you are.' She gave them each a couple of pound coins.

'You needn't have done that, Dora,' Eileen said when the front door had been shut and the house was quiet.

'I know, but I wanted to. They're such dear little children. Now that we're alone, I can tell you all about last night.'

Eileen looked up from her sewing. 'Goodness, Dora, what have you been up to now?'

'Put the kettle on and I'll tell you. No, second thoughts, I'll make us some tea while you carry on here. I'm hopeless at sewing.'

'You haven't had enough practice, that's your trouble.'

Dora had never had children and Eileen privately thought this was one of her friend's big regrets in life. Her first husband had left her for his secretary after eleven years of marriage and then her second husband had died six years ago. He'd been the love of Dora's life but she had picked herself up and bulldozed her way through her grief.

In her twenties, Dora had been a model, and it had given her a certain financial independence, but for all that, at the age of sixty-two, Dora couldn't imagine life without a man in it. She always believed that her Prince Charming was just round the corner. 'What I need,' she often told Eileen, 'is someone steady like Bob.'

Of course, Dora had no idea about Bob's affairs all those years ago and Eileen would never dream of telling her; that would be too disloyal. She reached for another name tag and thought of Bob. With each day that passed he was becoming more cool and distant. He just didn't seem able to move on. It was as if Felicity had died yesterday, not nearly five months ago. There were times when Eileen believed that Bob resented her because she was coping better than he was. But she was only coping because she knew she had to.

'Tea's up,' announced Dora. Rousing herself, Eileen made room on the table for the tray. Dora poured, and once she was settled, knees and ankles together, she said, 'I've joined The Soirée Club.'

'Heavens, what's that? It sounds like something Hyacinth Bucket would join. Do you have to give smart candlelit dinners?'

Dora laughed. 'As good as. Every other week there's a dinner party held in the house of one of the club's members—the gentlemen tend to use caterers—and you simply sign up for the one you want to go to.'

'It sounds expensive.'

Dora stirred her tea. 'What cost the price of a good man?'

What cost indeed, thought Eileen.

Annoyed that she couldn't get everything they needed in Kings Melford, Harriet drove on to Maywood. The woman in the shoe shop had all but laughed in her face when she'd asked if they had any plimsolls. 'We sold out of them weeks ago,' she'd said.

But Fuller's in Maywood still had some stock left. Twenty minutes later they emerged with the children each carrying a plastic bag. Relieved that she could cross the last item off her list, Harriet said, 'Let's have a drink now, shall we?' She thought they'd earned it. She took the children into Novel Ways where she could have not only a caffè latte but also a rare, self-indulgent browse among the bookshelves afterwards.

They queued for their drinks, then found themselves a table. They'd only been there a minute or two when a voice said, 'Hello, Harriet.'

It was Miles, looking his usual hurried self. He was the only person Harriet had ever known who walked as fast as she did. 'Hello, Miles,' she said warmly. 'You look busy.'

He rolled his eyes. 'Tell me about it.' Then more awkwardly: 'I've been meaning to ring you for ages. Mum and Dad told me you were back on a permanent basis now. Is that true?'

'It was the only answer.'

His gaze flickered over the children and Harriet was prompted to say something to bring them into the conversation. 'You remember Miles, don't you? His parents live in Maple Drive.'

Carrie looked thoughtful. 'Is this your bookshop?' she said. 'Did Mum bring us here?'

'I don't know,' Miles said carefully. 'Can you remember?'

Carrie shrugged. 'Maybe it was another bookshop.'

This was as close as Carrie had got to openly discussing her mother, and Harriet didn't know whether she ought to pursue the matter. But the moment was lost when Joel said, 'I need the loo.' They hurriedly finished their drinks and after the obligatory trip to the loos, Miles appeared again.

'Harriet, I don't suppose—' he broke off and swallowed nervously. 'Look, I just wondered if you'd like to go for a drink. That's if you're not too tied up with the children.'

She smiled. 'You mean a grown-up drink that doesn't include straws and endless trips to the toilet? You're on.'

While Eileen was busy with Dora, and Harriet was out shopping with the children, Bob was acting on an impulse. He stared down at the abandoned wire-haired fox terrier he had chosen from the dog refuge and saw the means by which he would be able to escape. Walking a dog twice a day would give him the ideal excuse to be out of the house. Latterly, he'd started to feel a stranger there. More than that, a stranger in his own life. He loved the children, yet the strain of having them under his feet every single minute of the day was making him feel claustrophobic. He longed for the old days, when he could hand them back. But, of course, what he really longed for was his daughter to be returned to him. As a parent you're not supposed to have a favourite among your children, but Felicity had always been special. He had never felt so close to Eileen as he had when she'd first handed Felicity to him to hold. He didn't so much as look at another woman from that moment on. The two affairs he'd had still haunted him. He wasn't proud of it; he didn't know what he'd do if Eileen ever found out. But it was only when he'd been with those other women that the pain of what he and Eileen were going through each time they lost yet another baby had lessened. On both occasions, the affairs had ended because deep down he loved his wife and didn't want to hurt her.

Eileen seemed to be coping far better than he was. It was irrational, but her one-step-at-a-time attitude annoyed him, as though her steady recovery somehow trivialised his pain, or worse, trivialised Felicity's death. She didn't seem to need to make sense of what had happened. Perhaps she had the right idea, because as far as he could see, it was a hopeless task. Maybe he should start sleeping his troubles away like her. He instantly felt guilty for this thought. It wasn't Eileen's fault that she needed to rest in the afternoon.

Bob walked back to the car with the dog and drove home. He got out slowly and, keeping the dog on the lead, went round to the back of the house, bracing himself for Eileen's reaction.

SEPTEMBER

*'Each player must accept the cards
life deals him or her.*

*But once they are in hand,
he or she alone must decide
how to play the cards
in order to win the game.'*

VOLTAIRE

IT WAS THE START of the autumn term, and the school was thronging with activity. Toby had to be left behind in the car while Harriet and the children walked across the playground, because it was against the rules to bring him into school, much to Joel's disappointment.

Coming home out of the blue with a dog was the best thing her father could have done for cheering up the children. Carrie had thought of the name Toby and they had all agreed that it suited the dog perfectly.

They were greeted in the noisy corridor by a tall, elegant woman who claimed to be Carrie's teacher, Mrs Kennedy. She swept Carrie away with her, pointing out Joel's classroom further down the corridor. Harriet glanced down at him. His eyes were pools of tear-filled wretchedness. She bent down to him and with his head resting against her forehead, he flung his arms round her neck. He wasn't crying, but somehow that made it worse. She knew that when he was silent he was most upset. All she could think to do was put her own arms round him. It was then, with a shock of tenderness, as she felt the trembling within his small body, that she realised this was the first time she could recall ever really hugging either of the children.

'Hello there. I'm Miss Rawlinson and you must be Joel Knight. I was wondering what had happened to you.'

Disentangling herself from Joel's vice-like grip, Harriet stood up to greet her nephew's teacher. 'I'm afraid he's a little nervous,' she explained.

'Why don't you come and meet all your new friends?' Miss Rawlinson asked. 'Everyone's waiting to meet you.'

His head moved from side to side.

'Don't you want to make lots of new friends?'

Another shake of his head.

'I think that's a no,' Harriet said. 'Perhaps we ought to give him a break and try again tomorrow?' She couldn't believe what she'd just said, but it seemed the simplest and kindest thing to do.

But the teacher shook her head. 'It would be a terrible mistake to give in to him,' she said. Then lowering her voice to a confidential murmur, she added, 'It's usually better if the mother just walks away.'

Her voice equally low, Harriet said, 'It's usually better if the mother isn't dead. My name's Miss Swift; I'm his aunt and legal guardian and I'd appreciate a little more thought on your part towards my nephew. Maybe you should acquaint yourself with his background.'

The woman looked flustered. Down on Joel's level once more, Harriet looked into his face. 'Joel,' she whispered, 'you've got to help me out here. I want you to be really brave and give today your best shot. I'll be back later this afternoon, and . . . and I promise I'll bring Toby with me. I'll even have your silky waiting for you in the car.' She leaned back. 'Do we have a deal?'

After a lengthy pause, he nodded. But only just.

'OK.' She straightened up again and walked away, not trusting herself to look back.

It was first break and Carrie searched the playground for Joel. She found him in the sandpit. When he saw her he ran to her. 'Is it time to go home now?' he asked. 'Is Harriet here?'

Holding his hand, Carrie walked him across the field. When no one could hear them, she said, 'Joel, we haven't had lunch yet. Look at your watch.' Then: 'You haven't cried this morning, have you?'

He shook his head solemnly. 'You said I wasn't to do that.'

'Good boy. And no thumb-sucking?'

He looked less sure. 'Um . . . I might have.'

'Joel, I told you, you mustn't do it. You'll get called names.'

'Is he your brother?'

Carrie spun round. A group of girls from her class had appeared from nowhere and were staring at her and Joel. 'Yes,' she said.

'He looks really sweet.' They moved in closer. One of them said, 'Is it true your mum and dad are dead?'

Carrie reached for Joel's hand.

'And is it true they were killed in a car crash and had their heads chopped off?'

Joel gasped. Carrie suddenly wanted to pick him up and run, but she knew she mustn't. She had to be strong. 'Yes,' she said. 'It is true. And do you want to know something else?' They nodded. 'Their heads rolled out of the car and onto the road. There was blood everywhere. Puddles of it. Great big enormous puddles of blood.'

It was lunchtime and Joel was doing his best to do everything Carrie had told him. Not to cry. Not to suck his thumb. But he couldn't help himself. He felt sick and he badly needed the loo, and all he could think of was Mummy's and Daddy's heads rolling in the road. Did the police find their heads or were they still somewhere in the bushes?

He shifted in his seat but couldn't hold on any longer and suddenly he felt the wet warmth spreading down his legs. He began to cry. Now Carrie would be cross. And Harriet too. Carrie had told him they mustn't make Harriet angry because they'd end up in an orphanage. But surely Harriet wouldn't do that to them. Harriet was nice.

Harriet was in a good mood. The morning's post had brought her a party invitation from Erin. The prospect of going down to Oxford shone like a beacon in the wasteland of Harriet's pitiful social life. She went upstairs to work on her CV. Now that she had some free time, she could get down to the business of landing a job. The plan was that her parents would do the afternoon school run (she would drop the children off early in the morning before going to work) and look after the children if either of them were ill. It seemed a flawless plan, and one that would, before long, give her the wherewithal to buy a house of her own.

She switched on her laptop. 'Here goes,' she said out loud.

'I'm sorry to keep you waiting.'

Harriet whipped round to face Miss Rawlinson. Without preamble, she said, 'Why didn't you ring to say there was a problem with Joel?'

She looked confused. 'I'm not aware of there having been a problem.'

'If Joel wet himself it sounds to me like there was a problem.'

'But they nearly all do that at this age. It's nerves.'

'Really? Well, the least you could have done was change his trousers for him. Have you any idea how humiliated he must have felt?'

'Unfortunately there wasn't much we could do. It's the start of term so there weren't any spare trousers. The lost-property box is empty, you see. Perhaps—' She hesitated. 'Perhaps it might be useful if you could send him in with a spare pair of his own trousers from now on. Just in case.'

I might even send him in with a spare teacher who can look after him properly, fumed Harriet as she went outside to the children. 'Come on, you two, let's get out of here.'

Nobody spoke until they were sitting in the car. Joel said, 'I'm sorry, Harriet. It just came out. I . . . I couldn't stop it.'

She looked at him in the rearview mirror. Oh, hell, that face.

'Please don't be cross with him,' Carrie said. 'It was an accident.'

Harriet yanked on the handbrake. She turned round to face them both. 'Whoa there! Who said anything about me being angry with Joel?'

Carrie said, 'You looked cross when you were talking to Joel's teacher.'

'That's because I have a tendency to get cross when I'm talking to a numpty-head who doesn't know her arse from her elbow.'

Carrie's eyes widened. 'You're not allowed to say bad words in front of us.'

'I'll say what the hell I like in front of you. Watch out, because here I go again. *Arse!*'

Carrie began to laugh. Harriet laughed too. But looking in the rearview mirror again, she noticed Joel wasn't joining in.

Even Eileen failed to get Joel to open up, and all during tea he just sat playing with his food. He was silent too during bedtime when Harriet read to them, and despite hovering by his bed for longer than usual, he still said nothing about his day at school.

Accepting there was nothing else she could do, she got ready to go out. She was meeting Miles at his parents' house before going for a drink.

'I just wanted to say how desperately sorry I was that I was too ill to come to Felicity's funeral,' Freda McKendrick said.

Harriet played along. She'd heard it all before; the list of mystery illnesses that had kept Freda away from every social engagement beyond her own doorstep was endless. 'These things happen,' she said lightly.

'And how are you all coping? Dear me, it seems like yesterday when you four children used to play together. Miles, dear, pass me that photograph of Dominic. It must be quite a while since Harriet last saw your brother. Here. Doesn't he look handsome?'

Freda's overly refined but vague manner had Harriet wanting to shake her. And that husband of hers wasn't much better. Harvey McKendrick had always given Harriet the creeps: he was so upright and formal.

Harriet gave the photograph a cursory glance. It was of Dominic,

Dr Dominic McKendrick, and he was dressed up to the nines in his Cambridge finery; black gown and fancy fur trim. He did look handsome. But then he always had. She muttered a suitable response and said, 'Well, Miles, shall we see what delights Kings Melford has to offer?'

She wanted to get out of the suffocating atmosphere. She had always been infuriated by the blatant favouritism that had gone on in the McKendrick household. Since for ever, Dominic had been considered the brightest son, the one destined for a stellar future. At the age of eleven he was sent away to boarding school where, apparently, his academic ability would be better nurtured. This might have left him excluded when he came home for the holidays, but there was no force on this earth that could exclude Dominic McKendrick. From an early age he'd believed the world revolved around him. The oldest within their gang of four—he was a year older than Felicity—he'd been their self-appointed leader. It had been Dominic who'd got them all drunk for the first time, and playing strip poker. Harriet's face coloured at the memory. She wondered if Miles remembered that night, too.

'Seeing as it's such a nice evening, I thought we'd go to The Navigation,' he said. 'That OK with you?'

The pub was heaving, and after queuing for their drinks, they spied a free table in the garden overlooking the canal. Further along, the towpath was busy with people mooring up for the night.

'Ever thought you'd like to have a boat and just cruise away?' she asked him. He looked back at her.

'We all think that at some time or other, don't we?'

'So why don't we do it? People dream of escaping, but rarely do.'

'The vast majority of people aren't brave enough. And, of course, there are those who are too tied down to do it.'

Harriet took a moment to observe him. He'd always been the quieter and more thoughtful of the McKendrick boys. He had a sensitive, intelligent face with pale blue eyes. In all the years she had known him they had never argued and she had never stopped respecting the way he'd handled living in the shadow of such a difficult and dynamic brother. Dominic had to be the ultimate pain when it came to older brothers. As a highly regarded English don with a couple of slim books of poetry to his name it wouldn't occur to him that Miles was his equal. Or that anyone else was, for that matter. Thinking about what Miles had just said, she asked him, 'So do you feel tied down?'

Again he looked back at her. 'Yes.' The starkness with which he uttered that one word made her sit up.

'But why?' she pressed. 'You're not married and have no real commitments. You could sell the bookshop and—'

'I have a mother who's ill, Harriet,' he interrupted.

'Your father can take care of her. She's not your responsibility.'

'You think I should just walk away? Like Dominic has?'

'It's an option.'

He looked her straight in the eye. 'Presumably that's the same option you could take. You could leave your parents to look after Felicity's kids.' For a moment she didn't know what to say. No one had ever suggested she had a choice. That she could turn her back on her family . . . could forget her promise to Felicity.

'I could walk away if I wanted to,' she admitted.

'You could, but you're missing the point. You won't walk because, like me, you have an innate sense of duty, a strong sense of right and wrong. It's called loyalty and it means we play with the cards we're dealt. We do the best job we can.'

She sat back in her chair and felt a rush of affection towards her old friend. 'You have no idea how refreshing it is to talk to someone who understands,' she said at length.

'I understand all too well. And I have nothing but admiration for you.'

Harriet took a long swallow of her lager. 'People think that because I loved Felicity,' she said quietly, 'it must follow that I'm crazy about her children. But I'm not. I can't help it, but that's the truth. Children have never interested me. Does that sound awful to you?'

'I have even less experience with kids than you, but my guess is the important thing is that they know they can rely on you. They need stability and I reckon you'd be better than most at providing that.'

She suddenly smiled. 'You know what? I think we should do this again. You're good for me. To be honest, I'd been feeling guilty that I didn't seem able to—' She broke off, distracted by the sight of a tall, slim man on the other side of the beer garden: Will Hart. He was with an attractive blonde girl who laughed when he kissed her on the top of her head. She had to be about half his age. Typical, Harriet thought with disgust.

'Someone you know?' asked Miles, following her gaze.

She explained who it was. 'Do you know him?'

'I know *of* him. His ex-wife's an auctioneer in Maywood; she runs Stone's. He used to be a hotshot lawyer, had some kind of breakdown, then got into the antique trade. He has a business here in Kings Melford.'

'He doesn't look the sort to have a breakdown. He looks too . . .' She sought to find the right words. 'He looks too laid-back and untroubled. How do you know so much about everyone?'

'I own a bookshop where people congregate to gossip over coffee and occasionally buy a book. Have you started looking for a job yet?'

'I spent today putting the finishing touches to my CV and now it's polished up, I'm going to email it out to as many agencies as I can.'

'You wouldn't consider a change of direction, then?'

'No chance. I love the geeky world of computer programming.'

He smiled. 'Felicity used to be so proud of you, you know. She once told me that she wished she had half your brains.'

Harriet frowned. 'When did she say that?'

'Earlier in the year when she was staying with your parents.'

'Felicity was far smarter than me,' Harriet said. 'She spoke three different languages, for heaven's sake. She was always in demand to do translation work. I don't know how she did it with the children around.'

'She must have been very organised. Like you, I expect.' After a pause, he said, 'Does it upset you to talk about Felicity?'

'No. Funnily enough, it feels good. Like she's still with us. That I could look over my shoulder and there she'd be, her old smiling self.'

He nodded and looked thoughtful, staring off into the distance. 'I know what you mean. I still can't quite believe she's gone . . . Dead. It's so final.' He swallowed and slowly turned his pale blue eyes back to Harriet. She was surprised to see the depth of sadness within them. 'I don't think I shall ever forget that day at the funeral,' he said. 'You handled it so well.'

'I was on autopilot. In too much shock to cry. But I do remember how glad I was to see you there.' She also remembered how upset he was, and that he made no attempt to hide his feelings. She liked his uncomplicated honesty. He was the complete opposite of his brother, who was the most devious person she knew. Felicity used to say that Harriet judged Dominic too harshly, that she expected too much of him. 'He can't help being the man he is,' Felicity said. 'We're all the sum of our experiences.'

In that case, Dominic must have had some pretty awful experiences, because he always behaved abominably.

'Another lager?' Miles asked.

'Why not?' She watched him go back inside the pub. It felt good spending the evening with someone who knew her so well.

It had been a successful day. It was Will's birthday and he was going home after an enjoyable afternoon spent at one of his favourite salerooms. To top it off, he was spending the evening with Gemma and Suzie. He'd suggested they eat out, but Suzie had said a meal in would be better. 'If you cook for us, I'll bake you a cake,' she'd said.

Will wasn't a great cook, but having lived on his own for as long as he had, he considered himself competent. Tonight he was knocking a chicken korma into shape. It was only at Suzie's insistence that he was celebrating his birthday. Forty-six, who'd have thought it? He'd been all for letting it slip by unnoticed, but Suzie had put her foot down.

'Just get in the car, Gemma! Honestly, sometimes I could kill you.'

Gemma banged the door shut. 'What's with the grumpy sister act?'

'I'm not grumpy,' snapped Suzie.

She snorted. 'Not much.' Gemma sank back into her seat. She dismissed her sister from her mind and thought of the letter she'd received that morning from Marcel. He'd written to say that he wanted to come and see her. Could he stay? The very idea of him under the same roof as Mum and Steve made her want to leave the country. Gemma didn't object to a bit of boat-rocking, but she was smart enough to know that a capsize was counterproductive.

Suzie gripped the steering wheel, trying to keep calm. It wasn't easy. She was about to tell her father something no father wants to hear. Usually daughters turned to their mothers when faced with a crisis, but Suzie had always turned to Dad when there was something she couldn't resolve on her own. She supposed it stemmed from those days when he'd chucked in being a lawyer and was at home with her and Gemma. Oh God, how could she have been so stupid? How could she have slept with a friend's boyfriend and ended up pregnant?

It was warm enough to eat in the garden so they'd carried the only table Will possessed—the kitchen table—outside. In the gathering darkness, listening to Gemma telling him and Suzie about something that had happened at school that day, Will thought of the birthday present they'd clubbed together to buy him: a pair of tickets to see Jools Holland at the Apollo in Manchester. Not exactly his first choice, but he appreciated it all the same.

Next thing he knew, Gemma was on her feet. 'Come on, Suzie,' she was saying, 'time to bring on Dad's cake.'

Their father groaned when he saw it. 'That looks horribly like a forest fire of candles,' he said.

'Go on,' urged Gemma, 'blow them out. Don't forget to make a wish!'

Suzie watched her father take a deep breath. Get it over and done with, she told herself. Just as he was about to lean forward, she said, 'Dad, I'm pregnant.'

Will's breath came out in one long exhalation and all but two of the candles spluttered and died.

It was Gemma who spoke first. 'Bloody hell!'

Very slowly, Will wetted his thumb and middle finger and snuffed out the two remaining candles. He was giving himself time to think.

'I'm sorry, Dad. Sorry for spoiling your birthday. But I had to tell you.'

'Of course you did.' He swallowed, tried to keep the shock and disappointment from his face. 'Er . . . Gemma, I wonder if you'd give us a moment? Maybe some coffee would be a good idea.'

When they were alone, Suzie said, 'Are you very cross with me?'

He shook his head. 'I don't know what to think. I'm too stunned. I'd never have thought . . . I mean, you've always been . . .' He broke off, knowing how absurd he was about to sound.

'You were going to say sensible, weren't you?'

He nodded. 'Let's go down to the end of the garden. It'll be easier to think in the quiet.'

Suzie sat on the bench overlooking the slick, unmoving surface of the canal; he joined her. 'Who's the father?' he asked.

'The father has nothing to do with it.'

Will raised an eyebrow. 'I think you'll find he does.'

'It's not straightforward. He's the boyfriend of a friend of mine at uni.'

Anger stirred inside Will. 'What kind of two-timing bastard is he?'

'You could ask the same of me. What kind of friend was I?'

'I'm sorry,' he said. 'So . . . how many weeks are you?'

'Four months. And before you ask, I hadn't sussed I was pregnant because I'm not that regular. I never have been. It was a mistake. A stupid, drunken mistake—'

Suddenly squeamish, Will interrupted her. 'It's OK, you don't have to give me the details. But are you sure you shouldn't be having this discussion with him?'

'No. It should never have happened between us. One bad decision on both our parts shouldn't mean his life is ruined.' She hung her head.

He put his arm round her. 'What does your mother say about it?'

'I haven't told her. I wanted to talk to you first. I'll tell her when I know what I'm going to do.'

'You mean whether you'll keep the baby or have a termination? Or even have it, then give it up for adoption?'

Suzie nodded and turned away. But not before Will saw her eyes fill. His heart went out to her. He drew her close. 'It'll be OK. Whatever you decide to do, I'll be there for you. You're not to worry.'

After a run of bad days, Eileen was having a good one. The lethargy that had swamped her this last week had lifted. Carrie and Joel were now into their second week at school and the workload was considerably lighter. However, now there was Carrie's homework to supervise and not for the first time since their lives had been turned upside-down, Eileen felt out of her depth. Thank goodness Joel only had reading homework to do each evening. That much she could manage. But Joel troubled Eileen. He was having nightmares. Night after night they were woken by his piercing screams. Try as they might, they couldn't get him to say what he was dreaming of. Eileen regretted now that the children's sessions with the grief counsellor had recently come to an end. Eileen listened to Harriet moving about upstairs. She was packing for her weekend away. Guiltily, Eileen wished she was going with her.

Less than five miles from home and Harriet could feel an explosion of relief rushing through her body. Freedom. What bliss. But then she went and spoilt it by recalling the look on Carrie's and Joel's faces when she'd told them that a friend had invited her to stay for a couple of days.

'How will we get to school?' Carrie had demanded.

'You won't be going to school. I'm away over the weekend.'

'But you can't go! You have to stay here with us! I don't want you to go.' This had been from Joel, and the squealed vehemence of his words had taken Harriet aback. They'd been upstairs sitting on the floor in Carrie's bedroom, reading the latest Harry Potter before bedtime.

'I'll only be gone two days,' she'd explained patiently.

'But you will come back?' Everything Joel said was peppered with buts.

'Don't be silly, Joel,' Carrie had said, 'of course she'll come back.'

While her niece's steely gaze elicited a suitably reassuring reply—'I'll be back before you've even missed me'—Harriet had felt a twinge of irritation that her movements were being monitored so thoroughly. It was like being a teenager again and being grilled by Mum and Dad.

Enough! No more thoughts about Carrie and Joel. Or Mum and Dad. She was off the hook. She swooped on towards Oxford.

Harriet suspected she was drunk, but not quite as drunk as the bleary-eyed bore she was talking to. With all the interrupted nights she'd had lately because of Joel's nightmares, if she spent another second in this man's company she'd nod off, no trouble. She decided simply to walk away. He probably wouldn't notice she'd gone.

She went to look for Erin. She knew Erin was embarrassed that only a handful of Harriet's friends had replied to the invitations and only two had bothered to turn up—Gary and Paula who used to live in the house next door. Holidays were blamed, which only served to remind Harriet of the gap that now existed between her and her friends. They could holiday out of term-time, whereas she was doomed for the rest of eternity to spend her precious time off with other young families in damp seaside cottages building sandcastles and pretending she was having a ball. Harriet suspected the real reason for her so-called friends not showing up was that she was still infectious, incubating a double whammy of those highly contagious germs of the recently bereaved and the out-of-work loser. Well, to hell with them!

Erin was otherwise engaged when Harriet found her, pressed against the combi boiler in the kitchen by a man who didn't look like a heating engineer. Back in the crowded sitting room, Harriet pushed through the noisy mob to help herself to another drink. She found the ideal tipple tucked in behind the vodka and Bacardi Breezers. A bottle of Baileys.

'Trust me; you don't want to touch that.'

Harriet swivelled round. Observing her was a man who looked like he was straight off the cover of *GQ*. 'Wouldn't you prefer a proper drink?' He produced a bottle of wine from somewhere about his person and began filling a pair of glasses that he'd also conjured up. 'My name's Titus by the way, as in—'

'The hero of Mervyn Peake's *Gormenghast*?' she interrupted him. She was reminded of Dominic—it had been one of his favourite books.

He bowed. 'Correct.'

'With a name like that I could almost feel sorry for you. I'm Harriet, by the way. I used to live in the flat downstairs.'

His glass hovered midway to his mouth. 'So you're the one whose sister snuffed—I mean died. Erin told me about it. What are you doing now?'

'I'm living in Cheshire looking after my sister's children.'

'That's rotten luck. And living in the North, too. When do you come back?'

She stiffened. How dare this patronising man denigrate what she was now doing. 'Children aren't like dogs,' she said sharply. 'You can't abandon them on the roadside like a bag of unwanted puppies.'

'Yeah, but they're not even yours.' He shook his head wearily. 'God, your life is so over. Because let's face it, when you're done with those kids, there'll be the ageing parents to wash and feed.'

'You know what,' she said, 'you're nothing but a shallow, gobby bloke who's just pushed me into mental meltdown.' She walked away, and not trusting herself to speak to anyone, she kept on walking until she was standing in Erin's tiny spare bedroom, where she was spending the night. She noticed the remains of a coke-fest on the bedside table and wondered what she was doing here. This was no longer her world. She felt like a spinster aunt who'd accidentally gate-crashed a students' party.

Harriet groaned and sank down onto the floor. After all the excitement of getting away, she knew she'd rather be back in Maple Drive than here. She'd prefer to be sitting on the bedroom floor reading to Carrie and Joel—Carrie absently winding a lock of hair round a finger and Joel pressing against her, his small body fresh from the bath.

A trilling sound came from her mobile. It was ten past one—who the hell was calling her at this time of night?

At the sound of her father's voice, she froze. It was too reminiscent of the night he'd called to say Felicity was dead. What had happened now?

'Thank goodness you're there, Harriet. We're at our wits' end. If he carries on like this we'll have to call a doctor out. He's cried so much he's made himself sick. Your mother's exhausted and—'

'Dad, slow down!' Harriet's head was spinning. 'Tell me what's happened. And take it slowly.' Her heart was hammering painfully.

'It's Joel,' her father said. 'Well, it's Carrie too. She started it.'

'You're still not making any sense, Dad.'

'We've discovered what's been causing Joel's nightmares. We had a phone call from the headmistress this afternoon; apparently Carrie's been telling everyone at school that her parents' heads were sliced off in the accident, that the police never found them and . . . because of that, Felicity and Jeff, dripping in blood, are forced to wander the streets at night searching for them. No wonder Joel's been so terrified.'

A chill ran down Harriet's spine. 'Carrie said all that? But why?'

'I've no idea, but she's said a lot worse. Stuff about her being able to make her parents haunt anyone she doesn't like. She's scared some of the children so badly that their parents have complained to the school.'

'To hell with them. It's Joel I'm concerned about. Do you think he'll talk to me?'

'That's why I've called. He keeps asking for you. Perhaps if you speak to him, he might calm down and go back to bed.'

Waiting for her father to put Joel on the line, Harriet thought of the nights she'd found her nephew drenched in sweat, his eyes squeezed shut, and the duvet wrapped tightly around his body as though it would protect him. Knowing what they knew now, she could understand his terror. Her chest tightened and she coughed, instinctively trying to force oxygen into lungs that were threatening to close down. She fumbled for her inhaler at the bottom of her bag.

'Harriet, are you still there?'

'Yes, Dad,' she wheezed. 'Put him on. Joel, can you hear me? It's me, Harriet.' In the ensuing silence, she put her inhaler to her mouth, pressed down on the canister and breathed in sharply.

'Wassat noise?' a small, husky voice asked.

Progress, thought Harriet. 'It's my asthma inhaler, Joel.'

She heard a sob catch in his throat. 'Are you . . . ill?'

'No, of course not. I'm as fit as a fiddle. How about you? I hear you've had another bad dream.'

Silence again. Then: 'Are you coming back?' His voice was a dried-up raspy whisper. He'd probably cried his throat raw.

'On Sunday. Don't you remember we discussed all that?'

'But I want you here. Why can't you come home?' He started to cry again.

'Oh, Joel, it's not as easy as that.' How could she explain that she was well over the limit? 'Listen to me, Joel,' she said as firmly as her breath would allow her. 'I know what's been causing the nightmares you've been having. But none of it's true. All that stuff Carrie's been saying—she was making it up.'

'But why would she say those things if they weren't true?'

'I haven't a clue.' She took another puff of her inhaler. Her heart was racing now, but she could feel her lungs expanding.

'Is that your inhaler again? You're not going to die, are you?'

His question shook her. 'Joel, now listen very hard. I've always told you the truth, and I'm not about to start lying to you now. I'm not dying, and your parents didn't die the way Carrie said they did. Ghosts don't exist and you have nothing to be frightened of. Unlike your sister who's going to get a good talking-to from me when I get home.'

After a lengthy pause, he said, 'Harriet? Please come home. I want you to come back. I don't like it when you're not here.'

Not for a long time had Harriet allowed anyone to manipulate her, but this boy could do it every time. Stupid thing was, she realised she didn't care; her planned day of watching *Sex and the City* DVDs with Erin had lost its appeal anyway. 'I'll be home some time after breakfast,' she said. 'How does that sound?'

As if by magic, he cheered up instantly. 'Will you take me to the bookshop? The one where your friend works?'

'I will.' Then seizing her opportunity, she added, 'But you have to promise me you'll go to bed right now. This very minute.'

Harriet was on the road by seven. Erin surfaced briefly, and said she completely understood that Harriet had to get home. 'No worries,' she said, 'we'll get together again soon.' But Harriet knew it wasn't ever going to happen. Those days had gone.

It was while she was tearing up the M6 that another truth hit her. When it came to the children's sense of security, it appeared that the buck stopped with her. It had been her, last night, that Joel had wanted. It felt oddly reassuring, as if she was finally getting something right.

But what on earth had been going through Carrie's head to make her say such ghoulish things? Harriet knew from experience that most children—usually rather older than Carrie—go through a phase of being fascinated by death. Certainly when she and Felicity had been teenagers it was a topic that had cropped up with morbid regularity, and invariably with Dominic and Miles. Harriet could remember one conversation in particular. It had taken place during late summer, the year Dominic had been offered a place at Cambridge. They'd been lying on the flattened grass in the corner of a field; Felicity had said that she wanted her body to be donated to medical science and that what was left had to be cremated. 'I don't want worms wriggling in and out of my eye sockets and centipedes crawling up my nose,' she'd explained. Rolling onto his side and running his hand over Felicity's stomach then letting it linger on her breasts, Dominic had said, 'I've got a better idea: why don't you donate your body to me to research.' It had always amazed Harriet that Felicity could let Dominic touch her like that. It upset her because she knew he was only doing it to annoy his brother—Miles had always had a bit of a crush on Felicity.

'What's wrong with what we do?' Felicity said to Harriet when she tackled her about it one day. 'Dominic knows I like it when he touches me. It doesn't mean anything.'

'But it drives Miles mad, and that's the real reason Dominic does it.'

'Miles knows better than to be upset by anything his brother does.'

It wasn't often that Harriet questioned her sister's judgment, but in that instance she did. Privately, she thought Miles minded a lot of things, especially the way Dominic would treat people. On one memorable outing to a club in Manchester, when Dominic was home from Cambridge for Easter, he had really excelled himself. With his black hair swept back from his broad forehead, his piercingly blue eyes and his easy nonchalance, he had an aura of glamour that attracted attention wherever he went. On that particular night, after several drinks he suddenly announced that he was going to make someone's night. 'And it's that girl there,' he said, indicating possibly the ugliest girl in the club. To their surprise, he sauntered over to where she was standing and started chatting to her.

'What the hell's he up to now?' muttered Miles. Minutes passed, then Dominic joined them where they'd been queuing for a drink. Intrigued, they then watched the girl come towards him. She tapped Dominic on the shoulder. 'Are you ready for that dance now?' she said.

Dominic swung round and said, 'Good God, you didn't think I was serious, did you? That I'd willingly dance with a fat cow like you?'

It was like watching a balloon being popped. The girl burst into tears and fled. It was one of the cruellest things Harriet had ever witnessed. Miles was so furious with Dominic that he dragged him outside, pushed him up against a wall and punched him hard. For days afterwards,

Harriet and Felicity refused to speak to Dominic. In the end, in a typically over-the-top gesture, he stood beneath their bedroom windows late one night and read out a letter of apology. That was Dominic all over. A clever, self-obsessed man who ruthlessly trampled others underfoot for his own pleasure and saw it as his right to be forgiven, no matter what the offence.

In danger of dozing off at the wheel—she'd only had three hours' sleep—Harriet stopped at Stafford Services. She bought a cup of coffee and a slice of toast. Half an hour later, feeling suitably revived, she went back out to the car park. Her car window had been smashed and the alarm was screeching. Her laptop had been stolen.

Carrie knew she was in big trouble. She just hoped that when Harriet started shouting at her she'd remember to tilt her head back and stare at the ceiling so that it was impossible for any tears to spill out. She'd learned to do this (and to blink a lot) when Mummy and Daddy had died and everyone kept asking if she was OK.

It felt like for ever since they'd died. Sometimes she had trouble remembering what they looked like. Part of her thought it might be easier to forget them, but then she'd suddenly think of something nice, like her birthday, when she'd unwrapped their presents and found the best one of all: Poppy. Poppy was an enormous fluffy polar bear and lying on the bed with her arms wrapped around her, Carrie suddenly wished that it was Mum she was cuddling. Mum had been nice to cuddle up to. She'd smelt nice and she always knew what to say or do to make her and Joel smile when they were upset. She hugged Poppy tightly. Harriet was going to be so cross. She reminded Carrie of Professor Snape sometimes, always scowling and looking serious. But then, just when you thought she was about to tell you off or be cross, she'd surprise you. Like that time in the car when she'd used that word Mummy said they weren't to say and had laughed her head off.

But there wouldn't be any laughing today. She shouldn't have told all those lies. She hadn't meant to but they'd just kept slipping out. She was sorry she'd frightened Joel, but she wasn't sorry about the others at school. They deserved it. Hadn't they started it by asking if Mum and Dad had had their heads chopped off? How would they feel if it was their parents who were dead? Burying her face in Poppy's white fur, she let herself cry, safe in the knowledge that no one was there to see.

With Toby off the leash and snuffling on ahead in the bushes, Bob followed slowly behind. It was only the second week of September, but already there was a soft gauze of mist hanging over the surface of the canal and a scattering of fallen willow leaves, yellow and wet, lay like a catch of slippery fish on the ground. There was no sign of Will this morning. It was Saturday after all; he was probably at work.

They had met while Will was hacking back the jungle of bushes at the end of his garden and Bob was out walking Toby, and had had several conversations since, all conducted over the gate. Disappointed, Bob pressed on. Perhaps they ought to have him over for a drink—put on a sort of belated 'welcome to the neighbourhood' do. Except that would mean fuss and bother, something he couldn't face. For now it was as much as he could do to keep treading water, his chin just skimming the surface. It'll change, he told himself. Things *will* get better. They had to.

Following the towpath as it curved away from the last of the houses in Maple Drive, Bob watched Toby chase a startled moorhen out of the undergrowth. At the sound of chugging, he turned. Coming towards them was a traditional tug-style narrowboat. When it drew level, a well-wrapped-up woman with an arm resting on the tiller waved at Bob. 'Beautiful morning,' she said. 'You wouldn't give me a hand, would you? I want to moor up for a brew. If I could throw you a rope, it would make things a lot easier.'

Surprised that she was apparently travelling alone, Bob went on ahead to the prow of the boat while the woman steered it towards the bank. She then cut the engine and tossed him a neat coil of rope. While he held the boat firm, she stuffed some mooring pins into her jacket pockets and hopped out with a coil of rope in one hand and a rubber mallet in the other. 'You OK to hang on while I bang this one in?' she called to him.

'No problem at all.' Bob watched the woman; she clearly knew what she was about. He wondered why she was travelling alone. Or maybe she wasn't. Peering through one of the brass-rimmed portholes, he could make out a cabin that looked invitingly snug. He had often been tempted to go on a canal holiday but somehow it had never happened.

'Right then, that's the back end sorted; let's see about relieving you.'

'You've done this before,' he said when she was finished.

Hot from all the exertion, she pulled off the woolly tea cosy of a hat she was wearing and revealed a head of curly pepper and salt hair. 'Just once or twice,' she said with a broad smile, unzipping her bulky jacket. She was less weather-beaten than he'd first thought. Slimmer and younger too. Late fifties he reckoned. She looked cheerful and robust. 'Thanks for the help,' she said. 'I appreciate it.'

'It's a large boat to manage on your own.' He was blatantly fishing, curious to know if there was a companion on board.

'It's not as difficult as you'd think. I can do locks on my own quite easily, which was my biggest worry initially. With the centre rope, it's not too bad.' She smiled again, revealing, he thought, a hint of pride.

'Well,' he said, 'I'd better leave you to your brew.'

She laughed. 'I'm afraid that was a euphemism for wanting the loo.'

'In that case, even more reason for me to take my leave. Come on, Toby, stop sniffing round that rope.'

Normally Bob would walk Toby as far as the bend just before The Navigation, but this morning, knowing that Harriet would be arriving home soon, he cut short their walk and within a few minutes was returning the way he'd come. *It's got nothing to do with chatting to that woman again, then?* he asked himself.

The mist had cleared when he spotted the boat. It was still moored where he'd left it. There were gaily painted pots of flowering chrysanthemums on the roof of the boat, which he now saw was named the *Jennifer Rose*. The flowers suggested that the woman was a live-aboard, not a casual holidaymaker. He pictured the curly-haired woman sitting in the cabin, cosily insulated from the outside world and planning where to go next. He suddenly wished he could do the same. Oh, to pretend he was someone else, that he had never known Felicity. The thought was such a betrayal of his love for his daughter that he had to fight to keep his composure. A tapping sound had him looking to one of the windows. Holding up a metal teapot, the woman was inviting him to join her in a cup of tea. *You'll tell her you haven't got time*, he said to himself, *that you're expected home*. But he didn't.

It was three days since Harriet's car had been broken into and she felt completely lost without her laptop. Rightly or wrongly, the theft had superseded her shock at the gruesome tales Carrie had been spreading at school. It was still a mystery to Harriet and her parents why Carrie had felt the need to tell such lies—no amount of careful questioning could make sense of any of the muttered answers the girl gave them. In the end, Harriet had concluded that her niece didn't know why she'd done it; she had promised, though, not to do it again. After a brief telephone call to the headmistress at school, it was accepted that in view of the circumstances, no more would be said on the matter.

It wasn't just the hassle of buying a new laptop that irritated Harriet, and the sense of violation, it was the loss of so much personal stuff that really bothered her; all those emails she and Felicity had exchanged. It was like losing a precious photo album.

In the meantime, she was using Felicity's computer. She switched it on now to access her own emails, hoping to hear from one of the job agencies, though in her heart she knew that if there was a job going, they would be in touch by phone. She missed work so much; it was her identity, she supposed. Resigned to another week of scanning the pages of *Computer Weekly*, she sighed heavily. 'Oh, Felicity, why did you have to die?' Suddenly filled with longing to feel closer to her sister, she wondered if it would be so wrong to read an email Felicity had sent to her— just to hear her voice, to feel her presence. She knew it would be like poking around in another person's personal diary, but she justified her need by telling herself that it wasn't the same, that reading something Felicity had already sent to her was perfectly all right.

She knew Felicity's password and had no trouble accessing her sister's Outbox. The list of sent emails was in date order and Harriet felt a chill run through her when she saw the last email had been sent the day before Felicity and Jeff had died. She also saw that the email address was Harriet_Swift@yahoo.co.uk. She stared at the address and those preceding it. Scrolling back over the preceding weeks and months, there were two names that appeared more regularly than any others: the Harriet_Swift@yahoo.co.uk address and MissTechie@btinternet.co.uk. A strange feeling crept over Harriet. She was all too familiar with who MissTechie was—it was her email address—but who was Felicity messaging under the name of Harriet Swift? She'd never had a yahoo account.

There was only one way to find out, but should she do it? Her hand hovered over the mouse . . . Click.

Whatever she'd expected, it wasn't this. The text was brief and made no sense. But as Harriet scanned the block of text she saw it for what it was: a code. And not any old code. This one had been used by Harriet and her sister when they were children. The trick had been not to leave any gaps between the words. Also, the letters of each word had to be substituted with the following letter of the alphabet—for instance, THE would be written as UIF. There could be only one reason why Felicity had used their code: she had wanted this kept private. She thought of Miles's words about her having a strong sense of right and wrong. 'Sorry to disappoint you, Miles,' she murmured, and began the painstaking process of decoding the email.

> I dreamt of you last night. You said your heart was breaking. That I was breaking it. Tell me that's not true. I couldn't live with myself if I ever thought I was causing you such unhappiness. You know how very much I love you—you always have—but you have to be patient. Trust me, please, it won't be long now. Just give me a little more time. You mean everything to me. EVERYTHING.

Felicity had been having an affair. Her very own sister, who she'd thought had never kept anything from her. Harriet's first thought was that she should wipe the computer clean. No one else must ever stumble across what she had. It would kill her father if he ever knew that Felicity had been leading this double life, that she had been less than perfect.

Her second thought was to wonder who Felicity had been seeing. She knew she would have to read more. She wanted to know who had mattered so much to her sister. Who had meant *everything* to Felicity?

Gemma was having trouble concentrating on that afternoon's philosophy lesson. It was two weeks since Suzie's revelation, but Gemma still couldn't believe her sister had made such a mess of things. How could she have got herself pregnant? But hadn't she and Marcel taken a similar risk in Paris? Each time she thought of that occasion—when they'd realised he'd run out of condoms—she shuddered. It had only happened the once, but of course, once was all it took. How crazy could she have been? She'd never make that mistake again. No way. And to make doubly sure, she'd replied to his letter saying there was too much going on for him to visit. 'It would be better to put your trip off until next year,' she'd written.

But the million-dollar question was what Mum would say about Suzie's pregnancy, other than going mental. Tonight was the night. Suzie had told Gemma and Dad that she was going to break the news to Mum during a family dinner, which Suzie would cook and to which Dad was invited. They were in for an evening of pure over-the-top melodrama.

Maxine was suspicious; she knew in her bones that something was going on. She called through to the en suite bathroom where Steve was brushing his teeth. 'The last time Suzie cooked for us was my fortieth birthday. I haven't missed an important date on the calendar, have I?'

Steve joined her in the bedroom. 'Maybe this is Suzie's way of apologising for what her father did to my car,' he said. 'Take it as an olive branch.' He kissed her neck and placed his hands round her waist, something Maxine wished he wouldn't do. She always felt as though he was checking to see if she'd put on any weight. And dammit, she had. She'd have to go on a diet. Joining a gym was out of the question as she simply didn't have the time. Work was crazier than ever at the moment; the saleroom had never been busier. And if everything went to plan, she'd soon be acquiring a second saleroom; one in Stafford. It was a shame her father wasn't around to see what she'd achieved.

She knew she wasn't overweight, but Steve didn't like the 'comely wench' look as he referred to any woman bigger than a size twelve. Just as well he'd never seen her when she was pregnant. She'd been enormous. Will used to pretend he couldn't get his arms round her, but then he'd kiss her, and they'd end up in bed. In those days, she and Will couldn't get enough of each other. What a lifetime ago that was. And how pig-headedly, how selfishly and how recklessly Will had thrown it all away. If she lived to be a hundred, she didn't think she would ever forgive him for what he did to her and the girls. She came back to the present with a jolt as the doorbell chimed. 'That'll be Will,' she said. 'I wonder if he knows what this evening's all about. I certainly don't buy your olive-branch theory.'

Will had promised Suzie that he'd be on his best behaviour. 'Don't worry,' he'd told her when she'd said what she was planning. 'I won't crack a single joke in poor taste.' In fact, as they sat round the late nineteenth-century French mahogany dining table Will was a bundle of nerves. He knew Maxine would be infuriated when she discovered she had been kept in the dark.

He and Gemma still didn't know what Suzie was going to do. Gemma reckoned that she would keep the baby and a small, indefinable part of him hoped that she would. Unbelievably, the idea of being a grandfather had grown on him. They were halfway through their desserts when Suzie announced that she had something to say. This was it, then.

Suzie took a deep breath. 'Mum, you'd better pour yourself another glass of wine; you're going to need it. I'm pregnant.'

'Oh my God!' Maxine muttered. Then more loudly: 'I don't believe it. How? I mean, how could you be so bloody stupid? You *stupid* girl!' This was exactly the response Suzie had expected, but even so the sharpness of her mother's tone made her feel like a naughty child.

'Maxine,' Will said firmly, 'will you show a little compassion?'

'Wishy-washy compassion isn't what's called for right now,' Maxine fired at him, her eyes blazing, her shoulders squared. 'Cool-headed detachment is what's needed. That's what will get this sorted out. How pregnant are you?' she demanded.

'Four and a half months . . . nineteen weeks to be precise.'

Maxine paused to take this in. 'OK,' she said, 'that still gives us time to deal with this mess.'

Suzie winced. She didn't like hearing the baby referred to as a mess. She was about to say something, but Dad beat her to it: 'Maxine, do you think you could sound just a little more like a mother and not the hard-bitten chairman of the board trying to—'

He got no further. Maxine rounded on him. 'The day you have something sensible to say, Will, I'll be in touch. For now, I suggest you leave the matter to me.'

'What about Suzie? Doesn't she figure in this?' piped up Gemma.

Maxine turned her attention to Gemma. 'Well, of course she does.'

She hesitated. Switching her gaze to Will and then back again to Gemma, she said in a more measured voice, 'Hang on, you two don't look or sound at all shocked by what Suzie's told us. Why's that?' A crashing silence roared round the table. 'You already knew, didn't you?' For a second, Maxine looked genuinely hurt. And oddly vulnerable. Something Suzie would never have thought possible. But it was only a flicker of emotion, then once more her mother was on the attack. 'And you didn't think to mention it to me?'

'I . . . I wanted to be sure in my mind what I was going to do before I spoke to you. I didn't want you worrying unnecessarily,' Suzie said.

'You're not telling me you've had to deliberate over this, are you? How the hell do you think you'll carry on at university with a baby hanging round your neck? And don't imagine for one second that I'm going to step into the breach and take care of it.'

'For God's sake, Maxine! Do you have to be so insensitive?'

'Dad's right, Mum,' joined in Gemma, 'you're out of line, talking like Suzie doesn't have any choice in the matter. It's her baby.'

'Gemma, I'd rather you didn't speak to your mother like that.'

'This is a family matter, Steve, so I'd rather you kept quiet,' said Will.

'How dare you speak to Steve like that?'

Feeling tearful now, Suzie had to shout to make herself heard above the din. 'Please!' she yelled. 'Please, will you all just calm down. This is what I plan to do.'

Will poured himself a generous glass of Glenmorangie and went out into his garden. The gate creaked noisily in the hushed stillness. He sat in the moonlight on the old bench and swished the whisky round his mouth.

Suzie had opted to have a termination and he was staggered how disappointed he was. Stupidly, he'd imagined a grandson. The son he'd never had. But it wasn't to be. And rightly so, he told himself. Suzie was much too young to go through motherhood. Of course it made sense for her to get rid of the baby, carry on with her studies and be glad that she'd been given a second chance.

All this, Maxine had put in her own inimitable way. She'd then gone on to say that she would go to the doctor in the morning with Suzie. Will was too stunned to speak, because it felt as though he was already going through some kind of weird grieving process for a child he would never know. For the first time ever, he felt distanced from one of his children, sidelined by the very fact that he was a man and this was women's business. He was clearly not needed. This was something that was going to take some getting used to.

He drained his glass, letting the last of the liquid slide down his throat and dull what was left of his senses. Aware of something moving along the path, he leaned forward to peer into the silvery darkness. A fox perhaps? He smiled. It was the Hedgehog, and beneath the peak of her baseball cap she looked as prickly as ever. What was she doing out at this time of night when all sensible people were tucked up in bed?

'Hi,' he said, making his presence known so that she wouldn't be startled. 'Where are you heading at this time of night?'

'I couldn't sleep.' She glanced at the empty glass on the arm of the bench. 'Whenever I see you, you have a drink in your hand.'

'It's the neighbourhood; it's driving me to it.' He waited for her to say something, but she didn't, just kept on standing there. 'You know; you really oughtn't to be out on your own so late at night. Luckily for you I'm not a crazed psycho on the lookout for a fresh victim, but who knows what excitement lurks further down the towpath for you?'

'I can take care of myself.' She bristled; every one of her hedgehog spikes was up and ready to repel him.

Will suddenly felt sorry for this young woman. Knowing more of her background from the conversations he'd had with her father, he said, 'Any luck on the job front, yet?'

'No.'

He admired her candour, the fact that she didn't give out any bull about there being any number of offers she was currently considering.

'By the way, I was being serious when I said you ought to be careful walking along the canal late at night.' He received a look that seemed to dare him to go on and annoy her further. Which, of course, he did. 'If you'd like, I could trail you by skulking along in the shadows and act as your bodyguard.' This at least elicited a smile.

'And there I was, thinking you were only good for sitting on benches and making out you were a dedicated wino,' she said.

'That's me; Jack-of-all-trades.'

'I heard you used to be a lawyer. Why did you give it up?'

A question from the Hedgehog? This was a new phenomenon. 'I had to,' he said. 'I was beginning to imagine myself running amok in the office with a machete and massacring anything with a pulse.'

She raised an eyebrow. 'So much for not being the crazy psycho on the lookout for a fresh victim.'

'Ah, but I'm all cured now. I put my unstable past behind me when I became a convert to the school of thought that believes tomorrow is but a dream and yesterday no longer exists. What matters is today and seizing the opportunities that come one's way. As a lawyer, you can't live like that; the two aren't mutually compatible. Would you like to sit down?'

She shook her head. '*Carpe diem* is a bit passé, don't you think?'

'Tell me that when you're all grown up.'

'You're very patronising, you know.'

'I'm sorry, I don't mean to be. It's just that you look so young.'

'I'm thirty-two.'

He smiled. 'OK, so you're older than I thought you were by a few years, but I guarantee one day you'll remember this conversation and think what a wise sage I was. You sure I can't persuade you to let me keep you company on your walk?'

'Thanks, but I need to think.'

'Tell me about it. That's what I was doing before you showed up.' Torn between wanting to respect Suzie's privacy and suddenly feeling the need to talk about his rotten evening, he chose his next words carefully. 'Someone very close to me has got herself pregnant and, well, the thing is she's very young and has decided to have an abortion. And for reasons I'm almost ashamed to confess, I hate the thought of her doing that. I know it's selfish, that the decision is hers, but I can't help it.'

'You're right, it is selfish of you. You can't dictate her life.'

'But what if she regrets the abortion?'

'That's the price of choice. *Her* choice.'

'Do you always see things so dispassionately?'

'If you mean do I always view things rationally and with an objective eye, then yes, I do.'

He folded his arms across his chest, beginning to feel the cold. 'You'd have made an excellent lawyer.'

'And you'd probably have hacked me to death.'

He smiled. 'There's still time. Anyway, I'm going in now; the cold's getting to me. It was nice chatting with you.'

Closing the gate after him, Will thought that if there were any psychos out there on the towpath, they were the ones who might need to take care. She was one formidable girl.

At last Harriet had a job interview. It had come her way not through an agency, but by word of mouth. Adrian, her old boss down in Oxford, called to say that he knew of a company in south Manchester that was desperate for someone with her level of expertise and in particular, her specific knowledge of AVLS—automatic vehicle location systems. 'Howard Beningfield, who runs the company, is one of the brashest, most straight-talking men I know,' Adrian had said. 'Get on the right side of him and he'll be your friend for life. What do you think? Shall I give him a ring and put in a good word for you?'

'Absolutely.'

Adrian had one final piece of advice for her. 'Whatever you do,

Harriet, don't underestimate Howard. It's his favourite trick, fooling people into thinking he's an idiot.'

So here she was, looking for a small business-park on the outskirts of Crantsford. This way lies my sanity, she told herself. Once she had a job, she'd be able to start making plans for the future. She was desperate to get a place of her own. Or rather, a place for her and the children. The thought of taking on the full weight of responsibility for Carrie and Joel still terrified her, but biting bullets was what she did best. Wasn't that why Felicity had entrusted her with the task in the first place?

A week had passed since Harriet had read the first of her sister's secret emails and she was still shocked at what she'd discovered. Felicity's had been no lightweight affair. It was obvious that she had been involved with whoever it was for some time. A lot of the emails they'd written to each other had been near-pornographic in content and Harriet had baulked at reading some of them, but wanting to discover the identity of Felicity's lover, she had forced herself to go on. All the while, she kept thinking of Jeff. Had he been such a terrible husband? Perhaps he'd been a little staid but he'd been devoted to Felicity. Felicity had always claimed that she fell in love with him the moment she set eyes on him, when they were at university. 'That's the man I'm going to marry,' she had said in a loud voice when they were standing in the dinner queue during a ball up in Durham. 'His name's Jeff Knight and he's my knight in shining armour. He doesn't know it yet, but he's going to sweep me off my feet.' It was nearly the end of the summer term and Felicity was drunk, as they all were—Miles and Dominic were spending the weekend with them—and they'd laughed at her, thinking her quite mad.

'But, darling,' Dominic had said, his voice overtly camp, 'he looks like one of those frighteningly hale and hearty types. Not our sort at all.'

As soon as Dominic had made the transition from boarding school to university, he'd come out as gay and delighted in shocking those who were uneasy about such matters. Including his parents. *Particularly* his parents. Had Harriet not seen for herself a set of moody black and white photographs of him lying naked in the arms of a man, she would have said it was another of his affectations.

'He's exceptionally hearty,' Felicity had said proudly. 'He has muscles you McKendrick boys can only dream of.'

'I can't speak for my brother,' Dominic had drawled, 'but for myself, I'm rather partial to something with a brain.'

'He has one of those too,' Felicity crowed. 'He's a maths scholar.'

Dominic shuddered. 'Another maths bore, just like Harriet. How extraordinarily dull.'

'I don't care what you think of him. He's the man I'm going to marry.'

So where had it gone wrong? thought Harriet. The only clue was that Felicity's new life as a wife and mother lacked the excitement of the life she'd led before. If Felicity was to be believed from the way she wrote to him, the lover made her feel whole again. But this conclusion didn't make Harriet feel sympathetic towards her sister. She was furious with Felicity for being so deceitful.

Had she really planned to leave Jeff? That last email certainly implied that she wanted to: '. . . *you have to be patient. Trust me, please, it won't be long now. Just give me a little more time.*'

But it wasn't only Jeff who had been cheated on. Harriet felt betrayed, too. She hated knowing that despite the closeness between them, Felicity hadn't confided in her. It was a hurtful blow, and it left her wondering if she had ever really known her sister.

She entered the modern offices of ACT—Associated Controlled Technology—with five minutes to spare and was shown through to an office by a receptionist, who told Harriet that Mr Beningfield would be with her in a minute.

At breakfast that morning, the children had presented her with a good luck card that they'd made. Harriet had been touched by their efforts. Now that the dust had settled on Carrie's handiwork at school, Joel's nightmares had stopped and he was sleeping properly. He was also opening up a little.

Harriet had to wait half an hour before Howard Beningfield walked in. Adrian's description of the man hadn't been reassuring. He was apparently garrulous and jocular, but a 'bit much' at times. 'You have to stand up to him,' Adrian had said. 'He likes nothing better than a good sparring partner.'

She saw before her a big man in his mid fifties; one of those who are as broad as they are wide. He plonked himself down behind the desk—the black leather chair exhaling a sigh of resistance—then looked up. 'Well, then, Harriet,' he said, 'may I call you Harriet?'

She nodded.

'You come very highly recommended. Why's that, do you think?'

'Because I'm very good at what I do.'

He leaned back into his chair, clasped his hands behind his enormous head and laughed. The chair groaned. 'That's what I like about you modern girls: more front than Blackpool and Southport put together.'

Oh, brilliant! He was one of those suffer-the-little-women-unto-me types. In other words, he was a honking great sexist pig. Adrian had omitted to mention that.

Howard sat forward and scanned Harriet's CV briefly, then he ripped it up. 'So much for the blah-di-blah,' he said. 'Let's get down to basics.' He fired off a salvo of questions which she returned with equal gusto, outlining various large-scale applications she'd been in charge of, until finally he said, 'We'll only know if you're any good when you've worked here for a while. The proof will be in the pudding, so to speak. When do you want to start? Adrian explained that you're keen to get going a-s-a-p.'

Wondering what else Adrian might have explained—had he mentioned the children and their obvious consequences?—she said, 'I'm available as of tomorrow.'

'I'll be straight with you, Harriet. Adrian told me to look no further than you, but I don't want to hire you if in nine months' time you waltz into my office and announce that you're pregnant. And don't give me any of that equal rights crap. I'm running a business, not a charity.'

Harriet knew that now was the moment she should raise the matter of being Carrie and Joel's guardian, that there might be times when, if her parents couldn't cover for her, she would have to take time off. But she didn't. Self-preservation made her keep quiet. Nor did she feel inclined to point out the glaringly obvious, that Howard Beningfield was committing the cardinal sin of discriminating against women who wanted to combine motherhood with a career.

'Mr Beningfield,' she said, adopting a firm but deferential tone, 'I think we can safely say that there is about as much chance of me becoming pregnant as the Pope.' Well, he hadn't asked straight out if she already had children, had he?

She drove away with a job offer under her belt. She couldn't wait to get home and share her good news. Better still, she'd be able to have a celebratory drink that evening with Miles—they were now meeting regularly for either a drink or a meal.

It was gone six when she turned into Maple Drive and parked. Across the road, she saw Will Hart getting out of his car. There was a young blonde girl with him—the same girl she'd seen him with at The Navigation, and presumably the 'someone close to him' who was pregnant.

Harriet hadn't been fooled by that guarded speech of his. Honestly, why didn't he just come right out and admit that he was having a relationship with a girl young enough to be his daughter and had got her pregnant?

Letting herself in at the back door, Harriet froze. 'Hello, Harriet,' said a voice that was all too familiar.

Her first thought was that he still had the same effect on her. But just as she had taught herself all those years ago, she stamped on the emotion. Stamped on it hard. She would rather die than let him have the pleasure of knowing she'd spent the best part of her childhood hero-worshipping him.

'Hello, Dominic,' she said. And wanting to hurt him, to twist the knife round in his heart just as he had with her so many times, she added, 'We missed you at the funeral. What happened? A college crisis that was more important than saying goodbye to your oldest friend?'

Will could hear Suzie being sick upstairs. It was the third time that morning. He was almost sick with nerves himself. He glanced at his watch. They would have to go. The clinic had told them to be there for ten o'clock. Originally Maxine had insisted that she would be the one to accompany Suzie, but then she and Suzie had had one almighty row and Suzie said she wanted Will to take her to the clinic.

It was raining during the journey and the wipers juddered in the awkward silence. Will couldn't remember a time when he and Suzie hadn't had a hundred and one things to chat about. But what could they discuss today? Anything, other than what Suzie was about to go through with, would seem trivial and insulting. He looked at Suzie in the passenger seat, her eyes closed. She's so beautiful, he thought, his heart bursting with love. She didn't deserve this ordeal. He started to hum to himself. Suzie opened her eyes. 'Sorry, love, were you trying to sleep?'

She shook her head. 'Sing it properly, with all the words. Like you used to when Gemma and I were little.' For the rest of the journey, the mournful tune of 'Scarlet Ribbons' filled the car.

From the outside, the clinic looked more like an up-market country hotel: cool, aloof and splendid. That was private healthcare for you. So efficient and professional were the members of staff, Will hardly noticed his daughter being spirited away, and as he settled in for the necessary wait, he flicked idly through a glossy car magazine.

Suddenly the door opened and Suzie came in. He leapt to his feet. The next thing he knew, she was in his arms, sobbing. 'I'm sorry, Dad, but I couldn't do it. I just couldn't get rid of it. I'm so sorry.'

Some things never change. Dominic had only been back in Maple Drive a matter of hours, but within no time at all he'd made himself the centre of attention. Harriet's drink with Miles had been postponed because Freda was in the mood for playing happy families and had insisted on both her sons sitting round the dinner table that evening.

Five days after his surprise arrival, he was still around, casting the shadow of his ferocious presence on their lives.

Harriet's parents had taken her to task over the sharpness of her greeting to Dominic. 'There was no need to be so rude,' her mother had said. 'Especially as he'd gone to the trouble to call in and apologise to us about missing the funeral.'

They might have succeeded in making her feel churlish had it not been for the fact that she knew Dominic better than they did. He revelled in making people eat their words. One minute he'd make people hate him, the next he'd be so contrite that he'd be instantly forgiven, somehow instilling a sense of guilt in those who had been so quick to misjudge him.

Carrie and Joel were fascinated by him. With his tall, lean frame, his Prince of Denmark attire and his propensity to swear at random, he was irresistibly charismatic. Once Carrie realised he was Miles's brother and had been a friend of her mother's, she wanted to know everything they had ever done together. Any of the stories Harriet and her parents had told the children were now forgotten, redundant in the face of this golden-tongued storyteller in their midst.

'Did Mummy really get caught for shoplifting?' Carrie was now asking Dominic, her face more radiant than Harriet had ever seen it. Joel was listening too, his eyes rapt with wonder.

'You bet to buggery she did! We all did; Harriet, Miles and me.'

It was Saturday morning, and they were in the kitchen. Shortly after Mum and Dad had gone to the supermarket, Dominic had called round. 'I'm bored to death,' he'd said. 'Let me in and talk to me. If you don't I shall have to shoot myself. Here, these are for you.' He thrust an extravagantly large box of champagne truffles at her. 'I thought you deserved something expensive and frivolous. And these are for the children.' From his coat pocket he produced a box of Maltesers. His thoughtfulness brought to mind equally unexpected gestures of kindness he'd made in the past—the large bouquet he'd sent to her mother when he'd heard about her being diagnosed with ME; the housewarming gift of a luxury food hamper for Harriet when she'd moved into her flat in Oxford. She smiled her thanks and took his coat.

Now, as Harriet listened to Dominic giving a riveting account of Edna Gannet catching the four of them with their pockets bursting with Cadbury's creme eggs, she wondered why he was here. Kings Melford was normally the last place on the planet he wanted to be.

'I hear you and Miles are practically inseparable these days,' he'd said after he'd caught up on gossip at Freda's family get-together.

'We've been out for drinks and the occasional meal, if it's any of your business,' she'd said.

'Is it serious, then? I always thought you two should get it together. You're perfectly suited.'

'Why? So that you could take pleasure in tearing us apart like you used to pull the legs off spiders?'

He had sighed. 'I'm getting bored with the diva bitch thing. Whatever's happened to you? You never used to be quite so touchy.'

'Losing the person who meant the most to me has changed me more than you'll ever know,' she'd said.

'Ah . . . Felicity,' he had said stiffly, sounding like the desiccated academic he was destined to be. 'I miss her too.'

She gritted her teeth. How glib he could be. Tuning back in to what Dominic was now saying, Harriet did a double take. To her astonishment, he was helping Joel to pull on his socks and telling Carrie to forget about her homework so they could all go for a walk.

'Keep away from the bank,' she yelled at the children as they scampered on ahead in their Wellington boots, squealing and laughing. The morning was bright and fresh, the sky clear as if washed clean by the heavy rain overnight. The sight of Dominic's sartorial elegance wrecked by a pair of her father's old gardening boots brought a smirk to her mouth. She rearranged her face. 'When are you going back to Cambridge? What about the start of term and freshers' week?'

'I dare say they can manage a few days without me.'

'But I thought the world revolved around you, Dominic.'

'It does. Which is why I can decide my own comings and goings. A bit like masturbation, you could say.'

Again she smiled to herself. The same old Dominic; buried in among all the flaws was his sharp wit and diverting turn of thought. They walked on in silence, passing Will's house. Harriet wondered if his girlfriend had had her abortion yet. Wondered too what its consequences would be on their relationship. What would her sister have done if she'd got pregnant by her lover? It occurred to Harriet, stealing a quick glance at Dominic, that maybe, because they'd been such close friends, he was the one person in whom Felicity might have confided. She was tempted to ask him if he knew anything.

Before that, though, she had something else to sort out with him. 'I still think you were a complete shit to miss Felicity's funeral,' she said.

After another pause, he said, 'She wouldn't have wanted it.'

'You mean *you* didn't want it. Funerals, after all, must be so wearisomely pedestrian for a distinguished don such as you.'

He suddenly turned on her, his face so savage that she took a step back. 'Don't be so bloody patronising!' he roared. 'Is it too much for you to understand that I wanted to remember my oldest and closest friend the way she was? That I didn't want to watch her mutilated corpse being shoved into a hole in the ground?'

'It's always about you, isn't it? You, you, *you*! And for the record, she was cremated and her ashes buried. She was not *shoved* into a hole!'

'You picky little cow! Just remember this: there are no exclusive rights to grief.' He turned and stalked in the direction they'd just come.

Her eyes brimmed with hot, stinging tears, and she rushed on to find the children. *Bastard!* Why had she allowed him to get to her? And how the hell had he managed to grab the moral high ground?

OCTOBER

*'Love may be a fool's paradise, but it is the only
paradise we know on this troubled planet.'*

ROBERT BLATCHFORD
Taken from *My Eighty Years*

IT WAS THE MIDDLE of October, and what had so far been a gentle and relatively mild autumn now consisted of strong wintry winds that shook the curling leaves from the trees, sending them rattling along the streets. A fence panel had blown over in the night, and under normal circumstances Bob would have been straight out to the garden to fix it. But he had other things on his mind this morning. He had an appointment to keep. A rendezvous, you could say. Jennifer had said she would be coming back to Kings Melford: she wanted to photograph this stretch of the canal when autumn had really settled in.

That day when he'd accepted her offer of tea and climbed down into the snug warmth of the saloon had been a turning point for Bob.

'Grief's a terrible thing,' she'd said matter-of-factly when he'd told her about Felicity—the words had come out before he could stop himself. 'I lost my husband two years ago,' she said, 'and for months after his death I could hardly bring myself to get up in the morning.'

'What changed?'

'You mean, how did I pull myself together? It sounds vaguely absurd, but I simply ran out of tears. Unlike a lot of people who bottle them up, I let it all go in one long, horrid outburst. Have you cried much?'

'Er . . . a bit.'

'In private, I'll bet.'

'Mostly at night,' he'd confessed, avoiding her gaze by bending down to Toby and scratching the top of the dog's head. 'I go and sit inside the Wendy house I made for my daughters when they were little,' he further admitted. 'It's the only place I can be alone.'

When he'd raised his glance, she'd said, 'Oh, that's so sad.'

'It's pathetic,' he shot back, his voice too loud and harsh.

'No, you mustn't ever think that. You do whatever it takes. How's your wife coping?'

'Better than me. She has her friend Dora to talk to. It seems to make all the difference to her.' Moving the subject on, he'd asked her what she was doing, cruising the inland waterways on her own.

'I'm satisfying a long-held ambition. Actually, it was something my husband and I had planned to do together, but when he died and I'd come out from under the duvet, I thought, what the heck, I'm going to do it anyway. I sold the house, moved to an isolated bungalow where my only neighbour is a grumpy old farmer who is much too busy to bother me with pitying looks, and I bought this boat and took off.'

She pointed to an expensive-looking camera on a shelf. 'I'm trying my hand at being a photographer.'

'Where are you heading next?' he'd asked, scarcely able to keep the envy out of his voice. Take me with you, he wanted to say.

'I'm on my way up to Yorkshire but thought I would stay here for a few days. I'm going to moor the boat this side of a pub called The Navigation. Do you know it?'

'You could say it's my local.'

The next day when he was out walking Toby, the *Jennifer Rose* had moved on. Approaching the mooring points near The Navigation, he saw that its owner was on the roof of the boat, sweeping leaves that had fallen from the nearby trees. She'd told him yesterday that she'd named the boat after herself; it was what her husband had planned to do.

'Hello,' she said, 'it must be about time for a cuppa. Why don't you go down below and put the kettle on?'

In all, she stayed moored in the same spot for four days. He visited her every morning and late afternoon. He came to believe that she was part of his healing process. He never once thought about touching her—he'd never make that mistake again—he just wanted to be with her.

Now that Harriet was working, it was his job to take the children to school, and after he'd done that he poked his head round the bedroom door. Eileen was having a lie-in; she hadn't slept well that night.

'I'm just off out with Toby,' he said softly. 'See you later.' Getting no reply, he assumed she was sleeping and crept quietly downstairs.

If he had been a younger and fitter man he would have sprinted to the towpath, but as it was, he lumbered along at his usual pace trying to keep the eager anticipation from showing on his face. Today was the day Jennifer had said she would be back in Kings Melford. And sure enough, as he rounded the curve of the canal, there was the *Jennifer Rose* moored just where it had been last month.

'Hello, stranger,' she said, when she emerged from the engine room, her face dotted with soot. 'I'm having a bit of trouble with the engine. Don't suppose you're any good with such things, are you?'

It was just as if the intervening weeks had never passed.

Carrie slid her fingernail under the gummed-down section of the envelope and opened it. She knew what it would say. With trembling hands and her heart hammering, she unfolded the piece of paper.

Nobody likes you because you're a nasty show-off. We don't want you here. We wish you were dead like your parents.

It was the same as the last note. And the one before that. Carrie ripped up the letter and dropped it into the loo. With her eyes fixed on the ground, she marched out of the toilets towards her classroom.

She felt hot all over. And sick. She wished she was at home. Anywhere but here.

She was just passing the main entrance when she noticed the door was open. Usually it was shut and anyone wanting to come in would have to press a button. How easy it would be to sneak out and spend the day wandering round the shops. It would be better than staying here listening to those spiteful girls. A glance over her shoulder told her that the school secretary, whose office was opposite, was talking on the phone. She slipped quietly through the open door and made a dash for it, beyond the gate and out onto the pavement. She'd done it!

Her first mistake, she realised, was not to have brought her coat. She was cold. Her school sweatshirt and grey skirt was also attracting attention. One woman had already asked her if she should be at school.

'I'm waiting for my mother,' she'd told the woman. 'She's in the cake shop.' Which was where she was now standing, her stomach growling for food as she breathed in the smell of freshly baked bread. It would be lunchtime at school. Next time she would have to bring some money.

Across the road, she saw a scruffy man in an anorak giving her an odd look. Carrie would have liked to stick out her tongue at the nosy man, but she didn't think it would be a good idea. Deciding she ought to keep moving to keep warm, she wandered down the main street and came to the cobbled area where Harriet had told her the original market used to be. Turning to her right, she came to a building with a green and gold sign above the door that said *Hart's Antique Emporium*. She was just making up her mind whether to go inside when she heard footsteps behind her. She spun round, suddenly scared that it might be the man in the anorak. But it wasn't him; it was the man who lived across the road from them.

'Hello, Carrie,' he said, 'what are you doing here?'

She swallowed. 'Um . . . I'm just waiting for Grandma.' She looked in the direction of the emporium.

He looked surprised. 'Why did she leave you outside?'

Carrie began to get flustered. 'Because . . . I didn't want to go in.'

'Well, you look frozen to death. Come on in out of the cold.'

She held back. 'It's OK. I'll wait here. I'm sure she won't be long.'

He smiled and she suddenly wished she wasn't lying to him. He was too nice to lie to. She saw that he was carrying two paper bags; one had a greasy patch on its side. She could smell food.

When she looked back at his face, she saw that the smile had gone and he was frowning. 'Your grandmother's not in there, is she, Carrie?'

She shook her head and looked hard at her shoes.

He bent down to her. 'And you're not in school where you should be, are you?'

Again she shook her head.

'Tell you what; I'll trade with you. You tell me what you've been doing and I'll share some of my lunch with you. How does that sound?'

She raised her eyes. 'Will you tell on me?'

He stood up and took her hand. 'Not exactly. But we will have to tell a few people where you are as otherwise they'll be very anxious and call the police. If they haven't already.'

She tightened her grip on his hand. She was beginning to realise how much trouble she was in. But she had a worse fear. 'I don't want to go back to school,' she said.

He smiled. He had a nice smile, she decided. It reminded her of Dad.

'Don't worry,' he said, 'I'll make sure you have the rest of the day off.'

He led her inside the emporium and at once she forgot all about being in trouble. She'd never been anywhere like it. Everywhere she looked there was furniture—tables, chairs, bookcases—and china and sparkling silvery things and lots and lots of ticking clocks.

She let go of his hand and wandered over to a chest that had a glass dome on top of it. Inside the dome was a brightly coloured bird. 'Is it real?' she asked.

'In a manner of speaking. It died a long time ago. It's stuffed.'

'What with?'

'Do you know, I haven't a clue!'

'Hello, hello, hello, and who have we here?'

Carrie turned round to see a very peculiar man coming towards them. He was wearing a suit the colour of Ribena with a spotty bow tie.

'Carrie, let me introduce you to Jarvis. Jarvis, this is Carrie, a friend of mine. Carrie's got herself into a bit of a fix and I am going to sort things out for her.'

'Well, my dear, any friend of Will's is a friend of mine. How do you do?' He leaned forward and held out his hand. Carrie giggled and held hers out just as she knew she was expected to.

'Enchanted,' he said. 'Now correct me if I'm wrong, but did I hear you enquiring with what this splendid creature is stuffed?'

She nodded, at the same time trying to get her giggling under control.

'Permit me to explain. You see, what you have to bear in mind is that the Victorians believed this to be a form of conservation . . .'

From inside his office, Will watched Jarvis carefully lift the glass dome. He reached for the phone book on the shelf behind him and within seconds was ringing the local primary school. The next call he made was to his neighbours, Bob and Eileen. There was no answer.

Harriet switched off her mobile and leapt to her feet. This couldn't be happening. What had got into Carrie? Shutting down her computer and gathering up her bag and jacket, she forced herself to take a steadying breath while she thought how to make an exit from her office without attracting attention from her new boss. She would have to feign illness.

A knock at her door made her jump. It was Dave Carter, one of the junior analysts.

'How's it going?' he said. 'I just thought . . . Hey, you OK? Only you look a bit pale.'

Pale? It must be shock. She covered her face with a hand. 'I'm really sorry,' she rasped. 'It's an asthma attack. I'm going to have to call it a day.'

'Will you be OK to drive?'

'I'll manage,' she said, already out of the door.

By the time she was driving out of the car park, she was beginning to worry that she really did have an asthma attack looming. There was a niggling tightness in her chest. But she couldn't reach her inhaler—it was in the bag on the back seat where she'd thrown it in her haste.

She tried to relax. Carrie was quite safe. That was what was important, as the headmistress had pointed out on the phone. Apparently school hadn't been able to get hold of Mum and Dad when they realised Carrie was missing, and when she'd tried Harriet's mobile there'd been no answer because, until ten minutes ago, she'd switched it off while she was in a meeting. But thank goodness their neighbour, Will Hart, had spotted Carrie in town and taken her in, then phoned school. She would for ever be grateful to him. Even if he was now probably wondering how a child in her care had so nearly come to harm.

I'm doing my best, was all she could say in her defence. Then suddenly it wasn't Will to whom she was defending herself, it was Felicity. 'Oh, Harriet,' she imagined her sister saying, 'I thought you'd take good care of Carrie. My precious baby could have been snatched by some vile perverted beast. Murdered because *you* didn't care about her!'

'But I do care about her!' Harriet said out loud, a rush of panicky sickness consuming her as the reality of what could have happened to Carrie sunk in. 'She's safe, Felicity.' Oh God, she was going mad. She was arguing with her dead sister.

She parked as near to Hart's Antique Emporium as she could and ran all the way. The tranquil scene that greeted her was totally at odds with the state she was in—sweating and out of breath, her chest wheezy, her mouth dry. But there was Carrie, polishing a silver teapot, concentrating hard on its spout, and humming.

'You must have driven like the wind.'

She turned to see Will sitting behind an untidy desk in a small, cramped office. 'The kettle's just boiled; would you like a cup of tea? You look like you could do with one.'

His kindness was too much, and overcome with relief that Carrie really was OK, she felt foolishly tearful and sank into the nearest chair. The tightening in her chest had worsened to such an extent that she fumbled for her inhaler in her bag. But she'd gone too long without it; her fingers were numb with pins and needles. Panic kicked in, which made her throat constrict even more.

Will was concerned. 'What is it, Harriet? What can I do?'

'Asthma,' she wheezed. She pointed to her bag. 'My inhaler.'

Will tipped the bag upside-down onto the floor, scattering pens, tissues, personal organiser, lip gloss, tampon, chequebook, wallet. And finally, an inhaler. He passed it to her.

'OK?' he asked, when she'd pressed it to her mouth a second time and he'd put everything back in her bag.

'I will be,' she rasped.

'How about a drink?'

She shook her head. 'I should take Carrie home.' They both looked over to where Carrie was oblivious to anything but the shiny teapot.

'I hope that's not too valuable,' Harriet mumbled, getting to her feet.

'Silver plate, *circa* yesterday.' He thought Harriet looked in no state to be going anywhere. 'It's no trouble, you know, that cup of tea. Come into my office and relax while I keep an eye on Carrie from the doorway.' After he'd flicked the switch on the kettle, he said, 'I realise it's none of my business, but I said she wouldn't get into too much trouble if she told me exactly what she'd been up to.'

'Well, of course she's in trouble. She can't expect to skive off school at her age and not realise there are serious consequences.'

He let it go. It wasn't his place to tell someone else how to go about the sticky business of parenting. He handed her a mug. 'Feeling any better?'

'Getting there. I'm sorry for snapping. It was rude of me. You've been very kind. I haven't even thanked you for taking care of Carrie.'

Her words were in the shape of an apology, but her tone was so stiff it sounded more like she was reading from a script. 'Oh, shucks,' he said good-humouredly, 'now you're embarrassing me.' He expected her to smile, but to his horror her face crumpled and she began to cry.

'I'm a failure,' she murmured, her head lowered. 'A total failure. I haven't got a clue how to bring up children. I feel so guilty. So useless.'

He looked about him for some tissues, but could only find a pack of muslin he used for polishing. He pulled out a sheet and passed it to her. 'You're not a failure,' he said, 'you're a hero for what you're doing. Your sister would be proud of you.'

'You're wrong. I've let her down. I'm a rotten sister and an even worse aunt, guardian, mother, whatever it is I'm supposed to be. Oh God, I don't even know who I am any more. What am I doing wrong? You're a parent; tell me how to do a better job.'

He put a hand on her shoulder. 'Don't be so hard on yourself. You're just on the steepest learning curve of your life. It'll get better.'

'That's OK for you to say; your children don't even live with you.'

Surprised at the vehemence of her words, and the implied criticism, he said nothing, just kept his hand on her shoulder.

In the silence, another voice spoke up: 'Will, have you got anything else for me to polish? Oh . . . hello, Harriet.'

Harriet shrugged off Will's hand and blew her nose hard as Carrie stepped into the office nervously. 'Are you crying, Harriet?'

Will could see that Harriet was fighting to keep what little composure she'd reinstated. 'Your aunt's just relieved to find you in one piece,' he intervened. 'Now then, Carrie, why don't we let Harriet finish her tea while I find you something else to polish?' Leading the way, he glanced back to check if it was OK with Harriet. But she wasn't looking his way. He thought he'd never seen anyone look more miserable.

Later that afternoon, in Maple Drive, Harriet was conscious that they were all distracted and uncomfortable. They'd already had the Big Scene, during which Carrie had been cajoled to explain what had got into her. But all they'd learned was that she'd been bored and fancied a walk. Harriet had decided it could well be true; she had entertained the same thought countless times when she'd been at school.

When tea was over and Harriet was upstairs supervising bathtime, Carrie said, 'Harriet? Are you going to punish me?'

'No. But I want you to write a letter of apology to school saying that you're very sorry for causing so many people to worry. I think you might even write a thankyou note to Will, too. He was very good to you.'

At this, Carrie's face brightened. 'I like Will. Do you like Will, Harriet?'

'I've never really thought about it. He's just one of our neighbours.'

'Why was he hugging you when you were crying?'

Taken aback, Harriet said, 'I wasn't aware that he was hugging me. *Or that I was crying,*' she added hastily, noticing Joel looking at her.

'He had his hand on your shoulder,' Carrie carried on blithely. 'I think he likes you. Maybe he could be your boyfriend.'

'Oh, don't be absurd! He's much too old for me. Besides, he has a girl-friend already.'

Joel couldn't sleep that night. Outside his window he could hear the wind rustling in the trees. He didn't like the sound the leaves made; it was like people whispering. They whispered at school; sometimes it upset him. He drew his legs up to his chest. Why had Carrie tried to run away from school? And supposing she did it again and disappeared completely? He'd be all alone. No one to cuddle up to in bed when he couldn't sleep. No one to tell him stories about Mummy and Daddy. And he really wanted to hear those stories because he was already beginning to forget what it used to be like.

With tears running down his cheeks, he slipped out of bed and tip-toed across the landing to Carrie's bedroom. He slid under the duvet next to her. Comforted by her warmth, he was asleep within minutes.

Disturbed by the sound of Joel creeping into Carrie's bedroom, Eileen stirred. She lay for a moment on her side, contemplating the day she'd had. She wished now that she hadn't taken up Dora on her offer to join her for lunch. It had been a mistake. And not just because if she'd been at home to answer the phone, Harriet wouldn't have been bothered at work and rushed home and given herself an asthma attack.

What Eileen most regretted was what she'd told Dora. It was wrong of her. It wasn't as if she had any proof, just a gut feeling to go on. And a history. Dora couldn't hide her shock that Bob, of all men, could have an affair. 'But how do you know?' she'd asked.

'I don't. All I have is a nagging sense of déjà vu.' She explained about the two affairs during the Wilderness Years and how she could see a pat-tern repeating itself. 'It's the way he always leaves the house making sure I have everything I need. That and the long absences.'

'But he's out walking the dog, surely?'

'Oh, Dora, don't you think I'd rather I was imagining it?' she'd said. 'But I just know. You see, there were days, last month, when he was out with Toby for hours at a time and he'd come home almost cheerful.

Then, I don't know why—perhaps she was away on holiday—the walks got shorter. But this morning he was out for ages again. I'm certain he's seeing someone.'

She turned over to look at Bob. But the other side of the bed was empty. She was about to go and see if he was downstairs when a glow of light in the garden caught her eye. Bob was sitting in the Wendy house in the light of a candle. Her heart sank. What was he doing out there? Talking to his lover on his mobile?

A week later, as she drove to work, Harriet knew she needed to make two apologies. Curiously, the two men to whom she needed to say sorry had become Carrie's favourite people. If she was watching television and an antique programme came on, she would hurl herself into a monologue: 'Ooh, look, that's just like Will's shop. When I grow up, I want to do a job like Will's. Do you know what Will—?'

On and on she'd twitter until one of the others, usually Harriet, would change the subject.

Unfortunately Carrie's other hot topic of conversation was Dominic McKendrick. To everyone's amazement, Dominic had sent Carrie an old photograph of Felicity and himself done up as a couple of teenage punks. The picture immediately became one of Carrie's most treasured possessions. She begged Harriet to buy her a frame for it and she placed it on her bedside table, next to her other framed photograph, the one of her parents. She then wrote and thanked Dominic.

When by return of post a further piece of correspondence for Carrie arrived from Cambridge—a postcard depicting a college gargoyle picking its nose, causing Carrie to hoot with laughter—Harriet began to have second thoughts about Dominic. Was it possible that he was finally showing a more genuine side that made him want to please a nine-year-old girl? If this was the case, then she owed him an apology. Within minutes of that awful scene on the towpath when she'd accused him of being incapable of real grief, she had regretted her words. Who was she to dictate how he should publicly mourn Felicity? Especially when they had been such close friends. It had been a friendship that Harriet had, at times, been jealous of. But so what if Dominic always favoured Felicity? she'd told herself. Why should she care when she had Miles? Miles was infinitely kinder than his brother and much easier to be around.

Although there was so much going on in Harriet's life just now, what with her new job and house-hunting, her thoughts were never far from wondering who Felicity had been seeing behind Jeff's back. She was systematically going through all of Felicity's emails late each night, looking for clues. She had gone way beyond feeling guilty about her actions.

Intriguingly and annoyingly, neither Felicity nor her lover had used their names in any of the messages.

For the most part, the emails were intensely serious and highly passionate. Harriet could see what Felicity saw in this man; his adoration must have been powerfully addictive. But it was evident that while Felicity wanted to be with her lover, she was not about to walk out on her children. 'If we're to be together,' she wrote, 'I have to bring my children; they're a part of me.'

'I know that,' he replied. 'And what's a part of you is a part of me.'

'You write as though it will be easy to wrench them away from their father. Believe me, it won't be. They love him and he loves them.'

'But you have to believe me when I say that this agony I'm in is far worse than anything he might feel. His feelings cannot compare.'

The arrogant, self-absorbed nature of this reply made Harriet think of Dominic; he fitted the profile perfectly. Except for the small matter of his sexual preference. True, he had spent part of his adolescence experimenting with Felicity—as Felicity had described what had passed between them—but his lifestyle, since those days, was all too clear.

All this Harriet put aside when she reached the business park. The good news was that she loved her new job. It was early days, but work with ACT was proving to be interesting and stimulating.

However, her efforts to find a house were failing miserably. The details the estate agents were sending her were either grossly misleading or well out of her price range. That was the trouble with wanting to stay in Kings Melford, where she would be close to school and her parents. The latter was imperative; they were her safety net.

Although they hadn't been much of a safety net when Carrie had performed her disappearing act at school. It still appalled Harriet to think what might have happened to her niece if Will hadn't come across her. Which brought her full circle: Will Hart. There really hadn't been any need for her to make that barbed comment about his children not living with him. Feeling decisive, she made a mental note to ring him and apologise. When she'd done that, she would ring Miles and ask him for Dominic's phone number so that she could wipe that slate clean as well.

Howard Beningfield pointed to a chair. 'How do you fancy a trip over to Ireland, Harriet?'

'A potential client?'

He nodded. 'That's right. I want you to convince the haulage company I've been chasing for some months now that we're the boys to give them what they want. Presumably there's no reason why you can't go?'

'No reason at all. When were you thinking?'

Back in her office, Harriet dug out her personal organiser and pen-cilled in the days she would be away. Her stomach rumbled, reminding her that it was now lunchtime. Which in turn reminded her that she had two phone calls to make. Will's number was engaged so she tried Miles.

'You're lucky you caught me,' Miles said. 'I'm just off for lunch.'

'I shan't keep you, but have you got Dominic's number to hand?'

'I have, but what on earth do you want that for?'

'I need to speak to him. Actually, I need to apologise. I was pretty hard on him when he was up here and I've been feeling bad about it.'

'Well, don't. Dominic's never felt bad about another living soul.'

After she'd rung off, having arranged to meet for a drink next week, Harriet tried Will's number again and got through. 'Hi,' she said, 'it's Harriet Swift, your neighbour from across the—'

He cut her off with a laugh. 'It's OK, I know exactly who you are. What can I do for you? Oh, by the way, how's your asthma? No further attacks I hope.'

Harriet stalled, picturing herself making an embarrassing fool of herself in his office. An apology over the phone, though convenient, suddenly didn't seem adequate. If she had any bottle at all, she'd do it in person. 'What time do you finish work?' she asked.

'About six. Why?'

Harriet steeled herself. 'If you're around this evening, I wondered if I could nip across and speak to you. I won't keep you long.'

'You can keep me as long as you like. I have nothing planned for the evening.' He laughed. 'Or for the rest of time, come to think of it.'

Mm . . . she thought, when she'd said goodbye, idly moving the cursor about on her computer screen. It sounded like the pretty blonde girlfriend was no more. Was there a danger, if Will was used to pulling girls much younger than himself, that he might try it on with Harriet?

Let him try!

It was a while since Will had had anyone other than Suzie and Gemma to the house, and after a hurried tidy-up and a blitz round with the Dyson and a duster, he deemed the place verging on the half-decent. Lately he hadn't had much time for the pinny and rubber-glove routine. Keeping the peace between Suzie and her mother was a full-time job in itself. When he'd driven Suzie home and explained the situation, Maxine had screeched, 'But she can't keep the baby! What about univer-sity? How does she think she's going to manage? Oh, this is madness!'

Unable to keep his temper in check a moment longer, Will turned on Maxine. 'I'll tell you how's she going to manage: she's going to have all the love and support she bloody well deserves.'

Since then, Maxine had calmed down, though Will knew Suzie was hurt that her mother had pointed out several times that it wasn't too late for her to have a termination. But he couldn't believe that Maxine wouldn't finally come round and be there for Suzie.

He gave the sitting room a final check, then opened a bottle of Merlot. He wondered what the Hedgehog wanted to discuss with him.

Harriet went downstairs after reading Joel his bedtime story. Her mother was in the kitchen. 'Dad out with Toby again?' she asked.

Eileen slammed the lid of the bin shut. 'Looks like it.'

Harriet could see how tired her mother looked, but she sensed it wasn't only her ME and Felicity's death that was bothering her. As she crossed the road to see Will, she turned it over in her mind. There was something else going on; but what? She was no good at subtexts. It was another reason she often preferred computers to people. You knew exactly where you stood with them.

While Will was in the kitchen fetching their drinks, Harriet took the opportunity to prowl round his sitting room. It was homely and comfortable. She had just picked up one of a pair of photographs on top of a writing desk when Will came in.

'Feel free,' he said, when she put it back guiltily. 'I'm totally biased, of course,' he went on, 'but I think they're beautiful.'

Harriet looked at the two little girls, dressed in their best party frocks. Their blonde hair was long and fine and Harriet had to admit they did indeed look beautiful. 'How old are they?'

'In the picture?'

'Yes.'

'Two and four.' He set their wineglasses on the desk and picked up the other photograph. 'This was taken of the three of us last Christmas. Suzie's nineteen and Gemma's seventeen.'

Harriet took the photograph from him. She paid particular attention to the taller of the two girls, then suddenly felt very stupid. The girl she'd thought was his girlfriend hadn't been anything of the sort. 'I'd imagined your children younger; early teens perhaps.'

'Ah, that will be on account of me looking so devilishly youthful. Come and sit down. I'd recommend the armchair, the sofa has wonky springs.'

Harriet settled herself by the fire, dwelling on the error she'd made.

'How's Carrie?' Will asked. 'No more break-outs, I trust?'

'Thankfully her attempt last week seems to have been a one-off.'

'Did you get to the bottom of why she did it?'

'She said she was bored.'

'And you believed her?'

Harriet bristled. 'Why wouldn't we?'

He opened his mouth to say something but then seemed to change his mind. He took a gulp of his wine and said, 'My mother once told me that becoming a parent provides you with the opportunity to make more mistakes than any other way she knew.'

'Are you saying I've made a mistake with Carrie?'

'Not at all. I'm suggesting, as I did before, that you shouldn't be so hard on yourself.'

Harriet didn't want to think about that day too much, but seeing as he'd brought up the subject, she said, 'You were very good to Carrie . . . and me, which is why I'm here. We're all really grateful for what you did. I don't think I expressed myself very well at the time.'

He waved a hand at her words. 'You were upset. I quite understood. Anyway, your father's already thanked me.'

'He has? He never said anything. But the apology still stands; there was no excuse for what I said to you.'

He raised an eyebrow. 'Remind me what you said.'

If she didn't know better, she'd say he was enjoying himself at her expense. 'I accused you of not knowing what you were talking about because your children don't live with you.'

'It's an accusation my ex-wife would be quick to agree with.'

'That's as maybe, but I had no right to suggest it. I'm sorry.' There. She'd done it. Apology made. She sat back in the chair.

'How's the new job going?' he asked after a moment's silence. 'What's a nice girl like you doing in the yawn-inducing world of computers?'

She rolled her eyes. 'And if I had a pound for every time I'd been asked that crass question, I'd be richer than Bill Gates.'

'Sorry to be so unoriginal.'

'Don't worry, I'm used to it. There's a theory that only a limited number of people are genetically predisposed to be programmers.'

'And you're one of them?'

'It would seem so. It's not a matter of intelligence, more a way of thinking. And actually, there aren't enough of the right brains out there.'

'So what's the fascination? They're just machines.'

'To you, maybe. But for someone like me, it's the perfect interaction. Computers don't answer back. You tell a computer what to do and it does it. Computers are very literal and as a programmer you get used to taking things, and people, at face value.'

'So if a Johnny Quick Banana came along and tried out something subtle on you, like a compliment, you'd blow a fuse and flash up, "Sorry, can't compute!"'

Knowing that he was making fun of her, she said, 'Except there wouldn't be the apology.'

He smiled. 'Unless you were feeling remorseful about something.'

'Are you trying to extract another apology out of me?'

'No. I think you've done splendidly in that department already. How about some music? Do you like R.E.M.?'

'Bring it on.'

Will put *Reveal* into the CD player. He decided that once the Hedgehog was relaxed and on safe ground, she was excellent company. Her enthusiasm for her work was charming. Yet it occurred to him that she probably expected Carrie and Joel to behave logically, like a computer would. And as any parent could tell her, kids just don't do that. Did he dare tell her this? No. He was enjoying himself too much to want to spoil a pleasant evening by antagonising her.

'I've got a confession to make,' she said, interrupting his thoughts, which had started to run along the lines that she was really quite pretty; her cheekbones seemed less sharp and her eyes softer, less wary.

'A confession? That sounds ominous. What have you done?'

'It's part of another apology I think I owe you. You see, one of the reasons I snapped at you last week was because I'd taken something at face value and misinterpreted it. I thought your eldest daughter, Suzie, was your girlfriend and that it was her you were referring to when you said someone close to you was pregnant and considering an abortion.'

'Bloody hell, I've done some shitty things in my time, but chasing girls less than half my age is not one of them. You must have thought I was a randy old git who couldn't keep it in his trousers.'

'I did. And I'm very sorry.'

He let out his breath. 'Wow. I don't know what to say, other than Suzie is definitely my daughter and she's definitely pregnant, but not by me.' He saw a look of surprise pass across Harriet's face.

'Your daughter's pregnant?' she repeated. 'But she's—'

'So young,' he finished for her. 'Yes. I'm all too aware of that.'

'And the abortion?'

'She changed her mind. She's not going through with it.'

'That's brave.'

'You're telling me.' Then, hearing the change of track on the CD, he said, 'Listen to this. Isn't it the best?'

'What's it called? I'm not familiar with it.'

He pulled a face. 'I knew you were too good to be true. It's "I've Been High". Now close your eyes and breathe it in.'

Harriet watched Will close his eyes and tilt his head back against the sofa cushion. What a surprising man he was.

The following Sunday Harriet drove the children to Maywood where they were meeting Miles for Sunday lunch at Casa Bellagio. Her efforts to apologise to Miles's brother had so far run aground on an answering machine. Her messages for him to call her back had all been ignored and she'd decided not to waste any more energy on him. Work was picking up and next week she was off to Dublin. Her trip coincided with half term which meant that Bob and Eileen would have to entertain Carrie and Joel all day. Will had very kindly offered his daughter as a baby sitter. 'Now that Suzie has quit university, she might be glad of something to do,' he'd said.

It was good to know that there were people close by to whom she could turn for help: Miles and Will, to name but two. Will had also recommended a good friend of his who was a solicitor and who could act on her behalf when she was ready to buy a house. Having got to know Will better, Harriet now realised just how unfairly she had judged him, especially when it came to bringing up children. He'd told her about his house-husband days. 'I can't tell you how much I enjoyed being at home with the girls,' he'd said.

Miles was already at the restaurant when they arrived. As soon as they were settled, Miles produced two small Novel Ways carrier bags. He passed them across the table to Carrie and Joel. 'I thought you might like these,' he said. Their faces lit up when they each pulled out a book.

'That was very kind of you,' Harriet said, after the children had thanked him and started to turn the pages.

When the waitress had taken their order Miles said, 'We're having a special Halloween event at the shop next week during half term; I don't suppose you'd like to come, would you, Carrie and Joel? We're making pumpkin lanterns followed by a story hour. Everyone has to dress up as a character from a book.'

Two eager faces stared at Harriet across the table. 'Can we go, Harriet?'

Harriet still found it weird that she was the one whose decision was sought on such matters. 'I don't see why not. What day is it, Miles?'

'Friday afternoon. You can come along as well if you like.'

She pulled a face. 'I might be able to join you. I'll be flying back from Dublin that morning and skiving off early could well be justified.'

They decided to walk off lunch with a stroll in the park. Carrie and Joel ran on ahead, kicking madly at the fallen leaves. Anyone looking at them would have taken them for the perfect nuclear family. The thought gave Harriet a curious feeling of pleasure. As crazy as it sounded, she could picture Felicity looking down on them and nodding her head approvingly.

Seeing the look of happiness on Carrie and Joel's faces as they ran off to the roundabout, it was hard to imagine they'd so recently gone through the trauma of losing their parents. They're moving on, Harriet thought. It's really happening.

Breaking into her thoughts, Miles said, 'They're great kids, aren't they? They've coped so well.' He stood beside her and put his arm round her shoulder. 'Felicity would be proud of them.'

'Jeff too.' She was beginning to realise how easy it was for everyone to forget her brother-in-law. A man she was feeling increasingly sorry for.

But there was another man she had started to feel sorry for. A man she didn't even know. Felicity's lover must have been distraught when he found out she was dead. How was he coping?

A squeeze on her shoulder made Harriet look up at Miles. He said, 'We should spend more afternoons like this.'

She smiled. 'I'd like that.'

He held her closer. 'And if you'd let me, I'd like to do more to help with Carrie and Joel. They feel like family to me anyway.'

Harriet thought about this later that evening when she was looking for a clean nightdress for Carrie in her chest of drawers. Was it possible that she and Miles could be more than just friends? She was on her way out of the room when she caught her foot on the wastepaper bin. She bent down to tidy the mess and noticed a screwed-up ball of paper. Without knowing why, she picked it up and smoothed it out. What she saw horrified her, and she cursed under her breath. She stuffed it into her jeans. She then recalled Will's words about getting to the bottom of Carrie's actions. Once again her respect for the man went up. It also explained the reluctance Carrie had started to display about going to school.

She said nothing about the note to Carrie when she tucked her into bed that night, but she found herself giving the girl an extra big hug.

'I enjoyed today,' Carrie said. 'Did you?'

'Yes, it was fun. And you've got Friday afternoon at the bookshop to look forward to now, haven't you?' She was conscious that Carrie needed as many things to look forward to as possible. School must have become a nightmare for her.

'Will you help us to make some costumes?'

'I've got a much better idea: why don't we ask Grandma to do that? She's better at that kind of thing than me.'

Carrie smiled and held out her arms. 'Can I have another hug, please?'

When Carrie was sure Harriet had gone downstairs, she got out of bed and tiptoed through to her brother's bedroom. 'Are you awake, Joel?'

He turned over and sat up. 'What is it?'

'Do you think Miles is Harriet's boyfriend?'

He shrugged. 'I don't know. What do you think?'

'I saw them holding hands in the park. If Harriet married him we could live with Miles in Maywood. And we'd always have books to read.'

'Would it be like having a proper mummy and daddy again?'

'Sort of. If we moved to Maywood, we'd have to change schools. You'd like that, wouldn't you? A new school with nicer people in it.'

Joel hugged his sister tight. If Carrie was right, and she always was, then everything would get better. If Carrie was happy in their new school, she wouldn't think of running away again and he wouldn't have to worry about being left all alone.

Bob knew it was selfish and unworthy of him, but he couldn't wait for half term to be over and the children to return to school. So long as they were around, it was difficult for him to slip away and see Jennifer. His feelings for her had intensified but not in the way he might have anticipated. She had made it very clear that she was not the sort of woman who would have an affair with a married man.

'That's not what I want,' he had said, taken aback by her candour, but at the same time, relieved. 'I find I feel better about myself when I'm with you,' he told her. 'You make all the bad stuff go away. All the anger. All the hopelessness. Am I making any sense to you?'

'You sound like a bereaved man who needs a friend,' she'd said simply. 'So long as we're both clear on that score,' she'd added. 'I'd hate for your wife to get the wrong idea about us.'

Today, at Eileen's suggestion, he was driving them all to the garden centre. He would have preferred to come on his own, but Eileen had said that while she was deciding which daffodil bulbs to buy, he could treat the children to a ride on the narrow-gauge railway train that ran through the garden centre.

Carrie and Joel were the only passengers as the train set off on its mammoth eight-minute trek. They waved at Bob—Carrie's hand barely moving, but Joel's waving frantically—and all at once he was overcome with a desperate sadness. Never had his grandchildren seemed more alone. Oh God, he thought as he returned the wave, I'm going to cry.

Carrie wished it could be like this always. No school, no horrid letter, no spiteful girls, just lots of lovely days out. After the train ride at the garden centre, and a beans and sausage lunch in a nearby café, they were now going into town. While Grandma was having her hair done, Granddad said he'd take them to his favourite type of shop.

'The thing about charity shops,' he said, as he pushed open the door, 'is that you never know what you might find. There's a section over there with books and toys; why don't you both go and have a rummage?'

Carrie took Joel to the children's area. 'Look, Joel,' she said, 'it's a train like the one we've just been on.'

'No, it isn't. It's broken. And it's . . . ooh, look what I've found.' He held up a clockwork mouse. He turned the winder, then let the toy loose. It scuttled across the dirty carpet, and disappeared into a small, curtained area. They chased after it and dived under the curtain to find themselves looking up at a pretty blonde girl; she was just pushing an arm through the sleeve of a jacket. 'I think it went under my bag,' she said with a friendly smile. Embarrassed, they both slid out the way they'd just come. Within seconds the girl appeared and handed them the clockwork mouse. 'I know you two, don't I? You live over the road from my father. I'm Gemma, by the way. I hear that my dad's offered my sister's services as baby sitter for you two.'

'Really?' asked Carrie.

'Don't look so scared. She's quite friendly. See you.'

Carrie watched her go. 'She was nice, wasn't she?' she said to Joel.

'Why do we need a baby sitter? We've got Harriet and Grandma and Granddad. We don't need anyone else.'

Carrie sighed. She was getting fed with Joel's constant worrying. 'Even when we had Mum and Dad, we still had a baby sitter,' she reminded him. 'Don't you remember Mum used to say it was important she and Dad went out without us sometimes? She called it grown-up time.'

As they went to find their grandfather, Carrie had a sudden memory of her mother getting ready to go out one night. Dad had been away, and Carrie had been surprised that her mother was going out on her own. 'This is Mummy time,' she'd said with a laugh. 'Do I look nice?'

'You look lovely,' Carrie could remember saying. 'Where are you going?'

'To see a friend. A special friend. Kiss me good night and be extra good for the baby sitter.' That night seemed a long, long time ago.

During the drive home, Joel kept thinking about what Carrie had said. That their parents used to go out without them. He had only one memory of them going out at night, and that was the night they never came back. Then, from nowhere, he recalled something he must have forgotten about that night. Dad had been angry about something. But what could Daddy have been angry about?

'Have you and your wife ever thought about bereavement counselling?'

Bob sat down on the bench seat. At the other end of the table, Jennifer was mixing herself a hot toddy. He'd been here for less than ten minutes, but already the strain of the day was slipping away. 'No,' he said. 'Eileen wanted to, but . . . but I couldn't bring myself to discuss something so personal, not with a stranger.'

'But you've done it with me.'

He thought about this. 'This may sound odd, but you've never felt like a stranger.'

She stopped what she was doing and looked at him. 'That's probably one of the nicest things anyone's ever said to me. Thank you.' She went back to stirring the hot toddy, then took a cautious sip.

'If you're not feeling well, I ought to leave you,' he said.

'Perhaps you're right. I do feel rather tired.'

He got to his feet reluctantly and kissed her for the first time. Just a fond peck on the forehead. 'Sleep well.'

Out on the towpath, the chill of night seeped into his bones. He buttoned up his coat and walked briskly. When he was level with Will's house, he looked up and saw a bedroom light on. There were no curtains and it was embarrassingly easy to make out the two figures and what they were doing. Bob hurried on. Good luck to them, he thought, with a stab of envy.

Will was doing his best, he just couldn't summon the energy for what Sandra expected from him. Disentangling himself from her voluptuous body, he rolled over onto his side.

'Oh, no, you don't,' she said, 'you come back here.'

'I need the bathroom,' he lied. He hotfooted it across the landing and locked the bathroom door. What the hell was he doing? Why had he agreed to see Sandra again, after they'd both admitted that the fun had gone out of their fling? Hearing Sandra calling to him, he closed his eyes and tried to prepare himself for a convincing performance.

He didn't know whether to be humiliated or relieved when twenty minutes later Sandra was throwing on her clothes in a huff of frustration. 'You know what your trouble is, Will? You're past it.'

'I think you might be right,' he murmured as she was clattering down the stairs and shouting that she never wanted to hear from him again.

He stood in the shower till the scalding water ran cold. In his bathrobe, he went and stood on the landing by the window that overlooked the front garden. He had long since decided that he liked living in Maple Drive and probably wouldn't sell the house on as quickly as he'd originally planned.

Looking across to number 20, he wondered how Harriet was. He'd enjoyed their evening together. Compared to the one he'd just had it seemed perfect. He wondered if he could get away with asking her out for dinner. Why not? he asked himself. *Because she's so much younger than you, you idiot!* It would only be dinner, he argued back.

But even as he thought this, his body betrayed him with a stirring that would have solved all his earlier problems with Sandra.

Shocked, he turned away from the window. What the hell was going on? Harriet Swift was not his type at all. She was too young. She was too thin. She wasn't blonde. So what was it, then? OK, she was smart, pithy and honest, attributes he did like in a woman. She was also fiercely detached, which he found oddly touching. And, of course, there was that whole hedgehog thing he'd found so amusing initially, and which he now found endearing, knowing that her prickliness was actually due to a need to disguise how vulnerable her new situation made her. He couldn't help but admire her. She had real guts.

So was that it? There was only one way to find out. He had to get to know her better. Would it be pushing his luck to say he had a spare ticket for the Jools Holland concert next month? He could always make out he was being neighbourly. Why not? The age gap wasn't *that* big.

The piercing pipping of the alarm clock woke Harriet and she lay for a moment in the darkness, unable to shake off a strange dream. It was one of those dreams that could persuade you it held some vital truth or significance. She had been insisting to Miles: 'I need to know what to do.' What had she been referring to?

By the time she was in the shower and thinking about the day ahead—her trip to Ireland—logic had kicked in. Of course! The anxiety in the dream had been about Carrie and school. Harriet still hadn't said anything to her parents about the letter she'd found. She didn't want them to worry. Especially not her mother, who worried Harriet almost as much as Carrie's latest problem. She was convinced there was something going on that Eileen was keeping to herself. But all that would have to wait. Today there was Dublin to concentrate on.

The children were already up when she went downstairs to grab a quick cup of coffee before driving to the airport to meet Howard. They were in the sitting room on the sofa when she popped her head round the door.

Joel saw her first. 'You look different, Harriet,' he said.

Carrie wrenched her gaze away from the television. 'You're wearing a skirt,' she said, a mixture of accusation and disbelief in her voice.

'Correction. I'm wearing a suit.'

'Are you going somewhere special?'

This was something else she'd learned; children only ever remember what's going on in their own world. 'Don't you remember I'm flying to Ireland today?'

Joel's eyes grew wide. 'How long for?'

'Come on, Joel, we discussed this yesterday. I'm only going to be away for one night.' To distract him, she added, 'You haven't forgotten about going to Maywood tomorrow to see Miles at the bookshop, have you?'

'You will be back in time, won't you?' There was an anxious tremor in Joel's question.

Harriet said, 'I'll try very hard to make sure I am. But I can't promise anything. If my flight's delayed or the traffic's bad, it's out of my hands.'

'But you have to be there!'

This was from Carrie. Surprised that her niece was being so insistent, Harriet stood up. 'Like I say, I'll do my best.'

When she was leaving the house, her mother said, 'Try not to let the children down about tomorrow. They really want you to be there.'

Harriet could never understand why people felt the need to reiterate the same point. One clearly made instruction was all it took.

Harriet was impressed. Howard was performing like a pro. He knew his stuff and was taking his time with the prospective client. There was no sign of the patronising buffoon she'd sat next to on the Aer Lingus flight who'd called the steward Mick and made an offensive joke about Irish time to a fellow passenger.

'What I suggest we do now,' he said, casting a look in her direction, 'is for Harriet to outline the kind of application we could do for you. That way you can get to know the expert who will look after the job for you.'

Several hours later, she and Howard were heading back to their hotel opposite St Stephen's Green. Harriet was looking forward to pampering herself in a hot, bubbly bath and then calling room service, but Howard was having none of it. 'Let's go for a drink to celebrate.'

'We haven't got the contract yet.'

'Are you always this optimistic?'

'I think—'

'No, I'll tell you how you think,' he said, forcibly leading her through to the bar. 'You think too literally. You programmers are all the bloody same. Now sit on that stool and let me buy you a drink.'

Welcome back the real Howard, Harriet thought with a smile as she tried to make herself decent on the stool—her skirt had ridden up somewhere on a level with her knickers.

'Stop wriggling,' he said, 'and leave your skirt where it is. It suits you.'

She blushed. 'Do you treat all your employees like this?'

He gave her a wink. 'Only the ones for whom I have high hopes.' Some champagne arrived and Howard insisted on pouring it. 'Cheers. And well done for today. You did brilliantly. Just as I knew you would.'

She accepted the compliment with as much good grace as she could muster. Howard was a fast drinker and while she had no intention of keeping pace with him, Harriet drank more than she'd intended. 'There's something I want to say, Hat. Can I call you Hat?'

Harriet nodded.

He smiled. 'Well, Hat, I think you're doing a great job. And I'm not just talking about work. I'm referring to the job you're doing at home. I think it's brilliant, what you're doing, bringing up your sister's children. And you've never once let it get in the way of your job.'

'How did you know?'

He tapped his nose. 'Adrian. He told me everything.'

'Before or after my interview?'

'Oh, definitely after your interview. So why didn't you tell me about the kiddies?'

'It was you who said you didn't want to employ one of those devious girls who'd get herself pregnant then sting you for maternity leave.'

'That's quite a different matter, Hat. How are you managing child-care wise?'

Seeing as he seemed genuinely interested, she told him about her parents and how she was now trying to buy somewhere to live.

'You've been on a hell of a learning curve. Now, Hat.' He leaned in close. 'I'm a fair man. If you need the odd afternoon off to pick up the children for some reason, just make up the hours another day. OK?'

'Thank you, that's very kind of you,' she said, and seizing the opportunity, added, 'Can I do that tomorrow afternoon when we get back?'

The next morning, Harriet was awake early. Unable to get back to sleep, she decided to go for a walk in the park opposite the hotel. She hadn't been walking for long when she noticed a figure on a bench ahead of her. Bundled up in a thick overcoat, he was leaning forward, his elbows resting on his knees. He looked like he was deep in prayer. As she approached, a prickle of recognition caused her to call out.

'Dominic?'

'Good God, Harriet. Is that really you, or am I dreaming?'

'Perhaps we're both dreaming. What brings you to Dublin?'

He waved a hand airily. 'I'm ransacking Trinity's library for a paper I'm doing on Yeats. The poet,' he added.

She sat on the bench next to him, noting how tired and dishevelled he looked. Like a man who hadn't been to bed perhaps. Certainly not his own bed. Same old Dominic, then. 'Yes, Dominic, I am aware who Yeats is,' she said tightly. 'I'm not quite that thick, you know.'

He ignored the gibe. 'So what are you doing here?'

'Work. I'm here with my boss. We leave this morning.'

'Who's looking after Carrie and Joel while you're away?'

'Who do you think? Mum and Dad, of course.'

'And they're well?'

These questions from Dominic enquiring about someone else wrong-footed her. So often it was only his own welfare he was concerned about. 'Sorry. Who?'

He turned sharply. 'Just what exactly is your problem?'

'All I was wondering was who you meant specifically.'

'Is it entirely beyond the realms of your feeble understanding that I might ask after the children as well as your parents? Or have you imposed some kind of embargo on whose health I might be interested in? Just as you have when it comes to displays of grief.' He shook his head. 'Who'd have thought you'd turn into such a fascist?'

'And who'd have thought you'd turn into an even bigger bastard than the one we thought you were destined to be.'

He glared at her, then suddenly tipped his head back and laughed. 'I'm disappointed in you. How could you have ever underestimated me? I'm the biggest bastard going.'

'Not entirely. You were very sweet to write to Carrie.'

He shuddered. 'If I ever hear you call me sweet again, I shall have to kill you. Now shut up, you obnoxious harridan, and give me a hug. I'm in dire need of one.' He held her fiercely then let her go. She saw that his eyes were moist and bloodshot.

'You OK?'

'As it happens, no, I'm not. I think I'm on the verge of a breakdown.'

The directness of his words shocked her. She didn't know what to say.

'I've been doing a lot of thinking,' he said softly. 'I've come to the only possible conclusion: life has as much point to it as a mote of dust.'

'You mean in the light of Felicity's death?' she asked.

His head snapped up. 'What the hell else could I be referring to?'

'If you're going to bite my head off every time I say something—'

He suddenly reached out to her. 'Please. I'm sorry.'

His voice was unbearably contrite and Harriet felt a wave of compassion for him. After a lengthy pause, she said, 'So tell me why you think everything's so futile.'

'It's because I'm completely and utterly alone in this world. If I was to die tomorrow, who would mourn my passing? Who would even care?'

'Aren't you forgetting your parents and Miles? And what about me? I'd miss you. There'd be no one to fight with,' she added lightly.

'I'm talking about love. Real love. The kind of all-consuming love Yeats understood too well.'

'You don't have the monopoly on not being loved, Dominic. I don't have a queue of people lining up to worship the ground I walk on.'

'But you have Carrie and Joel who rely on you. They need you. Who the hell needs me? What difference do I make to the world?'

Harriet wondered if he had been speaking the truth when he said he was on the verge of a breakdown. 'Have you seen a doctor?'

'No, but I have seen a priest. I'm worried about my spiritual welfare.'

She laughed, but immediately wished she hadn't.

'Sod you, Harriet. I was being serious.'

'It was so unexpected hearing you speak like that. I'm sorry.'

'So you should be. That was the difference between you and Felicity. Felicity was perfectly in tune with me. She never misinterpreted anything I said. She could always read between the lines.'

'You know what? I'm sick of people criticising me. I'm Harriet Swift. The way I think is the way I am. Why can't people accept that?'

'So who else has been having a go at you, besides me?'

She told him about Howard saying she thought too literally, not realising until now just how deeply his comment had resonated with her. 'Do you think I'm too literal?' she asked Dominic.

'Of course you are. You always have been.'

'Is it a bad thing?'

'Yes. You lose sight of the wider picture. You see only the detail. And why, I'd like to know, are we talking about you, when it's me we're supposed to be discussing? I'm hungry. Let's go to your hotel for breakfast.'

It was still early when they pushed open the door of the dining room. There was no sign of Howard. When a waiter approached their table, they ordered eggs Benedict for Dominic, scrambled eggs and bacon for Harriet and a pot of coffee with two rounds of toast.

When they were on their own again, Dominic said, 'Tell me something to cheer me up. How's my brother? Behaving himself, I trust?'

'The children and I spent the day with him on Sunday. We had lunch in Maywood then went for a walk in the park.'

'Ye gods! It sounds like something out of *Mary Poppins*. Take a tip from me, Hat. Please indulge yourself more. Treat yourself to some sinful pleasure now and then. It'll do wonders to thaw that frosty streak of self-denial that's ruining your life.'

She folded her arms and stared out of the window. Why did he always have to spoil things? She went on the attack, as she usually did whenever she was in his company. 'Why haven't you returned any of the messages I left you?'

'I've been too busy. Ah . . . at last, here's breakfast.'

When their waiter had left them, Dominic poured the coffee. 'This is very domestic, isn't it?' he said. 'I feel quite the husband.'

'That'll be the day,' she muttered, still cross with him.

He glanced at her. 'It must be exhausting being such a bitch. Why do you have such a problem with my lifestyle?'

'I've never been bothered by your sexuality; it's your promiscuity I have trouble with.'

'There's nothing illegal about the way I conduct my sex life. Why should you concern yourself with what a raging queer like me gets up to?'

She winced at his words. 'I'm not concerned.'

'You are. It's coming at me in great waves of disapproval across the table. Let's face it, you always were a prude. You used to hate it when Felicity and I went off for one of our experimental romps.'

In spite of herself, Harriet blushed. She hated knowing that he still had the power to do this to her. 'What if I did?'

'Was it because you were jealous? Jealous that it wasn't you I was experimenting with?'

His tone was uncharacteristically gentle, but even so she could have thrown her plate at him. 'I know you've always had a high opinion of yourself, Dominic, but really, take it from me, I'd have to have been two shades of crazy to fancy you.'

'I'm sorry if I've embarrassed you, but actually it was Felicity who told me you were jealous.'

'Never! Never in a million years would she have said that.'

He continued with his breakfast in silence, leaving Harriet to contemplate the inconceivable—had Felicity betrayed her to Dominic? Everything she'd believed in, when it came to Felicity, was falling apart. There were too many acts of betrayal going on. She glanced up at Dominic, and wondered just how many more confidences Felicity had shared with him. Was it possible that he knew about Felicity's affair?

'Do you think Felicity was happy in her marriage?' she asked.

His fork halfway to his mouth, he said, 'Good God, Harriet. The poor girl's dead. Have you no respect?'

Determined to make him answer her, she said, 'Do you think she was capable of an affair?'

He sighed. 'We're all capable of doing the unthinkable. But cheating on her husband wasn't Felicity's style. She was above such behaviour.'

He resumed eating as though the matter had been neatly dealt with. But still hurting from the assertions he'd made about her, Harriet wanted to get her own back, and the best way to do that was to openly criticise his precious Felicity. 'I know for a fact that Felicity was seeing someone behind Jeff's back.' She watched his face closely for a reaction.

'I don't believe it,' he said. 'Who was it? Who was she seeing?'

'I don't know yet.' She told him about the emails, taking a perverse pleasure in knocking down the plastered saint illusion Dominic had created.

His reaction was not to defend Felicity, as she'd expected, but to say, 'And you really can't think who her lover might have been? Who always had a thing for your sister? Who hated it whenever I embarrassed him in front of her. Who—?'

'You don't mean—'

'I do. My brother was always crazy about Felicity.'

'But . . . but she was never crazy about him. And surely Miles just isn't the type? He's certainly not a home-wrecker.'

'He's a man with as great a sexual appetite as the next. Gay or straight. Have you looked through Felicity's things for proof? There must be diaries, letters, or billets-doux you can mull over.'

'No. We got rid of most of the stuff like that. There are a few boxes left in the garage, but my guess is I won't find anything. She wouldn't have been silly enough to keep anything that would give them away. You really believe it's Miles?'

'Yes. In fact, the more I think about it, the more certain I am.'

Harriet thought about Miles's unconcealed distress at the funeral. Was his sadness out of proportion for mourning a friend? Seeing his face before her, a more recent memory came into Harriet's mind of her and Miles in the park in Maywood when she'd begun to think that maybe their friendship was developing into something deeper. And what of that comment he'd made about wanting to do more for the children? None of it made sense. If he'd loved her sister, why did he now want to spend time with her?

Harriet said, 'You don't seem shocked by what I've told you. After all, you did just say you thought Felicity was above such behaviour.'

'You expected me to be shocked? How odd. No—' His words stopped abruptly and his gaze shifted. 'Don't turn round, Hat, but there's the most hideous man looking this way. *Harriet!* I said don't turn round.'

Oh Lord, it was Howard.

While the girl with the dangling, light-up pumpkin earrings read to them, Joel watched the door anxiously. He wished Harriet would come. Maybe if he closed his eyes, held his breath and counted to twenty, the door would open and Harriet would be there. But when he got to sixteen he opened his eyes with a thought so terrifying it made his heart beat faster. What if Harriet wasn't coming? Because she'd had an accident like Mummy and Daddy? His lip began to tremble.

Bob left the car in The Navigation's car park and took the steps down to the towpath. He tapped on the side of the boat and was about to let himself in through the hatch doors as he usually did, when he heard the sound of a man's voice. He stepped into the saloon and was surprised to see a man shutting a large briefcase.

Jennifer said, 'It's OK, Bob, come on—' But her words were cut short by a racking cough that made her shoulders shake. 'Excuse me,' she managed to say, before disappearing to the prow, where Bob could still hear her coughing painfully.

The man, clearly a doctor, and one Bob didn't recognise from his own surgery, looked at him. 'Are you the friend she says is looking after her?'

'Yes. How is she?'

'Not good. Ideally, she needs to get off this boat. She has a chest infection and the damp will only make things worse.'

After the doctor had left, Bob helped Jennifer into bed. 'You need to do as the doctor says; you must go home. If you're worrying about the logistics, don't. You can leave the boat here and I'll drive you home.'

A small smile appeared on her washed-out face. 'But if I went, I'd—' Gripped by a bout of coughing, she covered her mouth with a hand.

'What were you going to say?' he prompted.

'No,' she said breathlessly. 'It's better I don't say it.'

He stroked her hand. 'Please tell me what it was.'

Her fingers became entwined with his. She met his gaze. 'I'd rather be ill here and still see you than go home to an empty house.'

Harriet was cutting it fine, but so long as the traffic kept moving, she'd make it to Maywood and catch the last half-hour with the children at Novel Ways. Howard had been great; he'd told her to shoot off the moment they'd got through passport control.

He'd surprised her in so many ways during the trip. Behind the crass, overtly chauvinistic exterior, was a reasonable and approachable man. The other surprise had been Dominic showing up in Dublin.

However, the extraordinary coincidence of their paths crossing hadn't amazed her as much as the content of their conversation had. Could Felicity really have told Dominic that Harriet had fancied him? Maybe, if she'd been drunk. It was too hurtful to contemplate Felicity deliberately laughing with Dominic over the time when Harriet had secretly, *stupidly*, longed for Dominic to love her. But far worse than any of that was Dominic's assertion that Miles could be Felicity's mystery lover. Surely it just wasn't possible. Or was it?

She arrived at Novel Ways in time to see Carrie being awarded a book voucher for her vampire costume. 'I sincerely hope that was nepotism,' she said to Miles, slipping in at the back of the applauding parents.

'Harriet, you made it!' The pleasure on his face gave her a warm glow. But then she thought of everything Dominic had said and the feeling passed. Miles and Felicity. Felicity and Miles. The more she said their names together, the more possible their affair seemed. But where did it leave her? Where she'd always been, she supposed. Miles's friend. She'd been stupid to imagine anything else. But there was no time to reflect on this. Joel hurtled across the shop and threw himself at her. 'You mustn't go away again,' he said breathlessly.

'Why ever not?' she asked.

'Because you might die. Just like Mummy and Daddy did.'

She looked into his tear-filled eyes and felt something like an earthquake inside her.

NOVEMBER

'Pleasure's a sin, and sometimes sin's a pleasure.'

'Don Juan', LORD BYRON

ON MONDAY MORNING the children went back to school and just as soon as she had a free moment, Harriet took a break from work to ring Mrs Thompson, the headmistress. A meeting, face to face, was probably a better way of dealing with the matter, but Harriet didn't want to take any more time off work unnecessarily. Nor did she want to take the easy way out by telling her parents what had been going on and off-loading the problem onto them. When the culprits had been dealt with, then she'd tell them. Or maybe she wouldn't. Just now her parents seemed distant and unreachable. Particularly her father. On Saturday he announced at breakfast that he was spending the day with an old work colleague who was going through a rough patch and needed taking out himself. He didn't come home until gone midnight.

'What can I do for you?' Mrs Thompson said, when she came to the phone. 'Is it about the parents' evening next week?'

'No, it's not that,' Harriet said, scribbling a note on her pad in front of her. Damn! How had she forgotten that? 'I'd like to know what your policy is for dealing with bullies. I'm assuming you do have one.'

'Can you be more specific?'

'Yes. Carrie has received what I can only describe as hate mail. Given her behaviour recently, I suspect it isn't the first that she has received.'

'Do you still have the letter?'

'Yes.'

'If you bring it in, I can take it from there. In my experience, a small but firm word in the right ear is all that is required.'

A small but firm rap round the ear seemed more appropriate, but Harriet let it go. 'I think this explains why Carrie skipped out of school the other week,' Harriet said, 'so I'd appreciate it if you would keep a close eye on her and make sure that the time she's in your care is a happy time.'

'I like to think that goes for all our pupils, Miss Swift. But we have to face facts. As unpalatable as it may seem, some children do single themselves out for treatment which is far from being socially acceptable.'

Harriet wasn't going to stand for this. 'I hope you're not suggesting that Carrie has brought this on herself because her parents are dead.'

'All I'm saying is that invariably there's a reason for these problems. Carrie didn't help herself with those terrible stories she told about her parents. We have to view the wider picture at all times. Have you talked to Carrie about the letter and that you were going to talk to me about it?'

'No. I didn't want her worrying that the bullying would get worse.'

'Mm . . . I'm not sure that's the best thing to do. But for now, as I said earlier, bring in the letter and we'll take it from there.'

Harriet rang off and considered the headmistress's comment about the *wider picture*. Was someone trying to tell her something?

Ever since his spectacular fall from grace, Will's life had jogged along quite nicely. The trick was to keep things simple. And he'd done that to great effect. Until now. Now there were complications coming at him from all sides. The biggest one was Suzie. She was six months pregnant and Maxine was still struggling to come round to the inevitable. But grandparents they were about to become, whether they liked it or not, and the sooner Maxine got used to the idea, the better for them all. He couldn't exactly say he was thrilled at the new persona he was about to adopt: grandfather. It put at least another twenty years on him, which he'd rather not feel right now.

And that brought him to the other equally unexpected complication in his life. Harriet. He wasn't used to being turned down by women and he wasn't sure he could handle it if Harriet said no. He still hadn't plucked up the courage to ask if she'd like to come to the Jools Holland concert. Every time he thought of Harriet—which he did frequently—he was reminded of that determined spirit of hers. There was something quite magnificent about her, he'd decided. Heroic even.

He was meeting Marty for lunch at Brian's burger bar. For once, Marty was late. Will wrapped his fingers around his polystyrene cup and scanned the market for Marty's approaching figure. Perhaps a client had overrun and kept him. He took a sip of his hot chocolate, glad of its sweet warmth. The forecast was that winter was on its way. Just as it should be. It was, after all, bonfire night in two days' time.

He caught sight of Marty hurrying over and waved. 'Sorry I'm late,' Marty said, his face flushed red from the cold.

'No worries.' Will turned to Brian. 'How are the burgers doing?'

'Ready when you are.'

They took their lunch and strolled through the market. 'How's Suzie?' Marty asked, as they stood absently browsing a CD and DVD stall.

'Other than not liking how pregnant she now looks, she's well. But are you OK? You don't seem your usual self.'

Marty picked up a CD of an old Sex Pistols album. 'Do you remember us thinking this was the last word in world-changing music?'

His voice low, Will said, 'Put the CD down and tell me what's wrong.'

Marty frowned. 'Who said anything was wrong?'

'It's written all over your face. Is it work?'

'No.' They walked on. 'It's no big deal,' Marty said quietly. 'I've just come from a doctor's appointment. That's why I was late. I have a lump where us chaps would prefer not to have such things.'

'Oh shit! Are we talking cancer?'

'Too early to tell. The doctor's now organising a visit to the specialist for some tests.'

'It'll be fine,' Will said. 'No worries. Absolutely no worries.'

She was not depressed, Eileen told herself firmly. Run down, fatigued, angry, yes. But depressed, no. It was Bob who was depressed. It was Bob who needed help. Not her.

She'd only agreed to come because of Dora. 'Perhaps, you know, in view of everything you're going through, you need some stronger medication. Just to tide you over,' Dora had said. Eileen didn't think stronger drugs were the answer. It was courage she needed. Courage to confront Bob and make him talk to her.

She reached for another magazine and flicked through the glossy pages, envying the young women their slim figures, their perfect faces and their come-hither eyes. She had been pretty once. But now she felt old and dowdy and worn out. She stopped turning the pages when she came to a piece about a grandmother of two having a make-over. There was a sparkle in the eye of the woman, a lifting of the corners of her mouth and chin. '*I did this for me*,' the caption read beneath one of the photographs. '*Not for my husband, or my family. For me.*'

Dora would strongly approve of this woman, Eileen thought. Dora who rarely left the house without full make-up, who, despite the heart-break in her life, always came bouncing back. She was currently bursting with happiness over a new man she'd met through her Soirée Club. 'You have to meet this one,' Dora had gushed. 'He's just the sweetest man alive. And so very interesting. He used to run his own wine-importing business. He wants to take me to Barcelona for a long weekend.'

For the first time Eileen felt envious of her friend. What did she have to look forward to each week, other than a husband who hardly spoke to her these days? If only Bob would share his grief with her. But that was never going to happen. Not now he'd found someone else to do that with. Another woman.

A buzzer above the receptionist's hatch went off. It was her turn to go through to the doctor. She remained in her seat though, suddenly aware that she was on the brink of an important decision. The way she saw it, she had three options. She could go and sit in that doctor's cramped room and pour out her problems and admit she was terrified her husband would leave her. Or she could simply lie and hold out her hand like a good little girl and accept those magic sweeties in the hope they would turn her head to cotton wool. Or, she could simply walk out of here and . . . do what, exactly?

She was still pondering this question outside in the cold November wind as she waited for Dora's car to appear round the corner. When it did, Dora said, 'You were quick. The surgery not busy today?'

'I didn't see the doctor. But I think I did see a chink of light. And I need your help.'

Bob would give anything to leap in his car and drive down to Warwick to see how Jennifer was. But he couldn't. In half an hour, when he'd finished cleaning the gutters, he had to fetch the children home from school, and then later he had to get things ready for the firework display he was putting on for them.

Climbing down the ladder, he stood on the patio and looked at the mess he'd created. Rotting leaves lay scattered all around him. He began sweeping them up and loading them into the wheelbarrow to take down to the compost heap. When he'd been working all hours he'd longed for days like this, when he could do nothing but potter in the garden. He must have been mad. How could he ever have thought that this nothingness would suit him? Where in God's name had Bob Swift gone?

Jennifer would have the answer. She always seemed to be able to answer his questions. When he'd left her on Saturday night he could have wept. She'd been close to tears herself and if she'd said the words 'don't go' he would have obeyed without a second thought. She had finally given in to common sense—and a rising temperature—on Friday evening and told him she was going home. 'You were right,' she said.

'In that case, I'll drive you home.'

'We are going to be sensible about this, aren't we?' she'd said when they were nearing the end of the journey.

'I'm not sure that I can cope with being sensible any more,' he said.

'But your marriage? You mustn't do anything to wreck that.'

'Perhaps it's wrecked already.' They both knew they were minutes away from saying goodbye, without knowing if they would see one another again. 'I'll ring you tomorrow morning,' he said. 'And don't worry about the *Jennifer Rose*. I'll arrange for her to be taken to the marina.'

Her last words to him were: 'Be kind to yourself, Bob. As kind as you've been to me.'

Harriet arrived home to find Joel and Carrie helping Eileen to butter some rolls. 'We're making hot dogs,' Joel told Harriet importantly. 'Granddad's in the garden setting up the fireworks.'

She put her bag down on the worktop. 'Anything I can do to help, Mum?'

'That's all right, love. We've got it all in hand. How was your day? Oh, I nearly forgot, I've invited Will. I thought it was time we had him over for a drink. Dora said she'd pop in as well. We'll be quite a little party. Oh, and there's some post for you.' She pointed to the microwave and the pile of mail on top of it.

Harriet wondered if she'd come home to the right house. Her mother was a different woman from the one she'd said goodbye to that morning. There was a sense of purpose about her that had been missing these last few weeks.

She took her mail upstairs and while she changed her work clothes, she checked out the house details two agents had sent her. One house in particular caught her eye; a cottage overlooking the canal, with vacant possession, on the outskirts of Kings Melford and on the Maywood road. It had already been renovated and had a small extension. It was too late now to make an appointment to view it, but it would be first on her list of jobs in the morning. She finished dressing, grabbing her favourite old black beret, then went downstairs.

With Marty's news still fresh in his mind, Will wasn't in the mood for a party, even a low-key firework party. But he reasoned it would be better than mooching around on his own. He'd been told not to bother knocking on the front door, but to go round to the back. It was there he found Bob pushing a row of rockets into the ground. Will helped; they worked steadily together and had just finished the task when Carrie and Joel appeared, each carrying a can of beer.

'Or would you prefer something else?' Harriet said, following behind. 'A glass of wine maybe?'

'No, this is great,' Will said. Better than great, he thought, unable to take his eyes off Harriet. She looked irresistible in that beret. Cute. Sassy. But most of all, incredibly sexy. If there had been any doubt that he had imagined his attraction to Harriet, the matter was now settled.

Ruby Hart was one of the nicest and most straightforward women Maxine knew and had always gone out of her way to make her ex-daughter-in-law still feel a part of her family. Today, she and Suzie and Gemma were taking Nana Ruby out for afternoon tea. Maxine parked in front of the neat little bungalow. Give him his due, Maxine thought, Will did his best when it came to his mother; he always kept an eye on her as well as doing whatever odd jobs needed to be done around the house.

Dressed to the nines in a smart knitted suit, Ruby greeted them with hugs and kisses and her usual stream of compliments and keen-eyed observations: 'Maxine, what a stunning trouser-suit, but how tired you look! You must be working too hard . . . Gemma, how colourful your hair is! And, Suzie! You look just like your mother did when she was pregnant—wonderfully voluptuous, just as nature intended! Now sit yourselves down while I finish switching handbags.'

Maxine recognised the handbag that Ruby was exchanging for her everyday one, and was touched; it was the bag she'd given Ruby for Christmas last year, the price of which would horrify the older woman if she ever knew. Maxine never begrudged a penny she spent on Ruby, not when she'd been such a loving grandmother to the girls.

'What do you think of this lipstick?' Ruby was saying to Gemma and Suzie, while puckering her lips. 'A bit too young for me, do you think?'

'No way, Nana,' Gemma said. 'It looks great on you.' The generosity of the comment gave Maxine a prickle of envy. Gemma never said anything nice about her appearance. But then rarely could Maxine think of any-thing nice to say about her daughter's attire. Last night Gemma had spent an hour in the bathroom ruining her lovely blonde hair by apply-ing garish pink streaks to it.

Will occasionally accused her of rampant snobbery, but was it so wrong to want better for, and of, her daughters? Was it so wrong to wish that Suzie's life didn't now revolve around antenatal visits, and that her youngest daughter wasn't such a surly, ungrateful mess? In the coming months Gemma would be going for university interviews. What chance did she have of securing a place at a decent one? It was beyond Maxine how her daughters could be so wantonly careless with their lives. If she'd been given the opportunity to go to university she would have grabbed it with both hands. She hadn't cared at the time that her father wanted her to go straight into the business, but just occasionally since then she had experienced regret that she'd missed out, which was why she'd been so damned determined her girls wouldn't lose out.

Gemma had always loved coming to the Maywood Grange Hotel. Dad used to bring her and Suzie here when they were little. It was the first time she could remember feeling grown-up; she'd loved being treated as an adult. Her mother could do with learning that. Gemma glanced across the table at her mother; she was boasting to Nana Ruby about the saleroom she'd recently bought. She doesn't care about anything but work, Gemma thought bitterly. Suzie and I don't mean a thing to her. All because we haven't conformed to what she thinks is perfect daughter behaviour. Gemma had no intention of sticking around at home. Once she got to university, that would be it. She supposed that she probably would want to come home now and then, but only to see Dad. Oh, and Nana and Suzie. And the baby—her niece, or nephew.

Gemma had written to Marcel, telling him about her sister being pregnant. He'd replied almost straight away, inviting her to come to Paris for Christmas. She hadn't answered his letter yet, but she knew that there was no way her mother would let her go.

While Maxine was off paying the bill and Gemma was in the loo, Nana Ruby said, 'So how are you, Suzie?'

'I'm OK,' she said.

'Good. You know, I'm so excited about this for you. I can't believe I'm going to be a great-grandmother. My friends are all so envious.'

Suzie felt a rush of affection towards her grandmother. It was lovely to be with someone who wasn't telling her how awful her life was going to be. She was sick of her mother's comments and of the hurtful remarks her supposed friends from school and university were making. Running her hand over her bump, she said, 'I wish Mum could be as pleased as you, Nana. I told her I couldn't get rid of the baby and run the risk of thinking in years to come that today my child would have been starting school, or, today my child would have been learning to drive. I don't want a life of what might have been.'

'And what did your mother say?'

'She said I already had that to look forward to, and that I would forever ask myself what might have been if I hadn't got pregnant.'

Gran looked thoughtful. 'I wonder if your mother often asks herself a similar question?'

'What? If she hadn't had Gemma and me?'

'No, of course not. But maybe there are things your mother regrets not having done.'

It was almost two in the morning, and with her bedroom door shut, Harriet was once again decoding her sister's emails. There were numerous references to Felicity's state of mind: 'trapped' was a word that appeared again and again, but not with regard to the children, as Harriet might have supposed, but by the lack of choice she had in her life. The depth of her sister's unhappiness was more disturbing to Harriet than the original discovery of the affair. But was the affair with Miles? Frustratingly, the emails had yielded nothing of any use. Nor had there been a chance to see Miles so that she could drop hints into the conversation and watch his reaction.

If she was honest, in the light of Dominic's assumption she felt uncomfortable imagining herself in his company. As well as being embarrassed that she had misinterpreted his friendliness towards her, she also felt angry with him, having come to the conclusion that he might have been using her as a way of still being close to Felicity. But there was always the chance that Dominic was wrong. In which case, it was important to keep an open mind. And her distance. Miles had phoned her this afternoon and invited her out to dinner. She'd used the children to put him off, then she tried to deflect him by saying she had an appointment to view a house tomorrow. 'I'm quite excited about this one,' she told him.

Except it had backfired and he'd said, 'Why don't I come with you? Another pair of eyes to check out the place might be useful.' It would have been churlish to say no, so she had agreed to meet him at the property in the morning.

When Carrie had learned that Harriet had seen Dominic in Dublin she'd wanted to know when he was coming to see them again. 'He didn't mention anything,' Harriet told her gently, 'and I know he's very busy at the moment.'

At the same time as fielding Carrie's questions about Dominic, Harriet had done some probing of her own, trying to ascertain how things were going at school. She had posted the bullying letter, with an accompanying note, through the letterbox at school on Tuesday, on her way to work. Later that afternoon she'd received a phone call from the headmistress saying that it hadn't been difficult to work out who had been behind the letters and that the group of girls involved had been spoken to, as well as their parents.

Harriet hadn't shared the headmistress's confidence that it was now behind them. 'Carrie has been made to feel like a social outcast. How are you going to rectify that situation?'

'It'll take some time, but let me assure you, Miss Swift, we'll get there, together.' Harriet had just picked up on the emphasis of the word *together* when Mrs Thompson said, 'It might help if you got more involved with school. Have you thought of joining the PTA? I know they're crying out for extra helping hands, what with the Christmas fair and the nativity play coming up next month.'

Harriet said, 'I'm sorry but I don't have the time.'

'Well, maybe you could take advantage of the parents' evening next week and meet some of the other parents.'

Once again Harriet was left with the uneasy feeling that the onus was back on her. Was that what being a parent was about? Always feeling that it was down to you to solve everything?

All she shoehorned out of Carrie was that she was bored at school. This didn't come as a surprise to Harriet. She knew her niece was quite bright. Will had said much the same the other night when they'd had their firework party. After a few glasses of wine, Harriet had found herself confiding in him about the bullying letter. He'd suggested having an all-out heart-to-heart with Carrie: 'Give her the opportunity to get it off her chest,' he'd advised.

'But I wanted to give her the sense of having coped with it by herself. I thought it would be more empowering.'

He'd frowned. 'Is that because that's how you always do things? Single-handedly taking on the world? It can be a tough and lonely business being such a courageous pioneer.'

It was an odd comment to make, but what he'd come up with later, when he was leaving, surprised her even more. 'I have a spare ticket for the Jools Holland concert at the Apollo in Manchester next week; I don't suppose you'd like to go, would you?'

Dora had been hovering at the door with them as Will had offered to walk her home, and she gave Harriet an embarrassing wink, at the same time giving Will a nudge with her elbow and saying, 'If Harriet doesn't want to go, I'm sure I could make myself available.'

Will had laughed in that easy way of his and said, 'I wouldn't want to come between you and Derek.' During the course of the evening, Dora had talked at length about Derek, her wine-importing boyfriend. Somehow Will had left without Harriet giving him an answer.

She rubbed her face hard and focused her thoughts on the coded email in front of her. Felicity's lover's language veered from euphoria that Felicity should want to be with him, to desperate and heart-wrenching despair that she might regret what they had got themselves into. Harriet had to wonder what it was about Felicity that could have brought a man to his knees like this. She couldn't imagine anyone feeling the same for her. Scrolling down, she came to a paragraph that had her senses on full alert. She slowly pieced together the coded words.

Do you remember that sweltering hot day when the four of us were lying in the cornfield and you were threatening to take off all your clothes and jump into the canal? That was the moment when I knew I loved you. You seemed braver and more vibrant than anyone else alive. It's how I've always thought of you.

There it was; the evidence. It really had been Miles with whom Felicity had been having an affair. She could clearly remember the day in question. She could also remember telling her sister not to be so stupid. How boring she must have seemed in comparison to Felicity.

As she pondered what she'd discovered, her cheeks suddenly burned fiercely at the thought of Miles and Felicity in bed together. She was surprised how much it hurt. She had only fantasised about Miles for a blink of an eye, but once more it was as if Felicity had spoilt things for her—first Dominic, now Miles. Oh, she'd never truly believed that Dominic would love her when they were teenagers, but if Felicity hadn't been there, he might have treated her as an equal and not as the younger sister permanently cast in the shadow of the prettier and more interesting older one. And now it had happened all over again with Miles. He had been heart, body and soul in love with Felicity, therefore Harriet could only ever be second best in his eyes. She wouldn't have believed it possible, but she suddenly hated her sister. And Miles.

Her thoughts turned to the coming day, when she would be seeing Miles. She decided it would be better to take the children with her. If she spent any time alone with Miles it was almost inevitable that she would end up telling him she knew about him and Felicity. In her current frame of mind, she didn't think this would be a good idea. She needed time to think about what she now knew.

Harriet and the children arrived at number 1 Lock Cottage ten minutes early. She took the children round to the back, which was the aspect of the house she knew they would appreciate most. Both children let out shrieks of delight when they saw that beyond the small, south-facing back garden, just the other side of the boundary wall, was the towpath and the canal.

The three of them took in the view. It was a glorious autumnal morning. After the last few days of frosts and freezing temperatures, the weather was unexpectedly mild. The sky was the palest of blues, and the shadows were long and ethereal. Freshly ploughed fields undulated gently into the distance. Harriet turned round to look at the cottage and thought of the views the bedrooms at the back would offer. A flicker of movement at the window in the next-door property had her hoping the natives were friendly. Because she knew this was where she wanted to be.

'What do you think?' she asked the children. It was important to her that they shared at least half her enthusiasm.

'Could we have a boat if we lived here?' asked Joel.

'Maybe a very small rowing boat.'

'We'd be like Ratty in *Wind in the Willows*,' joined in Carrie. 'We could go for picnics in the boat. And Miles could come with us, couldn't he?'

'He could indeed,' Harriet said guardedly. She'd been aware lately how frequently Carrie brought Miles into the conversation. Hearing the sound of a car, she said, 'Come on, that'll either be Miles or the man who's going to show us round.' It turned out to be both arriving in convoy. The man, brandishing a set of keys, let them all in.

Despite the echoing emptiness of the rooms, Harriet wasn't disappointed with what she saw. Leading off from a small hallway there was a downstairs cloakroom and a good-sized sitting room with a view of the tiny front garden, but it was the large kitchen and breakfast room at the back that gave her a shiver of excitement. The sun streamed in through the French doors that opened onto the rear garden. Harriet looked at the children to gauge their reaction. This could be their home for a very long time. This was where Harriet would have to guide them through all the dramas their combined lives would bring. Living here, she might just pull it off.

Carrie wanted to choose her bedroom, and with Joel chasing after her, she clattered up the uncarpeted stairs and crashed into the first room she came to. It was smaller than the room she had at Grandma and Granddad's, but much prettier. If she had a chair and desk right by the window, she'd be able to watch the boats going past. She couldn't think of anything nicer.

Except for having Mum and Dad back with them.

It was on a day like this, when something good was happening to her, that she really missed them. She used to love coming home from school to tell Mum about all the interesting things she'd done that day. But now Carrie kept everything to herself. Grandma was too tired to listen, Granddad was never around and Harriet was too busy. Although she had noticed that Harriet had asked her more questions about school this week than she normally did. She'd told Harriet that she was bored. She hadn't said anything about the letters, or how the girls had stopped writing them. One of the girls, Emily, had even tried to be friendly to her in the playground. Carrie had thought maybe she was quite nice after all.

'Carrie! Come and see what I've found.' She turned at the sound of Joel's shrill voice and hurried into the room next door. It was bigger than the one she'd claimed for herself, but didn't have a view as nice as hers. There was no sign of her brother and she was just thinking that maybe he was in another bedroom, when behind her a door flew open and Joel leapt out.

'It's a secret hiding place,' he said when he'd stopped laughing. Carrie knew that it was nothing more than a cupboard at a strangely low height, but she kept quiet; if Joel wanted this room, she'd be able to have the one with the brilliant view. 'Do you think Harriet will let me have this room?' he said.

'Let's go and ask her.'

They found her across the landing in a bedroom that was much bigger than either of theirs and had the same view as the room Carrie had picked out. Her aunt was talking to the man with the keys. Carrie noticed the happy smile on Harriet's face and thought that she should smile more often; it made her look pretty. More like Mum.

Carrie hadn't forgotten her plan to try to get Harriet to spend more time with Miles. With him around, Harriet didn't seem so serious or so snappy. 'Couldn't Miles come back with us for Sunday lunch, Harriet?' she said. 'Grandma wouldn't mind, would she?'

Bob carved, with Eileen supervising which bits of the joint to give everyone. Harriet offered to pour the wine so that she wouldn't have to talk to Miles. Or think about him. Because whenever she did, her brain automatically assembled graphic images of him and Felicity in bed together. It pained Harriet to admit it, but she envied her sister, for she had never felt that depth of passion for any man she'd been to bed with.

When everything was served and a hush had fallen on the table, Eileen said, 'Now then, tell us properly about the house.'

'It was brilliant,' Carrie rushed to explain. 'Completely mega brill. And the bedroom Harriet says can be mine is just *so* cool.'

'Carrie, please don't speak with your mouth full. And whatever has happened to your vocabulary?'

Angry that her father had pulled up Carrie so needlessly in front of Miles, Harriet said, 'Carrie couldn't have described the house better.' She shot her niece a quick smile, then turned to Miles. 'You thought it was great too, didn't you?'

'It certainly has a great location,' he agreed. 'Stunning, in fact.'

'But it's the location that concerns me,' said Eileen. 'How safe would it be? It's so close to the water.'

'A busy main road would be just as dangerous.'

'So are you going to make an offer for it?' This was from her father.

'She already has,' chipped in Carrie. 'On her mobile in the car.'

'I hope you weren't driving at the same time.'

Harriet frowned. Just what the hell was eating her father? 'No, Dad, it was a hands-free call as always. I wanted to get in quick. I've offered the full asking price; the agent sees no reason why the owners won't accept it. I'm going back to see it tomorrow evening. Do you want to come?'

'Sounds to me like you've made up your mind without our approval.'

'It's not a matter of seeking your approval. I thought you'd be interested.' Why was he behaving like a grumpy old man? She took a gulp of wine and got on with her meal. It was then that Carrie suggested they go for a walk with Toby after lunch.

'You'd like to come too, wouldn't you, Miles?' she asked him.

'You don't have to do everything bossy-boots Carrie asks of you,' Harriet said to Miles when they were crossing the road and heading for the footpath to take them on their familiar route to the canal.

'That's OK; I'm used to being bossed about by the Swift women.'

She laughed uneasily and was about to ask if there was one particular Swift woman who stood out from the crowd, when he said, 'All I was going to do this afternoon was depress myself by trying to write.'

'Oh? What are you writing?'

'I'm trying my hand at poetry. But please don't say anything to Dominic; he would only belittle what I'm doing. In his view there's only room for one poet in the family, and he's it.'

Harriet had once attempted to read one of Dominic's so-called epic poems but hadn't been able to make head nor tail of it. Felicity had told her that she was a philistine.

'What kind of poetry do you write?' Harriet asked Miles. Part of her wanted him to come right out and just say it—*I'm writing about my love for Felicity*. But the greater part of Harriet wasn't ready to have her hurt and disappointment further compounded by a confession. She hated the fact that those who had known her sister would always want to talk about Felicity in preference to her.

'Oh, you know, the usual,' he replied. 'Regret and lost opportunities.'

'And love? Surely that's a given. Every poet writes about that.' Stop it, she told herself, and quickened her pace to catch up with the children.

'Can we let Toby off the lead now?' Carrie asked.

'Yes. But the usual rules apply—'

'We know,' they both chorused, 'don't go near the water!' They charged off whooping and yelling.

Miles laughed. 'I know you won't believe me, but you really are turning out to be a great mother to them. They've become very fond of you.'

Reminded of what Dominic had said to her in Dublin—that the children relied on her and needed her—Harriet was brought up short by a bolt of self-pity. Very likely, because her situation made her as desirable as a bucket of fish eyes, the children's fondness for her would be the nearest she ever got to being loved. Being relied upon isn't enough, she wanted to scream. Self-pity morphed into stinging bitterness and she set off at a ferocious pace, wanting to put as much distance between herself and the man who had loved Felicity in a way she would never know.

But Miles was hot on her heels. He put a hand out to stop her. 'Harriet, what is it? What did I say?'

'The children,' she blurted out. 'We mustn't let them go too far without us.' Then, hearing Toby give off a loud bark, she turned her head sharply. Further up the towpath, chatting to the children, was Will Hart.

'Hi,' Will said when Harriet and her companion joined him and the children. He held out his hand to the other man. 'I'm Will Hart, the Maple Drive neighbour from hell.'

'Hi, I'm Miles.'

'Ah, one of the McKendrick boys.' He smiled, first at Miles and then at Harriet, and began to feel he'd walked in on something. Something between the two of them. If it was possible, Harriet looked more agitated than usual. 'Carrie tells me that you've found the *coolest* house ever,' he said.

She looked up at him. 'Yes. I've made an offer on it already and I've arranged to see it again tomorrow with Mum and Dad.' Her face suddenly brightened and she smiled one of her rare smiles. 'Why don't you come with us? We could make a party of it.'

Surprised at the invitation, he said, 'Thanks, I'd like that. What time?'

'Seven. Oh, and before I forget,' she said. 'That Jools Holland concert you mentioned—remind me of the date again?'

Will was thrown. He thought he'd blown it the other night, but now here she was bringing the matter up of her own accord. What lucky stars had brought about this stroke of good fortune?

Will knew from Gemma that Suzie was bored and missing her friends from university. To give her something to think about other than antenatal classes, the benefits of breastfeeding and the understandable fear of giving birth, he had asked her to help out in the shop if she wanted. He'd also offered her the chance to go round the salerooms with him. 'Any way to get out of the house would be fantastic, Dad,' she'd said. So today, Monday morning, they were heading north on the M6 to attend an auction in Lancashire.

The saleroom was filling up fast when they arrived. 'Can I do the bidding for you, Dad?' Suzie asked when the auctioneer took his place.

'If you want. But you stop when I tell you to. And be sure to hold up our card so the auctioneer's assistant can write down our number if we make the successful bid.'

'Is that it? No lecture about being careful not to rub my nose at the wrong moment?'

'That's a myth. It takes more than a nervous twitch to catch the attention of a busy auctioneer. OK, it looks like we're off.'

Later, when they were driving away with a full boot, wearing matching satisfied looks on their faces, Will said, 'You enjoyed that, didn't you?'

'It was great. I loved it. Will you bring me again?'

'If you're going to come and work for me, you'll have no choice.'

She smiled and his heart surged: it was good to see her so happy.

They were almost home when Suzie said, 'Dad, is there any chance I could move in with you when the baby's born?'

Will didn't need to think about his answer. 'Of course. But only if you sort things out with your mother. She has to be happy about it.'

Suzie rolled her eyes. 'She'll be glad to see the back of me.'

'Maybe a little distance between the two of you might help,' he said.

It wasn't until that evening, when Will was at home, checking through his post before going to see Harriet's house, that he experienced a pang of regret. If Suzie came to live with him, there would be no more seduction tricks in front of the log fire. Any future bedroom activity would have to be conducted with the volume turned down low. He was being selfish, he knew, but he couldn't help but wonder where it would leave him in his cause to get to know Harriet better. If he was going to make a move on her, he'd better do it soon, before the house was invaded. As love nests went, it would be a two-star romantic turnoff.

Carrie and Joel turned round to wave at Will every now and then as he followed behind Bob Swift's car. Will told himself that life would be a lot easier if he could put Harriet out of his mind. Why did he want to get involved with someone so complicated? How often would he be able to see Harriet on her own with Carrie and Joel on the scene? But he knew the attraction was more than a whim. He respected and admired her; something he hadn't felt for a woman in a long while. He genuinely thought she was one of the strongest people he knew. As far as he could see, in that split second when her sister's car had collided with another, Harriet's life had changed for ever and she had sacrificed everything she had created for herself to take on the challenge of a lifetime. She must have loved her sister an awful lot to do that.

It seemed par for the course that Harriet hardly spoke to him when they arrived at the house. But he didn't care: she was wearing that cute, sexy beret again; she could treat him any way she liked!

And like the headgear, he loved the house on sight. With Harriet busy showing her parents round—she seemed to have her work cut out jolly-ing her father along—Carrie and Joel voiced their eagerness to give him a guided tour.

He made all the requisite noises of appreciation when he saw their bedrooms, including showing thigh-slapping astonishment at Joel's secret hiding place. They then led him back out onto the landing and into the biggest of the bedrooms. 'This is Harriet's room,' Carrie said.

He went over to the window where he cupped his hands round his eyes in an effort to cut out the light so he could see the garden and view beyond. But it didn't work; it was too dark outside. When he turned round, the children had vanished but Harriet was standing behind him looking arch and remote. He started slightly.

'Sorry,' she said, 'I didn't mean to make you jump.'

'It's an age thing. When you get to be as decrepit as me, you have to watch the old ticker. I don't suppose I could tempt you into a drink with me when we've finished here, so I can congratulate you on finding such a great house?'

'Where were you thinking?' she said.

'How does The Navigation sound? We could go straight from here if your parents don't mind.'

The Navigation was so busy that they couldn't find a table and ended up standing around yelling into each other's ears above the swell of other voices.

'This is a complete disaster, isn't it?' Will shouted. 'Shall we give it up as a bad job?' He could see the relief in Harriet's face.

Once outside, they stood for a moment to settle their reeling senses. 'Not one of my finest ideas, I'll admit,' Will said. Then, fishing his keys out of his pocket, he led the way to the car. Five minutes later and he was apologising again, this time for a flat battery. 'I'm so sorry,' he said. 'This evening is going from bad to worse. I'll call a taxi.'

'No. Let's walk along the towpath,' said Harriet. 'It's a clear night, prac-tically a full moon. Besides, I know the way like the back of my hand.'

'Boy, are you my kind of girl! Intrepid as well as forgiving.'

He soon realised he had to alter his usually slow loping step to match her more hurried pace: he'd never known a woman walk so fast. Where did she get the energy from? 'How's your asthma?' he asked.

'It's fine. I seldom get any problems at this time of the year. It's pollen and mildew spore related.'

'And that day in the shop?'

'Ah. That was stress induced. It doesn't happen often. How's Suzie?'

Touched that she was interested, he said, 'Oh, she's blooming.' He told her about Suzie coming to work for him. Then he said, 'How's your father? I don't know him well, but he didn't seem himself when we were looking round the house.'

In the still night air, he heard her tut. 'He's being a complete pain. Nothing anyone says or does is right. I don't know what's got into him.'

'You don't suppose he's depressed, do you?' Will said. 'I only ask because when I went through my period of wanting to hack great lumps out of my colleagues, I blamed everyone else for how I felt.'

Her pace slowed. 'I can't imagine you being depressed.'

'It happens to more people than you'd think. I could try talking to your father, if you like?'

'I doubt it would do any good. By the way, how's the friend you mentioned during the children's firework party? Any news yet?'

He'd forgotten he'd told Harriet about Marty. 'He has an appointment with the specialist tomorrow. I'm meeting him for a drink in the evening.'

A long way off an owl hooted, followed shortly by the eerie screeching bark of a fox. Pointing to the hedgerow on their right, Harriet said, 'Felicity and I used to squeeze through the brambles there to get to the far side of the field and listen to the nightingales.'

'I've never heard a nightingale sing before.' He'd also never heard Harriet refer to her sister so readily.

'Once, during a particularly warm spell in early summer, we came here for a midnight picnic.'

'With Miles and his brother?'

She turned and looked at him. 'We didn't do everything with them. But yes, they were with us. Stupidly, Mum and Dad thought we'd be safer with them.'

'Are there still nightingales here?' he asked, wishing he hadn't provoked the sharpness in her voice. He was curious, too, about the 'stupidly' reference. Had something happened that night?

'I don't know if there are any here these days; it's years since I've been to listen to them.' Her tone had become soft and wistful now.

In the silence that followed, Will speculated on some of what Dora had told him the night of the fireworks about the intensely close friendship between the Swift girls and the McKendrick boys. According to Dora, the older brother, Dominic, whom she colourfully likened to a wily fox in a chicken coop, was the one they all followed, with Miles destined to be in his talented brother's shadow. 'Eileen and I used to feel sorry for him,' Dora had further explained. 'We blamed the parents, though. They shouldn't have treated the boys so differently. Their father had some very peculiar ideas. He could also be excessively strict. Cruelly so.'

Minutes later they were standing at the end of his garden. 'Well, then,' he said, playing for time, 'I'm sorry the evening was such a disaster.'

'Please don't keep apologising. I enjoyed the walk.' Her face curved in a soft smile. 'It brought back memories.'

'Not painful ones, I hope.'

She shook her head. 'Mostly happy memories.' But as she said this, the smile melted from her face and she looked ineffably sad.

He suddenly felt a tremendous surge of tenderness for her, and without thinking what he was doing, he put his arms round her and kissed her.

It was a colossal error of judgment. He knew it the second her body stiffened in his arms and her lips, cold and unresponsive, felt like stone against his. He lowered his arms and stepped away from her, and she simply stared at him with a look of such terrible blankness he felt more humiliated than if she'd slapped him.

'I'd rather you didn't ever try that again,' she said. She turned and walked away. He'd blown it. But then so what? What had he thought would come of it, anyway?

Halfway along the footpath, Harriet came to a stop. What the hell had happened back there? Why had he kissed her? And why had she reacted like that? There had been a sudden weakening sensation deep within her, as if something sore and tender inside her chest had been touched. She had been so startled by her reaction that she had frozen in his arms and forced her brain to evaluate what was going on. When this had failed, she had decided retreat was the best course of action.

Her breath forming in the cold night air, she mentally scrolled through the evening. Had there been earlier warning signs that he wanted to kiss her? She couldn't be sure. Spencer used to tease her that she wouldn't know a guy was coming onto her if he stripped naked and threw himself at her feet. Over the years, Dominic had frequently accused her of living like a nun. She suddenly felt crushed. Why wasn't she more sexually aware? More in tune with her body?

Once again she was reminded of the hurt of being rejected by Spencer. Was it possible that if she'd meant more to Spencer he wouldn't have walked away? The word 'love' had never been mentioned between them, but then nor had lust, or passion, or desire, or any of those other words Miles and Felicity had been so fond of using in their emails. She had to face up to the truth: she wasn't a very exciting or loving person. And the net result of that, surely, had to be that she was unlovable. She would never experience the adoration her sister had experienced for the simple reason that she was incapable of giving it out herself. If Dominic was to be believed, she lacked emotion and spontaneity. She was dull and unsexy. Yet Will had wanted to kiss her. Why? And why, more importantly, had it provoked that weakening sensation? Try as she might, she could not recall another man kissing her ever eliciting such a perplexing response.

There was only one logical way to find out what had caused it. She retraced her steps, all the way to the end of Will's garden. If she was going to do this, it had to be now or she'd lose her nerve. For the second time in the last two days she was acting out of character. Yesterday she had deliberately invited Will to see the house in front of Miles to get at him, to prove some twisted kind of point: See, I don't need you, I have plenty of other friends who don't lie and who don't treat me as second best. Within hours she was regretting freezing Miles out like that. It was no way to treat an old friend. Or a new friend, for that matter. Using Will to score a point was cheap and unworthy.

It was when they were at the house and Will had asked her to go for a drink with him that she had suddenly realised what it was about Will that she liked. He took her for who and what she was: Harriet Swift. He had never known her sister, therefore he hadn't and never would make a comparison. She would never be second best in his eyes. Spencer and Erin had both met Felicity and they had both independently made the same comments she had heard for most of her life—that Harriet was quieter than Felicity, that Harriet was shorter than Felicity, that Harriet was more serious than Felicity. But that would never happen with Will.

She pushed open the gate, walked the length of the garden and knocked on the back door. This is a first, she told herself, a spontaneous first. This would show Dominic! The door opened. 'May I come in?'

He looked confused. Alarmed, even. 'Yes. Of course.' He shut the door after her, then raked both his hands through his hair. 'Look, I'm sorry about what I did. I should never have tried it on. I don't know what I was thinking.'

'Please, I haven't come here for an apology. I need you to do something for me.'

'Oh. OK. What is it?'

She swallowed. 'I need you to kiss me again.'

He opened his eyes wide. 'What?'

'Please don't make this any more difficult for me than it already is. I want you to kiss me like you did before.'

'Is this some kind of crazy trick? Because if so, I ought to point out that entrapment's against the law.'

'Just kiss me, Will. And no funny business.'

He came towards her, slowly. 'You're sure about this?' he asked.

'Yes,' she murmured. She braced herself for his touch: first his arms and then his lips. They felt different this time, warmer and softer. His arms felt different. Firmer. More solid. Her heart gave a surge and an aching tenderness filled her chest. Next a flood of warmth swept through her. It was like the sun bursting through the clouds. It was at this moment, on the towpath, that Will had pulled away. She didn't want that to happen this time and so she put her arms round him, and now she was kissing him, opening her mouth wide against his, wanting the warmth to go further within her, wanting him never to stop kissing her.

But he did. 'Hey there,' he said, 'you've got to breathe sometime. First rule of kissing in this house. Especially for asthmatics.'

At the sound of his voice, she opened her eyes and found herself staring into his. They were the darkest shade of brown she'd ever seen. She took a deep breath, realising that he was right.

'I don't wish to appear nosy,' he said, while straightening her beret, 'but was there any particular reason why you wanted me to kiss you? After all, you did say I wasn't to do it again.'

'I . . . I wanted to know if I'd imagined something.'

He raised an eyebrow. 'And had you?'

'No.'

'Would you like me to do it again? Just to be sure?'

She nodded, slipped her hands round his neck and pulled him down to her. Almost immediately this time she was suffused with the euphoric warmth that seemed to fill her from head to toe. Without once ever letting go of her, he manoeuvred her out of the kitchen, along the hallway, and into the sitting room.

She had been undressed many times before, but never by a man as deft as Will. They were on the floor. Music was playing. He gently parted her legs with his hand and made her gasp as he slid a finger inside her. For a split second she tensed, but as his tongue pushed further into her mouth and the palm of his hand pressed against her, she relaxed and gave in to his touch. He carried on, slowly, rhythmically, expertly. His eyes, even darker now, had a strange look in them; an absorbed, mysterious look she couldn't fathom.

'But what about you?' she moaned as the wave came closer.

'Ssh . . . stop worrying. Concentrate on enjoying yourself.'

She did as he said and when it came, it was like nothing she had ever experienced before. It was a tsunami, the mother of all tidal waves. For minutes afterwards she lay quivering in his arms, fearing her body would never feel the same again. Finally, she broke the silence and said, 'What was that?'

'I think it's what we in the trade, Miss Swift, call a classic case of the earth moving.'

'But what did you do?'

'I'll show you again in a minute, if you like.'

True to his word, he did. And a lot more besides.

At work the following morning Harriet was having difficulty staying awake. She had just told herself for the umpteenth time that what she had done with Will had been nothing more than a night of proving that she was as spontaneous and sensual as the next person . . . when Howard came in.

'How are you fixed for Friday?' he asked. 'Any chance you can squeeze a trip to Dublin into your hectic schedule?'

She didn't need to check her diary; she knew the day was free: it was her birthday. 'No problem.'

'Excellent. I'll fill you in on the details later.'

He closed the door after him, and with the greatest of effort Harriet forced her brain to apply itself to the program she was working on. No more thoughts of Will, she warned herself. The trouble was, she knew that having experienced that pleasure, she wanted more of it. But she was going to be sensible. And firm. What had happened last night was a one-off. She would have to make that very clear to Will.

Don't kid yourself, Harriet Swift. You want that man to shag your brains out again, don't you? The voice—the voice of her conscience—belonged to Dominic. She could see him clearly mocking her. *'Oh, so Miss Prissy Boots gets it now, does she? Now she knows what all the fuss is about. So what are you going to do about it?'*

She knew exactly what she was going to do. Heaven help her, but she couldn't help herself.

'Oh, so you're going to use him, are you?' taunted Dominic's voice. *'How deliciously ironic. The girl who sat in judgment of my sexual proclivities has come a long way.'*

I'm not using him, Harriet told herself, and picked up her mobile. No more than he's using me. We're both adults, both getting out of this what we each want. It's called fun. After what I've been through, I reckon I deserve it. What's wrong with that?

In his office, while listening to the lunchtime news on the radio, Will answered his mobile. He sat up straight when he heard Harriet's voice. He'd wanted to speak to her for the pleasure of hearing her voice and because he knew women usually demanded a follow-up call, but he worried that she would think he was being pushy and getting above himself. 'Hi there,' he said, in his best George Clooney voice.

There was a pause before she spoke. 'You OK, Will? You sound like you're coming down with a cold.'

So much for George Clooney. 'It's exhaustion,' he said. 'I hardly slept a wink last night. But when I did drop off, I dreamt this incredibly sexy woman turned up on my doorstep and demanded I made love to her for hours on end. I know it was a dream because a guy like me could never be that lucky.' He crossed his fingers, hoping he hadn't overdone it.

'That's weird, because I had the same dream too.'

'You did? You mean the woman turned up on your doorstep as well? The two-timing little minx!'

Her laughter had him relaxing back into his chair. 'So, any chance we might get together again? I know it's difficult for you, what with—'

'How about later tonight? I've got a parents' evening at school, but I should be home by eight and with you by nine.'

'Sounds perfect. Oh, but hang on, I'm seeing Marty for a drink.'

'I could come over afterwards, when you're back.' Any fears he'd had that she'd regretted last night were now gone. She was as keen to see him as he was to be with her.

Bob was polishing the brassware on board the *Jennifer Rose*. One more porthole and then he'd ring Jennifer. He had to try to make her change her mind. She couldn't possibly have meant what she'd said during their last conversation.

'Bob, you've been so sweet to me, but really, it's time to be sensible. You're married. You have a wife and a family who all need you more than I do.'

'That's not true. They're all getting on with their lives without me.'

'What you mean is that they're getting on without Felicity and you can't bear that, can you?'

When he hadn't responded, she'd said, 'I'll always be at the end of a phone, Bob, but we can only ever be friends. I blame myself; I turned to you when I was feeling low and alone, but now I know better.'

Since then, he'd gone over and over what she'd said. Part of it was true: the bit about hating his family for being able to carry on without Felicity. It was callous and heartless of them. The worst of it was seeing Harriet so pleased about that house she was buying. Bob had almost aired the thought he'd vowed he never would: why couldn't it have been Harriet who had died? Why Felicity? Why his precious Felicity? He knew it was a bad thought, but he couldn't help it.

Satisfied that the brasswork was gleaming to perfection, he went down below. The boat was now safely moored at the marina, and as he'd promised Jennifer, he was keeping an eye on it for her. He'd got a rapport going with the older of the two men who ran the marina and they were quite happy for him to show up with Toby and potter about on the boat. He didn't have Toby with him today, because he didn't want any distractions when he told Jennifer just how he felt about her. That he couldn't go on if he didn't think she'd be there for him.

'You're absolutely sure you want to do this?' Dora said.

Eileen knew her friend was doubtful about what they were doing, but the time had come to think about herself. She was tired of always making allowances for Bob. It was her daughter too who had died, but the way Bob went on, you'd think no one had loved Felicity but him. Now that he had become so critical, she was damned if she was going to put up with it any longer. Felicity's death didn't mean the living were condemned to a slow death as well.

'Dora,' she said, 'I'm as ready as I'll ever be.'

The door opened and a plump, middle-aged woman came in, bringing with her a waft of strong perfume and slick professionalism. 'Eileen, forgive me for keeping you waiting. You don't mind me calling you Eileen, do you? Here at the Soirée Club, we like to keep things informal. Now then, I have your membership application here and I thought we might just run through it together. I think it would be advisable to pad out the section where it asks for hobbies and interests.'

Eileen was at a loss. It was the part of the form that had worried her most. It had also made her realise just how little she did beyond the four walls of her home. She'd become as good as institutionalised.

'Do you like to travel?' the woman asked her.

'Well, yes. But I haven't actually had the chance—'

The woman put a tick in the box opposite Travel. 'And I'll bet a pound to a penny that you're a fine cook.'

'Only very ordinary, everyday—'

A tick went in the box marked Cordon Bleu Cook. 'What about trips to the theatre?'

The last time she'd been to the theatre was to take the children to a Christmas pantomime. But now that she was getting the hang of the form, she said, 'Come to think of it, I've always enjoyed live theatre.'

'Excellent.' Another tick was added. 'That really has pepped things up nicely.' The woman turned the page of the application form. 'Ah, it says here that you're separated. May I ask what time span we're talking?'

Without batting an eyelid, Eileen said, 'My husband and I have been separated for some time.' She had no trouble with her conscience over this; after all she and Bob had been living separate lives for months now. 'Does it matter that I'm not actually divorced?'

'So long as you're honest with the gentlemen on our books and you explain your situation, we don't mind. We're not here to judge.'

'But what about the gentlemen? Supposing they're not honest? Supposing they're happily married and playing away from home?'

'We can only do our best. If people lie to us, what can we do?'

Eileen looked at Dora anxiously.

'There's always a risk involved, Eileen,' her friend said. 'You could meet the most perfectly charming man through a friend of a friend and still discover he's a lying, cheating good-for-nothing.'

Or you could be married to him, Eileen thought unhappily. She took out a pen from her handbag and said, 'Where do I sign?'

The last time Harriet had attended a parents' evening she had been in the lower sixth. She'd had to listen to her form teacher telling her parents that he thought Harriet would get more out of school if she was prepared to put more into it. 'School isn't just about academic success,' he'd told them, 'it's about joining in and helping to foster a sense of community.' The day she had received her A-level results, Harriet had mentally told Mr Forbes to go screw himself. With A grades in maths, advanced maths and physics and a B in chemistry she was all set for Durham.

That was the summer she'd ended up in hospital. It was the night she and Felicity had wanted to go on a midnight picnic and listen to the nightingales singing. Their parents had said they could only go if Dominic and Miles went with them. The minute Maple Drive was behind them, Dominic produced a bottle of vodka and proceeded to pass it round. By the time they'd made it to the nightingale field, they were all pretty drunk. Harriet was so drunk it was some time before she realised that she was having a full-blown asthma attack, and when she couldn't find her inhaler—it must have dropped out of her pocket on the towpath—Dominic had staggered over and told her not to worry. 'I know what to do,' he'd claimed. 'I'll give you the kiss of life.'

It showed the measure of how drunk and desperately ill she was that she believed it might work. But instead of kissing her, he'd been sick on her. Miles, probably the least drunk of them, had somehow got her home safely. Her mother had taken one look at her and called an ambulance; she spent two days in hospital. All of them, except for Dominic, who was beyond his parents' control now, were grounded for the rest of the summer.

Sitting in front of Carrie's form teacher, Harriet had a horrible sense of déjà vu. Carrie, she was being told, was going to have to make a bigger effort to join in more. 'Carrie's a bright girl and we'd love to see her really blossom,' Mrs Kennedy explained. 'But she has to understand that school isn't simply about sitting in front of the blackboard or reading books all day.'

'So, what you're saying is that Carrie has consistently come top in every subject, but you'd like more from her if she's to become a model pupil?' Harriet stood up and held out her hand. 'Good night, Mrs Kennedy, it's been most enlightening.'

If only, she thought angrily as she walked away. Seeing the head-mistress coming towards her with a group of parents in tow, Harriet let out a sigh of irritation. What now?

'Miss Swift, let me introduce some of the other parents from Carrie's class. Rebecca's parents, Mr and Mrs Simpson, and Emily's mother and father, Mr and Mrs Woodward.'

After a round of handshaking, the headmistress drifted away. One of the women, Harriet couldn't remember who it was, said, 'Perhaps we could get the three girls together sometime.'

'That would be lovely,' Harriet said quickly, keen to scotch any attempts at polite chitchat. 'I'll let Carrie know.'

She had started to inch away from them when one of the fathers said, 'We were thinking of going for a drink when we're finished here. You're more than welcome to join us.'

Her heart sank. Was this it, then? Being Carrie and Joel's guardian meant that she had a part to play herself when it came to oiling the wheels of their social lives? The thought appalled her.

'I'm sorry,' she said, tightening the scarf round her neck, 'but I have to get going. I promised I'd be home in time to read to Carrie and Joel before they went to sleep.' Little did they know that the real reason she wanted to get home, other than to read to the children, was to have a long soak in the bath before seeing Will.

Will had just finished changing the sheets on the bed when he heard the doorbell. His mouth was dry at the prospect of another night with Harriet. He'd spent the best part of the day anticipating her arrival. He'd confided in Marty at the pub about Harriet, and his friend had looked at him enviously.

'Bloody hell, Will! How do you do it? All I get is a doctor in rubber gloves fondling me.' The only news Marty had following his appoint-ment with the consultant was that he was now lined up for some tests.

Will pulled open the front door with a flourish, then dropped his arms in disappointment when he saw it wasn't Harriet standing on the doorstep. It was Gemma and Suzie.

'Hi, Dad,' they said in synchronisation. 'We thought we'd surprise you.'

'You have. Believe me.'

'What's wrong, Dad? Aren't you going to let us in?'

He ushered them in. 'What's brought this on?' he said, taking them through to the sitting room. Too late he realised it was set for an evening of seduction—a bottle of wine and two glasses on the coffee table, a few strategically placed candles.

Gemma took one look at the room and howled with laughter.

'Had we better go?' asked Suzie with a smile. At least one of his daughters was sensitive to his predicament.

The ring at the doorbell could not have been better timed. It was Harriet. He explained the situation. 'Just say hello to them and then they'll be on their way.'

'I could come back later, if you want.' She was already edging away.

'No!' he said, extending a hand and pulling her inside. 'You might change your mind and not come back. Let's get this over with.'

There was no mistaking the look of surprise on his daughters' faces when he introduced Harriet to them. Within minutes their curiosity was satisfied and they were saying their goodbyes. The last comment Will heard was from Gemma as she got in Suzie's car. 'I can't wait to tell Mum about this one. How old do you reckon?'

He returned to the sitting room, where Harriet was standing in front of the fire with her back to him. Observing her from behind, she looked no older than his daughters. He suddenly felt unsure. Don't do this, his head told him. She's too young. But then she turned round and looked at him with her pale, inscrutable blue-grey eyes and he was lost.

DECEMBER

'In the midst of life we are in death.'
Book of Common Prayer

A FORTNIGHT HAD PASSED since Suzie and her sister had shown up unexpectedly at their father's. The reason Gemma had been so eager to see him was to try to get him on her side with her plan to spend Christmas in Paris with Marcel. Suzie had told her it was selfish to keep using Dad this way. Gemma had said, 'That's rich coming from the girl who wants to move in with him when the baby's born. How do you think that'll work when he wants to bring some woman home?'

Gemma had a point, Suzie could see that. Which was why she was going to tell Dad that she'd decided to stay at home with Mum, just until she'd got herself sorted. If she thought about the future too much she became depressed. Nana Ruby said it was her hormones playing merry hell with her. Because her grandmother was always so positive, Suzie had taken to spending more and more time with her. It was lovely to be pampered by Nana. She had even said that if things got difficult with Mum, there would be room for Suzie and the baby in her tiny bungalow. 'It would be a bit of a squash,' Nana had said, 'but I want you to know there'd always be a welcome for you here.' Her generosity had made Suzie cry. Burrowing her head into her grandmother's shoulder, she'd wished her mother wasn't such a heartless bitch. 'You mustn't think so badly of her,' Nana had said. 'She has a lot on her plate. And there's that husband of hers to keep happy. Relationships are fragile things. Talking of relationships, I hear from Gemma that your father's seeing someone. What's she like? Gemma said she's very young.'

'I don't know how old she is for certain; she looks about thirty. She's got this intense, serious look about her. I can't imagine she'd be a laugh a minute. Not really Dad's type.'

'Perhaps it's time your father took on someone with a bit of substance. Would you be very upset if he did marry again?'

'It would take some getting used to,' she'd said guardedly.

'Your father would never stop loving you, Suzie,' her grandmother had said. 'He wouldn't ever let anything come between him and you. But you have to respect his right to be happy.'

Nana's comments combined with Gemma's criticisms meant that Suzie knew she couldn't move in with her father. It wouldn't be fair to him. But selfishly, she knew that she would be jealous of any woman who meant more to her father than she did.

This conversation, like so many between Suzie and her grandmother, had taken place while Nana Ruby was knitting and Suzie was flicking through a baby magazine trying to picture the baby she would be holding in a matter of weeks. She couldn't believe how huge she was now, but no matter how uncomfortable she felt, she didn't regret her decision. This baby was going to be the most loved child in the world. As though to make the days pass quicker, Nana Ruby had made a special countdown calendar to go on her kitchen wall and as each day came and went, her grandmother crossed it off with a red marker pen. Suzie's due date—January 15—was only six and a half weeks away.

Her friend, Sinead from University, had been in touch to see how she was getting on, but most of the phone conversation had been about her and breaking up with Richard. 'I found out he was seeing someone else behind my back,' she told Suzie. 'Can you believe it?' It proved to Suzie that she'd been right to keep her silence about Richard; he was not the kind of boy who would have stood by her. That much was obvious.

Sitting in her father's office—he was out for the afternoon—Suzie opened the box of Christmas decorations he had asked her to inspect. 'Throw out anything you think is past its sell-by date and use some money from the petty-cash box to buy some replacements,' he'd said.

It was good working for Dad. She liked it that he trusted her. It gave her a sense of responsibility. Something, as her mother had told her, she was going to have to get used to.

Will was at the hospital waiting for news about Marty. His friend had been in surgery for nearly two hours now as the only way forward, as Marty had put it, was to submit to the knife and be 'one man down'. Apparently, only by resorting to surgery could testicular cancer be confirmed or discounted. It was drastic stuff: Will didn't know what he'd do if Marty did have cancer and nothing could be done. To lose his oldest and closest friend would be like having both his arms ripped off. He tried to remind himself of the statistics. The cure rate for early testicular cancer was ninety-five to a hundred per cent. It could be beaten. That was the thought he had to hang on to.

He went to find the nearest payphone and tapped in Harriet's number. Disappointingly, all he got was her endearingly prim, self-conscious recorded voice telling him to leave a message. He didn't know how long this honeymoon period would go on for, but it wouldn't be him who ended it. He enjoyed having her in his life. Although, to be precise, it wasn't so much his life as his bed she was in. Last night, when they were lying exhausted and slick with sweat in each other's arms, he'd said, 'Let's go out on Friday night.'

'I'd rather be here in bed with you.'

'But I want to take you out for a special dinner, seeing as I wasn't able to help you celebrate your birthday in style.'

'I'll think about it. But not Friday night. I have to work late.' Then pulling the duvet up over their heads, she slowly slid down his body and the last thing on his mind was going out for dinner.

One of the things he liked most about her was that she had no inclination to change him. She wasn't interested in reorganising his kitchen or tidying up the bathroom like so many women had tried before. A woman he'd gone out with last year had kept on at him to resume his former life as a lawyer. When he'd told Harriet this, she'd said, 'People should learn to mind their own business. We are who we are.'

An elderly couple walked towards him, the man's arm resting protectively on the woman's shoulder, and Will stepped back to let them pass. Long after they'd disappeared round the corner he was still standing in the same spot, lost in thought. He was thinking the inconceivable—how he wanted to be an all-out couple with Harriet. He wanted her to meet his mother. Marty too. He wanted her fully in his life. And that, he suspected, would be his downfall.

Marty was wheeled back to his room a short while later, still groggy from the anaesthetic, but sufficiently awake to say to Will, 'What, no flowers?'

'Don't you dare go all Barbra Streisand on me.'

The doctor advised Will to stay for just a few minutes, and after learning that there would be no instant diagnosis, he left Marty to sleep.

He tried ringing Harriet again in the car and this time she answered. 'Sorry I missed you,' she said. 'I was in a meeting. How's Marty?'

'Sleeping soundly. Don't suppose you'd like to come over and cheer me up tonight?'

'I think I could manage that. How does eight thirty sound?'

Carrie listened to Harriet moving about in her bedroom. She was getting ready to go out. And Carrie knew she was going to see Will. She saw him nearly every night. Carrie knew because she'd watched her aunt through the gap in the curtains. One night, she'd actually seen Will kiss Harriet. The funny thing was Carrie had asked her if Will was her boyfriend and Harriet had told her he was only a friend. But friends didn't kiss the way she'd seen Will kissing her. He'd done it the way she'd seen people doing it on the telly; arms and bodies pushed together.

Carrie had given up wanting Harriet to marry Miles. She didn't mind because Will was just as nice and maybe Harriet would marry him. Maybe when they moved into the new house, Will'd be able to help with all those jobs Granddad was too old and grumpy to help with. Like putting up shelves and making wardrobes. She could remember a day, a long time ago, when Mum and Dad argued about a wardrobe they had bought and were trying to make. In the end, Dad had thrown a load of screws on the floor and shouted at Mum that seeing as she was so good at screwing things, she could do it herself. He'd sworn as well and had gone outside to sit in the garden, even though it was raining.

Grown-ups were peculiar, Carrie decided. They were always telling children not to use bad language, but they did it all the time. At school, Emily and Rebecca said their parents were the same. They also said they didn't like their parents, and sometimes wished they were dead. Emily had then said she was sorry for saying that. 'What's it like not having your parents any more?' she'd asked. 'And did they really die in a car crash?'

It was the first time she'd talked to anyone at school about Mum and Dad. Afterwards she felt upset. But also just a little bit happy. It was good talking about them because they felt real again, not just a sad memory.

During lunchbreak Emily had asked if she'd like to go to her house after school on Friday. 'Rebecca's coming too,' Emily had said. 'You could stay the night if you're allowed. Mum said we'll get the Christmas tree down from the loft at the weekend so you could stay and help put the decorations on it. It would be so cool if you could be there too.'

Carrie hadn't decided yet whether she wanted to go. If she did, it would be the first night she'd spent away from Harriet and Grandma and Granddad. She didn't know why, but the thought scared her. And what if Joel forgot she wasn't there and crept into her room and found her bed empty? Would he scream the place down?

She was still wide awake when she heard Harriet go downstairs and tell Grandma and Granddad that she was going out, that Will was having problems with his computer. She thought how lucky Will was that Harriet was around. If anyone could sort out a computer it was her.

Maxine's day was going from bad to worse. Bad enough that the police had come to the saleroom with allegations of stolen goods passing through it, but now she was stuck in traffic with the prospect of being subjected to one of Will's self-righteousness sessions when she finally got home. She had absolutely no desire to see him this evening, or any other evening for that matter. She was sickened by his behaviour. What kind of example did he set for Suzie and Gemma with all his carryings-on? Why couldn't he just remarry and have done with it? But he'd phoned to ask if he could call round after work. She'd agreed, albeit reluctantly, without asking him what he wanted to discuss. She didn't need to. It would be about Gemma and her crazy plan to spend Christmas in Paris.

The house was empty when she let herself in—Steve was down in London attending some conference and the girls had gone to see Nana Ruby. She went straight to the kitchen and made herself a gin and tonic. She gulped half of it down, then added more gin and a token splash of tonic. At least with Steve away there was no one to mutter about how much she was drinking. She took the glass upstairs to the bedroom, stripped off her clothes and took the remains of her drink with her to the en-suite bathroom. She looked at herself in the mirror. Nana Ruby was right; she did look tired. Though perhaps wrecked was a more apt description. She sighed, and stepped into the shower. Ruby was always telling her she worked too hard and for the first time in her life, Maxine was prepared to admit that this may indeed be true. 'Hard work never killed anyone,' her father used to say. 'It's idleness that finishes people off.' As if to prove his theory, exactly two years after retiring he dropped dead of a heart attack. At the rate she was going, Maxine reckoned she'd go the same way, probably before she retired.

Out of the shower she wrapped a towel round her and looked again at her reflection in the mirror. What wouldn't she give to be young like Suzie and Gemma? And how little they appreciated what they had. She'd worked damned hard to give them the kind of lifestyle they had and what thanks did she get? Bugger all! She slapped her hand down sharply on the surface, but cursed aloud when she saw her empty tumbler go flying. It dropped to the marble floor with a crash, scattering glass. Instinctively she stepped back, but it was the wrong thing to do. She let out a yelp of pain and bent down to see a piece of glass protruding from her heel. Steeling herself, she pulled out the shard of glass just as the doorbell rang.

Grabbing some toilet paper, she wrapped it round her foot, but by the time she had limped downstairs, the blood had seeped through.

'Don't even think about making a wisecrack,' she told Will.

'Anything I can do?'

'Yes. You can make me another gin and tonic while I get dressed.'

He looked at her foot doubtfully. 'You shouldn't be doing anything until we've put a proper dressing on that. Here, lean on me.'

She allowed him to help her into the kitchen. Pain had started to build now and she winced when he took her foot in his hands, mopped up the blood and put a dressing on the wound. Then he went upstairs to her bedroom and came back down with her bathrobe.

Once she had wrapped herself in it and Will had made her a drink, she allowed him to help her through to the sitting room. She felt both annoyed and grateful that he was here; the confident ease with which he was moving about her home irritated her, as did his appearance. He looked too damned well. Younger too. Was that what sex with a young girl did to a man? Rejuvenated him? There again, he didn't have the kind of responsibilities she had. Bitterness darkened her mood. Will had only ever played at life, opting out of anything that got too challenging.

He sat in the chair nearest her and she raised her glass to him. 'Sure you won't join me?'

'Better not. I'm driving. How's the foot doing?'

'It'll be fine. Why don't we get on with why you're here? I'm surprised you can spare the time,' she added tartly.

'You know I've always got time when it comes to the girls, Maxine.'

She sniggered. 'That's what I hear. It used to be women, but apparently now it's young girls you're chasing.' She could see he was angry; could see it in his mouth. She suddenly remembered how it used to feel to be kissed by him, and looked away.

'My private life is exactly that,' he said coolly. 'Private.'

'Then perhaps you shouldn't flaunt your young girlfriend so blatantly in front of our children. Have you any idea how much enjoyment Gemma gets out of rubbing my nose in it?'

He took a moment before saying, 'I'm sorry, but that's between you and Gemma. Have you tried talking to her about it?'

Maxine took a long swallow of gin, annoyed at the way her words had come out. She didn't want Will to know that she hated the fact that he was still on top of his game, while she was sliding into middle age. Pulling herself back to his question, she said, 'What do you think? She only ever speaks to me when she wants something. As with this proposed trip to Paris. Presumably she's wrapped you round her little finger and you've said she can go.'

'Wrong. I told her you and I would have to discuss it, which is why I'm here. What do you really think about her going?'

'She's not going,' Maxine said with finality. 'For the simple reason I'm not having another daughter coming home pregnant.'

Will let out his breath and shook his head. 'You don't think that's being too simplistic? She could be here in Maywood and get pregnant just as easily. And for the record, I'm not happy about her going either. It'll be the first Christmas without both of the children around and it feels like a milestone too far and too soon. Why don't we compromise and say she can go for New Year?' Smiling, he added, 'We could even give her a joint pep talk about the birds and bees. Just for the fun of making her squirm, of course.'

Maxine drained her glass and looked at Will. How did he do it? How did he always manage to make her feel so shitty? 'Maybe,' she demurred.

He relaxed into his chair and stretched his legs out in front of him. 'So how are things between you and Suzie?'

Determined not to lose any more ground to him, Maxine said, 'We're getting there. I'm organising for a decorator to turn the spare room into a nursery. I haven't told her yet.'

Will smiled. 'That's great. She'll be delighted, and if she's not too tired, she could help with some of it. I remember you being a whirlwind of activity in the last month of pregnancy. Do you remember when you were expecting Gemma and I woke up in the middle of the night and found you downstairs stripping the woodchip off the walls in the hall?'

Maxine cast her mind back and recalled her heavily pregnant self with a scraper in one hand and a cup of hot chocolate in the other. 'I'd forgotten about that,' she said faintly. I'm drunk, she thought. When she looked up, Will was on his feet. He was going. She suddenly didn't want to be alone. She thought how convenient it would be if Will was to stay and make her something to eat. But the thought of asking him for help was out of the question. However, in her experience there was a sure-fire way to get a man to do what you wanted: she loosened the belt on her bathrobe, knowing that the action would reveal a generous amount of cleavage. Will had always liked her breasts.

'Do you have to go so soon?' she asked, smiling up at him. She caught his glance skating over her body and congratulated herself on not having lost her old seductive powers. How pathetically simple men were!

'I'm . . . I'm afraid I can't stay,' he said. 'I'm . . . I'm meeting someone.'

'Can't you ring and put them off? I thought we could have something to eat. Or maybe we could . . .' She lowered her gaze coyly.

'Sorry,' he said more firmly, edging away. 'I can't. I'm taking Harriet out for dinner.' His words slapped her hard. Of course! His latest girlfriend.

When he'd shut the door behind him, she realised what a fool she'd been. How could she have thought of coming onto him like that? She blamed it on the gin. Steve was right; she really ought to cut down.

Will drove out of Maywood in a near state of shock. He didn't know what was scarier: a furious Maxine venting her spleen, or a tipsy Maxine coming onto him. What had got into her? But it wasn't his business. What was his business this evening was Harriet. He'd finally pinned her down—quite literally while in bed—and got her to agree to him taking her out for dinner.

Joel hovered anxiously outside Harriet's bedroom door. Everyone was going out except for him and Granddad. Grandma was going out with her friend Dora, Harriet was going out with Will, and Carrie had already gone to Emily's. Last night Carrie had told him to be good while she was away, and not to have any bad dreams. 'You mustn't spoil it for everyone,' she'd said. She made it sound like he did it deliberately. He didn't. He wished Harriet wasn't going out. She was different from Mummy, but reminded him of her. If he couldn't find his reading book to take into school, or his PE bag, she always seemed to know where to look. That's what Mummy had been like.

Carrie said that she thought Harriet and Will would get married. But then she'd said that about Harriet and Miles. It was difficult to keep up with Carrie. Now she thought school was great and that they would stay there for ever, even when they moved. He liked the idea of moving to that nice little cottage, but what if he forgot something? What if—

'Joel, is that you?'

He nudged open the door, went inside and sat on Harriet's bed. He watched her as she brushed her hair. She had nice hair, like Mummy's. He wondered if she would let him touch it.

'You're very quiet, Joel. You OK?'

He nodded. 'Harriet? You know when we move?'

'Yes?'

'Do you think everything will be safe?'

She turned round to look at him. 'Safe from what exactly?'

'From being lost.'

She put the brush down and came and knelt on the floor in front of him. 'Joel, I promise you, nothing will get lost in the move. I'll mark all the packing boxes with what's inside and you can watch every single one of them being loaded onto the van. Then at the other end, you can help me put them into your bedroom. How does that sound?'

He instantly felt better. He put his arms round her neck and hugged her tight. She smelt lovely. Once more he was reminded of his mother and he plucked up the courage to ask if he could brush her hair.

For a moment she looked as if she didn't understand him, but then she smiled. 'If you really want to, go ahead.'

He jumped off the bed to fetch the brush. 'I used to do this for Mummy.'

'Really?'

'Yes. Sometimes when she was upset, she asked me to brush her hair because it made her feel happy.'

'Was she often upset?'

'Just sometimes. Am I doing it right?'

'You're doing it brilliantly.'

Harriet opened the door to Will with mixed feelings. His calling for her made the evening seem too much like a date. 'Don't leave the poor man hanging about on the doorstep,' her mother said, coming down the stairs in a calf-length dress and high heels. Dora had asked Eileen to make up the numbers at a dinner dance—Harriet hoped her mother wouldn't overdo it.

Will said, 'Wow, Eileen! You look like a million dollars.'

Eileen blushed and laughed. 'You don't think this dress is pushing the bounds of credibility?'

'It suits you perfectly. You look terrific.'

Half listening to Eileen asking how Marty was—he was now at home resting—Harriet looked round the door of the sitting room and saw her father slumped morosely in front of the television. Perhaps Will was right and Dad *was* depressed. If so, he needed help. But it was difficult to feel sympathetic when he didn't seem to want to help himself.

Joel, on the other hand, had all Harriet's sympathy. Whereas Carrie had turned a corner and was making friends at school, Joel seemed ever more isolated and anxious. Worryingly, she suspected that the anxieties he actually expressed represented only the tip of the iceberg. Often she found herself wanting to scoop him up and make everything better.

His earlier remarks about his mother had been an encouraging sign that he was now prepared to talk more openly about his parents, but Harriet had been saddened by his account of brushing his mother's hair. As a consequence, Harriet now had a disturbing mental picture of

Felicity holding back the tears while her precious son tried to make her feel better. Was this before or during the affair with Miles?

Harriet had insisted she would drive, and as she was pulling away from the kerb, Will leaned over to kiss her. 'By the way, did I mention you're looking gorgeous?'

'No, you didn't. You were too busy schmoozing my mother.'

'I had hoped you might wear a skirt. Didn't you know that it's the law when a chap takes his girl out for dinner that she has to show her legs. It's a sexist thing.'

'Yes, and it's the kind of thing that will get you a bloody nose.' Her words were spoken with humour, yet she felt a tightening of anxiety in her stomach. What did Will mean by *when a chap takes his girl out*?

But she knew exactly what he meant and that was what frightened her. Without realising it, she had become hooked on this man. He was generous, amusing and endlessly diverting. The moment she stepped over his threshold she became another person. A happier and more alive person. And, of course, there was the sex. The intensity of it was mindblowing. Ironically, she now knew what had driven Felicity to become obsessed with Miles: she was just as obsessed with Will. But she knew she wasn't playing fair with him and that the decent thing to do was to end it. If he was beginning to see her as *his girl*—something she hadn't planned on—she had to act sooner rather than later. The basis of their relationship was skewed. For a start there was the age gap, but more importantly she despised her motives for wanting to sleep with him in the first place. She may well have proved Dominic wrong, and metaphorically stuck her fingers up at Spencer, but knowing that she had achieved it at the expense of another person upset her.

All during dinner Harriet kept looking across the table at Will and thinking how much she was going to miss him. But she mustn't weaken. He was too nice to use for her own selfish needs. Yet each time she resolved to say something, she just couldn't do it. She knew that he was concerned about Marty. What he hadn't told Eileen earlier, probably in deference to her good mood, was that the tumour had turned out to be cancerous and Marty was now set on a course of radiotherapy. Could Harriet really add to his problems?

'Hello, anyone at home on planet earth?' He put down his glass of wine and reached across the table. His fingers wrapped around hers.

Meeting his concerned gaze, she said, 'Will, I think we need to talk.' She knew that he was smart enough to recognise that contained within those few words was an unequivocal message.

He surprised her by raising her hand to his lips and kissing it softly. It was such a tender gesture. 'Please don't say anything else,' he said. 'It's

OK. I pride myself on knowing when to bow out gracefully. I guess it was the age difference, wasn't it?' She nodded. It wasn't the whole truth, but it was kinder to let him think it was.

Shortly after, when he'd paid their bill and they were outside in the car park, he put his arm round her. 'Don't look so glum, Harriet. I had it coming.' He then kissed her lightly on the mouth. It was a poignant farewell kiss that made her heart feel heavy. I must be mad, she thought wretchedly. How can I give him up?

She made a play of fishing around in her bag for her keys so that he wouldn't see how upset she was. She had just found them when the sound of a mobile rang out in the cold night air. It was Will's.

'Oh, hi, Mum,' he said, shrugging apologetically at Harriet. 'What . . .' There was a long silence while Will didn't speak. His eyes grew wide. 'I'll be right there,' he said. 'No, second thoughts, I'll go straight to the hospital. You just keep everyone as calm as you can. And thanks, Mum, you're a star.'

He hung up and let out his breath. 'It's Suzie. She's collapsed. It doesn't sound good. They've called an ambulance. Any chance you can rush me home so that I can get my car and go to the hospital?'

Opening the car door and pushing him inside, Harriet said, 'No way. You're over the limit. I'll drive you there instead.'

In between trying to reach Maxine—she wasn't responding to her mobile and the answering machine was switched on—and cursing every driver who got in front of them, Will kept replaying what his mother had told him: 'She crumpled, Will, fell to the floor. When she came round, she was obviously in pain. She keeps moaning and clutching her head and she says she can't move. She's been sick, too. Gemma's called an ambulance. I think you'd better get here, Will. I don't like the look of this.' Will didn't like the sound of it either.

When they arrived at the hospital, Harriet dropped him off at the entrance to A & E and went to find somewhere to park.

It was a while before Will could find someone to talk to inside. It was bedlam. 'Has my daughter, Suzie Hart, been admitted?' he asked a harassed woman behind the desk.

After an interminable wait, she shook her head. 'Sorry, there's no one of that name.' Not knowing what else he could do, he went back outside and called Gemma on his mobile

She answered immediately. 'Dad, it's a bloody nightmare here. The ambulance hasn't sodding well come and Suzie's completely crashed out. What the hell do we do now?'

'I'll ring for another ambulance,' he said, his hands shaking and his heart pounding. He was just putting his phone back in his jacket pocket when Harriet appeared.

'What's the news?' she asked.

'It's a total cockup! The ambulance hasn't arrived. I've just called for another.' He swallowed. 'Gemma says Suzie's unconscious. They can't wake her. I should have gone there. We could have got her here by now.'

'Let's go inside,' she said. 'You find us a vending machine for some coffee and I'll have a word with someone on the desk so they'll be ready for Suzie when she comes. We just have to wait now.'

It was twenty minutes later, almost midnight, when the sight of Gemma coming in behind the paramedics confirmed for Will that it was Suzie on the trolley. He rushed over but was pushed aside by a whirlwind of activity. Forced to stand back helplessly while Suzie was wheeled away, he caught snatches of what was said: 'Coma . . . preceded by vomiting and drifting in and out of consciousness . . . foetal heartbeat dropping . . .' Paralysed with shock, he stared after his daughter.

'Dad? She'll be OK, won't she?'

He turned. Gemma was standing next to him and the sight of her pale and dazed face brought him up short. He put his arm round her. 'She'll be fine, love. Once they've got her on the right medication.'

'Do you think she's going to lose the baby?'

'Let's hope not. I'm no expert, but it's probably strong enough to be born this early without coming to too much harm. Where's Nana Ruby? Didn't she come in the ambulance with you?'

'She's gone to Mum's. I got her a taxi and gave her my key. Mum should be here, Dad.'

He gave her another hug. 'Good thinking, Gem.'

'I don't understand why she isn't answering her mobile or phone. What's she doing?'

Will told Gemma about Maxine cutting her foot. 'She probably decided to have an early night,' he said.

Gemma sighed. 'I just wish I'd learned to drive. If I had, I could have got her here quicker. Oh, Dad, we felt so helpless. What if she—?'

Will cut her short. 'Don't even say it. Do you want a drink?'

No sooner had he spoken than he saw Harriet coming over with a plastic cup in her hand. 'I thought you might like this,' she said to Gemma. 'Hot chocolate.'

Gemma took the cup. 'Thanks.'

For the next few minutes they stood in awkward silence, watching the clock and waiting for news. When a young doctor approached them, Will tensed. He could see straight away from the man's face that the news was bad. Suzie must have lost the baby. His heart went out to her.

After a brief round of introductions, the doctor ushered Will through to a room that was as cramped as it was uninviting. 'Mr Hart,' he began gently, 'I'm so very sorry to have to tell you this, but your daughter suffered what we think was a ruptured aneurysm. We won't know until—'

Will's mouth went dry. 'I'm sorry, could you explain what that is?'

'Of course. It's a type of brain haemorrhage. In your daughter's case it was severe and sent her into a coma. We did our best to carry out an emergency Caesarean to save the baby, but I'm afraid—'

Will took in the deepening expression of sympathy in the doctor's face. 'The baby didn't survive?' he said helpfully. 'Does Suzie know?'

Confusion passed across the man's face. 'Mr Hart, I'm afraid that neither the baby nor your daughter survived. I'm so very sorry.'

Will heard the words but it was as if his brain wouldn't compute the information. He blinked hard. 'I . . . I don't understand. Dead? Are you telling me Suzie's *dead*?' Suddenly he was finding it hard to breathe. A convulsive trembling had seized him.

'I'm sorry, Mr Hart—'

Whatever else the doctor had to say, Will was deaf to it. A crashing noise had filled the space between his ears. His whole body seemed to have turned inside out and disintegrated.

The next thing he knew, Harriet and Gemma were in the room with him. Harriet was trying to hold him, but he was shaking her off. He looked around for the doctor and saw him standing in the corner talking to Gemma. Tears were streaming down her face. He knew he should go to her, but he couldn't. All he could think of was his beloved Suzie.

'Can I see her?' he said to the doctor. 'My daughter. Please.'

Harriet watched Will walk off hesitantly beside the doctor. It was a painful reminder of the night Felicity and Jeff had died, when she had accompanied her father to identify the bodies. No parent should ever have to go through this, she thought. Poor Will.

Minutes later, when the sound of raised voices broke the unearthly hush, Gemma's head jerked up. 'It's Mum,' she said.

Feeling nauseous with impotent shock, Harriet once more found herself standing helplessly in the background. Gemma and her mother embraced, while an older woman, presumably Will's mother, hovered to one side. With a burst of fresh tears, the girl broke the devastating news.

With tears in her own eyes, and unsure what part she could play in this horrific drama, Harriet decided to leave. She wouldn't be wanted here.

Eileen and Dora were taking it in turns to cook for Will. Each evening they would leave a plastic food container in his porch with instructions on how to reheat whatever was inside. A week had passed since Will's eldest daughter had died and Eileen wished she had the courage to knock on their neighbour's door and tell him just how well she understood the pain of his grief. But Will had made it very clear that he didn't want to talk when Eileen had called over with the first of the food parcels. Most days the curtains stayed shut; his car had moved only once from the drive and that was the day of the funeral. She had hoped that Harriet, on behalf of the family, would attend. But she hadn't. When Eileen had asked her why not, Harriet's reply had taken her aback. 'I think I'm the last person he'd want there,' she said.

'But you'd been such good friends,' Eileen pressed, keeping to herself that she and Dora had long since suspected that there was more than friendship between Harriet and Will. All Eileen could imagine was that there had been a disagreement between them. Probably the night Will's daughter had died.

That was the night Eileen had deliberately gone all-out to deceive her husband. She had gone with Dora and Derek to the pre-Christmas dinner dance put on by the Soirée Club, all set to have some fun. Disappointingly, the night did not prove to be the success she had thought it would be. Yes, it was lovely to be wearing a new dress and feeling happily light-hearted as they danced till midnight—one man even asked her for her phone number—but there was only one man she wanted to enjoy the evening with and that was Bob. But not the Bob he'd become. She wanted her old Bob back: the man she'd always loved and still did. Driving home, Eileen had realised that cheating on Bob to teach him a lesson would solve nothing.

'So what are you going to do next?' Dora had said when Eileen confided in her.

'I'm going to get Christmas over with and then I shall talk to Bob. Really talk. I'll tell him I know about the affairs all those years ago, that I forgave him then, as I will this time round.'

'Will you tell Bob about how you were tempted to do the same?'

'Yes.'

'And have you thought about the consequences if bringing everything out into the open gives him the courage to walk away?'

'Oh, Dora, I've thought of little else. But I have to risk it.'

When Dora dropped her off, the house was in darkness and there was no sign of Harriet's car. Bob was already asleep, and she found Joel sleeping peacefully in Carrie's bed. Back downstairs, she made a pot of tea, thinking how Felicity's death seemed to be a catalyst for change between her and Bob. She was still dwelling on this when she heard Harriet's key in the front door. As soon as she saw Harriet's face, she knew something awful had happened.

'What is it?' she asked.

'I've just come from the hospital. Will's eldest daughter died this evening. She had some kind of aneurysm and died, just like that.'

Eileen put a hand to her mouth. 'Oh, poor man. What about the baby?'

'Dead too.' Harriet pulled out a chair and sat down heavily.

Eileen poured her a cup of tea. 'How is Will taking it?'

'At a rough guess, I'd say it's damn near killing him. Oh, Mum, why do we have to go through so much shit? What's the point of it all?'

'I've no idea. I gave up wondering why and how a long time ago.'

'Will doesn't deserve this. He really doesn't. He's one of the nicest people I know. I wish I could turn back the clock for him.'

'None of us deserve it. But it happens, and somehow, don't ask me how, we find the strength to survive. Look at us. Look how we've coped.'

Harriet shook her head. 'I'm barely coping, Mum. Believe me.'

'Rubbish. Without you, your father and I wouldn't have managed at all. And the children, who have lost the most, really look up to you.'

'Only because I'm taller than them.'

They both smiled, but then suddenly they weren't smiling, they were both crying and hanging on to each other, just as they did the night Jeff and Felicity died.

Since that conversation, Eileen had felt as if a barrier had lifted between her and Harriet. They'd all been living their separate lives with the barriers firmly in place. The children had school, Harriet had work, she had Dora, and Bob, well Bob had had to go in search of something to distract him—first Toby and then this woman who was consoling him. From what she could see, however, Bob was anything but consoled.

It was Saturday morning, exactly a week before Christmas; Bob was out with Toby (allegedly), the children were upstairs playing—Eileen could hear them thrashing around in Joel's bedroom and shaking the floorboards—and Harriet was reading a letter from her conveyancing solicitor, a colleague of Will's friend, Marty, who was still covering for him while he was off work. It had been an eventful week: school had finished for the Christmas holidays and there had been the carol concert, several parties and the school nativity play. Harriet had made Joel's day by managing to get the afternoon off work to see him perform as one of the innkeepers. Watching Harriet slide the letter back inside the envelope, Eileen said, 'Everything still on track? No problems with the house?'

'It looks like we might be able to bring the completion date forward by a week,' Harriet answered. A sudden extra-loud thump from upstairs had them both glancing anxiously at the ceiling. 'I'll take them out with me. I need to do some Christmas shopping.'

'I don't suppose you'd take this box across to Will before you go out, would you?' Eileen asked. She had decided that whatever had caused the rift between Harriet and Will, it had gone on for long enough.

'I will, but only if I can leave it in his porch.'

In the spirit of openness between them, Eileen said, 'Look, Harriet, I know there was something a lot more than just friendship going on between the two of you, but whatever went wrong, I don't think—'

'*Mum!* How did you know?' Harriet spluttered.

'It wasn't difficult. You were spending nearly every evening together, often coming home with a glow that no amount of computer fixing could have put there. So what happened?'

'I ended it with him. It wasn't right between us.'

'Was it the age gap?'

Harriet frowned. 'It was more complicated than that, but that was the excuse I used.'

'That would have hurt him.'

'I think he's got more to worry about than me right now, Mum.'

'But you're upset about it, aren't you?'

'Yes. I behaved badly. I turned into the kind of person I've always despised. And please don't expect me to explain what I mean by that.'

Knowing she'd gone as far as she could with her taciturn daughter, Eileen said, 'I'd still like you to take this food over to him. It would be an olive branch of sorts.'

'You realise, don't you, that you're as subtle as Carrie when it comes to matchmaking? And if it's allowed, I'd appreciate a change of subject. Tell me what's going on with Dad. I think he's clinically depressed. In my opinion, he needs help. Will thought so too.'

Eileen reminded herself that openness was her new watchword. 'I agree with you. But it's not as straightforward as you think.' She took a deep breath. 'Your father's having an affair. It's not the first time it's happened. He did it years ago before Felicity was born, when I had all those miscarriages. It seems to be his way of handling grief.'

Harriet's jaw dropped.

Half an hour later, Harriet went upstairs to tell the children they were going out. Leaving them to tidy the war zone they'd created in Joel's bedroom, she went into her room and stood at the window that overlooked the garden. Her family was falling apart around her. Her father wasn't the man she'd believed him to be. No wonder Mum had decided to play him at his own game; but Harriet was glad Mum had thought better of it. There were some people in the world who had to be beyond reproach. While her mother had been telling her all this, it would have been the ideal opportunity to confide in her about Felicity's secret affair, but she hadn't. Her mother had enough to worry about as it was.

Coincidentally, Harriet had decided the previous night that she wanted to tell Miles that she knew about him and Felicity. As brief as her relationship with Will had been, it had taught her something vitally important: to be less judgmental of what Miles and her sister had done. She planned to go to Novel Ways in Maywood, to buy her parents Christmas presents and at the same time ask Miles out for a drink.

But before then she had to perform a far more difficult task. Leaving the children with one final mind-boggling challenge—to find their coats and put on their shoes—she took the plastic box of food across the road.

It was a gloomy, cold day with a sky the colour of pewter. She rang Will's doorbell just one short ring. Then, having got no response, she bent down to leave the box on the floor of the porch. At that moment, the door opened and Will stood before her. His face was gaunt and unshaven, his hair unwashed, his clothes crumpled. But it was the pain in his ravaged eyes that shocked her most.

Feeling stupid and inadequate, she held out the box like a gauche child delivering harvest festival boxes to the needy. 'Please just say if you'd rather my mother and Dora didn't keep on doing this,' she said.

He looked straight through her, his expression blank. The blankness hurt her as much as when he'd shrugged her away in the hospital. He took the box from her. 'Tell them no more after this. I'm OK.'

No, you're not! she wanted to shout. But all she said was, 'My mother wants you to know that if there's anything we can do, just call.'

Without another word, he closed the door.

After depositing Carrie and Joel in the children's section at Novel Ways, Harriet went to find the latest Alan Titchmarsh gardening book for her father and the new Delia for her mother. When she'd paid for them, she asked the teenage girl behind the counter if Miles was around. She was told he was upstairs.

'Harriet!' he said. 'How . . . how are you?'

There was no disguising his awkwardness. Which made her feel even guiltier. There he'd been, silently grieving for the woman he loved, and she'd come along and metaphorically kicked him in the teeth. How could she have been so insensitive? Perhaps Dominic was right and she really was incapable of genuine affection.

Realising that Miles was waiting for her to speak, she said, 'I think I must be suffering from a severe case of jingle-bells madness to be out shopping on the last Saturday before Christmas. How are you? The shop seems maniacally busy.'

'It's been like it for days. As if that wasn't enough, I'm organising an event here for the writing group I belong to.'

'What kind of event?'

'Poetry and short story readings. It's on Monday evening. I . . .' His voice broke off. 'I don't suppose I can interest you in a ticket?'

She smiled, filled with relief that a bridge was forming between them. 'Why not? And how about a drink afterwards? There's something we need to discuss, isn't there? And I think we'll both feel a lot better once we've got it over and done with.'

The tension disappeared from his face. 'A drink would be great. But you'll have to hang around after the event while I lock up the shop.'

'No problem. What time does it start?'

'Kickoff's at eight o'clock and tickets are available on the door.' He put a hand on her arm and kissed her cheek, sealing an end to their estrangement. 'Oh, by the way, Dominic's coming home for Christmas.'

Will opened the plastic box Harriet had delivered and without looking at the foil packages put them straight in the bin. As he'd done with all the others. He wished he could feel more grateful for what his neighbours were doing, but he couldn't. His feelings were centred on the one agonising and inescapable truth that would haunt him for the rest of his life: he'd failed Suzie. He knew in every fibre of his being that if he'd only acted differently that night, his daughter would still be alive. If only he hadn't insisted on taking Harriet out for dinner. If only he and Harriet hadn't thought it would be better to go directly to the hospital. If only he had gone straight to his mother's.

Jarvis, Marty and his mother kept telling him on the phone that it was futile to think this way, that Suzie's death had occurred after events that no one could have foreseen. As though it would make him feel better, his mother had pointed out that Maxine's guilt was far worse than his. Apparently, when Ruby had let herself in with Gemma's key, she had found Maxine lying comatose on the sofa.

But he didn't care a damn that Maxine had to live with the knowledge that she'd been so drunk she'd been oblivious to the constant ringing of the phone. That was her problem.

The post-mortem had revealed, as the medical staff at the hospital had suspected it would, that the cause of Suzie's death had been a ruptured aneurysm on the right side of her brain. There had been a fatal loss of blood and severe damage. Time, they had been told, was of the essence if there had been any chance of saving Suzie. The wheels of an official inquiry had been put into motion, and while Maxine was determined to fight tooth and nail to sue the ambulance service, Will knew it

wouldn't make any difference. Suzie was dead. No amount of legal wrangling would bring her back. Somehow he would have to learn to live with the incalculable weight of his grief. The gut-wrenching anguish he felt at times left him in a state of catatonic numbness when he could think of nothing but the futility of carrying on.

Feeling sick to his stomach, he filled the kettle to make some coffee. But he'd run out of coffee. It was just about all he was surviving on. That and toast. After checking the breadbin and finding just a pair of crusts left in the bag, he knew he had to summon the energy to go to the shops. He couldn't face going into town but thought he could manage the short walk to Edna Gannet's.

The light was fading; snow had begun to fall. A delicate flake landed on his nose, prompting a memory that made his eyes sting with tears. Suzie had been two years old when she'd first seen snow. She'd stood at the open kitchen door, a foot hovering cautiously on the brink of exploring the magical whiteness, but only when she'd taken his hand had she plucked up the courage to venture forth.

Edna Gannet's was empty when he pushed open the door. Her infamous steely gaze fell on him as he ducked behind a shelf to find some coffee. Then, picking some bread up, a packet of butter, half a dozen eggs and bacon—who knows, he might get round to eating it—he put his purchases on the counter, behind which Edna was now standing. He knew that she would know about Suzie; it had been front-page news in the local paper: YOUNG GIRL DIES BECAUSE OF AMBULANCE BLUNDER.

Avoiding any eye contact with Edna, he opened his wallet while she rang up his bill. To his annoyance, he found that it was empty. 'I'm sorry,' he mumbled, 'I don't seem to have any money with me. Will you take a credit card?' Without meaning to, his eyes had found hers and he flinched when he felt the full force of her scrutiny.

'I'll have to add on a charge if you pay that way.'

'So be it.'

'Cheaper not to. Why don't you pay me another day?'

Will had lived in Maple Drive long enough to know that this was an unheard-of proposition: Edna Gannet never put anything on a tab. 'No, really, I'd rather pay now.'

'It's a one per cent charge.'

'I don't care.'

'Any time you're passing.'

'I don't plan to be passing for some time,' he said, his voice rising. 'Please, just take my card and charge me whatever you want.'

'Suit yourself.'

Back out on the street, he walked home, his head down so as not to

attract any more eye contact with passers-by. He'd had enough of that from Edna. He recalled Harriet telling him how Edna had once tried to be nice to her and the children because of her sister's death. 'It's too much of a shock to the system if people you rely upon to behave brutally suddenly act out of character,' Harriet had said. 'Unexpected acts of kindness should be outlawed.'

She was right. Just as she'd been right to end things between them. He didn't know what he'd been thinking of to get involved with her. Perhaps he'd been trying to prove something to himself. He wasn't sure what, but it no longer mattered. Harriet was in the past. As was any semblance of a normal life. His mother and Jarvis had been on at him since the funeral that he should get back to work. How could anyone expect him to work when it was as much as he could do to get up of a morning? Sometimes it was hard to breathe for the pain.

This trip to Edna's was his first step beyond his front door since the day of the funeral. If it hadn't been for Jarvis and Marty he didn't know how he'd have got through the service; they'd sat either side of him in church, literally propping him up. He had no recollection of anyone else at the funeral. Not until afterwards, when everybody had assembled at Maxine and Steve's.

By this stage Maxine had disappeared; she'd gone to bed, too trauma-tised to talk to anyone. It had been down to Steve and Ruby to dole out drink and food. Despite the cold, Will had wanted to spend most of the time outside in the garden. But Marty, still not a hundred per cent from his operation and now embarking on a course of radiotherapy, had forced him to come inside for a drink. He'd been drinking solidly for some time when he'd caught sight of a group of youngsters—friends of Suzie's, Gemma had said.

'Who's the lad all done up in the suit and tie?' he'd asked, curious.

'His name's Richard,' Gemma had said. 'He used to go out with Sinead, Suzie's closest friend at university.'

Seized with a fury he didn't know he possessed, he had wanted to beat the shit out of him. 'You're the reason my daughter's dead!' he wanted to scream. But he didn't. He let the murderous sense of outrage pass. Blaming his daughter's death on anyone but himself wouldn't wash. She'd been his responsibility, no one else's.

When he let himself in there was a message on the answering machine from his mother. She phoned him every day. He wished she wouldn't.

Now that he'd been out, the house was making Will feel claustropho-bic, and after drinking a mug of coffee and managing half a slice of toast, he put on his walking boots and warmest fleece and went down to the end of the garden to walk along the towpath.

He'd been walking for no more than a few minutes when he saw Harriet's father coming towards him.

'How's it going, Will?' Bob asked when they were face to face.

'Oh, you know, each day as it comes.' It was a stupid thing to say.

Bob looked at him hard. 'I used to lie as glibly as that,' he said. 'What you really mean is that you wish you were dead yourself. Don't let anyone tell you it gets better. Take it from me, it doesn't.'

His words were like a knife thrust between Will's ribs. Will took a step back. He suddenly realised that he needed to believe what Marty, Jarvis and his mother had told him: that, given time, the pain would lessen. Whatever else, he didn't want his grief to turn him into an embittered old man like Bob. He made his excuses and walked away.

Bob watched him go, disappointed. He'd thought Will would appreciate some honesty. But apparently not. There was no helping some people. Jennifer was another person who was refusing his help. Whenever he phoned her to see if there was anything he could do for her, she would say he wasn't to keep ringing. For heaven's sake, she made him sound like a stalker! All he wanted to do was speak to the one person who had taken the trouble to listen to him.

'I can't just forget about you,' he'd said.

'But you must. You're a married man and I should never have encouraged you.'

'But it was so natural between us.'

'No, Bob, it was very unreal. Looking back on it, I behaved like a silly twenty-year-old looking for a holiday romance.'

He'd been reduced to begging and it had got him nowhere. In the end she had agreed that he could call her occasionally, especially if there was anything to report about the *Jennifer Rose*, which would be staying at the marina until the spring, when she planned to come up and travel home on it. It was this thought that kept his hopes alive. In the spring, he would see her again. Then he'd have the opportunity to make her understand just how real and natural it had been between them.

So far Miles hadn't shown so much as a flicker of annoyance, but Harriet felt it on his behalf. The last person in the world that he would have wanted to be in the audience was sitting on Harriet's left: Dominic. While Miles was managing successfully to ignore Dominic's presence, others were not. People—mostly women—were openly staring, some craning or twisting their necks to get a better look at this dark, saturnine and elegant figure in their midst.

After a hurried supper, and while Harriet was upstairs reading to the children, the doorbell had rung. It was Dominic. 'Hello, Hat. I've just

heard of the literary extravaganza my brother's putting on tonight,' he said, brushing her cheek with a careless kiss, 'and I've decided I would be letting him down if I wasn't there to offer him my inimitable support. I'll be back in half an hour. You will be ready then, won't you?' He cast a disapproving eye over her baggy trousers and hooded top.

'What about your father? Isn't he going?'

Dominic laughed. 'Good God, no. It's not his kind of evening at all.'

Thinking it might have been nice for Miles to have his father's support, just once, Harriet went upstairs to finish reading to the children. Sitting on Joel's bed and answering Carrie's excited questions about Dominic— how long was he going to be around and how often would they get to see him?—she had hoped he would behave himself at Novel Ways.

The wiry-haired woman, who had been reading out a lengthy, clichéd poem about growing old, finally sat down and the audience clapped enthusiastically. Perhaps because the poem had at last come to an end. Next to Harriet, Dominic scribbled something on the ticket he'd bought at the door. It said: *Save me from this freak show, Hat!*

She tried to keep herself from laughing but failed miserably. When Miles took his place behind the lectern, Harriet shot Dominic a warning look. 'Behave,' she whispered, 'or I'll stamp on your hat when we get out of here.' He blew her a kiss.

Even to Harriet's unappreciative ears, there was no mistaking the beauty of what Miles was reading out. It was a strikingly tender and poignant poem of love and longing, and knowing that he must have written it for Felicity, it moved Harriet almost to tears. When Miles read the last line of his poem, Dominic snorted loudly and a spontaneous burst of applause rang out. Hoping that Miles hadn't heard his brother, Harriet dug her elbow into Dominic's ribs. 'You pig!' she hissed. 'Don't say I didn't warn you.' She snatched his hat from his head, threw it onto the floor and stamped on it hard. His reaction was to slap her thigh, causing her to yelp loudly. This Miles did hear. As he remained at the lectern to invite people to stay and enjoy a mince pie and a glass of wine, he glared. Harriet sank down into her seat feeling like a naughty child.

The conversation Harriet had planned to have with Miles had been put on hold the second Dominic had muscled his way into the evening, and she was now resigned to the three of them going for a drink instead.

'So what did you think?' Miles asked when they were settled at a table in the wine bar. The question was directed at Harriet, but before she could answer, Dominic said, 'It was a violation of the English language.'

'Dominic, can't you ever stop living up to your reputation as an insufferable bastard?'

'It's OK, Harriet,' Miles said matter-of-factly, 'a great scholar like my

brother is welcome to his erudite opinion. How else would he view a homespun writers' group? Even if one of our members has probably outsold anything he's ever had published. Our novice scribbler has made it onto the bestseller lists in no less than seven different countries.'

'Don't make it so easy for me, Miles. You of all people should know that it's rarely the well-written novels that make it onto those lists.'

'Yes, but it's those books that subsidise most of the unreadable stuff you'd have everyone reading.'

Harriet had heard enough. 'Shut up and be nice, you two!' she said, 'or I shall walk away right now.'

Miles looked shamefaced but Dominic raised his eyebrows sardonically.

'You're beginning to annoy me, Harriet. First you massacre my hat, now you tell me how to talk to my own brother. Motherhood clearly doesn't suit you; you're far too bossy these days.'

Miles rolled his eyes. 'Not funny, Dominic.' Then addressing Harriet: 'How's your friend Will? I read about his daughter in the paper.'

Momentarily wrongfooted, Harriet took a sip of her wine before saying, 'It was the suddenness of it that made it so devastating. I was there at the hospital when it happened.'

'That must have been a comfort to him, at least,' said Miles.

Dominic clicked his fingers. '*Hello*. Remember me? Who's Will?' he demanded. 'And what happened to his daughter?'

'Will is Harriet's boyfriend,' Miles explained patiently, 'and his daughter died recently. OK?'

Dominic sat up straight. 'Boyfriend? You never said, Hat. How long has that been going on for?'

'It hasn't.'

'But Miles just said—'

'He's wrong! So just leave it.' More gently, she said, 'Sorry, Miles, it wasn't really anything as heavy as a girlfriend-boyfriend situation—'

'Hey,' interrupted Dominic. 'Who the hell is this Will character?'

'He lives in Maple Drive, in the house opposite Harriet and her parents.'

A calculating look in his eyes, Dominic said, 'Come to think of it, Mum and Dad have mentioned something about a new neighbour. The daughter who died was nineteen, wasn't she?'

'Yes,' Harriet said.

'Which must mean this Will, the father, is . . .' Dominic pursed his lips. 'Gosh, Hat, exactly how *old* is he?'

'Forty-six,' she said, staring fixedly at Dominic's hateful, smug face and wondering if anyone in the wine bar would notice her strangling him with her bare hands. 'Do you have a problem with that?'

He shrugged. 'No problem at all.'

'I'd advise you leave it right there, Dominic,' Miles said in a low voice.

'It's OK, Miles, I'm quite capable of answering for myself.' She leaned across the table. 'What exactly do you want to know, Dominic? Did I sleep with him? Is that it? Did I have a fling with the man? Well, yes, I did. Put a tick in all of the above boxes. There! Satisfied?'

'How disagreeably suburban you make it sound. Miles? You've gone awfully quiet. Don't you have anything to say on the matter?'

Ripping a beer mat in two, Miles said, 'I'd say it's none of our business.'

'Really? I'd have thought it would have been very much *your* business. After all, the last time I was home you were practically falling over yourself for a bit of action in the sack with our frigid little Harriet.'

Seeing the look of horror on Miles's face, Harriet did the only thing she could have done. She picked up her wineglass and threw its contents in Dominic's face. 'You vicious bastard!'

The office Christmas party had never been one of Harriet's favourite pastimes. In years gone by she had devised all manner of excuses why she couldn't attend, but Howard had warned her yesterday that he'd make her life a living hell if she so much as thought of not joining in. And when it came to organising a Christmas lunch, Harriet had to hand it to him; he spared no expense. He'd not only organised a bus to ferry everyone into Manchester, he arranged taxis for people to share on their way home, and he was treating them all to a meal at his favourite Chinese restaurant. With Dave Carter, the junior analyst, on her left and Tina, a lively fifty-year-old from accounts getting more raucous by the minute on her right, Harriet had somehow found herself entering into the spirit of the occasion. She was one of the few sober people, because she had brought her car and would be driving home, so she was probably the only person who would remember Howard's appalling jokes in the morning. But God love 'em, she thought with surprising affection, he knows how to instil a sense of loyalty in his employees and she counted herself lucky to work for him.

Much later in the evening, she felt a hand clamping down on her shoulder. 'There you are, Hat! Having fun?'

'This might surprise you, but, yes, I am.'

Howard laughed. 'Excellent. Now, come and sit with me.' He grabbed her by the arm and pushed her towards his table. Most of the chairs were empty, people having got up to wander around and chat. Howard pulled out the chair next to his. 'Drink?' he offered.

'No, thanks, I'm driving home later.'

'You mean you're sober and still enjoying yourself! So tell me how the kiddies are. Looking forward to Christmas, I'll bet. When mine were little they would write wish lists to Santa that were as long as my arm.'

'They're pretty much on the case,' Harriet said lightly. This was a huge understatement. Carrie's requests included a pair of purple rollerskates that lit up with flashing lights, a bike with at least ten gears, a CD player, some kind of disco-babe game (like Emily has), and a hamster (like Rebecca's). In contrast, Joel's list was heartbreakingly short; he'd asked for a new pair of slippers.

'But I guess their excitement must be tempered by knowing this will be their first Christmas without their parents,' Howard said. 'The same must be true for you; you'll miss your sister, won't you?'

Touched by his solicitude, she said, 'We'll cope.'

'Of course you will. But it won't be easy. How's the house move going?'

'All set for the 4th of January. I've booked a day off, by the way.'

'Only the one? Take two, at least.' He filled his wineglass and took a mouthful. 'So how's your love life? Is that bloke in Dublin still keen?'

Alarmed, she said, 'Dominic's an old friend. Nothing more. As I recall telling you at the time.'

'My sources tell me that you were heard talking to a guy called Will on the phone. Who's he? Another *friend*?'

'Have you been tapping the phones?'

'No, just listening to office gossip. Come on, talk to Uncle Howard. You know you want to. I've noticed a few changes in you recently; one minute you're fizzing away like a nun who's just been snogged, and next you're looking like the mother superior who wasn't so lucky.'

Harriet shook her head in bewilderment. Was there nothing this man didn't know? But the extraordinary thing was, she was actually tempted to talk to Howard about Will—about how much she missed him, how she wished she could spend an evening with him just to make sure he was all right. Before she could stop herself the words were leaping from her mouth and she was unburdening herself.

When she'd finished, he said, 'The poor devil. I don't know what I'd do if anything happened to either of my children. So why didn't it work out between you two? Was it the age gap?'

'Yes,' Harriet lied.

'You want to know what my advice is? It sounds to me like you still fancy the bloke, but I'd advise you to put him out of your mind. After what's just happened to him, he's seriously damaged goods. Best keep away from him altogether. Start offering your shoulder for him to cry on, as you girls love to do, and you'll end up in big trouble.'

'You really think so?' Harriet was surprised at Howard's take on the situation.'

'Trust me, he's in no fit state to get involved with anyone right now.'

Harriet drove home with Howard's words echoing in her ears. The thought of rekindling her relationship with Will hadn't crossed her mind, but it had certainly gone through her mind to provide him with a shoulder on which to lean. If Howard was right and Will was vulnerable, her being there for him could well make matters worse. Howard's advice struck her as being shrewd. All the same, she felt disappointed. She missed Will and hated the thought of him suffering.

As for her so-called friend, Dominic, after his foul behaviour the other night he could go to hell. His interest in Will had been nothing more than a malicious desire to make Harriet look stupid. And why had he tried to make out that Miles had been interested in her, when it was Felicity who had been the love of his life? OK, Dominic didn't know it for sure—Harriet hadn't told him about the email that had given Miles away—but what kind of twisted mind continually made him want to provoke and embarrass people? Had he got a kick out of pushing her until she flipped, just to see if he could make her lose control? It had struck Harriet in bed that night that maybe Dominic, given that he suspected Miles had had an affair with his perfect Felicity, was jealous, knowing that he couldn't have Felicity in the way that Miles could.

The following morning Miles had phoned her on her mobile and apologised again for Dominic's behaviour. 'That comment he made about you and me, it . . . it was totally out of order. I hope you didn't—'

This constant apologising from Miles was getting on her nerves and Harriet had cut him short by saying, 'Dominic isn't your responsibility, so don't keep saying sorry on his behalf.'

'You're right, I know. I don't suppose there's any chance we can get together for that chat, just the two of us, is there?'

Harriet said, 'Not for a while. Let's do it in the New Year when Dominic's gone back to Cambridge.'

'But I'll see you over Christmas, won't I?'

'Sure. I'm counting the days until your parents' New Year's Day sherry fest.'

He groaned. 'Promise me you'll be there. I don't think I could hack it without you.'

She'd ended the call feeling happier that her friendship with Miles seemed to be back on track.

Gemma was in town, wandering aimlessly. She had thought a look round the shops in Maywood would cheer her up, but it wasn't working. Every morning she woke feeling the same intense loneliness. But the mornings were nothing compared to the nights, when just as she was nodding off she would relive the terrifying journey to the hospital in the ambulance. With the siren wailing and the paramedic bent over Suzie's inert body, she had tried to convince herself that Suzie was going to be OK, that any minute her sister would wake up and wonder what all the fuss was about. Then there were all the questions the paramedic kept firing at her—and with each one that was asked, Gemma dreaded getting something vital wrong that might save her sister.

Later, when Dad had been taken away on his own, she'd thought the same as him, that the doctor was going to break the news that Suzie was OK but the baby had died. Had it been wishful thinking on their part—let the baby die so that Suzie might live? Even if it was wrong, Gemma didn't care. If it happened all over again, she'd wish for exactly the same, for her sister to be alive and looking forward to Christmas.

There would be no Christmas this year. And certainly no going to Paris to see Marcel. Mum had thrown away all the cards they'd received; Gemma had found Steve fishing them out of the bin one night and asked him what he was doing. 'These people don't know about Suzie,' he'd said. 'Someone has to write and tell them.'

She'd always despised Steve for being unimaginative and interfering but now Gemma was grateful for his rock-steady help. He was endlessly patient and kind with Mum and Gemma could see that it wasn't always easy. Sometimes Mum would shout at him as if she was taking it out on him that Suzie had died. She had gone back to work the day after the funeral, which Gemma had thought was a mistake. Steve had said she ought to take a leaf out of Will's book and stay at home for a while. 'Don't you dare tell me what to do!' she'd yelled. 'And don't ever compare me to that man.' She was being scarily irrational.

Dad's behaviour was equally scary. Gemma had tried many times to go to see him but whenever she phoned he'd say, 'Not today, love. I'm not very good company just now.'

The only person Gemma was able to talk to was Nana Ruby. Out of them all she was the one who seemed to be coping best. 'Don't worry about your father,' she told Gemma. 'He has to sort this out himself. He'll get there. Just be patient with him.'

But Gemma didn't want to be patient; she wanted her father *now*. She decided she wouldn't ring Dad; she'd just turn up on his doorstep.

Twenty-five minutes later, she was getting off the bus and heading for Maple Drive. It was dark and the houses had their lights switched on and some hadn't drawn the curtains. Through the windows she could see Christmas trees decorated with lights and baubles. Not knowing why, she began to cry. Dragging her hands across her eyes, she turned at the sound of a car behind her. As it drew level, she recognised the driver; it was her father's girlfriend. Except Gemma had the feeling she wasn't his girlfriend any more. He hadn't mentioned her since the night Suzie died.

Harriet stopped the car when she realised who she'd just driven past. With no traffic behind her, she reversed the short distance and lowered the passenger window. 'If you're going to see your father, would you like a lift?'

'It's OK, I can walk.'

'It's freezing out there. Go on, hop in. It's no trouble.'

When the girl had strapped herself in, Harriet drove on in silence. She badly wanted to find the right words of sympathy and support for Will's daughter, but could think of nothing helpful to say. She suddenly felt sorry for all those people who had tried to be nice to her in the aftermath of her sister's death. In the end she said nothing until she had pulled onto her parents' drive. 'I know how it feels to lose a sister you're really close to,' she said quietly. 'My sister died earlier this year . . . She was my best friend, too.' Her words were received with a crashing silence. Gemma released her seat belt, and as she fumbled in the darkness for the door handle, Harriet quickly reached for her bag and dug out a business card. 'Look, any time you think a chat might help, just give me a ring.'

'Thanks,' Gemma said, putting the card in her pocket. 'But I'm OK. Really I am. It's my parents who are going to pieces.'

Harriet watched her cross the road to her father's house. Poor kid, she thought. She was far from OK.

It was Christmas Day and Maxine felt sick. 'We have to do something for Christmas,' Ruby had said with her customary reasonableness, 'so let's do it differently. I want you all to come to me. Will too. There won't be much room but it will do you both good.'

'I don't think it will work,' Maxine had said. Her ex-mother-in-law was deluding herself if she believed she and Will could be united by a bond of grief. She hadn't bargained on Ruby's no-nonsense determination.

'I'm doing this for Suzie,' the older woman had said firmly. 'For one day you and my son will put your differences aside. You'll do it for Gemma's sake as well. She needs her family to act with solidarity.'

So here she was reluctantly sitting in Ruby's cramped dining room. Will didn't look well. But then nor did she. She'd lost weight and was only managing to sleep for a couple of hours each night. Maxine hadn't told anyone, but she'd hidden some of Suzie's unwashed clothes; they still smelt of her and when she was alone she would take out a piece of clothing and bury her face in it. Sometimes she cried, but more often she sobbed dry-eyed, her head aching with every scrap of memory connected with Suzie. There was regret too. All those sports days she'd missed. Even a birthday party one year. She'd been a lousy mother. She hadn't deserved a daughter like Suzie. But it was too late now to put it right. Maxine would never be able to say how sorry she was.

'Red or white wine, dear?'

Maxine looked up. 'None for me, Ruby,' she murmured. She hadn't touched a drop of alcohol since Suzie had died. The shameful memory of Ruby rousing her from her drunken stupor was still palpable. As was the memory of her disgusting behaviour with Will that night.

When lunch was over, Will insisted on doing the washing-up. Glad to be alone at last, he unbuttoned his shirtsleeves and took stock of the mess. He had just cleared a space round the sink, when the door opened and Maxine came in. 'Your mother suggested you might like some help.'

'It's OK. I've got it covered. You go and relax with the others.'

'She said you'd say that, but I'm under orders to stay.'

'It's not like you to do something against your will,' he said irritably. At once he realised how petty he sounded. 'I'm sorry,' he said, meaning it. 'It's just that I wanted to be on my own. I find it's easier that way.'

'Me too.' He saw that her face—so often resolutely proud and hostile—was clouded with tiredness and misery.

'I'll wash, you dry,' he said.

They worked in silence until Maxine said, 'How's Marty coping with the radiotherapy?'

'You know Marty; it would take more than a bit of cancer to get to him. How about you? How are you coping with everything?'

'People at work say I'm doing brilliantly.'

'And what does Steve think?'

'He thinks I'm burying myself in my work.'

'I never thought I'd say this, but Steve's not a bad bloke. I'm not sure how either of us would have got through this if he hadn't been around.' Out of the corner of his eye, he watched her putting the cutlery in the drawer. He'd forgotten that Maxine didn't put cutlery away like most normal people did; she lined everything up neatly, the spoons and forks all layered with precision, the knives blade-side down.

Her hand jolted, sending the forks askew that she'd just lined up. 'Damn!'

He looked away, disconcerted at seeing her so flustered. This wasn't the Maxine he knew of old. But what else could he expect? They were both changed. Everything they ever experienced from now on would be affected by Suzie's dying. Suzie would be there in every piece of music they heard, every conversation they had, every sleepless night they suffered. For the rest of their lives there would be a bottomless pit of memories to refer to: that was the way Suzie liked her toast . . . Oh, Suzie used to love that film . . . Do you remember the doll Suzie used to take everywhere she went? He didn't know whether it was a relief or a comfort, but already Suzie's presence seemed to be greater in death than when she was alive. It was as if he'd been made raw from grief and his mind, body and soul were sensitive to everything he'd ever known about her.

The most painful memory was of him kneeling by the side of her bed on her third birthday. She was still overexcited from an afternoon of too much sugar and a houseful of squealing friends, and he had soothed her by singing to her. His heart thumped as he pictured her small, restless body gradually relaxing. But without warning, the picture changed and it was a grown-up Suzie he was looking at—Suzie dead in the hospital, the lights bright, the ground rising up to meet him as he pitched forward, hands reaching out for him, voices asking if he needed to sit down, did he want a drink? No, he silently screamed, I want my daughter back. Give me back my daughter! He lowered his head, squeezing his eyes shut against the burning tears.

'Will, are you OK?'

Fighting hard to regain his composure, he forced himself to swallow. He didn't want Maxine to see him like this. It was too reminiscent of a lifetime ago, when she had despised and scorned him for his weakness.

'Here, try this.' He turned round; Maxine was holding out some kitchen roll towards him. He took it but was careful not to look at her. 'Thanks,' he muttered. 'Sorry to let the side down. You never did like seeing me when I was upset, did you? In your eyes men should behave like real men. As your father did.' His tone was bitter.

She shrugged wearily, and once again he realised how changed she was. She looked haggard, thoroughly defeated.

'I'm sorry,' he said, 'old habits die hard. I keep having a go at you, and I shouldn't. Not now when we're going through—'

She raised her hands. 'No, please, don't say any more.' She looked terrified that he might offer her sympathy.

It upset him to think how divided and entrenched they'd become. How could they have created a beautiful child like Suzie, only to end up hating each other? Surely, for Suzie's sake, they could learn to be kinder to one another. Couldn't they? Or had they left it too late?

It had rained steadily over Christmas, but the day after Boxing Day, the sky suddenly brightened, and Harriet phoned the estate agent to ask if she could borrow the key to number 1 Lock Cottage to do some measuring. The biggest surprise of the move so far was how much Carrie was looking forward to it. To Harriet's amazement her niece spoke of little else and was constantly on at Harriet about when she could invite her new friends to see the cottage and when they could have their first sleepover.

As to be expected, Joel was more reticent about the move. Harriet had lost count how many times he had asked her how he would get home from school. His anxiety was contagious and whenever Harriet found herself beginning to worry too much about her nephew, she reminded herself of something Will had once told her; that as soon as Joel had made a special friend at school, everything would come together for him. She hoped he was right. It really mattered to her that Joel was happy. He wasn't a strong, resilient child the way Carrie was; he was quiet and sensitive and too prone to introversion. He was entirely his father's child, Harriet had come to realise.

Harriet had seen Will only twice during the Christmas period, and that was when he came and went from his house. Mum had wanted to invite him over for a drink, but Harriet had begged her not to. 'It's far too soon,' she'd told Eileen.

Their own Christmas had, of course, been overshadowed by Felicity and Jeff's absence, and Harriet knew that at times her parents had struggled to keep a brave face on the proceedings. It was particularly palpable when it came to the children opening their presents. Harriet's father had left the room abruptly.

'It was their faces,' he told Harriet later. 'There was such joy and excitement in their expressions. And poor Felicity not here to see it. It's so bloody unfair. It's like they've forgotten her already.'

'They'll never forget their mother,' Harriet had said, quick to defend her niece and nephew. 'They're just adapting faster than us.'

These had been almost the only words exchanged between Harriet and her father since she had learned of his double life, and she could muster up little sympathy for him.

The children had wanted to come and help her measure up at the house and just as they were climbing into the car, a voice had Harriet turning round. She hadn't seen either Miles or Dominic since the evening at Novel Ways, but here was Dominic coming towards her. 'Just the person I wanted to see,' he said. 'Are you going anywhere interesting?'

'Yes, my new house.'

'Excellent. I'll come with you.'

She moved away from the car so that the children couldn't hear her.

'You're not coming anywhere with me until you've apologised.'

He raised his eyebrows. 'It would help if I knew what it was I'm supposed to be sorry about. Remind me what heinous crime I've committed.'

Staggered at his glibness, she tightened her scarf round her throat. 'I suggest you cast your mind back to last week when I threw my drink in your face,' she said, 'and in particular, the reason why I did it.'

'Surely you're not still cross about that? A silly off-the-cuff remark about my little bro fancying you?'

She looked at him hard. 'You called me frigid.'

'And is that what you want me to apologise for? For you having an underdeveloped sexuality? Not for my teasing you about Miles swapping his affections from one sister to another? Which was, I admit, rather cruel of me. By the way, presumably you've now proved me right; that it *was* Miles with whom Felicity was having an affair?'

'Dominic, I'm warning you. You apologise or I'll—'

'Or what?' he interrupted her. 'What will you do, Harriet?' He suddenly flung his arms out wide. 'What can anyone do to me?' To her horror and amazement, he started to cry, and lurching towards her, he wept uninhibitedly, his sobs catching in his throat.

Stunned, and wondering if he'd been drinking, Harriet stood in his arms not knowing what to do. She tried to slip out of his grasp. 'Dominic,' she said. 'Please stop. You'll upset the children.'

To her relief he let go of her, but with tears streaming down his cheeks, he said, 'I don't give a damn about anyone else. I'm beyond that. Please let me come and see your new house.' He was pleading with her.

What could she do but give in? She bundled him into the passenger seat of her Mini.

By the time they'd picked up the keys from the estate agent and Harriet had driven to the house, Dominic had calmed down. 'I'm sorry,' he murmured, when at Harriet's instructions the children had taken the keys and gone round to the back of the cottage. 'I warned you in Dublin that I was losing it.'

'Dominic, have you thought seriously about seeing a doctor?'

'No!' He slammed the car door. 'Come on. Show me your house.'

His mood swings were so difficult to keep up with. Not for the first time, Harriet wondered if drugs were responsible. But whatever the reason, Harriet couldn't stay cross with him for long. She never had been able to. That was the trouble with him; he was his own constellation. You couldn't judge him by normal standards.

Leaving the children to give Dominic the guided tour, she worked out where all the larger pieces of furniture would go. He made no comment on the house until they were locking up.

'Felicity would approve.' From nowhere, a smile appeared on his face. 'Let's go for lunch,' he said. 'One of those dreadful family pubs where they pander to the whims of diminutive savages. Any chance of there being some kind of quicksand pit in which these two can be thrown, thereby allowing us to have a quiet conversation?'

There was no quicksand, but there was the next best thing: a pit of brightly coloured plastic balls. The children's eyes lit up when they saw it.

It was a surreal experience having lunch in such an environment with Dominic: only the Queen could have looked more out of place. 'Felicity told me these places existed,' he said, pushing aside his half-eaten plate of beef and ale pie. 'Whoever came up with the idea for this one clearly couldn't decide whether it was to be a crèche or an S and M dungeon.'

'What's an S and M dungeon?' asked Carrie.

Harriet jumped in smartly. 'Nothing you need ever think about, Carrie. Have you chosen what you want to eat for pudding?'

Carrie puffed out her cheeks. 'I'm too full to eat anything else,' she said. 'Can we go and play?'

'If you like. Carrie, keep an eye on your brother for me, please. And make sure you don't forget where you've left your shoes.'

Joel immediately looked uncertain. 'Why don't you come and watch us?' He leaned against her, his small body heavy against her side. '*Pleease*.'

'OK, just until you're settled in.'

His face instantly brightened and he slipped his hand in hers and pulled her to her feet. 'You can either stay here on your own,' she told Dominic, 'or you can come and watch as well.'

'I wouldn't miss it for the world. What do you think, kids, shall we throw Harriet in too? She's no bigger than a child, is she?'

Carrie and Joel laughed, but Harriet scowled back at him. 'Don't even think about it.'

He ruffled her hair and laughed. 'I'll think exactly what I want to.'

Fifteen minutes later, she and Dominic were still standing next to the ball pit. Each time Harriet tried to move away, Joel would come over to make sure they were staying. 'I'm sorry,' she said to Dominic.

He shrugged. 'Lunch with my parents in Maple Drive would be a hundred times worse, I assure you. And for the record, I'm sorrier than I can say for what I said to you that night with Miles. Am I forgiven?'

'I'll think about it.'

He smiled. 'So now we've got that behind us, why don't you fill me in on what you've found out about Felicity and her lover.'

Harriet hesitated. In his current state of mind, would he think that Miles had defiled his dearest friend in some way?

But it had been a mistake to hesitate. He leapt on it. 'You've found something, haven't you? Come on, don't hold back.'

It was pointless even to think about lying to Dominic. So she told him about the last email she'd read.

'I knew it. I knew it from the moment you told me in Dublin. Well, well, well. What did Miles say when you confronted him?'

'I haven't spoken to Miles about it.'

'Really? And yet, if I'm not mistaken, there was a moment not so long ago when you had hopes for Miles, didn't you? Is that why you had a fling with this Will character? To get back at Miles?'

The accuracy of his guesswork was breathtaking. But it was only guesswork, she told herself. 'Stop fishing, Dominic,' she said firmly. 'What passed between Will and me was private, and I'm not going to tell you anything. Will deserves that much respect from me, if nothing else.'

'How honourable. I wish I could be more like you, but there isn't an honourable bone in my body. My father saw to that.'

His voice echoed faintly with something that, coming from him, didn't add up. It was regret. Harriet studied his face closely.

'Don't look surprised,' he said. 'I was always going to blame my father for my behaviour at some time. After all, he's made me the man I am.'

'That's a cop-out.'

'Perhaps so in your eyes. However, it's the truth. I knew a long time ago that I had to distance myself from Dr Harvey McKendrick, local do-gooding general practitioner. Ironically, he destroys people rather than heals them. He used to make me look at porn magazines when I was a boy. You see, he suspected then that I wasn't normal. He once caught me brushing my mother's hair and he beat me senseless afterwards. That's when he decided I had to go away to school. Stupid old fool thought an all-male environment would cure me of my tendencies and I'd have it knocked out of me. I was raped three times in my first week by the head boy and his cohorts. I was eleven.'

Harriet was appalled. How could any parent victimise their child so cruelly? And what would he have done with a sensitive boy like Joel . . . who also liked to brush his mother's hair? She shuddered. Let anyone lay a hand on that boy and she'd kill them. 'But we all thought you were sent away because you were so bright,' she said.

He let out a short, bitter laugh. 'A convenient enough cover. And it had the added bonus of making me even more of an outsider. My father was and still is an overbearing, sadistic bully.'

'Did Felicity know all this?'

He nodded. 'Felicity knew everything about me. It's why I miss her so much. Oh, Hat, it feels good being able to talk to you. Hey, you know what we should do? We should get married. We could bring up Carrie and Joel together.' He tilted his head back and looked deep into her eyes. At once his proximity aroused in Harriet a dangerous mix of emotions—love, hate, admiration, affection, fear, but most of all confusion.

'I'm being serious,' he said. 'You could come and live in Cambridge. You'd easily get work there.'

'Mm . . . so while you were off having sex with the entire male population of Cambridge, I'd be doing what exactly?'

He grinned. 'I'd leave that to your imagination. You do have one of those, don't you?'

He was mocking her now. 'Believe me, Dominic, there's nothing wrong with my imagination.'

JANUARY

A mermaid found a swimming lad,
Picked him for her own,
Pressed her body to his body,
Laughed; and plunging down
Forgot in cruel happiness
That even lovers drown.

'The Mermaid', W.B. YEATS

IT WAS NEW YEAR'S DAY, the day of the McKendricks' drinks party. Upstairs the children, having minutes earlier pulled back the curtains, were going crazy with excitement. Overnight, a heavy fall of snow had covered the garden. Bob filled the kettle and plugged it in, hoping the weather would not delay Harriet's move. Her leaving with the children heralded the start of their lives getting back to normal. Or rather, a life that resembled some kind of unreal normality, for he knew that nothing would ever feel truly normal again. Jennifer had told him that his life had been changed irrevocably and that he had to accept that. But how? How did one go about that? Others were all too willing to consign Felicity to the past—and how he hated them for it—but he would not betray her.

After Harriet had helped the children build a snowman, she told her father she wanted to sort through some of Felicity's things in the garage.

'You haven't got much time,' he muttered, glancing at the clock above the fridge. 'We're expected at Harvey and Freda's in two hours.'

'The sooner I get started, the sooner I'll be finished,' she said, and before he could invent another reason why she shouldn't touch Felicity's things, she slipped out of the kitchen. She regretted not doing it sooner; there was so little time left before the move.

An hour later, knowing she ought to go and change, she opened one last box. It contained a selection of photograph albums. One of the albums had a discoloured photograph stuck on the front of it. Harriet recognised herself in the picture, along with Felicity and Dominic. How young they looked, Harriet thought as she opened the album to revisit those days. She turned a page and out fluttered a photograph; it landed at her feet. She stooped to pick it up. Holding her breath, she took in the naked bodies. It must have been taken using the camera's timer device and it was graphically explicit, yet at the same time wholly erotic. Putting the photograph face down in the palm of her trembling hand, she saw that Felicity had written on the back of it—'*Soul and body have no bounds.*' Underneath was a date; it was February last year.

Harriet felt sick. How could she have been so stupid?

From his sitting-room window, Will watched another carload of guests arriving for the McKendricks' drinks party. An invitation had been slipped through his letterbox, but he'd thrown it in the bin. He stayed watching the road until a car he recognised appeared. She was here.

He opened the door to Maxine and surprised her with a kiss. She looked startled, as if he'd pinched her. 'What's that for?' she asked.

'Happy New Year,' he said. 'I'll make us some coffee.'

He was just filling the cafetière when Maxine cleared her throat and said, 'OK, Will, what was it you wanted to say?'

He took a deep breath. 'Maxine, I know this is going to be hard for you to believe but I want us to be friends.' His words came out in a nervous rush. 'I want to feel comfortable around you and I want you to be comfortable around me.'

'Why?'

'It might sound crazy, but by being emotionally close to you again I think I'll feel closer to Suzie. To put it bluntly, I'm terrified I won't survive this mess unless you help me.'

'Nothing will bring her back, Will. Don't delude yourself.'

'I'm not. I just know that she was a part of you and me and that by bringing the two of us together—' But his nerve failed him and he hung his head. Moments passed and then: 'Look, Maxine, I'll admit it, I'm desperate, I can't do this alone.'

'You are only talking about being *friends*, aren't you?' she said more gently. 'You're not suggesting we get back together again?'

He looked up. 'I think that would be a challenge too far, don't you?'

For the first time since she'd arrived, her expression softened. 'You're right. And Steve might have something to say on the matter too.'

He swallowed his relief that his plea for help hadn't been met with an outright rejection. 'I've lit a fire in the sitting room; why don't you go and sit down in the warm?'

She did as he said and minutes later, he joined her with the coffee things. He found her holding a photograph: it was of Suzie and Gemma as toddlers; all blonde hair and best party frocks. 'I never meant to be such a bad mother,' she murmured.

He put a hand on her shoulder. 'You haven't been a bad mother, Maxine. Don't ever say that.'

She put the photograph back with the others. 'What I regret most is that she never knew how much I loved her. I never took the time to tell her. I . . . I was always too busy. Too busy trying to be the person I thought my father wanted me to be.' Her voice caught in her throat and she put a hand to her mouth.

'Come and sit down,' he said.

'I idolised him, Will,' she said, making no attempt to move. 'I wanted to be just like he was: all-powerful and invincible.' Tears filled her eyes. 'I sacrificed everything for him. The teenage dreams I'd had for myself. You. And now Suzie. If I hadn't been so obsessed with following in his footsteps, to prove myself to him, Suzie would still be alive. It's all my fault. I know it is.' The tears really flowed now and Will took her gently in his arms. With tears filling his own eyes, he let her cry it out. He'd only ever seen her cry once before, and that was when her father died.

Half an hour into its stride, the McKendricks' sherry fest had looked as though it would be as tedious as it always was. Harriet had no intention of causing such an almighty scene, but when it happened—when she found herself alone with Miles and Dominic—the red mist came down.

'There's something I want to discuss with you two,' she said. 'Let's go outside where no one will hear us.'

'Harriet, are you quite mad? It's about minus six out there.'

She took hold of Dominic's elbow. 'Move it,' she snapped. 'And you too, Miles.'

She slammed the front door shut after them. 'Right, I'll start with you, Miles. How long had you been having an affair with my sister before she died? To the nearest month will do.'

Miles stared back at her in horror, just as Harriet had expected him to. 'Don't be shy, Miles,' she said. 'After all, it's not the big secret you think it is. Your brother had it all worked out ages ago. Isn't that right, Dominic?'

Dominic looked at her warily, his eyes slightly narrowed.

'Lost for words, are you?' she said nastily. 'Wow, that must be a first.'

'Look, will somebody tell me what the hell's going on here?' Miles said.

'Well, Miles, in view of your brother's refusal to speak, allow me to fill in the gaps. Several months ago I discovered Felicity had been having an affair, and when I mentioned it to Dominic, guess who he suggested as being the most likely candidate to be her lover. Yes, that's right. You.'

Miles's jaw dropped. He turned to his brother. 'Why?'

'Oh, I think that's obvious,' Harriet said. 'Don't forget he's the master manipulator. What better way could there be to prevent me from viewing you as anything more than a friend, than to put the idea into my head that you'd been screwing my sister on the quiet?'

If it was possible, Miles looked even more horrified. 'But that's sick.'

'It gets a whole lot worse,' Harriet said. 'He couldn't handle the thought that anyone else might find happiness when he couldn't. I blame myself for being so gullible. It never occurred to me that he could be bisexual.' Reaching into her trouser pocket, she pulled out the incriminating photograph she'd found among Felicity's things. She pushed it under Dominic's nose. 'See anyone you recognise?'

Before he could reply, Miles snatched the photograph out of Harriet's hand. He stared at it, first in disbelief, then in understanding. 'You! You and Felicity. Oh, you bastard! You complete and utter bastard.'

The first punch knocked Dominic backwards and he lost his footing. As he scrambled to stay on his feet, Miles came at him again, this time throwing all his weight against him; the powdery snow softened their fall. His fists smashed into Dominic's face, and spots of blood began to splatter the snow. It was then that Harriet realised Dominic was making no attempt to defend himself.

Behind them the front door suddenly flew open and Harvey McKendrick's voice shouted, 'Stop it at once!'

Miles was getting to his feet now and straightening his clothes, but Dominic continued to lie in the snow, blood trickling from his mouth. A crowd of guests had gathered at the door behind their host.

'For once, Dr McKendrick,' Harriet said, 'I've actually enjoyed one of your miserable drinks parties.' And she walked away.

Bob helped Harvey get his eldest son to his feet. He was just gathering up the loose change that must have fallen out of the brothers' pockets when something caught his attention: it looked like a photograph half-buried in the snow. He bent down to pick it up and froze. He turned the photograph over and looked at the date on the back.

'Perhaps it would be better if you gave it to me.' Miles's bloodied hand reached out for the picture, but Bob stepped away from him. It was just the two of them in the McKendricks' front garden now. In the silence of the snow-muffled day, Bob could feel an enormous bubble of anger rising within him. 'Is this what you were fighting about?' he said breathlessly.

'It's part of it,' Miles said.

'Felicity would never have an affair,' he whispered. 'She wasn't . . . she wasn't that sort of a girl. She was so good. She was a loving and devoted mother. Your brother must have forced her. It's the only explanation. Where's that filthy bastard? I'm going to finish off what you started!'

He marched back inside the house to the sitting room. 'Where is he?' he roared. 'Where's that conniving bastard?'

Everyone looked at him, startled. He crashed his way up the stairs and found Eileen and Freda in the front bedroom with Dominic. They were tending to the cuts to his face.

'I want to speak to you, Dominic McKendrick,' Bob said.

'Can it wait, Bob?' asked Eileen, exchanging a look with Freda.

'No. It's got to be said now.'

'What's got to be said now?' It was Harvey and he looked furious. He must have followed Bob upstairs. 'Isn't it bad enough that your daughter has embarrassed my wife and me by provoking my sons to brawl?'

'Your son,' Bob inclined his head towards Dominic, 'he's nothing but a marriage wrecker. See for yourself.' He held out the photograph.

A stunned silence fell on the room. Freda began to cry and Harvey looked with disgust at his son. 'I knew all along that you weren't gay,' he said. 'It was just an act to annoy and disappoint me.'

At this, Dominic suddenly sprang to his feet. 'You, you, YOU! It's always about bloody you, isn't it, Dad? And for the record, I'm bisexual. I fuck women as well as men.' He towered over his father and prodded him in the chest. 'Tell me, is that more acceptable for you? Or is that equally shaming and disappointing?' He came towards Bob now and before Bob could stop him, he had snatched the photograph out of his hands. 'And if it's any concern of yours, I loved Felicity. I always did and I always will. She was my life. My dearest friend *and* my lover. Now I have nothing.' He stalked out of the room.

Will had witnessed the extraordinary commotion in the McKendricks' front garden; it had taken place only minutes after Maxine had left. He'd also seen Harriet leave and make her way home.

With nothing else to do, he remained at the window. First an angry-looking, dark-haired man marched past, and just as a flurry of fresh snowflakes began to fall, Harriet reappeared. This time she was wrapped in a purple duffle coat along with a scarf, gloves, boots and a hat—the famous black beret. His heart, so heavy these days, gave a small surge. She crossed the road in the direction of the footpath. In an instant, he made a decision he hoped he wouldn't regret.

Bob went round to the back of the house. He knew exactly what he was going to do. He'd spent far too long covering up his feelings, pretending to the world that he was OK.

161

The door at the back of the garage was open and going inside he found what he was looking for: his old spade. His first act of destruction was to obliterate the snowman Harriet and the children had made that morning. From there he went over to the wooden bird table and took a hefty two-handed swipe at it. Pain ripped through his shoulders as he made contact, but it toppled to the ground with a thud. In his mind he was smashing Dominic McKendrick's skull to a pulp. And that joy-riding bastard who'd killed his beloved Felicity.

The bird table dealt with, he moved onto the rose bed. In no time he was flattening the area. The first blow was for all those unborn babies he'd never know. The subsequent strikes were for cheating on his wife. For not being a better husband. Next he attacked the pergola he'd made three summers ago. That was for making a fool of himself over Jennifer. For being so pathetically weak.

Petrified by cold and fear, the snow settling on and around her, Eileen stood shivering on the patio, watching Bob systematically decimate the garden to which he'd devoted so much of his life. She was glad she'd had the sense to leave the children in Dora's care before she'd left the McKendricks'. Bob was oblivious to her presence, but she would stay watching over him until he'd unleashed every last demon of grief-fuelled anger and frustration.

That moment came when the light began to fade and at last, spent, Bob fell to his knees and covered his head with his arms. His cries were terrible to hear. She prayed that they signalled the end of her husband's nightmare. 'Please let him be at peace now,' she murmured as she walked stiffly to where Bob was crouched like a wounded animal.

'Harriet?'

'Yes, Joel.'

'Carrie says Granddad's got flu. When will he be feeling better?'

'I don't know. He's very poorly at the moment. He needs a lot of rest.'

While he continued to help Harriet put his toys and books into a box, Joel suddenly felt sad. And a bit frightened. Things kept changing. He blamed it on that boring party the day it snowed. Ever since that day things had been different. First he'd overheard Dora talking to someone about Will and what a shame it was about his daughter dying. Hoping it wasn't that nice girl they'd met in that funny old shop, he'd asked Grandma about it. She'd hugged him and said he wasn't to worry about anything. But he was worried. *Everyone* was dying. Who would be next? Granddad? Carrie said that Granddad had caught his flu germs at the party and that was what had made him go mad and wreck the garden. But Joel didn't believe her. Granddad must have drunk too much wine at the party, like Dad did that time when he got cross with Mummy and threw all her books out of the window. She cried because they were ruined. She said they were her favourite books of poems. He hadn't liked seeing Daddy like that, all angry and using bad words.

'Come on, Joel,' Harriet said brightly, 'a little faster with those toys or we'll still be here when the removal men arrive in the morning.'

They worked together for another twenty minutes, until finally every last cuddly toy, book and game had been sealed up in a packing box. 'There,' she said, 'all done. You've done a fantastic job, Joel. I don't know how I would have managed without you.'

He gave her one of his wobbly smiles. 'Can I have my bath now?'

'You'll have to see if Carrie's finished in there.' She listened to him talking to his sister through the closed bathroom door and yawned. She was exhausted. She had spent most of the day getting ready for the move. A blessing really, because it had taken her mind off the events of the last forty-eight hours.

The first she'd known about Dad's breakdown—and that he knew all about Felicity's affair with Dominic—was when she'd come home later that evening and found Miles in the kitchen drinking tea with her mother. Mum had told her she'd had to call out the doctor for Dad.

Her mother had then taken her outside and shown her the garden. What hurt most was the sight of the Wendy house—it was the only thing her father had left standing. It stood there bleakly in the snow and shadows, like a lone, traumatised survivor of a massacre.

At no stage did Eileen ask where Harriet had been for the last three hours, for which she was grateful. Perhaps her mother had guessed where she'd been and was saving Miles's feelings. Harriet offered to go back out into the cold and fetch the children, who were still with Dora. Across the road, the curtains were drawn at Will's and she pictured him sitting by the fire where she'd left him earlier.

Immediately after leaving the McKendricks', she had decided that only a walk in the cold would make her feel better. She had come across Will clearing the snow from the bench at the end of his garden. It had seemed an odd thing to be doing, seeing as a fresh fall of snow was now coming down. When he saw her, he'd stopped what he was doing and, without a word, started walking beside her in unnerving silence. Several minutes passed before she asked him how he was.

'I've been better,' he replied. 'How about you? I saw punches being thrown at the McKendricks'. Was there a problem with the sherry?'

She stopped walking and looked at him. 'I've missed you, Will.'

'I've missed you too.' The snow was falling faster and heavier now. He glanced up at the sky and catching sight of the vulnerable paleness of his skin above his scarf she felt an urge to kiss his neck. 'We need to make a decision,' he said, stamping his feet in the cold. 'We either brave this snowstorm or we turn for home.'

'I don't want to go home. Not yet.'

'Then come back to my place. I could do with the company.'

While Will threw some logs onto the fire, Harriet knelt in front of it gratefully. 'How's Gemma?' she asked when he was settled in a chair.

'Difficult to say.'

'Did she tell you I gave her my mobile number? In case she wanted to talk to someone, other than family.'

'That was kind of you.'

'I know how it feels to be the surviving daughter—the daughter who gets overlooked in favour of the one who's died.'

He visibly bristled. 'She isn't being overlooked. I'd never do that.'

'Good. Because it's the worst thing that can happen to her.'

'I'll keep your advice in mind,' he replied coolly. She could see from his expression he'd taken her comment as a criticism. She was just about to apologise when he said, 'Tell me about the fisticuffs. What was that all about?'

She sighed. 'I realised this morning that I've been manipulated in a way you wouldn't believe. And I hate myself for having been so naive. I seem to have a singular lack of talent for reading between the lines.'

'Would I be right in thinking that your old friend Dominic, the one on the receiving end of the punches, is at the bottom of this?'

She nodded. And then she told him the whole unedifying story, the lies, the secrets, the betrayals. She poured everything out: how she'd grown up with a love-hate relationship towards Dominic, and how her and Miles's friendship had begun to change when she moved back home. 'I suddenly saw him in a different light,' she explained.

'No longer as a friend but as a potential boyfriend? A lover?'

'Yes. It suddenly seemed the perfect answer. Almost as though this was what Felicity might have wanted for us; you know, two people who had been really close to her coming together to bring up her children. But Dominic couldn't bear for anyone else to find happiness if he couldn't. So he deliberately set out to scotch whatever feelings Miles and I were beginning to have for each other.'

'But all you had to do was confront Miles about his alleged affair.'

'I couldn't bring myself to do it. I felt angry with him for a while, and—you probably won't understand this—but believing him to be in love with Felicity made me feel second best. And of course I believed Dominic when he said that unless I had proof, his brother would probably deny the affair.'

'So instead of questioning Miles, you went on the hunt for evidence?'

She nodded. 'I kept going through Felicity's emails while all the time keeping him at arm's length.'

'Meanwhile I came along. I might be jumping to conclusions, but did I become part of what you were going through?'

Ashamed, she turned and looked into the flickering flames. 'On top of being ditched by my last boyfriend because I now came with two non-negotiable complications, and feeling second best, I felt horribly rejected. Pathetically, I needed to prove to myself that I was attractive, a person in my own right. Does any of that make sense to you?'

'Yes,' he said. She could see the hurt in his eyes, though.

'I'm sorry. I soon realised I'd got myself into a situation that was all wrong. I was getting too fond of you and I hated myself for having used you to bolster my stupid ego. You deserved better. You're the nicest, kindest, funniest, most generous and straightforward man I've ever met and I shall always regret the way I treated you.'

'I'd have made do with just being the sexiest man you've ever met.'

She gave him a tentative smile. 'That's a given. And before you ask, there was no faking on my part. Every moment we spent in bed together was genuine.'

He briefly closed his eyes. 'What more could a guy ask for?'

She said, 'So how have you been? The truth.'

'Bloody awful. I don't think I'm handling this at all well, if I'm honest. Some mornings I wake up feeling like I'm made of glass: one bump and I'll fracture into a thousand pieces. When does it start to get better?'

'I can't answer that. But some day soon you'll catch yourself thinking about something else, and then you'll feel as guilty as hell because you'll think it's wrong to be happy. Or even distracted.'

She'd left him a short while later, sensing that he wanted to be alone. She may have escaped the immediate aftermath of her public confrontation with Dominic for those few hours she'd been with Will, but it was waiting for her when she got home. As indeed it had been ever since.

Two days on and her father was in bed suffering from mental exhaustion; she and her parents would never be welcome at the McKendricks' again; and there was still Miles to talk to. And Dominic. She hadn't finished with him yet. Which was why she'd hurried Joel with his packing; she'd arranged to meet Dominic later that evening. Unbelievably he was staying with Miles in Maywood.

He was waiting for her in the same wine bar they had used the night she'd thrown her drink in his face. He looked dreadful. Bruised and battered, his nose was swollen, his right eye blackened, his top lip sporting a couple of stitches. 'You look awful,' she said matter-of-factly.

'But perhaps not as bad as if you'd got your hands on me.'

'You're right; you could have wound up dead with Felicity.'

'I'm impressed; you said that without a hint of remorse.'

'What can I say? I've learned at the feet of the master.'

'OK,' he said in a bored voice, 'it's official, I'm a monster. Can we move on?'

'Yes, but on my terms. For starters, I want to know exactly what was going on inside that twisted mind of yours when you made me suspect Miles was Felicity's lover. Did it give you some kind of sick pleasure knowing that you were playing God with our lives?'

'You know me; I get my pleasure any which way I can.'

She drummed her fingers on the table impatiently.

'Why pretend you were gay when you're clearly not?'

He smiled. 'I unnerve you, don't I? That's the great thing about a strong sexuality; it delivers such a powerful punch. You see, Hat, I've always known I could have had you in bed any time I wanted.'

His arrogance made her want to get up and leave right away, but she had to know everything. 'So why didn't you *have* me?' she asked.

'I don't know. It's a mystery that's puzzled me for some time. Perhaps I was leaving the best till last.'

She snorted. 'Rubbish! It's because your so-called prowess never really worked on me. I'm the one person who could see through you.'

'But not entirely.'

'True,' she conceded, knowing that would always annoy her. 'But answer my question. Why pretend you were gay?'

'Queer. Straight. Gay. Bi. They're all just words. I'm me. This is the way I am.'

'You're not answering my question.'

'OK. It was part of the subterfuge. A game Felicity liked to play. I could openly kiss her in front of Jeff and there wasn't a damn thing he could do about it. Gay men are notorious for flirting with women.'

'But you professed to be gay before Jeff came into Felicity's life.'

'True. I guess I hadn't made up my mind just where I stood until she got serious about another man. I was shattered when she told me she was going to marry Jeff. I could have killed them both. I asked her to marry me instead but she said no, that like Maud, the only woman Yeats ever really loved, she wanted to have my love for the rest of her life. She believed that marriage would kill what we had.'

'So why all the secrecy in your emails?'

'Again it was what Felicity wanted. She got a thrill out of creating a special world in which only the two of us existed. She loved secrets. She also loved the power she had over me. So long as she was in the world

I could only ever be truly happy when I was with her. There was a wildness about her that only I saw.'

'When did the affair start?'

'Do you mean when we first made love?'

'I'm assuming you did that before we all went away to college. No, when you started sneaking around behind Jeff's back.'

'That was the day they returned from their honeymoon.'

Harriet nearly choked on her wine. 'You're joking!'

'No. I was there waiting for her. Jeff had to go away on a course and I made love to her in their bed. It was what she wanted, in case you're thinking I forced her to do it. You see, what you never realised about your sister was that she was a lot like me. She had an intensely strong sexual nature. So strong that it emasculated dull old Jeff.'

'Were you faithful to her?'

'In mind, yes. In recent years I only slept with men. To sleep with another woman would have seemed unfaithful.'

'How did you feel knowing that Felicity was having sex with Jeff?'

'I hated it.'

'And the children. When they came along, how did that make you feel? After all, they were a special bond between Felicity and Jeff that you couldn't deny or take away from them.'

'You think so?'

His voice was so sure, his face so composed, Harriet stopped in her tracks. It's another of his twisted games, she told herself.

But the damage was done. She had to know. 'Tell me. Was Jeff Carrie and Joel's father? And make it the truth or you'll wish you'd never asked to meet me.'

'It's possible Carrie is my daughter.'

'And?'

'And what? What do you want of me? A paternity blood test right here?' He pushed back his sleeve and pressed a finger to a prominent vein. 'There, cut me open.'

'Oh, stop being so melodramatic. Just give me a straight answer.'

'I can't. This is real life: ends don't always get neatly tied up.'

'Bullshit! Who did Felicity think was Carrie's father?'

'Because she couldn't be sure, she decided to keep it that way. She once said she thought I'd make a terrifyingly inconsistent father. That was something Jeff was good at, apparently.'

'Was it why she stayed with him?'

'One of the reasons. She thought the children would have more stability that way.'

'What about Joel? Why don't you think you could be his father?'

'Basic biology. We didn't see one another during the time he was conceived.' He drained his glass in one long swig.

'How often did you get to see each other? And where?'

'It varied. Once a month. Sometimes twice a month. I always went to her. We had our lovers' trysts in some hellish places, I can tell you. Oh, shit, Hat, I miss her so much.'

'Do you think she would have approved of you lying and manipulating me? How you deliberately set out to destroy a potential relationship between Miles and me?' It was only now that Harriet trusted herself to acknowledge that her original instinct about Miles wanting more than friendship with her had been correct. 'You still haven't told me why you did it. Do you really hate your brother so much?'

'It's got nothing to do with hate. It's about love and happiness and being deprived of it. Why should you and Miles have what I couldn't?'

'You admit it, then? That it was purely a selfish motive? As soon as you suspected Miles might be interested in me, you put a stop to it.'

'But of course. What else could it have been? If you're dying from a disease, why would you wish others good health?'

'Destroying my chance of happiness would have made you feel better?'

'Does making me explain my feelings for Felicity make *you* feel better? Yes, it does, doesn't it? Inflicting pain on others is quite pleasurable.'

'That's the most depraved thing I've heard you say.'

They sat in silence for some minutes. It was getting late, the wine bar crowd was thinning out, and by rights Harriet should be making a move herself, but she still had questions she needed answering. 'How long did you think you could keep the lie going for?' she asked.

He smiled, even though it must have hurt his mouth to do so. 'Which lie? I've told so many.'

She didn't return the smile. 'The one about Miles being Felicity's lover. The game would have been up the moment I confronted him.'

'Ah, but the damage would have been done. Would you have believed his denial? Every time he kissed you, you'd have wondered if his lips had kissed your sister's before yours. I know how you hated the thought of being second best to Felicity.'

Determined not to rise to the bait, she said, 'It was clear from the last few emails that she was going to leave Jeff for you. Why the U-turn?'

'She'd had enough. It was a snap decision. Plus Jeff had started to suspect that she was having an affair. He was becoming irrational. He got drunk once and threw some of Felicity's things out of the window. He was also accusing her of being unfaithful in front of the children.'

'Did he suspect you?'

He suddenly held up a hand. 'Enough! More than enough of you playing the grand inquisitor. Now it's my turn to ask a question. I don't want to carry my suspicions alone any more. Have you ever wondered about the accident that killed Felicity and Jeff? If it was an accident that could have been avoided?'

'You're not suggesting—'

He leaned forward, his battered face inches from hers. 'I'm convinced Jeff deliberately made no effort to avoid that car. I think he was mad at Felicity because she'd finally told him she wanted to leave him, and he took matters into his own hands.'

A tremor of fear ran through Harriet. She swallowed. 'You have no proof of that.' Her voice was little more than a whisper.

'I have the memory of the last conversation I ever had with Felicity. She said she'd just told Jeff that she wanted to leave him.'

The tremor grew. The thought of Felicity knowing, in the last seconds of her life, that she had driven her husband to kill them both was too horrifying to take in. 'Then you must accept your part in their deaths,' she said, fighting hard to keep her composure. 'If you hadn't been so obsessed with Felicity they'd both be alive today.'

'You think I don't wake up every morning reminding myself of that?'

She shook her head wearily. 'How do you live with yourself?'

'I exist, Hat. Nothing more. I'm the swimming lad the mermaid took for her own, and now I'm drowning.'

'Have you told anyone else about this?'

'I just told you, I've kept it to myself all this time.'

'Good. I don't want the children ever doubting their parents. I want them to grow up feeling proud of their mother and father. You must swear on whatever is most precious to you that you will never utter to another living soul a word of what you've just said.'

They left the wine bar at chucking-out time. Harriet offered to give Dominic a lift to Miles's flat down by the river, but he refused. 'I need some fresh air,' he said. 'Unless that was a subtle attempt on your part to see Miles. He'd probably appreciate seeing you.'

'No. I'll talk to him another time. I'm too tired now. I'm amazed he's let you stay at all.'

'That's because he's one of life's incorrigible optimists. He'd love nothing better than to prove to me his way is better than mine.'

'His way is infinitely better than yours, Dominic.'

'But it hasn't got him what he wanted, has it?'

'I don't know. What is it he wants?'

'Oh, Hat, haven't you figured that out? He wants you, of course.'

She frowned. 'Is that one last try to stir things up?'

'You really are hopeless when it comes to matters of the heart, aren't you? Why do you suppose Miles did this to me?' He raised a hand to his face. 'Think also of the poem he read that night at Novel Ways. It was written for you, when you were shagging Will and he thought he'd lost you. Now give me a gentle hug goodbye so that I know we're friends again. Goodbye, sweet thing.' In spite of everything that he'd said and done, Harriet put her arms round him. He was such an integral part of her life—and her sister's—she couldn't say goodbye without making her peace with him.

Harriet watched him unbuttoning his coat as he walked away. A sadness came over her as she wondered what would become of him. And what had he meant by that reference to the mermaid?

FEBRUARY

This sugarcane
this lemonade
this hurricane, I'm not afraid
C'mon c'mon no one can see me cry.
This lightning storm
this tidal wave
this avalanche, I'm not afraid.
C'mon c'mon no one can see me cry.

'Imitation of Life', R.E.M. BUCK, MILLS, STIPE

AT WEEKENDS, and when the children's social engagements permitted, Harriet liked to sit up in bed and look at the view from her bedroom window. This particular bright and sunny Saturday morning a light frost was melting in the sun. There were drifts of snowdrops along the towpath and their delicate flowers were swaying in the breeze.

A month had passed since she and the children had moved into number 1 Lock Cottage; a month, too, since she had last seen Dominic and he had said that life's loose ends weren't always tied up. She had to accept she would never know what had really happened that night when Jeff and Felicity died. If Jeff really had been so out of his mind with jealousy that he had decided, in a split second of madness, to kill them both, he had taken the truth to his grave.

She knew, though, that she had to let go of the thoughts Dominic had planted in her brain. If she allowed them to grow she might well go mad. But what he'd said went a long way to explaining his episodes of inexplicable behaviour; the unpredictable mood swings. How he would learn to live with the knowledge that he may have been instrumental in killing the woman he'd loved, Harriet didn't know. He needed help, but she doubted he'd seek it. She felt enormous pity for him.

As to him being Carrie's father, whether he was or not was immaterial for now. It was one of those loose ends that had the potential to come together when the time was right. She had asked him if he wasn't curious to know the truth. 'What's the point?' he'd replied.

'The point is, it could be important to Carrie.'

'I'd be a hopeless father, Hat. I'd only screw her up.'

Despite the apparent indifference, he appeared, in his own way, to be adopting the role of avuncular uncle to Carrie and Joel. He'd sent them both cameras and a photograph album with instructions to fill them with pictures of things they thought he'd approve of. He'd also sent Harriet a book of Yeats's poems. The accompanying card read: *Time to educate yourself! Best wishes from your oldest friend, Dominic.*

'What does he mean?' Joel had asked. 'Pictures that he'd approve of?'

'He wants us to think before we stick any old picture in our albums,' Carrie had said, perceptively.

'Well, I'm going to put a picture in of Tom and me in the garden.' Tom was Joel's new best friend. He was two months older than Joel and lived in the house three doors down the terrace of cottages. It turned out Tom's father, Stewart, was a programmer like Harriet and his wife, Diana, was a freelance graphic designer. Harriet took to them straight away; they were friendly and welcoming without being at all pushy. The perfect neighbours, in fact. Especially as their son Tom, who, although he attended a different school, was doing wonders for Joel's self-confidence. He still worried over the slightest thing, but she was getting better at winkling out his concerns and anxieties and dispelling them for him.

All in all, the move to number 1 Lock Cottage was proving to be the refuge she'd hoped for. Miles had been a godsend, too; he was always offering to help with any odd jobs that needed doing. The children enjoyed his company and he often had supper with them. He was joining them this evening for a takeaway after he'd finished work.

There had been a lot of cautious sidestepping around each other in the days after New Year's Day, particularly on Harriet's part. She kept thinking on what Dominic had said about Miles and his feelings for her. Wanting to be sure just how she felt, she was determined to take things slowly. Having rushed into things with Will, she didn't want to make a similar mistake. Once they'd opened up to each other and had put the misunderstandings and embarrassing memories of New Year's Day behind them, they were again able to talk more freely, just as they used to. She had showed him the decoded email that she had thought proved he had been Felicity's lover. 'Like the fool I am, I simply leapt to the conclusion I wanted to. I've been very stupid,' she'd admitted.

'No, you haven't. Anyone would have made the same mistake. And for the record, I got over my crush on Felicity a long time ago.'

'I always suspected that you had a thing for her. What changed?'

'I grew up.' He then shyly confessed to having had a soft spot for Harriet for some years.

'Why did you never say anything?' she'd asked.

'Don't laugh, but I was also a bit scared of you. You were so fearless.'

She'd told him the reasons she'd got involved with Will, and in turn he said he regretted not being more forcible in making his feelings known to her before, particularly that day on the canal. 'I'd been trying to pluck up the courage for weeks to tell you how I felt,' he'd said, 'and when you started asking me about what I wrote in my poetry, whether I wrote about love, I thought perhaps you were hinting that you knew how I felt. But then you went rushing off and the next thing, you and Will were organising a cosy evening out. I was crushed.'

'I'm sorry,' she'd apologised. 'I was scared that you might tell me about your affair with my sister. I grabbed at the easiest and nearest thing to shut you up.'

The first time Miles kissed Harriet, Carrie walked in on them in the kitchen. 'This isn't going to be easy, is it?' he'd said with a half-smile as Carrie turned bright red, giggled loudly and thumped her way back upstairs to share the big joke with Joel.

Not surprisingly, Harriet and Miles had spoken a lot about Dominic and how they were both worried about him. Without Felicity in his life, he seemed dangerously adrift. Thinking of Felicity now, as Harriet watched a colourful barge chug steadily by her bedroom window, she no longer felt as though she knew her sister. Harriet wasn't even sure she liked the person her sister had turned into. She hadn't been fair to Jeff, and her treatment of Dominic—a man who was obsessed with her—wasn't much better; she'd kept him dangling for far too long.

Although Harriet didn't really believe in heaven, she sent up a silent message to her sister. 'It's time to let Dominic go, Felicity. You couldn't do it in life, but you must do it now or he'll never know peace of mind.'

It was a while before Bob could look at his garden without being consumed by a humiliating sense of shame and sorrow. The grief counsellor he was seeing said it was quite common to lash out at that which meant most to you when the chips were down, and he saw now that the therapist wasn't only referring to the terrible madness that had over-taken him on New Year's Day. The affairs he'd had—including the one he'd tried to have with Jennifer—had been a way of punishing poor Eileen. He'd never properly grieved for those babies he and Eileen had lost, and he had blamed her for the miscarriages. Perhaps, more dis-turbingly, he'd also blamed her for not being able to keep Felicity alive.

The worst counselling session he'd had to sit through had been the one with Eileen present. They had openly discussed his affairs and he'd been devastated to learn that Eileen had always known about them and that she had suspected he'd met someone more recently. Humbled and broken-spirited he'd wept in her arms that night in bed—how could she be so forgiving?

'It's called love, Bob. No matter what, I'll always love you.'

'I'm a lucky man.' The words echoed in his head as he stared at the garden. He knew now that he was. His breakdown had been a blessing in disguise. He was now able to put his grief into context. It was still there, but it was no longer the constant focus of his thoughts.

It pained him to know that Felicity had been so unhappy in her mar-riage, but nothing could help him to understand the relationship she'd had with Dominic McKendrick. How could she have been attracted to such a freak of nature? The therapist had suggested this was a typical father's reaction to an unsuitable suitor. 'But I accepted Jeff,' he'd told her.

'Very likely you saw him as someone who would never outshine you in your daughter's eyes,' the woman had said.

They had scarcely touched on his relationship with Harriet, but Bob knew there was a lot to be said on the matter. He hoped that one day she would forgive him. He was also glad that he'd never gone ahead and had a full-blown affair with Jennifer. With Eileen's knowledge he had written to Jennifer and apologised for his behaviour. By return of post he received a card wishing him all the best for the future. The therapist had suggested that his attraction for Jennifer had really been to do with the sense of freedom she represented. It was with this new understanding in mind that he had a surprise in store for Eileen. He'd been planning it for the last few days.

It was Saturday evening at Bellagio's. Gemma didn't know whose idea it had been to go out for dinner, but it was good seeing her parents together like this. She wished Suzie was here to see it. Sometimes, late at night, when she couldn't sleep, she imagined herself writing a letter to her sister, as though she was away on a long holiday rather than dead. She would tell Suzie how school was going, how Marcel had stopped writing to her because he'd got a girlfriend, how Nana Ruby was having a hip replacement next week and that Mum was paying for her to go privately, *and* that Dad had actually kissed Mum when she'd told him what she was doing.

Hearing her name mentioned, Gemma tuned in to what her parents were saying, realising that they were no longer talking about Mum and Steve's long weekend away in a few weeks' time. 'Here's to you,' her father said. 'Congratulations on the offer from Durham.'

Gemma frowned. 'It's only an offer; I've got to get the grades yet.'

'You'll do fine,' her mother said.

'And if you don't,' her father said after glancing quickly at her mother, 'that'll be fine too. Whatever happens in the summer with your exams, we'll be right behind you, won't we, Maxine?'

Gemma could see what they were up to and cringed. *Dear Suzie*, she imagined writing, *Mum and Dad are driving me mad with their consideration and support. Help! Who will crack first; them or me?*

After dropping Maxine and Gemma off, Will drove on to see his mother. She never went to bed early so when he rang the doorbell at half past ten he did so confident that she would still be up.

'Been dining out, have you?'

'With Maxine and Gemma.' He caught the twinkling smile in his mother's eyes. 'And yes, before you ask, Maxine and I really are making an effort these days,' he said.

'Good. Does she know about Steve's surprise for her?'

'No, she doesn't have a clue. She thinks he's taking her to London and then on to a health spa for a few days.'

'Oh, I'd love to see her face when he tells her they're going to Rome and Florence. She'll be thoroughly made up. All those art galleries and museums to lose herself in. It'll be just the ticket. Now come and sit down.' Ruby pulled out a kitchen chair for him. 'I want to get a good look at you. You still look like you're not eating enough. How are you sleeping?'

'Mum, I'm forty-six years old; can you drop the parent routine for a bit and let me ask how you are? How's the hip?'

She sat down with a wince and a sigh. 'Sore.'

He mentally thanked Maxine for what she was doing for his mother. It was only in the New Year that they had realised just how much pain Ruby was in. She'd kept it from them because she didn't want a fuss.

'So how's business at the shop?' she said.

'I'm gradually getting back into the swing of it.'

'And your love life? How's that?'

'That's the last thing on my mind.'

'Then you're making a big mistake. A kiss and a cuddle would go a long way to making you feel better right now. What was that girl's name you were seeing before . . . before Suzie died?'

'Harriet.'

'I liked her.'

'Don't be ridiculous! You never even met her.'

'I heard about her from Gemma and I did see her at the hospital that night. She looked a sweet little thing.'

'She wouldn't thank you for that description.'

Ruby tutted. 'These modern girls are all the same: toughened exteriors with silky soft centres. Gemma's the same. You'll need to keep a careful eye on her this year. She's got a lot on her plate, what with grieving for her sister and the pressure of exams in the summer.'

'You're a wise woman, Mum.'

'I know. I'm also weary. I think I'll go to bed now. And you look even more worn out than me. Better you push off home and get some sleep.'

Tired as he was, Will didn't go straight to bed when he got home. There was a message from Marty on his answering machine. It was almost midnight but he returned the call anyway. They had an agreement; no matter what time it was, if either of them needed to talk, the other would be at the end of a phone. Marty had finished the course of radiotherapy but Will still feared that the all clear his friend had been given would turn out to be a hospital error.

'Everything OK?' he asked Marty when he picked up.

'Everything's fine. More than fine, actually. That's why I rang. I wanted to . . . well, the thing is . . . I've met someone. She's the specialist who's been treating me.'

'Is that ethical?'

'It is now I've finished the treatment.'

'That's brilliant! When do I get to meet her?' It was good to hear Marty sounding more like his old self; Will was pleased for his friend.

Lying in bed later, he thought about Harriet. He closed his eyes and a whole series of memories came to him: the night he'd mistaken her for a boy; the day she'd had an asthma attack in the shop; the first time they made love. But the best memory of all was the one of her sitting by the fire with him after their New Year's Day walk had been snowed off. Her company that afternoon had meant more to him than she would ever know. It didn't matter that she had confessed to using him—bizarrely, he admired her for having the guts to be so honest with him. But that was her all over. After she'd gone, he'd put on R.E.M.'s CD *Reveal*. When he listened to Stipe singing about not being afraid and no one seeing you cry, he suddenly found himself weeping uncontrollably.

One of the things he hated most about mourning the loss of Suzie was that he had to do it alone. Was there anything more pitiful than crying alone? His mother was right: a bit of affection would be nice. He wondered what Harriet was doing right now. Whatever it was, it had to be better than him lying here in the dark realising just how much he missed her.

'Come on, Harriet, the kids are fast asleep; they'll never hear us.' Miles went back to unbuttoning her shirt and kissing her. She closed her eyes and tried to relax. But she couldn't.

'Harriet, are you OK?'

She opened her eyes and realised that Miles was staring down at her hands, which were balled into fists either side of her. 'I'm sorry,' she said, 'I'm finding it hard to concentrate. You know, with the children upstairs.'

He frowned. 'Married couples manage it all the time.'

'I know; that's what makes me feel so silly. I'm sorry.'

The frown disappeared and he smiled again, kissing her once on each eyelid and then on the lips. 'Let's try it on the floor.'

It'll be fine, she told herself. She kissed him on the mouth and began undoing his trousers. He gave a groan of pleasure as her hands touched him. 'Now yours,' he said. Unzipping her jeans and kicking them off, she suddenly felt shy. He lay on his side and ran his hand the length of her thigh, then put it between her legs. She almost jumped at his touch. He then parted her legs and lay on top of her. 'I love you, Harriet,' he whispered into her ear. 'I always have.' He was breathing heavily now.

Oh God, she suddenly thought, squeezing her eyes shut. He loves me. But I don't love him. Why don't I? Why do I keep thinking this is so wrong? She opened her eyes, and as if looking down at herself she realised it felt as if she were having sex with a brother. She felt enormous affection towards Miles, but no desire. She began to panic. What should she do? If she backed out now, she would hurt Miles's pride. She couldn't do that to him. Oh, why couldn't it be like when she'd been in bed with Will?

Her heart gave a small leap. Was that the answer? Could she imagine it was Will making love to her? She closed her eyes and pictured him. At once her body relaxed and she felt his smooth, firm hands caressing her. She put her arms round his neck and moved her body against his. 'Oh, Will,' she murmured, 'I've missed you so much.'

She suddenly heard what she'd said. Will. *Will!*

Miles heard it too. He rolled away from her and sat bolt upright. For a while neither of them spoke. She reached for her clothes. 'I'm sorry, Miles. It just came out. I don't know what to say.'

'Is that what the problem's been all these weeks?'

'I don't know what you mean.' But she did. It was all too clear to her now. The prevaricating had had little to do with the children and every-thing to do with Will: her feelings for him had never gone away.

'You've been putting off sex with me because you've still got a thing for Will, haven't you?'

'I didn't know it until just now,' she said. 'You must believe me, Miles. I would never consciously do anything to hurt you.'

He sighed. 'Either way, it's obvious to me we're not going anywhere, are we? What was I? A shoulder to cry on?'

All she could do was repeat how sorry she was.

While Eileen was in the shower, Bob got the fire going and made a start on cooking breakfast. He felt glad to be alive. His plan had worked. When he'd been working out how to spring his surprise on Eileen, he'd been scared that she would turn him down. But the risk had paid off and yesterday afternoon, after giving Eileen no more than an hour to pack a bag, he had driven them, plus Toby, to the marina and intro-duced her to their home for the next week.

'You're sure you want to do this?' he'd asked her. 'It could turn out to be a disaster.'

She'd kissed him and said, 'We won't know until we've tried it, will we?'

The man from whom Bob had hired the narrowboat had instructed them on how it worked and explained how to operate a lock, and they were soon unpacked and off. They didn't have much daylight time left and before long they were mooring up for the night. It didn't matter that they'd only travelled a couple of miles north of Kings Melford; just to be away from Maple Drive was enough to make Bob feel free.

After supper they'd sat with their cups of coffee in the soft light cast from the lamps, listening to the sounds of the night. They'd talked too, as they did all the time now. He still felt he didn't deserve Eileen's for-giveness; she kept reassuring him that he had to stop thinking this way. 'What we should do is pretend we've just met for the first time,' she'd said in bed last night, smiling shyly at him. 'That we know nothing about each other and have to learn to get to know one another.'

He was still thinking about her remark and his response to it when Eileen appeared in the saloon. 'Mm . . . that smells wonderful,' she said.

Eileen watched her husband spooning hot oil over the eggs in the frying pan. The transformation was incredible. Bob was looking and sounding just like the man he used to be. If one night away from home could bring about such a miracle, maybe they should consider spending the rest of their lives on board this boat and just float away.

When they had tidied breakfast away, Bob got the boat ready to move on: they were doubling back on themselves today and heading south.

They stood side by side, Bob's arm resting on the tiller as he steered their course, his expression one of contented purposefulness. Eileen had no idea how far she and Bob would travel in the week ahead, but she didn't care so long as they were together and as happy as this.

Harriet wasn't a gambler by nature, and she'd spent all of the last week agonising over the risk Miles had urged her to take.

After he had recovered his composure and they were both dressed, he'd sat with her at the kitchen table, and as was so typical of him, had given her the opportunity not just to apologise but to talk about Will.

'I don't seem to be able to get him out of my mind,' she confessed.

'What do you think the attraction is?' Miles had asked.

'I don't know.' But she did. It was everything. The way his eyes crinkled at the corners when he smiled, the way he wore his hair—just a bit too long—the way he tried not to wear his glasses in front of her because he was vain and thought they aged him. And then there was the way he held her, the way he kissed her.

'Do you want to get back together with him?' Miles had asked.

'I don't think it's possible,' she'd said. 'Or even a good idea.' She was thinking of Howard's advice to leave well alone.

'You can tell me to mind my own business,' Miles had said, 'but if I were you, I'd talk to him. Tell him how you feel. If he agrees with you that it's not a good idea, and there's every chance he might, then so be it.'

'But what if—?'

'There are always going to be what-ifs, Harriet,' he interrupted. 'But for once in your life, stop analysing the situation and just go for it. If it all comes to nothing, so what? What will you have lost?'

It was only now, a week on, that she had convinced herself to do as Miles had suggested. She would go to see Will and tell him how she felt.

It was six o'clock when Will let himself in that evening. It had been a busy afternoon in the shop. Now that he could face people, including regular customers with their sympathy, the shop seemed a better option than being at home on his own. It was progress, he acknowledged.

He checked to see if there were any messages on his answering machine. There was only one, from Jarvis, saying he wouldn't be in until after lunch the next day—'Just in case you were thinking of having a lie- in, laddie.' Will felt like ringing Jarvis back and telling him to stop worrying; he could be trusted to make it into work these days. Even so, he was touched that the old man was still looking out for him. He went upstairs for a shower and he'd just changed into some clean jeans when the doorbell rang.

His first thought when he opened the door and saw Harriet was that he was glad he'd cleaned himself up. His second thought was to tell himself not to be so stupid and vain. She wasn't interested in him. Trouble was, just one look at her and he knew he'd never lost his desire for her.

'Hello, Will,' Harriet said. 'Is it a bad time to drop by?'

He stepped back to let her in. 'It's perfect timing. You can help me choose what to cook for supper. Here, let me take your coat.'

Their hands brushed as he took it from her and she knew she hadn't imagined what she still felt for Will.

'Where are the children, by the way?' he asked.

'They're with some neighbours.'

'Come on through to the kitchen and I'll open a bottle of wine. You've settled in OK, then?'

'Yes, it feels like we've always been there. You must come and see us. Carrie and Joel would love to see you again.'

'I'd like that. Chardonnay OK for you?'

'Thank you.' While she watched him take out the cork and pour the wine, she wondered if she could go through with what she'd come to say. The fear of being rejected, of being rebuffed, were making her nervous.

'There you go,' he said. 'Cheers. Good to see you.'

They clinked glasses and she took an enormous swig of Dutch courage.

'How are your parents?' he said, leaning back against the worktop and crossing his legs at the ankles. 'Your father in particular.'

'They're well.' She told him about them going off in the boat Dad had hired. Then she chewed on her lip. As happy as she was for her parents, their unexpected holiday was the last thing she'd come here to talk about.

'You OK?' he asked. 'You look on edge. Something bothering you?'

Tell him. Go on, just say the words.

'Oh, you know me, always something on my mind.'

He smiled. 'Let's go and sit down and see if that will have the required calming effect. I'm afraid I haven't lit the fire yet. In the sitting room, she watched him light the fire and after he'd put the box of matches on the mantelpiece, the phone rang.

Will made his excuses and disappeared out to the kitchen to answer the telephone. Within seconds he had replaced the receiver—it was one of those wretched overseas cold calls—and was wondering what to do about Harriet. It was obvious that she'd come here to tell him something, but at the rate she was going, she'd still be here at midnight trying to get the words out. He decided to give her a helping hand.

Back in the sitting room, he said, 'Sorry about that. It was one of those polite but annoyingly persistent women from a call centre somewhere along the banks of the Ganges.' He sat on the sofa next to Harriet, just inches from her, but kept his gaze on the fire straight in front of them. 'I told her to call later when I'd finished entertaining an ex-girlfriend of mine. She was most intrigued and asked why you were an ex. I said it was complicated. She asked if there was any way of starting afresh and I said I didn't know, that I'd have to look into it. She suggested I get right back in here and ask you straight out if there was any chance of us getting it together again.' He tutted and shook his head. 'I don't know, these call centres, they have some nerve. Poking into other people's lives.'

There was a slight pause before Harriet said, 'Did the woman say anything about you being particularly vulnerable at the moment and maybe a relationship would be unwise?'

Picking up his glass of wine and turning to face her, he said, 'Actually, she said it would be the best possible answer. That having someone special in my life would stop me from feeling sorry for myself.'

'She sounds like she knows what she's talking about. What do you think we should do?'

'I think that rather depends on you, doesn't it?'

Harriet took his glass from him and kissed him softly on the mouth. 'I can't stop thinking about you. I tried to, but you wouldn't go away.'

'Are you saying I'm like a bad smell?'

She smiled. 'No. You're the kindest, funniest—'

He put a finger to her lips. 'I told you before; I'd make do with being the sexiest.'

'Care to prove it?'

Later, in bed, he said, 'I'm nothing but a sex toy to you, am I?'

'You mean far more to me than that, Will.'

Hearing how serious she sounded, he said, 'I was joking.'

'For once I'd like you not to.'

He leaned over, suddenly needing to hear the words. 'Tell me what I mean to you, then.'

She swallowed. 'You mean more to me than anyone has before.'

'Does that scare you?'

'Yes.'

'Imagine how I feel. Definitely the wrong side of forty and totally blown away by you.'

'It's not the age thing that bothers me.'

'What, then?'

'It's . . . it's the logistics of being together.'

'Stop worrying. We'll sort it. There's always a way to do these things.'

'It doesn't sound like a lot of fun for you, though. Seeing someone in my position.'

He raised an eyebrow and took in her naked body. 'Frankly, Miss Swift, your position seems perfect to me. And you can give up trying to talk me out of being a part of your life. Real men pick women with a challenge to them. So tell me, what is it about me that got you hooked?'

She slapped his chest playfully. 'No way am I going to play that game!'

'Spoilsport. But I'll tell you what did it for me. First off it was the wrath-and-brimstone looks you gave me—Oh, no, you don't,' he laughed as she began to protest. 'No interrupting or denying. And then it was your fierce love for your sister and her children that touched me.'

'No, you've got it all wrong. Every decision I made was done out of a sense of duty and the fact that I didn't have a choice.'

'That may have been true in the beginning, but what about now? Those kids really mean something to you, don't they?' When she didn't reply, he became aware that they were getting too serious. 'And on a lighter note, I'd like it to be known that regarding my attraction for you, there was one more thing that clinched matters for me.'

'What was that, then? My razor-sharp wit? My scintillating intellect?'

'Um . . . actually, it was the sight of you in your beret. Any chance you could wear it in bed for me some time?'

When Harriet had gone, Will remembered he hadn't had anything to eat. He rustled up an omelette, ate it hungrily, then checked what time it was. Another twenty minutes, he reckoned, and then he'd ring her.

On the stroke of eleven he was back in bed and phoned Harriet. 'Hi,' he said. 'Are we on for some phone sex now?'

She laughed. 'Is this how it's going to be?'

'Yes, every night when we're not together, this is what we'll do. Mornings are good for me too. Right then, fire away. Say something smutty.'

'You're insane.'

'And you're blushing, aren't you?'

'Certainly not. I was just putting on my beret.'

He groaned exaggeratedly.

'Good night, Will. I'll speak to you tomorrow.'

Smiling, he switched off his mobile. Harriet was right about her situation being complicated. Could he really picture himself with two young children along with Gemma and the grieving process he still had to get through? He didn't know, but what he could picture was being with Harriet. He turned out the light and within minutes he'd nodded off.

At work the next day, shortly after Harriet had taken a call from Will, Howard came into her office. 'You've got that look on your face, Hat. You're seeing that bloke again, aren't you?'

'And which bloke would that be?'

'The one I said you should leave well alone.'

'Perhaps you were wrong. Let's face it, it can't be a first.'

'Hah! I knew it. I knew I could rely on feminine logic.'

'What do you mean, "feminine logic"?'

'I knew if I told you not to do something, you'd do it. I haven't worked with women and computers as long as I have to know that unlike a computer, a woman doesn't function to the accepted rules of logic. You've got to employ reverse psychology to make them do what you want. I knew I'd get you and that bloke back together.'

'Get out! Out of my office, you conceited, horrible man!'.

That evening, while Harriet was getting the tea ready, she asked Carrie and Joel how they'd got on with Dora doing the afternoon school run. With Eileen and Bob away, Dora had stepped into the breach.

'Auntie Dora took us to Maywood,' Joel answered.

'We saw Miles in his bookshop,' joined in Carrie. 'I asked him if he was coming to help you with any jobs this week and he said if there was anything you needed doing, you knew where he was.'

Later, during their bedtime story, Joel said, 'Carrie thinks you're going to marry Miles. Is that true?'

Harriet decided to be completely honest with them. 'Miles and I have always been very close. But friends is all we'll ever be.'

'But I saw you kissing him.'

'Yes, Carrie, you did. But—'

'You don't want to shag him, is that it?'

Harriet's eyes opened wide. 'Carrie! Where did you get that from?'

Her niece didn't even blush. 'Is shag a very bad word?' she asked.

'It's not a word you should repeat in front of Grandma.'

'What does it mean?' asked Joel.

'It means to be sexy with someone,' Carrie informed him importantly.

The definition was near enough for Harriet to let it go. Joel said, 'Auntie Dora says she thinks you're more likely to marry Will than Miles. Are you sexy with Will?'

Harriet felt the colour cover her from top to toe.

'Is he your boyfriend?' asked Carrie.

Thinking that she must stick to her policy of being honest with the children, she said, 'Sort of.'

Her niece looked at her doubtfully. 'What does *sort of* mean?'

'I suppose it means yes. Is that OK with you two?'

Both of the children smiled.

Later, when Harriet was lying in bed, her mobile went off. It was Will.

'Hi,' he said. 'How was your day?'

'It kicked off with an obscene caller, followed by an interrogation by my boss on my love life and then this evening the children gave me a thorough grilling. Carrie has picked up the word "shag" from somewhere and wanted to know if that's what we get up to.'

'She knows about me?'

'Apparently she had her information from Dora.'

'So am I officially your boyfriend now?'

'I thought that was a given.'

'Excellent. It makes me sound at least ten years younger. So when do I get the chance to show off my girl round town?'

'That'll have to keep for a few days, but you can come for supper tomorrow evening if you like.'

'Count me in.'

When they'd said good night, Harriet thought she heard a noise coming from Carrie's bedroom. She got out of bed and crossed the landing. 'Are you all right, Carrie?' she said softly at her open door.

Carrie raised her head from the pillow. 'I heard you talking to someone. Who was it?'

Harriet went and knelt by the side of her bed. 'It was Will. He's coming to see us tomorrow evening. Is that OK with you?'

Carrie nodded sleepily. 'Mm . . . that'll be nice. Will's fun.'

'Yes, he is.' Bending down to kiss her niece good night, Harriet thought that the word 'fun' summed up Will best.

'Harriet?' Her niece didn't sound so sleepy now.

'Yes, Carrie?'

'You won't . . . you won't ever leave us, will you?'

'Hey there, kiddo, what kind of a question is that?'

'You might if you got bored with us. Or if we did something really bad.'

Harriet sat down on the edge of the bed and mentally rolled up her sleeves to get to the bottom of what was on her niece's mind. 'Are you worrying about something, Carrie? Has something happened at school?'

Carrie shook her head. 'It's nothing to do with school. It's just that everything feels . . .' She hesitated and gave a little shrug. 'Everything feels so nice since we moved here . . . and it makes me feel happy.'

A flutter of understanding made Harriet say, 'And that worries you, doesn't it?'

'Yes, because what if it stops being nice?' Raising herself onto her elbow, Carrie sat up. 'What if it all turns nasty and horrible again?'

The flutter of understanding became a surge of heartfelt love for this young girl who had so bravely learned to live through the pain of losing her parents, but who was afraid to trust the happiness she was now experiencing. Swallowing back the lump in her throat, Harriet put her arms round her niece and hugged her tight. 'I'll make you another promise,' she said, leaning back so that Carrie could see her face in the half-light. 'I'll do my absolute best to make sure nothing ever turns nasty and horrible for you again. Now, come on; it's way past your bed-time. And mine too, for that matter.'

Will was right about the children, Harriet thought as she looked in on Joel a few minutes later. They did mean the world to her. She stroked her nephew's cheek gently and felt a jolt of tender love for him, just as she had with Carrie. She still experienced moments of paralysing fear when she remembered that she was totally responsible for these two children, but she was learning to enjoy rising to the challenge. She was also learning that while the buck stopped with her, she wasn't as alone as she'd initially felt. But it was the awesome trust Carrie and Joel put in her that frequently knocked her sideways. Could she really live up to their hopes, needs and expectations? Only time would tell.

ERICA JAMES

When I met Erica James in London on a bitterly cold January day, she breezed into the restaurant, swathed in what she jokingly calls her 'Goofy' coat, as it completely dwarfs her small frame. 'It's funny,' she told me, as we settled down to chat, 'but when I meet my readers at book signings, the one comment I hear going around the room like a Mexican wave is: "isn't she small? I was expecting someone much bigger!" Perhaps it's because I write big books!'

Erica may be petite physically, but in publishing terms her success has been huge and marked by an impressive ten best-selling novels in as many years. Surprisingly, she is nonetheless very insecure about it all. 'Each time I deliver a book to my publisher, I am always convinced that this one is going to be the turkey,' she tells me, with a self-deprecating laugh. 'My sons have got tired now of listening to my worries, but I know that in publishing you are only as good as your last book. It's a fragile world out there.'

Life's fragility was very much on Erica's mind when we met, as she and her two sons, Edward and Samuel, had just returned from a Christmas break in Hong Kong and Thailand, and had been on Phuket when the tsunami hit. 'I feel quite a fraud talking about it, in a way,' Erica told me, 'because I am here. We were very lucky. We were not hurt at all and all we lost was a book I was reading. After the second wave hit the hotel, it looked like a scene from a dis-aster movie and, of course, all I could think about were the "what-ifs". Most days, my son Samuel and I had gone down to the gym and had we been in there that day we would not have heard the water coming . . .'

Her experiences in Thailand have not put Erica off travelling. 'You have to be philosophical, don't you? I travel as part of my book research and also to take time out from the novel I'm currently writing, so that I can plan the next one. I write down any ideas I have and then put them to one side. Then, when I've finished the work in progress, I delve into my pot of thoughts. Long before I started work on *Love and Devotion* I knew that I wanted to write about how it would be to take on someone else's children. You love your own, of course, but someone else's? I had my two main characters, Harriet and Will, worked out and I gave Will my love of antiques.'

When Erica moved house, over two years ago, she decided to furnish it with antiques and has since become quite adept at picking up bargains. 'The house has also fuelled my passion for gardening. When I first saw it, there was just a large expanse of lawn but I had a picture in my head of how I wanted it to look.' Erica's interest in gardening has been the spur for the novel she is now writing, entitled *Gardens of Delight*.

As our lunch comes to an end, I ask Erica if she ever manages to find time to relax? 'Relax?' she laughs. 'What's that? Obviously I love going on holidays but I spend a lot of the time away researching or planning. As a writer, you are never fully off duty—you are always eavesdropping on conversations and looking for great locations as settings for your novels. I listen to music when I write and you may have noticed from reading *Love and Devotion* that I love R.E.M. I also enjoy a glass of wine and trashy television. What more could a girl want?'

Jane Eastgate

WHERE
RAINBOWS
END CECELIA AHERN

Ever since their first day at school
Rosie and Alex have stuck by each
other through thick and thin. It's only
as they reach adulthood that their
close friendship becomes strained
as both begin to wonder whether
they are meant to be more than
just good friends.
The question is, which one of them
will be brave enough to make
the first move?

PART ONE

To Alex
 You are invited to my 7th birthday party on Tuesday the 8th of April in my house. We are having a magician and you can come to my house at 2 o'clock. It is over at 5 o'clock. I hope you will come.
 From your best friend Rosie

To Rosie
 Yes I will come to your brithday party on Wensday.
 Form Alex

To Alex
 My birthday party is on Tuesday not Wednesday. You can't bring sandy to the party because mum says so. She is a smelly dog.
 From Rosie

To Rosie
 I do not care wot your stupid mum says sandy wants to come.
 Form Alex

To Alex
 My mum is not stupid you are. You are not aloud to bring the dog. She will brust the baloons.
 From Rosie

To Rosie
 Then I am not going.
 Form Alex

To Alex
  Fine.
  From Rosie

Dear Mrs Stewart,
  I just called by to have a word with you about my daughter Rosie's birth-day on the 8th of April. Sorry you weren't in, but I'll drop by again later this afternoon and maybe we can talk then.
  There seems to be some sort of little problem with Alex and Rosie lately. I hope you can fill me in on the situation when we meet. Rosie would really love if he came to her birthday party. I'm looking forward to meeting the mother of this charming young man!
  See you then,
  Alice Dunne

To Rosie
  I would be happy to go to your brithday party next week. Thank you fro inviting me and sandy.
  Form Alex your frend

To Rosie
  Thanks for the great day at the party. I am sorry sandy brust the baloons and ate your cake. See you at skool tomorrow.
  Alex

To Alex
  Thanks for the present. Its ok about what sandy did. Mum says she needed a new carpet. Dad is a bit mad though. He said the old one was fine but mum thinks the house smells of poo now, and its not baby Kevin.
  Look at Miss Casey's nose. It is the biggest nose I have ever seen.
  Rosie

To Rosie
  I no. She is the ugliest alien I have ever seen. I think we should tell the police we have an alien as a teacher who has smelly breath and—

Dear Mr and Mrs Stewart,
  I would like to arrange a meeting with you to discuss how Alex is pro-gressing at school. Specifically, I would like to talk about the problem of his note-writing during class. I would appreciate it if you called the school to arrange a suitable time to meet.
  Yours sincerely,
  Miss Casey

To Alex

I hate that we dont sit together anymore in class. I'm stuck beside stinky Steven. What did your mum and dad say about Miss Big nose?
From Rosie

To Rosie

Mum did not say much because she kept laffing. I dont no why. It is really boring up the front of the class. Smelly breath Miss Casey keeps on lucking at me. Have to go.
Alex

To Alex

You always spell know wrong. It is KNOW not NO.
From Rosie

To Rosie

Sorry miss prefect. I no how to spell it.
Form Alex

Hello form Spain! The weather is hot and sunny. There is a swimming pool with a big slide. It is cool. Met a freind called John. He is nice. I broke my arm coming down the slide. I went to the hopsital. I would like to work in a hopsital like the man that fixed my arm because he wore a white coat and had a chart in his hand and was really nice and he helped me to feel better. I would like to make people feel better and wear a white coat. My freind john signed my cast. You can too when I get home if you like. Alex

To Alex. Hello from Lundin. My hotel is the one in the picture on the front. My room is the one that is 7 up from the ground but you cant see me in the post card. I would like to work in a hotel when I grow up because you get free chocolates everyday and people are so nice that they tidy your room for you. The buses here are all red like the toy ones you got last Christmas. Everyone talks with a funny voice but are nice. Have met a frend called Jane. We go swimming together. Bye. Love from Rosie

To Alex

Why amnt I invited to your birthday party this year? I know all the boys from the class are going. Are you fighting with me?
Rosie

Dear Alice,

I'm sorry about Alex's behaviour this week. I know that Rosie is upset about

*not being invited to the party. I have tried to talk to Alex but I'm afraid I can't
get inside the mind of a ten-year-old boy!*

*I think it's just a case of his not being able to invite her because the other
boys don't want a girl to go. Unfortunately, he seems to be at that age . . .
Please give my love to Rosie.*

Best wishes,
Sandra Stewart

To Rosie
The party was not very good. You did not miss anything. The boys are
stupid. Brian threw his pizza in Jameses sleeping-bag and when James
woke up he had tomato and cheese stuck in his hair and my mum tried
to wash it and it would not go away and then Jameses mum gave out to
Brians mum and my mum went red and my dad said something I didn't
here and Jameses mum started to cry and then everyone went home.
Alex

To Alex
Sorry about your party. Brian is a weirdo anyway. I hate him. Brian the
Whine is his name. Look at Miss Casey's skirt it looks like my granny's.
Or it looks like sandy puked up all over it and the—

Dear Mr and Mrs Dunne,
*I was hoping to arrange a meeting with you to discuss Rosie's note-writing
during class. How does Thursday at 3 p.m. sound?*
Miss Casey

TO ALEX
HAPPY VALENTINE'S DAY!
MAY THERE BE SEX IN YOUR LIFE AND . . . LIFE IN YOUR SEX!
LOVE FROM YOUR SECRET ADMIRER XXX

To Rosie
You wrote that card didn't you?
From Alex

To Alex
What card?
From Rosie

To Rosie
Very funny. I no it was you.
From Alex

To Alex

I really don't know what you're talking about. Why would I send you a Valentine's card?

From Rosie

To Rosie

Ha ha! How did you no it was a Valentine's Card! The only way you could no is if you sent it. You *love* me, you want to *marry* me.

From Alex

To Alex

Leave me alone I'm listening to Mrs O'Sullivan. If she catches us passing notes again we're dead meat.

From Rosie

To Rosie

What happened to you? You've turned into such a swot.

Alex

Alex

Yes Alex and that's why I'll go places in life, like going to college and being a big successful business person with loads of money . . . unlike you.

From Rosie

Dear Mr Byrne,

Alex will be unable to attend school tomorrow, the 8th of April, as he has a dental appointment.

Sandra Stewart

Dear Ms Quinn,

Rosie will be unable to attend school tomorrow, the 8th of April, as she has a doctor's appointment.

Alice Dunne

Rosie,

I'll meet you round the corner at 8.30 a.m. Remember to bring a change of clothes. We're not wandering around town in our uniforms. This is going to be the best birthday you ever had, Rosie Dunne, trust me! I can't believe we're actually getting away with this!

Alex

PS. Sweet 16 my arse!

St James's Hospital
10 April

Dear Mr and Mrs Dunne,
  Enclosed is the medical bill for Rosie Dunne's stomach pumping on 8 April.
  Yours sincerely,
  Dr Montgomery

Rosie,
  Your mum is guarding the door like a vicious dog so I don't think I'll get to see you for the next ten years or so. The kind big sis you love so much (not!) has agreed to pass this on to you. You owe her big time . . .
  Sorry about the other day. Maybe you were right. Maybe the tequila wasn't such a good idea. Told you that fake ID my mate got would work, even though yours did say you were born on the 31st of February!
  Just wondering if you remember anything that happened the other day . . . write to me. You can trust Stephanie to pass it on. She's mad at your mum for not letting her drop out of college. Phil and Margaret have just announced that they're having another baby so it looks like I'll be an uncle for the second time round. At least that's taking the attention off me, which makes for a change. Phil just keeps laughing at what you and me did because he says we remind him of himself ten years ago.
  Get well soon, you alco! Do you no I didn't think it was possible for a human being to go *so* green in the face. I think you have finally found your talent, Rosie, ha ha ha ha.

Alex/Mr Cocky,
  I FEEL AWFUL. My head is pounding, I have never had such a headache, I have never felt so ill before in my life. Mum and Dad are going ape shit. I'm gonna be grounded for about thirty years and I'm being 'prevented' from seeing you because you're 'such a bad influence'.
  Anyway, it doesn't really matter what they do because I'm gonna see you at school tomorrow, unless they 'prevent' me from going there too, which is absolutely fine by me. Can't believe we have double maths on a Monday morning. I would rather get my stomach pumped again. Five times over. See you on Monday then.
  Oh, by the way, in answer to your question, apart from my face smashing against that filthy pub floor, flashing lights, loud sirens, speeding cars and puking, I can't remember anything else. But I bet that just about covers it. Anything else I should know about?
  Rosie

To Rosie

Glad to hear everything is as normal as usual. Mum and Dad are driving me crazy too. I can't believe I'm actually looking forward to going to school. At least no one will be able to nag us there.

From Alex

Dear Mr and Mrs Dunne,

Following the recent actions of your daughter Rosie, we request a meeting with you at the school immediately. We need to discuss her behaviour and come to an agreement on a reasonable punishment. Alex Stewart's parents will also be in attendance. The scheduled time is Monday at 9 a.m.

Yours sincerely,

Mr Bogarty, Principal

From	Rosie
To	Alex
Subject	Suspended!

Holy shit! I didn't think that old bogey would go ahead and suspend us! Oh, this is the best punishment *ever*. I get to stay in bed for a whole week nursing a hangover instead of going to school!

From	Alex
To	Rosie
Subject	I'm in hell

Glad life is going so wonderfully for you these days. I'm emailing you from the worst place in the world. An office. I have to work here with Dad for the entire week, filing shit and licking stamps. I swear to God I am NEVER EVER going to work in an office in my life. The bastards aren't even paying me.

From	Rosie
To	Alex
Subject	Re: I'm in hell

Ha ha ha ha ha ha ha ha ha em . . . I've forgotten what I was going to write . . . oh yeah . . . ha ha ha ha ha ha ha ha ha ha ha ha ha.

Lots of love from an extremely comfy, snuggy, warm and happy Rosie typing from her bedroom.

From	Alex
To	Rosie
Subject	Lazy

I don't care. There is an absolute babe working in this office. Her name is

Bethany Williams and she is seventeen (older woman!), blonde, has a massive pair of boobs and the longest legs I have ever seen. I am going to marry her.
 From the sex god

From   Rosie
To   Alex
Subject   Mr Sex God (puke puke gag vomit)

She sounds like a giraffe. I'm sure she is a really nice person (not!). Have you even said hello to her or has your future wife yet to acknowledge your existence? (Apart from handing you memos to photocopy, of course.)

You have an instant message from: ALEX.

Alex:	Hey there, Rosie, got some news for you.
Rosie:	Leave me alone, please. I'm trying to concentrate on what Mr Simpson is saying. Excel is so exciting.
Alex:	Oh, you're turning into such a bore.
Rosie:	I WAS JOKING, YOU IDIOT! But go away anyway.
Alex:	Do you not wanna hear my news?
Rosie:	Nope.
Alex:	Well, I'm telling you anyway.
Rosie:	OK, what's the big exciting news?
Alex:	Well, you can eat your words, my friend, because virgin boy is no longer.
Alex:	Hello? You still there?
Alex:	Rosie, c'mon, stop messing!
Rosie:	Sorry, I seem to have fallen off my chair and knocked myself out. I had an awful dream you said you are no longer virgin boy.
Alex:	No dream.
Rosie:	Uuuugh! So who's the unlucky girl? Please don't say Bethany please don't say Bethany . . .
Alex:	Tough shit. It's Bethany.
Alex:	Hello?
Alex:	Rosie?
Rosie:	What?
Alex:	Well say something.
Rosie:	I really don't know what you want me to say, Alex. I think you need to get yourself some male friends because I'm not gonna slap you on the back and ask for gory details.
Alex:	Just tell me what you think.
Rosie:	To be honest, from what I hear of her, I think she's a slut.
Alex:	You no that's not true.

Rosie:	You keep spelling KNOW wrong. It's KNOW not NO.
Alex:	Shut up with the 'know' thing. You've been going on about that since we were about five!
Rosie:	Yeah, exactly, so you think you would listen by now.
Alex:	Oh forget I said anything.
Rosie:	Are you two going out with each other?!
Alex:	Yes.
Rosie:	YES?????
Alex:	You sound surprised.
Rosie:	I just didn't think Bethany went out with people, I thought she just slept with them.
Mr Simpson:	You two, get down to the principal's office now.
Rosie:	WHAT??? OH, SIR, PLEASE, I WAS LISTENING TO YOU!
Mr Simpson:	Rosie, I haven't spoken for the last fifteen minutes. You are supposed to be working on an assignment now.
Rosie:	Oh. Well, it's not my fault. Alex is an awful influence on me. He just never lets me concentrate on my school work.
Alex:	I just had something to tell Rosie and it just couldn't wait.
Mr Simpson:	So I see, Alex. Congratulations.
Alex:	Eh . . . how do you know what it was?
Mr Simpson:	I think you two would find it interesting if you listened to me every now and again. You can really learn some useful tips, like how to keep an instant message private so everyone else can't see.
Alex:	Are you telling me other people in the class can read this?
Mr Simpson:	Yes, I am.
Alex:	Oh my God.

From   Rosie
To   Alex
Subject   Julie's house party

Hiya, long time no see . . . I hope they're not working you to death down there at 'the office'. I've hardly seen you at all this summer. There's a party at Julie's house tonight so was just wondering if you wanted to go.

From   Alex
To   Rosie
Subject   Re: Julie's house party

Rosie, this is just a quick email. Real busy. Can't go out tonight, promised Bethany would go to cinema. Sorry! You go and have fun.

Rosie, hello from Portugal! Weather here really hot. Dad got sunstroke and all Mum does is lie by the pool, which is really boring. Not much people here my age. Hotel quiet (on front of postcard) and it's right on the beach, as you can see. You would love to work here! I'm bringing home a collection of those little shampoos and shower caps and stuff that you love. See you when I get back. Alex

From   Rosie
To   Alex
Subject   Catching up?

How was the holiday? Haven't heard from you since you've been back. Fancy going out tonight to catch up?

From   Alex
To   Rosie
Subject   Re: Catching up?

Sorry have been so busy since I got back. Got you pressie. Can't go out tonight but will drop your pressie by before I head out.

From   Rosie
To   Alex
Subject   Re: Catching up?

Didn't see you last night. I want my little shampoos, ha ha.

From   Alex
To   Rosie
Subject   Re: Catching up?

Heading to Donegal for the weekend. Beth's parents have a little 'hideaway' there. Will drop your pressie by when I get back.

To the most inconsiderate asshole of a friend

I'm writing you this letter because I know that if I say what I have to say to your face I will probably punch you.

I don't know you any more. I don't see you any more. All I get is a quick text or a rushed email from you every few days. I know you are busy and I know you have Bethany, but hello? I'm supposed to be your best friend. Whenever you cancel nights out I end up staying home with Mum and Dad watching TV. Stephanie's always out and even Kevin has more of a life than I do. It's so depressing. This was supposed to be our summer of fun. What happened? Can't you be friends with two people at once?

I know you have found someone who is extra special, and that you both have a unique 'bond', or whatever, that you and I will never have. But we have another bond: we're best friends. Or does the best friend bond disappear as soon as you meet somebody else? Maybe it does, and I just don't understand that because I haven't met that 'somebody special'. I'm not in any hurry to either. I liked things the way they were.

In a few years' time if my name ever comes up you will probably say, 'Rosie. Now there's a name I haven't heard for ages. We used to be best friends. I wonder what she's doing now; I haven't seen her in years!' Well, I don't want to be one of those easily forgotten people, so important at the time, so special, so influential and so treasured, yet years later just a distant memory. I want us to be best friends for ever, Alex.

I'm happy you're happy, really I am, but I feel like I've been left behind. Maybe our time has come and gone. Maybe your time is now meant to be spent with Bethany. And if that's the case I won't bother sending you this letter. And if I'm not sending this letter then what am I doing still writing it? OK, I'm going now and I'm ripping these muddled thoughts up.

Your friend, Rosie

From   Alex
To   Rosie
Subject   Buttercup!!

Hey, Buttercup, you OK? (Haven't called you that for a *long* time!) I haven't heard or seen you in a while. I'm sending you this email because every time I call by your house, you're either in the bath or not there. Should I begin to take this personally? But knowing you, if you had a problem with me you wouldn't be too shy to let me know all about it!

Anyway, once the summer is over we'll see each other every day. We'll be sick of the sight of each other then! I can't believe this is our last year in school. It's crazy! This time next year I'll be studying medicine and you will be hotel manager woman extraordinaire! Things at work have been frantic. Dad kind of gave me a promotion so I've more to do than just filing and labelling. (I answer phones now too.) But I need the money and at least I get to see Bethany every day. Anyway, email me or call me back or something.

From   Rosie
To   Alex
Subject   Moonbeam!

It's not because I hate Bethany that I'm not seeing much of you (although I do hate her) it's just that I think Bethany dislikes me just a little. It could have something to do with the fact that a friend of hers told her what I wrote about her in that (not so) private instant messaging thingy in computer class last year. But I suppose you already know that. I don't think she liked being called a slut, I don't know why . . . some women are just funny like that.

Anyway it's your birthday soon! You will have finally reached the grand old age of eighteen! Want to go out and do some legal celebrating (well, legal for you, anyway)? Let me know.

PS. Please STOP calling me Buttercup!

From   Alex
To   Rosie
Subject   18th Birthday

Good to hear you're alive after all. I was beginning to worry! I would love to celebrate my 18th with you but Bethany's parents are taking me and my parents out for dinner to the Hazel. (How posh is that?) It's so we can all get to know each other. Sorry, another night definitely.

~~Dearest Alex,~~
~~Well whoopdeedoo for you.~~
~~Fuck Bethany.~~
~~Fuck her parents.~~
~~Fuck the Hazel.~~
~~And fuck you.~~
~~Love your best friend Rosie~~

From   Rosie
To   Alex
Subject   Happy Birthday!

OK then. Well, enjoy the meal. Happy birthday!

From   Rosie
To   Alex
Subject   DISASTER!

I can't believe this is happening! I was just talking to your mum; called over for a chat and she told me the bad news. This is the *worst* news *ever*! Please call me when you can.

This is so terrible. I feel awful!

Dear Mr Stewart,

We are delighted to inform you that you have been accepted to fill the position of Vice President of Charles and Charles Co. We are thrilled that you will be joining the team over here and we look forward to welcoming you and your family to Boston.

I hope the relocation package we are offering is to your satisfaction. If there is anything further that Charles and Charles Co. can do for you, please do not hesitate to ask. Maria Agnesi, personnel executive, will call you to discuss a suitable date for you to begin work.

Welcome to the team!

Yours sincerely,

Robert Brasco

President, Charles and Charles Co.

From   Alex
To   Rosie
Subject   Re: DISASTER!

I'll call you when I get home. It's true. Dad was offered a job doing something that sounds incredibly boring . . . I don't really know, I wasn't listening when he told me exactly what. I can't understand why he has to go all the way over to Boston to do a boring job. There's plenty of them right here.

I'm so pissed off. I don't want to go. I only have a year left in school. This is such the wrong time to leave. I don't want to go to a stupid American high school. I don't want to leave you.

We can talk about it later. We have to think of a way that I can stay. This is really bad, Rosie.

From   Rosie
To   Alex
Subject   Stay with me!

Don't go! Mum and Dad said that you could stay here for the year! Finish school in Dublin and then we can both decide what to do after that! Please stay! It will be so brilliant, us living together. It'll be just like when we were young and we used to keep each other up all night with those walkie-talkies! Remember that time on Christmas Eve absolutely *years* ago when we had a 'Santa' watch? We planned it for weeks, drawing little diagrams of the road and maps of our houses just so we could cover every angle and not miss him. You were on the 7–10 p.m. watch and I was on the 10 p.m.–1 a.m. watch. You were *supposed* to wake up and take over from me, but—surprise, surprise—you didn't. I stayed awake all night, screaming down into that walkie-talkie, trying to wake you up! Ah well, it was your loss. I saw Santa and you didn't . . .

If you stay with us, Alex, we'll be able to talk all night! It would be so much fun. Talk to your mum and dad about it. Convince them to say yes. Anyway, you're eighteen so you can do what you like!

Rosie,

I didn't want to wake you so your mum said she would pass this on to you. You no I hate goodbyes, but anyway, it's not goodbye because you're going to come over and visit all the time. Promise me. Mum and Dad wouldn't even let me stay with Phil, never mind you. I couldn't convince them. They want to keep their eye on me for my final year of school.

I have to go . . . I'll miss you. Ring you when I get there.

Love, Alex

PS. I told you, I was awake that Christmas Eve. My battery just went dead on my walkie-talkie . . . (and I did see Santa, I'll have you no).

From   Rosie
To   Stephanie
Subject   Urgent sisterly advice needed

I can't believe he's gone, Steph. I can't believe you're gone. Why is everyone leaving me? Surely you could have 'found yourself' a little closer to home? But France? Alex left only a few weeks ago but I almost feel like he's dead . . .

Why did he have to break up with Slutty Bethany just two weeks before he left? Then I wouldn't have gotten used to him being around so much again. Things really got back to normal, Steph. It was brilliant. We spent every second together and had so much fun!

Brian the Whine threw a going-away party for Alex just last week; I think it was just an excuse for Brian the Whine to get permission from his parents to have a party, to be honest, because the two of them *never* liked each other. Not since that pizza in James's hair incident. Anyway, Whine held the party in his house and invited all of his friends, and me and Alex knew hardly anyone in the entire place! The people we did know we can't stand, so we left and headed into town. You know O'Brien's where we held your surprise 21st? Well, we went there and the more drinks we had, the more me and Alex ended up getting all weepy about him moving away . . . Apart from that the night was brilliant. I miss the times we had, just us together like that.

You can't imagine how lonely it is at school these days. I'm just short of getting down on my hands and knees and begging for someone to be my friend. How pathetic. No one really cares. I spent the last few years ignoring them so they don't feel like they really have to talk to me. I think some of them are even enjoying it. I'm horrified that things have gotten so bad that I actually pay attention to the teachers. They're the only people who even talk to me from one day to the next. How depressing.

I wake up in the morning and I feel like I'm missing something. I know that there's something not right, and it takes me a while to remember what it is . . . then I remember. My best friend is gone. My only friend. It was silly of me to rely so much on one person. It's all coming back on me now.

Anyway, sorry for whinging on and on all the time. I'm sure you have enough problems of your own to worry about. Tell me how my sophisticated big sis is doing over in France. Strange you're over there—you always hated

French class. At least it's only for a few months, right? And then you're coming back? Dad's still not happy about you dropping out of college. Why you had to go away to find yourself is beyond me. Just look in the mirror. What's the restaurant like? Have you dropped any plates yet? Are you going to work there for long? Any nice men? There must be; French men are yummy. If there are any spare men that you don't want, send them my way.

Love, Rosie

From   Stephanie
To   Rosie
Subject   Re: Urgent sisterly advice

Hello, my darling little sister.

Don't worry about Alex. I've thought long and hard about it and I've come to the conclusion that it's a good idea he's not there for your final year of school because at least for the first year EVER you may not get suspended. Think of how proud you would make Mum and Dad.

I definitely know how you feel right now. I'm alone here too, but just stick the year out and when you're finished maybe Alex will move back to Ireland, or you can go to college in Boston!

Aim for something, Rosie, I know you don't want to hear it, but it will help. Aim for what you want and the year will all make sense. Go to Boston if that will make you happy. Study hotel management like you've always wanted.

You're only young, Rosie, and I know that you absolutely hate to hear that but it's true. What seems tragic now won't even be an issue in a few years' time. You're only seventeen. You and Alex have the rest of your lives to catch up together. After all, soul mates always end up together. Silly Bethany won't even be remembered then. Ex-girlfriends are easily forgotten. Best friends stay with you for ever.

Take care. Tell Mum and Dad I said hi and that I'm still looking for myself but may have found someone else in the process. Tall, dark and handsome . . .

Dear Ms Rosie Dunne,

Thank you for your application to study Hotel Management with us at Boston College. We are delighted to inform you that you were successful in your application . . .

From   Rosie
To   Alex
Subject   Boston here I come!

I GOT IN!! Boston College, here I come!!! WAHOOO! The letter arrived just this morning and I am soooo excited! You'd better not move a muscle, Mr Stewart, because I am finally coming to see you. It'll be great, even though you and I won't be studying at the same college. (Harvard is far too distinguished for the likes of me!) But I think it's just as well because I don't think we can really afford to get suspended again . . .

Email or call me as soon as possible. I'd call you but Dad put a block on long-distance calls, as you know, after the last bill. Mum and Dad are so proud, they're phoning all the family to tell them. Dad keeps warning me not to go trying to 'find myself' anywhere like Stephanie did. By the way, it doesn't look like Steph is coming home anytime soon. She met some chef that works at the restaurant she's waiting at, and she's officially 'in love'.

The phone hasn't stopped ringing all day with congratulations! Honestly, Alex, the house is buzzing! Kevin is happy I'm leaving so he can be even more spoilt than usual. I'll miss the brat even though he never talks to me. I'll miss Mum and Dad even more, but right now everyone is just so excited I've been accepted that I haven't stopped to think about the fact that I won't be living here any more. I suppose the enormity of it will hit me the day I wave goodbye, but in the meantime we'll continue to celebrate!

PS. One of these days I can run a hotel and you can be the doctor-in-the-house who saves the lives of the guests I poison in the restaurant, just like we always planned. Oh, this has all worked out wonderfully . . .

From   Alex
To   Rosie
Subject Re: Boston here I come!

This is *brilliant* news! I can't wait to see you too! Harvard isn't too far away from Boston College (well, in comparison to being a whole ocean apart—can you believe Harvard accepted me? It must be the intellects' idea of a hilarious joke). I'm too excited to type—just get over here. When are you coming?

From   Rosie
To   Alex
Subject September

I won't be over till September, only a few days before the semester starts, because I have got so many things to sort out you wouldn't believe!

The debs are at the end of August—will you come over for them? Everyone would love to see you, and I need someone to go with! We will have so much fun and we can annoy all our teachers, just like old times . . . Let me know.

From   Alex
To   Rosie
Subject Re: Debs

Of course I'll come home for our debs. I wouldn't miss it for the world!

Where r u??? I'm waiting at airport. Me & Dad have been
here for hours. I tried ur house phone & mobile. Don't know
where else 2 call. Hope everything's ok.

Hi Rosie. Just got ur text. Sent u an email explaining. Can u
check email at airport? Alex

From   Alex
To   Rosie
Subject   Sorry!

Rosie, I am so sorry. This whole day has been a nightmare. There was a foul-
up with the flight. I don't no what happened, but my name wasn't in the system
when I went to collect my ticket. I've been here all day trying to get another flight.
They're all booked because of people flying home from holidays and students
returning home, etc. I'm on standby, but so far there's been nothing.

From   Rosie
To   Alex
Subject   Flight tomorrow

Dad's talking to the lady at Aer Lingus ticket desk. She says there's a flight
that leaves Boston tomorrow at 10.10 a.m. It takes five hours to get here so
that will make it 3 p.m., then we're five hours ahead, which will make it
8 p.m. We could collect you from airport and go straight to ball? Or maybe
you'd prefer to go to my house first? You can't wear your tux on the plane.

From   Alex
To   Rosie
Subject   Flight

Rosie, bad news. That flight is fully booked.

From   Rosie
To   Alex
Subject   Flight

Shit. Think, think, think. What can I do? Somebody up there really doesn't
want you to get on that plane. Maybe it's a sign?

From   Alex
To   Rosie
Subject   My fault

It's my fault, I should have double-checked with the airline yesterday—they
always say you should reconfirm your flights but whoever does? I no I've

messed up your night but please go to the debs anyway. You still have the whole day to find someone else to go with you. Sorry, Rosie.

From   Rosie
To   Alex
Subject   Re: My fault

It's not your fault. I'm disappointed but it's not the end of the world. I'm gonna be in Boston in a little over a month and we'll be seeing each other EVERY DAY! We'll have a brilliant time. I better go searching for a man now . . .

From   Alex
To   Rosie
Subject   Manhunt

Any luck finding a man?

From   Rosie
To   Alex
Subject   Man found

What a stupid question!! Of course I found a man. I'm insulted you asked.

From   Alex
To   Rosie
Subject   Mystery man

Then who is it?

From   Rosie
To   Alex
Subject   Secret man

That would be absolutely none of your business.

From   Alex
To   Rosie
Subject   Invisible man

HA! You didn't find a date!! I knew it!

From   Rosie
To   Alex
Subject   Big strong man

Yes I did.

From   Alex
To   Rosie
Subject   What man?

THEN WHO IS IT?

From   Rosie
To   Alex
Subject   Almost a man

Brian.

From   Alex
To   Rosie
Subject   Brian?

BRIAN? BRIAN THE WHINE? Ha ha ha ha ha ha, you're going to the debs with Brian the Whine?! Talk about scraping the barrel! Brian who lifted your skirt when you were six, in front of everyone in the school yard, to reveal your knickers? The Brian who spilt his beer all down your new top at my going-away party? The Brian you hated all throughout school? And now you're going to the last school dance ever, *with Brian?*

From   Rosie
To   Alex
Subject   No, the other Brian

Yes, Alex, *that* Brian. Now may I ask that you please stop emailing me as my darling mother is currently tying knots in my head trying to make me look half decent? She has also been reading your emails and wants you to know that Brian the Whine won't be lifting up my skirt tonight.

From   Alex
To   Rosie
Subject   Re: Brian

Well, it won't be for lack of trying. Have fun! May I suggest that you wear your beer goggles tonight?

From   Rosie
To   Alex
Subject   Re: Beer goggles

The beer goggles will be well and truly on! Brian was the only person I could get last minute, thanks to you. All I have to do is stand in with him for the photos so that Mum and Dad can have lovely memories of their daughter going to the debs all dressed up with a man in a tuxedo. The tables seat ten so I won't have to talk to him at dinner. You're enjoying this, aren't you, Alex?

From   Alex
To   Rosie
Subject   Re: Re: Beer goggles

Not really. I'd love to be there instead. Don't do anything that I wouldn't do . . .

From   Alex
To   Rosie
Subject   Debs

How were the debs last night? No doubt you're nursing a hangover. I'll wait to hear from you tomorrow but I'll wait no longer! I want to know *everything*!

From   Alex
To   Rosie
Subject   Debs

Did you get my last email? I keep calling and there's no answer. What's up? Email me soon, please.

You have an instant message from: STEPH.

Steph   Rosie, stop avoiding Alex and tell him how the debs went. Alex is even emailing me wondering what happened, and I'm certainly not going to tell him! The poor guy missed out and all he wants to know is who did what, where and when.
Rosie: Well, I certainly won't be telling him who did who.
Steph: Ha ha.
Rosie: It's not funny.
Steph: I think it's hilarious. Come on, it's been three weeks now!
Rosie: Are you sure it's three weeks?
Steph: Yeah, why?
Rosie: Holy shit.
Rosie has logged off.

From   Alex
To   Rosie
Subject   Please, Rosie?

Are you mad at me? I'm very sorry I couldn't go to the debs ball, but I thought you understood. Things with whiny Briany can't have gone that badly, can they? What have you been doing all month? This is ridiculous.

Why doesn't anyone answer the phone at your house when I call?
Answer me. Alex

Dear Sandra,
   Alex has been leaving messages with us all week and he's terribly concerned about Rosie. I know you're worried about him worrying about Rosie so I'm just writing to let you know the situation . . .

From   Alex
To   Rosie
Subject   You're not coming to Boston?

My mum told me today that you're not coming to Boston. Please tell me what's happening. I'm so worried. Did I do something wrong? You no that I am always here for you when you need me.
   Whatever it is, Rosie, I will understand and will always be here to help you. Please let me no what is happening. I'm going out of my mind here.
   Love, Alex

Dear Miss Rosie Dunne,
   Thank you for your recent letter. Boston College acknowledges that you will not be accepting your position this year.
   Yours sincerely,
   Robert Whitworth

Rosie, can't believe this is the decision u have made.
You know I am not in support of it. I'm moving away
as I had already planned. Hope everything works
 out well 4 u. Brian.

From   Rosie
To   Alex
Subject   Help

Oh God, Alex, what have I done?

Alex,
   It was good to see you again. Please don't be a stranger—I'm going to need all the friends I can get right now. Thank you for being so supportive last week. I honestly think I would go mad without you sometimes.
   Life is funny, isn't it? Just when you think you've got it all figured out, just when you finally begin to plan something, get excited about it and feel like you know what direction you're heading in, the paths change, the signs change, the wind blows the other way, and you're lost.
   There aren't many sure things in life, but one thing I do know is that you

have to deal with the consequences of your actions. You have to follow through on some things.

I always give up, Alex. What have I ever had to do in my life that really needed to be done? I always had a choice, and I always took the easy way out—we always took the easy way out. A few months ago, the burden of double maths on a Monday morning and finding a spot the size of Pluto on my nose was as complicated as it ever got for me.

This time round I'm having a baby. A baby. And that baby will be around on the Monday, the Tuesday, the Wednesday, Thursday, Friday, Saturday and Sunday. I will have no weekends off. No three-month holidays. I can't take a day off, call in sick or get Mum to write a note. I am going to be the mum now. I wish I could write myself a note.

I'm scared, Alex.

Rosie

From   Alex
To   Rosie
Subject   Baby talk

No, it's not double maths on a Monday morning. It will be *far* more exciting than that. You will learn masses more from this experience than a maths class can ever teach you.

I am here for you for whenever you need me. College can wait for you, Rosie, because you have far more important work to do now.

I no you will be just fine.

From   Rosie
To   Alex
Subject   Re: Baby talk

You KNOW I will be fine. Watch the spelling, Mr Stewart!

You have an instant message from: ALEX.

Alex: I thought you said you'd keep an eye on Rosie for me, Phil.
Phil: How do you feel about it?
Alex: Everyone keeps asking me that and I have no idea. It's weird. Rosie is pregnant. She's only eighteen. She can barely take care of herself, let alone a baby. She smokes like a chimney and refuses to eat greens. She stays awake till 4 a.m. and sleeps till one o'clock in the day. I don't think she's changed a nappy in her life. I don't think she's ever held a baby for more than five minutes. What about college? What about working? How will she ever meet someone? She's just trapped herself into a life that's her worst nightmare.

Phil: Believe me, Alex, she'll learn. Her parents are supporting her, aren't they? She won't be alone.

Alex: Her mum and dad are great but they will be at work all day. If only I'd gotten on that flight and made it to the debs . . .

Dear Stephanie,

Let me help you find yourself. Allow my words of wisdom, from the sister who greatly loves and respects you and wishes for nothing but happiness and great fortune in your life, to rain down on you and shower you with knowledge. Please take my advice. Never get pregnant. Or enceinte, as you would say over there. Look at the word, say it out loud, familiarise yourself with it, repeat it in your head and learn to never ever want to be it.

Trust me, Steph, pregnancy is not pleasant. I'm not feeling at all at one with nature, I'm not radiating any sort of magical motherly signals, I'm just fat. And bloated. And tired. And sick. And wondering what on earth I am going to do when this little one is born and looks at me.

Alex has started his wonderful life in college, people who were at school with me are out tasting what the world has to offer and I'm just expanding by the second, wondering what I have got myself into. I know it's my own fault but I feel like I'm missing out on so much. I'm not allowed to smoke and the doctor says I have to start eating properly. I'm going to be a mother yet I'm still being spoken to like a child.

Lots of love,
Rosie

Mr Alex Stewart,

You are invited to the christening of my beautiful baby daughter, Katie. It's on the 28th of this month. Buy a suit and try to look presentable for a change, seeing as you're the godfather.

Lots of love,
Rosie

From   Alex
To   Rosie
Subject   Re: Christening

It was great to see you. You look amazing! And you are NOT fat! Little Katie was a girl of few words but I am already besotted with her. I almost felt like stealing her and bringing her back over to Boston.

In fact that's a lie. I really felt like staying in Dublin. I almost didn't get back on that flight. I love it here in Boston and I love studying medicine. But it's not home. Dublin is. Being back with you felt so right. I miss my best friend.

I've met some great guys here, but I didn't grow up with any of them

211

playing cops and robbers in my back garden. I don't feel like they are *real* friends. I haven't kicked them in the shins, stayed up all night on Santa watch with them, hung from trees pretending to be monkeys, played hotel or laughed my heart out as their stomachs were pumped. It's kind of hard to beat those sorts of experiences.

However, I can see that I have already been replaced in your affections. Little Katie is your whole world now. And it's easy to see why. I even loved her when she threw up on my (new and very expensive) suit. That must mean something. It's weird to see how much she looks like you. She has your twinkling blue eyes (I sense trouble ahead!) and jet-black hair and a little button nose. Though her bum is slightly smaller than her mother's. Just joking!

I no that you are incredibly busy at the moment but if you ever need a break from it all, you're welcome to come over here and relax. Let me no when you want to come—the invitation is always open. I realise things are tricky for you financially so we could help out with the cost of the flights. Mum and Dad would love you to come over too. They've got photos of you and Katie from the christening all around the house already.

There's also somebody I would like you to meet when you come over. She's in my class in college. Her name is Sally Gruber and she's from Boston. You would both get along.

College is a lot tougher than I thought it would be. There's just so much studying to do, I barely have a social life. I've got four years here in Harvard altogether, then I've to do about five to seven years in a general surgical residency so I'm estimating that I'll be fully qualified in my specialised field (whatever that will be) by the time I'm one hundred years old.

So that's all I do here. I wake up at 5 a.m. and study. Go to college, come home and study. Every day. Not much more to report really. It's great that Sally and I are in class together. She takes away from the feeling of dread I get every morning at having to face another day of study, study, study. It's tough, but then I don't need to tell you that. I bet it's a hell of a lot easier than what you're doing right now. Anyway, I'm going to sleep now, I'm shattered. Sweet dreams to you and baby Katie.

Bonjour Stephanie!

How's my beautiful sister doing? Sitting in a café drinking a café au lait, wearing a beret and a stripy top while stinking of garlic, no doubt! Oh, who says stereotypes are dead and gone?

Thanks for the present you sent Katie. Your goddaughter says she misses you very much, and she sends lots of drool and sloppy kisses your way. I think I could make those words out of the screaming and wailing bellowing out of her tiny little mouth, anyway. Honestly, I don't know where all the noise comes from. She is the tiniest and most fragile little thing I have ever seen, so that sometimes I'm afraid to hold her, but then she opens her mouth and all hell breaks loose. The doctor says she's colicky. All I know is that she doesn't stop screaming.

I'm so knackered, Stephanie. I feel like a complete zombie. I can barely read the words I'm writing (apologies for mashed banana on bottom of page, by the way—small breakfast-time accident). Katie just cries and cries and cries through the night. I have a constant headache. All I do is wander around the house like a robot, picking up toys that I trip over. I still look like a balloon. All I wear are the most unflattering track suits. My bum is huge. My stomach is covered in stretch marks; there's all this flab that just won't seem to go away, and I've had to throw all my belly tops out. My tits are HUGE. I don't look like me. I don't feel like me. I feel like I'm about 20 years older. I haven't been out since the christening. I can't remember the last time a member of the opposite sex even looked my way (except the people who glare at me angrily in cafés when Katie starts to scream). I think I am the world's worst mother. I think that when Katie looks at me she knows that I haven't a clue what I'm doing.

She's almost walking now, which means I'm running around saying, 'NO! KATIE, NO! Katie, do not touch that! NO! Katie, Mummy says NO!' I don't think Katie cares about what Mummy thinks. I think Katie is a girl who sees something she wants and she goes for it. I dread the teenage years! But time moves so fast that she'll be grown up and moving out before I know it. Maybe then I'll have some rest. But then again that's what Mum and Dad thought.

Poor Mum and Dad, Steph. I feel so bad. They have been so fantastic. I owe them so much and I don't just mean money. I don't know how I'm ever going to move out and work and look after Katie.

Alex has met someone over in Boston, she's the same age as me and has enough brains to be studying medicine at Harvard. But is he really happy I ask myself? Anyway, I have to go. Katie is wailing for me.

Write soon.

Love, Rosie

To Rosie

I'm glad all is well with Katie; the photos you sent of her on her third birthday are beautiful. I framed them and they're on our mantelpiece in the house. Mum and Dad were delighted to see you when they visited Dublin last month. They can't stop talking about you and Katie. We're all so proud of you at having created such a perfect child.

Hope you had a happy 22nd birthday. Sorry I couldn't make it home to celebrate with you, but things have been crazy at college. Because it's my final year here there's just been so much work to do. I'm dreading the exams. If I fail I don't no what I'll do. Sally was asking after you. Although you've never met, she feels like she nos you from me talking about our old times so much.

From Alex

To Alex

It was Dad's birthday last weekend and we splashed out and went out for dinner to the Hazel restaurant where I believe you went with slutty Bethany and her rich parents all those years ago for your 18th. I hired a baby sitter for Katie, so that was my treat for the weekend.

Rosie

From	Alex
To	Rosie
Subject	(none)

Ah come on, Rosie! You're letting the side down! You better have something wild to tell me about next time!

From	Rosie
To	Alex
Subject	3-year-old child

In case you didn't know, I have a three-year-old child, which makes it rather difficult for me to go out and drink myself silly, otherwise I wake up with an awful headache and a screaming child who needs me to look after her and NOT to be sticking my head down the toilet.

From	Alex
To	Rosie
Subject	Sorry

Rosie, I'm sorry. I didn't mean to come across as insensitive. I just meant that you should remember that you need to enjoy life too. Sorry if I hurt you.

From	Rosie
To	Stephanie
Subject	A moment to whinge

Oh, Stephanie, sometimes I just feel like the walls are closing in on me. I love Katie. I'm glad I made the decision I made, but I'm tired. So bloody tired. All of the time. And that's how I feel with Mum and Dad helping me. I don't know how I'm going to cope on my own. And I'm going to have to do that eventually. I can't live with Mum and Dad for ever. Although I really want to.

But I think it's time for me to grow up now, Steph. I've been putting it off, running away from it for so long. Katie will be starting school soon. Imagine! It's all happened so quickly. Katie will be meeting new people and beginning her life and I have left mine behind. I need to stop feeling sorry for myself. Life is hard—so what? It's hard for everyone, isn't it? Anyone who says it's easy is a liar.

As a result of all that, there's this huge divide between me and Alex right now because I feel like we're living in such different worlds, I don't know what to talk about with him any more. And we used to be able to talk all night. He phones once a week and I listen to what he's been up to during the week and try to bite my tongue every time I launch into another Katie story. Truth is, I have nothing other than her to talk about and I know it bores people. I think I used to be interesting once upon a time.

Anyway, I've decided I'm finally going to visit Boston. I'm going to finally face up to what my life could have been like had Alex gotten on that plane and made it to the debs with me instead of . . . well, you know who. I could have a degree by now. I could have been a career woman. I know it seems silly to put all that's happened down to the fact that Alex couldn't make it to the debs, but if he had come then I wouldn't have gone with Brian. I wouldn't have slept with Brian and there would be no baby. I think I need to face what I could have been in order to understand and accept what I am.

All my love,
Rosie

Stephanie,

Honey, Mum here. I was wondering if you would be able to get in touch with Rosie and maybe have a word with her. She just returned from Boston a week earlier than we expected and she seems upset about something, though she won't say what it is. I was afraid this would happen. I know she feels that she has missed out on huge opportunities. I just wish she could see the positive side to what she has now. Will you get in touch with her? She always loves hearing from you.

Love you, sweetheart,
Mum

You have an instant message from: STEPH.
Steph: Hey, you, you're not answering your phone.
Steph: I know you're there, Rosie. I can see that you've logged online!
Steph: Hellooooo!
Rosie: Hi.
Steph: Well, hello there! Why do I get the feeling I'm being ignored?
Rosie: Sorry, I was too tired to speak to anyone.
Steph: I suppose I can forgive you. Everything OK? How was the trip to Boston? Was it as beautiful as it looks in the photos Alex sent us?
Rosie: Yeah, the place is really gorgeous. Alex showed me around everywhere. He really took care of me.
Steph: As he should. So where did you go?
Rosie: He showed me around Boston College so I could see what it

would have been like for me to study there, and it is so beautiful and the weather was just fabulous . . .

Steph: Wow, it sounds great. I take it you liked it then?

Rosie: Yeah, I liked it. It would have been a nice place to study . . .

Steph: I'm sure it would have been. Where did you stay?

Rosie: I stayed in Alex's parents' house. They live in a very posh area, not at all like around here. The house is really lovely: Alex's dad is obviously making loads of money in that job.

Steph: What else did you and Alex get up to?

Rosie: Well, we went looking round the shops, he brought me to a Red Sox game in Fenway Park and I hadn't a clue what was going on but I had a nice hot dog, we went out to a few clubs . . . sorry I've nothing that interesting to tell you, Steph . . .

Steph: Hey, that's a hell of a lot more interesting than what I did all week, believe me! So how is Alex? How does he look?

Rosie: He looked really well. He's got a slight American accent although he denies it. But he's still the same old lovable Alex. He really spoilt me. It was good to feel free for a while.

Steph: You are free, Rosie.

Rosie: I know that. I just don't feel it sometimes. Over there I felt like I hadn't a care in the world. I haven't laughed so much in years. I felt like a twenty-two-year-old, Steph. I haven't felt like that much lately. I know this probably sounds weird but I felt like the me that I could have been.

I liked that I didn't have to look out for somebody else while I walked down the street. I liked laughing at a joke without my sleeve being tugged at and being asked to explain. I liked having adult conversations without being interrupted to cheer and applaud a silly dance. I liked that I was just me, Rosie, not Mammy. Isn't that awful?

Steph: It's not awful, Rosie. It's good to have time to yourself. But if things were so great then why did you come home a week early? Did something happen?

Rosie: It's too embarrassing to explain.

Steph: What do you mean?

Rosie: Oh, I just made a show of myself one night.

Steph: Don't be silly. I'm sure Alex didn't mind! He's seen you make a show of yourself plenty in your lifetime.

Rosie: No, Steph, this was a different kind of making a show of myself. Trust me. Not the usual kind of Alex and Rosie thing to do. I kind of threw myself at him.

Steph: WHAT? Do you mean that . . .? *Did you and Alex . . .?*

Rosie: Calm down, Stephanie!
Steph: I can't! This is too bizarre! You can't have!
Rosie: STEPHANIE! WE DIDN'T!
Steph: Oh. Then what happened?
Rosie: Well, it's really far more innocent than you think but equally
           embarrassing. I kissed Alex.
Steph: *I knew it!* And what happened?
Rosie: He didn't kiss me back.
Steph: Oh. And did you mind that?
Rosie: The unsettling thing is that yes, I did.
Steph: Oh, Rosie, I'm so sorry . . . but I'm sure Alex will come round.
           He was probably just shocked. Oh, I'm sure he feels the same!!
           This is so exciting! I always knew something would happen
           between you two someday. Tell me more.
Rosie: Well, at first we had so much to catch up on we were barely
           even listening to the ends of one another's sentences before
           moving on to the next. And there was lots of laughing. Then
           the laughing stopped and there was this silence. This weird
           comfortable silence. What the hell was it?
               It was like the world stopped turning in that instant. Like
           everyone around us had disappeared. All we could do was
           look at each other. It was like he was seeing my face for the
           very first time. He looked confused but kind of amused. Exactly
           how I felt. Because I was sitting on the grass with my best
           friend Alex, and that was my best friend Alex's face and nose
           and eyes and lips, but they seemed different. So I kissed him.
           I seized the moment and I kissed him.
Steph: Wow. And what did he say?
Rosie: Nothing.
Steph: Nothing?
Rosie: Nope. Absolutely nothing. He just stared at me.
Steph: So how do you know he didn't feel the same?
Rosie: At that very moment, Sally came bounding over. We had been
           waiting for her before going out. She was all excited. Wanted
           to know whether Alex had told me the good news or not. He
           didn't seem to hear her so she told me herself. They're getting
           married. So I came home.
Steph: Oh, Rosie.

Phil: What kind of a silence?
Alex: Just a weird silence.
Phil: Yeah, but was it good or bad?

Alex:	Good.
Phil:	And that's bad?
Alex:	Yes.
Phil:	Because?
Alex:	I'm engaged to Sally.
Phil:	Did you ever have 'the silence' with her?
Alex:	We have *silences* . . .
Phil:	So do Margaret and I. You don't always have to talk, you know.
Alex:	No, this was *different*. It wasn't just a silence, it was a . . . oh, I don't no.
Phil:	Bloody hell, Alex.
Alex:	I no. I'm all over the place.
Phil:	OK, so don't marry Sally.
Alex:	But I love her.
Phil:	And what about Rosie?
Alex:	I'm not sure.
Phil:	Well then, I don't see a problem here. If you were in love with Rosie and not sure about Sally *then* you'd be in trouble. Marry Sally and forget about the goddamn silence.
Alex:	Once again, you've put my life into perspective, Phil.

Dear Rosie,

I am so sorry about what happened. You didn't have to leave Boston so soon; we could have worked this out . . . I'm sorry I didn't tell you about Sally before you got here but I didn't want to tell you over the phone. Maybe I should have . . .

Please don't distance yourself from me. I haven't heard from you in weeks. It was wonderful seeing you . . . please write soon.

Love,
Alex

To Alex, or should we say Dr Alex!
CONGRATULATIONS!
GIVE YOURSELF A BIG PAT ON THE BACK . . .
YOU MADE IT!! WE KNEW YOU COULD DO IT!
Congratulations on graduating from Harvard, you genius!!
Sorry we couldn't be there,
Love Rosie and Katie

You have an instant message from: ALEX.

Alex:	Rosie, I wanted you to be the first person to no that I've decided to become a heart surgeon!
Rosie:	Great, does it pay well?

Alex: Rosie, it's not about the money.

Rosie: Where I come from, it's *all* about the money. Probably because
            I don't have any. Working part time at Randy Andy Paperclip
            Co. isn't really as financially rewarding as it sounds.

Alex: Well, in my world it's all about the lives you save. So what
            do you really think? Do you approve of my choice of
            employment?

Rosie: Hmmm . . . my best friend, the heart doctor. You have my
            approval.

From   Alex
To   Rosie
Subject   Thank you!

The last time we spoke I forgot to thank you for the congrats card you and Katie sent me. It's about the only thing I actually have here in the new apartment. Sally and I just moved in a few weeks ago.

The apartment is small but because I've such long shifts at the hospital, I hardly get to be here anyway. I've got another lifelong sentence here at Boston Central Hospital before I can actually call myself a heart surgeon. In the meantime I'm being paid a pittance and slaving away till all hours.

Anyway, that's enough about me. I seem to be just talking about myself these days. Please write to me and let me no how things are going for you. I don't want there to be any awkwardness between us, Rosie.

Keep in touch,
Alex

To Alex
Merry Christmas!
May the festive season be filled with love and joy for you
and your loved ones.
Love Rosie & kAtIe

Rosie and Katie
HAPPY NEW YEAR!
May this year bring you lots of fun, love, and happiness!
Love Alex and Sally

TO ALEX
YOU ARE IVNITED TO MY 7TH BIRTHDAY PARTY ON THE 4TH OF MAY. WE ARE HAVING A MAJICIN. I CANT WAIT. IT IS ON AT 2 O'CLOCK AND YOU CAN LEAVE AT 5 O'CLOCK.
LOVE
KATIE

Dear Katie,

I'm sorry I can't come to your birthday party. The magician sounds like he will be lots of fun. You will have so many friends you won't even no I'm not there! I have to work at the hospital. I told them it was your birthday but they still wouldn't listen!

However, I have sent you a little something so I hope you like it. Happy Birthday, Katie, and take care of your mummy for me. She is very special.

Lots of love to you and Mum,

Alex

To Alex

Thank you for my brithday present. My mummy cried when I opened it. I never had a locket before. The photos of you and Mummy are very small.

The majicin was good but my best freind Toby said he new he was cheating and showed everyone where the man hid the cards. The man was not very happy and he got mad at Toby. Mummy laffed so loud I do not think the majic man liked her eether. Toby likes Mum.

Mummy and me are moving howse soon. I will miss Grandma and Granddad so much and I no Mummy is sad because I heard her crying last night in bed. But we are not moving too far away. You can get the bus form Grandma and Granddad to our new house. It does not take too long and we are nearer to all the shops in town so we can walk.

It is much smaller than the howse we are in now. Mummy is funny she calls it a shoe box! There are 2 bedrooms and the kitchen is tiny. Mummy said that I can paint my room whatever colour I want. I think I'll paint it purple or pink or blue. Toby says we should paint it black. He is funny.

Mummy has a new job. She works only a few days a week so sometimes she can collect me from skool and other times she cant. I play with Toby until she comes home. I don't think Mum likes her job. She is always tired and crying. She said she would perfer to be back in skool doing dubble matts. I don't no what she means. Me and Toby hate skool but he always makes me laff. Mummy says she is tired of having to keep going back to my teacher Miss Casey. Miss Casey has the biggest nose ever. She hates me and Toby. I do not think she likes Mum eether.

Mum has a new freind. They work in the same building but not in the same office. They met outside in the cold because they have to smoke outside. Mum says she is the best freind she has had for ages. Her name is Ruby and she is real funny. She and Mum are always laffing. I like it when Ruby is here because Mum doesn't cry.

When are you coming to see us? Mummy says you are getting married to a girl named Bimbo. That's a funny name.

Love, Katie

You have an instant message from: RUBY.

Ruby: Hey, you, happy Monday. What did you do over the weekend?

Rosie: Oh, *wait* till you hear this! I was just *dying* to tell you all morning, it's *so* exciting! You'll *never* believe it, I—

Ruby: I sense sarcasm here. Let me guess: you watched TV.

Rosie: Introducing Ruby . . . and her psychic powers!! I had to listen to it with the volume blaring just to drown out the couple next door screaming their ears off.

Ruby: Honestly, don't some people understand the meaning of the word DIVORCE?

Rosie: Ha ha, well, it's a magic word for you.

Ruby: I would appreciate it if you wouldn't make fun of a devastatingly difficult time in my life.

Rosie: Oh, please! Getting that divorce was the happiest day of your life! You bought champagne and we went out clubbing.

Ruby: Ah well, people have their different ways of grieving . . .
       So when are you going to *ever* go out with *someone, anyone*?

Rosie: Ruby, we are *not* having this conversation again. Everyone you have tried to set me up with has been a complete weirdo! Anyway, you can't talk. When exactly was the last time you went out on a date?

Ruby: Ah, that's a very different matter altogether! I'm a woman ten years your senior who has just been through a very difficult divorce from a selfish little bastard of a man and I have a seventeen-year-old son who only communicates with me in monosyllabic grunts. I think he is the son of an ape (actually, I know he is). I have no time for a man!

Rosie: Well, neither do I.

Ruby: Rosie honey, you're twenty-six years old. You should get out there and enjoy yourself, stop letting the weight of the world rest on your shoulders. And stop waiting for him.

Rosie: Stop waiting for who?

Ruby: For Alex.

Rosie: I am *not* waiting for Alex!

Ruby: Yes you are, my dear friend. He must be some man because nobody can ever measure up to him. And I know that's what you do every time you meet someone: compare. I'm sure he's a fabulous friend and I'm sure he always says wonderful things to you. But he's not here. He's thousands of miles away, working as a doctor in a great big hospital and he lives in a fancy apartment with his fancy doctor fiancée. I don't think he's thinking of leaving that life anytime soon to come back to a single mother who's living in a tiny flat working in a crappy part-time job in a paperclip factory with a crazy friend who emails her every second. So stop waiting and move on.

Rosie: I have to get back to work now.

Rosie has logged off.

Dear Rosie and Katie Dunne,

   Shelly and Bernard Gruber proudly invite you to the marriage ceremony of their loving daughter, Sally, to Alex Stewart.

From   Stephanie
To   Rosie
Subject   Re: No way in the world I'm going to that wedding!

I am so angered by your last letter! You cannot miss Alex's wedding! That would be completely unthinkable!

This is *Alex* we're talking about! Alex, the boy who you used to chase down the road and shoot at with a banana for a gun! Alex who sat beside you in class for twelve years!

He was there for you when you had Katie. He was so supportive throughout the entire thing when I'm sure it was difficult for him to adjust to the fact that little Rosie, who had slept in a sleeping-bag on *his* floor, was having a *baby*.

Go over to him, Rosie. Celebrate this with him. Share in his happiness and excitement. This is a huge step for him and he needs his best friend by his side. Learn to get to know Sally too, as she is an important person in his life now. Just as he has learned to get to know Katie—the most important person in your life. I know you don't want to hear it, but if you don't go you will be ending what was once and what still is one of the strongest bonds of friendship that I have ever seen.

Make the right decision, Rosie.

Dear Rosie,

   Hey there! I have no doubt you have received our wonderful wedding invitation that took Sally three months to choose. Why, I don't know, but it seems that a cream-coloured invite with a gold border was so much more different than a white invite with a gold border . . . you women . . .

   I don't no if I should be worried or not, but Sally's mom hasn't seemed to have received a reply yet! Now I no I don't need one from you because I'm just presuming you will be there!

   The reason why I am writing and not ringing is because I want to give you time to think about what I'm asking you. Sally and I would be honoured if you would allow Katie to be our flower girl at the wedding. We would need to no quite soon so that Sally and Katie can pick out a dress.

Whoever thought this would be happening, Rosie? If someone had told us ten years ago that your daughter would be a flower girl at my wedding we would have just laughed at the ridiculousness of it all.

The second question I have to ask you is the one I'm sure you will need to think about. You are my best friend, Rosie; that goes without saying. I have no best friend over here, no one that measures up to what you mean to me, therefore I have no best man. Will you be my best woman? Will you stand beside me at the altar? I no I will definitely need you there! And I trust you will organise a better stag night than any of my male friends over here!

Think about it and let me no. And say yes!

Love to you and Katie,

Alex

My 'best woman' speech.

Good evening, everyone. My name is Rosie and, as you can see, Alex has decided to go down the non-traditional route of asking me to be his best woman for the day. Except we all know that today that title does not belong to me. It belongs to Sally, for she is clearly his best woman.

I could call myself the 'best friend', but I think we all know that today that no longer refers to me either. That title too belongs to Sally.

But what *doesn't* belong to Sally is a lifetime of memories of Alex the child, Alex the teenager and Alex the man that I'm sure he would rather forget but that I will now fill you all in on. (Hopefully they will laugh.)

I have known Alex since he was five years old. I arrived on my first day of school teary-eyed and red-nosed and half an hour late. (I am almost sure Alex will shout out, 'What's new?') I was ordered to sit down at the back of the class beside a smelly, snotty-nosed, messy-haired little boy who had the biggest sulk on his face and who refused to look at me or talk to me. I hated this little boy.

I know that he hated me too, him kicking me in the shins under the table and telling the teacher that I was copying his school work was a telltale sign. We sat beside each other every day for twelve years, moaning about school, moaning about girlfriends and boyfriends, wishing we were older and wiser and out of school, dreaming of a life where we wouldn't have double maths on a Monday morning.

Now Alex has that life and I'm so proud of him. I'm so happy that he's found his best woman and his best friend in ~~perfect little brainy and annoying~~ Sally.

I ask you all to raise your glasses and toast *my* best friend, Alex, and his new best friend, best woman and wife, Sally, and to wish them luck and happiness in the future.

To Alex and Sally!

OR SOMETHING LIKE THAT. WHAT DO YOU THINK, RUBY?

You have an instant message from: RUBY.
Ruby: Gag gag puke puke puke. They'll all love it. Good luck, Rosie.

Dear Rosie,

Greetings from the Seychelles! Rosie, thank you so much for last week! I had such a good time. I never really thought I could actually enjoy my wedding day but you made it so much fun. Don't worry, I don't think anyone noticed you were drunk for the entire ceremony (maybe they did for the speech—but it was funny), but I don't think the priest was too impressed when you hiccupped just as I was about to say 'I do!'

I can't quite remember the stag night but I hear it was a great success. The boys just keep going on and on about it. I think Sally is a little angry that she had to marry a man with one eyebrow and I don't care what anybody says, I no it was you who did it!

The wedding went really well, didn't it? I thought I was going to be a bundle of nerves all day but you just made me laugh so much I think it helped to get rid of the nervous energy. Sally's dad thought you were great. Is it true you made him knock back a shot of tequila?!

Everyone agreed your best woman speech was brilliant. I think all my friends have a crush on you. And no, you can't have their phone numbers. By the way, Rosie, you were my best woman that day and you still are my best friend. Always will be. Just to let you no.

Married life is going well so far. We've only been married ten days so we've only had, let's see . . . ten fights. Ha ha. I'm sure somebody told me that was healthy in a relationship . . . The place we're honeymooning in is fabulous, which I'm glad about because it's costing us an absolute fortune. We're staying in this little wooden hut-type building on stilts high up over the water. It's beautiful. The water is that turquoise-green colour that you can see through right down to the multicoloured fish below. It's paradise; you would love it. Now this is the hotel you should work at, Rosie. Imagine your office being the beach . . .

Well, I better go. Apparently people aren't supposed to write letters while they're on their honeymoon (according to Sally—so I must go). I think she wants to do something crazy like be dragged around on water-skis by a dolphin. God help me, what have I gotten myself into?!

Love, Alex
PS. I miss you!

Dear Katie,

Thank you for being my flower girl at my wedding last week. Everybody said that you looked beautiful, just like a real little princess.

Myself and Alex are now on holiday in a place called the Seychelles. It is lovely, very hot and sunny, and you can show your mummy the photograph of me and Alex lying on the beach so she can see what it looks like here. We are very happy and very much in love.

Love, Sally

Dear Sally,

Thank you for your letter. I'm glad you liked my dress, but if I were you I would have worn a pretty dress like my mum's for my wedding day. Everyone said that it matched Alex's tuxedo really well. They looked so nice together, don't you think? I showed Mum and Toby (my best friend) the photograph of you and Alex on the beach and Toby says that he hopes that your sunburn doesn't hurt too much.

I have to go now because Mum's new boyfriend is coming to the flat soon. Tell Alex that me, Mum and Toby said hi.

Love from Katie xxx

From   Alex
To   Rosie
Subject   Secret boyfriend

You sly little lady, you never told me about this new boyfriend of yours! Sally couldn't wait to tell me, which I thought was rather sweet. I didn't realise Katie and Sally were writing to each other, did you?

Anyway, why didn't you say a word about this guy at the wedding? You usually tell me everything. So come on! What's he like? What's his name? Where did you meet him? What does he do for a living? I'll have to get back to Dublin to meet this guy; make sure he gets the best friend approval. Anyway, let me no all the details.

From   Rosie
To   Alex
Subject   Re: Secret boyfriend!

Oops, my little secret is out now, thanks to Katie and her big mouth! Well, I didn't say anything about Greg (that's his name) at your wedding, because at that stage we hadn't even gone out yet! We met in the Dancing Cow nightclub just before I went over to you in Boston, and he took my number and asked me out but I said no! So I must have gone all gushy after your wedding because when I came back I rang him up and asked him out!

Oh, Alex, I've been wined and dined like never before! He's taken me to restaurants I've only read about in magazines and he's terribly romantic . . . OK, so you wanted to know all about him, here goes. He is thirty-six, works at the bank in Fairview. He's not exactly tall (my height), which isn't exactly small either, but . . . OK, if he was to stand beside you, you would have a fantastic view of his scalp. But he has sandy-coloured hair and wonderful twinkling blue eyes.

He is always bringing Katie little gifts, which I know he shouldn't do, but I love seeing her being spoilt. I can't believe I have finally met a man who doesn't mind that I have a daughter.

Anyway, he is a very generous, caring and thoughtful man, and I think I am very lucky to have met him. It may not last for ever but I'm enjoying myself, Alex. I know I've been such a misery guts for the past, oh, I don't know . . . ten years or so (!) but now I have realised that Katie and I are a team and if they can't love us both then they can get lost.

But I *think* I may have met a man who does. Fingers crossed.

From	Alex
To	Rosie
Subject	Oooh Rosie's in love!

Oooooh! Rosie sounds like she's in love! With a bank manager who goes clubbing in a place called the Dancing Cow? What kind of bank manager (or any man, for that matter) goes to the Dancing Cow? I'm not yet convinced this man is the right one for you.

And I have to say I was slightly insulted by your last email. What do you mean by the statement, 'I have finally met a man who doesn't mind that I have a daughter'? I think that I have always been supportive of you and Katie—in fact I no I have. Whenever I can, I visit you and bring you out to all your favourite restaurants and bring my goddaughter presents.

Anyway, I'd better go. Just worked a double shift at the hospital so I'm feeling really tired.

From	Rosie
To	Alex
Subject	Thanks, Mr Supportive

Well, thank you, Mr Supportive, for being so happy for me. In case you haven't noticed, you and I are not involved in a romantic relationship. Yes, you are a wonderful friend (supportive and generous), but you are not here every day with me. I'm sure you will understand when I say that finding a friend and finding a partner are two very different things. You accept me warts and all, some men don't. But you're not here.

OK, well, that's all. Hope married life is going wonderfully!

You have an instant message from: RUBY.

Ruby: Katie told Sally what??
Rosie: I know, it's crazy, isn't it? And Katie wrote that letter after I had only been on *one* date with Greg!

Ruby: Wow, she must really like him to be telling people about him so soon. Ah well, maybe Sally won't feel like you're trying to get your grubby little mitts on her husband now.

Rosie: Ah, who cares anyway? I have my Greg!

Ruby: Ugh, you make me sick. You've turned into one of those sickening couples that we hate. I think I'll have to find a new single friend so that I don't feel like a gooseberry the next time we go out . . . Oh, by the way, that guy called me last night. His name is Ted (a real teddy bear), he's overweight but then so am I. He's a truck driver and he seemed like a nice guy because he kept buying me drinks, which puts him up pretty high on my Decent Man scale. Plus he was the only person who wasn't ignoring me in the pub that night.

Rosie: Oh, I'm so sorry, but you know what it's like when you meet someone new: you want to know *everything* about them.

Ruby: No, I don't quite want to know everything about Ted . . . I don't want to be put off him.

You have an instant message from: GREG.

Greg: Hello, gorgeous. How's your day going?

Rosie: Oh, hello! Oh, it's the same as usual . . . better now, though! Sorry, Greg, just a second. I'm chatting to Ruby online too!

Ruby: Hello? Are you still there or has Randy Andy attacked you?

Rosie: Sorry, Ruby, Greg is messaging me too, so bear with me for a few minutes.

Ruby: Can you two not live without each other for a few hours?

Rosie: No!

Ruby: Oh, I miss Rosie. Who are you and what have you done to my man-hating friend?

Rosie: Don't worry, she's still here, just taking a well-deserved break.

Rosie: So, Greg, what are you doing tonight?

Greg: Rosie, my dear, I am all yours! Why don't we get a bottle of wine, some takeaway and stay in? We can get Katie a DVD.

Rosie: Yep, that sounds like a great idea!

Ruby: So should I call him?

Rosie: Call who?

Ruby: TED!

Rosie: Oh, yeah, of course! Ask him out. I can get Kevin to baby-sit and then we can all go on a double date. I've always wanted to do that! How does next Friday sound?

Ruby: Friday's fine.

Greg: I hope Ruby is OK with us after the other night; we were kind of in a world of our own.

Rosie: Don't be silly, she didn't mind at all. She met some guy called Teddy Bear. Oh, and by the way, are you free to go out on a double date thingy for dinner on Friday night?

Greg: A dinner date with Ruby and a man named Teddy Bear. Sounds interesting.

Rosie: Greg said he's free for dinner on Friday.

Ruby: Well, that's all very well but I haven't asked Ted yet. What did Alex say about you and Greg being *in love*?

Rosie: Well, I didn't say I was *in love*, Ruby! But Alex sent me some weird email telling me that he thinks that Greg sounds like a freak of nature and that he's insulted that I don't think that he's supportive of me and Katie. He just went on a bit of a rant, to be honest, but I won't take any notice because he had worked all night at the hospital and he was tired.

Ruby: Uh-huh.

Rosie: What's that supposed to mean?

Ruby: This is just as I suspected. He's jealous.

Rosie: Alex is *not* jealous!

Ruby: Alex is jealous of Greg; he feels threatened.

Greg: So what time should I call over to you tonight? Seven or eight?

Rosie: No, Alex is *not* jealous of my relationship with Greg! Why should he be? He's married to perfect pretty little Sally— happily, might I add (at least according to Sally). I gave him a chance to be part of Katie's life and mine and he chose to remain my friend, which I have now come to terms with. It's fine. Now I am in a relationship with Greg, he's wonderful and I no longer care about Alex in that way *at all whatsoever*! I am over Alex, he is not interested in me and now I am in love with Greg! So there!

Greg: Well . . . thank you for sharing all that with me, Rosie. I can't tell you how thrilled I am to hear that you are no longer in love with a man named Alex '*at all whatsoever*', as you so articulately put it.

Rosie: Oh my God, Ruby!! I just sent Greg the message that was supposed to be for you!! Fuck fuck FUCKETY FUCK! I TOLD HIM I LOVED HIM!!!!

Greg: Em . . . that, eh . . . went to me again, Rosie. Sorry . . .

Rosie: OK, so that has to be the singularly *most embarrassing* thing
           that has ever happened to me, with NO exceptions!!!

Ruby: What about the time you wore that white dress out to a club
           with no underwear on, and someone spilt water all over you
           and it was suddenly completely see-through?

Rosie: OK, so that was pretty embarrassing.

Ruby: And what about the time—

Rosie: OK, that's enough, thank you! Maybe it was not *the* most
           embarrassing thing ever, but it's pretty much up there with the
           all-time classics. The number-one embarrassing moment being
           the time I kissed Alex.

Ruby: Ha ha ha ha ha ha ha.

Rosie: The joy of having supportive friends. I'm going now; Randy
           Andy is glaring at me. His nostrils are flaring and he's
           breathing quite heavily.

Ruby: Are his hands above the desk?

Rosie: Uuugh! Ruby, stop!

Ruby: What? You don't think they call him Randy Andy for nothing,
           do you?

Rosie: Oh my, now he's staring at my legs.

Ruby: Rosie, you really need to get out of that office. It's not healthy.

Rosie: I know, I'm working on it, but I can't quit until I get another job
           and that's proving to be rather difficult. Apparently no one
           really cares about whether or not you work as a secretary in a
           paperclip factory.

Ruby: How odd . . . and it *sounds* so glamorous.

Rosie: Oh my God, he has now moved his chair over so he can get a
           better look. Hold on a minute while I send him a message. I've
           had enough!

Ruby: Rosie, don't.

You have an instant message from: ROSIE.

Rosie: Stop staring at my tits, you pervert.

Rosie: OK, Ruby, I sent it.

Ruby: Oh, you are so fired.

Rosie: Screw him! He can't fire me for that!

Ms Rosie Dunne,

   Andy Sheedy Paperclip & Co. will no longer be requiring your services, which means that your contract will therefore not be up for
renewal next month as was previously discussed.

You are, however, entitled to remain as an employee of Andy Sheedy Paperclip & Co. until the end of the month, i.e. 30 June.
Yours sincerely,
Andy Sheedy
Owner of Andy Sheedy Paperclip & Co.

From   Rosie
To   Alex
Subject   Is my CV OK?

Attachment: CV.doc

Please, please, please help me with my CV or my poor daughter and I will starve to death. How do I make all my crappy jobs look impressive? Help! Help! Help!

From   Alex
To   Rosie
Subject   Re: CV

Attachment: CV.doc

As you can see (by the attached document) I have been over your CV. The one you sent me was practically perfect as it was, of course, but I just fixed the grammar and a few spelling mistakes . . . you no how great at spelling I am!

By the way, Rosie, you haven't been doing a 'crappy job', as you so nicely phrased it. I don't think you understand the difficulty of what you are doing. You are a full-time *single* mum who has a job as a personal secretary to a very successful businessman. I only changed the words around; I didn't alter the truth in any way.

Don't underestimate yourself, Rosie; don't play down what you do. When you go into your interviews keep your head held high and feel confident. You are wonderful, beautiful, smart and intelligent, and if you knew anything about coronary heart diseases I'd hire you myself.

Just one more thing. I *strongly* suggest that you apply for a job that you actually *like* this time. How about finally trying to find a place in a hotel? You've wanted to do that since you stayed in the Holiday Inn in London when you were seven, remember?

Go for it and let me no how you get on.

From   Alex
To   Rosie
Subject   Boston visit?

Just taking a sneaky break from performing 'lobotomies' to send a quick email to see how you're getting on with the job search. You have one week left till

Randy Andy throws you out of his paperclip empire, so there's still plenty of time, and if by any chance something hasn't caught your eye by then, I can send a cheque to help tide you over for a while (but only if you *want* my help).

I would love to go home right now and go to bed, I am so tired. I've worked a double shift so tomorrow I have the day off, such bliss . . . The problem is that when I get home Sally will be getting ready to go on her shift. We don't have the most sociable hours in the world and Sally and I don't really get to spend a lot of time together, and when we do we're usually so tired we just pass out.

Here's a good idea. If you come over with Katie and whatshisname then I'll take a few days off and we can see all the sights, eat out, enjoy ourselves and I can *sleep*. And I'll finally get to meet whatshisname. I've had a lousy few weeks; I really need your comic relief! Work your magic, Rosie Dunne, and make me laugh.

From   Rosie
To   Alex
Subject   Rosie is here!

Hello there, misery man. Have no fear, Rosie is here! Sorry things have been shit for you lately. I think life likes to do that every now and again and when you feel like you can't take any more it smooths out again. But until then, my dear friend, I will try to humour you by explaining the events of my life.

OK, firstly you are a bad, bad influence on me. After I read the master-piece that was my CV, and after I read your email I felt so motivated that I proceeded to drop my CV into every single hotel I've ever wanted to work in but was always too afraid to try. Shame on you for giving me strength, because it quickly disappeared and I found myself faced with a million billion interviews with a million billion snotty companies that hated me and my cheek for even *thinking* I could work for them.

So let's see, which embarrassing interview should I tell you about first? Hmm . . . there are so many to choose from. Well, let's start with the most recent, shall we? Yesterday I had an interview to work at the reception in the Two Lakes Hotel—you know, that really posh one in the city? The front of the building is made entirely of glass so you can see the big bright glistening chandeliers dripping down from miles away. It really is very beautiful.

I was seated at The Longest Table Ever for the interview. Two men and a woman sat at one end—at least I think that's what they were; I was so far away I could barely see (I almost felt like asking them to pass the salt).

So I thought that I would try to make myself sound interested in the company, like you told me to. I asked them how the hotel got its name as I wasn't aware of any lakes in that part of the city. The two men started laughing and introduced themselves as Bill and Bob Lake. They own the place. How embarrassing.

So I basically just kept talking about what you told me to say: how I like working as part of a team, that I'm good with people, how I'm very interested in the running of a hotel . . . bla bla bla. And then I waffled on about how I've loved hotels since I was a child and have always wanted to work in one. (Well, the luxury is in *staying* in one but we both know I can't afford *that*.)

And then they go and spoil it all by saying something stupid like: 'So, Rosie, from the time you spent working at Andy Sheedy Paperclip & Co. what have you learned that you think you can bring to the table here at the Two Lakes?'

Please, like that's even worth asking.

OK, I have to go now, actually, because Katie just got home from school with the look of evil on her face and I haven't made dinner yet.

From   Alex
To   Rosie
Subject   Two Lakes Hotel

It's a shame you had to rush off. I was enjoying that email. Glad to hear your interviews are going so well—it's cheered me right up!

But I'm dying to no, what was your answer to that question they asked you?

From   Rosie
To   Alex
Subject   Re: Two Lakes Hotel

Alex, isn't it obvious? Paperclips!

(They just laughed so I got myself out of that one easily.) OK, so I'm really going now. Katie is shoving pictures that she drew in school in my face. Oh, by the way, she drew one of you . . . you look like you've lost a bit of weight. I'll scan it to you . . .

Dear Ms Rosie Dunne,

It is our pleasure to inform you that we are offering you the position of head receptionist at the Two Lakes Hotel.

On a more personal note, we are very excited about having you here following the success of your interview last week. You come across as a bright, intelligent and witty young woman; the kind of person we like to have working at the hotel.

We take pride in hiring people we ourselves would like to be greeted by in a hotel and we have great faith that the smiles you brought to our faces when we met will also be brought to the customers of the hotel when they arrive at reception. We are pleased to have you as a member of the team, and hope our working relationship will develop successfully over many years in the future.

We ask that you get in touch with Shauna Simpson at reception with regard to your work uniform.

Yours sincerely,

Bill Lake   Bob Lake

PS. We would also appreciate it if you would bring those paperclips with you—office supplies are rather low!

From   Rosie
To   Stephanie
Subject   Congratulations

I'm delighted to hear that you and Pierre got engaged! I know we spoke for hours last night but I wanted to send you this email too. Congratulations!

Something rather bizarre is happening in my life, Stephanie. I have a boyfriend who loves me, and who I love back, I'm about to start work in the hotel of my dreams, Katie is beautiful and healthy and funny, and I finally feel like a good mum. I feel happy.

This is not something that will 'just do', this is perfect; this is exactly what I wanted. I wanted to feel loved by someone, I wanted Katie to stop wondering if it was all her fault that she didn't have a daddy like all the other kids, I wanted to feel that the two of us not only belong together but that someone else would accept us in his life too, I wanted to feel like *somebody*, I wanted to know that if I called in sick to work that I would be *missed*. I wanted to stop feeling so sorry for myself, and I have.

Things are going great. I'm feeling really good about myself and I'm not quite used to that. This is the new Rosie Dunne. Young and confused Rosie is gone. Phase two of my life now begins . . .

PART TWO

Dear Alex,

Thank you so much for the holiday! I had such a fantastic time. Boston was even more beautiful than I remembered, and I'm glad I didn't have to run home early in embarrassment this time round. Katie just loved the whole experience, and will not stop talking about you!

Greg really enjoyed it too. I'm glad you finally got to meet him. It was such a treat to have my two favourite men in the same country at last, never mind in the same room! So what do you think of him? Does he get the best friend seal of approval?

So apart from the fact that your wife absolutely hates me, everything else was very comfortable and enjoyable. But I actually don't mind, Alex; I'll just accept it. It just makes it official and confirms what I've already thought: for some unknown reason, any girlfriend or wife of yours will forever hate me. And that's fine with me. I'm over it.

I just hope she lets me see your son or daughter when he or she is born. Now there's something else I never imagined! Alex Stewart is going to be a daddy! Every time I think about it I just have to laugh out loud. God love your child to have a father like you! Just joking—you know I'm thrilled! Although I can't believe you kept it a secret from me for so many months. Shame on you.

By the way, I'm really sorry Katie spilt her drink over Sally's new dress. I don't know what got into her; she's usually not so clumsy! I've told her to write a letter of apology to Sally.

Anyway, my few weeks of fun are over now; it's back to reality again. I start work at my new job on Monday. All my life I've wanted to work in a hotel and I've put the thought away, with the rest of my dreams.

There's one more thing I forgot to tell you. Greg has asked me and Katie to move in with him. I'm not quite sure how I feel about it. Things are going so well at the moment between us but it's not just me that I have to think about. Katie really likes Greg, and she loves to spend time with him (it may not have been that obvious in Boston because she was so excited to see you), but I don't know if she would be ready for such a huge change in her life. Well, I suppose all I need to do is ask her.

Thanks again for the break. I really needed it.

Love,

Rosie

Dear Rosie,

Welcome to your first day at the Two Lakes. I'm sorry I'm not there to greet you but I am currently in the States finalising a few things at our new Two Lakes Hotel in San Francisco.

In the meantime, Amador Ramirez, the hotel assistant manager is there to show you the ropes. Let me know if you have any problems.

Once again, welcome!

Bill Lake

Dear Sally,

Sorry I spilt my orange juice on your new dress when we visited a few weeks ago. It is just that when I heard you slagging my mum's new dress I got a shock and my juice went all over you. Just like you laughed to your friend the next day about my mum having me, accidents happen.

I hope your dress doesn't stain, seeing as it was so expensive and all. I hope you will come to visit us sometime in our new house. We are moving in with Greg. It's bigger than your apartment. We had so much fun in Boston when Mum and Alex got new passport photos done for my locket. I'll keep the two of them together in it for ever.

Love,
Katie

From   Alex
To   Rosie
Subject   Moving in with Greg?

So I take it you're moving in with Greg? Sally got a letter from Katie during the week, but she wouldn't let me read it.

In answer to your question about Greg, yes, he's a nice man. Not the kind of person I expected you to settle down with, he's very quiet and reserved. A lot older than you as well. He's what . . . thirty-seven? And you're twenty-seven. That's ten years, Rosie. How will you feel when he's old and decrepit and you're still young and beautiful? How will you ever look into those faded watery eyes and kiss those wrinkly dry cracked lips?

These are the things you need to worry about, Rosie.

You have an instant message from: ROSIE.
Rosie: Are you on drugs???
Alex: Only the little pink ones . . .
Rosie: OK, I take it that you don't like Greg. Well, to let the truth be known, I can't stand Sally. Ta-da!
           I hate Sally and you hate Greg. Now we have learned that we all can't love each other. Katie and I are moving in with Greg next week. Everything is wonderful. We are blissfully happy, blah blah blah. Now stop annoying me and get over it. Greg is here to stay. So what have you got to say to that?
Alex has logged off.

Rosie, Katie and Greg,
Merry Christmas and a Happy New Year!
Love from Alex, Sally, and baby Josh

To Alex, Sally and baby Josh!
Warm wishes for the New Year!
With love,
Katie, Rosie, and Greg

Hello, sis,

Stop worrying! You have me more stressed out than you! Rosie, for the last time, it is absolutely normal for friends not to get along with each other's spouses/partners. There's never going to be anyone good enough for your best friend, Rosie. Alex is probably thinking that you could do far better than Greg and you think the same of Sally. Greg knows that Alex was the most important man in your life (he also knows that you once had a crush on him, which doesn't make things any better). And Alex knows that he's been replaced. So both Greg and Alex are going to be a bit competitive with each other.

By the way, if you don't like Pierre, I don't care. I love him, so keep your opinions to yourself!

Send me your measurements over, will you? And don't lie, Rosie. This is for your bridesmaid dress and if you pretend you're two stone lighter than you actually are and the dress doesn't fit, tough, you have to wear it because I can't afford to get you another one. Do you prefer red or wine? Let me know.

Love,
Your agony aunt

To Rosie,
Birthday wishes from us to you!
Happy 28th—you're catching up on me!
Love, Alex, Sally and Josh

To Katie,
YOU ARE 9 TODAY!
Best wishes! I hope you can buy something nice with this!
Love, Alex, Sally and Josh

From	Rosie
To	Alex
Subject	Great news!

Alex Stewart, why don't you ever answer your phone? I have become best friends with Josh's nanny now and we both agree that you and your wife work far too much. Does poor little Josh even know who Mummy and Daddy are?

Anyway, the reason why I'm emailing you is because I have something brilliant that I really want to tell you and I refuse to announce it to you on a computer! So ring me when you get this message.

From	Alex
To	Rosie
Subject	Re: Great news!

I am refusing to ring you on the grounds that I am far too angry over your attacking my parental skills. Things are tough at the moment because of my and Sally's working hours. The majority of the time we arrive home when Josh is asleep and I have to stop myself from waking him up just to say hello. We never have the same days off together and we just can't seem to spend any quality time together.

It's not the greatest situation for Josh to be in but we can't afford to stop working to be there for him all the time. And, by the way, *never* get married.

From   Rosie
To   Alex
Subject   Surprise!

Oh, shucks, you've gone and spoilt my surprise.

From   Alex
To   Rosie
Subject   Re: Surprise!

Rosie Dunne, are you getting married?! How did it all happen? When's the big day? I thought whatshisname didn't want to get married.

From   Rosie
To   Alex
Subject   Re: Marriage at last!

Oh, Alex, you don't have to pretend to be interested in all the little details, it's OK. And his name is Greg, by the way. You've plenty on your mind now so I'll bore you another time. I just want to let you know that the 'big day' won't be so big. It's only going to be a small gathering with close friends and family. Greg doesn't really want anything too OTT and I'm happy enough to go along with that.

Katie is my flower girl/bridesmaid-type person and I want you to be my best man. If Greg is allowed to have one then so should I. Please say yes. Sally and Josh are more than welcome too. Make it a family holiday. You can finally spend a few days together as a family.

I won't go into any detail about the proposal; I knew it was going to happen so it wasn't that amazing . . .

Ruby: He proposed to you in Bogger-reef?
Rosie: Yes, it's a cute little village—
Ruby: You HATE cute little villages!
Rosie: But we stayed in this sweet little B&B owned by the nicest—
Ruby: You HATE B&Bs! You are obsessed with hotels. You work in
          one. You want to run one, own one, live in one. The biggest
          treat for you is staying in a hotel and he took you to a crappy
          B&B in the middle of nowhere.

237

Rosie: Oh, but if you had just seen the little restaurant. It was called the Fisherman's Catch—

Ruby: You gag whenever you see people eating oysters (which, by the way, is very embarrassing in restaurants). You think smoked salmon is the work of the devil, and prawns make you vomit.

Rosie: I had a nice salad, thank you very much.

Ruby: You always say salad is for rabbits and supermodels!

Rosie: Anyway, we finished the evening by strolling hand in hand in the moonlight alongside the lake—

Ruby: You LOVE the SEA. You told me you want to live on a beach.

Rosie: Oh, please, *stop* it, Ruby!

Ruby: No! You please stop *lying* to yourself, Rosie Dunne.

Rosie has logged off.

From	Rosie
To	Alex
Subject	SOS

Alex, please save me from my family and friends. They are driving me absolutely demented.

You have an instant message from: ALEX.

Alex: Snap. What's the problem?

Rosie: I don't really want to talk about it. I want to take my mind off them.

Alex: That's fair enough, I can understand that. So why don't you tell me about whatshisname's proposal?

Rosie: OK . . . here I go again. *Greg* took me to a quiet little village. We stayed in a gorgeous little B&B. We ate in a lovely restaurant called the Fisherman's Catch. He proposed while I had my mouth full of chocolate profiteroles, I said yes, we took a walk along the lake and watched the moon shimmering along the water. Isn't that romantic?

Alex: Yes, romantic.

Rosie: That's all you have to say??

Alex: Could have been better.

Rosie: How much better? What would you have done to make it so much better? I'm just *dying* to know!

Alex: OK, that sounds like a challenge! Well, firstly, I would have brought you to a *hotel* along the coast so that your *suite* would have the best possible *sea view*. You could fall asleep listening to the waves crashing against the rocks, I would sprinkle the bed with red *rose petals* and have *candles* lit all around the room, I would have your favourite CD playing.

	But I wouldn't propose to you there. I would bring you to where there was a huge crowd of people so they could all gasp when I got down on one knee and proposed.
Rosie:	Oh.
Alex:	That's all you can say? I get down on bended knee and ask that you'll spend eternity with me and you say, 'Oh'? You have to do better than that!
Rosie:	OK, so that would *also* be a very nice proposal. Did I go on about proposals so much, Alex?
Alex:	All the time, my friend. All the time. Anyone who nos you half well would realise that is more or less the kind of thing you have always dreamed about.

To Alex, Sally and baby Josh
DENNIS & ALICE DUNNE
Proudly invite you to the marriage of their
beloved daughter
ROSIE TO GREG COLLINS
on July 18th of this year

Dear Rosie,

So you went ahead and did it. You married whatshisname. You looked beautiful, Rosie, I was proud to stand beside you at the altar, and I was proud to be your best man, but just as you said at my wedding, I wasn't the best man that day, whatshisname was.

I got the oddest feeling when you turned your back to me to walk down the aisle with Greg. Could it have been a pang of jealousy? Is that normal? Did you get that feeling on my wedding day, or am I going completely crazy? I just kept thinking over and over in my head: Everything is going to change now. Greg is the man for you, now he gets to hear all your secrets, and where does that leave me? It's not like I was jealous because I wanted to be your husband, it was just . . . oh, I don't no how to explain it. I suppose I just felt left out, that's all.

I'm glad Josh finally got to put his feet on Irish soil—well, actually mostly his bum but he's almost there. I meant to bring him home a long time ago but work got in the way. I think Katie was happy enough to mind him all week.

I'm not quite sure how your plan to unite me, Sally and Josh went. As you could probably tell, Sally wasn't in the friendliest of moods. I thought the break away would help us, but apparently not. It just gave us a chance to talk to each other too much. And that's not the best thing when neither of you have anything nice to say. I think I can safely say that the honeymoon period is over. We're together nine years now.

Anyway, I hope you and Greg are enjoying your honeymoon. I always thought you wanted to go to an exotic beach location for your honeymoon, I never new you were interested in seeing all the sights around Rome. Although I'm sure they are beautiful, I just thought you were too shallow to care! Just teasing.

Get in touch with me when you get back. Prove to me that at least some things never change.

Love,
Alex

From   Rosie
To   Alex
Subject   I'm baa-aack!

Just got home a few minutes ago from our honeymoon and I read your letter. You sounded down so I called and guess what? Surprise, surprise, you weren't there. So I'm emailing you once again.

I know I never really liked Sally much, but I want you two to get over whatever it is that's bothering you. It's a big change when a baby comes along—I know that only too well—and I can understand that it's difficult for two people who work harder than anyone I know to deal with a new addition in their lives.

I certainly don't pretend to be a know-it-all but just stop talking to me about how you feel and start telling Sally. I am always here for you, Alex, married woman or not.

Dear Alex,

I hope you are well. It was good to see you at the wedding. Josh is really cool. Mummy looked lovely and so did you. Me and Toby are fighting. He is ten next week and he thinks he is so cool just because he is a little bit older than me. He didn't invite me to his birthday party and I didn't even do anything wrong.

Mum thinks that it is really, really mean of Toby and that I will be motionally scared when I grow up, from the xperience of not being invited to a birthday party. She says you no what she means.

Love,
Katie

Dearest Katie,

Your wise and extremely intelligent mother is correct, as always. I agree that Toby is being terribly cold and calculative. It is an awful thing not to invite your best friend to your tenth birthday party. I do believe it should be a crime. He is selfish and it is an unforgivable act that will haunt him for years to come, no doubt—maybe even until he is nearly thirty years old, in fact.

I think that there is no punishment bad enough to inflict on him and he should not get away with this. So tell your mother and tell Toby that I shall do my best to make sure that he and I redeem ourselves.

Love,
Alex

Dear Toby,
It's Alex here (Katie's mum's friend from America).

I heard that you're going to be ten next week. Happy birthday! I no you probably think that me writing to you is really weird but I heard that you didn't invite Katie to your party and I couldn't believe my ears.

Katie is your best friend! I no for a fact that your party won't be much fun without Katie there. It once happened to me. Who cares if your best friend is a girl? Who cares if the other guys laugh? At least you have a best friend and, trust me on this, it's really hard to live your life without a best friend, especially if you're in boring school with Miss Big Nose Casey. If you don't invite Katie then you will really hurt her feelings and that's not very nice. Let me no how you get on.

Alex
PS. Hope you can buy something nice for yourself with this present . . .

From	Toby
To	Katie
Subject	KNOW not NO

Your mum's friend spells 'know' wrong, just like you. He says NO instead of KNOW. By the way, do you wanna come to my party next week?

From	Rosie
To	Alex
Subject	Dunne women

Very clever, Mr Stewart, but you haven't quite redeemed yourself yet. Us Dunne women are pretty hard to please, you know . . .

From	Alex
To	Rosie
Subject	Done woman

So I see. You're a done woman all right. Well, I have a theory that I wish to share with you. OK, if I *had* invited you to my tenth birthday party then Brian the Whine wouldn't have been invited. If Brian hadn't gone then he wouldn't have thrown pizza all over James and his sleeping-bag and if he hadn't done that then you and I wouldn't have hated him so much and you

241

wouldn't have had to drink so much in order to be able to accompany him to the debs. If you hadn't have done that . . . Well, perhaps you wouldn't have been quite so drunk and your darling little Katie wouldn't have been born. Therefore I did you a favour!

From   Rosie
To   Alex
Subject   My theory

Very clever, Alex, very, very clever. But you needn't have gone that far back to accept responsibility for Katie. Here's my theory.

   Had I not been stood up by you at the debs, I wouldn't have had to go with Brian the Whine at all. Had you showed up at the airport that day our lives could have turned out very differently.

From   Alex
To   Rosie
Subject   Life

Yeah, that's something I'm beginning to wonder about.

Ruby:	They WHAT? They *split up*??
Rosie:	Yeah, they're finished. Sad, isn't it?
Ruby:	Well, not really, actually. Why did they split up?
Rosie:	Irreconcilable differences.
Ruby:	So who has Josh?
Rosie:	Sally took him and went to stay with her parents.
Ruby:	Oh, poor Alex. So come on, spill the beans.
Rosie:	Well, I don't know everything—
Ruby:	Liar. Alex tells you everything, which is probably the reason in itself.
Rosie:	Please do not accuse me of being the reason for his marriage breakup.
Ruby:	So when are you going over to him?
Rosie:	Next week.
Ruby:	Are you planning on coming back?
Rosie:	RUBY! QUIT IT!
Ruby:	OK, OK. It's sad, though, isn't it?
Rosie:	Yes, it is. Alex is devastated.
Ruby:	No, I didn't mean that. The irony of it all makes *me* sad; I can't even imagine how *you* must feel.
Rosie:	What irony?
Ruby:	Oh, you know . . . you wait and wait for years for him until you

finally give up and marry Greg and weeks later, Alex splits up with Sally. You know, you two have the worst timing ever.

From   Rosie
To   Alex
Subject   Happy 30th

I can't believe you're not having a thirtieth birthday party! Or are you having one and you're just not inviting me? I know you've been inclined to do things like that in the past. Imagine that was a whole twenty years ago. I never thought we would reach the time when we could remember anything happening that long ago. Anyway, Happy Birthday. Have a slice of cake on me.

From   Alex
To   Rosie
Subject   Thanks

Sorry I haven't been in touch, I'm almost ready to finish up my residency here so I can move on to do two more years of cardiothoracic residency program. My one hundred years of study are almost up! No celebrations for me this year, too busy trying to pay back my million-dollar student loan.

You have an instant message from: GREG.

Greg: Hi, honey, how's your day going?
Rosie: Oh, it seems to be one of those never-ending days. My face is sore from smiling and my eyes are stinging from staring at this bloody computer screen. I'm thrilled I've got the weekend off! I can't remember the last time I had a Saturday off, or two days in a row, for that matter. It means we can go out tonight and I won't have to worry about getting up in the morning.
Greg: Oh, Rosie, I'm so sorry but I have to go to Belfast tonight for a seminar. I only found out this morning so it's completely last minute. I'm sorry.
Rosie: Oh no! Do you *have* to go? Will they even notice if you're there?
Greg: No, they wouldn't notice, to be honest, but I want to go. I have to stay ahead of my game.
Rosie: How much more could you possibly learn about bloody banks?
Greg: I'm sorry, Rosie.
Rosie: This is so annoying. Of all the bloody weekends Bill gives me off, it's the one you have to go away for. You do know that I will not get a weekend off for another year, don't you?
Greg: I love the way you never exaggerate, Rosie. Listen, I have to go, OK? Talk to you later. Love you.

From   Kevin
To   Rosie
Subject   My favourite sister

Hello, my most favourite big sister in the whole entire world. It's Kevin here. How's Katie? Tell her I was asking for her. How's Greg? Tell him I was asking for him. How's Alex? Tell him I was asking for him. Anyway, that's all from me, take care of yourself and keep in touch.

    PS. Any chance you could ask your boss for a job for me?

From   Rosie
To   Kevin
Subject   A-HA!

A-HA! I knew there had to be a catch! You never usually care about what's going on in my life. Katie is fine, thank you, so is Greg, and so is Alex. You could see how they are with your very own eyes if you ever bothered to call round. I'll try to help you out, but I'm not promising any miracles. Don't mess this up, Kevin, or Bill will hold it against me and it'll ruin my grand master plan of taking over this hotel.

Dear Alex,

OK, so as you probably no, it's Mum's thirtieth next month, and me and Toby are arranging a surprise birthday party for her. So will you come? You can bring Josh too. We need more people anyway. Aunt Stephanie can't come because she is due next month and I don't think the pilot will let her fly because she's too heavy or something. Grandma and Granddad are going over to visit her, Pierre, and the new baby if it comes. Uncle Kevin can't come because he's starting his new job as a chef in a new hotel down the country. So far it's just Ruby, Toby and me.

I wanted it to be kinda special for Mum, because she's been really sad again this week. I think it's because the telephone is broken. Every time the phone rings and Mum answers it, no one is there. It happens when I answer it too. It doesn't happen when Greg answers it.

Greg said he would get someone to fix the phone and Mum just spilt her drink on him. I don't really think it's broken. I think that whoever is ringing wants to speak to Greg and not me and Mum.

It would be good if you came over—you're loads of fun. You can even sleep here but you can't sleep in the spare room because that's Greg's room now, I think. You can sleep on the couch, or I have a pull-out bed in my room. Remember, don't ring because it's a secret and Mum just keeps hanging the phone up without saying hello anyway. Email me if you want.

Love, Katie

From   Alex
To   Katie
Subject Re: Rosie's 30th

Thanks for the letter. That's a good idea of yours and Toby's but I won't wait until your mum's birthday, if you don't mind. I'll be over as soon as I can.

Rosie,

I'm returning to Boston tomorrow but before I go I wanted to write this letter to you. All the thoughts and feelings that have been bubbling up inside me are finally overflowing from this pen and I'm leaving this letter for you so that you don't feel that I'm putting you under any great pressure. I understand that you will need to take your time trying to decide on what I am about to say.

I no what's going on, Rosie. You're my best friend and I can see the sadness in your eyes. I no that Greg isn't away working for the weekend. You never could lie to me; you were always terrible at it. Your eyes betray you time and time again. Don't pretend that everything is perfect because I see it isn't.

Greg is the luckiest man in the world to have you, Rosie, but he doesn't deserve you and you deserve far better. You deserve someone who loves you with every single beat of his heart, someone who thinks about you constantly, someone who spends every minute of every day just wondering what you're doing, where you are, who you're with and if you're OK. You need someone who can help you reach your dreams and who can protect you from your fears. You need someone who will treat you with respect, and love every part of you, especially your flaws. You should be with someone who can make you happy, really happy, dancing-on-air happy. Someone who should have taken the chance to be with you years ago instead of becoming scared and being too afraid to try.

I am not scared any more, Rosie. I am not afraid to try. I no what that feeling was at your wedding—it was jealousy. My heart broke when I saw the woman I love turning away from me to walk down the aisle with another man, a man she planned to spend the rest of her life with. It was like a prison sentence for me—years stretching ahead without me being able to tell you how I feel or hold you how I wanted to.

Twice we've stood beside each other at the altar, Rosie. Twice. And twice we got it wrong. I needed you to be there for my wedding day but I was too stupid to see that I needed you to be the reason for my wedding day.

I should never have let your lips leave mine all those years ago in Boston. I should never have pulled away. I should never have panicked. I should never have wasted all those years without you. Give me a chance to make them up to you. I love you, Rosie, and I want to be with you and Katie and Josh. Always.

Please think about it. Don't waste your time on Greg. This is our opportunity. Let's stop being afraid and take the chance. I promise I'll make you happy.

All my love, Alex

From   Alex
To   Rosie
Subject   More time?

Alex here. It's been a while since I've heard from you . . . I was hoping you would have been in touch by now. If you need more time, I understand. Please let me no what's going on.

From   Rosie
To   Alex
Subject   Re: More time?

What do you mean, do I need more time? It doesn't take very long to accept I'm thirty! Thanks for coming over for my birthday, by the way. It was really sweet of Katie and Toby to organise it, even if you and Ruby were the *only* people there. Sorry I was a bit of a sourpuss. I suppose I was just down because I turned thirty and most people were away. It just would have been nice if more people had come, but never mind. You were there and that was good enough for me. I was so happy to see you.

So, how are things with you? How's Josh? Give him a big hug from me.

From   Alex
To   Rosie
Subject   My letter

Didn't you get my letter?

From   Rosie
To   Alex
Subject   Letter?

What's this about a letter? Maybe it's just delayed in the post; I'll probably get it soon. When did you send it?

From   Alex
To   Rosie
Subject   My letter

I didn't post the letter; I put it on the kitchen table in your house just before I left to go to the airport. Didn't you get it? I wrote some really important things in there and I would love you to read it if you can. Please try to find it.

From   Rosie
To   Alex
Subject   Your letter

Hi, Alex. I searched the house from top to bottom yesterday when I got home from work. No sign of it. Can you just email me what it said? Oh, hold on, Greg is online. I'll see if he's seen the letter.

From   Alex
To   Rosie
Subject   My letter

Don't bloody well ask *him*!

You have an instant message from: ROSIE.

Rosie: Greg, Alex is online asking about a letter. Did you see a letter on the kitchen table for me?
Greg: A letter? No, I think there was just the electricity bill.
Rosie: No, I'm not talking about this morning; I'm talking about two weeks ago, the weekend of my birthday.
Greg: But, Rosie, you didn't want me around that weekend. I stayed on the couch in Teddy's flat, remember?
Rosie: Of course I remember. I thought you might like it, seeing as you've been sleeping in everybody else's houses for the past while. I'm not stupid, Greg.
Greg: Honey, I—
Rosie: Don't honey me. Did you see the bloody letter or not? You were home on the Monday just after Alex left.
Greg: No, I honestly didn't see it.
Rosie: Well, there's a reason not to believe you, Mr Honesty.
Greg: Look, Rosie, we can't move on if you don't forgive me.
Rosie: Greg, I don't have time for another one of these conversations with you. This is very simple. I've got Alex online waiting for me. He left a letter for me. He wants to know if any of us found it. So I'm asking you one more time, Greg, did you see the letter?
Greg: No, I promise you that I didn't.

From   Rosie
To   Alex
Subject   Your letter

Alex, Greg didn't see the letter. Maybe you can just write me another one or ring me later when I'm at home. Got to go now before I get fired.

From   Greg
To   Alex
Subject   Your letter?

I was told you were online so I hope I caught you in time. I happened to have stumbled across something I believe you're looking for. I would appreciate it if you would stop sending my wife love letters. You seem to have forgotten that she's a married woman. Married to *me*, Alex.

Rosie and I have had our troubles like all marriages do, but we are willing to put all that behind us now and give it another chance. You need to understand that none of your letters is going to change that. You said it yourself: you had your chance but now the moment has passed you by.

Let's be realistic here for a minute, Alex. You and Rosie are both thirty. You've known each other since you were five. Don't you think that in all that time, that if something was supposed to happen between you two, if it was so *meant to be*, that it would have happened by now? Think about it.

From   Alex
To   Greg
Subject   Rosie

Do you think your ridiculous attempt to scare me off is going to work? You are a pathetic sad little man. Rosie has a mind of her own and she doesn't need you making those decisions for her.

From   Greg
To   Alex
Subject   Re: Rosie

So what are you going to do if she says yes, Alex? Move to Dublin? Leave Josh behind? Expect Rosie to uproot Katie, leave the job she loves and move to Boston? *Think*, Alex.

You have an instant message from: ALEX.
Alex: She didn't get the letter, Phil.
Phil: Oh, bloody hell, Alex.
Alex: Greg found the letter.
Phil: The idiot husband? I thought they were finished?
Alex: Evidently not. But it doesn't change anything. I still love her.
Phil: Yeah, but she's *still* married, isn't she?
Alex: The guy cheated on her. He's all wrong for her.
Phil: Yeah, but the difference between now and before is that *now* Rosie knows he cheated on her. But she's still with him. She must really love him, Alex. Just my opinion but I'd say back off.

Alex: I don't agree with that, Phil.

Phil: Fine! I know you want the best for Rosie but you're being selfish here. Look, if the marriage is a disaster, then it's a disaster and in a few months it'll end and Rosie will come to you. Just don't be the prick that tries to break up her marriage. She'll never forgive you for that.

Alex: So you think I should let it happen naturally? Let her come to me when she's ready?

Phil: Something like that. I'm thinking of starting one of those advice shows that they have on telly.

Alex: You'd have me on it every week, Phil. Thanks.

Alex has logged off.

From   Rosie
To   Alex
Subject   Letter?

Alex, I searched high and low in the kitchen for your letter, I left no stone unturned and Greg and Katie swear they didn't lay a finger on it so I don't know where else it could be. Are you sure you left it there? We were in such a rush to get you to the airport that morning, maybe you forgot. I checked the spare room you were sleeping in. All I found was a T-shirt you left behind, but it's mine now so you're not getting it back!

So what was in the letter? You didn't call me when I got home from work yesterday. You're really keeping me in suspense, Alex!

From   Alex
To   Rosie
Subject   Letter

How are things with you and Greg? Are you happy?

From   Rosie
To   Alex
Subject   Greg

Wow, talk about a change of subject. That's a very direct question.

OK, I know you can sense that he and I are going through a bad phase and you're worried. And I also know that you absolutely can't stand him, which is really difficult for me because I would really *love* you to see him how I see him.

Deep down, underneath *all* his layers of stupidity, he's a really good man. He may act out far too many selfish thoughts, say all the wrong things at all the wrong times, but behind closed doors he's a best friend. I *understand* that he has idiotic tendencies and I can still love him for it. He's someone that I feel comfortable sharing my life with. When I get my hair cut, he notices. When I dress up to go out at night, he compliments me. When I cry, he wipes my tears. When I feel lonely, he makes me feel loved.

We all follow our own rules. Taking Greg back was my decision to make and I wouldn't have if I hadn't felt that Greg, and most importantly that I, had learned something. I *know* that what has happened will never happen again and I really, really believe it. Because if I didn't feel so sure about our future, there's no way that I could go through with this.

I have a feeling that's what was in your letter, Alex, but don't worry about me. I'm fine. Thank you, thank you, thank you, for caring about me so much. There aren't enough friends like you in the world.

From	Alex
To	Rosie
Subject	Greg

And that's all I've ever wanted. For you to be happy.

From	Mum
To	Stephanie
Subject	Is this working?

I think I've just about figured out this email thingy. Anyway, I just wanted to see if our plans are still in place for your father's sixtieth. He thinks it's a few quiet drinks with Jack and Pauline, so don't email me back on this address because he can read it too. Call me on my mobile. I really would love you to come. It would be nice for us all to be together again and I think it would be good for Rosie. I'm worried about her, she's so upset about Greg that she's lost so much weight. Your father is only two steps away from punching Greg in the face, which won't do anyone any good. Especially not your father's heart.

Dear Alex,

I think I'm going to organise a search party. Have you fallen off the edge of the earth? Are you still alive?

I called your mother the other day and she hasn't heard from you very much either. Is everything OK? Because if it's not, I have a right to know. You're supposed to confide in me because I'm your best friend and . . . it's the law. And if things are OK then contact me anyway. I need gossip. It's section two of the same law.

Everything here is as crazy and unpredictable as usual. Katie is eleven now, as you know. Thank you for her present. She is so grown up that she tells me that she doesn't need to inform me where she is going during the day or when she'll be coming home. Unimportant information like that, which a mother apparently doesn't need to know. I thought I had another few years left until she became a monster. I am now under instructions to knock on her bedroom door three times before I'm allowed to enter, just so she can identify the intruder. (I'm quite jealous because Toby only has to knock once. Greg, on the other hand, has to knock thirteen times. Poor Greg.)

I'm not sure if she is still writing to you, but if she fills you in on any interesting aspects of her terribly busy and secretive life, please let me know. I'm her mother and that is definitely the law.

How is Josh? I would love to see him again. We must make arrangements to meet up soon. I don't want him not knowing who I am.

Write to me, ring me, email me or fly over and visit me. Or you could do all of those things. Just do anything to let me know that you're still walking the earth.

Miss you.

Love,

Rosie

Dear Rosie,

Just to let you know I'm still alive—just about. Sally seems to be sucking all the life out of me these days. We're finalising the divorce . . . it's a nightmare.

So that's what's going on with me. Give my love to Katie.

Alex

From   Rosie
To   Alex
Subject   Grown-ups

What are the two of us like? I was going to say who knew we'd be going through so much 'grown-up stuff', but I don't consider you going through a divorce and me trying to pick up the pieces of my marriage is necessarily grown up. I think we both had it pretty much sussed when we were playing cops and robbers in the back garden. It's all been downhill from there!

The weather has been beautiful over here for the past few weeks. I love June in Dublin. The sound of laughter is in the air, everyone is full of smiles, there's a bounce in their step. The verandah of the hotel is busy with people taking drinks out in the sun: Long Island iced tea, gin and tonic, tangy orange with crushed ice, lime-green concoctions, fruity cocktails and bowls of ice cream. Clothes are being discarded and hung on the backs of chairs. Days like this don't come often and you can tell everyone wishes they did.

And I sit here and think of you. I send you my love.

From   Alex
To   Rosie
Subject   Happy!

You sounded happy and very poetic! I've just returned from a weekend with Josh. He's a feisty little thing now, Rosie. He's running around trying to grab anything and everything. Seeing him always lights me up, as if a switch is flicked somewhere in my body. I could watch him for ever. Watch how he learns, how he eventually finds a way to do things without help from anyone. Josh always takes that extra step when he nos he shouldn't. He does it anyway and he learns. I think we adults have a lot to learn from that. Perhaps to be not so afraid and over-sensible about reaching for goals.

So I am following Josh's lead. An eminent heart surgeon is giving a talk during the week. It's a few days of seminars about a new procedure he has developed. I'm going to try to meet him—me along with the other thousand or so wannabe heart surgeons who will be there. Rumour has it he's from Ireland and has moved here to develop his studies—and needs some help.

Cross your fingers and pray for a miracle.

From   Rosie
To   Alex
Subject   Mysterious meeting

I have a mysterious meeting with Bill, my boss, next week. I have no idea what it's about, but I'm quite nervous about it. He flew over yesterday in a not-so-good mood and has had a series of secret meetings all day. Lots of suspicious-looking people, dressed in dark suits, have been arriving to talk to him on the hour every hour. What makes it even worse is the fact that his brother, Bob, is flying over tomorrow morning. They only ever get together to do the hiring and firing. I hope they don't fire me. I don't know what I would do. I think I would sleep with him to keep working here. That's how much I love it. Or how scared I am about having to search for a job elsewhere. Or how desperate I am to sleep with a man other than Greg for a change. I love him but, bless him, he's a sucker for routine.

Better go and look like I'm really busy so that they will have absolutely no grounds to fire me. Cross your fingers for me, and I'll cross mine for you.

From   Alex
To   Rosie
Subject   Chill out!

For Chrisssake, Rosie Dunne, I love you with all my heart but you need to chill out! Everything will be fine. Just about to leave the apartment now to go to a seminar. Good luck to the both of us!

Kevin,

Hi, son. I know I'm not one to write letters, but I'm not sure if you gave your mother and me the correct phone number of the staff barracks. Whenever I call it just keeps on ringing and ringing and that's at all hours of the day and night. You either gave us the wrong number, there's something wrong with your phone, or everybody is working so hard they're not there to answer my calls.

It's a shame you couldn't make it home for my retirement party. The company invited the entire family. They really treated us well for the night—treated me well for over thirty-five years, in fact. Stephanie, Pierre and Jean-Louis made it over from France. Rosie, Greg and young Katie were there too. It was a good night. I'm not picking on you, son—just wished you had been there too, that's all. It was an emotional night. If you had been there you would have seen your old man cry.

So no more early mornings for me. I caught up on a whole load of sleep I never even thought I needed. The garden is spotless, everything in the house that was once broken is now fixed. I've played golf three times this week, visited Rosie twice, took Katie and Toby out for the day, and I still feel like hopping into my car, speeding down to the office and teaching the rookies a thing or two about how to do business. But they won't care; they want and need to learn it for themselves.

So I thought I would join the Dunne women in writing. It seems that's all they do. Keeps the phone bills down, I suppose. Let me know how things are going for you, son.

Did you hear about our Rosie's job?

From Dad

From	Kevin
To	Stephanie
Subject	Dad

How are things? I just got a letter from Dad today. Dad writing a letter is weird in itself. Is he OK? He sounded like another man altogether. Not necessarily a bad thing. Sorry I wasn't there for his retirement do. Should have made more of an effort to be there.

Tell Pierre and Jean-Louis I was asking for them. Tell Pierre I'll beat his culinary skills hands down next time I see him! Dad mentioned something about Rosie's job? What has she done now?

From	Stephanie
To	Mum
Subject	Kevin and Dad

Something must be in the water over there in Ireland because I just received an email from your son, my little brother Kevin—yes, Kevin, the guy who never keeps in touch with family unless he needs to borrow money. He was writing to tell me that Dad had written to him and he was worried! Did you even know that Dad could lick a stamp?

I'm assuming Dad is just feeling very contemplative now that he has entered a new era in his life. Now at least he has *time* to think. The both of you have worked so hard all your lives. Now Kevin your baby is gone, Rosie and Katie are gone, I'm gone and the house is finally all yours. I suppose I can understand how it's difficult for Dad to get his head round it. You were both used to a house full of screaming kids and bickering teenagers. When we finally grew up along came a crying baby and you were so good to help Rosie out. I know it was hard for you financially too. Now it's time to treat yourselves.

Kevin mentioned something about Rosie's job; I don't want to call her until I've heard from you about it. She was so worried that she was going to lose it. Let me know.

From   Mum
To   Stephanie
Subject   Re: Kevin and Dad

You're absolutely right. I think your father has a lot of thinking to do and enough time in the day to do it now. I love having him home! He's not rushing off all the time or thinking about a problem at work while I'm trying to have a conversation with him. It's like he's all here with me now—body and mind.

I'm amazed you didn't hear about Rosie's job. I thought you would have been one of the first people she'd have told (apart from Alex, of course). That girl has me so worried at times. Honestly, she kept telling me all week that she was going to lose her job, then finally she calls me to tell me that she had a meeting with her bosses and she's got a promotion!

Oh, Stephanie, we were so thrilled for her! I'm surprised she hasn't told you the good news yet, but it was only a few days ago. Anyway, I'll let her tell you herself or else I'll be in trouble for spoiling the surprise. I'd better go now; your father's calling me. We're about to go down to the garden centre. If he plants any more flowers or trees in that garden, we'll have to apply for planning permission for a jungle!

Take care, love, and hugs and kisses to baby Jean-Louis from Grandma and Granddad!

From   Stephanie
To   Rosie
Subject   Job promotion!

I know you're at work so I won't ring you. Received an email from Mum today. What's this I hear about a job promotion? Email me ASAP!

From   Rosie
To   Stephanie
Subject   Job promotion

Can't believe Mum opened her big mouth! YES!! The job title is 'Hotel Host', and before you get overexcited like our beloved parents did, it's not the manager's job. I will be the primary source of information for guests to ensure maximum client satisfaction (or so they tell me . . .)!

It was the surprise of *all* surprises. I really had convinced myself that Bill and Bob Lake were going to ask me to quietly and calmly return to my desk, gather my belongings, leave the premises and never return.

But they were so generous to me. They pumped me full of confidence as they went through what the job would entail. They said that they were delighted with my 'performance' within the hotel over the past few years (and I really hope they weren't referring to the time when I lay across the piano and sang Barbra Streisand songs after all the residents had gone to bed). There they were, telling me I had an abundance of charm and confidence, when deep down I was just waiting for the moment they would break into a smile, look at me as though I was a fool for believing them before telling me the promotion was all a joke. I kept looking round for the hidden camera.

But it seems that I will be moving to a new hotel that's yet to be built (hence all the secret meetings with men and women in dark suits). But if they *are* serious, then my job is to be solely responsible for the running of all aspects of the resort and I'll have to liaise with head office and provide weekly reports. I've never had to 'liaise' before. It sounds sexy and dangerous.

Apparently I have a flair for organising and have good communication skills. Anyone who has seen me rushing to get all my Christmas shopping done in the last hour on Christmas Eve knows the truth. But we all have our different ways of seeing things.

From   Alex
To   Rosie
Subject   Congratulations!

I am so proud of you! If I was there, I would twirl you around and give you a great big sloppy kiss! You see, Rosie, things *can* happen for you, all you need is a lot more faith and to stop being so negative all the time!

From   Ruby
To   Rosie
Subject   Cork?

What do you mean, the bloody hotel is being built down in Cork? And they only tell you now? Did they think that piece of information was *irrelevant* to you? For Chrissake, Rosie, how are you going to drag your family down to *the other side of the country?*

Do you even want to move? Oh my God, I think I'm going to have a heart attack! Email me back ASAP!!!

From   Rosie
To   Ruby
Subject   Re: Cork?

Oh, Ruby, I don't know what to do. I know that I want this job but there are two other people to think about. I'll have to have a chat with Katie and Greg about it tonight. Pray for me!

PART THREE

Dear Alex,

I was so happy when I finally got round to shutting the door on this horrible day. 'It's only a job,' Greg said. Well, if a job is so unimportant then why is he so adamantly refusing to leave his own? It's not only a job, though. So they offered me a promotion, but with it they offered me confidence and a little bit of self-belief.

But this time I wasn't even given the choice to screw it up myself. That decision was made for me. Katie won't leave Toby and I'm not quite hating Greg enough to storm off to Cork in a huff on my own. Although, I'm pretty close to it. God, does that man make my blood boil!

In his opinion, he has a great job here that pays well and I have a good job that pays OK. Why on earth would he want to move to a city where his wife will have a brilliant job and earn great money? Oh, I forgot. They don't have any banks in Cork so there's no way he could ever find a job or be transferred.

On the other hand, I can honestly say that Katie's friendship with Toby is possibly the most important thing to her. He's a great supportive force in her life; he makes her happy and keeps the innocence in her eyes. Children need close friends to help them grow up, to discover things about themselves and about life. They also need close friends to keep them sane.

So I can't accept the job of my dreams because my family won't move with me. Big deal. It's not as though I arrange my life to revolve around them. It's not as though I come home from work tired and still have dinner on the table for them, it's not as though I perform wonderful supportive wifely chores when there's a million other things I could be doing. It's not as though I defend my daughter at school, constantly fighting with the teachers about how she is not Satan's daughter. It's not as though I tolerate Greg's mother for dinner every Sunday and listen to her whinge about how the food isn't cooked right, about my hair, about the way I dress, about the way I have chosen to raise Katie.

Just as well I don't do any of those things.

But who cares? I get burnt toast and milky tea one morning once a year on Mother's Day as thanks. And that should make up for it, shouldn't it? Greg always tells me I'm forever chasing rainbows. Maybe I should stop now.

Love, Rosie

From   Alex
To   Rosie
Subject   Rosie Dunne!

I hate to see you miss out on another opportunity. Isn't there anything you can do to convince whatshisname?

From   Rosie
To   Alex
Subject   Family

Thanks, Alex, but no. I can't force my family to leave their home if they don't want to. I can't live my life pretending it's just me in the world. But how much easier it would be! Anyway, it's just another missed opportunity.

So enough about me—how are all those lectures going? Find out who Mr Fantastic Surgeon is yet?

Thanks for your support, as always.

From   Alex
To   Rosie
Subject   Family duties!

You and your 'duties' to your family. I just don't want you to be the only person following the rules, that's all.

The lectures are going great. You will never believe who the surgeon is! Your very favourite man—Reginald Williams.

From   Rosie
To   Alex
Subject   Reginald Williams!

Pass me a bucket while I puke. You mean Slutty Bethany's father? So do you think you're in with a chance to be one of the 'chosen few' to work with him, seeing as you were an almost-son-in-law? There's nothing like a bit of nepotism to keep the world a just and equal place.

From   Alex
To   Rosie
Subject   Nepotism!

I think the chances of that happening are fairly slim. I think I sealed my own doom when I dumped his favourite and only daughter!

From   Rosie
To   Alex
Subject   Slutty Bethany

Oh, I don't know about sealing your doom. I think it may have been the *best* move you have ever made. Come to think of it, I haven't seen Slutty Bethany for about ten years! What is she up to I wonder . . .

From   Rosie
To   Stephanie
Subject   Best friends stay with you for ever

Oh, wise and wonderful sister Stephanie, you were right! When I was seventeen you told me that girlfriends come and go but best friends stay with you for ever. I found myself saying today, 'I wonder what Slutty Bethany is doing these days . . .' The exact statement I never wanted Alex to have to say about me. I didn't believe you at the time but I sure do now!!

FOR A SPECIAL FRIEND ON HER FORTIETH BIRTHDAY
MAY THIS BE THE BEGINNING OF A HAPPY AND SUCCESSFUL YEAR FOR YOU!

Sorry, Ruby, this was the only half-decent card I could find that didn't go on about how your life is almost ending. Thanks for always being there for me, even though you'd rather not be! You're a fantastic friend to have. Let's enjoy this birthday and good luck in your new year.
Love, Rosie
PS. I hope you like your pressie.

This voucher entitles the bearer to ten lessons in Salsa dancing.
Ricardo will be your teacher every Wednesday @ 8 p.m. in the school hall of St Patrick's Secondary School.

You have an instant message from: RUBY.
Ruby: I'm all salsa'd out! I can't remember the last time I was in

this much pain! It took me twenty minutes to get out of bed. But thank you for the gift, Rosie; we had fun in the class, didn't we? I can't remember ever laughing so much in my life, which is probably why my stomach is so sore. Thank you for reminding me that I'm a woman, that I have hips, that I can be sexy, that I can laugh and have fun. And thank you for bringing the sexy Ricardo into my life. Can't wait to feel this way again next week. Now, after all my whinging and moaning, how do you feel?

Rosie: Oh, fine, thanks. No complaints.

Ruby: Ha!

Rosie: OK, OK, so I feel a little stiff.

Ruby: Ha!

Rosie: Oh, OK, so the bus had to lower the wheelchair ramp for me this morning because I couldn't lift my legs.

Ruby: That's more like it . . . So what's Alex up to these days?

Rosie: He's still hanging around Slutty Bethany's dad, trying to get a job chopping people's bodies up.

Ruby: Oh . . . kay, who is Bethany, why is she a slut and what business is her father in?

Rosie: Oh, sorry. Bethany is Alex's first love, she's a slut because I say so, and her dad is a surgeon of some sort.

Ruby: How exciting—the return of one of Alex's ex-girlfriends. This will be a page turner.

Rosie: No, she's not around any more; Alex is just attending some lectures being held by her father.

Ruby: Oh, Rosie Dunne, expect the unexpected, for once. Maybe this time you won't get a shock when things don't go your way.

IRISH SURGEON TO JOIN WILLIAMS
by Cliona Taylor

Irish surgeon Reginald Williams, who recently achieved success with his much-publicised new cardiac surgery, today announced he would be welcoming fellow Irishman Dr Alex Stewart to the award-winning team. The 30-year-old Harvard graduate says, 'I have always followed Dr Williams's studies with great interest and admiration,' and that he is both 'delighted and honoured to become a new member of this ground-breaking and, most important, life-saving new surgery'.

Dr Stewart is originally from Dublin, and moved to Boston at age 17 when his father accepted a post with the prominent US law firm Charles & Charles. Dr Stewart completed five years in Boston Central Hospital on a general surgical residency training programme before joining Dr Williams for further cardiac surgery studies. Pictured above (from left to right) are Dr Reginald Williams with his wife, Miranda, and his daughter, Bethany, who accompanied Dr Stewart to the Reginald Williams Foundation for Heart Disease charity ball last night.

From   Rosie
To   Alex
Subject   Congratulations!

Heard about your good news. You've made it into every newspaper over here today. We're all so proud of you. I think Toby wants to be a doctor when he's older, because he'll get his photograph in the newspaper just like you. Katie is now insisting she wants to be a dance club DJ. You've had no effect on her in that department whatsoever; she'll be in a business that *gives* people heart attacks.

I'm still at the Two Lakes Hotel. Still at reception; still providing the big bad public with a glass roof over their heads. Alex, please write me a letter and let me know what's going on in your life.

Love, Rosie

Rosie,

Sorry I've been so distant recently, but I've been so busy. Still, it's no excuse for not being in touch.

I have good news! I'll be coming back to Ireland to visit next month. Mum and Dad are coming back too, and Sally has agreed to let me take Josh for the fortnight, seeing as she had him last Christmas. It's been a long time since the entire family has been back together and Mum decided she wanted to be with Phil, his twenty kids and the rest of the family and all her friends, for their fortieth wedding anniversary. Forty years—imagine! I don't no how they did it. You're doing well, though. How long have you and whatshisname been together? Long enough, I would imagine.

I can't remember when I last spent Christmas in Dublin. But soon we'll be reunited, Rosie.

Alex

From   Rosie
To   Alex
Subject   G. R. E. G.

Hmm . . . Alex, you're going to have to learn my husband's name before you come over. It's Greg. G. R. E. G. Try and remember it, please.

Did I tell you that Ruby and I are salsa dancing queens? I got the first batch of classes as a present for Ruby's fortieth a few months ago and we enjoyed it so much we kept it up. In fact, Ruby's started taking the classes twice a week now but I can't go on Mondays because I have to take Katie to basketball practice. Ruby insists that it's not as much fun without me, because she has to dance with tutu-wearing Miss Behave, a six-foot-tall drag queen with the longest legs and blond hair, who's trying to learn salsa for her show, which is on at the local gay club.

Anyway, Ruby and I are really enjoying ourselves, and I hope you're having some sort of life, Alex, and that you're not overworking yourself. Go on any dates recently?

From   Alex
To   Rosie
Subject   Dating?

I might have . . .

You have an instant message from: ROSIE.
Rosie: I'm all ears now. Anyone I know?
Alex: Maybe . . .
Rosie: Oh, please tell me it's anyone but Slutty Bethany.
Alex: Well, I'd better rush off because I have to get ready for tonight.
Rosie: You got a date?
Alex: Maybe . . .
Rosie: Well, whatever you're doing, enjoy it. But not too much.
Alex: I wouldn't dare dream of it!

You have an instant message from: ROSIE.
Rosie: Was just instant messaging Alex a few seconds ago.
Ruby: Yeah? Did he say anything interesting?
Rosie: No. We were just catching up on old times.
Ruby: Good for you both. You and Greg have any plans for tonight?
Rosie: He's going on a date, Ruby.
Ruby: Who is? Greg is?
Rosie: No! Alex.
Ruby: Oh, are we still talking about him? Who's he going out with?
Rosie: I don't know. He wouldn't tell me.
Ruby: Well, he's allowed to have a private life, isn't he?
Rosie: Yeah, I suppose.
Ruby: And it's good that he's able to finally move on after having his heart broken and going through a divorce, isn't it?
Rosie: Yeah, I suppose.

Ruby: Well, it's good that you feel that way. You're a great friend,
           Rosie, always wanting the best for Alex.
Rosie: Yeah. Yeah, I am.

You have an instant message from: ALEX.
Alex: Hi, Phil. What you doing?
Phil: Surfing the internet, searching for a crank hole cover for a
           1939 Dodge Sedan. It's a rare car.
Alex: Right.
Phil: Something on your mind, Alex?
Alex: No, no.
Phil: Well then, did you message me for any particular reason?
Alex: No, just wanted to catch up with my big brother.
Phil: Right. How's the job?
Alex: I'm going on a date tonight.
Phil: Really? That's good.
Alex: Yeah, it is.
Phil: Meeting someone new will stop you from working so much.
Alex: Yeah.
Phil: Does Rosie know?
Alex: Yeah. Just was chatting to her there by instant message before
           I messaged you.
Phil: How's that for a coincidence? Well, what was her reaction?
Alex: Not much of one, actually.
Phil: She wasn't angry?
Alex: No.
Phil: Or jealous?
Alex: No.
Phil: She didn't beg you not to date other women?
Alex: Nope.
Phil: That's good then, isn't it? You've got a good friend there. One
           that wants you to move on, and find happiness.
Alex: Yeah. That's good. Good to have a friend like that.

You have an instant message from: KATIE.
Katie: I look like a goofball.
Toby: You do not look like a goofball.
Katie: You don't even know what a goofball looks like.
Toby: They're only braces, Katie. Could you do me a favour?
Katie: What?
Toby: Just say sizzling sausages one more time.
Katie: TOBY! That is so not funny. You said you wouldn't laugh. I'm
           gonna be stuck with these stupid train tracks for years now,

and it's not my fault they're giving me a lisp. I'll even have them for my thirteenth birthday. *Everyone's* coming to my party, people I haven't seen for yonks, and I want to look nice.

Toby: Let me guess, you'll be trying to look nice in black again.

Katie: Yep.

Toby: You're so morbid.

Katie: No, Toby, I'm sophisticated.

Toby: Whatever. Who's going, anyway?

Katie: Alex, Aunt Steph, Pierre and Jean-Louis, Grandma and Granddad, Ruby, Teddy and her weirdo son that never speaks, Mum, of course, and a few girls from basketball.

Toby: Well, yippee. What about your uncle Kevin?

Katie: Does he ever come to anything? He's still working in that posh hotel down in Kilkenny. He said he's sorry he couldn't come but he sent me a card with a tenner inside.

Toby: Well, that's all you want anyway. What about Greg?

Katie: Nope, he's working in the States for a week. He gave me thirteen euros. A euro for every year.

Toby: Cool. So is there anyone under the age of eighty coming that's not on your crappy basketball team?

Katie: Alex is bringing Josh.

Toby: Josh is four years old, Katie.

Katie: Exactly. You'll have lots in common. Same brain power.

Toby: Oh ha ha, metal mouth.

To my wonderful daughter
You're a teenager!
Happy birthday, darling.
Lots of love,
Mum

To Katie
You're a teen today,
Hip hip hip hooray!
It's a joyous day,
You're a teen today!
Greg

You're a groovy chick!!
Happy birthday, pet.
Love you lots like jelly tots!
Love, Grandma and Granddad

Happy birthday, Glitter Girl!
Take this money and buy yourself an item of clothing that's not
black. I dare you.
Love, Ruby, Teddy and Gary

For my niece
Bon Anniversaire!
Love, Stephanie, Pierre and Jean-Louis

To my Goddaughter
Happy 13th, you little adult!
I'm so happy to share the day with you.
All my love,
Alex

You may be a teenager but you're still ugly.
From Toby

From   Kevin
To   Rosie
Subject   Secret visit!

Kevin here. Sorry I couldn't be home for Katie's birthday, but it's absolutely crazy at work. The golf open is being held here this week and all the world's greatest golfers have booked in.

Anyway, the reason I'm emailing you is because I can't believe you kept it a secret from me that you have the honeymoon suite booked out for the weekend! Good ol' Greg's a bit flash, paying for all that, isn't he? Anyway, I'm glad you're finally coming down to see me. It's about time. I'll make sure the staff treat you extra specially, and I'll even tell the lads in the kitchen not to spit in your food.

From   Rosie
To   Kevin
Subject   Secret visit

Sorry, my baby brother, but it must be another Rosie Dunne. I wish it *was* me!

From   Kevin
To   Rosie
Subject   Secret visit

There's only one Rosie Dunne! No, the booking is actually under Greg's name. Shit! I hope I haven't spoilt a surprise. Just FORGET I said anything. Sorry.

From   Rosie
To   Kevin
Subject   Secret visit

Don't worry, Kev—what day is the booking for?

From   Kevin
To   Rosie
Subject   Secret visit

Friday until Monday. Oh, please don't tell him I told you. What an idiot Greg is. He should have known I work here.

You have an instant message from: RUBY

Ruby: I have to admit that I'm surprised. That's very romantic of him!

Rosie: I know! I'm so excited, Ruby. I've dreamed of staying in that hotel for years. Oh, I bet the little shampoos and shower caps in the bathrooms are just the most beautiful things.

Ruby: Christ, Rosie, you could open your own shop with the amount of hotel products you've stolen.

Rosie: It's not *stealing*. They're not just there to be *looked* at. Although, they do seem to be nailing down the hair dryers a lot more these days.

Ruby: Rosie, you have a problem. Swiftly moving on, when are you being whisked away to the lap of luxury?

Rosie: Friday. I can't wait! I'm so pleased that he's made this effort. I am really, really happy.

From   Rosie
To   Greg
Subject   Coming home?

It's Friday and I was just wondering what time you'll be home?

From   Greg
To   Rosie
Subject   Re: Coming home?

Hi, love. I told you I'd be here in the States until Monday. I should be home in the evening sometime. Sorry if there was some confusion. I'm sure I told you it was Monday and not Friday. I wish it was today, darling, I really do.

From   Rosie
To   Kevin
Subject   *This* weekend?

Do you think you could be mistaken about that booking for *this* weekend?

From   Kevin
To   Rosie
Subject   Re: *This* weekend?

It's definitely correct, Rosie. Greg checked in this morning. Aren't you here?

From   Rosie
To   Alex
Subject   Whatshisname

Whatshisname is gone. For good.

From   Alex
To   Rosie
Subject   Re: Whatshisname

I'll book flights for you and Katie to come over here immediately. I'll let you know the details within the next hour. Don't worry.

From   Rosie
To   Alex
Subject   Please wait

Just give me a little time before you book those flights. There are a few things I want to tie up here before I leave. And once I go over to you in Boston I'm *never* coming back here. Just please wait for me.

Hi, it's me, Alex.

Look, I'm really sorry but I'm not going to be able to make it out for dinner tonight. I'm sorry to tell you in a letter but it's the best way I no how. You're a wonderful, intelligent woman but my heart lies with someone else. It has done so for many, many years. I hope that when we meet we can remain friends at least.

Alex

Dear Bill Lake,

It is with great sadness that I submit my resignation. I will remain working in the Two Lakes Hotel for the next two weeks as I'm contracted to do so.

On a more personal level, I would like to thank you for five great years of allowing me to work in your company. It has been an honour.

Yours sincerely,

Rosie Dunne

From   Toby
To   Katie
Subject   Disaster!

YOU WHAT?? You CAN'T be moving away! This is awful! Ask your mum if it's OK for you to stay with me for a while. I'll ask my mum and dad too. They'll definitely say yes. You can't leave.
What about school?
What about the basketball team?
What about wanting to DJ for Club Sauce?
What about me?

From   Katie
To   Toby
Subject   Re: Disaster!

I can't change her mind. I can't stop crying. This is the worst thing that's ever happened to me in my whole entire life. I don't even want to go to Boston. What's so good about Boston?
Oh, I hate Greg so much. It's all his fault we have to move away. It's all his fault Mum is upset. I hate him, I hate him, I hate him.
At least Alex and Josh are in Boston. That's something. I think we're gonna stay with them for a while. So we're really going, Toby. She's not just threatening. Mum said you can visit us all the time. Promise me you will. You may annoy the hell out of me, Toby, but you're my best friend in the whole entire world and I'll miss you so much. Even if you are a boy.
We can write to each other all the time. That's what Mum and Alex did when they were younger and he had to move away.
Love,
Katie

You have an instant message from: RUBY.
Ruby: So you're leaving in two weeks.
Rosie: Yep.
Ruby: You're doing the right thing, you know.
Rosie: Funny. You're the only one who seems to think that.
Ruby: I'm the only one who knows how you feel about him.
Rosie: Oh no, I'm not in the mood to go jumping into another relationship. I hate all men right now.
Ruby: Including Alex?
Rosie: Including Alex, my father, George the lollipop man, and my brother for telling me.
Ruby: You would have wanted to know, though.
Rosie: Yes, and I'm not blaming him. He hadn't a clue Greg was

	messing around. Again. The lying little . . . aaaah! I don't think I've ever been so angry in my life.
Ruby:	So who am I going to go to salsa lessons with now?
Rosie:	I'm sure Miss Behave will be delighted to be your partner.
Ruby:	I finally get to dance with a man and he wears tights. Oh, I'll miss you so much, Rosie Dunne. It's not often in life a woman finds a friend like you.
Rosie:	And I you, Ruby, but as much as Greg has hurt me, he's given me an opportunity to start from fresh.

You have an instant message from: ALEX

Alex:	You were right, Phil. She's coming over to me. I just had to leave it and let her come at her own pace.
Phil:	Lucky for me I was right! It was a good guess, wasn't it? So did she tell you that she loves you, that she never should have married that idiot and that she only wants to be with you and all that other stuff that they say in the movies?
Alex:	No.
Phil:	She didn't tell you she loves you?
Alex:	No.
Phil:	Did you tell her?
Alex:	No.
Phil:	Then what's she going over for?
Alex:	She just said that she wanted to get out of Dublin and that she needed a change of scenery and a friendly face.
Phil:	Oh.
Alex:	What do you think that means?
Phil:	Probably exactly what it says.

From	Alex
To	Rosie
Subject	You and Katie

I'm so excited that you'll be here so soon. Josh is practically running up the walls with excitement. He loves Katie and is delighted about your decision to come live with us for a while. I've a friend who has a friend who owns a hotel and they are looking for a manager. You are more than qualified for the job.

I can help you through this, Rosie. Remember I've been in your shoes. I no how it feels to go through a marriage breakup. I'm here for you one hundred per cent. Moving to Boston may be fourteen years later than you planned but it's better late than never. Josh and I will be here waiting. See you next week.

You're moving away!
Good luck, Rosie. We'll all miss you here at the Two Lakes.
Bill, Bob, Tania, Steven, Geoffrey, Fiona, Tabitha, Henry and Grace

Sniff, sniff. I'll miss you, Rosie Dunne.
Good luck with your new life. Send us an email every now and
again. Lots of love, Ruby

Rosie and Katie,
We are so sorry that you feel you have to go. We are so sorry this has hap-
pened. We will miss you both so, so much, but we hope you can find eternal
happiness. No more tears for our two girls. Let the world be good to you.
Phone us when you land.
Love, Mum and Dad

Good luck with the move. My fingers are crossed for you and Katie.
We're all here for you, if you need us.
Love, Stephanie, Pierre and Jean-Louis

Sorry you had to go.
Good luck.
Kev

Katie—Good luck in your new home. I'll miss you.
Love, Toby

Dear Rosie,
Before you rip this up please give me a chance to explain. Firstly, I sincere-
ly apologise from the bottom of my heart for the years gone by. For not being
there for you, for not supporting you and giving you the help you deserved. I
am filled with regret and disappointment with myself for the way I have
behaved and chosen to live my life. I know there is nothing I can do to change
or make better the years I acted so foolishly and mistreated the two of you.
But please at least give me a chance to build a better future, to make right
what's wrong. I can understand how you must feel so angry, betrayed and
hurt, and you must hate me so much but there's not just yourself to think of.
I look back on my life and I wonder what have I to show for all these years?
I haven't done many things in my life that I'm proud of. I have no stories of
success to tell. There is only one thing in this life that I'm proud of. And that's
my little girl.
The fact is that I have a little girl, who isn't even 'little' any more. I'm not
proud of the way I've treated her. I woke up one morning a few weeks ago on
my thirty-second birthday and suddenly it was as if all the sense that's been

missing for the past thirty-two years came to me in an instant. I realised I had a daughter, a teenage daughter who I know nothing of, and who knows nothing of me. I would love the chance to get to know her. I'm told that her name is Katie. That's a nice name. I wonder what she looks like. Does she look like me?

I know I haven't shown any signs of deserving this, but if you and Katie are willing to let me into your lives I can prove to you it won't be a waste of time. Katie will meet her father and I will see my daughter—how could that ever be considered a waste?

Please contact me, Rosie. Give me a chance to undo all the mistakes of my past and to help create a new future for Katie and me.

Best wishes,
Brian

You have an instant message from: ROSIE

Rosie: No no no no no no no no no.

Ruby: Rosie, calm down. You're upset.

Rosie: Too right I'm upset! Where the hell has he been for the past thirteen years? Where did he disappear to for the most important years of Katie's life—or *my life*, for that matter? And he has the cheek to stroll back into our lives after thirteen years, with a little shrug of the shoulders and a pathetic little sorry, just after I decide to move to Boston where I should have been anyway had it not been for him ruining my plans, turning my life upside-down and legging it off to another country. Fuck him. This time it's about me, Rosie Dunne, and no one else.

Ruby: But, Rosie, you're wrong. It's about Katie too. She needs to know he wants to see her.

Rosie: But if I tell her, then she's going to want to see him. She'll be so excited to meet him and he'll probably let her down again.

Ruby: But, Rosie, it could turn out really well. He may have really changed. You never know.

Rosie: You're right, you *never* know. EVER.

Dear Stephanie,

Congratulations on the pregnancy! I'm thrilled for you and Pierre. I'm sure baby number two will be a joy as Jean-Louis has been. I'm assuming Mum has told you the news. She's delighted I'm not moving to America any more. Alex isn't. He cursed and swore and screamed every bad word under the sun at me. He thinks I'm giving in again and letting everyone walk all over me so now he's in a huff and won't speak to me. I may have let people walk all over me *before but not this time. Katie is number one in my life and my reason for being is to ensure she gets the best chance at happiness possible.*

I don't quite know where I should go from here. I have no job, no home and I'm back living with Mum and Dad again. Everything about this house brings back a time when I wasn't happy. I had a wonderful childhood but the years with Katie were so difficult, they're the strongest memories I have of this house—the smells, the noises, the wallpaper, the bedrooms all remind me of late nights, early mornings and worrying.

Anyway, forgive me for not being in contact over the past while but I've been trying to get my head round all of this. I'm trying to make some sense out of the phrase 'everything happens for a reason', and I think I've figured out what the reason is—to piss me off.

Rosie

My sincerest apologies for that ridiculous note I sent you last week. Just put it down to a momentary lapse in concentration, I'm a complete fool (as you're already aware) and I have absolutely no idea what I was thinking. But you'll be pleased to no (I hope) that I've landed back on earth with a thump and I'm willing and able to give us another go. So let's not waste any more of our valuable time but get down to the important stuff. Are we back on for tonight?

Alex

You have an instant message from: RUBY.

Ruby: How was your meeting with Brian?

Rosie: OK. He booked a flight over here as soon as he got off the phone from me so it seems he is very serious about his new role of fatherhood. He tells me he's been living in Ibiza for the past thirteen years, where he now owns a nightclub.

Ruby: How did you feel when you saw him?

Rosie: I had to muster all my strength to stop myself from punching him. Katie was so nervous about meeting him that she was shaking like a leaf and clinging to me. We met him in the coffee shop in Jervis Street Shopping Centre and, I have to admit, as we were approaching his table I felt sick. Sick with anger that the miserable little man who I was going to have to force myself to be nice to for the next hour, and help to become a part of my daughter's life, was the very same person who had caused me so much heartache in the past. *But,* for the sake of Katie's relationship with Brian, whatever feelings of resentment I have for him need to be kept to myself.

Ruby: You've done a good thing, Rosie. It must have been difficult. How long will he be around for?

Rosie: A few weeks and then he'll have to head back to Ibiza. The summer months are obviously when he's at his busiest. He'll be back a few times to visit Katie, of course, and then he's going to hire someone else to run the club so he can stay in Dublin for the winter. He really seems to be taking this seriously and I'm glad for Katie's sake.

Ruby: Any luck finding a job?

Rosie: Well, I had just switched on the computer to search the internet when you messaged me.

Ruby: Oh, OK, well, I'll go now and let you become the responsible parent you should be. By the way, I'm making my Gary come to salsa dancing classes with me. Miss Behave drank one too many sangrias at the summer party last week and turned her ankle in her twelve-inch platforms.

Rosie: Oh God, poor Miss Behave. But how on earth did you get Gary to agree to go to dance classes with you? Did you threaten his life or something?!

Ruby: Yes.

Rosie: You evil, evil woman.

Ruby: Thank you. Now go find a job. In a hotel. You hear me?

Rosie: Loud and Clear.

Dear Alex,

When will you stop giving me the silent treatment? You must understand that I can't make decisions to suit myself. I've Katie to think about too. It is important for her to get to know Brian. You of all people should know how it is to want and need to be there for your child. Brian has finally realised that he wants to be here for Katie. It's better late than never, as you always say. Some things are.

Let's not allow your disapproval of my decision to stay affect our friendship. Perhaps sometime, someday we can be reunited in the way we planned when we were seven years old. I'm lucky to have a friend like you, Alex Stewart; you really are my moonbeam—guiding the way for me all the time. I don't know how unrealistic the promise we made to each other as children was, to stay together side by side for ever, but we have remained friends from across the seas for over twenty years, and that, I'm sure, is some feat.

I've been job hunting all week. My aim was to try to get a job in a hotel, surprise, surprise, but it seems that as the summer has already begun students and immigrants only too willing to be underpaid have already taken every-thing for the next few months. Unfortunately, my position at the Two Lakes Hotel has been filled. Brian has offered to pay child support but I don't want his money. I managed before without him; I certainly don't need his help now.

There hasn't been a peep out of whatshisname lately. That man is too afraid of his own shadow, never mind of me. I filed for a divorce last week; I need him out of my life for good. I'll dance around the streets naked when the divorce is final.

Did you hear that Stephanie is pregnant? She's due in November so all the family are naturally thrilled. Mum and Dad are in great form, always asking for you and Josh, and they're very much enjoying their retirement together. They're actually talking about selling their house and moving down to the country where it's cheaper so they can use the extra money to travel the world together for the rest of their years. I think it's a great idea. But it means I have to hurry up and find a job so I can move out with Katie.

My friend Ruby is taking her son, Gary, to salsa lessons from this week, which should be funny. You've met Gary, and I'm sure you'd agree he's not the most expressive or emotive person in the world. But it's a good idea, I suppose. Katie and I should do something together. She gets to go out for the day with her father but we never spend any time like that together. I'll think of something good she'll like, maybe bring her to a concert. With Greg in the house I was always the cool mum that came to the rescue, but now with Brian here, he's the cool new dad who runs the trendy nightclub and I'm the boring mum who makes her clean her room. Of course, knowing that Brian has a nightclub has only strengthened Katie's desire to become a DJ.

Anyway, that's all my news. I'm getting through each day slowly, taking each day as it comes and all those clichés. Please return my calls. The last thing on this earth that I would want to happen is to lose my best friend. Even if he is a man.

All my love, Rosie

Dear Rosie,

I'm sorry, Rosie. I know these have been the worst few weeks of your life and I should have kept in contact. Sometimes I just get so frustrated watching your life but I no I can't control it for you. You have to make the decisions. I wasn't angry at you at all; I was just disappointed for you. I want to see you happy all the time and I new that whatshisname wasn't making you happy. I could see it for years. As crap as it feels right now, not being with him is a blessing in disguise. Anyway, I'll speak more about this over the phone during the week because I could rant about whatshisname for ever.

Speak soon, Buttercup. I no you'll be OK.

Alex

From   Rosie
To   Alex
Subject   Re: Messages

Alex Stewart, you KNOW I'll be OK.

Katie:	Cool, isn't he, Toby?
Toby:	Yeah.
Katie:	When I finish school I'll be able to move over to Ibiza and work as a DJ in his club. It's so perfect.
Toby:	Did he say you could work in his club?
Katie:	No, but he's hardly gonna say no, is he? You can come too.
Toby:	Thanks. Would you want to live in Ibiza?
Katie:	To start off with I would, yeah. First I'd get the experience in his club and then I could travel the world and work in loads of different clubs in each country. Imagine being able to play and listen to music for a living? It sounds like heaven.
Toby:	You need to get decks then, don't you?
Katie:	Yeah. My dad said he'd get them for me. Cool, isn't it?
Toby:	Yeah. It's weird—you calling him Dad.
Katie:	Yeah, I no. I don't really say it to him, though, just to other people. It feels odd. I expect I'll get used to it.
Toby:	Yeah, I suppose. Has your mum got a job yet?
Katie:	No, but she's been going to interviews every day.
Toby:	Are you going to the orthodontist guy soon?
Katie:	Yeah, Granddad is taking me tomorrow. Why?
Toby:	Can I go with you?
Katie:	Why do you always want to come? I've got blisters all on the inside of my mouth and he hacks away at me while you sit there sucking lollipops.
Toby:	I like going. So can I go tomorrow?
Katie:	What is your obsession with braces, you weirdo?
Toby:	They're just interesting.
Katie:	Yeah, about as interesting as this geography test. So come on, what's the capital of Australia? Sydney?
Toby:	Yeah, Katie, it is.

Dear Mr and Mrs Dunne,

Hyland & Moore Auctioneers received your request and we would be more than pleased to act on your behalf for the sale of your home. Thank you for choosing Hyland & Moore to represent you.

Yours sincerely,

Thomas Hyland

You have an instant message from: ROSIE.

Rosie:	Hi, it's me.
Rosie:	Helloooo?
Rosie:	I know you're there. I can see that you've logged online.
Alex:	Who is this?

Rosie: Oh, ha ha, you're so funny. What is this? Let's annoy Rosie day?! Tough luck, I am sharing the sob story of my miserable little life with you whether you like it or not. OK, here I go.

    I was offered a job. But I turned it down because I didn't think I was desperate enough to have to accept it. It turns out I was wrong. Suddenly Mum and Dad tell me that they've put the house on the market, and people start trampling in and out of the house, talking about which walls they'd knock down, and which of my cuddly teddies they would like to burn in a bonfire in the back garden while they danced around it hollering, with stripes of animal blood on their faces (OK, so they didn't say *that*). So then a couple put in an offer of full asking price, can you believe! Mum and Dad thought about it for approximately twenty seconds and then said yes!

Alex: No!

Rosie: Yes! Apparently the woman is eight months pregnant and they're living in a very small flat and they need to move house before the baby is born and has to bathe in the sink and play on the balcony.

Alex: No!

Rosie: Yes! Mum and Dad were really apologetic and everything, but I don't blame them because it's their life after all, and frankly they should've had to stop worrying about me. So all within a matter of days they've sold the house, everything has been boxed up, they bought a house for practically next to nothing in Connemara. Mum and Dad have already bought tickets to go on a cruise for two months and they're leaving on Monday.

Alex: No!

Rosie: Yes! This means that I had to call back the people who offered me the job that I already turned down—not too politely, I might add. I had to apologise profusely and try to convince them that I wanted the job after all. They were really pissed off and said they didn't need me until August. So today Katie spent the day with Brian while I went house hunting.

Alex: No!

Rosie: Yes! Everywhere that was affordable was disgusting. So Mum and Dad were discussing my personal problems (as they generally do) with the young sickeningly happy couple who are about to embark on blissful family life while butchering my childhood home. And they suggested that I move *into* the flat they just moved *out* of and had decided to rent out.

Alex: No!

275

Rosie: Yes! But the only thing is that they have already rented the place out for a few weeks to a group of male students so I have to wait until they move out. By which time it will no doubt be disgustingly smelly and dirty.

Alex: No!

Rosie: Yes! So who do I stay with while I wait, I hear you ask. Well, let's see, Mum and Dad have moved to Connemara, as you now know. Kev lives in the staff quarters of the Two Lakes Hotel in Kilkenny, Steph lives in France, Ruby has only two bedrooms and no space for me and Katie, and you're in Boston, which isn't convenient commuting. So who is the only other human being in Dublin that I know right now (and don't even think of whatshisname)? None other than Brian the Whine.

Alex: No!

Rosie: Yes! I am afraid so. How much lower can I go? And that's not even my worst news. I haven't even told you who my new boss is. None other than Miss Big Nose Smelly Breath Casey.

Alex: No!

Rosie: Yes! I am now secretary to the woman we most hated while growing up, the woman who made my daughter's life hell while in school and who is now principal of St Patrick's Primary School, and my boss.

         So what do you think of all that?

Rosie: Hello, Alex?

Rosie: Alex?

Alex: Em . . . sorry, Alex isn't actually online.

Rosie: Oh, ha ha. Well then, how is his name on my screen and I am typing to him?

Alex: You're not. I logged on using his home computer. I guess his name automatically comes up on your system. I've never come across this little system, it's fun. Sorry, I didn't know you were looking for him.

Rosie: What?? You think I just rant about my private life to all strangers on the computer??? Who is this?

Alex: Bethany.

Rosie: Bethany?

Alex: Bethany Williams? Remember me?

Rosie: What the hell are you doing on Alex's home computer?!

Alex: Oh, I'm sorry, it all makes sense now. Alex didn't tell you, did he? I thought you two told each other everything. I'll let Alex explain this one to you. By the way, Alex is working with my

father now. He's doing very well for himself. Perhaps if you're that stuck for money he could give you a loan.
Rosie has logged off.

From   Stephanie
To   Rosie
Subject   Miss Casey!

I cannot *believe* you're going to be working with Miss Casey! Mum told me over the phone and I could barely understand her through all her laughing.

Whatever persuaded you to take this job? What does Alex think about all this? I'm sure he's got some very interesting views on the subject!

Dear Stephanie,

I'm probably nuts taking this job, but to be honest it's the best one with the most attractive pay packet by far. It's Monday to Friday 9 a.m. to 3.30 p.m. which is great, because I had to work all hours and weekends with my last job. I really don't intend working there for very long, just until a job in the hotel industry opens up. But the main reason for me taking the job is the fact that I have very little choice. I have a week left here in purgatory (Brian's flat) before I can move into my rented flat, which is a dump.

Strange things have happened to Katie over the years, but none of them as bizarre as her mother and father living in the same house as one another. What may be a way of life for some children is something for Katie to laugh hysterically at. Actually, it's not as if Brian and I dislike each other, it's just that we know absolutely nothing about one another. We are two complete strangers who got together once in our lives (and only for a few minutes, trust me) in a moment I can barely even remember, to make the most incredible thing ever. How could two fools like us create something as great as Katie?

I still feel angry at Brian now, but it's a different kind of anger. Before I felt angry at him because he left me. But now when I look at him joking around with Katie I just think what a waste. That's all he had to do while she was grow- ing up—be there for her and she would have accepted him, as children do, no matter what he was like. I feel angry at him for not being there for her. I've finally lost that selfish part of me.

Once again, I don't quite know where I'm headed, Steph. It seems that every few years I'm shovelling up the pieces of my life and starting from scratch all over. No matter what I do or how hard I try I can't seem to reach the dizzy heights of happiness, success and security, like so many people do. And I'm not talking about becoming a millionaire and living happily ever after. I just mean reaching a point in my life that I can stop what I'm doing, take a look around me, breathe a sigh of relief and think: I'm where I want to be now.

And in answer to your question about Alex, I don't know what he thinks of

*my new job because I haven't heard from him in a long time. He's so busy sav-
ing valuable lives and attending charity functions that I couldn't possibly
expect him to get in touch with a friend like me. He's far too busy hooking up
with 'old' friends. Slutty ones at that.*

You have an instant message from: ALEX.

Alex: Hello.

Rosie: Oh, so he *is* still alive. Where have you been for the past few
        weeks?

Alex: Hiding.

Rosie: From whom?

Alex: You.

Rosie: Why?

Alex: Because I'm dating Bethany again and I was afraid to tell you
        because you hate her with a passion, and then you found out
        from *her* first, which made things even worse. So I was hiding
        from you.

Rosie: Why?

Alex: Because you think she's a slut and that she's no good for me.

Rosie: Why?

Alex: Because you're my overprotective best friend and you've
        always hated my girlfriends (and wife) and I've always hated
        your boyfriends (and husband).

Rosie: Why?

Alex: Because he was an absolute fool and he didn't no how lucky
        he was. Because I'm your best friend and I care about you.

Rosie: Why?

Alex: Because I've nothing better to do.

Rosie: Why?

Alex: Because it's the unfortunate way that my life turned out.
        Whatever happened made me care about you and yours.
        Anyway, it's great that I don't have to hide any more.

Rosie: Why?

Alex: Because I've apologised.

Rosie: Why?

Alex: Because I'm tired of not hearing from you and I miss you.

Rosie: Why?

Alex: Because (and I'm now saying this through incredibly gritted
        teeth) You. Are. My. Best. Friend. But I have to warn you, I'm
        not going to listen to any of your bitchy remarks about her this
        time round.

Rosie: Why?

Alex: Because I really like her, Rosie, and she makes me happy. I feel like the little boy working in Dad's office again. And just think, if it wasn't for you getting so drunk on your sixteenth birthday that you had to get your stomach pumped, we never would have been caught, we wouldn't have been suspended and I wouldn't have been punished so severely by having to file every piece of paper in the world in Dad's office, where, I might add, I would never have met Bethany. So it's all down to you, my dear friend!

Rosie: OH, WHYYYYYY??? Dear God, why?

Alex: Ha ha. I'm really glad we had this discussion and that we've cleared the whole Bethany thing up. So I'm forgiven?

Rosie: No.

Alex: Great stuff, thanks.

Rosie: By the way, you *still* haven't said anything about my job.

Alex: Job? You got a job? When? Where? What are you doing?

Rosie: Alex, I've only left approximately 22,496 messages on your answering machine explaining this. Don't you listen to them?

Alex: Sorry. So what's the job?

Rosie: Promise not to laugh.

Alex: I promise.

Rosie: I'm starting in August as a secretary in St Patrick's Primary School.

Alex: You're going back . . . *there*? Hold on a minute . . . that means that you're going to be working with Miss Big Nose Smelly Breath Casey! Why?

Rosie: Because I need the money.

Alex: Wouldn't you rather starve? Why on earth did she hire you?

Rosie: I'm wondering the same thing.

Alex: Ha ha ha ha ha.

Rosie: You said you wouldn't laugh.

Alex: Ha ha ha ha ha.

Rosie: You promised!

Alex: Ha ha ha ha ha.

Rosie: Oh, bugger off.

Rosie has logged off.

Dear Rosie and Katie,
   Greetings from Aruba! Having a wonderful time here in paradise!
   Hope all is well with you,
   Lots of love,
   Mum and Dad

You have an instant message from: RUBY.
Ruby: Watch out, Ireland, here we come!
Rosie: Here who come?
Ruby: Gary and Ruby Minnelli.
Rosie: Minnelli?
Ruby: OK, so I changed our name to something far more superstar-like. Gary doesn't mind because it means that he's in disguise and none of his friends will recognise him. The All-Ireland Salsa Dancing Championships are on in a few months from now. A couple from each county goes forward and whoever wins becomes the Ireland champions, then there's the European Championship and the World Championship.
Rosie: So you're going for total world domination?
Ruby: Well, not quite the *world* but Gary and I are willing to take on Ireland. The competition's on in a few weeks—will you be there?
Rosie: I'm insulted you even had to ask!
Ruby: Thanks.

Ba'ax ka wa'alik from Mexico!
  What an adventure this is taking us on. Hope you're both happy.
  Love, Mum and Dad

Happy Fourteenth Birthday, Toby!
  Hope you like the remote-control car I got you. The guy in the shop said the Rally ones are the best (and they're the most expensive too). They're really fast!
  Anyway, here's to another year. Maybe ten years from now you'll be poking at people's teeth. Why you want to be a dentist is beyond me, but you were always weird.
  Katie

From   Toby
To   Katie
Subject   Re: Happy birthday

Thanks for the car. I'm gonna bring it to the crappy dance thing on Sunday. You girls can paint your nails and watch them dance while I drive my car out in the corridor.

Aloha from Hawaii!
  Having a ball. Heading to Samoa and Fiji next. Can't wait!
  Love to you and Katie, Mum and Dad xxx

Ruby and Gary Minnelli!
Good Luck!
I was going to say 'break a leg' but I don't think it's appropriate for the occasion. You will both be brilliant and we'll be cheering for you.
Love Rosie, Katie and Toby

You have an instant message from: ROSIE.

Rosie: Congratulations, you Dancing Queen! I'm so proud of you! Are you still glowing from your win?

Ruby: I'm not too sure how I'm supposed to be feeling, to be honest. I really don't think that we should be the winners.

Rosie: Oh, don't be silly! The two of you danced brilliantly.

Ruby: But we didn't even get through to the final round . . .

Rosie: Well, it's not your fault the couple who came first were practising out in the corridor. Anyone could have slipped on Toby's stupid remote-control car. It was their own fault.

Ruby: Yes, but technically we shouldn't have won at all, Rosie. Only the two couples who got to the final round were supposed to battle it out. The second couple who were in the final really should have won . . .

Rosie: Yes, but once again that wasn't your fault. It was the woman in purple who tripped over Toby's car (they're very fast, aren't they?), knocking the drink out of Katie's hand, causing the second woman in yellow to slip and land on her backside. That automatically put you through. It's not your fault. You should be delighted!!

Ruby: Well, I am in an odd kind of way. Me and Gary are performing our winning dance in Miss Behave's show in the George.

Rosie: That's fantastic! I'm delighted for you, Ruby. My friend the superstar!

Ruby: Oh, I wouldn't even be doing all this if you hadn't got me the vouchers for my fortieth birthday. Thanks so much, Rosie. And thanks for cheering for me so loudly. I heard you the whole way through the dance. And I'm really sorry you, Katie and Toby were asked to leave the dance hall . . .

Ni hao from China!
Sorry we're not there to help you with the move. We wish you luck in your new apartment. We're sure it will bring you lots of happiness.
Love, Mum and Dad xxx

You have an instant message from: ROSIE.
Rosie: The place is disgusting, Ruby. Absolutely disgusting.

Ruby: Oh, stop. It can't be any worse than mine.

Rosie: Worse than yours multiplied by one hundred.

Ruby: Such a place exists? God bless you. What's so bad about it?

Rosie: Well, let's see, where should I start? Hmm . . . should I tell you about the fact that it's a second-floor apartment over a group of shops, among them a tattoo parlour and an Indian take-away which has managed to leave the stench of tikka masala all over my clothes already?

Perhaps I should tell you about the *gorgeous* 1970s green and grey floral wallpaper which is just *dangling* off the walls, and I wouldn't want to forget the fact that there're matching curtains. The kitchen is so small that when two people stand in it, one person has to back out to let the other leave. But *at least* the water works and the toilet flushes. No wonder the rent is so ridiculously cheap; no one in their right mind would want to live here.

Ruby: You are.

Rosie: Yes, well, I won't be here for long. I'm going to magically save loads of money and get us out of here.

Ruby: And open a hotel.

Rosie: Yes.

Ruby: And live in the penthouse.

Rosie: Yes.

Ruby: And Kevin can be the head chef.

Rosie: Yes.

Ruby: And Alex the in-house doctor so that he can save the lives of those you poison.

Rosie: Yes.

Ruby: And you'll be the owner and manager.

Rosie: Yes.

Ruby: So what can I be?

Rosie: You and Gary could be the evening entertainment. You can salsa till you drop.

Ruby: Sounds like heaven to me. Well, Rosie, you better get your ass in gear and get this hotel business off the ground before we're all old and grey. What are your plans for the week?

Rosie: Well, I'm trying to make this tip of a place look like a home. Brian the Whine has been very helpful, believe it or not. He's hired out a sander for the day and tomorrow we're going to rip up the smelly carpets and sand and varnish the floors in all the rooms.

We're going to paint the walls white, because even with a

million-watt bulb the place still looks like a cave. It needs brightening up and I'm going for the minimalist look, not because I'm trendy and fashionable but because I don't really have that much furniture. I'm going to pull down the old curtains and burn them in a ritual.

My darling brother Kevin was only too delighted to come to Dublin and raid whatshisname's house for all my leftover belongings. I even got the black leather couch which was in the house before I married him but, hey, I deserve it.

Ruby: It sounds like it's going to be lovely, Rosie. A real home.

Ei Je from Singapore!
Having such a wonderful time. We don't want to come home!
Good luck with your new job this week, love. We're thinking of you here as we lounge by the pool! (Just joking.)
Love, Mum and Dad

You have an instant message from: ALEX.

Alex: Have you a minute to chat?
Rosie: No, sorry, I'm busy licking stamps.
Alex: Oh, OK. Can I call you sometime later?
Rosie: I was only joking, Alex.
Alex: How's the job?
Rosie: It's OK. I've been here a few weeks now so I've settled in and it's going OK. Nothing to write home about.
Alex: Sorry I wasn't in touch sooner. I hadn't realised it had been so long. Time has been flying by once again.
Rosie: It's OK. I assumed you were busy. I've moved into my apartment now and everything.
Alex: Oh, gosh, that's right. How is it?
Rosie: It's OK. It was absolutely dire when we first moved in, but Brian the Whine was a really good help. He fixed all that was broken and cleaned what was dirty. Just like a regular little slave.
Alex: So are you and he getting along then?
Rosie: Better. I only have the urge to strangle him ten times a day now.
Alex: Well, it's a start. Any romance?
Rosie: What? With Brian the Whine? You need your head examined.
Alex: Oh. Anyone else in your life?
Rosie: Yes, actually. A thirteen-year-old daughter, a new job and a drawer stuffed with bills. My hands are pretty full at the moment. Although my neighbour did ask me to go out on a date with him this weekend.

Alex: So are you going out with him?

Rosie: Let me tell you a little bit about him. His name is Sanjay, he's sixty years old, and he's married, lives with his wife and two sons, and owns and runs the Indian takeaway downstairs. And guess where he invited me for dinner.

Alex: Where?

Rosie: His takeaway. He said he would pay.

Alex: So what's the dilemma?

Rosie: Very funny.

Alex: Well, at least you have friendly neighbours.

Rosie: Anyway, why all the personal questions about my love life?

Alex: Because I want you to find someone, that's why. I want you to be happy.

Rosie: Alex, I've never found happiness with another human being and you know it. I'm separated from my husband; I'm not looking for another victim just yet. Possibly never.

Alex: *Never?*

Rosie: Possibly. Well, I'll never marry again, that's for sure. I'm getting used to my new life. I have a new apartment, a new job, a teenage daughter, I'm thirty-two years old and I'm entering a new phase of my life. I think I'm finally growing up. Anyway, there's nothing wrong with being single. Being single is the new black. You should know.

Alex: I'm not single.

Rosie: Not *yet*.

Alex: No, I'm not. I won't be.

Rosie: Why, surely it's about time you broke up with Slutty Bethany?

Alex: Please don't call her slutty. And I'm not about to end mine and Beth's relationship. But, what I am saying is that I want me to be happy with Bethany and you to be happy with someone and then we'll both be happy with people.

Rosie: I know what it is. You just don't want me to be single because I'm a distraction to you. If I'm with a man then you think that *perhaps* you just might be able to keep your hands off me. I've sussed you out, Alex Stewart. You love me. You want me to have your babies. You can't stand another day without me.

Alex: I . . . don't no what to say . . .

Rosie: Relax, I'm joking.

Alex: Bethany's pregnant.

Rosie: Oh, dear God. Sometimes, because you're my best friend, I think that you're normal, like me. Then every now and again you remind me that you're a man.

PART FOUR

Welcome home, Mum and Dad! (Fáilte go h-Eirinn!)
Glad you arrived home safely and in one piece! Can't wait to hear all the
stories of your adventures and see all the photographs.
See you at the weekend.
Love, Rosie and Katie

Dear Stephanie and Pierre!
Congratulations on the arrival of your new baby girl!
We can't wait to meet little Sophia. In the meantime here are a few little
outfits to keep her as trendy as her mother!
Lots of love,
Rosie and Katie

Happy 5th Birthday, Josh!
Lots of love,
Rosie and Katie

DR WILLIAMS REWARDED

Reginald Williams was honoured last night at the National Health Awards in Boston. He was nominated through a highly selective process that recognises those who have made major contributions to the advancement of the medical sciences and public health.

This award is considered one of the highest honours in the fields of medicine and health. He was accompanied to the ceremony by his wife, Miranda, his daughter, Bethany, and her newly announced fiancé Dr Alex Stewart, cardio-surgeon at St Jude's Hospital in Boston. See page four of the Health Supplement for Wayne Gillespie's report.

You have an instant message from: ROSIE.

Rosie: You get engaged and you let me read about it in a newspaper? What the hell has happened to you these days?
Alex: I'm sorry, Rosie.
Rosie: Do you love her, Alex?

Alex:	I suppose.
Rosie:	Well, that's convincing.
Alex:	I shouldn't have to *convince* anyone.
Rosie:	Only yourself, Alex.
Alex:	There's a baby involved now.
Rosie:	The Alex I know wouldn't marry a woman he doesn't love for the sake of the baby. That's the worst thing you could do to the poor child—raise it in an environment where the parents don't even love each other. What's the point of that? You're not with Sally and things with Josh work out fine.
Alex:	I'm a weekend dad to Josh; I don't want a repeat of that. It's not right.
Rosie:	Marrying someone you don't love is not right.
Alex:	I'm extremely fond of Bethany; we have a great relationship and get on well.
Rosie:	Well, I'm glad you and your future wife 'get on well'. If you don't think this through properly, Bethany will be another Sally. Another failed marriage is not what you want.
Alex:	Why should I take advice from you, Rosie? What on earth have you done in your life that makes you such an expert on telling me how to live mine? You lived with a man that cheated on you for years and you kept taking him back time and time again. What do you no about marriage?
Rosie:	I know enough not to go racing up the aisle with someone else I barely know or love.
	So what would good old Reginald Williams have done if he had learned that his daughter was pregnant and that the fool who was responsible wouldn't marry her? Oh, the shame that would bring on the family, how the people would talk.
	But at least now she's got the ring on her finger, and you've got the job promotion, and we can all live happily ever after.
Alex:	Not everybody walks away, Rosie. They might in your life, but not in mine.
Rosie:	Alex, for Chrissake! Not marrying Bethany isn't 'walking away'. As long as you're there for the child then you're not walking away. You don't have to *marry* her!
Alex:	Look, I'm fed up with all this, Rosie, with you constantly checking up on me, me having to explain everything to you. You're not my wife or my mother, so give it a rest. Who says I have to run all my life decisions by you, anyway? I can make decisions on my own, you no. I'm a grown man.

Rosie: Then for once in your life ACT LIKE ONE!

Alex: Who are you to insult *me* and lecture *me* when you haven't done a thing right in your life yourself? Just do me a favour and don't bother getting in touch until you have something decent to say.

Rosie: Fine! Well then, I think you'll find you'll be waiting a long, long time.

Rosie has logged off.

Alex: No change there then.

You have an instant message from: ALEX

Phil: Why are you marrying *Bethany*? Is her dad putting pressure on you?

Alex: No, no, no. There's no pressure. I want to do this.

Phil: Why?

Alex: Why the hell not? Why did you marry Margaret?

Phil: I married Margaret because I love every inch of the woman with all my heart and plan to be with her for the rest of my life, in sickness and in health, till death do us part. She is my best friend, we have five beautiful children and as much as they drive me up the walls sometimes, I couldn't live a day without them. I don't sense you have this with Bethany.

Alex: Not all relationships are like yours and Margaret's.

Phil: No, they're not but the intention should be there at the beginning. Was there the silence thing with Bethany?

Alex: Oh, shut up about the silence, Phil.

Phil: So, was there?

Alex: No.

Phil: Then you shouldn't marry her.

You have an instant message from: KATIE.

Katie: You look very interested in learning about the female reproduction system.

Toby: I'm not. I'd rather figure it out for myself the practical way.

Katie: Oh, funny, but you'll be old and grey before anyone lets you get your hands on them.

Toby: My best friend is a comedienne. So what do you want?

Katie: Well, not that you deserve to be asked, but I'm going to the orthodontist again later if you wanna come. You can ask him a million questions about everything he's doing, as always, and annoy the hell out of him.

Toby: Sorry, I can't go. Monica is coming around to my house to watch the football.

Katie: Monica, Monica, Monica. I'm sick of hearing about stupid Monica Doyle. So why aren't I invited to your house?

Toby: Because you have to go to the dentist.

Katie: Yes, but you didn't no that until a second ago.

Toby: OK then, would you like to watch the football, the sport that you absolutely hate with a passion, at my house today?

Katie: I can't. I'm busy.

Toby: You see? Now don't say I never ask you out anywhere.

Katie: How long have you known that I'm going to the dentist?

Toby: All of five minutes.

Katie: How long ago did you invite Monica Doyle to your house?

Toby: Last week.

Katie: My point exactly!

You have an instant message from: KATIE.

Katie: Mum, I hate men.

Rosie: Congratulations, dear. Welcome to the club. Your membership is in the post. I'm so proud of this moment.

Katie: Please, Mum, I'm serious.

Rosie: And so am I. So what has Toby done this time?

Katie: He's invited Monica Doyle to his house to watch the football and he didn't invite me. Well, he did, but only after he new I was busy.

Rosie: Oh dear, he's caught the bug already. Is this moany Monica we're talking about? The little girl who cried all day at your tenth birthday party?

Katie: Yes, but she's not a child any more, Mum. She's fourteen, got the biggest chest in the school, dyes her hair blonde, leaves the top buttons of her shirt open and leans down so the boys can see down her top. She hates talking about anything other than shopping so I don't no why she's going to watching football. Well, actually I do no why.

Rosie: Sounds like she's got a case of the Slutty Bethanitis to me.

Katie: What? What do I do about Monica?

Rosie: Oh, that's simple. Assassinate her.

Katie: Please, Mum, for once in your life be serious.

Rosie: I am an incredibly serious woman. The only way to deal with this is to silence her. Because if not, she'll only end up coming back to haunt you when you're thirty-two years old. Death is the only thing for it.

Katie: Thanks, but I'm open to any other suggestions you may have.

Rosie: You said he invited you?

Katie: Yes, but only because he new I couldn't go.

Rosie: My dear sweet innocent daughter, an invitation is an invitation.
            It would be rude to turn him down. I suggest you turn up on
            his doorstep this evening.

Katie: But I've got an appointment with the orthodontist.

Rosie: Well, the dentist can wait. I'll make another appointment for
            you. This is a very important football match, you know. I
            wouldn't want you to miss it just because of a silly little thing
            like getting your teeth fixed. Now, get off the computer before
            Mr Simpson catches you and reports me to Miss Big Nose
            Smelly Breath Casey and gets me fired.

Katie: You wish, Mum. I don't no how you work with her every day.

Rosie: Actually, I'm surprised to admit it myself but she's not so bad.
            As far as bosses go she's been really, really pleasant. Her name
            is Julie. Can you believe it? She actually has a first name. And
            it's a nice, normal name too; I would have thought it was
            something more like Vladimir or Adolf.

Katie: Ha ha, me too. But is it not really awkward working with
            someone who used to give out to you every day?

Rosie: Things are a little awkward between us. But each day we talk
            more and more. Do you know that she thought Alex was your
            dad?!

Katie: Did she?!

Rosie: Anyway, I told her that Brian was your father and she couldn't
            stop laughing . . . Actually, perhaps this isn't a story to tell you.

Hi, love,

Hope all is well. It was great to see you at the weekend. Thanks for coming
over to us in the west and joining us. I promise the house will be in better order
next time you come to see us, but I'm finding it so difficult to settle down after
travelling for months.

Settling into a new home, in a new village, in a new county is an adventure
for us. Everybody is so friendly here and our Irish is gradually coming back
to us. We don't have neighbours as exciting as you seem to have in your new
apartment though.

You're my wonderful brave baby girl, Rosie, and your dad and I are so, so
proud of you. I hope you know that. You never allow anything to knock you
back and you're the best mother to Katie. She's a feisty young lady now, isn't
she? She's definitely her mother's daughter. I'm sorry Dennis and I left you at
such an important time of your life, it just broke my heart having to leave you
and Katie when you were going through all that stuff with whatshisname. But
you're a tough cookie and what doesn't kill you only makes you stronger.

It would be such a shame for you to miss Alex's wedding. I was talking to Sandra earlier on and she was telling me that they're planning a very big Christmas wedding. They want to be married before the baby is born, and Bethany doesn't want to be showing too much in her dress. Sandra would love for you and Katie to be there; they've watched you grow up over the years too. I get the impression she's not a huge fan of Bethany's herself, but she loves Alex and she wants to support him.

Sandra said that Dennis and I are invited but unfortunately we can't go because we are spending Christmas with Stephanie and Pierre in Paris, as you know. Christmas in Paris will be beautiful, no doubt, and I'm excited to meet granddaughter number two! It's such a shame that you and Katie can't come too, but I understand she wants to spend her first Christmas with her dad, and I know she wants to get to know her 'other' grandparents too. I can't help feeling jealous, though, that they'll be seeing my Katie on Christmas Day, and I won't!

Kevin has met a girl, would you believe, and he's spending Christmas with her and her parents in Donegal! It must be serious! I think she's a waitress in the same hotel as him or something, but I'm not too sure. You know Kevin: he's not too good at giving information out.

Your dad says hello. He's tucked up in bed with a nasty flu. He's been very tired since we returned from the trip. I can't believe we're both in our sixties, Rosie. How time went by so fast I'll never know. Anyway, I'd better go because he keeps calling me. Honestly, you would think he was on his deathbed by the way he's acting!

I'm so proud of my two girls in Dublin.

Love you.

Mum

Dr Reginald & Miranda Williams
invite **Katie Dunne**
to join them in celebrating the
marriage of their beloved daughter
Bethany
to
Dr Alex Stewart
at
the Memorial Church of Harvard University
on 28th December
at 2 o'clock
& a reception at
the Boston Harbor Hotel
RSVP Miranda Williams

From   Julie Casey
To   Rosie
Subject   Fax for you

Don't want to disturb you while you're so 'busy' working (how is Ruby?), but a fax just arrived in my office a few minutes ago. It wasn't addressed to you but on reading it I discovered that it could *only* be for you, as which of my other employees would give out *my* fax number for *their own* personal use? I think I can just about make out a 'Form Josh' signed at the bottom. Come into my office and collect it. Oh, and while you're at it, divert all your calls to my office; bring two cups of coffee and a packet of cigarettes in with you.

SOCIAL LIVES
by Eloise Parkinson

For those of us who were lucky enough to attend the wedding of the year (or surely, *at least*, the wedding of the week) we have lived to tell the tale of extravagance and sophistication that was displayed for the lucky 300 guests of Dr and Mrs Reginald Williams at the marriage of their daughter, Bethany, to Dr Alex Stewart.

No expense was spared at the wedding ceremony, which took place at the Memorial Church of Harvard University, where vibrant displays of red roses and red candles lined the aisle, like lights illuminating a runway for the couple to take off to their future life together.

Bethany, 34, was looking flawlessly stunning, as always, in a white dress designed for her by the famous friend-of-the-stars (and mine) Jeremy Durkin. The boned bodice was embellished in ten thousand pearls (and disguised that pregnancy everybody is whispering about). The ballerina-style full skirt, made up of layers and layers of soft tulle, swished as she floated up the aisle on the arm of her proud father, prominent surgeon Dr Reginald Williams.

Miranda Williams looked every bit the perfect mother of the bride in her scarlet red Armani trouser-suit, teamed with a fabulous Philip Treacy hat. Catwalk models Sara Smythe and Hayley Broadbank acted as Bethany's two bridesmaids and wore sexy red silk spaghetti-strapped dresses that clung to their barely there curves. The bride's bouquet was made up of half a dozen red roses and half a dozen white roses.

At the top of the aisle a confident-looking Prince Charming looked down on his princess with pride, dressed in a classic black cutaway coat with white wing collar and red tie, accompanied by a single red rose in his lapel. Everything was certainly 'rosie' on this day.

The extravagant reception was held at the Boston Harbor Hotel where the finest speech by far was made by the best man, five-year-old Josh Stewart, son of the groom from a previous marriage.

Rosie,
Happy Birthday, friend.
Another year—here we go again.
Ruby

Dear Alex and Bethany,
Congratulations on the birth of your baby boy.
We wish you every happiness for the future and are delighted that Josh
has the brother he wished for!
Rosie and Katie

Happy fourteenth, my little angel!
Have a good night at the disco tonight and remember no drinking, no sex,
and no drugs.
Lots of love, Mum

You have an instant message from: RUBY.

Ruby: So what are you going to do for the next two months now that
          the kids are off school?

Rosie: I'm not too sure. Julie mentioned something about taking an
          adult course at the school in hotel management like I always
          wanted to do. Like it's that simple.

Ruby: Why *can't* it be that simple? Look, Rosie, you don't know until
          you try.

Rosie: Julie said that if I don't take the course she'll fire me. And she
          said that when I finish the course she's firing me anyway.

Ruby: You need to listen to her; she's been a good teacher to you
          over the years.

Rosie: But, Ruby, it takes two years to get a diploma, and it's
          expensive, and I'll have to work by day and study by night.
          It'll be tough.

Ruby: Oh, but, but, but, Rosie Dunne. Have you got anything
          better planned for the next three years of your life?

Hi, Mum.

Winter *again*. It's scary how the months fly by so fast. They turn into years without me even noticing. Katie is like my calendar, watching her grow and change. She is growing up so fast, learning to have opinions of her own, learning that I don't have the answers to everything. And the moment a child begins to understand that, you know you're in trouble. I know that Katie is going to leave in a few years and she won't need me like she does now.

I have to set up my own life for when Katie goes. I *need* to do that because I don't see any Prince Charmings coming along to rescue me. Fairy tales are such evil little stories for young children. Every time I'm in a mess I expect a long-haired posh-speaking man to come trotting into my life (on a horse, of course, not literally trotting himself). Then I realise I don't want a man trotting into my life because men are the ones who put me in the bloody mess in the first place.

I'm like Katie's coach right now, gearing her up for the big fight that is adult life. She's hardly thinking of life after me. Sure, she has her dreams of travelling the world and DJ-ing for a living *without me*, but the *without me* part hasn't hit her yet. And so it shouldn't—she's only four-teen. Anyway, she is not up to making her own decisions yet, and I've put my foot down on the quitting school idea.

Although lately I haven't had to force her out of bed in the mornings because of John, a new boyfriend of hers. The pair of them are insepa-rable; they go to discos every Friday night at the GAA club near where he lives. He's a real GAA man and plays hurling for the Dublin minors.

I haven't seen or heard much of Toby lately, but I saw his mother at the school and she told me he was acting more or less the same as Katie with his new girlfriend, Monica.

I never dated when I was fourteen. The youth of today are really growing up fast . . . (I sounded SO OLD there!) OK, OK, Mum, I can hear you fuming from here. I did become pregnant at the age of eigh-teen without having a job or education or man, and almost gave you a nervous breakdown, but in some countries of the world that's old, so you should thank your lucky stars that I didn't get started even sooner.

Kevin called up for the weekend; he brought his girlfriend with him. Did you know that they've been going out for over a year now and that they are buying a house together? Honestly, that brother of mine is so secretive; you practically have to beat the information out of him! You never know, there could be more wedding bells in the air for the Dunne family!

Notice I'm typing to you today and not emailing. That's because I'm pretending that I'm studying. We both have Christmas exams coming up and I told Katie she needed to take them more seriously. Well, I walked myself straight into that one. So here we both are, crammed at the kitchen table with our books, folders, papers and pens, pretending to look intellectual.

I still haven't spoken to Alex and it's been over a year now. I think this is really it this time. All we've been doing is sending stupid cards back and forth to each other. It's like we're having a staring competition and neither of us wants to be the first to blink. I miss him like crazy. There are so many things that happen to me, silly little everyday things that I itch to tell him. Like the postman this morning was delivering across the road and that stupid little Jack Russell dog called Jack Russell was attacking him again. So I looked out of the window and I saw the postman shaking the dog off his leg as he does every morning but this time he kicked the dog in the stomach by mistake and the dog fell over and didn't move for ages. Then the owner came outside and I watched as the postman pretended that Jack Russell was like that when he got there. The owner believed him and there was pandemonium as they tried to help the dog. Eventually Jack Russell got up and when he took one look at the postman he whimpered and ran away into the house. It was so funny. The postman just shrugged and walked off. He was whistling by the time he got to my door. Things like that would have really made Alex laugh, especially as I had told him all about the wretched dog keeping me awake all night barking, and always stealing my post from the poor postman.

Hang on a sec, Katie is trying to sneak a peek off my page . . .

MASLOW'S THEORY OF HIERARCHY.

Ha ha, that'll put her off the scent. OK, I better go now and actually do some work. See you both soon.

Oh, by the way, Ruby has set me up on a blind date on Saturday night. I nearly killed her but I can't cancel it. Cross your fingers for me that he's not some sort of serial killer.

Lots of love, Rosie

You have an instant message from: ROSIE.

Rosie: Hi, Julie. I've signed you up to be one of my instant message buddies. Whenever you're online I can send you messages.

Julie: Why would you set up an instant messaging service with me when I am in the next room?

Rosie: It's what I do. It means I can multi-task. I can speak to people on the phone and also do business with you online. Anyway, what is it that you actually do, Miss Casey? All I see you doing is terrorising innocent children and having meetings with pissed-off parents.

Julie: That's about all I do, Rosie, you're right. Believe me, you were one of the worst kids to teach and one of the worst parents to meet with. I hated calling you in.

Rosie: I hated coming in.

Julie: And now you've added me to your messaging list. How times change. By the way, how was your blind date? Come on, spill the beans, what was he like?

Rosie: His name is Adam and he is a very, very attractive man. All evening he was polite, a terrific conversationalist and very funny. He paid for the meal, the taxi, drinks, everything. He was tall, dark and handsome, dressed impeccably. Plucked eyebrows, straight teeth and not a nose hair in sight.

Julie: What does he do for a living?

Rosie: He's an engineer.

Julie: He sounds too good to be true. Are you meeting again?

Rosie: No.

Julie: Are you crazy?

Rosie: Probably. He was such a good man but there was just nothing there—no sparkle.

Julie: But it was only your first date. You can never really tell these things by a first date. What did you want, fireworks?

Rosie: No, actually, quite the opposite. I want silence, a perfect moment of quietness.

Julie: Silence?

Rosie: Oh, it's a long story. But last night only proves that you can put me with a guy who's perfect and I'm still not ready.

Julie: Changing the subject. How's the studying going?

Rosie: It's tough working, studying and being a mother.

Julie: Is there anything I can do to help?

Rosie: Yes, actually. A pay rise would be a terrific help.

Julie: No chance. How's the saving going?

Rosie: It would be going fine if I didn't have to feed, clothe, educate my child as well as pour rent into the shoe box I'm living in.

Julie: That always seems to get in the way of things, that whole looking-after-your-child part. Have you spoken to Alex yet?

Rosie: No.

Julie: Oh, Rosie. I spent my life trying to separate you two from each other but now the fun is over for me. Tell him Miss Big Nose Smelly Breath Casey has given you both permission to sit beside each other again.

Rosie: That'll never work; he never listened to you anyway. And it's not like we're not in contact at all. Katie emails all the time and I send cards for every occasion under the sun and he does the same back. So we're not completely ignoring each other. It's a very civilised kind of argument we're having.

Julie: Yes, apart from the fact that you don't talk. Your best friend has a six-month-old baby that you haven't even met. All I'm saying is that if you let this carry on much longer, the years will multiply and before you know it it'll just be too late.

Dear Rosie and Katie Dunne,
Season's Greetings from St Jude's Hospital.
My wife, two sons and I hope that the year ahead brings you
and your loved ones good health and happiness.
Merry Christmas and a Happy New Year from the Stewarts.
Dr Alex Stewart MD

To Dr Alex Stewart
May the coming year be filled with health, wealth and happiness
for you and your family.
Best wishes,
Rosie Dunne

You have an instant message from: ALEX.

Alex: Your card arrived this morning.

Rosie: Oooh, talking to me now, are you?

Alex: It's been long enough. One of us should be adult enough to make contact. Remember I'm not the one who started this in the first place.

Rosie: Yes, you did.

Alex: Rosie, no, I didn't.

Rosie: Yes, you did!

Alex: Oh, *please*! Last year I told you Bethany was pregnant, at which point you went crazy. And, for your information, I proposed to her before we went to that award ceremony. Bethany said yes, and being excited, she told her parents at the table (as any normal person would do). Her father was presented with his award and during his speech he announced that his daughter had just gotten engaged (as a proud father would on just learning that his daughter was to be married).

　　　The press were there; they went back to their desks and reported on the evening in time to make the next day's papers. I went out and celebrated my engagement with my fiancée and her family. I got home to bed and woke up the next day to phone calls from my family wanting to no why the hell I hadn't told them I was getting married. My in-box was full of emails from confused friends and I was just about to deal with them when I got an instant message from you.

　　　So I sent you and Katie wedding invites anyway, thinking that even though you disapproved of my choice of wife and concocted pathetic stories about why I was marrying her, you might still have behaved like the friend you claim to be by attending my wedding and being supportive.

Rosie: Wait a minute, I didn't receive any wedding invite!
Alex: What?
Rosie: I got no invitation to your wedding. There was one for Katie all right, but none for me. And Katie couldn't very well go because she was only thirteen and where would she stay?
Alex: Stop! Now let me think about this for a moment. You didn't receive a wedding invite?
Rosie: No. Just one for Katie.
Alex: What about your parents?
Rosie: Yeah, they received one but they couldn't go because they were visiting Steph in Paris and—
Alex: But my parents—didn't they tell you?
Rosie: They said they would love me to go but they don't control the invites, Alex. You never asked me to go.
Alex: But you were on the list. I even *saw* your invite on the kitchen table.
Rosie: Oh.
Alex: So what happened?
Rosie: Don't ask me! I didn't even know there was an invite for me! Who posted them?
Alex: Bethany and the wedding planner.
Rosie: Hmm . . . OK, so somewhere between Bethany walking to the postbox and the invite actually going in the slot, something happened to my invite.
Alex: Oh, don't start, Rosie. It wasn't Bethany. She's got much better things to be doing with her time than hatching plans to get rid of you.
Rosie: Like doing lunch with the ladies?
Alex: Stop.
Rosie: Well, I'm in shock.
Alex: So you thought all this time that I didn't want you at my wedding?
Rosie: Yes.
Alex: But why didn't you say something? An entire year and you didn't say anything? If you didn't invite me to your wedding I would at least *say* something!
Rosie: Excuse me, why didn't you ask me why I wasn't there? If I invited you to my wedding and I noticed that you hadn't turned up, I think I would at least say something.
Alex: I was angry.
Rosie: Me too.
Alex: What I want to no is where your wedding invite went to. The

wedding planner had everything arranged. Unless it was . . .

Rosie: Who?

Alex: Not *who* but *what* . . .

Rosie: *What*, then?

Alex: Jack Russell the Jack Russell. Next time I see him I'm going to wring his neck.

Rosie: Oh, you can't do that. He's dead. The postman kicked him in the stomach a few mornings in a row and one morning, Jack just stopped moving.

Alex: I'm not sorry to hear that.

Rosie: I'm sorry though, Alex.

Alex: Me too. Friends again?

Rosie: I never stopped being your friend.

Alex: Me neither.

For our beautiful daughter
We love you with all our hearts. Here's to a new year.
Happy Birthday, Rosie!
Good luck with your exams in June.
Lots of love, Mum and Dad

For my sister
You're finally catching up on me, Rosie! Best of luck with your
exams. I'm sure you'll fly through them!
Happy Birthday.
Love, Stephanie, Pierre, Jean-Louis, Sophia

Happy Birthday, Mum
Hope you like your present. If it doesn't fit you, I'll have it!
Love, Katie

To a special friend
Happy 35th Birthday, Rosie! I'm working on a new experiment to
slow down time. Fancy joining in with me?
Enjoy your day and I hope to see you soon!
Alex

To Rosie
Happy Birthday again! After this celebration there will be no more
distractions. You have to pass these exams with straight A's. You can do
it and you're my only hope of getting out of here. I'm still dreaming of
that job as an entertainer at that fine hotel of yours.
Love, Ruby

You have an instant message from: ROSIE.

Rosie: Sixteen. My little angel sixteen! When I think of the things I did
            on my sixteenth birthday . . . actually, I can't remember
            exactly what I did!
Ruby: What did you do?
Rosie: Me and Alex forged our mums' signatures and wrote notes to
            school saying we would both be absent for the day.
Ruby: Coincidentally.
Rosie: Exactly. We went to some old man's pub in town where ID
            wasn't a necessity and we drank all day. Unfortunately it was
            ruined by the fact that I fell and hit my head, had to be raced
            to hospital in an ambulance where I received seven stitches and
            my stomach was pumped. The parents were none too pleased.
Ruby: I bet they weren't. How did you fall? Were you doing some of
            your funky moves on the dance floor again?
Rosie: Actually, no. I was only sitting on my stool.
Ruby: *Only you* could fall on the floor while you were sitting down.
Rosie: I know, that's weird, isn't it? I wonder how it happened!
Ruby: Well, you should ask Alex. I'm surprised it's never occurred to
            you to ask him before.
Rosie: Good idea! Ooh, he's online now so I'll ask.

You have an instant message from: ROSIE.

Rosie: Hi, Alex.
Alex: Hi there. Do you ever do any work? Every time I log on you're
            on too!
Rosie: I'm just chatting to Ruby. It's cheaper this way. Internet use is
            unlimited if you pay a monthly charge and, besides, typing
            makes us look like we're busy. Anyway, I just wanted to ask
            you a quick question.
Alex: Fire ahead.
Rosie: Remember on my sixteenth birthday, I fell and hit my head?
Alex: Ha ha, how could I forget? Are you thinking of this because
            Katie's birthday is coming up? Because if she's anything like
            you, you should be afraid, be very, very afraid.
Rosie: Age is only a number, not a state of mind or a reason for any
            type of particular behaviour.
Alex: O . . . K then. What's your question?
Rosie: How on earth did I manage to fall and hit my head on the floor
            while I was sitting down on a stool at the bar?
Alex: Oh my Lord. The question. *The* Question.
Rosie: What's wrong with my question??

Alex: Rosie Dunne, I have been waiting nearly twenty years for you
           to ask me that question and I thought you never would.
Rosie: What??
Alex: Why you never asked is beyond me, but you woke up next day
           and claimed to have no knowledge of what had happened.
Rosie: Alex, *tell me!* How did I fall off my stool??
Alex: We were kissing.
Rosie: We were *what??*
Alex: Yep. You were leaning across on your high stool, kissing
           me; the stool was very wobbly and lodged unsafely between
           the cracks of the uneven tiled pub floor. And you fell.
Rosie: WHAT??
Alex: Oh, the sweet nothings you whispered into my ear that night,
           Rosie Dunne. And I was gutted the next day when you woke
           up and forgot.
Rosie: *Alex! Why didn't you tell me?!*
Alex: Because we weren't allowed to see each other for a while and
           I didn't want to tell you in a note. And then you said you
           wanted to forget everything that had happened that night
           so I thought that maybe you remembered and regretted it.
Rosie: I can't believe it. Because I fell, we got caught and I had to stay
           home for a week while your punishment was to start work in
           your dad's office, where you met Bethany. The girl you said you
           were going to marry . . .
Alex: Well, I actually said that just to test you but as you didn't seem
           to care too much I went out with her anyway. That's funny. I
           had forgotten I had said that! Bethany would love to hear that!
           Thanks for reminding me.
Rosie: No, no, thank *you* for reminding *me* . . .

You have an instant message from: RUBY.
Ruby: You find out what happened yet?
Rosie: Yes, I found out I'm the biggest idiot in the whole entire world.
Ruby: I could have told you that ages ago.

Dear Katie,
Happy sweet sixteenth!
Love, Mum xxx

For our granddaughter,
Happy sweet sixteenth birthday!
Lots of love, Grandma and Granddad

For my girlfriend
Happy Sweet 16!
Lots of love,
John

To Katie
Happy birthday, you pain in the ass. A few months and those braces
will be off. Then I won't be able to tell what you've eaten for dinner.
Toby

For my daughter
Congratulations, Katie. Happy sweet sixteen!
Love, Dad

From   Rosie
To   Alex
Subject   Dad

Something awful has happened. People at work said you were in surgery
but, please, as soon as you get my messages and this email, ring me?

Mum called me just a minute ago in tears; Dad has had a massive heart
attack and has been rushed to hospital. She's in huge shock but she told me
not to travel over to her because my first exam is starting tomorrow. I don't
know what to do. I don't know how serious it is, the doctors won't tell us
anything yet. Can you maybe ring the hospital and see what's going on? You
understand all that stuff.

Oh God, Alex, please help. I don't want to lose my dad.

From   Alex
To   Rosie
Subject   Re: Dad

I tried calling you but you must be on the phone. Just stay calm. I rang the
hospital and had a word with Dr Flannery there. He's the doctor looking after
your dad and he explained Dennis's condition to me.

What I suggest you do is pack a bag for a few days and get on the
earliest bus you can to Galway. Do you understand what I mean?

Forget about your exam, this is more important. Keep calm, Rosie, and just
be there for your mum and dad. Tell Stephanie to come home too, if she can.
And Kevin. Keep in touch with me during the night.

Dear Alex,
Coffin sizes can be no wider than 76 cm; can be made of chipboard
with approved veneers and plastics for cremation purposes. Did you

know that? Ferrous screws are acceptable in small numbers and wood braces will give extra strength but must *only* be placed in the inside of the coffin.

The coffin must have the full name of the deceased on the lid. Wouldn't want to get anyone mixed up, I suppose. The thing that I really wished I hadn't learned was that the coffin should be lined with a substance known as 'Cremfilm', or use absorbent cloth or cotton padding because apparently fluid can leak from a body.

I didn't know any of this.

There were forms. Lots and lots of forms. Forms A, B, C, F and all the medical forms. No one mentioned anything about D and E. I didn't know you needed so much proof to show you were dead. I thought the fact you've stopped living and breathing was a huge giveaway. Apparently not.

Mum hasn't stopped shaking since it happened and she looks like she's aged twenty years. Yet she seems younger. Like a lost little child who looks around her and doesn't know where to go, like suddenly she's in a whole new place and she doesn't know the way.

I'm thirty-five years old and I've never lost anyone close to me. I've been to ten funerals in my life and they were of distant relatives, friends of friends and family of friends whom my life is none the worse off without. But Dad going? God, that's a big one.

I'm still over in Galway with Mum. In the wild, wild west. But it's a beautiful summer and it doesn't feel right. The atmosphere doesn't suit the mood, there's the sound of children's laughter floating up from the beach down below, there are birds singing and dancing around the sky. It reminds you that life goes on. People come and people go and we know this happens, yet we get such a shock when it does. To use that old cliché, the only certainty in life is death. It's a certainty, it's the one condition of living that we're given but we often let it tear us apart.

I don't know what to do or say to Mum to make her feel better; I don't suppose there really is anything that would accomplish that, but watching her crying to herself all day tears me apart. I can hear her pain in her tears. Maybe she'll just run out of tears.

Thanks for coming over to the funeral. It was so good to see you. It was just a shame that it was under these circumstances. It was good of your parents to come as well. Mum really did appreciate it. Thanks for getting rid of whatshisname too; I really wasn't in the mood to have any discussions with him at the church. It was good of him to come but if Dad had seen him he would have leapt out of that coffin and thrown him in in his place.

Stephanie and Kevin headed home a few days ago but I'm going to stay on for a little while longer. I just can't leave Mum alone. The neighbours are being so kind to her. I know she will be in good hands when I do finally leave. I've missed all my exams and by the sounds of things I'll have to repeat the entire year if I do want to complete the course. I don't think I could be bothered doing it all over again.

Thanks for being there for me once again, Alex. Isn't it typical of us that it's a tragedy that gets us together?

Love,
Rosie

From	Rosie
To	Alex
Subject	Dad

I just returned home from Connemara to be greeted by an overflowing mailbox. Among a pile of bills was the following letter. It was posted the day before Dad died.

Dear Rosie,

I hope you're over the trauma of your daughter becoming a fully fledged teen. I remember the day that happened with you. I think it hit you before Stephanie! You were always eager to try new things and go new places, my fearless Rosie. I thought that when you finished school you were going to set off around the world and we would never see you again. I'm glad that didn't happen. You were always a delight to have around the house. You and Katie. I'm only sorry we had to leave you when you needed us both. Your mum and I questioned our actions time and time again. I hope we did the right thing.

I know you always felt that you were in the way, but that's far from the truth. It just meant that I got to see my little girl grow. Grow from being a baby to an adult and grow as a mother. You and Katie are a great team and she is a fine example of the good parenting she received.

Life deals each of us a different set of cards and out of all of us there's no doubt that you received the toughest hand of all. But you shone through the tough times. You are a strong girl and you grew even stronger when that idiot of a man (whatshisname, your mother told me to say) let you down. You picked yourself up, dusted yourself off and started all over again, set up home with Katie, found yourself a new job, provided for your daughter and did your dad proud once more.

And now you're only days away from your exams. After all you went through you'll now have a diploma. I'll be proud watching you accept that scroll, Rosie; I'll be the proudest dad in the world.

Love,
Dad

From   Rosie
To   Alex
Subject   Diploma

There's no way I'm giving this college course up now. In the wise words of Johnny Logan, what's another year? I'm going to do these exams and I'm going to get this diploma in Hotel Management. Dad wouldn't want himself to be the reason for me missing out.

It's the goodbye I needed, Alex. What a wonderful gift to be given.

You have an instant message from: RUBY.

Ruby: Hello, stranger.

Rosie: Oh, hi, Ruby, sorry it's been so long; I've had a lot on lately.

Ruby: No apologies needed, you know that. How's your mum?

Rosie: Not great. That tear reservoir still hasn't dried up. She's coming to stay with me for a little while.

Ruby: In the flat?

Rosie: Yes.

Ruby: How's that going to work? You don't have any spare rooms.

Rosie: Oh, gosh, it has been ages since I spoke to you. After many days of deliberations with Brian the Whine I eventually gave in and have decided to allow Katie to stay with him in Ibiza for the summer. I must be crazy because no matter how much Brian the Whine assures me that he's a responsible father, I can't stop thinking of the fact that he ran off when he found out I was pregnant and only returned when she was thirteen. I'm not too keen on his definition of responsible.

Ruby: The good thing about Brian being her father is that he's the owner of a seedy nightclub where he's used to seeing what exactly sixteen-year-olds get up to. He will not want his daughter joining in with that kind of fun. Trust me.

Rosie: Anyway, John is going to join her for a few weeks and Toby and Monica are going over for a holiday too. But I can't put up too much of a fight because Brian said he would make sure she gets a bit of experience DJ-ing while she's there, which would be brilliant for her.

Ruby: Have you convinced yourself enough yet?

Rosie: God, does it really sound like that?

Ruby: Yep.

Rosie: Well, without wanting to sound like a complete moan (because we all know I'm not one to moan), this summer is going to be really lonely for me. Everyone will be gone. Dad, Katie, Steph, Kev, Alex. Even Mum is only staying with me a short while before she's off again. A few people Mum and Dad met while they were on their cruise got in touch with Mum. They're planning a trip to South Africa and they're going to stay for a month. That was the next place Dad wanted to go to. He always used to watch National Geographic and swear he would one day go on a safari. Well, he's going now because Mum is taking his ashes and scattering them with the tigers and elephants. So, I'll be all alone and because it's the summer and the school is closed, all I have to do is to study.

Ruby: You think that maybe this is a sign to meet more people?

Rosie: I know, I know.

Ruby: Sooner or later you're going to have to start enjoying yourself again. You recognise that word, Rosie? *Enjoy*. To have fun.

Rosie: Never heard of it.

Dear Mum,

Sorry I didn't write sooner but I've been so busy ever since I landed that I haven't had the chance to pick up a pen. It's really hot here at the moment so I'm trying to work on my tan before John comes over. I want to meet him at the airport looking like a complete beach babe!

Dad collected me from the airport, which was a weird experience. Weird to see him dressed up, or I should say dressed down *in shorts and flip-flops. I didn't know he had legs. You'd have laughed if you'd seen him. He was wearing this navy-blue Hawaiian-style shirt with yellow flowers splattered over it.*

He has an electric-blue convertible, which is pretty cool as I've never been in a convertible before. The island is so beautiful. He lives in a really nice complex just outside the busy part of town and there are about ten white-painted villas that share a swimming pool.

Toby and Monica are coming over next week, which should be good fun as long as Monica keeps her gob shut. They're both staying in a hotel in town and there's loads of cool clubs around them. But before you go ape shit let me tell you that the day I arrived, Dad brought me up and down the street of bars and clubs and introduced me to all the bouncers and managers. I thought he was doing it so that they'd recognise me and let me in, but when I tried the bars last week not one of them let me in. Not one. I thought maybe they hated Dad and were trying to piss him off or something, but yesterday a bouncer from the club down the road came up to Dad's club with his fifteen-year-old son who was staying with him for the summer too, and introduced him to Dad and all the head doormen. Then I heard Dad tell the guys at the door to remember the boy's face and not to let him in.

So I've just been going to Dad's club most nights. Last night I was allowed to stand in the DJ box. The resident DJ is DJ Sugar (He. Is. Gorgeous!) and he was showing me what to do all night and he even let me take over for a few minutes. The entire point was for the crowd not to notice because I wanted to sound as good and professional as Sugar, but I looked up and everyone was staring at me because Dad had a massive camera in his hand. It was so embarrassing.

I also met Dad's girlfriend. She's twenty-eight, her name's Lisa and she's a dancer in the club. She dances on a podium that's about ten feet off the ground in the centre of the club, and inside a ring of fire in a tiger-print piece of material that she wraps around her body (I wouldn't call it a dress).

She's talking about bringing a snake into her act next because she bought a new snakeskin costume and she thinks it'll look cool. Anyway, Dad thinks she's crazy and refuses to get her a snake and they've been arguing about it all week. I didn't have the heart to tell her that everyone is so drunk in the club I don't think they'd notice if Lisa was dancing with an elephant, never mind a snake.

I've just realised that you and I have never been on a proper holiday together. In fact, apart from visiting Steph and Alex have you ever been away away? You and me can go away next year when I've finally finished school and I'm enjoying my freedom. You'll have finished your diploma by then too so the two of us can celebrate! I hope your studying is going well. At least you don't have me there distracting you from your work.

I'll write again soon. I miss you!

Love, Katie

Dear Rosie,

I'm writing to you from Cape Town in South Africa, which is so stunning. The rest of the group are taking good care of me so don't you worry about that. And because they all knew Dennis from the cruise it's nice to be able to talk to them about him and remember the funny times we had. There's another lady here who has also lost her husband and this is her first holiday alone, so we both tend to get teary-eyed together at times.

I miss Dennis very much. He would have loved this holiday. But in a way he is here with me. I've scattered your father's ashes. Some into the air, some into the water and some into the ground. He's all around me now. I know this is what he would have wanted. This way he's floating through the air all around the world. Seeing more of it than me now. His final adventure.

I hope Katie is getting on well in Ibiza and that Brian is taking good care of her. He seems to have turned into a decent, hard-working man so I wouldn't worry, my dear Rosie. Could you please pass on the enclosed letter for Katie? I wasn't sure of her address.

Good luck with the studying, love.

I love you and miss you.

Mum

You have an instant message from: TOBY.

Toby: I bet you had a salad sandwich for lunch.

Katie: How do you no?

Toby: It's KNOW not NO. I can see the lettuce hanging out of your braces.

Katie: This time next week you won't be able to slag me any more. For the end of an era has come. The braces are coming off. After three and a half years behind bars, my teeth, my now *straight* teeth, may I add, will be free.

Toby: Well, it's about time. I can't wait to see how they come off. I *need* to see how they come off.

Katie: You don't actually *need* to no everything *before* you study it at college, Toby. The general idea is to learn it there.

Toby: Well, I haven't been accepted yet, have I?

Katie: You'll get in, Toby.

Toby: We'll see. Have you figured out what you're going to do yet?

Katie: How the hell are we expected at the age of sixteen (and seventeen, in your case) to decide what we want to do for the rest of our lives? Right now all I want to do is get *out* of school, not start planning to get into another one. You're lucky you've always known what you want to do.

Toby: Only thanks to you and your manky teeth. Anyway, you've known what you wanted to do for longer than I have. Be a DJ.

Katie: I can't study that in college, though, can I?

Toby: Who says you have to go to college?

Katie: Everyone. The career guidance teacher. My mum. My dad. All the teachers.

Toby: Well, I wouldn't listen to the career guidance teacher because his job is to take you for a half an hour every week and discuss college courses to his heart's content. Do you think he really cares what you do? Your dad is only agreeing with your mum, and your mum is only saying you should go because she thinks you want to.

Katie: But Mum has worked so hard to finally get round to studying what she wants and it's been such a struggle for her. She wanted this opportunity so much at my age and I kind of got in the way and now it's my turn and I've nothing in the way. I think Mum thinks I should be jumping for joy at the idea but it feels more like a prison sentence. Dad said that I could go over to him for the summer and work behind the bar in the club a few nights a week. Sugar will train me the other nights. He says if I want to do it I might as well start taking it seriously.

Toby: He's right.

Katie: Well, you don't sound like you're going to miss me too much!

Toby: Of course I won't. If you don't go, then I'm the one who has to listen to you moan for the rest of my life. Look, if your mum knew you really wanted to DJ, seriously, then she'd tell you to go for it.

Katie: I never thought of it like that. But how could I move away from Mum and Grandma. Oh my God, what about John?

Toby: John'll be able to fly to Ibiza and see you. I noticed you didn't mention me there. Will life be that easy without me?

Katie: Yes, of course it will. No, but honestly, aren't there any dentistry colleges in Ibiza?

Toby: Not where you're going, unless you include extracting people's teeth using your fist.

Katie: Well then, I guess it's Ibiza for just me and Dad then.

To Katie and Rosie
Good luck to the both of you in your exams.
I'm praying for my girls.
Love Mum/Grandma

To Rosie and Katie
Good luck!
Love, Steph, Pierre, JeAN-LOuiS and Sophia

To Rosie and Katie
My best friend and goddaughter, best of luck in your exams. You will both excel as you always do. Let me no how the first one goes.
Love, Alex

To Rosie
I know I encouraged you to go for this diploma but if you fail these exams this year and have to repeat I'm giving you the official warning that I have the firm intention of making a new friend.
So absolutely no pressure there.
Good luck!
Ruby

To Mum
Here we go. In a fortnight we'll both be free.
Best of luck.
Katie

WHERE RAINBOWS END

To Katie
Good luck, honey. Thanks for being my study partner.
No matter how you do, I'm proud of you.
Love, Mum

Exam results: Rosie Dunne.
Student number: 4553901-L
Course: Diploma in Hotel Business Management
Recognised by Irish Hotel & Catering Institute (MIMCI) & Catering
Managers' Association of Ireland (MCMA)

Subject	Grade
Accounting	B
Computer Applications and Data Summary	B
Economics	B
Hospitality Ethical and Legal Studies	B
Financial Control and Marketing	B
Human Resource Management	A
Enterprise Development	A
Languages (Irish)	A
Tourism and Hospitality Industry Studies	A

Graduates qualify for membership of a period of professional
internship in the hospitality industry.

YES! YES! YES! YES! YEEEEEESSSSSS! ALEX I DID IT! I FINALLY DID IT!!

Rosie I'm so happy 4 u! Congratulations!

From   Rosie
To   Ruby
Subject   Let's celebrate!

Now we can definitely go out! By the way, Katie is coming out with us too
so get your dancing shoes on (of course in your case I don't mean that
literally. No one wants to see those scary-looking salsa shoes in a nightclub).
She did well in her exams and got accepted to a few college business
courses but she's going to stick to her original idea of trying out DJ-ing. Toby
got enough points for Dentistry at Trinity College, which is wonderful news
so overall everyone is happy, happy, happy!

You know when I was eighteen I missed out on going to Boston and I
thought my world had ended. While all my friends were partying and studying I was cleaning dirty nappies. I thought my dream was lost. Never in a
million years did I think that I would be able to share this special moment
with my teenage daughter.

309

Everything does happen for a reason. I'll just be so sad to see my baby go away. The day I've been preparing for has finally arrived, Katie is spreading her wings and moving on and I must do the same. *Finally.*

Dear Rosie,

On behalf of all of us here at St Patrick's Primary School I congratulate you on your recent exam results. You have proved yourself to be a true achiever and should feel proud.

Keeping my promise, I am delighted to inform you that your services are no longer required. Your contract with us will not be up for renewal in August.

We are sorry to see you go but you have to. My retirement was one year later than planned but it was worth hanging around to see you succeed. Rosie Dunne, you have been the longest project of my life, my eldest and longest-serving student, and although we may have had a rocky start and an even rockier middle, I am so glad to see you succeed at the end.

Your hard work and dedication is an inspiration to us all and I wish you the very best for the future. I do hope you keep in touch and I would love to see you attend my retirement party, for which you will receive an invitation shortly. I ask that you forward on an invitation to Alex Stewart too.

Congratulations again.

Keep in touch.

Julie (Big Nose Smelly Breath) Casey

Katie,

My baby girl is moving away! I'm so proud of you, love. You are so brave to be doing this. Make sure your dad doesn't forget to feed and clothe you.

I'll miss you so much. I loved having you here with me but I hope I'm welcome to visit you lots!

If you need me, just call and I'll come running.

Lots of love,

Mum

Dear Brian,

This is a huge responsibility. Please take care of Katie and don't let her get up to anything stupid over there. You know what eighteen-year-old males are like—you yourself were one. Keep her away from them as best you can. She's over there to learn, not party and make babies.

Let me know *everything* that's going on with her. Even the stuff she's afraid to tell me. A mother needs to know. Please listen to her and be there for her all the time. If you even sense that something is wrong and she won't confide in you, just let me know and I'll subtly find out.

And last but not least, thank you so much for giving my baby, *our* baby, her dream.

Best wishes,

Rosie

Dear Rosie Dunne,

Congratulations on completing your Diploma in Hotel Business Management. We are pleased to inform you that your professional internship in the hospitality industry will be undertaken at the beginning of August. Each graduate's employment has been randomly selected and chosen by a computer without discrimination or prejudice. Once a placement has been made the graduate cannot change.

The contract of twelve months is for the position of assistant manager and is to be held at the Grand Tower Hotel in Dublin's city centre. You will begin on Monday, 1 August at 9 a.m. For more information regarding your placement please contact Cronin Ui Cheallaigh, manager and owner of the Grand Tower Hotel. The phone number, details and map of directions to the hotel are provided overleaf.

We wish you luck in your new venture and hope it brings you success in the future.

Yours sincerely,

Keith Richards
Hotel Business Management Course Director
St Patrick's Primary School Night Courses

Alex: Very impressive, Rosie. The Grand Tower Hotel?
Rosie: Oooh, I know! I feel like a kid on Christmas Eve! I haven't felt like that for a long, long time. I know the job is temporary and that I'm only in training but I've waited a long time for this.
Alex: You've waited too long for it. I of all people no how much you've wanted this. I used to hate it when you made me play Hotel.
Rosie: Ha ha, I remember that. I was always the person in charge and you had to be the customer!
Alex: I hated being the customer because you would never leave me alone. You kept fluffing my pillows and lifting my feet up on stools 'for the customer's comfort'.
Rosie: My God, I'd forgotten all about that! I used to try to be like the guy on *Fantasy Island* who looked after his guests so much he would use magic to give them their dreams.

Alex:	I don't call tucking me in so tight that I could hardly breathe, a comfort/dream-providing service! I don't no what type of manager you were trying to be but if you behave like that with your real customers then a few of them will have restraining orders taken out against you.
Rosie:	Well, at least it was better than playing Hospital. All that game consisted of was you tripping me up on concrete and then tending to me.
Alex:	Yeah, that was fun, wasn't it?
Rosie:	Well, you have a distorted idea of what fun is.
Alex:	Hotels and hospitals. Sounds like some dodgy porn movie.
Rosie:	You wish!
Alex:	I do wish. I have a three-year-old son who likes to sleep in between me and Beth.
Rosie:	Well, I could join the nunnery and I don't think it would bother me in the slightest.
Alex:	Oh, I disagree!
Rosie:	No, really, trust me, Alex. After the men I've been with, celibacy would be like a *gift*.
Alex:	It wasn't the celibacy I was referring to; it was the vow of silence that would kill you.
Rosie:	Funny. Well, believe me, Alex, there are certain silences that make you walk on air. And on that note, I'll leave you.

Rosie has logged off.

| Alex: | Those silences I no. |

Hi, Mum,

Just a quick note to wish you luck (not that you need it) on your first day of work tomorrow. I'm sure you'll knock 'em all dead!

Best of luck,
Love,
Katie

You have an instant message from: RUBY.

Ruby:	Well, Ms Assistant Manager, tell me all about it. How's work going?
Rosie:	Very, very sl o o o o o wly.
Ruby:	Should I ask why?
Rosie:	Are you ready for a rant?
Ruby:	Fire ahead.
Rosie:	*OK,* so I arrived on the road the hotel was situated on nice and early and proceeded to walk up and down the street for three-quarters of an hour trying to find the very beautiful and *Grand*

Tower Hotel. I asked shop owners and stall owners but none of them had any idea where this hotel was.

I rang the course director almost in tears, but he kept on repeating the same address over and over again, which I told him couldn't be possible because the building in question was completely derelict.

Eventually he said he'd ring the hotel owner and double-check the directions with him so I sat down on the filthy front steps of the derelict building (dirtying the bum of my new suit). Suddenly the door of the building behind me opened and this *thing* looked out at me. The thing spoke in a very strong Dublin accent, introduced himself as Cronin Ui Cheallaigh, the owner of the building, and insisted I call him Beanie.

He brought me inside to the ancient, damp building and showed me around the few rooms on the ground level. He then asked me if I had any questions and I, of course, wanted to know why I was in this particular building and when was I going to see the hotel. To which he replied proudly, 'Dis is de bleedin' hotel. Nice, wha'?'

He then asked me if I had any ideas on how to improve the hotel after my first impression and I suggested displaying the actual name of the hotel on the actual building so as to make it easier for the guests (although not doing so was also a good marketing ploy). I also suggested spreading the word of its existence among the surrounding businesses so they could help advertise the hotel (or at least be able to help give directions to completely lost tourists).

He studied my face very hard to see if I was being smart. Which, by the way, I absolutely wasn't. I'm currently waiting on a sign for the front of the hotel to arrive.

How this so-called hotel has remained open up until now is beyond me. It is one of those beautiful houses that in its time would have been extremely grand but that has been left to rot away. It has four levels and on the underground level, I have now learned, is a lap-dancing club also owned by Beanie.

As you enter the ground level of the hotel, you are greeted by a tiny little desk made of dark mahogany wood. Small lantern-like lights adorn the walls and throw out absolutely no light at all. The place is like a dungeon.

A long corridor leads down to a large bar area, which contains paisley-covered stools and chairs and when the sun shines through the tiny, paint-flaking window all you can see is the air thick with wisps of tobacco smoke.

The dining area has twenty tables and a limited menu. There are brown velvet curtains, and net blinds; the tables are covered in what were once white but are now yellow lace tablecloths with rusty, food-stained cutlery. The glasses are misty, the walls are white, which makes it the only light room, but no matter how much the heat is turned up it feels cold.

There are sixty rooms. Twenty on each floor. Beanie proudly announced that half of them are en suite. You could imagine how happy I was to hear that!

I was also beginning to wonder what kind of customers a hotel like this would attract but it all became clear to me as I worked the late shift one night. As the lap-dancing club finished downstairs, the party continued upstairs.

Rosie: Ruby? Ruby, are you there?
Rosie: Hello? Ruby, did you get all that?
Ruby: Zzzzzzzzzzzzzzzzzzzzzz
Rosie: Ruby!!
Ruby: Oh, what?! Did I miss something? Sorry, I must have nodded off when you *started* telling me about your job.
Rosie: I'm sorry, Ruby, but I warned you. It's been one of those months.
Ruby: Not all jobs turn out to be what you think they're going to be. Anyway, would you rather be a secretary at Randy Andy Paperclip Co. or assistant manager of the Grand Tower Hotel?
Rosie: Oooh, definitely assistant manager of the Grand Tower Hotel.
Ruby: Well, there you go, Rosie. Life could be worse then, couldn't it?
Rosie: I guess so. But I do have one other slight problem.
Ruby: Can you tell me what it is in less than one thousand words?
Rosie: I'll try! Alex is coming over for Julie Casey's retirement party in a few weeks and he's bringing Bethany, and they've booked themselves into the hotel for the weekend. You see, I kind of told him that it was really nice . . .
Ruby: Oh dear . . .

You have an instant message from: ALEX.
Alex: Hi, Rosie, you're up late.
Rosie: So are you.
Alex: I'm five hours behind, remember.
Rosie: Katie's debs ball is on tonight. She's there right now, in fact.
Alex: Oh, I see. Can't you sleep?
Rosie: Are you mad? Of course I can't sleep. I helped shop for the

dress, helped her get ready with her make-up and hair, took photographs of her being so excited on her special night. The night when she will see friends she probably won't see again for years, or never again, despite promises of keeping in touch. It was like turning the clock back twenty years.

I know she's not me, she's her own person with her own mind, but I couldn't help but see myself walking out that door. Arm in arm with a man in a tuxedo, excited about the night, excited about the future. Excited, excited, excited. I was so bloody young. Of course, I didn't think I was at the time. I had a million plans. I knew what I was going to do. I had the next few years of my life all figured out.

But what I didn't know was that within a few hours all those plans would change. I just hope Katie comes home tonight when she should.

Alex: She's wise, Rosie, and if you've raised her the way I think you have, then you have nothing to worry about.

Rosie: I can't fool myself. She's been with her boyfriend for over three years now so I don't exactly think they've been holding hands all this time. But for tonight at least, on the night that changed my life, I wish her home early.

Alex: Well then, I'll just have to distract you until she comes home, won't I?

Rosie: If you wouldn't mind.

Alex: So how is our hotel room set for when we're over? I certainly hope the manager can arrange the very best for us!

Rosie: I'm actually only the *assistant* manager, remember, and the hotel isn't exactly . . .

Alex: Isn't exactly what?

Rosie: As snazzy as the ones you're used to when you travel.

Alex: This one will be extra special because my best friend runs it.

Rosie: I wouldn't want to take much credit for the general running of the hotel . . .

Alex: Oh, don't be silly. You never give yourself enough credit for what you do.

Rosie: No, *really*, Alex. I wouldn't want to accept any responsibility for this hotel *at all*. You know, I'm only there a few months. I haven't had a chance to put my stamp on it.

Alex: Nonsense. I can't wait to see it. How funny would it be if someone was poisoned in the restaurant and I had to be the in-house doctor that saved the day? Remember that was our plan when we were kids?

Rosie: I remember all right, and it may not be far off a possibility.

Alex: It'll be weird seeing Miss Big Nose Smelly Breath Casey again. It's about time she retired. The children of the world need a break from her.

Rosie: Her name is Julie, remember that, and do *not* call her by the other name. And she has been very good to me over the past few years so please be good to her.

Alex: I will, I will. Don't worry, I do no how to deal with people.

Rosie: Of course you do, Mr Socialite Surgeon extraordinaire.

Alex: Oh, shut up! So how's your mum these days? Any word back from the hospital about those tests?

Rosie: No, not yet. They really don't seem to know what's wrong with her. I'm really worried. I looked at her the other day and it was as though I hadn't seen her properly for years. Without even noticing it, my mum has gotten old. It was a shock. Anyway, I just hope they find out what it is and fix it. She's really not feeling well at all.

Alex: As soon as you find out, let me know.

Rosie: I will. It's tough having to travel to Galway on my days off. As much as I love Mum, it's a bit of a trek for me. Between working incredibly unsociable hours, travelling to Mum, helping her, I haven't had any real days off for the past few weeks and I am tireder than tired. Hold on, a coach pulled up outside. Wait while I run to the window and check.

Alex: Is Katie in it?

Rosie: No.

Alex: Oh. She'll be—

Rosie: Oh, *thank God*, there she is. I'd better switch off the computer and dive into bed. I don't want her thinking I was waiting up. Oh, thank you, God, for bringing my baby home. Night, Alex.

Alex: Night, Rosie.

Mother dearest,

Thanks for last week. It was so good to be home again with you. I bring good news with this letter! Tony Spencer, an English bloke who owns Club Insomnia down the road, was here in Dad's club last night when I was doing my set, and he asked if I'd like to work for him! How cool is that?! He also organises summer dance festivals so I'll be off around Europe during the summer, playing at those. I'm really excited!

I don't no when John is coming over. Ever since he started college in September it's been really weird with the two of us. I thought I'd be with him for ever but the rate we're going I can barely imagine being with him until the end of the summer.

Meanwhile, I haven't heard from Toby in a long, long time. It's entirely my fault because he rang me loads of times at the beginning when I moved over here and I just didn't get round to calling him back. Time just ran away. I keep on saying I'll call him tomorrow but it's been months and now I'm embarrassed. The last time I spoke to him he was having a great time at college, making friends with lots of teeth, no doubt. I'll call him tomorrow, promise I will.

Alex wrote to me a while back and told me what happened when he and Bethany stayed in the hotel when they were over for Miss Big Nose Smelly Breath Casey's retirement party. How funny! Didn't you no it was going to be the lap-dancing club's Christmas party? I don't think Alex seemed too disturbed by the sight of red-and-white-fluffy-bikini-clad Mary Clauses dancing around the bar. I can't believe Bethany refused to stay the night. That woman really doesn't have a sense of humour. I don't no what Alex sees in her. I've only met her a few times but she's so uptight and he's so laid-back I really don't see them lasting together for much longer. I can't believe Alex had to tend to one of the guests in the restaurant—was the man poisoned? What kind of food is your restaurant serving?! Just as well there was a doctor in the house.

I miss you so much but whenever I'm lonely I just look at the photos of you and Alex in my locket. You're both close to my heart. Always.

Love,
Katie

You have an instant message from: RUBY.

Ruby: I've been dumped.

Rosie: *What?* By Teddy?

Ruby: No! Don't be silly, that man doesn't know how to put the bins out, never mind dump me. No, the culprit is in fact my adoring son. He has informed me that my salsa services are no longer required and he's traded me in for a younger model.

Rosie: Oh, no, Ruby, I'm so sorry. Who's the other woman?

Ruby: Actually, I pretend to be mad but I'm not really. Well, that's a lie. At first I was *really* angry and ate an entire chocolate cake myself—Gary's favourite cake that I had bought for him, coincidentally. Halfway through it I was just angry and then while I was spooning the last mouthful into my mouth I began to think rationally (that's what it does to me, you see). So I devised a plan whereby I was going to invite this 'other woman' into my home for dinner so that I could poison her.

I needed to find out who she was, why on earth Gary left

me for her. As it turns out she's only in her late twenties, is from Spain, teaches Spanish at the school (that's where Gary met her, where he works as a custodial engineer), she's thin, pretty and is a very beautiful person.

Rosie: She's everything you would usually hate, right?

Ruby: *Usually*, yes. But this time it's different because she and my Gary have found love.

Rosie: Ooooh!

Ruby: I know! Isn't it great? So I had no problem stepping aside and hanging up my dancing shoes. To tell the truth, I was thinking of parting with Gary soon anyway. I'm not far off fifty now. I need to dance with someone more my own age, who won't have the energy to be flinging me across the other side of the room. I'm not up to it any more. I'm just happy Gary has finally found someone. Maybe Maria will make him move out of my house and in with her.

Rosie: Would you be upset by that?

Ruby: As upset as I would be if I found a million euros under my bed.

To Josh
Happy 10th birthday.
Lots of love,
Rosie

To Rosie
  Thanks so much for my present and card. It's really cool.
  Wherever Katie is tell her I said hi. She sends me postcards all the time from different countries and she sounds real happy. She's got the coolest job!
  I never hear about her old friend Toby any more. I guess they lost touch or something. Anyway, thanks again for the present. I'll be able to buy a new computer game with it.
  See you soon,
  From
  Josh

To Mum
  Hello! I'm in Amsterdam!
  Met a gorgeous guy who picks strawberries for a living. Doesn't speak English but we get along just fine.
  Everything here is great. Got loads of gigs and the cafés are nice too!
  Love,
  Katie

To Rosie
Happy thirty-eighth!
How scary is it that we're so close to forty?! Have a drink for me.
Love,
Alex

Rosie, if you think thirty-eight is bad, just imagine how I must feel, pushing fifty. Aaaah! We'll have a huge party. Just you and me invited.
Happy birthday again.
Ruby

Hi, Mum,
 I'm in Andorra. Met this gorgeous guy who's my ski instructor, who's trying to teach me how not to break my neck. He doesn't speak a word of English but we get along just fine. Everything is great here. The winter festival is going really well, got a few small gigs to do. I'll be home for Christmas so we can catch up on all the gossip! Can't wait to see you!
 Love,
 Katie

Hi, Mum,
 Do you want to stay with me for Christmas? Katie is coming home and it can be the three of us. I think it would be really nice, you can have Katie's room and I'll set up a sofa bed for her. I'm so excited about the idea. Beanie has given me Christmas Day off so please say yes!
 Rosie

Rosie,
 I'd love to come over, honey. Thanks for the invite. Can't wait to see little Katie. Not so little any more, I suppose!
 Love,
 Mum

From   Katie
To   Mum
Subject Coming home

Thanks so much for Christmas dinner. It was absolutely yummy, as always. It was good for us three to be together again. Just the girls!
 Grandma has changed a lot since the last time I saw her and you look tired. I was thinking of coming home for a few weeks to help out. Maybe I could get a job around Dublin? I want to help. (Plus there's the added bonus of meeting up with that guy I met while I was there!) Let me no.

From   Rosie
To   Katie
Subject   Re: Coming home

Do *not* come home! That is an order! Everything is just fine here. You need to live your life too so you can continue on with your travels, work hard and enjoy yourself! Don't worry about your grandma and me. We're fine!

I'm really enjoying the job and I don't mind the long hours. It's also nice to be able to go away every week to breathe the fresh air of Connemara. I do have one favour to ask, however. Ruby and I would love to come over to you for a week sometime in February if you could fit us into your schedule. Ruby said she wants to go to a foam party and win a wet T-shirt competition before she's fifty!

Let me know when a good week is for you.

From   Rosie
To   Steph
Subject   Mum

I've a favour to ask. Do you think you might be able to take Mum for a week in February? I'm sorry, I know you're really busy too, but Beanie has finally given me a week off and I really wanted to get over to Katie to check out how she's living these days. I want to meet her friends and see where she's working; you know, annoying things that mothers do.

If you can't then I understand. Perhaps I could twist Kevin's arm into caring about someone else for a change.

Give my love to the family.

From   Steph
To   Rosie
Subject   Re: Mum

Of course I'll take Mum. In fact, I'll go one better and take the family over to Connemara for the week. Pierre dragged me to his mother and father's for Christmas dinner so I think I'm entitled to have my turn!

You deserve a break, Rosie. I'm so sorry you're stuck doing everything. Have fun with Katie and enjoy the week with Ruby. I need to spend some quality time with Mum anyway.

From   Alex
To   Katie
Subject   Surprise 40th

I don't no where you are in the world right now, but I hope you're still checking your emails! Seeing as your mum is going to be forty next month and you are going to be twenty-one, I thought it would be a good idea to have a double birthday party. But I was hoping that we could fly you home and surprise your mum with a party?

You can invite all your friends and we can organise all of Rosie's friends too. Perhaps we can bring Ruby in on this for help? I think she would love it.
Let me no if you think it's a good idea.

You have an instant message from: ROSIE.

Rosie: I'm forty in a few days. *Forty*. The big 4–0.
Ruby: So?
Rosie: So it's *old*.
Ruby: Then what does that make me, ancient?
Rosie: Oh, sorry, you know what I mean. We're not exactly twenty years old, are we?
Ruby: No, thank God for that, because then I would have to go through a shit marriage and a divorce all over again. We would have to go out and look for jobs, be all uncertain about our lives, care about dating and how we look and what car we're driving, what music we're playing in it, what we wear, whether we'll get into certain clubs or not, blah blah blah. What's so good about being twenty? I call them the materialistic years. Then we cop on when we hit our thirties and spend those years trying to make up for the twenties. But your forties? Those years are for enjoying it.
Rosie: Hmm, good point. What are the fifties for?
Ruby: Fixing what you fucked up on in your forties.
Rosie: Great. Looking forward to it.
Ruby: Oh, don't worry, Rosie. You don't need to make a song and dance about the fact that the world has spun around the sun one more time. So what do you want to do for your fortieth?
Rosie: Nothing?
Ruby: Good plan. Why don't we go down to my local on Friday night?
Rosie: Sounds perfect.
Ruby: Oh, hold on, though. It's Teddy's brother's birthday that night too, and we're all gathering in the Berkeley Court Hotel.
Rosie: Oh, very snazzy! I love that hotel!
Ruby: I know, I think he's on the fiddle again. Honestly, you would think he'd know the *gardaí* are watching him after he's just got out of prison. Some people never learn.
Rosie: Oh well, would you rather change it to Saturday night then?
Ruby: No! Will you collect me from the hotel and we can head to the pub together?

Rosie: OK, but I don't want to get stuck talking to Teddy's brother. The last time I met him he tried to put his hand up my skirt.

Ruby: He had only been out of prison a few days, though, Rosie; you can understand how he was feeling.

Rosie: Whatever. So what time should I pick you up at?

Ruby: 8 p.m.

Rosie: Are you joking?! What time does it start at?

Ruby: 7.30 p.m.

Rosie: Ruby! You'll have to stay a lot longer than that! I'm not arriving to take you away after only a half an hour; everyone will think I'm so rude! I'll come at 9.30 p.m. At least that way you'll have two hours.

Ruby: No! You *have* to come at eight!

Rosie: Why?

Ruby: Well, for one thing the party is in the *penthouse suite* of the Berkeley Court Hotel.

Rosie: Oh my God, why didn't you just say so? I'll be there at 7.30 p.m.

Ruby: No! You can't!

Rosie: What is wrong with you? Why can't I?

Ruby: Because you're not invited and they'll think you've a cheek just turning up like that. If you come at eight then you can quickly see the place and then leave.

Rosie: But I want to stay at the penthouse. Have you any idea how much that would mean to me?

Ruby: Yes, I do . . . but I'm sorry, you can't stay. Anyway, once you meet the rest of Teddy's family you'll want to leave straight away.

Rosie: OK, but I hope you know that you're breaking my heart—and I don't care what you say, anything in the bathrooms that isn't nailed down is going in my handbag. Actually I think I'll bring my camera!

Ruby: Rosie, it's a birthday party. I'm sure lots of people will have cameras.

Rosie: Yes, I know, but I'll take some photos for Katie too. She'd love to see what it looks like. I was hoping she would be able to come over but she can't. It's her twenty-first birthday a few weeks after my birthday and I was hoping we could celebrate it together but unfortunately it's not to be. Mum is going over to stay with Stephanie again so she'll miss it as well. I was a bit upset about that but she's been so ill lately I didn't want to cause a fuss. I was just glad she said she wanted to go somewhere, even if it was on my birthday.

So it will just be you and me once again, but at least this year I'll get to sneak a peek at the penthouse suite! I'll steal a few ideas for my own hotel. What a treat!

Ruby: Looking forward to seeing your face, Rosie. See you at 8 p.m., room 440.

Penthouse Suite
440

SURPRISE, ROSIE!
HAPPY BIRTHDAY, ROSIE & KATIE!!

Happy fortieth, Rosie!

I had a wonderful weekend at your party, we really did surprise you, didn't we?! It broke my heart pretending to you that I was staying with Stephanie but it was worth it to see the look on your face (and the tears in your eyes). Alex arranged the entire thing. He's a lovely, lovely man, Rosie. Shame about the wife, though! Do you know, I always thought you and he would get together when you were children. Silly, isn't it?

Anyway, thank you, thank you for being a wonderful daughter and for all of your help over the past few years. Your father would be proud of you. I'll be sure to tell him all about you when I see him!

You are a beautiful young woman, Rosie Dunne. Your father and I did well! Lots of love, Mum

Happy seventieth, Mum!

You made it to the big 7–0 and you look as beautiful as ever! We'll have you out of hospital as quick as we can; in the meantime here are some grapes to make you feel really sick!

Love you always and for ever, Mum,
Rosie

Hi, Kev, Steph here. Texting as can't get you on the phone. You might want to come to Connemara now. It's time.

Hi, love, get in touch with ur dad asap. He's booked u a flight home 2morrow. I no it's short notice but grandma asking 4 u. Kev will collect u from airport & bring u here. C u 2morrow. Love, Mum

Dunne (née O'Sullivan) (Connemara, Co. Galway and formerly Dundrum, Dublin 10)—Alice, beloved wife of Dennis and loving mother of Stephanie, Rosie and Kevin; will be missed by her grandchildren Katie, Jean-Louis and Sophia, son-in-law Pierre, brother Patrick and sister-in-law Sandra. Removal at 4.45 p.m. today from Stafford's funeral home to Oughterard Church, Connemara. May she rest in peace.

'Ar dheis lamh De go raibh a anam uasal.'

THIS IS THE LAST WILL, dated the 10 day of September 2000, of ALICE DUNNE
Of
HEREBY REVOKING all former Wills and Testamentary Dispositions made by Alice Dunne.
If my husband survives me by thirty days **I GIVE DEVISE AND BEQUEATH** the whole of my estate to him and appoint him my executor. If my husband does not survive me by thirty days the following provisions shall apply:

1.   **I APPOINT** Rosie Dunne (hereinafter called 'my Trustee') to be executor and trustee and appoint her trustee for the purposes of the Settled Land Acts, Conveyancing Acts and Section 57 of the Succession Act.
2.   **I GIVE, DEVISE AND BEQUEATH** to my Trustee the whole of my estate upon trust to sell the same (with power to postpone such sale in whole or in part for such time as they shall think fit) and to hold the same or the proceeds of sale thereof on the following trusts . . .

You have an instant message from: STEPH.
Steph: How's my baby sister holding up?
Rosie: Oh, hi, Steph. I'm not sure. There's an eerie silence in my world these days. I find myself switching on the TV or radio just to fill the background. Katie had to head back to work; people have stopped ringing and calling around to offer their sympathies. Everything is calming down and I'm left with this silence.

I'm not quite sure what to do with myself on my days off. I'm so used to hopping on the bus and travelling over to Mum. Life is strange now. Before even when she lay in bed looking frail and weak she still managed to make me feel safe. Mothers do that, don't they? Their very presence can help. And even if I ended up mothering her in the final days, she still was taking care of me. I miss her.

Steph: I do too, and at the oddest times. It's only when you get back
            to the normal routine of life that you really feel it. I keep on
            having to remind myself that when the phone rings it's not her.
            Or when I get a free moment in the day I pick up the phone to
            call her and then I remember that she's not there to call. It's
            such an odd feeling.

Rosie: Kevin is still in a huff with me.

Steph: Ignore Kevin; he's in a huff with the entire world.

Rosie: Maybe he's right, though, Steph. Mum has put me in such an
            awkward position by leaving me the house. Perhaps I should
            sell it and split the profits three ways. It's fairer.

Steph: Rosie Dunne, you will not sell that house for me and Kev. She
            left it for you for a reason. Kev and I are both financially
            secure—we both have houses. We really don't need the
            Connemara house. Mum knew that so she left the house to
            you. You work harder than the two of us put together and you
            still can't get out of that flat. Obviously I didn't tell you, but
            Mum discussed it with me before and I agreed with her. Don't
            listen to Kev.

Rosie: I don't know, Steph; I'm not hugely comfortable with it . . .

Steph: Rosie, trust me, if I needed the money so badly I would tell you
            and we could work something out. But I don't. Neither does
            Kevin. It's not like we were forgotten about in the will. We're
            both fine, honestly. The house in Connemara belongs to you.
            You do with it whatever you wish.

Rosie: Thanks, Steph.

Steph: No problem. So what are you going to do over there on your
            own, Rosie? I hate you being all alone. Do you want to come
            over here for a while?

Rosie: No, thanks, Steph. I have to work. I'm going to throw myself
            into this job and make it the best damn hotel in the world.

Grand Tower Hotel
Tower Road,
Dublin 1

Dear Mr Cronin Ui Cheallaigh,

Following our visit to the Grand Tower Hotel we at the Department
of Public Works are sending you an emergency order due to an immi-
nent and substantial hazard to the life, health and safety of occupants.

After their visit last week, the Department of Building Inspection
listed more than one hundred code violations including missing smoke
detectors, water damage and inadequate lighting.

According to our records you have received many warnings over the years to improve the maintenance of the building. These warnings were ignored and we have no choice but to shut you down.

Please be in touch with our offices as soon as you receive this letter.

Yours sincerely,
Adam Delaney
Office of Public Works

From   Katie
To   Mum
Subject Your job

I'm so sorry to hear about you losing your job. I no you hated it, but still, it's never nice to have to leave when it's not your own decision. I couldn't reach you on the phone—you've either been on the phone all day or they've cut you off. Either way, I thought I'd email you instead. I completely forgot to tell you that when we returned to Dublin after the funeral, whatshisname called round to the flat to see you.

I didn't want to call you because you were upset enough as it was, so I took a message. He dropped in some post that had been delivered to his house for you and said that he hoped that they would be some sort of help to you now that your mum and dad are gone. He said he understood how you felt, as his mum died last year and he didn't want to be the cause of your loneliness.

He seemed sincere, but who can ever tell with him? It was odd seeing him after so many years. He's really aged. Anyway, I hope whatever is in the envelopes isn't too important but let me no what they are all the same. I left the two envelopes in the bottom drawer of the living-room cabinet.

Dr Reginald & Miranda Williams
invite **Rosie Dunne**
to join them in celebrating the
marriage of their beloved daughter
Bethany
to
Dr Alex Stewart
at
the Memorial Church of Harvard University
on 28 December
at 2 o'clock
& a reception at
the Boston Harbor Hotel
RSVP Miranda Williams

Rosie,

I'm returning to Boston tomorrow but before I go I wanted to write this letter to you. All the thoughts and feelings that have been bubbling up inside me are finally overflowing from this pen and I'm leaving this letter for you so that you don't feel that I'm putting you under any great pressure. I understand that you will need to take your time trying to decide on what I am about to say.

I no what's going on, Rosie. You're my best friend and I can see the sadness in your eyes. I no that Greg isn't away working for the weekend. You never could lie to me; you were always terrible at it. Your eyes betray you time and time again. Don't pretend that everything is perfect because I see it isn't.

Greg is the luckiest man in the world to have you, Rosie, but he doesn't deserve you and you deserve far better. You deserve someone who loves you with every single beat of his heart, someone who thinks about you constantly, someone who spends every minute of every day just wondering what you're doing, where you are, who you're with and if you're OK. You need someone who can help you reach your dreams and who can protect you from your fears. You need someone who will treat you with respect, and love every part of you, especially your flaws. You should be with someone who can make you happy, really happy, dancing-on-air happy. Someone who should have taken the chance to be with you years ago instead of becoming scared and being too afraid to try.

I am not scared any more, Rosie. I am not afraid to try. I no what that feeling was at your wedding—it was jealousy. My heart broke when I saw the woman I love turning away from me to walk down the aisle with another man, a man she planned to spend the rest of her life with. It was like a prison sentence for me—years stretching ahead without me being able to tell you how I feel or hold you how I wanted to.

Twice we've stood beside each other at the altar, Rosie. Twice. And twice we got it wrong. I needed you to be there for my wedding day but I was too stupid to see that I needed you to be the reason for my wedding day.

I should never have let your lips leave mine all those years ago in Boston. I should never have pulled away. I should never have panicked. I should never have wasted all those years without you. Give me a chance to make them up to you. I love you, Rosie, and I want to be with you and Katie and Josh. Always.

Please think about it. Don't waste your time on Greg. This is our opportunity. Let's stop being afraid and take the chance. I promise I'll make you happy.

All my love,

Alex

You have an instant message from: ROSIE.

Rosie: Ruby. I just came across a letter that was written just after my thirtieth birthday. A letter that was meant for me but never made it into my hands. It was from Alex.

Ruby: What did he say in the letter?

Rosie: He said he loved me.

Ruby: Oh. My. God. So where did you find the letter?

Rosie: Greg returned it to me. He 'didn't want to be the cause of my loneliness any more', he said.

Ruby: So have you spoken to Alex?

Rosie: How can I speak to him? Knowing what I know, how can I even *think* of him?

Ruby: Very easily, I would imagine. He's just told you that he loves you!

Rosie: No, Ruby, he told me over *ten* years ago that he loved me. Before he got married, *before* he had his son Theo. I just can't bring myself to talk to him. He's been writing and phoning but the thought of that missed opportunity makes me so sick to the stomach that I can't respond to his messages.

Ruby: You have to tell him you know!

Rosie: I was going to. But this morning his annual Christmas card arrived in the postbox. With the photo of his wife and two sons on the cover of the card, all wearing colourful knitted Christmas jumpers: Theo with his two front teeth gone, Josh with his beaming smile just like his dad, Bethany hand in hand with Alex. And I couldn't tell him. What would he care now? He's happy. He's over me, and even if he's not, I wouldn't expect him to jump out of that perfect Christmas photo for me. The possibility of me and Alex being together has faded, just like those old photos of us in Katie's locket.

Ruby: So what *are* you going to do?

Rosie: Move to Connemara.

Ruby: But *why*?

Rosie: I have my reasons, Ruby. There's nothing here for me in Dublin. Apart from you, of course. I have had a string of unsatisfactory jobs, have no family here, had my heart broken twice, I have no money and no man. I don't see a reason why I should stay.

Ruby: Well, forgive me for being the bearer of bad news but you have no family and no man in Galway, and no job.

Rosie: I may not have all those things but I have a *house*.

Ruby: Have you gone nuts, Rosie?

Rosie: Probably! But think about it. I have a great big modern four-bedroom house right on the coast in Connemara.

Ruby: Exactly! What are you going to do all on your own with no job, in a four-bedroom house, hanging off the cliff in Connemara?

Rosie: I'm going to open up a bed and breakfast! And I know I've always said I hate B&Bs, but I'm planning on turning the house more into my own mini-hotel. And I am going to be manager/owner extraordinaire! What do you think?

Ruby: I think . . . wow. I can't think of anything sarcastic to say, actually. I think it's a great idea. But are you sure?

Rosie: Ruby, I've never been surer in my life! I've done my research. With my inheritance from Mum and Dad I can afford the insurance. I've asked all the B&Bs around and the place is *crawling* with tourists.

Ruby: Well, I think it's a great idea, Rosie. Congratulations, you little genius. I hope that you will finally be happy, even without Alex.

Rosie Dunne will be your hostess in Buttercup House. The building is a modern four-bedroom home approved by Bord Failte, the Irish Tourist Board. All of the rooms are en suite, centrally heated, and also have telephones. Double, twin and family rooms are all available.

Buttercup House is the ideal location to explore Connemara, and enjoy hill walking, mile-long sandy beaches, sea angling, and fishing in Lough Corrib, Ireland's largest natural inland water mass, a favourite with fishermen for salmon and brown trout. Scuba diving, sailing and surfing are accessible along the coastline.

Connemara National Park is a 2,000 hectare state-owned conservation centre, with mountains, bogs, grasslands and spectacular wildlife. Traces of ancient settlements can be seen, including 4,000-year-old megalithic tombs. There are golf courses aplenty, with rocky hills and ocean inlets providing the ultimate challenge for the keen golfer. Walking, horse-riding and cycling are wonderful ways to explore the terrain, and mountaineering is also popular.

The television lounge is comfortably furnished, with log fire, board games and plenty of books for our guests to relax with after their active days. Traditional Irish breakfast is served in the conservatory, which offers panoramic views of the mountains and Atlantic Ocean.

Rates are 35 euros per person per night.

Contact Rosie Dunne to make your reservation.

From   Katie
To   Mum
Subject   Wow!

Wow, Mum, the photographs are beautiful. You are finally Rosie Dunne, general manager and owner of Buttercup House! Grandma and Granddad would be so proud of you using the house like this. They always said it was such a waste of space only having the two of them there.

Well done! See you next week.

Dear Rosie,

I just wanted to no if everything between us is OK? You've been sounding a little, well, odd on the phone lately. Have I done something to upset you in any way? I can't think of anything that I may have said to piss you off but do tell me. It seems I have to do nothing these days in order to succeed in upsetting the women in my life. Bethany starts a fight with me if I even look at her. If I have unintentionally done the same to you, Rosie, please let me no.

Bethany is going crazy about organising Theo's tenth birthday party next week. She has invited more of her own friends than Theo's, and Josh keeps stealing my car and driving it around all night with his new girlfriend. He's a madman. I can't seem to get him to settle down and study (I sounded like my own dad just then). He's supposed to be starting college next September but considering the fact he hasn't applied for anywhere and can't figure out what he wants to do other than drive my car, I'm presuming that he'll be taking a year out before he heads off to educate himself further.

Luckily Theo thinks Josh is nuts. He's actually afraid of him. So we're hoping that Theo can be the son that we can talk about and admit to having. That, of course, is a joke.

Things at the hospital are going well. I'm still doing the same old thing but my life has been made massively easier, due to the retirement of Reginald Williams. I can breathe now without having to explain it. Working with your father-in-law is as advisable as living with his daughter. Joking once again, of course. Well, kind of, but we won't go into that.

I have to go now but I wanted to make sure things were OK between us. The brochure for the B&B looks fantastic! I wish you well with it, Rosie. You deserve the best!
 Love,
 Alex

From   Rosie
To   Alex
Subject   Sorry

I apologise for sounding off with you on the phone. I was a little distracted by a few things that popped up from the past in my life. They were holding me back for a while, but they've let go of me now and I'm back on course.

I'm ready to move on and spend the next ten years of my life tending to my quest for greatness and happiness. You are more than welcome to stay with me *whenever* you are ready to.

From   Alex
To   Rosie
Subject   Thank you

Thank you very much for that generous offer, Rosie. I'll be sure to take you up on that whenever my wife isn't looking.

From   Rosie
To   Alex
Subject   Flirt

Now, now, are you flirting with me, Alex Stewart?

From   Alex
To   Rosie
Subject   Re: Flirt

Why, Rosie Dunne, I do believe I am.

PART FIVE

You have an instant message from: KATIE.
Katie: Happy birthday, Mum! How does it feel to be fifty?
Rosie: Hot.
Katie: Are you having another flush?
Rosie: Yes. How does it feel to be almost thirty-one? Any sign of my only daughter settling down, getting a decent job and giving me grandchildren?
Katie: Hmm . . . I'm not sure, although there was a little baby boy playing on the beach making sandcastles this morning and for

the first time ever I thought it was cute. It's possible that I'm coming round to the rest of the world's way of thinking.

Rosie: Well, that sounds hopeful.

Katie: How's the B&B going?

Rosie: Busy, thank God. I was just in the middle of updating the web site when you messaged me. Buttercup House now has *seven* en suite bedrooms.

Katie: I no, the place looks terrific.

Rosie: It's KNOW, not NO.

Katie: Sorry, us DJs don't need to be able to spell. OH MY GOD, I almost forgot to tell you! You'll *never* guess who I met in the club last night!

Rosie: Well, if I'll never guess I don't think I want to play this game.

Katie: Toby Flynn!!

Rosie: Never heard of him. Is he an old boyfriend?

Katie: *Mum!* Toby Flynn! *Toby!*

Rosie: I don't see how repeating his name is going to help.

Katie: My best friend from school! *Toby!*

Rosie: Oh my Lord! Toby! How is the little pet?

Katie: He's fine! He's working as a dentist in Dublin just like he wanted, and he's over here in Ibiza for a holiday for two weeks. It was so weird, seeing him after ten years, but he hasn't changed a bit!

Rosie: Oh, that's fabulous. Tell him I was asking for him, will you?

Katie: I will. He had lots of lovely things to say about you. Actually I'll be seeing him again tonight. We're going out for dinner.

Rosie: Is it a date?

Katie: No! I couldn't date Toby. It's Toby! We're just going to catch up.

Rosie: Whatever you say, Katie dear.

Katie: Honestly, Mum! I couldn't date Toby—he used to be my best friend. It would be too odd.

Rosie: I don't see anything wrong with dating your best friend.

Katie: Mum, it would be like *you* dating *Alex!*

Rosie: Well, I would think that would be perfectly normal too.

Katie: Mum!

Rosie: What? I don't see the big deal. Anyway, have you been speaking to Alex lately?

Katie: Yeah, just yesterday. He's on the couch again, so to speak. Bethany is tormenting him again. Honestly, I think they're both stupid to wait until Theo heads off to college.

Rosie: Well, they were both stupid for getting married in the first place. You know what Theo is like, though, Katie—he's such a softie. His parents splitting up would break his little heart. But he's going to have to deal with it from Paris at art college, so I'm not quite sure why they feel that will be better for him.

Katie: Well, the sooner the better. They're a match made in hell, I've said it all along. Josh says he can't wait for Alex and her to split up. He can't stand her.

Rosie: Still, they lasted longer than anyone thought they would. Tell Josh I said hi.

Katie: Will do. I better go and tell Alex about Toby. He'll never believe it! Don't work too hard on your birthday, Mum!

You have an instant message from: KATIE.

Katie: Hi, Alex.

Alex: Hello, my wonderful goddaughter. How are you and what do you want?

Katie: I'm fine and I don't want anything!

Alex: You women always want something.

Katie: That's not true and you no it!

Alex: How's my son? I hope he's working hard over there.

Katie: Still alive at least.

Alex: Good. Tell him to phone me a bit more often. As good as it is hearing from you and all, it would be nice to hear about his life from him.

Katie: I understand; I'll pass it on. Anyway, the reason why I'm messaging you is because you'll never guess who I met in the club last night!

Alex: If I'll never guess then I don't want to play this game.

Katie: That's exactly what Mum said! Anyway, I met Toby Flynn!!!

Alex: Is he an ex-boyfriend or someone famous? Give me a clue.

Katie: Alex! Honestly, you and Mum are getting forgetful in your old age. Toby is my best friend from school!

Alex: Oh, that Toby! Wow, there's a blast from the past. How is he?

Katie: He's fine. He's working as a dentist in Dublin and he's just over in Ibiza for a few weeks' holiday. He was asking about you.

Alex: Great, well, if you see him again give him my regards. He was a good guy.

Katie: Yeah, I will. I'll actually be seeing him again tonight; we're going out for dinner.

Alex: Is it a date?

Katie: Honestly, what is it with you and Mum? He used to be my best friend. I couldn't go out with him.

Alex: Oh, don't be stupid. There's nothing wrong with dating a best friend.

Katie: That's what Mum said too!

Alex: She did?

Katie: Yeah, so I tried to put it into perspective for her by explaining that would be like *her* dating *you*.

Alex: And what did she say to that?

Katie: I don't think she was particularly put off by the idea. So you see, Alex, whenever you get your lazy behind out of that house of yours, you no that there's one woman at least who'll have you. Ha ha.

Alex: I see . . .

Katie: Jesus, Alex, lighten up. OK, I gotta go and get ready for dinner.

You have an instant message from: ROSIE.

Rosie: Hello, old woman, what are you up to?

Ruby: Sitting in my rocking chair, knitting. What else? No, Gary, Maria and the kids just left and I'm knackered. I can't run after them like I used to.

Rosie: Do you really want to anyway?

Ruby: No, and stiff muscles are a great excuse for not having to play hide-and-seek 24/7. What are you up to?

Rosie: I'm just taking a break from clearing away all the dust from the builders. Honestly, have they ever heard of the words 'vacuum cleaner'?

Ruby: No, and neither have I. Is it a new invention? How is the new wing looking?

Rosie: Oh, it's great, Ruby, I'll have so much more privacy now. I can stick to my side of the house and the guests can have theirs. I've decorated a room just the way you like it so it can be yours when you stay. Let me know when you can come over.

Ruby: I will. I heard that Alex's marriage had ended.

Rosie: Ruby, his marriage barely even started, never mind ended.

Ruby: How do you feel about it?

Rosie: Sad for him. Happy for him.

Ruby: Now you can tell me the truth. How do you *really* feel?

From   Katie
To   Rosie
Subject   Oh, Mum

Oh, Mum.
   Oh my God, Mum.
   The most bizarre thing has happened.
   I've never felt so . . . *odd* in my whole entire life.

Last night I met up with Toby and we went to dinner at Raul's restaurant in the old part of town. The manager of Toby's hotel suggested the restaurant and it was such a good choice because it sat on a mountaintop overlooking the island on one side and the sea on the other. The air was warm, the stars were twinkling, a man played on the violin. It was like something out of a movie only so much better because it felt real and it was happening to me.

We chatted and chatted and chatted for hours until well after we had finished eating and eventually we were asked to leave at 2.00 a.m. I don't think I've ever laughed so much in my life. We continued talking as we strolled along the beach and the air felt so magical!

Mum, I don't no if it was the wine, or the heat, the food or just my hormones but there were some forces in motion last night. Toby touched my arm and I felt all . . . *zingy* from head to toe. I'm almost thirty-one years old and I've never felt that before. And then there was this silence. This really weird silence. We stared at each other as though we were seeing each other for the very first time. It was like the world stopped turning just for us.

Then he *kissed* me. *Toby* kissed me. And it was the best kiss I have ever had in all my thirty years. And as our lips pulled apart my eyelids opened slowly to see him staring at me, looking as though he was going to say something. And in true Toby form he said, 'I bet there was pepperoni in your dinner.'

How embarrassing. Immediately my hands flew to my teeth, remembering how he used to always tease me about the food stuck in my braces. But he grabbed my hands and pulled them gently away from my mouth and said, 'No, this time I could taste it.'

My legs nearly buckled from underneath me. It felt so odd that it was Toby that I was kissing but in another way it felt completely natural.

We spent all day together again today and my heart is beating so hard the vibrations are practically causing my locket to bang against my chest. I now no what all my friends were talking about when they tried to describe this feeling. It's so good it's indescribable.

Toby asked me to move back to Dublin, Mum! Not to live with him, of course, but just so that we could be closer. And I think I'm going to. I'll throw caution to the wind and leap into the darkness and all those clichés, and we'll see where I land. Because if I don't follow this feeling right now who nos where I will be twenty years on from now?

How crazy does all this seem? What a twenty-four hours it's been!

From   Rosie
To   Katie
Subject   Yes!

Oh, it's not crazy at all, Katie! It's really not crazy at all! Enjoy it, love. Enjoy every second of it.

From   Katie
To   Alex
Subject   In love!

So Mum was right, Alex! You *can* fall in love with your best friend! I've packed everything up and I'm heading home to Dublin with my heart filled with love and hope, and my head filled with dreams!

Mum told me about the silence she experienced years ago. She kept telling me when I felt that silence with someone, it meant they were 'the one'. I was beginning to think she made it up but she didn't! This magical silence does exist!

You have an instant message from: ALEX.
Alex: Phil, she felt the silence too.
Phil: Who, what, where, when?
Alex: Rosie. She felt that silence too, all those years ago.
Phil: Oh, the dreaded silence thing is back to haunt us, is it? I haven't heard you talk about that for years.
Alex: I new I wasn't imagining it, Phil!
Phil: Well then, what are you doing talking to me? Get off the internet, you fool, and pick up the phone. *Or the pen.*
Alex has logged off.

My dear Rosie,

Unbeknownst to you I took this chance before, many years ago. You never received that letter and I'm glad because my feelings since then have changed dramatically. They have intensified with every passing day.

I'll get straight to the point because if I don't say what I have to say now, I fear it will never be said. And I need to say it.

Today I love you more than ever; tomorrow I will love you even more. I need you more than ever; I want you more than ever. I'm a man of fifty years of age coming to you, feeling like a teenager in love, asking you to give me a chance and love me back.

Rosie Dunne, I love you with all my heart. I have always loved you, even when I was seven years old and lied about falling asleep on Santa watch, when I was ten years old and didn't invite you to my birthday party, when I was eighteen and had to move away, even on my wedding days, on your wedding day, on christenings, birthdays and when we fought.

I loved you through it all. Make me the happiest man on this earth by being with me.

Please reply to me.
All my love,
Alex

EPILOGUE

ROSIE READ THE LETTER for what seemed like the millionth time in her life, folded it into four neat squares and slid it back into the envelope. Her eyes panned across her collection of letters, greeting cards, email print-outs and scribbled notes from her schooldays. There were hundreds of them spread across the floor, each telling its own tale of triumph or sadness, each letter representing a phase in her life.

She sat on the sheepskin rug in front of the fire in her bedroom in Connemara. She had spent the entire night reading over them, and her back ached from stooping and her eyes stung from tiredness and tears.

People she had loved had come alive so vividly in her head during those hours as she reread their fears, emotions and thoughts. She had relived her life all over again that night in a matter of hours.

Without her even noticing, the sun had risen, the seagulls calling with excitement as the waves crashed against the rocks. Grey clouds still hung outside her window despite the early-morning rainfall.

The delicate shades of a newly formed rainbow rose from the sleeping village, stretched across the wakening sky and fell into the field opposite Buttercup House. A vibrant vision of candy-apple red, buttermilk, apricot, avocado, jasmine, oyster-pink and midnight blue against the grey sky. So close Rosie wanted to hold her hand out to touch it.

The bell from the front desk downstairs rang loudly. Rosie tutted and glanced at her watch: 6.15.

A guest had arrived.

She rose to her feet slowly, wincing at the pain of being crouched in the same position for hours. She held on to her bedpost and pulled herself up to her feet. She slowly straightened her back.

The bell rang again.

Her knees cracked.

'Ouch, coming!' she called, trying to hide the irritation in her voice.

She had been so stupid to stay up all night reading those letters. Today was a busy day, with five guests leaving and four more arriving, and she couldn't afford to be tired.

She carefully tiptoed between the mess of letters scattered around the rug, trying not to step on the important papers she had saved all her life.

The bell rang again.

She rolled her eyes and cursed under her breath.

'Just a *minute*,' she called cheerfully, holding on to the banister and hurrying down the stairs. Her toe hit against the luggage that had been placed by the bottom stair and she felt herself falling forward, before a hand grabbed her firmly by the arm to steady her.

'I'm *so* sorry,' the man apologised, and Rosie's head shot up. She took in the man that stood before her, nearly six foot in height, with dark hair that had greyed along the sides. His skin was wrinkled around the eyes and mouth. His eyes looked tired, as would anybody's who had just spent four hours in a car to Connemara after a five-hour flight. But the eyes sparkled and glistened as the moisture inside them began to well up.

Rosie's eyes filled up also. The grip on her arm tightened.

It was him. Finally it was him. The man who had written the final letter she had read that morning, begging her for an answer.

Of course, after she had received it, it hadn't taken her long to reply at all. And as the magical silence once again embraced them, after fifty years, all they could do was look at each other. And smile.

CECELIA AHERN

In 2004 the success of her debut novel, *PS, I Love You*, turned Irish author Cecelia Ahern into a publishing phenomenon. The book quickly became a number one best seller in the UK and Ireland and was chosen as a *Richard and Judy Summer Reads* selection; just recently the film rights were sold. So the first thing I wanted to know was how surprised had Cecelia been by her novel's runaway success. 'There is no way that I could have prepared myself for the reaction *PS, I Love You* received. You cross your fingers and hope that it will be a success of some sort but never in a million years did I expect it to take off as it did. The "Richard and Judy" endorsement was the icing on the cake and as a result of that and the fantastic review they gave, even more people became aware of the book in the UK. And I was delighted because I watch *Richard and Judy* all the time with my mom, so to watch them talking about me on that couch made us laugh.'

Where Rainbows End is written in a completely different style to her first novel and I asked Cecelia where the idea to write it as a series of letters and emails had come from. 'I'm a great hoarder of letters, postcards, old school journals, exam results, bank letters and just about anything that marks an important time in my life. During the early days of *PS, I Love You*, I printed off every email and kept them all in a folder. I have the first email where my agent introduces herself to me; the one in which I send off the first few

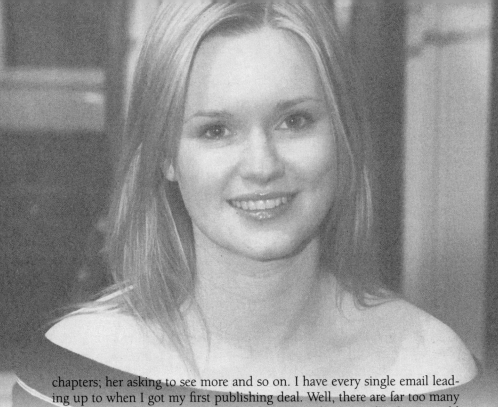

chapters; her asking to see more and so on. I have every single email leading up to when I got my first publishing deal. Well, there are far too many
emails now to keep, but when I read back over them, I realised you could
just make a book of letters and emails and they would tell the story themselves. So that's what I did. I knew that I wanted it to be two characters
writing to each other over the course of their lives. I wanted to include
spelling mistakes and bad grammar to really make it feel realistic. Two
people's lives, all in their own words really excited me.'

Cecelia is adept at getting under the skin of her characters—so much so
that Rosie Dunne caused her many a sleepless night. 'That woman was in
my head so much that with everything I looked at and every situation I was
in, I found myself thinking of how Rosie would deal with it. She has an
opinion on absolutely everything and she would scream at me very loud at
night when I was trying to sleep, just so I would put it down on paper!'

With *Where Rainbows End* now also hitting the best-seller lists, I asked
Cecelia what book number three was about. 'I would love to tell you, but
being quite superstitious, I hate to reveal story lines before the book has
even been printed. All I can tell you is that I have finished it and I loved,
loved, loved every single moment spent working on it. Like when I'm
reading a book that I'm hugely enjoying, I really didn't want to finish it,
but then there's that side of you that's on overdrive to get to the end. It's a
special story for me and I really hope people will love it as much as I do.'

Jane Eastgate

339

The Reluctant Landlady

Bernadette Strachan

Actress Evie Crump has been struggling
for years to get by on a succession
of small stage roles. She's desperately
hoping for her big break when an
unexpected inheritance – a dilapidated
old house complete with lodgers – casts her
in the role of landlady.
Not exactly the break she had imagined,
perhaps, but before long Evie finds
herself caught up in an exciting
number of dramas

One

EVIE CRUMP WAS SICK of hearing that she had a funny name. Bank cashiers said so. Telephonists said so. The woman in the dry-cleaner's had been saying so for years. Even her dad said so, and he had given it to her.

Just that morning Evie's acting agent, the magnificently monikered Meredith de Winter, had been banging on about it. 'I mean,' she'd wailed down the phone, with a voice steeped in half a century's worth of gin and Silk Cut, 'how am I supposed to find work for an actress named *Evie Crump*? What do you see when you look in the mirror, darling? You see a girl in her twenties with big blue eyes and woefully untidy hair, you do *not* see an *Evie Crump!*'

In fact, what Evie saw as she squinted into the dressing room's cracked mirror was a threadbare fun-fur badger, whose plastic left eye was hanging by a thread and whose paws smelt faintly of curry. God, she hated this costume.

An equally moth-eaten squirrel shuffled agitatedly in and said, 'Mfllllurg blllllhmph,' rather angrily.

'Oh, get your mouthpiece in the right place, Simeon,' snapped Evie.

'Sorry.' The squirrel didn't sound sorry. The grubby mask sported a whimsical woodland smile, but the drama graduate inside it was furious. As usual. 'I *said*, you missed your cue for the song and if you do that again you're *out!*'

'Oh, no!' Evie clasped her paws to her furry head in horror. 'Don't say that! Don't throw me out into the woods alone! How could I cope without you and all the other neurotic cuddly animals?'

There is always good-natured banter backstage. But this was not good-natured banter.

343

'I said all along you were wrong for the part,' yelled the squirrel, delving into a nearby rucksack and extracting a bottle of Jack Daniel's. 'Why won't you take this seriously?'

'Maybe because the script is crap, the costumes are crap and the set is crap.' Evie didn't add that Simeon was crap, but he was. He made John Inman look like Laurence Olivier.

The big squirrel was shaking with fury. Really, thought Evie, this was too easy. Any minute now he'd come out with his no-place-for-cynicism-in-the-theatre line.

'There is no place for cynicism in the theatre,' he shouted, for once right on cue. He began to swig noisily from the bottle.

'We're not in a theatre,' Evie pointed out wearily. 'We're in a community hall in the arse end of nowhere, performing anti-sexist, anti-racist, anti-class-distinction, anti-any-fun-whatsoever playlets for an audience of bored five-year-olds who, by the looks on their little faces, would rather be having rabies jabs—' She broke off as the headmistress of the audience put her head round the door.

'Do you think you could come back onstage?' she asked tentatively. 'Your friend the mole was halfway through a most delightful dance when he slipped and put his head through a plywood tree. There's blood everywhere.'

One day this would make a great story to tell over a glass of wine, Evie thought, but today wasn't that day. She could certainly appreciate that anybody glancing into Casualty and spotting a giant squirrel and a giant badger propping up a giant mole, who was bleeding profusely and muttering, 'I turned down *Crimewatch* for this,' would laugh. But not her. Not just now.

She sighed and closed her eyes. If she was honest with herself, she admitted that she had become an actress because she wanted to be famous. But that sounded shallow so she didn't admit it too often.

'*Crimewatch* wanted me,' whimpered Mole, with a concussed slur. 'I turned them down. I'm a fool; a mad, crazy fool.'

'Ssssh.' Evie stroked his latex head as he slumped against her. She tried to ignore the computerised sign informing her that there were a mere three hours and fourteen minutes to wait as she recalled how Meredith had described this job to her: 'A riot! A romp! You'll love it! All those smiling little faces! Being one of the happy band of a touring company!' The reality was being crammed into the back of a medieval Ford Transit with various rejects from the acting world who kept up their spirits by drinking, bitching, and being terribly, terribly serious about their craft.

That computerised sign had been optimistic. Four hours had crawled by before they were allowed to fold up the bandaged thespian and stuff him into the back of the van. Evie sat wedged against the window in the front passenger seat, cradling an immense bush that they'd had to take out of the back to make room for the prostrate mole, as the vehicle reached frightening speeds of up to thirty miles an hour on the M25 towards London, home, bath and fluffy towels.

Sums buzzed in her head as she gazed out at the rain-sodden dual carriageway. These days, she always came back to sums as soon as she was unoccupied. The equation went something like *wages minus rent minus bills minus a little bit of fun equals* . . . She could never do it so that it equalled anything at all. In fact, the answer was usually an offensively large minus figure.

If I don't get some sort of a break soon, thought Evie miserably for the thousandth time, I'll have to get a proper job. The very idea made her break out in a cold sweat. The truth was that she had the attention span of a toddler tanked up on E-numbers, and reacted to authority the way pit-bull terriers react to a poke with a sharp stick. Besides, she *had* to make it in acting. She would never give her mother the satisfaction of gloating over her often-prophesied failure.

But those sums. They couldn't be ignored for ever . . .

'Do you need me to take you to your door?' asked Simeon.

'Yes. That was the deal, after all,' replied Evie, as she did every day. Muttering bad things about Simeon into the bush helped to pass the rest of the journey until Simeon—again, as usual—braked unnecessarily sharply and snarled, 'Here we are. Your elegant town house.'

Evie gave him a long, hard look, then opened the door and hopped down onto the pavement.

The van roared away, leaving Evie alone outside her elegant town house. All twenty-six of its floors shot up into the darkening sky. The elegant steps were pockmarked with cigarette butts and strewn with takeaway wrappers. 'Something is very wrong with my life if I can't even earn enough to keep this place,' mused Evie.

It was hard to stab her floor number in the lift until she took off one paw. Then she crossed her uncovered fingers tightly and was rewarded with an ancient hum. She held her breath against the whiff of urine until the eighth floor.

As she put the first of her five keys into the door (security was para-mount at Dickens Tower) she allowed herself a tiny reckless daydream: the sound of a deep, warm, male voice calling, 'Evie, darling! Is that you? I've missed you!'

Instead the smell of garlic almost felled her, badger suit and all, in the tiny hall, and a male voice yelled, 'Where have you been? Get your arse in here and open this bottle of wine.'

'Oh dear,' exclaimed Bing, her flatmate, when she shuffled into the kitchen. 'I don't have to ask what kind of day you've had.'

Evie slumped into a rickety chair and grabbed the humungous glass of red wine on offer. 'Do you *have* to cook in the nude?' she enquired, after her first heady slurp of *vin ordinaire*.

'I like the air to get to my skin. Don't worry. I always wear an apron.'

Bing was a golden, glowing, tanned, toned, six-foot-two bundle of promiscuity. He managed the enviable trick of being outrageously homosexual without losing an iota of masculinity, thanks in part to his impressive physique and manly bearing. The only pastime he considered comparable to sex was gazing at his blond self in a mirror, something he was managing to do even as he stirred the Bolognese sauce, thanks to the reflective sheen of the eye-level grill.

Evie smiled over the rim of her glass at her lodger, his buttocks clenching and unclenching in perfect time to the Carpenters' song blaring tinnily out of the radio. She loved Bing. He was loyal, funny and decorative, all-poof but all-man. Damned annoying too, with his nuclear-strength campery and vicious tongue. But he loved Evie right back. When he had moved in, the small, damp flat had instantly perked up. The plan had been that Bing would live with her for a reduced rent while helping her tackle the countless home improvements that needed doing.

It had been a good plan. It had only one flaw. They'd been living together for six months now and the sole home improvement was a new glitterball hanging above the sagging three-piece suite. Tonight, cold, tired and disillusioned, Evie was finding it difficult to rise above the cracked seventies lino, the windows that had been painted shut by some gormless tenant long ago, and the astonishingly accurate map of India the damp had traced on the kitchen wall. Even these humble surroundings would be out of her reach if she didn't get a break soon. The sigh broke into the warmth of her wineglass and died there.

'It's being so cheerful that keeps you going,' remarked Bing. 'Now, what am I forgetting?' He struck a thoughtful pose in his pinny. 'Oh, yes!' He whirled round and thrust a tomato-smeared wooden spoon at Evie. 'A solicitor called! You've got to call him back!'

'A solicitor?' echoed Evie dumbly. 'Called me?'

'Yes. Yes. The number's by the phone. Quick, it's getting on for six.'

Evie stood up slowly. Why would a solicitor be after her? 'Do you think somebody's going to sue me?' she asked Bing.

'Typical. Always look on the black side.' Bing ushered her into the sitting room where the suite jostled for space with the widescreen TV he insisted on. 'Of course nobody's suing you,' he reassured her, as he handed her the receiver and dialled the number, adding, 'unless they saw your Lady Macbeth in Leamington Spa, that is.'

He returned to his saucepans, muttering distractedly, 'Now, what else was I supposed to remember?' as he tossed handfuls of spaghetti into foaming water.

A few minutes later Evie trudged back into the kitchen. 'I . . .'

'Yes?'

'I . . .' She looked shell-shocked.

'Don't make me use violence.' Bing raised the wooden spoon. 'I what?'

'I've been left something in a will. I've been left something *substantial* in a will.' Evie turned wide eyes to Bing. 'I've been left—'

'I get it, I get it. That's fantastic! What can it be?'

Evie was too busy wondering who had heard her desperate prayers to muse on that. There must be a patron saint of stressed-out actresses up there. 'I need a bath,' she announced.

'Make it quick,' said Bing sternly.

Still lost in wonderment, Evie opened the bathroom door and was surprised to discover that it was already warm and steamy.

''Allo!' beamed the cherubic dark boy from the bath, where his perfectly coiffed head just cleared the bubbles. 'I eez Raoul.'

From the kitchen Bing shouted, 'Ah, *that's* what I forgot.'

TWO

THE NEARBY PARK was a relief after the staid stuffiness of the offices of Snile & Son, solicitors. Evie sat on a bench by the pond while Bing paced to and fro in front of her. She had the dazed look of one who had been dropped from a helicopter but Bing was crackling with excitement.

'A house!' he exclaimed, for the fiftieth, or hundred and fiftieth, time. 'Out of nowhere! Doors, windows, walls, the whole shebang! You realise what this means? You're rich, babe!'

Evie smiled distantly. 'You're forgetting the conditions, Bing,' she said, holding up an envelope. 'I'm certainly not rich.'

'What conditions?' Bing snatched the letter from her and peered it. 'I stopped listening after he said some old dear had left you a house.'

Evie closed her eyes. Belle O'Brien had been no old dear. Warm, laughing, mischievous and always smelling deliciously of roses with just a hint of gin, she had been a big part of Evie's childhood.

Back in the twenties Evie's grandmother and Belle had sat beside each other on their first day at convent school in Dublin, and they'd sat together on the ferry to England when they were giggling, blue-eyed twenty-year-olds.

The two young women had had very different ambitions. Marriage and multiple motherhood meant that Gran's qualifications as a nurse had lain unused. But Belle had never been distracted from her dream: ever since her first trip to a panto, Belle had known she was an actress. Constantly touring in revues, plays and musicals, she had been careful to keep in touch with her old friend. Her career—never stellar—had waned long before Gran found herself bemused by the freedom that widowhood and a grown family afforded her.

The two old women had plenty of time for each other again and it was the Belle of this period that Evie had got to know. Evie, seven years old, had been allowed to drape herself with Belle's store of old stage costumes, and to plaster herself with heavy Leichner stage make-up.

Belle and Gran had been an enthusiastic audience for countless melodramatic improvisations about princesses, witches and Victorian heiresses. These performances took place at Belle's house in the basement, which Evie remembered as large and dramatically furnished with velvet chaises longues, ostrich feathers and rich, dark colours. The floors above, divided into self-contained flats, were let to lodgers.

Then Gran—dear loving, forgetful Gran—with her ever-present handbag and inexplicable devotion to Terry Wogan, had gone and died. Belle had excused herself from the funeral, explaining that she didn't want to think of her dearest friend and companion in the ground, she wanted to remember her alive and happy. All perfectly sensible, even to a child, but Evie's mother had embarked on one of her marathon huffs and Evie had never seen Belle again.

Bing was folding the letter. 'Hmm. Strange conditions. It looks to me as if the old bird left you something valuable, then tried to make damn sure there was no way you could profit from it.'

Evie reckoned she knew better. 'Listen. There's something I have to do. Are you on tonight?'

'Yes. I'll be giving my all upon the London stage.' Bing was in the chorus of the latest revival of *Joseph* at the Palladium. 'I'll bring a pizza home and we'll mull this over, OK?'

Very much OK. A kiss, a waft of Paco Rabanne, and he was gone.

Evie found the station and bought a ticket to Surbiton. Or, as she liked to think of it, the Gates of Hell. Surbiton was where her parents lived.

Now, don't get the wrong idea about Bridgie and John Crump. Nobody else thought of 25 Willowdene Gardens as the threshold of the underworld. Even Evie was slavishly devoted to her pipe-smoking, cardigan-sporting father. It was just that if *you* had grown up as the younger, relentlessly underachieving daughter of Bridgie Crump, you wouldn't recognise her as the mild-mannered, respectable citizen that everyone else saw: you would know her as an ambassadress of Hades.

'Well, hello, stranger!' yelped Bridgie, passive-aggressively as she opened the door. 'To what do we owe this honour?'

'Hi, Mum. I need to talk to you and Dad about something.'

'About what?' Bridgie gripped the door in alarm, the duster falling from her fingers. 'Work? Money? You're not . . . ?' She glanced in terror at her daughter's stomach.

'Er . . . can I come in?' As Evie performed the comprehensive shoe-scraping and mat-stamping that was a condition of entry, she attempted to reassure her mother. 'Don't panic. It's good. I think.'

'Come on through, then,' said Bridgie. 'You've caught me on the hop, so excuse the mess.'

As ever, the house was clean enough for Evie to have taken out her mother's appendix on the *faux*-bamboo coffee table.

'Tea?' queried Bridgie, with the certainty of the second-generation Irish: not so much a question, more a command. 'Sit yourself down while I see what I have.' The vocabulary and style was all Dublin, handed down from Gran, but the accent was hyper-polished suburbia.

Tea never arrives alone in an Irish house. It is chaperoned by a fondant fancy or a little sandwich. On this strange day Evie found the prospect of a cup of tea and a nice little something rather comforting. Less comforting was the migraine-inducing swirly carpet, the countless bowls of potpourri, the mystical flicker of the orange bulb from within the moulded-plastic coal-effect fire. Evie burrowed into the obscenely comfy sofa, taking care not to disarrange the artful cushion display.

A dent in the armchair nearest the fire signalled the absence of the man of the house. 'Where's Dad?' asked Evie, as her mother steered a course between occasional tables and pouffes, bearing her laden tray.

'Taking a turn in the gardens.'

Noting that the medium-sized patch of grass housing the bins and a sagging washing-line had been promoted to 'the gardens', Evie swiftly translated this information as 'Your father has sneaked out to have a quick puff of his pipe as I am too much of a heartless witch to allow him to smoke it indoors.'

'Now,' said Bridgie briskly, settling herself down and swinging into action with the teapot, 'what's this important news?'

'*Henry!*' Evie sank to her knees and threw her arms round the fat neck of the elderly black mongrel who had just ambled into the room. She was deaf to her mother's squawks of 'Aw, no, he'll get hairs all over your jumper. There's no need to ruin it.'

'Oh, Henry Henry Henry!' gabbled Evie, who had never found another male to match him for love and loyalty.

But something was wrong. There was a downcast look in Henry's eye. 'Henry, what is it?' Evie drew back, panic-stricken, and took a good look at him. 'Oh, dear God, Henry, you're *clean!*'

'As you well know, Henry's always clean,' snapped Bridgie. 'You could eat your dinner off that dog.'

Evie had an unwelcome flash of intuition. This could mean only one thing: 'Who's coming to visit?'

'Beth and the twins. And *Marcus*.' Marcus was Evie's dentist brother-in-law, who Bridgie worshipped for his conservative appearance, his effortlessly posh accent and his ability to install her elder daughter in a *4 recep/5 bed/3 bath(1 ensuite)/swmmng pl/extnsve grnds* near Henley.

'Thanks for the invite.' Evie's skin thinned perceptibly around Bridgie.

'You don't need one,' said Bridgie. 'It's on Sunday. I'm doing beef.'

A deep, merry voice rumbled, 'Can't wait,' from the doorway.

'Dad!' Evie stretched to accept the whiskery kiss he was offering. 'Oh, Dad, it's so good to see you.'

And it was. It was good to see his thick grey hair, his warm blue eyes, his quietly amused expression and his general, all-round daddishness. At twenty-seven, Evie was a good ten years younger than Beth and her parents had always been a touch older than other people's. She hadn't noticed it until recently. Her mother's thick Irish hair now had threads of startling silver. They were both slowing down. Dad looked—or was this just her imagination?—ever so slightly smaller.

'I've got a house!' Characteristically Evie leapt straight in.

When the what-do-you-means had subsided, she went on to explain more fully.

Bridgie sniffed meaningfully. 'Huh! Belle! That woman was mad as a hatter. There'll be a drawback.'

'Now, now, Bridgie,' began John, in the sort of voice vets use to calm hysterical horses, 'Belle was eccentric but perfectly harmless. And she was a good friend to your mum. If she's decided to make this generous bequest to our daughter we should be grateful to her.'

Bridgie looked chastened but, rallying, found another negative point to raise. 'You won't want to live in a big old dump like that. You'll sell it?'

John Crump was beaming. 'Looks like those money worries are over, you lucky girl.' He winked at his little girl.

'Well, no, not really.' Evie sighed and produced the letter. She smoothed it out on her lap and continued, 'There are conditions.' She ignored Bridgie's snort and read out the letter that Mr Snile, Jnr had given her, which Belle had written a few weeks before she died. Her Dublin lilt came clearly across the divide.

'Dear Evie,

How very peculiar it is to write a letter that will only be read out after I have perished! But perished I have and it is time to redistribute my possessions. My biggest and most significant possession I leave entirely to you, the granddaughter of my beloved friend. I loved to have you in the house and to listen to your stories and chatter. How your gran and I relished those impromptu productions when you played every part. I could see the love of performing in what you were doing even then, and I could also see some real talent.

I lost touch with you after we lost our mutual dear one. But I've seen you occasionally on my crackly TV, in commercials and walk-ons. And I knew you were struggling, because that's what we actresses do, unless we're stars. So I leave you my house.

My dear, I hand you the key to 18 Kemp Street, as security in the fraught but magical life you have chosen. I bought this house for what now seems small change back in the fifties. I had a plan. When the work dried up—my slender talent was never going to outlive my dimples—I would have an income from letting the rest of the house. And that is how I came to be living here, in my warm basement, with my lodgers in their flats above me. From the day I first put up a "rooms to let" postcard in the local newsagent I have felt that only the folk who were really meant to live here have approached me.

So, if you accept ownership of this house, you accept responsibility for the lodgers too. None of them must be turned out and the house must not be sold until the last of them has left of their own accord.

If you accept my bequest, I dearly hope that it will be of use to you.

Love to you, from wherever I am,

Belle O'Brien.'

Bridgie opened her mouth, but her husband shot her a look and she shut it again noiselessly. 'She obviously cared about you, Evie,' John said. 'But do you feel able to take on a house full of lodgers?'

'Yes.' The certainty in her voice surprised Evie. 'Yes, I do. I don't know why,' she added lamely, 'but I do.'

In reality, she did know why. One hopeful, star-struck, dedicated, slightly nutty actress had reached out to another across the years. It was a vote of confidence from one of her own.

Bridgie could never be quelled for long. 'This will just prolong the acting nonsense,' she proclaimed, returning to a well-worn theme. 'If you sold the house you'd have financial security and you could retrain for something useful.'

'There's a codicil—if that's the right word—to the will. If I don't accept Belle's conditions, the house passes to the local housing association, with in-built protection for her tenants.'

'I say good luck to you!' Evie's father stood up. 'And good luck to old Belle too. I'll dig out the sherry and we'll toast you both.'

It had taken a while to winkle the information out of Bridgie, but once Evie had ascertained that an invitation to the funeral had arrived and been ignored she was determined to visit Belle's grave. According to Bridgie, Belle had bought her plot decades ago in the Catholic corner of Brompton Cemetery in South Kensington. 'Morbid,' she had said, and sniffed, but Evie considered it canny and sophisticated. Of course a sexy young actress would want to make sure her well-applauded bones rested for ever in a chic part of town.

How does a cemetery achieve that stillness? Through the gates, it was as if the hectic traffic on the other side of the wall was now on tiptoe. Clutching a bunch of dusty pink roses to her chest, Evie looked at the plan posted for first-timers like herself, then set off purposefully down an asphalt path that shimmered hotly in the June heat.

In a corner, shaded by ancient yews, Evie spied a newish grave. Her pace slowed. She was not 'good' at cemeteries. The infrequency of her pilgrimages to her grandparents' graves was a source of tension between her and her mother. This visit had seemed different, though, more a thank-you to an old friend.

She knelt at the foot of plot 443N. Too recent for a headstone, the grave's only decoration was the dry funeral wreaths and bouquets.

'Hello, Belle.' Crazy to feel self-conscious, but she did. She coughed and raised her voice. 'It's me, Evie. I'm a bit older than the last time we met.' She hesitated, unsure how to go on. 'I'm sorry you had to die.' God! What a stupid thing to say! 'What I really want to say, Belle, is thank you. Thank you from the bottom of my heart. I know why you left me the house and I hope I can live up to it. And don't worry about your lodgers. They'll be safe and secure with me.' Evie leaned forward and laid down her roses.

'Oh.' There was one other fresh token. A small bunch of lavender, tied clumsily with ribbon of the kind you see looped round thick, shiny pigtails: navy, with yellow smiley faces dotted along it. Evie pushed a clod of earth from the luggage label attached to the lavender. *I miss you*, she read.

The sun bounced a spark off something at the edge of her vision. Evie turned to see a flash of dark fabric dart behind a tree. The movement was furtive and she sprang to her feet. 'Hello?' she sang, in a voice she hoped didn't sound too alarmed. The fabric appeared again as a young woman with a basket raced off between the trees and statues. Perplexed, Evie stared after her.

To Evie, North London was a foreign land. Fulham born, she regarded Camden as a forbidding alien landscape out of which erupted huge brutal houses full of, well, North Londoners.

Now she was the owner of one such brutal house.

'Eighteen Kemp Street,' announced Bing unnecessarily, looking up at the grey-brick house in front of them. 'It's handsome.'

'It's falling down,' Evie corrected him.

They were both right. The tall, austerely uniform windows were peeling and rickety, the front door was wantonly allowing a peek at its last three colours. The most recent had been pale blue.

'Good-sized front garden,' said Bing.

Knee-deep in brambles as she hacked her way to the wide steps that led to the front door, Evie snapped, 'What are you, the gay happy estate agent? It's like Borneo.'

Looking up, she came face to face with a girl who had emerged from the front door and stood scowling on the decaying top step, a toddler saddled neatly on her hip.

'You the new landlady?' asked the girl, in a fruity Lancashire accent. She managed to sound both belligerent and uninterested.

'Yes. I'm Evie Crump.' She bounded up the steps and held out her hand like a good little landlady.

The girl walked past her down the steps. 'I'm Caroline and this is Milly,' she threw over her shoulder, as she braved Borneo to get to the lopsided wrought-iron gate. 'I know I owed the old biddy a week and a half. Don't wet yourself. You'll get it.'

As they watched her progress down Kemp Street, Bing said, 'I *like* her.'

Evie laughed. 'Why was Belle concerned about *her*? She's a right madam.'

'Maybe she improves when you get to know her,' Bing suggested philosophically, and leapt up the steps to join her at the front door. 'Although she'd have to work very hard just to achieve "horrible".' He leaned over and pulled the creaking door shut.

'No, you don't,' he said. 'First time. Use your key, Ms House Owner.'
'Here goes.' Evie flourished it.

'No, hang on.' Bing swept her up into his arms as if she were a Victorian invalid. 'Let's do this properly. You open the door and I'll carry you over the threshold.'

Evie leaned over, key in hand, just as the door flew open.

'Oh,' said the unkempt man standing there.

'Oh,' echoed Evie. 'I mean hello. I'm Evie Crump, your new owner. Oh, God—no, I'm your landlady. Sorry, that sounded awful.' Her feet thumped on to the floor as Bing gratefully put her down.

'Yes,' said the second of her new tenants. 'Quite. Well. Ah. Now.' He was a tall, strawberry-blond man of impressive untidiness. Each item of his clothing—tweed jacket, check shirt, *brogues*, for heaven's sake— might have been donated by a vastly larger or smaller friend. His soft, educated voice gave him an air of other-worldly, baffled academia. 'I am so dreadfully sorry,' he gasped, 'I've spoilt the start of your honeymoon!'

Evie blinked hard. Bing guffawed heartily. 'I'm not married to *that*', he whooped ungallantly. 'Look. Let's start again. Evie here is moving in today. She's your new landlady. I'm her friend, Bing, and I am deeply— thank God—gay.'

A visible jolt rippled through the other man at the G-word. He recovered and informed them that he were Bernard Briggs, then flattened himself against the wall, as if he was expecting a herd of large horned things to rush past him, and in they went.

Evie looked around her at the maroon-painted communal hallway, which was high and spacious with original mouldings, heavy-looking doors and dark-stained floorboards.

Bing closed the door after Bernard, who had fled, and squealed glee- fully, 'You own all this?'

'I own the damp. I own the rotting door jambs.'

Bing's wide shoulders sank. 'Cheerful as ever,' he said. 'Have you any idea how much I envy you?'

'You? Envy? Me?' echoed Evie idiotically.

'Yes. I might have natural good looks, unbridled talent and all the sex I can eat, but I don't own a thing. The only security I have is the certain knowledge that *Joseph* closes in six months and it's back to auditions and waiting tables. Whatever happens in your career, you have bricks and mortar in your name. What a fantastic safety net. How lucky you are. Right!' Bing slapped his hands together in a workmanlike way. 'Lecture over. I'll start bringing the boxes up.'

Evie knew he was right. She was acting like an ungrateful baggage. The unexpected bequest of a house was a godsend. So why did she feel so oppressed by the dark, damp air of this house? *Her* house. Why did she feel so daunted?

Before she had time to formulate anything approaching an answer, Bing was staggering back up the steps to join her in the main hall with an overflowing box marked CLOTHES. 'Get the bloody door to the basement open. What have you got in here? Chain mail?'

Confused, Evie gazed about the gloomy hallway. Which *was* the bloody door to the basement? There were two doors leading off the hallway marked 'A' and 'B' with brass letters that didn't quite match. Presumably flat C was up on the first floor.

'I can't support this many size fourteens indefinitely,' warned Bing, his legs beginning to buckle.

'Sorry,' muttered Evie, and fumbled with the unfamiliar keyring. She heaved open the sticky door to flat A and stood back to allow Bing to stagger through it.

And fall down the stairs, all eighteen of them.

'It's a long time since I was here! I forgot!' wailed Evie, racing down to him and trying to sound contrite and sympathetic, rather than laughing like a chimp.

Bing recovered speedily and gazed around him. All the doors in the basement flat were open, so they could see into the two small bedrooms, the ancient bathroom, the poky kitchen and the dim sitting room. The maroon upstairs had evidently been Belle's favourite colour, for variants of it were repeated down here. Nosing gingerly through the doors, Evie saw purple, mauve, lavender, heather and indigo everywhere, gobbling up the scanty light that penetrated the fussy lace curtains. Playbills, publicity shots and carefully framed reviews still smothered the dark walls. Even the bathroom was a deep purple.

'Come and get a load of this.' Bing sounded awestruck. He was, as ever, ahead of her, and she followed his voice into the sitting room. It was a long room, running the length of the side of the house, and its purple expanse culminated in a large conservatory, which opened out to three steps that led in their turn up to a wide, wild and gloriously green garden, heavy with shrubs and shaded by decorous old trees. The June sun throbbed through the glass.

Evie was amazed. She hadn't remembered a garden. Then she frowned and opened her mouth but Bing was across the room with one *jeté* to put his finger on her lips. 'No! Don't say it! Don't say'—here he adopted a whiny mew—'"but it's purple. And the glass is cracked. And I can't look after a garden."' He reverted to his normal baritone. 'OK? Don't.'

'I wasn't going to,' said Evie, who had been going to.

Bing shot back up the stairs for more boxes. 'A lick of paint and some curtains and you won't know the place. Honestly, Crump, what are you going to do without me?'

The answer to that was probably 'Reverse my cirrhosis of the liver.' But there was another. Evie thumped up the stairs to the hall, puzzled as to why the idea hadn't occurred to her during the previous night's long orgy of chianti, crying and promising to keep in touch that she and Bing had indulged in.

'Bing!' she shrieked, from the front door.

'What?' came the ungracious response from the back seat of Bing's ancient Beetle, where he was trying to stuff knickers back into a box.

'Look at me! I can't talk to your arse,' commanded Evie.

'Hundreds have.' Bing straightened up obediently. 'Whaddyawant?'

'*Live with me!*' bellowed Evie, bouncing on her trainers with excitement. '*Give up that revolting flat and live here with me!*'

For a moment, Bing attempted to look reluctant. But, despite his training, he wasn't much of an actor so he threw the knickers into the air and screeched, '*I thought you'd never ask!*'

The only person who had exhibited unalloyed joy at Evie's news was her friend Sacha. Extremes of reaction were commonplace with Sacha, however. Although she'd been to drama school with Evie, she had never made any progress in the profession, mainly because her emotions were less restrained than any part called for.

'You'll be so near to me!' Sacha had barked joyfully. 'We can see each other every day.'

'Yes.' Evie had managed a smile. If she had to see Sacha every day she'd end the year in a box. Much as she loved her friend, she had learned over the years to protect herself from her demands.

Tinkling New Age music filled Calmer Karma, Sacha's tiny shop in Camden Market. The place was stuffed with New Age trinkets, all designed to promote serenity and wisdom. Evie had helped Sacha to hand-paint the sign, while noting with an inward smile that her chum's own karma was anything but calm.

'Just go through to the back and pop everything off,' said Sacha now, by way of hello.

'Er, why exactly?' asked Evie warily.

'I want to try out my new skill on you. Go on, go.' Sacha flapped her hands impatiently. 'I'm just showing this customer how to heal herself with this crystal.'

Shivering beneath a thin sheet on the wallpaper-pasting table that Sacha had reincarnated as a treatment couch, Evie sniffed the air with trepidation. It was impossible to guess which skill Sacha had acquired now, but they usually involved aromatic oils. Evie hated aromatic oils.

Sacha's voice drifted through to the back. 'A blue crystal is best for pains in the groin area,' she was explaining, with the confidence of a girl with a trust fund. Sacha's double-barrelled kin were of the truly, madly, overwhelmingly posh variety. Evie's mother had been keen to meet her upper-class friend from LAMDA and had been disappointed to encounter Sacha in jeans and jean jacket, looking exactly like her own unmistakably non-posh daughter. Sacha was embarrassed by her family's wealth, but had spent rather a lot of it in setting up Calmer Karma, a business that wavered but would never collapse so long as Daddy's arms were long enough to reach into Daddy's pockets.

'Stones!' declared Sacha, with dramatic emphasis, as she swished back the beaded curtain. 'Stones are what we're doing today. Hot stones,' she elucidated, rolling up the sleeves of her shirt. 'I'm going to lay hot stones on the energy points of your body to release your negative flow and realign your *chakras*. But, first, a massage with aromatic oils.'

Surprisingly, Sacha was a skilled, sensitive masseuse, so Evie lay on her front and closed her eyes as Sacha turned down the lights, lit a few beeswax candles and switched on her whale-sounds CD.

In her low, soothing, treatment voice Sacha cooed huskily, 'So tell me about the house and your tenants.'

Eyes shut as Sacha's small, strong hands kneaded at her chubby bits, Evie recounted what she knew. 'I'm down in the basement,' she began, 'with Bing. He's got two days off from the Palladium, so he's getting busy with the white paint. Up on the ground floor, in eighteen B, is Caroline Millbank and one-year-old Milly, who is gorgeous. Mind you, her mother must have been scowling when the wind changed 'cos now she's stuck like that. She's very pretty, I think, with china-doll features and long shampoo-advert black hair, but she's got a real problem with people. Probably needs her *chakras* realigned. *Ow!*' Sacha didn't take kindly to Evie's open disbelief. 'That bloody hurt. Anyway, up the stairs to eighteen C and we have the bachelor boy, Bernard. And, before you ask, you wouldn't want him. He's a rumpled academic type, but we're not talking *Brideshead Revisited*, although there is something lovable about him. A complete mess—shy, awkward, stooped. Ginger too.'

'Just because I'm twenty-seven doesn't mean I'm *interested* in every man I hear about,' said Sacha, whose voice sounded as though it was struggling to be gentle and soothing. 'You'll turn me into a cliché.'

'And how do clichés become clichés? By being true.'

'I'm heating the stones now. Just lie there and relax.'

Had there been the teeniest hint of a threat in that gentle suggestion? 'Anyway,' Evie gabbled on, to cover the ominous hiss from a candlelit corner, 'I'm having a little drink-up in the garden so that I can meet them properly. I've put an invite through both their doors. Seven o'clock tomorrow. You'll pop round, won't you?'

'Oooh, yeah.' Sacha was never knowingly under-drunk. 'Now, I'm going to place the first stone on your main *chakra*. You'll be suffused by an intense feeling of well-being.'

Much later, when Evie had stopped crying and they'd used up a whole bottle of lanolin, Sacha admitted she'd lost the instructions.

Three

NO PARTY IS TOO SMALL or too odd to circumvent the traditional pre-party paranoia. And parties don't come any smaller or odder than the one for which Bing was tearing open Twiglet packets on that warm evening.

He had partly tamed the back garden with a scythe and his dancer's shoulders while Evie had been out depressing the children of a Rotherhithe junior school with Simeon and their replacement mole.

'That was a quick shower,' commented Bing, as she emerged through the conservatory bearing boxes of wine, clad in her one good dress. It was black. Obviously.

'I didn't have one. I'd rather be hot-stoned again than face that boiler.'

The kitchen table, dragged outside and draped with a newly laundered ancient white sheet, was home to an eclectic selection of nibbles. The ubiquitous sausage-on-a-stick was well represented, and its humble seventies compatriot, cheese-and-pineapple-on-a-stick, was putting in an appearance too. There were shallow tubs of dip, surrounded by some carrots, and sufficient Twiglets to satisfy their most ardent admirer.

'What if nobody comes?' Evie blurted out, while she fiddled with the cheese-and-pineapple combo to create a more pleasing effect.

'We've only invited two people and a little girl. It's not Mardi Gras. Of course they'll come.'

'Three people, actually. Sacha.'

Bing pulled a face, his handsome features contorting into a gurn of annoyance. Evie knew that Bing and Sacha were chemically designed not to get on and that everything Sacha said and did made Bing want to buy a rifle. Evie also knew that Sacha, typically, had no idea of this and considered Bing a buddy. 'Well, *she*'ll definitely come. The Black Death wouldn't keep her indoors when there's a wine-box open somewhere.'

'But if the others don't come we'll just look like three alcoholics floundering in a sea of Twiglets.'

'The others will come. They've only got to walk down some stairs—they don't even have to go out into the street. The most dedicated, anti-social party-hater could manage that.'

'S'pose.' Evie wished that some of Bing's insouciance would rub off on her. He looked a model of self-assurance as he deftly poured wine into two glasses.

'Here you go.' He seemed to have read her mind. 'Confidence in a glass.'

Evie pulled a face, but accepted the offering. 'There's the door!'

'I didn't hear anything.'

She was already sprinting through the purple sitting room. She had definitely heard a knock.

She dashed upstairs to the door, yanked at the still unfamiliar locks and was rewarded with the sight of Sacha and Bernard chatting. Well, Sacha was chatting. Bernard was trying hard not to look as if he'd rather have his leg down the garbage-disposal unit. The poor man is shyness personified, mused Evie.

'Oh. Ah. Our hostess.' Bernard smiled widely and stuck out his hand with a kind of desperation.

'Hello there, Bernard.' Evie shook it. Bernard's arm was rigid.

'Bernard let me in,' announced Sacha. 'He's just told me he's a Leo, so he's full of passion and fire. A real big cat!' She punctuated her unlikely analysis with a loud roar and a swipe with a paw-shaped hand. Bernard laughed, or it might have been a cough, and attempted a little growl of his own, and Evie decided she rather liked him. She left the door to her flat ajar and led Sacha and Bernard down the stairs and out to the garden, where Bing handed round wine and topped up Evie's glass.

Then, as so often happens around the shy, silence descended. Bernard's self-consciousness blighted the little group and they were reduced to smiling inanely, raising their glasses and looking about them, until Evie rescued them by saying, far too loudly, 'Look, here's Caroline!'

'Haven't you got any soft drinks?' Evidently Caroline mistrusted formal greetings. 'I can hardly give Milly wine.'

'Oh Lord, of course not.' Bing squatted before the small visitor. 'Sorry, kiddo. Forgot about you. What would you like?'

Milly mumbled something and then laughed and stuck her finger in Bing's eye. 'Ribena. Toothkind,' her mother translated flatly.

'Right.' Bing was no wiser. 'I'll be two ticks.'

He made his way down the side of the house and disappeared through the garden door that led to the front garden and the pavement beyond.

'You made it!' gushed Evie, on hostess automatic pilot.

'It were hardly far,' Caroline pointed out, with disdain. 'Your friend, is he a poof?'

'Yes.'

'Right.'

Evie could only ponder what that exchange had meant. The girl should ask for a full refund from her charm school. 'Would *you* like some wine?'

'OK.' She said it as if she was doing Evie a huge favour.

Sacha sidled up, her glass to her cheek, and said knowingly, 'You look like a virgin to me.'

'You what?' Caroline's face blackened to match her leggings and T-shirt. 'What are you trying to say? What do you think *she* is? A bloody immaculate conception?' She motioned at Milly's curly dark head.

Unfazed, Sacha ploughed on: 'I can always tell. You are, aren't you?'

Before Caroline got any more het up, Evie said, 'She means she thinks you're a Virgo, born in September. This is Sacha. She prides herself on being able to spot star signs.'

'Oh.' Only slightly mollified—her default setting was 'disgruntled'—Caroline told them that she was a Gemini. 'And I don't believe in all that astrology rubbish.'

'No, Geminis never do,' said Sacha maddeningly.

Perhaps emboldened by the special-offer Pinot Grigio, Bernard ventured an opinion: 'Isn't it fascinating, though, to speculate that the movements of the heavens, by dint of laws discovered centuries ago, could dictate our fate?'

'It's all cock.' Caroline was succinct.

Before Sacha could trot out her defence (and it was a defence that had been trotted out more times than Red Rum), Bing reappeared in the garden bearing two big bottles.

'Toothkind for Mademoiselle Milly!' he roared, making the child clap her hands and squeal. 'Don't stop, I live for applause!'

'Oh. Are you a thespian, er . . . . Bing?' Bernard had trouble with the unusual name but he straddled it manfully.

Bing topped up everybody's glass. 'I'm a dancer and singer. I'm swing in *Joseph* just now. That means I cover various small parts on a rota.'

'Getting paid for singing and jumping around! You're lucky,' said Caroline.

'You're right. I am.' Bing raised his glass to her without smiling. 'But I've trained and worked hard to be this lucky.'

The sky dimmed to a pink wash as the awkward little party continued.

A surfeit of wine and the lack of any substantial food conspired to make Evie's head hot and her brain useless.

'A toast!' she said suddenly.

Four expectant, slightly tipsy faces turned towards her. Milly was engrossed in dropping leaves into her Ribena. 'We're all together here tonight because of one special woman. One very special woman.'

'Don't cry,' hissed Bing, who was familiar with the nuances at every stage of Evie's drunkenness.

'I won't,' she hissed back, as her eyes started to glisten. 'Let's raise our glasses to a friend who has gone but is certainly not forgotten. Belle O'Brien!'

'Belle O'Brien,' echoed the others, raising their glasses solemnly.

Caroline remained mute, staring into her wine.

Evie moved towards her, but Bing, who knew that belligerence surely followed tears, put out a hand to stop her. 'Won't you toast Belle with us?' he asked Caroline gently.

Caroline stuck up her chin. Her face was pink. 'She's gone, isn't she? Dead. Finished. Why should I toast her? She's history.' As the silence thickened around her she reached down to take her daughter's hand. 'Come on, Milly, you should be in your bed, pet.'

As Caroline walked away Evie shook off Bing's restraining arm and said, a little louder and with more emotion than was strictly necessary, 'She's not history. She was loved. There's a little note on her grave saying she was missed. Who'll miss somebody like you when you're gone?'

Caroline didn't break her step or turn.

Nobody said anything until Sacha intoned sadly, 'That girl's *chakras* are way out.'

Evie counted to ten and her friend's life was spared yet again. As Sacha interrogated a tipsy Bernard about his spiritual health, she leaned against Bing and whined, 'Why did I say that? What kind of landlady am I? That was the worst possible start, wasn't it?'

Bing folded his strong, tanned arms round her. 'Shut up whingeing,' he counselled, kissing the top of her head. 'You can apologise in the morning. She deserved it, if that's any consolation. I think the evening's been a roaring success. I mean, look at Bernard, he put on his best shapeless tweed jacket just for you!'

Evie giggled, then stopped abruptly as the front-door bell buzzed. 'My date!' Bing dropped Evie and leapt off upstairs.

Too sozzled to be miffed by his desertion, Evie wondered who it could be. It wasn't only the volume of Bing's dates that amazed her, it was the variety. He was fond of saying, 'The whole world is gay and you know it,' and judging by the taxi-drivers, boxers, policemen, security guards and at least one soap star who had found themselves under his duvet, he might be right.

After Bing had whisked his new friend off to the bright lights of Old Compton Street, Bernard showed signs of wanting to go home, but Sacha was enlightening him about Buddhism and the Chinese zodiac.

Bernard's eyelids were drooping. Even his ebullient hair was wilting. It was time to save him.

'Right. Shut it, Sash. Let this man get to bed.' It wasn't elegant but it was effective.

Bernard mumbled politely, 'Oh, no, no, I'm fascinated,' then scuttled at warp speed towards the house. 'Good night. Thank you so much for a lovely party.'

'Oh dear.' Sacha shook her head regretfully at his rapidly disappearing back.

'Oh dear, indeed,' laughed Evie. Bernard did cut a comic figure racing through her sitting room.

'You noticed it too!' gasped Sacha. 'God, what am I going to do? Not again. This is awful.'

'What is? What are you on about?'

'He likes me. He *really* likes me.' Sacha smiled ruefully. 'I'll have to let him down gently.'

Evie stared at her. At last she managed to say, 'Yes, that would be best.'

Bing had done Evie's bedroom first. It still smelt of paint, but with the window open it was bearable. He had rehung the photos and playbills on the freshened walls so Belle's young laughing face was everywhere. Boxes spewing crumpled clothes, books, make-up, even a teddy, were scattered across the varnished floorboards. They were a job for tomorrow, Evie decided, Scarlett O'Hara-style, as she launched herself onto the high, rather squeaky brass bed. She shivered. An old eiderdown lay bundled on top of the wardrobe. If she stood on the bed she could reach it. She swung it down and its cosy weight knocked her flat.

Evie burrowed into it, its scent enveloping her: lavender, lilac, roses, a sweet, mood-enhancing dustiness. 'Good night, Belle,' she whispered.

The Kidz!OK! van stopped just long enough for Evie to be spat out of the side door, then roared off. Bing was floating down the steps of number 18 Kemp Street as Evie darted past him.

'Break your legs tonight, cherub,' she sang.

'Oh, by the way, ring your agent,' Bing called over his shoulder. 'She said it was urgent.'

Evie was sitting beside the phone in the basement before Bing had got out the last syllable. Like all actors, she would wait for a message to ring her agent the way a dog waits for you to open a can of his dinner.

As Evie stabbed at the digits she glanced at her watch. Damn. Six twenty. Never what a doctor would describe as sober, after six o'clock Meredith had G&T administered intravenously.

'De Winter Associates. Good evening.' The voice was straight out of prewar RADA.

'It's Evie, Meredith.'

'Evie?'

'Yes, Evie.' Don't make me say my surname.

'I know no Evies. Kindly state your business.'

'Meredith, it's Evie Crump. I'm returning your call. You represent me?'

'And how am I supposed to represent an actress with a name like that?' She was off. 'I mean, do you *feel* like a fucking Crump, darling? Now, Redgrave, there's a name. But . . . Crump?'

'What was it you wanted, Meredith?' asked Evie calmly.

'God knows.' There was the jangle of a great deal of costume jewellery and the breathy rustle of papers. Meredith's office always had the look of a newly burgled crime scene but she could usually nail what she was after with one of her scarlet talons. 'Ah, yes. Here we are. An audition.'

Evie stood up. 'Really?' she whimpered.

'Hmm. Well, more of a go-see, really. For a commercial.'

Evie sat down. 'Oh. Right.' Go-sees were cattle calls. Hundreds of actors called in by a casting director for one or maybe two parts in an ad. 'Now, I've sorted all this out with Kidz!OK! They're giving you the day off. How's that going, by the way?' enquired Meredith, with all the sincerity of the Queen asking a flag-waving Brownie if she had come far.

'It's an experience,' said Evie carefully.

'Well, so is a fucking vaginal scrape. Are you *enjoying* it?'

'Of course.' Never look a gift agent in the mouth. Especially not such a foul mouth.

'Good, good.' There was a deafening crash, rather like a shelf of files collapsing. 'Oh Jesus. Barry's just pulled a shelf of files down on top of him. Must shoot. 'Bye.'

Evie giggled as she replaced the receiver. What a wonderful mental image. Barry, the office assistant, was even older than the Jurassic Meredith, but had the unlined face of a schoolboy, thanks, he claimed, to the fact that he hadn't been sober since 1963. His mishaps in the office were legendary.

The basement was looking, well, *younger*, decided Evie, as she gazed around her. The sitting room was half white now. She ventured into the kitchen. Still purple, unfortunately. There was a piece of paper on the grill above the cooker, with *Apologise to Caroline* written on it in Bing's loose scrawl.

Sighing, Evie mentally straightened her shoulders. It had to be done. What if the surly piece slammed the door in her face? I'll take an unfinished wine-box, she thought. Then she remembered Milly. What on earth did children like? She looked desperately around the kitchen. Ah! The remaining Ribena stood on the worktop. Perfect.

'Who is it?' The voice behind the door of 18B sounded every bit as belligerent as it had the night before.

'Evie.' No response. 'With a peace offering.'

After a couple of beats the door opened a sliver.

'Hmm. More crap wine.' But the door opened all the way.

Stepping into flat B was like entering the kingdom of the toddler. Toys were strewn all over the floor, a line of tiny dresses and dungarees was visible drying over the bath, and racing through it all, at a speed unlikely for somebody so small on all fours, was Milly.

'She's always laughing, isn't she?' said Evie, crouching down to smile at her.

'I'd laugh if I had no problems,' commented Caroline, preceding Evie into the tiny kitchen. 'Coffee?'

Evie was a touch disappointed not to be offered her own wine, but tried not to show it. 'Blimey!' she exclaimed, looking about her. 'This kitchen's new!'

The fitted whitewood cupboards, integrated appliances and gleaming chrome cooker contrasted strongly with the primitive cooking arrangements downstairs.

'Belle had it put in.' Caroline was not the sort to overwhelm with information, but she added, 'She thought it was better for Milly if I had a decent kitchen.'

While managing without one herself, thought Evie. Once they were seated on the threadbare sofa in the middle of a sea of Fisher Price, she embarked on the speech she'd speedily composed on her way upstairs. 'I want to apologise for being so rude last night. I was a bit nervous about taking responsibility for this house and I probably drank rather too much wine because of it. If you didn't want to toast Belle that was entirely up to you.' Evie paused, then added, 'Belle's generosity meant a lot to me and I know how much she cared about her tenants,' because she didn't want this sour girl to get off scot-free. Finally, swallowing hard, she pronounced, 'I'm sorry, Caroline. Can we start again?'

Caroline looked into the middle distance—seemingly her favourite place—and after a loud slurp of instant said, 'S'pose so. Yeah.'

'Great.' Evie produced a false, toothy smile. She had come to the wrong person for effusive proclamations.

A silence, not a comfortable one, hung around them like wet knitting until inspiration struck: 'She's gorgeous, isn't she?' Evie cooed, pointing at Milly. Indeed the little girl did look gorgeous as she chattered eagerly about important toddler business affairs on a toy telephone.

'Yeah. She's everything to me.' Caroline buried her face in her mug, possibly alarmed by her own enthusiasm.

Evie, who viewed life as one big soap opera, was itching to know where Milly's dad was, and why Caroline was bringing her up on her own, but Caroline's tetchy guardedness meant that she had to content herself with innocent-sounding queries.

'Where's your accent from?' asked Evie, and qualified her nosiness with, 'I often have to do accents in my work so I'm always fascinated by a new one.'

'Bury.' One-word answers were Caroline's speciality.

'So what made you come to London? I'm sure it's lovely in Bury. Are your family still up there?'

'My family are all dead.'

As conversation stoppers go, this was a beaut. Evie crumbled. 'Oh, I'm so sorry, Caroline.' She fidgeted a moment or two, allowing the raspberry colour in her cheeks to cool, then stood up and said, 'I'd better go down and get myself some dinner. I've got an audition tomorrow.'

'Have you.' Caroline left out the question mark.

Evie backed away. 'So, that's our fresh start, er, started, then! Knock on the door if anything goes wrong with—well, with anything, really. You know, plumbing or . . .' Evie's mind raced.

'Don't walk on my daughter,' warned Caroline evenly.

Evie wheeled round to see Milly right behind her, holding up her arms expectantly. 'Oooh, are you coming to the door with me?' Evie tried to sound pleased, but she'd never been comfortable around kids. Clasping Milly awkwardly she manhandled her off the ground. Christ, she was heavy! Did she have bricks in her nappy?

She smelt nice, though. And the messy kiss she planted on Evie's cheek was unexpectedly delightful. Evie grinned at her passenger, who settled comfortably on Evie's hip like a koala on a eucalyptus tree. 'Here we go, then!' It was a voice Evie had never heard coming out of her own mouth before. It was reminiscent of *Playschool*, *circa* 1973.

Caroline followed, presumably to ensure that Evie didn't maim her daughter on the short trip to the front door. 'See you, then.'

'Yeah. See you.' Evie passed Milly back to her mother. For the first time the similarity in their looks struck her. There was no similarity in their clothes, though. Caroline was in her drab uniform of faded black jeans and faded black T-shirt, while Milly was a riot of clean, pressed gingham. Her little socks were blindingly white with a gingham trim, and her floppy dark curls were held back with a colourful ribbon. Navy ribbon with yellow smiley faces on it.

As the door closed on flat B, a number of pennies dropped with a clunk.

The brief was 'young, carefree, playful'. When Evie had checked herself in the mirror at home she had been satisfied that white Capri pants and a sky-blue camisole looked young, carefree, playful. Haring through Soho after three-quarters of an hour in a stalled tube, she felt old, care-worn, murderous. Screeching to a sweaty halt outside the Green Room casting suite in Argyll Street, Evie was relieved to find that she was only five minutes late.

Evie gave her name to the receptionist, who had excelled at Indifference and Deep Boredom at reception school, then perched on the arm of an oatmeal sofa. A hasty scan of thirty other girls in the waiting room reassured her that she didn't know a soul, thank God, and she leaned back in relief.

Then the door opened and her name was called.

The audition room was a small, blank oblong with a chair, execution-style, at one end. Facing it were a lighting rig, a video camera on a tripod and three other chairs supporting three men. One—bearded, bald and trendy of trouser—rose and said wearily, 'I'm Greg, the director. Please sit down and go through your drill for us.'

Obediently Evie arranged herself as neatly, yet casually as possible. Endeavouring to sound young, carefree and playful, she said into the camera, 'I'm Evie Crump, and I'm with Meredith de Winter at Meredith de Winter Associates.'

'Okey-dokey.' Greg had the manner of a man who had been waiting for a bus for the last fourteen years. 'You've seen the script?'

'Ooh, dear. No, I haven't.' Evie couldn't bluff that.

Greg looked up at the heavens. Or the polystyrene tiles on the ceiling. 'Give the girl a script, someone.'

His assistant scurried over and handed her a dog-eared script.

Greg droned on: 'Right. You play "Woman". "Man" has already been cast, with Dan here. You stay seated and Dan'll read with you out of shot. OK?'

'Er, oh, yeah.' Evie could have been forgiven for her distracted reply, for when Dan rose, smiling, out of the dusky edge of the room, his appearance should have been accompanied by a heavenly choir, complete with harps. Dan was . . . well, handsome didn't cover it. Mills & Boon writers would have thrown down their pens in defeat. He really did have hair as black as a raven's wing, a chiselled, manly jaw, eyes like twin chips of sky and a devastating smile.

Afterwards she couldn't remember a word of the script. She had been too busy fantasising about what Dan looked like in the bath.

'We'll let you know. You'd have to be available the twentieth through the twenty-second. It's location. We'll get in touch with your agent if we're interested. Thank you, sweetheart, goodbye.' Greg's hand in the small of her back had propelled her out.

She came to. It was hot in Argyll Street. The Palladium's white frontage loomed in front of her. Bing! Today was a matinée. She'd take refuge in his dressing room.

Surrounded by eight, practically perfect, almost naked, undeniably homosexual male bodies, Evie perched on a Formica table and described Dan in minute detail. 'So I have to, *have to*, HAVE TO get this job, but I think I was lousy,' she finished.

'What's the commercial for?' asked Bing, rearranging his fluorescent-green loincloth.

'Some kind of dog food.'

'Class.'

'Don't knock it, green loincloth boy. I did my sums this morning. Belle kept the rents so low they're hardly worth collecting. I need a break, especially if I want to get started on all the house improvements.'

'Not to mention the shag you're crying out for. I thought you had a no-actors rule.'

'I do. But . . .'

'Tremendous strength of character as usual.' Bing put a small red dot in the corner of each eye with a scrubby old Leichner pencil. Then, as if obeying some secret call of the wild, he and his eight fellow chorines jogged out to be back onstage for the big dance number in the second act. Left alone with a smell of feet and make-up Evie ruminated, not for the first time, that it was a funny old way to make a living.

They were back in the garden and back on the booze. The sun had long since left them to it and gone to bed, but Evie and Sacha were still sipping wine in the warm air on mismatched kitchen chairs. Their swaying figures were lit by the soft glow of the fairy lights they'd rigged up outside the conservatory.

'Congratulations,' said Sacha. Again. She'd already congratulated Evie many, many times. They were drinking to celebrate the fact that Evie, against all the odds, had got the commercial. 'And he's really, *really* handsome and dead shexy? Are you going to . . . you know?'

'If I get the chance I intend to you-know him until I can you-know him no more.' This *bon mot* set them cackling like deranged fowl. Sacha toppling off her chair tipped them over into full-blown hysteria.

Bing approached them up the garden steps. 'Blimey! What a lovely vision of modern femininity,' he remarked. 'At a guess I'd say that you two might have had a mouthful or two of *vino*.'

'Oh, Bing!' yelled Sacha, from where she lay on the grass. 'You're gorgeous from this angle. Why aren't you straight?'

'Because I've got too much taste. Up you come.' Bing hoisted her back on to her rickety seat. She slithered down again.

Bing sighed. Both women were laughing now as if the Official Funniest Joke Ever had just been unleashed on them.

'Leave her,' gasped Evie. 'When she gets to this stage she can't stay upright. Oh, Sash!' She was choking again. 'Do you remember the time you—' she was finding it nearly impossible to talk '—launderette . . . Funny hat . . . The leg fell off—'

Incredibly Sacha did remember. A fresh bout of side-splitting commenced, with Sacha kicking her legs in the air and Evie sounding as if she was being strangled.

Bing, exhausted by two shows and a virtuoso snog with the new understudy, stomped back to the house for fresh supplies of wine. When he returned an eerie silence had fallen over the two drunks. He stepped over Sacha and took her seat.

Suddenly Evie asked, in the little-girl voice that she knew Bing disliked, 'Would I be an almighty bitch if I put the rents up?'

'Yes,' burbled Sacha emphatically from the ground, 'you would be an almi'y bish if you put the rentsh up,' and fell asleep.

Bing was more diplomatic. 'Leave things as they are for a while. Let them get used to you. Worried about money, Funnyface?'

'Just for a change.'

They sat in companionable silence, the night air filled with the soft swoosh of distant traffic and the insistent bass line of Sacha's snores. Finally Bing said, 'This house is growing on me.'

'Mmm.' Evie leaned back and looked up at it. All the windows were dark, and the outlines of the roof were smudged so that it seemed to melt into the sky.

'It feels kind of secure even though it's practically falling down.' Bing rubbed his face. 'Am I making any sense? It's been a long day.'

'Yeah, you are. I know exactly what you mean. It's solid. It's a . . . refuge.' Evie raised her eyebrows at her vocabulary after a surfeit of wine. Although it was in the middle of murky old Camden, the garden felt like a secret one, with its unrestrained trees and hedges. The only door out to it was through Evie's flat, so there was no danger of meeting a lurking tenant, and Bing had fitted a new lock on the garden door. 'My mum's been on at me about living in a basement. "It'll be damp and it'll be dark and it's the first place burglars go for," but it's cosy. And it's getting whiter every day, thanks to you.'

Bing sighed. 'Nothing I can do about that cooker, though. It's on its last legs. The fridge might be worth something to an archaeologist. As for the bathroom . . .'

'I know, I know. That's why I mentioned the rents,' said Evie sorrowfully. 'Belle kept them so low that the income will never pay for what needs doing, never mind give me the financial security she meant it to.'

Bing narrowed his eyes. 'That's not the only reason she left it to you. Maybe it's not even the main one.'

'Eh?' Evie squinted at him. His strong features were blunted by the glow from the fairy lights.

'Well . . .' He seemed unsure whether to embark on meaningful conversation with someone two bottles ahead of him. Evidently he decided to give it a go. 'I didn't know you back when you and Belle and your gran were all hanging out together but I suspect you haven't changed much. You like finding out about people, you enjoy sorting them out, you're never without a collection of lame ducks.'

Evie snorted.

'Snorteth not, Crump. I'm right. On the rare occasions you have a job, whose dressing room do all the little actresses who've had rows with their boyfriends end up in? How many times do I come home to find some tear-stained idiot who's "having a bit of a difficult time at the moment" taking up the sofa? And what about . . .' Bing pointed at the figure on the ground, whose snores had settled down into a disco mix of gurgles. 'You hold her hand through all her doomed love affairs, all her phases and crises. And what about me?' Bing pointed at his chest. 'Can you remember what a mess I was when we met?'

Evie remembered it well. A huge party in a tiny flat. Dozens of thespians, with trained diaphragms, shouting, laughing, drinking and flirting at ear-splitting levels. A fairly typical Edinburgh Fringe wrap party.

That day Bing had been chucked out by his Dutch lover of three years for (whisper it) a woman, and he was the wrong side of a bucket of Jack Daniel's.

'I was sobbing like a new Miss World and there was a six-foot exclusion zone round me—people were scared my misery was contagious. What did you come up to me and say?'

'You can stay at my place if you like.'

'Exactly.' Bing kissed Evie's forehead. 'You love a challenge. I moved in, cried it all out, and a fortnight later I was right as rain and thanking God I'd met you.'

'Aw. Really?'

'Yes, really, but don't go all dewy-eyed. I can't do drunken sentimentality just now. I'm sober. What I'm trying to say is that Belle knew her little band of misfits would be in safe hands with you.'

'Ho, ho, no. No, sirree.' Evie waved her glass around, slopping some of its contents over Bing's Armani trousers. 'I am *not* getting involved with this bunch.'

'Not even with irresistible raw material like Bernard?' He nudged her. 'You haven't been thinking, "If only Bernard smartened himself up a bit he could get himself a girlfriend?" Or itching to see inside his flat?'

'Absolutely not,' Evie lied.

As if prompted by a secret signal, a bare bulb sparked into life on the first floor. 'Our guinea pig is awake!' hissed Bing. He hollered, 'BERNAAAAAARD!'

'Ssssh! He is *not* our guinea pig. I'm not interested in him. Shut it!' commanded Evie, but the chrysanthemum-like outline of Bernard was already at the window.

'Er, helloooo?' he ventured, like a prewar schoolmarm.

'It's us, Bing and Evie! Come and join us!'

Bernard evidently didn't want to, but Bing's powers of persuasion were irresistible and soon he was sitting between them, having brought down his chair as instructed.

'We want to know all about you, Bernard,' said Bing, without preamble.

'Ooooh.' Bernard winced, but enquired mildly, 'What would you like to know? There isn't much to say about me.'

Evie, who had forgotten her resistance to this idea, decided to ease him in with a straightforward question: 'What do you do for a living?'

'Ah. That's easy. I collate statistics.'

There was a respectful pause while Bing and Evie tried to think of something interesting to say about statistics.

'Do you enjoy it?' enquired Evie finally.

'Oh, yes!' Bernard's pallid face lit up. 'The statistic is a marvellous thing. Packed with information. Surprising, yet reassuring.'

'Right.' Bing sounded unconvinced. 'What do you do for *fun*, Bernard?' He leaned towards him. Bing was the king of fun. This was his territory. 'What twiddles your knobs? What pushes your buttons?'

Bernard looked blank. If he had any knobs they remained, presumably, untwiddled.

Bing simplified his question. 'What do you look forward to doing?'

'Going to work,' Bernard said apologetically.

Evie smiled. There was something about Bernard that touched her. 'Don't you have a . . . ladyfriend?'

'Nooooo.' Bernard giggled nervously. 'I'm not much of a ladies' man.'

'Oh, come on.' Evie risked a pat on his arm.

Bernard gulped. 'No. No. Honestly. I've never, erm, never had what you'd call an, erm, relationship. As such.'

Bing and Evie had the same thought at the same instant, as if the fairy lights had suddenly rearranged themselves to read BERNARD IS A VIRGIN.

'Would you like a relationship? As such?' Evie's tipsiness made her bold.

'Of course he bloody would,' snapped Bing. 'Wouldn't you, Bernard?' he said encouragingly.

'I don't know,' said Bernard mildly. 'You don't miss what you've never had.' He went on, in a rare burst of eloquence, 'Mother used to keep me pretty busy and since she died I've kept myself to myself.'

'Do you miss your mother?' Bing's voice was gentle.

'Every day.' Such sincerity. Such sadness. 'She did everything for me, you see. I was a bit lost after . . . Sometimes I wish she'd shown me how to do things like cooking and so on.'

'Don't you cook?' asked Evie.

'No. She did everything. After she died I took to getting a very acceptable saveloy and chips from the nice takeaway round the corner.'

Bing, whose body was a temple, said hopefully, 'But not every night?'

'Oh, yes, every night. With a big bottle of pop.'

That explained the ghastly pallor. 'Bernard,' said Evie decisively, 'I'm going away for three nights, but when I come home you're coming to me for dinner. OK?'

Bernard nodded, more terrified than grateful.

'And, what's more, you're going to cook it.'

After Bing and Evie had seen Bernard to his door, they sauntered arm in arm back down to the basement. 'You've got the bit between your teeth now, girl,' Bing said. 'It only took half an hour to reel you in, and now you're planning cookery lessons for the poor sod.'

'Not just cookery lessons,' pronounced Evie. 'There'll be another guest at that dinner party. Someone nice-looking, who needs a decent, honest, solvent man. Someone who lives *there*.' Evie gestured at the floor above them.

'Caroline?' Bing lowered his voice. 'She'd eat him alive.'

'Nonsense. She's soft as butter underneath. All her family are dead so

371

she needs a man to stand by her and help bring up Milly.'

Bing shook his head. 'Does she *really* need a man who seems to have been raised in a growbag by a domineering mother who led him to believe that making a cup of coffee required a degree in the black arts?'

'We can work on all that.' Evie waved away such trivia.

'You'll also have to work on the clothes, the hair, the body language. One other thing—I suspect that our friend is not exactly a demon between the sheets.'

'God, can you imagine it?' Evie had to laugh. 'All sorrys and oh dears and him leaning on your hair.'

'What have I done?' mused Bing, looking down at his drunken land-lady. 'You've really taken the ball and run with it, haven't you? Good night, doll.'

'Night.'

A good hour had passed before, giggling hysterically, they raced out-side in their dressing gowns to retrieve Sacha from the damp grass.

Four

SUNDAYS AREN'T REALLY SUNDAYS any more. High streets are open for busi-ness; garden centres are lively with bickering couples; cinemas, estate agents, sex shops are all there for our delight. (Plus the odd church, of course.) However, sit down to a plate of roast beef with all the trim-mings and suddenly, magically, Sunday is just like it used to be, with delicious aromas creeping round the house.

Not to mention bone-crushing boredom and a passionate desire to burn the family home to the ground, thought Evie ungratefully, as she sat on the sofa, a three-year-old twin at either side of her and a huge photograph album open on her lap. Bridgie was leaning over her, enthusiastically pointing out the glorious highlights of their latest trip to the time share in Normandy.

Charles and Julius were leaning hotly into Evie, seemingly transfixed by the mundane parade of out-of-focus snaps of their grandmother.

'Nana's booootiful,' cooed Charles inaccurately, gazing at a shot of Bridgie in what seemed to be a French high-rise car park.

'And you're obviously destined for a lucrative career in PR, Charles.'

Evie gave her tiny nephew a squeeze and wondered for the squillionth time why Beth, who came from a long line of Marys, Johns, Catherines and Roberts, had gone berserk at the font and named her children Charles and Julius. On reflection maybe it was all Marcus's fault. No doubt there was a smattering of Jonquils and Hermiones in his pedigree.

'I can't stand around like this all day.' Bridgie sounded almost angry, as if the family had nailed her court shoes to the carpet. 'I have to get back to that roast.' She regarded a joint of beef as a wily opponent. She had to show it who was boss with constant basting and poking.

The anticipation of gravy made Evie feel so mellow she was emboldened to ask, 'Any chance of a drink, Mum?'

'Squash? Or Coke?'

'I was thinking of something a bit stronger.' A reckless request, but Evie kept hoping that a little French *je ne sais quoi* might creep into Surbiton, as a result of the annual fortnight across the Channel, in the welcome shape of a bottle of wine.

But no. A very small sherry was thrust into her hand. Then the twins were promptly removed.

Beth sat down beside Evie, tucking her espadrilles beneath her, and the glass was snatched out of her hand and downed in one. 'You don't drink!' hissed Evie, amazed.

Beth replaced the glass in Evie's still schooner-shaped hand as Bridgie cruised past with a groaning tray of appetisers.

'Finished already?' she yelped. 'Oliver Reed had nothing on you!'

Evie scowled at Beth, who mouthed, 'Sorry.' She was as blonde as Evie was auburn, with a lean, rangy silhouette quite unlike Evie's comfortable curves. It was incredible that Evie had waded through the swamps of adolescence without developing insane jealousy of her sister's brains and beauty. This was in no way thanks to their mother, who had heaped praise on Beth, along with a running commentary on Evie's shortcomings.

By rights Evie should have resented her high-achieving, good-looking elder sibling. Perhaps the reason she didn't was because Evie had never yearned for academic honours. Or perhaps it was because Beth's looks only seemed to attract the kind of bloke Evie would cross the street to avoid; they were always handsome, always wealthy, always buttock-clenchingly boring. They had culminated in Marcus, who was dark, loaded and loved to talk teeth. In Evie's opinion, dentists were to be avoided, but Beth had chosen to share her life with one.

Or perhaps the sisters' relationship had survived because Beth had a level head and kind heart. They were not close—the elder sister was as sensible and organised as the younger was reckless and disorganised—

but there was a comfortable familiarity between them.

'Congratulations,' Beth was saying. 'Mum told me about the house.'

'She doesn't approve.'

'Mum never approves of anything. Don't let that worry you. Are you all moved in?'

Evie brought her up to date, noticing that Beth was absorbed in the story to an unusual degree.

'And is it full?' Beth asked. 'Do you have enough tenants?'

'Yeah.'

'I'm really, really glad for you, sis. A homeowner!'

Evie shrugged. 'You're a homeowner too, you know.'

'Nooooo.' Beth drew the word out like a fat lady's knicker elastic. 'He is.' She cocked her head at her husband who, by virtue of his accent and his penis, was being awarded a *large* sherry by Bridgie.

'Same difference.'

'Well . . .' Beth changed the subject. 'When are you going to bring a bloke home to meet us?'

'Do *not* get me started!' Evie thumped a cushion.

'I'd been married seven years when I was your age,' Beth said dreamily.

'Don't I know it. I spent your wedding day mummified in fuchsia taffeta, and the sash was too tight.'

'Will you please get over it? It was seventeen years ago!'

Evie laughed, then gave in and returned to the thorny subject of the opposite sex. 'Look, I'm on the shelf. Past my sell-by date. Surplus. Redundant. When Charles and Julius grow up I'll be their eccentric spinster aunt and they won't want to kiss me because I'll take my dentures out to suck boiled sweets.'

'Come off it, Evie, you're in your prime. If I was you, with your youth and all that freedom, I'd be shagging like a rabbit.'

'Eh?' Evie's big sister was not supposed to talk like that. She was respectable. She was reserved. 'You wouldn't.'

'Wouldn't I?' murmured Beth, her face an unreadable mixture of sadness and secrecy. 'Everybody else seems to.'

Evie frowned, then followed Beth's glance to Marcus. 'I see,' she said, in her best lady-detective voice. 'Trouble in Paradise?'

The look Beth flung her way was uncharacteristically hard. 'Don't talk about things you don't understand,' she said, then stood up and strode out of the room. Evie stared after her. Not only did Beth never drink and never say 'shagging', she never strode out of rooms either. Something was eating Evie's big sister.

Marcus was skirting the dining table and heading for Evie. He threw himself down on the sofa and grinned toothily at his sister-in-law.

'How's it going?' he asked.

Evie took a moment to answer. An unwelcome thought buzzed round her head like a trapped bluebottle. *You're having an affair.* 'Fine, fine,' she said eventually. She was inspecting him with new eyes. She was looking at him as a man, not as her brother-in-law. He was still handsome, she was surprised to note. That touch of grey in his thick black hair was— sexy. Viewed objectively, Marcus was a very attractive man. His hands were manicured, he had a wide smile and clear blue eyes, which still held a boyish innocence.

But he wasn't innocent. Her sister's new bitterness could only stem from some terrible disappointment. It had to be a betrayal. Nothing else would cut that deep. Her brother-in-law had turned into an adulterer.

'Come on, come on. Lunch is served.' Bridgie wasn't a patient woman. Only Marcus's presence saved Evie from being exhorted to get her fat behind to the table.

Ah, the table. The heavy lace tablecloth—only ever seen on Sunday—was practically invisible beneath crocheted doilies, ceramic coasters, wedding-present crystal glasses, silver-plated cutlery, a cande-labrum worthy of Liberace's campest moment (the candles were lit despite the blazing afternoon sun), and an immense display of roses.

Evie sat between her nephews, opposite Marcus and Beth, who had returned from her brief exile in the hall. She searched her sister's face for signs of tears, but Beth was hard to read as she lunged, spooned and poured with the rest of them. It was always a complex matter to fill your plate from all the Sunday serving dishes.

'Peas, Marcus!' Bridgie yelled hysterically into his face. 'Evie, give Marcus the peas! Beth, pass Daddy the Yorkshires! *The Yorkshires!*'

Finally, every plate had a bit of everything on it and John said, almost tetchily for he was only human, 'Perhaps you can sit down now, Bridgie, and take that apron off'.

Bridgie snorted. Her apron-at-the-Sunday-lunch-table routine was one of her favourite parts of the week. The apron was her badge of mar-tyrdom: it reminded them all of how she toiled so that they might eat.

'This is *good*!' declared Marcus.

Evie wanted to empty the jar of horseradish over his head.

'Evie!' Bridgie's squeal made her jump. 'Don't let Julius rub roast potato into his hair!'

What was it with kids? 'Sorry, sorry,' she muttered, dabbing at the squirming child with her napkin.

'We're going to see you on the box soon, eh?' said John.

'Yes!' squeaked Evie. 'It's a commercial for dog food. It'll be shot on location in Dorset. Two nights in a hotel!'

Bridgie turned to Beth. 'How's the extension coming along? Did you decide about the skylight?'

Loyally Beth pretended to find the tablecloth fascinating and John asked Evie, 'When will it be on the screen?'

'I dunno. A few weeks, probably. They'll let me know and then I'll warn you, Dad.'

Marcus leaned across the table. 'Will you get a bundle for it? They're jolly lucrative, I hear.'

Beth cut in: 'What I'd like to know is, when are you getting back to *real* acting, *proper* acting?'

'Who knows?' Evie's tone was light, but she felt crushed. Why was Beth directing her anger at her?

Meredith had given Evie a first-class (first-class!) train ticket to Lyme Regis, a twenty-pound note for her cab ride to the Bayside Hotel and a call sheet, detailing the schedule of the production and the names of everybody on it. Through careful questioning Evie had ascertained that Dan Dan the Handsome Man was travelling down later in the day and would meet the rest of the crew at the hotel. Bing had said, in the manner of a stern Victorian grandparent, 'Now, young lady, I expect you to return home covered in lovebites. Do not let me down.' But, then, Bing saw sex as the great panacea.

Evie wasn't so sure. No, despite the drunken bravado with which she had pledged to Sacha that she would you-know-what Dan, Evie had a different plan. Simple, but—for her—unique. She would *get to know him*. She would *take things slowly*. She might not like him when she took the trouble to find out what he was like. But he just might be very nice and he just might fancy her and they just might embark on one of those things—oh, what were they called? That's right. A *relationship*.

Some instinctive part of Evie knew that one of those was ultimately much more nourishing than a shag. The problem was, she'd never achieved one. Knowing you want one is a start, though, surely?

The Bayside Hotel was quaint but it nestled spectacularly right in the middle of the wide sweep of Lyme Regis bay. Evie liked what she had seen of the town from the window of her (paid-for—oh, bliss!) minicab. Absurdly small and pretty houses hugged steep roads that all dribbled down to the bay, which was lined with fishermen's cottages, fish-and-chip shops and the hotel.

Evie wasn't used to hotels. She had been hoping for cutting-edge modernist, minimalist, funky chic. She had got Fawlty Towers. Reception was a large, panelled room with a log fire (despite the heat).

There was a high wooden desk with a brass bell on it, standing beside an open leather ledger.

The abrupt tinkle of the bell brought about the almost immediate materialisation of a stout woman through a door marked STAFF.

'Yes?' she said, by way of greeting.

'I'm Evie Crump, and I've been booked in by Gem Productions,' said Evie hopefully.

The woman glanced at the ledger and said, 'Yes. Sign in, please.'

Evie scribbled her name, and was informed that she was in room 34, that the shower was 'temperamental' and that she was to dial 101 if she needed any help.

'Right,' Evie said. She bent down for her bag but a hand was already upon it.

Another member of staff had materialised, presumably through a trap door. 'Allow me.' The porter was about her age, with a blunt but friendly face, and Evie followed him into the lift.

It's never easy to talk in a lift, is it? Evie adopted the commonplace tactic of looking at the floor numbers as they lit up, as if there might be some surprise waiting there.

The porter preceded her down the narrow wallpapered landing to room 34, and stepped back while she opened the door. It was a small, austere but pretty, pink room, as dated as Reception.

Oh Gawd, Evie thought, as the porter put down the bag and turned to her with a smile. *A tip.* She was bad at tipping. Working out how much, when and *if* was riddled with possibly insulting miscalculations.

Resolving to be cool and elegant about it, she delved into her huge suede sack and, unusually, put her hand straight onto her purse. She extracted a pound coin (Was that enough? Was it too much?), held it out with a big smile and said, 'Thank you very much.'

The porter just looked at it. Oh God. He was insulted. He was going to tell all the other staff and they would spit in her soup.

But he didn't seem insulted, he was smiling. A big smile that lit up his green eyes. 'We seem to have got off on the wrong foot. My name's Aden. I'm the assistant director.' He reached out and took the coin. 'But thanks very much.'

The door closed behind him. Evie collapsed onto the bed and buried her face in the pillow. It was dense but not as dense as she was.

On the phone Bing had said, 'Was he dressed like a porter?' Unless porters wear jeans and sweatshirts the answer had to be no. Evie looked at her call sheet. There he was. Aden Black, assistant director. Assistant directors are important on shoots. They do all the bits the big important director doesn't want to do, which can mean positioning the actors for lighting, running through the scene with them, checking camera angles, liaising with props people and so on. They work hard and their good-will is vital to actors if they want to be lit flatteringly, directed sensitively and generally treated more like human beings than cattle.

He looked like a nice man, mused Evie, as she glossed her lips in preparation for the 'Cast and Crew Drink in Reception' as detailed on her call sheet. Not at all the sort of bloke who would mind being mis-taken for a porter. She cringed. *Even though he's assistant director.*

He probably won't have mentioned it to anyone, Evie reassured her-self in the lift. As the doors opened on to the hubbub of people laying into the free drinks, the first face she saw, devastatingly, was Dan's. 'Carry your bags, Miss?' he said, in a jaunty Cockney accent and every-one laughed.

Evie must have looked sheepish. Dan swooped on her and hugged her as if he had known her all his life. 'Sorry. Couldn't resist it. Great to see you again, gorgeous,' he said, in a husky whisper that coiled like smoke right into her ear. Then he planted a kiss on her cheek. It was warm and delicious and temporarily robbed Evie of the power of speech. Whatever I do, she thought, I mustn't drink.

Aden handed her a glass of wine with an apologetic smile, and she drained it as if she had spent the last forty days and nights in the desert.

They were a nice bunch, a great bunch, she decided, as they sat down to dinner in the dining room. But, then, everyone's a great bunch when seen through the distorting curve of a glass. Some tiny voice of reason prevailed when the waiter came round and Evie found herself covering her glass with her hand.

The reason for her self-control was seated next to her. Dan was a tem-plate for the kind of man Evie found irresistible. It wasn't just the stun-ning looks, it was the devilish smile and the racy air. He was confident, outgoing. Worst of all, he made her laugh. A quick shag (if one was on offer—there was no real evidence so far) was very, very tempting. But a relationship . . . Imagine a relationship with someone who made you sweat with sexual anticipation *and* made you laugh. Now, that would be worth having.

Aden was sitting opposite her across the white linen tablecloth. He seemed nice too. A bit quiet, probably happily married. He had that air of settled-downness, with his short brown hair and unremarkable clothes. She was grateful to him for making a joke of the mistaken iden-tity: it wasn't going to affect their working relationship at all.

Dan's clothes and hair were just right. A moss-green linen shirt hanging over well-cut khakis. A David Beckham-style quiffy crop.

What was far from just right was that on the other side of all this funkiness was the make-up girl, Melody. Pretentious name, scoffed Evie to herself, which meant: she's got tits that should be fake but aren't and she's blonde and she's got the legs for that micro-mini she's almost wearing. And—and this was the worst bit—everybody always fancies the make-up girl.

Melody was laughing. A lot. 'What's so funny?' Evie leaned over, the wine already in her bloodstream emboldening her.

'Oh, it's him!' said Melody, in a deep brown Welsh accent. 'He's a one!'

Evie and Dan exchanged the tiniest look and she felt reassured. 'That's nice. I always look for that in a man,' said Evie.

'Oh, anybody can make me laugh. I think the world would be a better place if all the politicians got together and told jokes, don't you?' Melody theorised.

This time Dan's look had the faintest hint of a smirk and Evie knew, just knew, that Melody didn't have a chance.

'I don't know that politicians can tell jokes,' said Dan. 'I mean, can you imagine Margaret Thatcher doing stand-up?'

'Or Bill Clinton.' Evie laughed, pleased that Melody was looking puzzled. 'Knock knock. Who's there? *I did not have sexual relations with that woman . . .*'

'Perfect!' Dan sniggered.

'Crap Clinton impression, though,' said Aden.

'Oi, leave her alone.' Thrillingly, Dan had defended Evie's skills. 'I thought Bill Clinton was actually sitting here beside me for a moment. Obviously,' he went on as Evie simpered, 'not *the* Bill Clinton.'

Evie belted him with her napkin. Dan grabbed it and tickled her under the arms. She squealed before she recalled that they were in a hotel dining room. Sure enough, a few heads had swivelled their way. 'Whoops! We're lowering the tone,' she whispered to Dan.

'That's what they expect from actors,' he reminded her.

Evie felt high, breathless. They'd barely been introduced and they were already on tickling terms.

'So, what are you working on?' asked Aden. 'Apart from this I mean.'

'I'm the envy of Judi Dench. I'm in a children's educational piece with a group called Kidz!OK!.' Evie felt secure enough to work her pitiful job up into a funny story.

'That'll be with two exclamation marks, I presume?' said Aden.

'Spot on. If they spent a bit less on exclamation marks and a bit more on costumes I might not have to cross the stage with my arse hanging out of my badger outfit.'

'Not altogether a bad thing,' Dan murmured, so that only Evie could hear him.

Evie's cheeks—all four of them—went hot, and she squirmed on the hard chair. That was a signal. She was getting signals from Dan that he fancied her! She was breaking out into exclamation marks herself!

The little aside so diverted her that Aden had to repeat his question. 'What do you think the kids you play to *really* want to see? What would you give them if you had the chance?'

It was a good question, an interesting and thought-provoking one, but Evie wanted to shout, 'Oh, shut your face! Dan's got his hand on my knee!' She managed to say, in a high-pitched voice she wouldn't have recognised as her own, 'Something fun, something lively. And something that related to their own experiences.'

Aden nodded thoughtfully.

Dan's hand caressed, then squeezed her thigh. She caught his eye. There was a twinkle in it that could have floodlit Wembley Stadium.

Aden put down his coffee cup. 'Now, about tomorrow—'

'Aw, come on. The night is still young,' cajoled Dan.

'I just want to make sure you all know your call times. It's my job.' Aden was unapologetic.

Dan turned to Evie. 'He was just like this at school, you know.'

'You were at school together?' That was a surprise. Evie had presumed they'd met on this production. 'Oh.'

'Yeah. I know it sounds unlikely. Square old me and hunky leading man him, but it's true,' said Aden, with a smile.

'Oh, no, I didn't mean that.' Evie grinned. 'Well, not exactly . . .'

Dan leaned back and placed his hands behind his head. His linen shirt gaped across his tanned, taut chest. Evie dug her nails into her palms as he said, 'Even then Aden was always looking through a lens.'

'And Dan was always looking in a mirror.' Aden ducked as a piece of meringue came his way. 'Hey! You'll get us chucked out. We're in Lyme Regis, not Soho.'

'All right, all right, Head Boy.' Dan stood up, with an abrupt, clean motion. 'Why don't we explore the Lyme Regis nightlife? See what the glittering south coast has to offer?'

'If anything,' said Evie. 'Unless you fancy bingo.'

'Two little ducks!' shouted Melody, relieved that they had strayed into her area of expertise. 'Two fat ladies!' She'd been drinking while they'd been chatting.

Aden looked dubious. 'We've all got six a.m. alarm calls.'

Dan ignored him. He looked into Evie's eyes. 'What do you say? Do you want to paint the town?'

'Yeah!'

'Unlucky for shome—fourteen!' burbled Melody, as she followed them out into Reception.

Aden folded his arms and watched them as they stepped out onto the front. 'You make sure you get enough beauty sleep. Oh, and, Dan,' he said, as the door swung shut behind them, 'look after the ladies.'

It was cold. The sea snatched the warmth out of the night and flung spray back at them. The waves were right up against the promenade. It might have been romantic but for 'Key of the Door—twenty-one!' The cackling Melody was hanging on to Dan's arm as if she was drowning. Evie walked along beside them. She wanted—no, make that needed—to take Dan's other arm. But she was unsure and hung back, despite the unspoken invitation she had received at the hotel.

Painting the town red was going to be difficult. Even light pink was tricky. The pubs split cleanly into two camps. There were the touristy ones, garlanded with lobster pots, and the old-man pubs, smoky and lined with septuagenarians. The two styles of pub had one thing in common: they were all closing.

Dan shrugged. 'We might as well—'

'Go back?' Evie finished for him. 'Yeah. Might as well.'

'Ooooo-er! Me guts are bad.' Melody lacked the poetry of her Welsh forebears but she was certainly informative. It took both of them to haul her along the seafront and back to the hotel.

'You get off to bed.' Dan draped the rubbery Melody over his shoulder, as they got into the lift. 'I'll look after this one.'

'Are you sure?' Evie was relieved not to have to take responsibility for a girl who was threatening to spray-paint her surroundings with bile at any moment. But she was sorry to leave Dan. 'Night, then,' she said, like an awkward fourteen-year-old, and stepped out on the third floor.

'Night, gorgeous.' The lift doors closed, and Evie thought it was safe to scream and do a little dance. Kemp Street and all its dull, everyday problems seemed a million miles away as she pirouetted into her room.

'Night, gorgeous!' she squeaked at the girl in the mirror. Her reflection had the pink-cheeked look of someone who might, just might, be about to embark on a *relationship*.

On the beach Evie yawned. It was early. Very early.

'None of that!' chided Aden cheerfully, from where he stood behind a gigantic camera. He looked disgustingly healthy. 'Melody, could you touch up Evie's nose?'

Melody staggered across the sand and, with an effort, lifted a small powder brush to Evie's face. 'I feel dreadful, me,' she groaned. 'And I hardly touched a drop, an' all.'

Evie flinched. Melody's breath could have stripped wallpaper. 'Was I, you know,' Melody's voice sank to a whisper, 'embarrassing?'

Depends, thought Evie cruelly, but she had suffered from morning-after amnesia many times and decided to be generous. 'No, don't worry, you were fine.'

'Really? Oh, ta!' One last blast of dragon breath, and Melody dragged herself back to the other side of the cameras.

Making a TV commercial is a silly experience, but it's one that needs many people to accomplish it. The finished film for Toby Small Dog Food would last only ninety seconds, but huddled together on Lyme Regis beach were two cameramen, two lighting guys, a continuity girl, a make-up girl, a wardrobe mistress, two caterers, a dresser, three runners, two writers, an art director, three PAs, a dog wrangler and the assistant director. Plus, of course, two actors.

Only two players were missing. One was Greg, the director, who was making a heated phone call inside the hotel to the client—the big cheese at Toby Small Dog Food, who had asked for last-minute script changes—and the other was Tootsie, the real star of the production. Tootsie was a West Highland white terrier, a veteran of four commercials, one *EastEnders* and a *Crimewatch* reconstruction. Tootsie was . . . where?

'Where's the dog?' enquired Evie innocently.

'Ssssh!' Aden rounded on her. 'I don't want to start a panic, but it looks like Tootsie has . . . stepped out of her office for a moment.'

Dan found this irresistibly amusing. 'Oh, Aden, we're making a dog-food commercial and *you've lost the dog.*'

'I have not lost the dog,' hissed Aden, his habitual cool slipping. 'Oh, Jesus. Here's Greg.'

Evie felt for Aden. Greg had the look of a man with a sea urchin down his pants as he strode across the sand, the sun glinting off his John Lennon glasses. Aden met him halfway and whispered in his ear. A roar echoed around the bay: '*You've lost the fucking dog?*'

With the impeccable timing of a true pro, Tootsie rounded a rock and raced, barking joyously, into their midst.

Betty, the wrangler, followed close behind, her face wet with tears. Evie saw Aden take her to one side, listen intently for a moment, then wrap both arms round her.

Evie scuttled over. 'Why on earth is Betty crying?'

Aden's mouth was twitching, but he was trying hard to look grave. 'She's upset,' he said evenly. 'Apparently Tootsie had a, er, romantic adventure while she was AWOL. With *that.*' Aden pointed in the direction of a breakwater, where the filthiest, scruffiest mongrel sat looking nonchalant.

'Ooh dear.' Evie put her hand over her mouth. 'And Betty's scared that Tootsie might be a single mother?'

Dan, of course, thought the whole thing was hilarious. 'So, the leading lady's run off and had a quick how's-your-father in the sand dunes.' He gave Evie an undeniably saucy look. 'Pity we can't follow her lead.'

Aden said briskly, 'You don't have time. Not even the way you do it, Dan.' He stalked off to find the clapperboard.

'Oooooooh, bitch,' lisped Dan, and minced to his mark.

Evie stood alongside him, holding the sluttish Tootsie's lead.

'Hold hands, you two,' Greg barked. 'You're in love, for God's sake. I need you to walk from your mark to past that one. Carefree, please, and happy. Brainlessly, imbecilically happy. Tootsie, I'm assured, will romp alongside you. OK. Roll.'

Evie and Dan began to stroll. They covered the thirty-yard stretch ten, twenty, umpteen times. They did it fast, slow, and at every speed in between. Evie's face ached from smiling and Dan murmured increasingly violent and imaginative threats against Greg's person.

Lunch was a picnic laid out on the rocks. It was as if the contents of a London deli had come to the seaside. Goat's cheese lolled alongside rocket and Parmesan, and bottles of sparkling water peeked out of ice buckets lodged in the pebbles.

Melody plonked herself down beside Evie. 'I'm feeling a bit better now,' she said. 'The squits have tapered off, anyway.'

'Oh,' said Evie. 'Er, well done.' She was looking around for Dan and wasn't remotely interested in Melody's innards.

'If you're wondering where loverboy is,' said Melody, with just a squeeze of lemon, 'he's over there with Aden. Getting a telling-off.'

Dan trudged over, baguette in hand and a wickedly schoolboyish look on his face. 'Just been ticked off by Head Boy.'

'What for?' Evie might have added, 'Pompous squirt.'

'Flirting with my costar.' Dan lifted an eyebrow. 'It's not good for the production, apparently.'

'Dunno,' Evie mumbled. 'I think it might be.'

They held each other's gaze for a long moment. Then Dan passed his hand over his face in a quick gesture. 'You're dangerous,' he muttered.

Dan reckoned *she* was dangerous! Evie grew an inch right there and then. The atmosphere was dense with sexual excitement.

It was a relief when Dan broke the spell. 'Hungry?' he said, and stood up to fetch her a sandwich. Evie watched his ten-out-of-ten bum as he strode away, with the utter confidence that she would see it naked.

The plot—if you can have a plot ninety seconds long—was simple and cutesy. Loving couple and their adorable dog walk along a beach. The guy produces a metal detector, which promptly detects something. The adorable dog digs it up excitedly and—whaddyaknow? It's a tin of dog food, specially formulated for little fellas like him. The last scene shows the couple huddled cosily together by a campfire on the beach, sharing a chicken leg. At their feet the dog is tucking into a bowl of Toby.

Aaah.

To achieve the requisite light, airy, carefree mood on film, Greg behaved like an African tyrant. 'No! *No!* You people are cretins!' was one of his gentler instructions to the crew. 'Look *happy!*' he bellowed into Evie's face. 'You remember happy, don't you?' In common with a lot of actresses, Evie's most accomplished performance was managing not to look as if she loathed her director.

A downpour, in complete contradiction to the weather forecast, scattered the crew. Dan, Evie and Aden all scarpered to a broken-down bathing hut. No windows, no doors, but if they huddled together they were out of the driving rain.

Aden sighed. 'The sand will be wet. Continuity will be shot to hell.'

'Did Wardrobe bring a fresh set of clothes for us? We're drenched.' Evie shook her hair, scattering droplets over the two men.

'They'd bloody better have.' Aden glanced down at Evie's T-shirt. Something flickered across his face.

Evie's eyes followed his. Her nipples were standing out like doorknobs through the thin, damp material.

'I'd better, erm, get off and find the wardrobe mistress,' he said, and rushed out into the deluge.

Evie thought Aden's embarrassment was sweet.

Dan was not embarrassed at all. 'God,' he said slowly, focusing his mesmeric eyes on hers, 'you look soooo horny.'

He didn't touch her. He didn't speak. There was no sound except the rain. An overwhelmingly sexy situation. Yet Evie felt disappointed. 'Horny' was definitely a horny word, but it was also impersonal. Did Dan find *her* sexy?

His next utterance made her heart leap and blew away any disappointment. 'What would you say to dinner one night when we get back to London?'

'I'd say yes, please, and thank you very much.'

The night shoot went smoothly. Although tired from a day that had started with illicit sex and included fourteen baths to wash the damp sand from her rough, white coat, Tootsie behaved impeccably. At about

10 p.m., Greg said, 'That's it, people. I'm satisfied,' and went straight to a waiting chauffeur-driven car. He was going back to London, as befitted a VIP. The rest of them had another night in the hotel. Or, more accurately, the hotel bar.

Wrap parties are always wild. However short the shoot, there's always an air of release, of being—to be frank—let's-get-drunk-and-snog-somebody. The careful application of mineral water meant that Evie was comfortably settled in a big leather wing chair at the edge of the action, and not go-go dancing on the bar top in her bra. Unlike Melody.

'Top marks for enthusiasm. Technique needs work, though,' Evie murmured in Dan's ear. He was perched on the arm of her chair in a pleasingly proprietorial way.

The wardrobe mistress was yelling, 'Tonight, Matthew, I'm going to be Cher', with a handful of bedraggled ostrich feathers stuck on her head.

'Tonight, Matthew,' said Aden, from where he sat on the other arm of Evie's chair, 'I'm going to get completely pissed because I'm so glad this shoot's over. Thank you, you two,' he clinked glasses with Dan and Evie, 'for being so professional and so *nice*, for making it easy, in fact.'

'Aw.' Evie felt warmed. 'You're too nice to make it as a director, Aden. You'd better go for some bastard lessons.'

Aden was a touch *rosé* as he went off to warn one of the runners that cider and liqueurs don't mix.

'He's a nice guy, my friend,' mused Dan. '*Too* nice.'

Evie risked a flippant, 'You're nice too.'

'Boy, have you got me wrong!' Dan laughed at her stricken face. 'Joke,' he enunciated carefully. He pulled her to her feet. 'Come on. Betty the dog wrangler's being Posh Spice. This we've got to see.'

The crowd had thinned out, and only the hardened party animals—plus Evie, who had drunk enough Evian to refloat the *Titanic*—were still in the bar. Dan hadn't left her side all night. Evie had heard snatches of the gossip that was rolling like a wave around the room: she felt smug at having her name linked with his. She felt even more smug that he was holding her hand behind her back, where no one could see it.

Aden move unsteadily across the room to say good night. 'Cabs to the station at nine sharp. Don't be late or we go without you.' His authority was somewhat undermined by the fact that he couldn't focus on them.

'Yessir!' barked Dan, saluting and pinching Evie's bum.

Evie yelped. Aden shook his head disapprovingly.

'Oh, go to bed, you Puritan.' Dan gave him a shove in the direction of the lift. He turned to Evie and said, 'He's got us all wrong. We couldn't be more innocent, could we?'

Evie opened one eye. During the night elves had apparently superglued it shut. The morning sun was blinding, careering in off the sea. Her limbs were heavy, as if pressed like wild flowers beneath a great weight. Moving was difficult. And why would she want to move anyway? she reasoned. Far simpler to lie here and die.

Where had the evening gone wrong? It had been all happy faces, laughter, jokes, the odd sizzling glance from Dan.

Ah. She remembered where the evening had gone wrong. At the exact moment someone had popped up behind the bar and shouted, 'I've found some tequila!'

Only vague snatches of the intervening hours were coming through on Evie's scrambled reception. Snapshots of varying horror tumbled through her mind. She saw herself ram a piece of lime into her mouth and throw back the shot of tequila. She heard herself say, 'No, one's enough for me, thanks,' then saw herself throw back another shot. And another. She saw Dan yelling with delight as she tossed down a fourth.

Dan. Oh, Dan! Evie winced. Her forehead hurt.

Another unwelcome batch of images filtered through. Had that really been her leading a staggering conga line in and out of the toilets? Yes, it had. It had also been her dinging the brass bell dementedly and shouting, 'Cooeee! Mrs Hotel Ladeeeee!'

Evie went hot as she recalled how Dan had shut her up by kissing her full on the lips. That part of the night was in very sharp focus indeed. Her determination had drifted off over the bay on a raft of tequila fumes. Now, if she had the strength to pull the covers over her head she would have done, as she remembered how the others had silently cleared a path for them. It had been that predictable.

How had she undressed? The details were sketchy. Perhaps her mind wasn't letting her remember because the truth would drive her insane. Evie pleated her brain in the effort to conjure up the sequence of events once they had got upstairs.

The kisses were clear enough, burned on her mind. She squirmed with a mixture of pleasure and agony as she remembered them. The light, fluttering ones on the small of her back. The hot ones at the top of her thighs. The brazen hungry ones on her mouth. Evie groaned. And then . . . then they had had sex. 'Oh, Dan,' she whimpered miserably, as she relived how he had looked, how he had *felt* when he was on top of her. It should all have been so special. She should have felt every electric moment to the full, but she had been in a drunken fog.

And it had crippled the 'relationship' before it had begun. The relationship that never was. *Another* one.

Too hung over to cry, Evie lay desolate until another recollection, a distinctly more welcome one this time, started to develop.

She could remember, hazily at first and then more clearly, that at one point in their sweaty, glorious tussle, she had pushed him back onto the pillows and straddled him. Silencing him with a finger to his lips, she had said wildly that this hadn't been meant to happen.

'Oh, yes, it was.' His voice had been heavy with lust and he had reached up to her, but she had roughly pushed him down again.

'No, no, it wasn't! We were just getting to know each other, but we've gone too far too quickly. It's ruined everything.'

Now it was time for Dan to take the upper hand. He flipped her effortlessly onto her back, raised himself on one elbow and gazed down at her. Cupping her chin in one hand, he stared straight into her troubled eyes. 'Listen to me,' he began gravely, 'This is incredibly special. I've respected you since the moment we met and I'll always respect you. Tonight just *had* to happen, we both know that. We'll still go out in London for that dinner I promised you. I have a feeling that you and I are going to mean a lot to each other. Now, shut up.'

Evie sighed. Thank God their scramble to get naked hadn't ruined things. She felt absurdly grateful to Dan for putting her mind at rest. It had been as if he knew what she was thinking. In a way it made it a little less deflating that he wasn't there beside her now . . .

Groaning with exertion she turned her clanging head to peer at the clock radio. It was just coming up to half-past minicab.

Five

BORNEO WAS LOOKING a little less wild. A scythe dumped on the gravel was testament to Bing's hard work while she'd been away. When she opened the front door his labours were even more apparent: the hallway was bright, brilliant white. She peered up the staircase. He'd finished right up to the first floor. What a man!

Still moving like an OAP under water—tequila hangovers were the worst—Evie fumbled to open the door to her flat, then stumbled down the stairs to the basement. She looked around at the overflowing washing basket, the sink full of mucky dishes, the pile of unopened mail, and decided the best thing to do was go straight to bed.

Those little men with their hammers were still doing their damnedest in her head. Her limbs felt as if they'd been through a mangle. The pillows and the duvet on her bed beckoned to her like sirens. They had never looked so plump and alluring. She drew the curtains and sighed with anticipation as she pulled back the bedclothes.

A knocking, loud and urgent, echoed through the flat. Evie almost managed to ignore it, but it was too dramatic. Growling, she paced the hall, unable to work out where the noise was coming from.

The conservatory! Suddenly alarmed, Evie looked about wildly for something to protect herself with. In films vulnerable women always had a revolver stashed in the bedside table, or they picked up a poker. All Evie could lay her hands on was the telephone directory.

She crept through the gloom of the sitting room. Bing had left the curtains drawn. The knocking was frenetic now. Holding up the phone book menacingly, she swished back the curtain with a flourish.

It was Sacha, grinning like the village idiot.

'Jesus!' Evie unlocked the glass door with bad grace. 'What are you doing round the back?'

'I was trying to make your life easier by coming through the garden door. You'd have had to climb the stairs to let me in if I'd come round the front.'

'Well . . .' Evie couldn't carry on being a grouch in the face of such thoughtful reasoning, but she threw in for good measure, 'You can't do anything like a normal person, can you?'

'I've shut the shop. I want to hear all about Dan.'

The little men in Evie's head took up heavier hammers. 'Oh, not now, Sash.' She folded her arms resolutely. 'I'm off to bed.'

Sacha tailed her, crouched and wheedling. 'Please, pleeeease. I'll sit on the end of the bed. You won't even know I'm there.'

It was not Sacha's style to sit on the end of anything, and soon they were tucked up together with the duvet up to their chins.

'This is cosy!' squeaked Sacha.

'No, this is *not* cosy.' Evie wondered how Sacha, with all her dippiness, always got the better of her. 'You're hogging the bedclothes.'

'Sorry.' Sacha snuggled down. 'Now, tell me all about Mr Big.'

'I didn't say he was Mr Big.'

'You did!'

'I said he might be.' It was a weak point but it had to be made.

Sacha badgered her until Evie gave in and told the story of the last few days. She found she was enjoying reliving all the saucy exchanges and smouldering eye-contact, and Sacha was an excellent audience. She made Evie repeat the asking-her-out-to-dinner bit twice, with explicit instructions to phrase and pitch it *exactly* as he had.

It was only when they came to the tequila moment that Evie ran out of steam.

'Go on!' Sacha prodded her under the duvet. 'And then?'

'And then I ruined it,' she whispered. 'I slept with him.'

Sacha sat bolt upright. 'Why would that ruin it? Oh, my God!' Her voice dropped. 'He couldn't, er, rise to the occasion?'

'Believe me, that was not a problem,' said Evie nostalgically.

'So it was just crap? Were you inhibited?'

'If only.' Evie's cheeks burned. 'No, the sex was brilliant. We did it three times. I think.'

'Oooh.' Sacha looked envious. 'That's more sex than I've had since Christmas.' She thought for a moment. 'But how did that ruin it?'

'You know exactly how. Now it's just an opportunistic shag when it looked like it was going to *be* something.'

'It can still be something!' insisted Sacha. 'See how your dinner date goes.'

'You think he'll ring?' Evie gulped. 'Now that he's got what he wanted?'

'But he really liked you. It wasn't just about sex. You've got to have more confidence in yourself than that.'

Caroline was bumping the buggy down step by step. Milly was jiggling about like a jumping bean.

'Let me help you.' Evie put her foot on the steps.

''S all right. Don't need any help.'

'OK.' Evie took her foot off the steps. 'What do you think of the new paint on the walls?'

''S all right,' Caroline repeated, pushing Milly to the gate.

'You still on for Friday night? . . . The dinner party?' Evie prompted, seeing her blank look.

'Oh. Yeah.'

'I'm having a cooker delivered later in honour of it.' Evie was acutely aware that she talked too much when she was around Caroline. 'Belle's old one was a health hazard.'

Caroline paused before she stepped out into the street. 'The white does look good, Eve,' she said. 'Like the house is waking up after a long sleep.' The gate banged shut behind her.

'Hasseerung?' Sacha had used the phrase so much in the past two days that now, to Evie's ears, it sounded like one nonsensical word.

'No.' Evie braced herself for the spirited defence of Dan that always followed her answer.

'Well, he's busy. He's probably going out early, leaving your number at home, and getting back too late to disturb you. That's a *good* sign—he's thoughtful. Did he mention anything about going abroad?'

They were sitting in their new favourite café, and Evie knew Sacha meant well, but she wanted to drown her friend in a sack. 'Look,' she said, in a small voice, 'Dan is not going to call. It's been two whole days.'

'It's *only* been two days,' corrected Sacha, with the certainty of the unhinged. 'He said he would, didn't he? He *made a point* of saying it. And you told me yourself he sounded sincere.'

Bing joined them, setting down a chipped mug of strong tea. 'Ladies, allow me to introduce a note of reality. Dan is a sexually attractive man, fully aware of his appeal. He spots our Evie here and is delighted that there's going to be an attractive bint on this job with him. She obviously fancies him right back but is keeping her distance. But aforementioned bint gets sloshed and Dan moves in for the kill. A wonderful slice of sex happens. In the middle of this sex the girl gets jumpy, pulls the I-bet-you-think-I'm-a-tart-now move on him. He reassures her because he does not want the sex to stop. The next morning he's out of there so fast you'd think his Nikes were greased. That is how the Dans of this world operate.' With an air of finality, like a hanging judge, he ended, 'He will not ring.'

Evie looked wounded.

'So why did he bother to ask her out to dinner?' Sacha demanded. 'He must have wanted to or why would he say it?'

'Have you two just landed from the Planet of No Men? He asked her out to dinner because he guessed that that was what she wanted to hear. And he was right, wasn't he?'

Evie slumped, beaten down by the ring of veracity of Bing's unvarnished rendering of events.

Before Sacha could leap in with her sanitised world-view Bing said, 'You know what? It's his loss. He'd have the time of his life with you if he did go out with you. That's not what he wants, though, and that's his choice.' Bing reached over and took one of Evie's hands. 'You haven't come out of the deal so badly, have you? You had two days of flirting and getting your bum pinched, all rounded off nicely with some sex courtesy of a superstud.'

Evie had warmed up. 'You're right,' she said, and almost meant it.

'She's still owed a dinner.' Sacha was like a stubborn parrot. 'He promised to take her out to dinner.'

Bing ran a hand over his face. 'For God's sake, give the guy a break.'

Sacha turned back to Evie. 'I bet he's working out where to take you before he calls.'

Two burly men were manhandling the new cooker into the kitchen. Evie leaned against a door jamb, arms folded, wondering how come she was spending a hefty portion of her TV fee on a *cooker*, of all things.

The gleaming new oven put the rest of the kitchen to shame. It looked even dingier than before. With revulsion Evie realised that she'd have to *clean* it. What was her life coming to? She snapped on a pair of Bing's rubber gloves.

The trouble with cleaning, Evie discovered, was that as soon as you washed one thing it made the thing next to it look filthy. You were locked onto an endless merry-go-round of Vim and scouring pads. She had only another half-hour before Simeon would arrive and she hadn't even started on the skirting boards.

The cavalry arrived, in the unexpected shape of Caroline. 'Just wondered if you'd like an 'and.'

'You any good at skirting boards?'

Soon Caroline was crouched with a bucket of her own, while Milly stayed trussed up in her buggy. It was quite restful, mused Evie, being around somebody who preferred not to talk. They toiled away companionably until interrupted by the phone.

Evie stiffened. She hated herself for the way her heart was suddenly fluttering like a caged bird.

'Aren't you going to get that?' Caroline was staring at her.

'Of course!' Evie leapt up and dashed into her room where she snatched up the phone and stared at its tiny screen. *Number withheld.* She cleared her throat and punched the OK button. 'Hello,' she said, trying to cram sexiness, sophistication, intelligence, wit and firm breasts into the one small word.

'Evie? It's Beth. Is that you? You sound funny.'

'Oh.' The crushing, right-down-to-her-toes disappointment was swiftly replaced by panic. Beth *never* rang her. 'What's happened?'

'What? Nothing's happened.'

'Right. Sorry. How are you?'

'I'm fine, but I need a favour, actually.' This was yet more unusual behaviour. Beth had never needed anything from Evie before. 'I've got an appointment in London on Friday. Can I dump the twins with you for an hour or so? About ten?'

'What sort of appointment?' Evie's antennae were twitching. 'Is it with a solicitor?'

There was a shocked moment of silence, then Beth said tetchily, 'Look, does it matter? Can you watch them or not?'

Evie said of course she could and the conversation finished abruptly. Evie felt uneasy. It had been a shot in the dark about the solicitor. She hadn't wanted to be right. Bloody Marcus! It would take a lot to push somebody as placid as Beth towards divorce.

Tugging the outsize Marigolds back on she rejoined Caroline, who had graduated to worktops.

'That was my sister. She's coming over on Friday. She never visits me, so I know something's up. I think her marriage is in trouble, and I don't know what to do. Families! Sometimes they're more trouble than they're worth, aren't they?'

Caroline's sponge landed in the bucket with an angry splash. She banged the Vim down on the new cooker, picked up the buggy, and was up the stairs and out of the flat in a trice.

Evie was just about to call her a very bad name indeed when she remembered: Caroline had no family to get impatient with. She was alone in the world. Evie slapped her face with a rubber glove smeared in soapy grease. She figured she deserved it.

The phone shrieked. Evie slammed it to her ear. 'Hello?' she said breathlessly, forgetting to be sexy or intelligent.

'Hasseerung?'

She reckoned she deserved that too.

The supermarket was vast, and packed to the rafters with food, but still Evie couldn't decide what Bernard should be forced to cook. She was severely hampered by her own lack of kitchen skills. She was browsing the deli section, when her mobile rang.

She dropped her wire basket and fumbled through her bag. 'Hello?'

'Where are you? I'm standing outside your front door. They both want a wee!' Beth was not her usual cool self.

'Ohmigod! I for—tunately am only round the corner.' Evie didn't want to offend her sister by admitting that she'd forgotten their arrangement. 'Be there in two shakes of a lamb's tail.' Make that a rather lumpen, slow lamb.

Evie looked about wildly. A row of fat, pale birds caught her eye. Chicken! Of course. She bunged a bog-standard one into the basket, then raced round the vegetables, snatching up various green things. 'Stuffing!' she muttered, then, 'Gravy!' She was knackered by the time she screeched to a halt at the checkout. How did normal women manage this every day?

The twins were cross-legged and bulging-eyed by the time Evie reached them. 'Smart suit,' she said to Beth, as the three-year-olds careered towards the bathroom like Exocet missiles.

'Thanks.' Beth was distracted. 'I'll be a couple of hours at the most.'

392

'Good luck.' Evie was rather proud of herself for asking no questions. She had vowed to be silently supportive of Beth.

A tentative knock at the door announced Bernard. He was sporting a spotlessly clean, obviously brand-new stripy apron. His strawberry hair was more manic than ever, evidently having been shampooed for the occasion. Evie longed to sedate him and get some scissors to it. It wasn't just roast chicken on the menu tonight: there was love for dessert, and the current hairdo was unlikely to set Caroline's loins a-tingle.

First things first. 'Come into the kitchen and meet your victim.' The chicken crouched in the middle of the table.

'Oh dear,' said Bernard, with feeling.

'I'm bored,' said Charles, pulling at Evie's jeans.

'Me too. Read us a story,' pleaded Julius.

Luckily a shambling figure, newly resurrected from his bed, was shuffling past the door in Calvin Klein pants.

'Look!' trilled Evie gaily. 'It's Uncle Bing! Let's go and play with him!' The twins dashed ahead.

Uncle Bing hadn't shaved. Uncle Bing smelt of alcohol.

'Uncle Bing! Uncle Bing!' The twins leapt wildly up and down.

'Yuk,' he said vehemently. 'Put them away.'

Evie gabbled her predicament. 'The future happiness of Caroline and Bernard could hang on your cooperation,' she concluded. 'Please. Just amuse them for an hour until Beth comes back.'

Bing couldn't refuse. But he did. He refused until Evie agreed to forget the twenty quid he owed her.

'Where were we?' Evie marched into the kitchen.

'We were staring at the chicken,' said Bernard.

'First we have to wash it.'

'I can't!' Bernard was aghast. 'I'd have to touch it.'

'How did you imagine you were going to cook a chicken without touching it?' Evie picked up the bird and thrust it hard into Bernard's middle. His hands automatically grabbed for it.

'Uuuurgh!' His pale face was mottled with distress.

Evie propelled Bernard towards the cold tap. He certainly brought out the schoolmarm in her. 'Rinse it!' she commanded.

Enjoying her new role just a little too much, she prodded and bullied Bernard through the rudiments of preparing a chicken for the oven. He took all this treatment mildly, presumably as a result of all those years with his mother. 'You're not serious!' He was outraged by her suggestion that he put a halved lemon into the cavity.

'Bernard, it's a chicken, not a date.' She grabbed his hand. 'Just pull up the flap and thrust the lemon in.'

Bernard looked at his fingers in horror.

Bing stuck his head round the door. 'They didn't like the story,' he reported. 'Maybe they're just too young for Jackie Collins. What shall I do with them now?'

'Errr . . . Run about the garden screaming. They're really into that.' Evie returned her attention to Bernard. 'Now, peel the potatoes with this peeler and cut them into smallish chunks.'

Evie gave him a crash course in peeling and he finished off all the potatoes, managing to cut them into quarters without severing any major arteries. Then she introduced him to a packet of sage-and-onion stuffing and guided him through the intricacies of kettle-boiling. 'We'll make the gravy now and warm it up later.' Evie took a jar of own-brand economy granules from a cupboard.

Bing appeared, balancing a twin on each shoulder. 'This is too tough,' he moaned. 'They don't do drugs. They probably don't care for porn.'

'How about hide and seek?'

Beth raised an eyebrow when her precious offspring were retrieved from a cupboard. Their blond crops smelt strongly of dust.

'Everything OK?' Evie saw signs of strain around her sister's eyes.

'Of course.' Beth smiled glassily and was gone. 'I owe you one,' she shouted, through the car window.

'Yeah. You can look after Bing next time I go out.'

Bernard was intrigued to learn that the oven had to be warmed up before the chicken went into it. He was moving more confidently about the kitchen now, toying fearlessly with the utensils. He had even allowed Evie to tame his hair and she had coerced him into a plain blue shirt of Bing's.

'It brings out the colour of your eyes and complements your skin.'

'Does it?' Bernard peered uneasily at the man in the mirror.

'Yes, it does.' Evie was firm. If Bernard was to find true love he had to learn to brush his hair and brave pastels occasionally.

She supervised his dainty arrangement of tortilla crisps on a platter with a tub of salsa. 'Very good. It's not so hard, is it?'

Bernard didn't seem to agree wholeheartedly. 'Shouldn't we start boiling the peas? Mother always boiled vegetables for hours.'

'Ooooh, no. They go on at the last minute.'

The front doorbell rang. 'Our first guest!' Evie hugged Bernard for luck. He felt like an ironing board.

It was only as Evie put her hand on the latch that she remembered their guest lived on the floor above and wouldn't arrive by the front door.

She swung the door open and there was Aden.

He held out a bottle of wine. 'I've come to say sorry,' he said, looking all boyish with his denim jacket and his shiny hair.

'What have you got to say sorry for?' Evie was puzzled by his sudden appearance on the doorstep. She hadn't thought of Aden since the shoot ended. 'Oh, and hello.' She took the bottle. 'Thank you.'

'Sorry for leaving you in the hotel on the last morning. It wasn't very gallant. And sorry for not warning you.'

'About what?'

Aden shifted from foot to foot, adding to the boyish vibe. 'About Dan.'

Evie felt cold. She hesitated, fighting the desire to slam the door and stick her fingers in her ears.

'Come in,' she said quietly.

Caroline, clutching Milly, was coming out of her flat. She had put on some make-up and tied up her glossy black hair. What with that and the black peasanty top she was wearing she looked lovely.

Evie introduced Aden, then said to him, 'We're just about to have dinner. Do you want to join us?'

'Er, yeah, if that's OK.'

'Of course it is.' Evie led the way downstairs, hoping that the chicken would stretch to one more mouth.

Bing had dragged the kitchen table into the sitting room. A cloth had been procured, glasses had been polished and candles lit. He hastily moved everything to make another place. Bernard emerged from the kitchen with his salsa and crisps, grimly intent on them.

Evie introduced Aden to the others. She really wanted to scream, 'Whaddyamean warn me about Dan?' at him but that would have to wait. The purpose of this evening was to ignite something between two of her tenants: nothing must get in the way of that.

She went out to the kitchen to check on the chicken, and leaned against the wall, her head drooping. Why had Aden turned up now? She slammed the oven door so hard that the chicken trembled in its tin.

The front doorbell rang again. Glad not to have to return to the sitting room just yet, Evie took the stairs two at a time. 'Sacha?'

'Hi, hi.' Sacha swooped in, kissing and fussing, handing over a bottle. She was wearing her favourite poppy-red lipstick. 'Am I late for dinner?'

'You're not invited to dinner.'

'As if I need to be invited.' Sacha swept down the stairs to the basement, to leave scarlet marks on the cheeks of all present.

Bing glared at Evie as he moved everything on the table yet again. 'We'll be squashed up like Japanese commuters,' he hissed at Evie. 'You didn't say your insane friend was coming.'

'My insane friend wasn't invited,' said Evie. 'Bernard—*peas!*' she ordered, and he scuttled off, rubbing at the lipstick stain on his face.

Bernard, looking frazzled from the exertions of putting the peas on, sidled over to Evie.

'I've burned the gravy,' he confessed.

Evie followed him back to the kitchen, pursued by Sacha, who was plainly oblivious to any resentment directed at her. 'Your hair looks much nicer tonight,' she said in a seductive voice to Bernard.

'Shut up, Sacha, and get out of the way.' Evie was brisk: she had to save the gravy. 'Take the chicken out of the oven, Bernard, and put it on that big plate so we can carve.'

It almost goes without saying that the chicken ended up on the floor.

'He's nervous around me,' whispered Sacha, who had not got out of the way, to Evie as they dusted down the bird.

Evie stared blankly at her, silenced by such arrogance. 'Get out,' she advised eventually, 'and don't tell anyone what just happened.' She picked up the dish of steaming, perfectly roasted chicken and carried it aloft into the dining room. 'Dinner is served!' she announced.

The huddled diners grinned in anticipation. The food was passed round. Milly lolled on the sofa with a little bowl of her own while the adults tucked in at the table. The chicken sportingly managed to feed them all.

Evie didn't feel like the life and soul of the evening so she acted it. Somehow she encouraged both Caroline and Bernard to join in with the conversation, slyly topping up their glasses. But all the time the coldness inside her refused to melt. She looked at Aden, who was nodding at Caroline's tale of Milly's latest naughtiness. He looked so innocent, but he had come to shatter her dream.

'Who looks after Milly for you if you want to have an evening out?' Aden was asking, with real interest.

'There isn't anyone to baby-sit.' Caroline fiddled with the stem of her glass. 'There used to be, but . . .'

'Bing and I can baby-sit!' Evie offered enthusiastically, and ignored a sharp kick beneath the table. She turned to Bernard. 'You could take Caroline out somewhere nice one evening, couldn't you?' she prodded.

Caroline saved him from answering: 'I can arrange me own social life, you know.'

'Of course you can. It was just a suggestion,' Evie said meekly.

'Time for afters.' Bing ended the silence that had cloaked the table.

'It's just ice cream.' Evie rose. 'I'll get it.'

As Evie wrestled with the soft-scoop, Sacha whispered, 'Did you notice Bernard staring at me? God, it was so embarrassing.'

'Was it really?' Evie had been here before and knew better than to try to dissuade Sacha that Bernard was nuts about her.

'I'll have to be honest with him at some point. I just don't fancy him. How do you think he'll take it?'

'He'll cope.'

As they juggled plates and spoons Sacha nudged her dangerously. 'Aden's a bit of a dish.'

'Aden?' Evie had never spotted any dish-like tendencies in him.

'Yes, he's nice.'

They went back into the sitting room just as Bing flung open the conservatory doors. 'Let's have pudding outside.'

It was a good idea. The night air was warm and sweet, heavy with the scent of next door's magnolia. Sacha switched on the fairy lights. 'Don't you wish your whole life could be lit by fairy lights?'

Bernard and Caroline, dragging their chairs outside, gave her a wide berth. At least they had something in common: they both considered Sacha worth avoiding.

Aden was investigating the flowers in a stone urn near the house. Evie strolled over to him with leaden feet. It was time to hear what he had to say. Her gut lurched. 'You know what you said earlier about warning me?' She ushered in her own unhappiness. 'What did you mean?'

'Ah.' Aden sat down heavily on a large empty flowerpot. 'It's difficult. I mean, I don't want to spoil the party.'

'I've news for you. You already have.'

Aden looked hurt. 'I thought very hard before I came round. I told myself it was none of my business, but . . .' He paused, apparently casting about for the best way to express himself. 'You didn't deserve it.' He looked directly at her. 'Am I a patronising sod? Shall I go away?'

'No, no, Aden. Spit it out.'

'OK. Dan and I have been mates for years. He's a top bloke, I love him, but he has one huge flaw: his attitude to women. Dan was every bit as handsome as he is now when he was seven. The playground was full of girls crying over him. It's been that way ever since.'

'I haven't cried over him,' lied Evie.

'Good.' Aden didn't look as though he believed her. 'Dan has never had a serious relationship. He thinks falling in love would get in the way of his career. He's deeply ambitious. I can relate to that. What I *can't* relate to is the way he treats women. He likes . . .' Aden faltered, unable to look at Evie '. . . conquests. That's why I was so disapproving on the shoot. I knew he was pulling out all the stops to get you into bed.'

Evie swallowed. She even managed a smile.

'Well, anyway, knowing him as well as I do I asked him to lay off.

When you didn't show up on the last morning and Dan had dark circles under his eyes it was obvious what had happened. I really am sorry that I didn't wait for you. But Dan reckoned you'd be unconscious for hours.'

''S fine.' It was the least of her worries.

'On the way home Dan told me he'd promised to take you out for dinner.' Here Aden dried up.

'He didn't mean it, did he?' Evie helped to put herself out of her misery.

'No, Evie, he didn't. I thought you should know, so you could just get on with things and not hang around for him.'

Evie felt as a if a large frying-pan had hit her smack in the face. But her acting muscles were still warm: 'You're very sweet to do this, but there was no need. It was just a bit of fun as far as I was concerned.'

'Good. Although I feel a fool.'

'Don't! It really was sweet, like I said.' And it was. She just wished she hadn't had to hear it.

'Do you think Bernard enjoyed the experience?' Evie asked Bing, as they tidied up with Aden's help.

'I hate to admit it, but I think you did him some good,' replied Bing. 'He was trying desperately not to look proud when we all complimented him on the chicken.'

'If we can lure him away from the chip shop his complexion might improve,' mused Evie.

'I don't think the matchmaking is going to be a success.' Bing was carrying a teetering pile of plates out to the sink.

'What matchmaking?' Aden was incredulous. 'Caroline and Bernard?'

'We'll see,' said Evie, in a mysterious manner. She wasn't about to give up. Caroline needed someone to take care of her and Milly, and Bernard needed somebody to blossom with. 'You off, then?'

Aden was pulling on his jacket.

'Early start tomorrow. Just a low-budget film. Arty crap. But I'm directing, so I have to get my beauty sleep.' Aden kissed Evie's cheek. His lips were soft. 'Sorry I was such a party-pooper. May I come round again *without* tidings of doom and gloom?'

Evie nodded. Aden was a relaxing person to be with. 'Any time.'

''Night, then.' He pointed a directorly strict finger at her. 'No pining for Dan, now!'

'Dan who?' Just then her mobile buzzed into life. 'See? I didn't even jump.' She put the phone to her ear and said, 'Hello,' without a trace of intelligence or sexiness.

It was a bad line but she heard, 'Hi, gorgeous, it's Dan.'

Six

WHEN EVIE WAS UNHAPPY she over-ate. When Evie was happy she *really* over-ate. 'More biscuits!' she yelled at Bing. 'Jammy ones this time, not those plain bastards!'

It was 2 a.m. and they were still up. Evie couldn't go to bed because she was too excited and Bing couldn't go to bed because Evie was too selfish to let him.

'Ask me again,' she ordered, as Bing joined her on the sofa with a topped-up biscuit barrel.

'Hasseerung?'

'*Yes!*' She crammed a Jaffa cake into her mouth. 'And what were you?'

Bing rolled his eyes. 'I was wrong. And that's the last time I'm saying it,' he added grumpily.

'He rang, he rang, he rang, he rang,' sang Evie to an improvised tune, showering her companion with damp crumbs.

'I'm glad you hardly ever have sex if this is how it affects you.' Bing took a Club orange. 'If I went on like this every time some bloke fancied me I wouldn't hold down a job.'

'He's not "some bloke". He's Dan. Isn't that a lovely name? Manly. Strong. *Dan.*' Evie underlined its qualities by thrusting her fist in the air.

'Mmm. Very manly. Like Danny La Rue.'

'Wait till you see the way he dresses.'

'Is that anything like Danny La Rue?'

'He's really cool, really stylish, but kind of casual, you know?'

'I'm very happy for him.'

'And he's mine, all mine!'

Bing gave her what used to be called an old-fashioned look.

'Hang about, doll,' he said. 'He's taking you out for a bowl of pasta, he hasn't proposed.'

'I know. But it must mean something.'

She had been flabbergasted to hear his voice. Instead of answering his 'Hi, gorgeous,' she had mouthed, 'It's Dan,' at Aden, whose face had matched hers as an illustration of extreme shock. His jacket froze, half off half on, as they faced each other like waxworks.

'Are you there?' asked Dan.

'Yes, I'm here. Sorry. A—a thing just happened,' ad-libbed Evie ineptly. 'How are you?'

'Knackered. I've been on another commercial shoot in Spain. It came up the day I got back to London. That's why I didn't ring before. Left your number in my flat.'

Evie was flooded with warmth. The explanation healed her sore heart. Waving away Aden, who was listening too intently for her liking, she retreated into her bedroom, closed the door and sat on the bed. 'I thought you'd forgotten all about me,' she teased.

'As if. You're not an easy girl to forget.'

Evie didn't turn on the light. The world had shrunk to the darkness and Dan's deep voice. 'Really?'

'Really. Have you been thinking about me?'

'Occasionally. I lead the full life of a modern young woman, but you've crossed my mind.' She laughed. 'Oh, I saw Aden tonight, though.'

'Aden?' Dan sounded surprised and not all that pleased. 'Didn't realise you two were so cosy.'

'It was only dinner.' Evie trembled at the sound of Dan's jealousy. She loved it, but didn't want him to back off. 'There were six of us.'

'Right. Well, anyway,' Dan continued, 'you know why I'm ringing. I owe you dinner. When are you free?'

Unless you counted her promise to do Bing's roots Evie was free every night from now until the end of the world. 'Let me think . . .' It was important to sound sought-after, a party girl rather than a sofa-and-soap-operas girl. 'I could do Monday, if that's any good.'

'Nah. What about next Saturday?'

Next Saturday. But that was over a week away. Mind you, it *was* a Saturday. That's a special night, the night you save for your special bird. 'That would be perfect.'

'Where would you like to go?'

Anywhere. A hole in the ground as long you're in it. 'Why don't you call for me and we'll see what we feel like?'

'OK. As long as we eat as well.' Dan took down the address. 'That's a date. I'll pick you up at seven. Night, gorgeous.'

'Night.'

He was gone and Evie was alone on Belle's overstuffed bed but it was floating high above the Camden chimney-pots.

It was debatable as to whether Dan would have thought gorgeous the dishevelled, unwashed creature with sleep in its half-closed eyes that dragged itself into Simeon's van the next morning.

'Jesus. Save your screams till you see its face,' sneered Simeon.

'Just drive, why dontcha?' Evie was too happy, despite her lack of sleep, to let this bargain-basement John Hurt get to her.

'Good morning, Crumpy.' The mole who had replaced the replacement mole stuck his head over the front seat. 'Want a bacon roll?'

'Do I?' Evie was suddenly awake.

This newest mole was called Terry. He was short, squat and easy-going.

'I wish you'd remember there's a vegetarian in your midst,' said Simeon loftily. 'The smell of slaughtered pig is unbearable.'

'I know,' sympathised Evie. 'Really makes you want one, doesn't it? So, where are we headed today?'

'Is there any point in giving you a schedule? We're taking our politically corrected *Winnie-the-Pooh* to Hayward's Heath.' He swivelled nervously towards Evie. 'You did remember to bring your Piglet costume?'

'Of course.' She hadn't.

Two subjects were now jostling for space in Evie's already rather crowded head. One, obviously, was Dan. The other was her Piglet outfit, which was hanging in her wardrobe, miles back. 'I'll get in the back with Terry,' she said suddenly.

'Why?' Simeon was testy.

Not feeling up to the honest answer ('So I can beg him to help me botch together a Piglet costume from the odds and ends in the back of the van'), Evie said simply, 'I just want to.'

'Oh, all right. Wait till I can pull over.'

'Pull over? We haven't moved in ten minutes.' Evie opened the door and dropped to the tarmac. As she clambered into the back she whispered her dilemma to Terry, who went pale.

'We'll do it somehow,' he vowed bravely, throwing open the lid of the wicker basket that contained the oddments they used for improvisation. 'Look!' He put his hands on an Edwardian bathing suit made of stripy material with a vest top and legs. 'Piglet has a stripy body, doesn't he?' A little more digging produced a swimming cap and a rubber glove. Terry waggled them triumphantly.

'Sorry. Don't get it.' Evie frowned.

'We can cut the tops of two fingers off, stick them to the swimming cap and that's Piglet's ears!' Terry was enjoying this.

Evie wasn't. 'I don't think it'll work. Maybe I should just tell Simeon.'

Just then Simeon bellowed out of the window. 'Move, move, you soulless scum, and let the artists through!'

Evie tugged on the swimming cap.

'Obviously we'll have to paint you pink,' said Terry solemnly.

The traffic meant they had only minutes to spare when they got to the primary school. Simeon, who had cast himself as Pooh, zipped himself into his yellow fur all-in-one and rushed onstage, while Terry rammed on his latex Tigger mask.

'I'll paint your legs as well. For realism,' said Terry enthusiastically, squatting down.

'Realism?' marvelled Evie. The Edwardian swimsuit was tightly belted but still hung in folds.

From the stage she heard her cue and ran on.

Meredith didn't often laugh. At first Evie wasn't sure what the gurgling sound at the other end of the line was. 'Well, darling,' gasped Meredith, 'you're fired but at least it sounds as if it was fucking worth it.'

Bing couldn't stop laughing either. Admittedly, Evie was still in costume when she told him. 'You went on stage like that? What did the children do?'

'Most laughed, some screamed.'

'But—you're *painted pink*! And that swimming cap is all bunched up on the top of your head!' Tears were sprouting from his eyes.

Evie angrily snatched off the cap. 'The audience had to be led out. They were all either laughing or sobbing.'

Wiping his eyes, Bing did his best to console her. 'At least you got a reaction. That's what every actor wants.'

Evie sighed. 'I didn't want the sack.'

Bing had opened a bottle of wine while she was in the shower, depinking. 'It's not quite—here's some plonk.' His landlady's glowering face warned him that she did not need to be told that the pink paint was not all gone. 'I've ordered a pizza. Extra everything.'

'I can't afford it,' said Evie miserably.

'I can, so shut your trap.' Bing was holding an envelope. 'I don't suppose it's the right moment to show you this, but it has to be faced up to.'

'What is it?' Evie stared at the piece of paper. 'It looks like a bill.'

'It's an estimate. For sorting out the damp.'

'What damp?' yelped Evie. 'Bloody hell. A grand! A *grand*?'

Bing held the glass to her lips. 'Drink. Trust Dr Bing. I got these guys in to give us a quote 'cos there's signs of damp all over the back of the house. It could wait, of course, but it's worst in Caroline's flat.'

'Milly!' said Evie immediately.

'Exactly. It ain't good for a little one. So we've got to find the money somehow. But it *is* we—you and me. You don't have to do it on your own.' Bing spoke lightly, stuffing his gym clothes into a nylon bag.

Evie appreciated that. He was wrong, though. It was her house and her responsibility. She couldn't accept any money from him.

Bing paused on his way out to refine his toned body and his flirtation with his personal trainer. 'Anyway, who cares? You're having dinner with Dan next Saturday.'

That did the trick. She was grinning again.

'Have you realised that every flat in this building has its fair share of strange occupants? Caroline's bad moods could well be from Satan himself.' Bing clutched the towel round his neck as Evie smothered his head with noxious peroxide paste.

Nimbly Evie defended her. 'Don't be horrible. Caroline's all alone in the world,' she said dramatically, adding with less drama, 'Do you want me to do your nails?'

'Oooh, yes!' Bing could never resist a beauty treatment. 'What does that mean, all alone in the world? You make her sound like a heroine in a Victorian melodrama.'

'I can't help that. She *is* all alone in the world. All her family are dead.'

'Poor cow,' said Bing, with feeling.

'She's a lot softer than you think.' Evie lowered Bing's hand into a cereal bowl of warm milk and lanolin. 'Do you remember me telling you about my visit to Belle's grave?'

Bing didn't. After a short huff, Evie carried on: 'I visited Belle's grave the day we got the keys to the house. I was a bit nervous—cemeteries and all that—but it was peaceful and I felt close to Belle. I wasn't the only one there. Somebody, a young woman, flitted off when I arrived. I disturbed her while she was putting a bouquet, just a simple one, on Belle's grave. There was a note on it: "I miss you."'

'Aw.' Bing melted.

'And that young woman was Caroline.'

'How do you know?'

'The flowers were tied up with a ribbon with little smiley faces on it. Who wears ribbons like that? Milly does. Round her bunches.'

'Hmm. Sherlock Crump. I'm not convinced. It's not Caroline's style. She never mentions Belle, except to say that she's dead and we should all forget her.'

'Denial,' said Evie. 'I think Belle mothered Caroline. Her heart went out to her because she was a single mother with no relatives to rely on.'

'So, of course, Caroline misses her.' Bing admired his newly buffed fingers. 'Am I ready to rinse yet?'

'Oh Gawd, yes. Hurry or you'll be like a billiard ball.'

Bing dashed off, saying over his shoulder, 'Belle knew what she was doing when she put you in charge.'

Evie hoped he was right.

On Tuesday morning there was great excitement in the basement. There had been a sighting of Bernard with a carrier bag from a man's clothes shop. True, it had been only a fleeting glimpse, but Evie was prepared to swear that the bag had looked fairly full and was from Top Man.

'Hugo Boss would have been better.' Bing was in nit-picking mood.

'Top Man's a good start. Don't you see what this means? My gentle persuasion to improve himself is working.'

'Gentle persuasion? Oh, you mean the psychotic bullying. I saw what went on over that chicken last week and that was not gentle persuasion.'

'No pain, no gain.' Evie snapped open a bag of Monster Munch.

'That's your third,' warned Bing.

'If I don't care why should you? Anyway, I intend to work them off.'

'How?' Bing looked dubious. 'By watching a *This Morning* special on exercise?'

'No. By going for a run. Now that I don't have a job I have lots of time to get fit. That's why I'm in my workout clothes.' Evie did a little twirl in her grey leggings and sweatshirt. Like the trainers on her feet, they were pristine. She had bought them at the time of her last speech on getting fit, about a year ago. 'I'm running over to Sacha's shop in a mo.'

'Why don't you go now?'

'I've got to wait for the damp men.'

'That's all right. I'll look after them. Off you pop.'

Evie narrowed her eyes at her usually unhelpful flatmate. 'Look after them? Is that what they call it nowadays?'

'It's a fair cop. The guy who came to do the estimate was absolutely *stunning*,' gushed Bing.

'So you're hoping love will blossom over the putty?'

'Not love.' Bing pulled a face. 'Plenty of time for that when my looks go. But a bit of slap and tickle with a builder is definitely my idea of home improvement.'

Evie took the pavements at a gentle pace. Even so, she was wilting by the corner of Kemp Street. When she reached Bernard's beloved chippy she was struggling to catch her breath. However, she arrived at Calmer Karma composed and breathing evenly. The thirty-six was a handy bus.

Sacha was pleased to see her, coming to greet her and dumping an American tourist who was inspecting a crystal as big as his fist.

'Er, excuse me, ma'am, how much is this?' asked the tourist meekly.

'Seventy pounds,' answered Sacha absent-mindedly, not even looking his way.

'*Seventy pounds?*' mouthed Evie, in silent disbelief, shooing Sacha away to deal with the customer.

When seventy pounds had been transferred from the gullible tourist's wallet to the till, Evie got down to the real business of her visit. 'Shoes.'

'No.'

'You don't even know what I'm going to say.'

But Sacha did know. 'You're going to ask to borrow my Prada shoes.' This knowledge wasn't due so much to Sacha's psychic abilities as to the fact that every time Evie saw Sacha's red Prada shoes she salivated.

Sacha carried on: 'Your feet are bigger than mine, so no. Remember when I let you wear my stilettos to that wedding? They came back like wellies.'

'That was years ago! We were still at drama school! Your feet have probably grown to catch up with mine by now.'

This pathetic line of reasoning was never going to get her anywhere. As Evie jogged back to the bus stop she experienced the first pangs of panic about what she would wear on Saturday. It was four days away and she was proud that she had staved off the first twinges until now.

'You're on! You're on!' Bing was yelling, as she put her key into the door lock.

Forgetting to feign breathlessness she dashed into the sitting room in time to see herself on the TV screen, strolling across the sand with Dan.

'Fuck me!' said Bing elegantly. 'I see what you mean. He's eleven out of ten.'

The voice-over was burbling on about pasta shapes over a pastiche of Elvis's 'Hound Dog'. Evie policed the images of herself on the screen with a severe eye. Did she look fat? 'Do I look fat?' she interrogated Bing.

'Oh, give it a rest.'

'That means yes, doesn't it? Urrgh!' She pulled a face at the cheesy fireside scene. 'I don't look like that when I smile, do I?'

'They've lit your chins with especial care. The dog looks sensational.'

Undoubtedly Tootsie was the star. Which was the way it was meant to be. 'Second billing to a West Highland white terrier. Great.'

'Aw, diddums. Massage the cheque into the wound.'

'Meet me for a glass of wine by the canal.' Sacha had made it sound so inviting: a summer evening, the sparkling water and a chilled glass of something nice. This was Camden, however. A filthy duck floated past, balanced on a rusty crate. The scraggy stretch of canalside outside the Weaver's Arms looked like Dunkirk late on D-Day.

'Plenty of blokes!' whispered Sacha excitedly, as one knocked her elbow and sent half her wine over another.

'I'm not interested in blokes. I'm interested in Dan and Saturday night.' Evie guided Sacha to a couple of wrought-iron chairs.

'Are you putting all your eggs in one doodah?' queried Sacha anxiously. 'I mean, are you going out with Dan just for a bit of fun or do you want something to come of it?'

'I want something to come of it.' That was an easy one.

'Aden didn't make him sound very nice,' said Sacha, choosing her words carefully for once.

'Aden made him out to be a monster so I wouldn't be too upset if he didn't call me.' Aden had been so certain that Dan wouldn't ring *but he had*. That meant something, right?

'Aden came across as a really straightforward person,' Sacha muttered. 'Dan's the one who likes playing games.'

'How can you say that about someone you've never even met?'

'All right, all right!' Sacha sounded alarmed by the passion in Evie's response. 'I'm only trying to protect you.'

'I don't need protecting, thank you very much.' Evie snarled.

'Can you do a nice York accent?' barked Meredith down the line.

'A York one? Yes.' Evie felt confident.

'Good. You've got a voice-over, then. It's tomorrow. Midday. Get yourself along to Miracle Sound Studios, 14 Little Row, Soho. Ask for Derek. It's an airlines ad, I think.' The phone went dead.

The date outfit was chosen and ready a whole two days ahead of time. Evie turned this way and that in front of the mirror, scrutinising herself.

She was all in black, chosen partly for its slimming effect and partly because almost every garment she owned was black. Her tight-fitting jersey V-neck showed just enough cleavage: sexy without overtones of a butcher's shop window. It fitted neatly to the waistband of her longish black jersey skirt. Her feet were nestling happily in a pair of pointed black suede boots. (Yes, all right, she shouldn't have spent money on suede boots when she was unemployed but she had.)

The detail that pulled the outfit together was the fitted black leather jacket that cinched in her waist and showcased her boobs. It was a triumph, and it was Sacha's. Poor Sacha had been so overwhelmed by guilt for refusing to lend the red shoes that she had practically begged Evie to borrow her new jacket.

Bing had to see the outfit. It was almost ten and he hadn't emerged from his room yet. When Evie threw open his door she realised why. He had company. 'Oh Gawd! Sorry!' Evie staggered backwards, blushing.

'Don't be silly.' Bing was propped up on pillows, like an Eastern potentate. 'Say hello to Georgie.'

'Hello, Georgie. Er . . . nice hat.'

Georgie, kneeling on the bed in a gold loincloth, sported a wide-brimmed straw hat laden with huge silk roses. 'Ta very much!'

Evie backed out again. 'See you later, guys.'

'No, wait!' Georgie was laughing so hard that his hat fell off, revealing a turquoise crop. 'You haven't met Mick yet.'

Another man popped up from under the covers at the foot of the bed, rather close to Evie. She jumped as his Chippendales torso rose from the duvet. 'Good morning,' he said politely.

'Good morning, Mick,' said Evie politely. 'Cup of tea, anyone?'

The laughing Georgie was folded into a minicab. 'Hope he doesn't give his old gran any trouble,' commented Bing.

'He lives with his gran? With turquoise hair?' Evie's remaining gran was still being shielded from the fact that Evie had pierced ears.

'His gran doesn't mind the hair, but she'll kill him for borrowing her hat,' said Mick. His chest and arms were bronzed, gleaming and superbly muscled. It took Bing an age to assemble the bacon sandwiches as he kept pausing to slap or caress him.

When the sandwiches had been consumed and patently insincere promises exchanged to do this again sometime, Mick went to Bing's boudoir to finish dressing.

The doorbell rang and Evie went upstairs to find Bernard, rent in hand. 'I'm terribly sorry that this is a few days late. I forgot all about it.'

'That's all right, Bernard. Better late than never. New clothes?'

Bernard squirmed. ''Fraid so.'

'Ver-ry nice,' said Bing, coming upstairs and stepping into the hall.

And so they were. True, Bernard had been drawn to his faithful cords, but the slate grey went well with the blue shirt, still in its shop creases.

'Although you mustn't tuck yourself in like that,' chided Bing. He yanked Bernard's shirt out of his trousers and straightened it.

Bernard stiffened. His face wore an expression hovering between consternation and terror. Human contact clearly unsettled him.

'There. Much better.' Hands on hips, Bing surveyed his handiwork.

'Thank you.' Bernard's voice was as feeble as an old lady's.

Evie's heart went out to him in his struggle to fit in.

Mick emerged through the door of the flat and Bernard looked at him sideways. 'Well, I must get off to the office,' he mumbled.

'Goodbye, tiger,' said Mick, wrapping his beefy arms round Bing. 'Something to remember me by.' He kissed Bing full and sensuously on the mouth. They drew apart and he said cheerfully, 'Goodbye, all!' and left, tapping Bing on the behind for good measure.

''Bye!' sang Evie.

Bernard had turned into a crimson statue. He was blushing so violently that it must have hurt, and staring at the space where Mick had been.

'Bernard? You OK?' asked Evie.

'Bernard,' Bing slapped him on the back, 'you've got to get out more!'

There was something about being on the top deck of a bus—peering down at the unsuspecting heads of pedestrians below, nosily inspecting first-floor flats along the route, watching the drunken waddle of passengers making their way down the aisle—that always made Evie feel schoolgirlish. She was on her way to her voice-over and Bing was on *his* way to a *Joseph* matinée. They were discussing Bernard.

'He must have. We're everywhere,' Bing pointed out.

'Bernard hardly goes out. He might have seen gay men on television, but he's obviously never seen one in the wild before. Were you insulted by the way he reacted?'

'No.' Bing was too robust to be disturbed by that kind of thing. 'Bernard didn't mean any harm. I know homophobia when I see it and he was just being provincial. He'll get over it.'

'He'll have to, living two floors above you. It's kill or cure. Oi! You didn't say what you thought of the date outfit.'

'Very good. Perfect. Just enough bosom, and the sharp boots add a hint of sexual tension. Leave the jacket on for a while, then slowly remove it, unzipping seductively.'

'Thank God for gay men.' Evie gave his arm a little squeeze. She had grown up hearing her father say, 'Very nice, dear. Are you sure you'll be warm enough?' in response to her mother's 'How do I look?'

'Nervous?' he asked.

'About Saturday?' Evie considered the question. 'Not really. Just excited.'

'What's your plan? Toy with him, then dump him? Lead him on, then cross your legs?'

Evie pulled a face. 'Why would I do any of that?'

Bing studied her. 'You're . . . serious about him?'

'Not *serious*,' corrected Evie. 'We hardly know each other. But, yes, I think I'd like to see him for a while. I don't just want a one-night stand.'

'You're a night in already.' Bing shook his head. 'I don't get this, doll. Aden—who seems like a regular guy—gave Dan the worst character reference a woman could hear, yet you're planning to go out on Saturday and sleep with him *again*?'

'Too bloody right I am.'

'But he didn't even ring to see if you were OK after he abandoned you in a West Country hotel.'

It sounded awful when he put it like that. 'He was in Spain,' she reminded him.

'And he didn't have *one minute* to make a quick call before he went?'

'It was all very last-minute. You know how it is.' Evie's voice was becoming shrill. A woman in a headscarf two seats ahead was discreetly swivelling her head, trying to listen in. Evie lowered the volume. 'The thing is, he's kept his word. He's taking me out to dinner. If he meant that bit, why wouldn't he mean the bit about me meaning a lot to him?'

'It's 'cos he's good-looking, isn't it?' Bing accused her. 'You wouldn't take this treatment from Aden, but you're so flattered that a sex god's coming back for seconds you're going to open your legs again.'

The headscarf woman jumped and risked a quick peek to see what they looked like.

'What is all this psychoanalysis shit?' asked Evie. 'Why aren't I just allowed to have a bit of fun for once?' She couldn't help it. She was loud enough now for Headscarf Woman to listen in comfort. 'I'd like to get away from the fact that my career is going nowhere, that my house is falling apart and eating money as it goes, that my tenants are sociopaths that I can't get rid of. But, oh no, my two so-called best friends want me to turn down the handsomest man I've ever met and live like a nun!' The bus had reached Oxford Street. She stood up and pushed roughly past Bing, even though she knew it was his stop too. 'I can't believe I'm getting all this puritanical shite from a man who spent last night in a threesome with a body builder and a laughing gnome!' Evie stomped furiously down the stairs.

Before Bing made for the stairs he leaned forward and whispered in the ear of Headscarf Woman, 'Episode two, same bus, same time, next week.'

Bing escorted Evie to the door of Miracle Sound. 'Just let me say this and then I'll shut up, I promise.'

'Good,' snapped Evie, still fizzing. 'All I've got to look forward to is Saturday and you're ruining it.'

'I don't want to rain on your parade. I'm just looking out for you because I *care*, you rancid old bat. Dan sounds like a perfect one-night stand, but he's not boyfriend material. Any sensible woman would know that. Belle left her house to you 'cos she trusted you to be strong and to take care of her misfits. What would she think of you falling for someone like Dan?'

'Maybe she'd understand. Maybe she would have fallen for him too.' Evie was in fighting mood.

'And she died alone, right?'

That was below the belt. Suddenly Evie felt tearful. 'What you and

Sacha aren't taking into account is how I *feel*!' she spluttered. 'I'm mad about him! Being with him makes me happy! I can't wait to see him again! Why aren't I allowed to feel that?'

'Oh, baby!' Bing could be soft as butter. He enveloped Evie in a big warm hug that smelt of expensive aftershave. 'I'm sorry. You have a great time on Saturday and fuck the lot of us with our advice. I mean, if Sacha's agreeing with me I must be wrong. Right?'

Evie managed a giggle. 'Don't!' she commanded, as Bing tried to disengage himself. So they stood there, rocking gently, as Soho whirled around them.

'I'm Evie Crump and I'm here to meet Derek.'

'Derek . . .' The receptionist looked blank beneath her highlights. 'Take a seat!' she said brightly, pleased with this plan.

Evie walked across the blond-wood floor and sat down in a low, squashy black leather chair. Very low. Her knees were earrings. Getting up was going to be a challenge.

Two actresses she vaguely knew from the box, and a man with a red-veined nose, were sitting much more comfortably on the other seats.

Suddenly, without any warning, Derek was towering over Evie, extending his hand. Except he was Eric. 'Your agent is a little hard of hearing,' he said.

'Well, she's hard,' agreed Evie, extricating herself from the chair.

She followed Eric downstairs to studio three. It was a small, dark room, rendered timeless and seasonless by the lack of windows and the hum of air conditioning. A leather sofa lined one wall, and opposite was the mixing desk. The writer—a trendy, cute guy wearing a Phat Farm T-shirt—and the client—a large man in a suit who owned a chunk of Southern Cross Airlines—were on the sofa. Evie was introduced to them, then said hello to the sound engineer, who was skinny and pale. Engineers are always skinny and pale (it's called a studio tan) because they spend their lives manacled to their mixing desks.

Eric shepherded her into the voice-over booth. It was a claustrophobic space with carpeted walls, separated from the studio by a glass partition. Evie sat down, put on her headphones, looked over the four lines of script and took a sip of water.

Eric flicked the talkback button, which relayed conversation in the studio through to Evie's headphones.

'OK, my love, if you're ready just give us a quick read-through in your best New York accent.'

Evie stared rabbit-like through the glass at Eric.

With her best *New* York accent. Unfortunately her best New York accent was the same as her worst New York accent. She couldn't do one.

'In your own time.' Eric was smiling encouragingly through the glass.

Evie, her mouth as dry as a Saharan sandal, looked down at the script. The words were dancing like paralytic ants.

The talkback clicked. 'Can we get you anything? Cup of tea? Quick massage?'

She heard the others' polite laughter before the button was pressed and she was back with her own silent terror.

Think. *Think.* What do New Yorkers sound like? She conjured up Robert de Niro, Woody Allen, the girls from *Sex and the City*, but they all mouthed mutely at her, like silent movie stars.

Right. There was nothing else for it. Evie had to open her mouth and *go.* With the all-purpose American accent that she and Bing used when they made up Oscar acceptance speeches, she read the script with all the energy, confidence and insight that her training could supply.

When she'd finished she looked up slowly through the glass.

They looked confused. Eric pressed the talkback. 'Can we have that again, just like that—it was a perfect read—but with your New York accent this time?'

Evie stared at him, a beseeching look in her eyes.

Eric was not a stupid man. 'That *was* your New York accent, wasn't it?'

Evie nodded. The click of the button banished her into silence again. It didn't look as though the burly man from the airline was commenting thoughtfully on her intelligent performance.

The engineer slipped into the booth beside her. 'It might be best if you go out this way,' he suggested, opening a concealed door.

Out in Reception he heard how Evie had turned up expecting to do a York accent. 'You've made my day,' he told her, trying not to smile. 'They thought you were doing Welsh.'

Only intravenous chocolate can revive a spirit as battered as Evie's was after her voice-over. She parked herself at a window table in the nearest café and ordered a slice of chocolate cake with a large hot chocolate.

Having hoovered up a slice of cake the size of her overdraft, Evie spotted a face she knew in the street. 'Aden!' She banged on the window.

Aden was distracted, worried-looking, but he smiled broadly when he saw her. 'You've got chocolate on the end of your nose,' he pointed out as he slid onto the plastic bench opposite her.

'Thought I'd missed a bit.' Evie noticed the circles under his eyes. 'You tired?'

'Shattered. I've been editing in a basement. You look perky, though.'

'Thank you. Do you want some cake? I'm going to order another slice. I'm eating to forget.' Evie recounted the tale of her voice-over.

Aden laughed and sympathised, and let her eat half of his cake too. 'How's the children's theatre thing going?'

'Gone.' Evie told him what had happened. 'How's your arty film going?'

'Just finishing it. That's what I've been editing. Next I'm assistant director on a meaty telly drama, filming here and in the States.'

Evie was pierced with envy, and hated herself for it. 'You're lucky.' She corrected herself: 'No, you're not. You're good at what you do.'

Aden wasn't too hot at accepting compliments. He ran a hand through his sandy hair. 'So, anyway, you and Dan, what's the score?'

'Well, we're having dinner on Saturday.' Evie smiled. 'Thanks for the warning but it doesn't look like it was necessary.'

Aden coughed. The tortured body language told Evie that he was uncomfortable with the subject. 'I'm sorry. I can be a sanctimonious schmuck sometimes.'

Evie couldn't disagree, but she could say, with complete sincerity, 'You did it for the right reasons. You can tell the story in your speech at our wedding.'

Aden raised his eyebrows.

'Joke! It's a joke! Blimey! Why can't girls make jokes about weddings without blokes taking them seriously?' complained the girl who had already chosen the dress and her bridesmaids.

'Have a great time. Let me know how it goes.' Aden was making a visible effort to be nice about it, despite his reservations. 'I'd better get off.' He stood up and bent to kiss Evie's cheek.

'Happy editing!' trilled Evie.

Aden didn't walk away. He was toying anxiously with his mobile. 'Look,' he said, 'I was hard on Dan. Don't pay any attention to me. It was only because . . .'

Evie smiled. 'I know. You two have history. You were only trying to protect me. Although,' she wagged a finger at him in mock sternness, 'you could have told me he'd been in Spain since we got back from Lyme.'

Aden said gravely, 'Yes. I should have told you.'

And then he was gone, leaving Evie with nothing to do but lick the plates and look forward to telling Sacha and Bing that the tales of Dan's dastardliness had been greatly exaggerated.

'Why did you lie about being able to do a New York accent? You made me look like a complete imbecile. We only narrowly escaped being liable for the studio time.'

Evie took her telephone ticking-off like a man. 'I'm sorry, Meredith, I misheard you.'

'Don't mishear this—*do that again and you're in fucking trouble!*' yelled Meredith, and added '*darling!*' as an afterthought.

'Is that all?' asked Evie hopefully.

'No. Amazingly you have an audition. For what you would call a proper job.'

'Eh?' This was out of the blue.

'Quite. I don't have the details, don't ask me, but it's a big telly, prestigious, costume drama. The director is Hugh Thomas and he's interested in you.'

'Hugh Thomas?' squeaked Evie. 'How come he's interested in me?'

'Fuck knows.' Meredith coughed operatically. 'Darling.'

Fabulous new man—tick.

Potentially fabulous audition—tick.

Things were looking up at Kemp Street.

'Oi!' yelled Bing, from where he stood frozen, willing his fake tan to dry. 'Your mother rang.'

Refusal to ring witchlike parent—tick.

Sacha was there on the dot, clutching a wine-box in one hand and the *Best Music in the World 107* in the other. She stationed herself on the bed. 'Shower! Chop-chop!'

Evie rinsed all her bits and anointed herself with Calvin Klein body lotion. This expensive product rarely saw the light of day, but tonight was worth it. Then she brushed her teeth vigorously.

'Hurry up!' Sacha yelled. 'I want to start your nails!'

Evie speeded up, teasing the tangles out of her wet hair, then pulled Bing's shortie robe off the hook on the bathroom door.

'You're behind,' chided Sacha. 'French?' she queried.

'Yeah.' Evie stuck out a hand and let Sacha get·cracking with the base coat. Holding a glass in her free hand, she sipped her wine.

'Do you know,' began Sacha, trying but failing to keep the whinge out of her voice, 'the only man to ask me out since Christmas is the bloke from the newsagent's? Why don't I get asked out?'

Bing was passing the open door. 'Do you want that alphabetically, in ascending order of importance, or just as it comes?'

Sacha attempted a dignified silence.

'Bing!' Evie scolded, trying not to laugh.

'Sor-ree. I have news!' He had just seen Bernard leave the house, resplendent in yet more new clothes.

'I told you. We're getting through to him!'

Sacha tutted and reached for the varnish. Bing enlarged on the sighting.

'Nice chinos. Cute white tee. *But* he was headed towards the chippy.'

'Aw, *no*,' Evie said despairingly. 'Right. Keep an eye out for him. If he comes back with chips, we'll jump him and confiscate them.'

'Maybe I should just give in and go out with him,' Sacha remarked gloomily, as she worked on Evie's nails.

Evie and Bing exchanged an eloquent glance over her bowed head, but wisely pretended not to have heard her.

'You should be on hair-drying now,' Sacha scolded, as Bing withdrew.

Her hair cooperated, much to Evie's surprise. She positioned herself in front of Belle's chipped dressing-table mirror, opened her make-up bag and gazed at her bare face in the mirror. She wondered how many times Belle had looked at hers in it, watching herself age. She touched the cold surface of the glass. 'Kylie!' she snapped, and sipped her wine.

Sacha was a few glasses ahead, so dancing inevitably broke out. 'I love Kylie!' she declared euphorically, shimmying past Evie who was now patting translucent powder onto her cheeks.

'Mind the—' A slosh of Sacha's wine slopped over. '—carpet.'

Slowly, glamorous Evie emerged. Don't overdo it, she cautioned herself. She could be heavy-handed with the lip-liner at times like this.

'Ooooh, you look lovely!' cooed Sacha, leaning shakily over her shoulder before getting back into the groove with Atomic Kitten.

Is this right? Evie asked herself, watching Sacha whirl by in happy uncoordination in the mirror. Wasn't it rather *sad* for two girls in their late twenties to be *still* getting excited about what to wear on a hot date?

There was no point in posing this question to Sacha. There she was, using a hairbrush as a microphone, giving it loads. Her answer would be a resounding, *Yes, of course this is right!*

Evie, clicking herself into a front-loading Wonderbra, wasn't so sure. It would be nice, wouldn't it, to go out just once without hoisting her boobs up? It might even be nice to stay in, sober, with a man she knew well.

'Oh, don't wear black,' pleaded Sacha, coming over to wrestle the skirt out of Evie's hands as she took it from the cupboard. 'Black brings bad vibes! It's the colour of darkness!'

'It makes me look slimmer.'

'Oh, yeah.' Sacha relinquished her grasp.

A shout came from the hallway. 'I have a prisoner! Come and get him, girls!'

Bernard was standing with his hands behind his back, looking even more sheepish than usual. 'What's—' he began, but got no further.

'Silence.' Bing held up his hand. 'You may not know this, Bernard baby, but your landlady has certain rights over you. One of these is the right to rifle through your carrier bags. If they contain tweed or chips she has the right to hang you by the neck until you are dead.'

Bernard gulped. 'Er . . .'

'Don't pay any attention to him,' Evie reassured Bernard, delving into the bag. She pulled out a bag of apples and some broccoli. 'This is *good*!' She retrieved a bag of rice and . . . an organic chicken. There wasn't a chip in sight. 'Oh, Bernard, I'm so proud of you!' She held the bag aloft like an Olympic medal.

Bernard left, looking bewildered.

'He's making real progress.' Evie sighed happily.

'Did you see how he was undressing me with his eyes?' asked Sacha.

'They'd have to be bloody big eyes,' muttered Bing.

'Oi, Date Mate!' Evie nudged Sacha. 'My glass is empty.'

'Sorry.' Sacha beetled off to find the wine-box just as Evie's mobile began ringing.

'That's Dan cancelling!' prophesied Sacha, reappearing with the wine.

'Don't say that!' Evie snatched up the phone. For perhaps the first time in her life she was glad to hear her mother's voice. 'Hi, Mum. Bing told me you rang. Sorry I didn't get back to you.'

'You've got a man, I hear,' said Bridgie, without preamble. 'Bing told me all about it. You're seeing him tonight so I won't keep you. I'm sure it will take time to make yourself presentable. Daddy's bought a barbecue.'

'Oh . . . good.' Bridgie was always steering conversation round hair-pin bends.

'So invite him tonight and we'll have a barbie next Saturday.'

The thought of sexy, smouldering, virile Dan balancing a plate on her mother's scrap of lawn was all wrong. 'It's much too soon for that!'

'Soon? I've been waiting *years* for this.'

It was settled. 'I'm doomed,' pronounced Evie, switching off the phone and reaching for the larger glass, filled with wine, that Sacha had thoughtfully provided.

'If you want a relationship with him he'll have to meet your parents,' said Bing.

'Why? *I* don't even want to meet them. He'll never have sex with me again once he's got a load of my mother.'

'He probably won't last that long anyway,' slurred Sacha. 'What? What did I say?' She was baffled by Evie's thunderous look. 'I'm only trying to be philosoph—'

Evie left Sacha to conclude the rest of what she was only trying to be and went to finish getting dressed.

Just as she applied the final slick of lipstick the doorbell rang. She inhaled deeply and pulled back her shoulders.

It had begun.

Seven

'SUSHI?' EVIE STARED up from the pavement at the neon-lit chopsticks.

'It's my favourite food.' Dan dropped her hand. 'Oh, no. You hate it.'

'I don't. I love it. Mm-mmmm. Lovely, lovely sushi.' Evie picked up his hand. 'Just let me get at all that raw fish.'

The restaurant was busy and bright. Booths lined the walls and a long white oval counter stood in the centre of the room, surrounded by high stools. Dan guided her to one, saying anxiously, 'Is this really OK? We can go somewhere else.'

Evie was touched. 'This is perfect,' she reassured him, hoisting herself on to the seat, legs dangling like a country-and-western singer. She was transfixed by the tiny conveyor-belt that ran round the counter at nose level, transporting plates of various foodstuffs. None of what was trundling past under plastic covers looked good. None of it looked *edible*.

'It's all so delicious I don't know where to start,' drooled Dan. 'Squid, I think.' He reached for a plate as it passed by. 'What about you?'

Still reeling at the mention of squid, Evie pointed at the nearest strange pale thing. 'Er, what's that?'

'Raw eel.'

'*Aiee*.' Evie emitted an unusual noise she'd never made before, and retracted her finger. Raw? Were the Japanese mad?

'I think you need a drink.' Dan pressed a red button on the table top. 'Some *sake* will get you in the mood.'

Evie watched him eat his squid with a kind of appalled fascination.

'Ow!' A tiny trolley had careered into her.

'The robot waiter,' Dan informed her, and leaned down to pick up a pottery flask and two tiny beakers. 'Cool, isn't he? It's radio controlled.'

'God. Boys *love* gadgets.'

'And girls are wimps about sushi.'

'Is that a challenge, Daniel?'

'I'm only saying that most girls I know come over all squeamish in a sushi bar.'

'That *is* a challenge. Get me down that lump of raw . . . whatever.' Evie gestured at a piece of flesh the colour of putty.

Dan set the dish in front of her. 'It's a sea urchin. Even I don't eat those.'

'Then *you*'re a wimp.' Evie fumbled it into her mouth.

If Dan was watching her with interest, it wasn't surprising. The expression that illustrates a mouthful of cold, salty snot is rarely seen. 'Oh, God!' she grabbed her drink. She'd never tried *sake* before and this wasn't a great time to be introduced to it. '*Yaaargh!*' She had invented a word to celebrate drinking nail-varnish remover. 'Dan,' she whispered.

His face, close to hers, was grinning widely. 'What, gorgeous?'

'I don't like sushi.'

Evie sighed with contentment at the sight of a big plate of spaghetti and the big hunk of bloke on the dog-eared banquette opposite her. They were in Pepito's, where the waiters were fat, the prices were lean and the food-poisoning was free of charge.

'I'm sorry,' said Evie.

'What for? I don't care what I'm doing as long as it's with you.' Dan looked down at his meatballs in murky sauce. 'Besides, I've never been rushed to Casualty before. It might be fun.'

Evie sniggered. 'When everywhere else is full you can always get a table at Pepito's.'

'I wonder why?'

A waiter coughed unselfconsciously over a basket of rolls. Dan and Evie pulled a face at each other and pushed aside their bread plates.

'Something's on my mind.' Dan's abruptness halted a forkful of spaghetti on its way to Evie's mouth.

'What?'

'I need the answer to a very important question or I won't be able to relax. At this moment it's the most important thing in the world.'

The hairs on the back of Evie's neck were standing on end. 'Ask me.'

'Are you coming home with me tonight?'

There it was, the electric stillness that Dan could throw over them like a cloak. This man thrilled her to the core. 'You try and stop me.'

'Ooooh, goody.' Dan spun the words out in his deep, dreamy voice, like a cat stretching. 'I have plans for you and me.'

Plans? Sexual ones—or relationship ones? Somehow Evie suspected them to be more concerned with tying her up and covering her with cream than with opening a joint bank account. That was fine by her.

'I'd love to see you act,' said Dan. 'That commercial didn't stretch either of us. I suspect you're a good actress. I can see it in your face.'

'You're making me blush.'

'Good. I like to see your face go pink. Women's faces flush when they orgasm, you know.'

'Really?'

'Yours certainly did.'

'*Dan!*' Evie looked round to see if anyone was eavesdropping.

'And will again in about . . .' Dan looked at his watch '. . . an hour and a half. Unless you want dessert.'

Evie laughed, embarrassed but loving it. 'I bet you're a good actor.'

'Well, you're wrong, gorgeous. I can't act. Don't get me wrong. I'm going to have a great career. But I definitely can't act.'

'You're very frank.' She'd met countless actors who couldn't act, but not one who admitted it. 'Here's to success, whether we can act or not.' She held up her glass for Dan to clink.

'Here's to being famous and rich!' Dan threw back his wine in one gulp. 'Let's have one for the road, then go back to mine.'

'There's nothing wrong with that plan, as far as I can see.' Evie was becoming long-winded, a sure sign that she had drunk too much. 'Make mine a coffee for the road, though.'

Dan pulled a face, but Evie stood firm. She wanted to remember this encounter. As a waiter put a coffee and a sambuca before them she said, 'I bumped into Aden yesterday.'

Dan cracked a knuckle. 'Oh, yeah? Chat about me, did you?'

This was irresistible. Evie assumed a serious expression. 'Oh, yes, we chatted about you, all right.'

Dan was darkly silent, glaring at his sambuca as if it had insulted his mother. Evie bit her lip. She'd only meant to tease him, not ruin the atmosphere. Frantically she rifled her mind for something innocuous to lighten the mood; something that was nothing to do with Aden.

Ah! She had it. 'How was Spain?'

Dan's reaction was as extreme as it was unexpected. 'I knew it!' he roared. 'That little shit had to, didn't he? He just *had* to,' Dan ranted, leaning towards her. 'St Aden. That's what we called him at school. It's about time he fucking grew up.'

Evie drew back. Dan's face, contorted with anger, scared her.

'Why couldn't he keep his mouth shut? So I didn't go to Spain. It was none of his business.'

Evie felt as though a bucket of cold water had been chucked over her. Everything changed. As if she were looking at a photograph, she saw herself and Dan: the seducer and the victim; the liar and the idiot. She swallowed hard, stood up, picked up her borrowed jacket and her handbag, and made for the door. She knew that tears were on the way. She had to be far away from Dan when they arrived.

Dan scrambled after her, fumbling for notes in his pockets and flinging them at the waiters. 'Wait! Hang on, gorgeous!'

Evie, now marching like a storm trooper, was at the corner before he caught up with her. She did not intend to waste a word on him.

Dan was dancing sideways awkwardly, gabbling, 'Will you let me explain? I made up the story about Spain because I— *ouch!*' A lamp post stopped him painfully in his tracks. He recovered and ran after Evie, who was on the kerb, peering up and down the street for a taxi. 'Listen, I lied about Spain because I didn't want to hurt your feelings. I'd been busy, I'd had loads of, er, stuff to do and I kept meaning to ring you but suddenly three weeks had gone by. I knew you'd be upset so I made up a little white lie. I did it for you!'

Evie kept scanning the road, willing the tears to stay back.

'Come on, give me a break,' Dan cajoled. 'You're behaving like a girl.'

That did it. 'How dare you? You lied to me and now you're trying to tell me you did it for my sake! You're just trying to make sure your target for the evening doesn't get away.' A memory from Lyme Regis popped into her head. She muttered, 'Melody was right about you.'

'Brilliant.' Dan threw his arms up into the air. 'Aden told you about her as well.'

Evie's mouth fell open.

'She meant nothing to me.' Dan was carrying on, unaware that he was hanging himself. 'She was drunk. She was a slapper. You weren't playing ball. It was just a bit of fun.'

More than anything, more than world peace, Evie wanted a taxi to appear. And one did. As she tugged open the door, evading Dan's restraining lunge, she said, 'Aden didn't tell me a thing.' She got into the cab and said, 'Kemp Street, Camden, please,' just as the first tears fell.

The taxi pulled away, leaving a shell-shocked Dan on the pavement.

Would you prescribe an open-air handicrafts fair for a bruised heart? Well, neither would Evie, but that was where she found herself on Sunday afternoon, strolling in Sacha's wake.

Note that Evie only considered her heart bruised. She was realistic enough to admit that it was nowhere near broken. A long night without either Bing or a bottle of red to lean on had led to some unusually clear-sighted introspection. An uncomfortable question or two had come up. Was she really so easily blinded by a pert buttock and a saucy smile?

The answer was an uncomfortable 'yes'. When she replayed the time she had spent with Dan, it was apparent that his louse-like tendencies had always been there. Shame crept over Evie as she remembered sneering at Melody's drunkenness. She'd thought she'd been in cahoots with Dan, when actually he'd been busy making a fool of them both.

Worse, much worse, was the knowledge that brainless Melody was much more clued up than she was. She hadn't entertained any virginal notions of a 'relationship'. She had guessed that Evie was the next notch on Dan's bedpost.

'I'm desperate,' concluded Evie miserably.

'No, you're not desperate.' Sacha had pooh-poohed *that* idea when they'd met at the handicrafts fair.

Evie's shoulders had relaxed in relief, until she reminded herself that she considered *Sacha* desperate. One-hundred-per-cent, top-quality, no-doubt-about-it desperate. So, could she trust the opinion of a certified desperate person on her own status as desperate?

Sunday-night telly as undemanding and comforting as a favourite aunt was just what the doctor would order, if he were around. Evie snuggled down on the couch to let a brainless costume drama wash over her.

The television was so loud that at first she didn't hear the knocking.

Caroline looked as if she had been standing on the step for some time. 'You deaf?'

Evie was used to these greetings by now. 'Evening, Caroline.'

'I want to talk to you about my flat.'

'Right. Come in.'

'No, I'm fine here,' said Caroline. 'It's about the damp you sorted out.'

'There's no need to thank me. I'm your landlady, I was just doing my duty. Honestly,' said Evie magnanimously.

'I know that. I was going to say that now my bedroom needs redecorating where they stripped off all the wallpaper.'

Evie was gobsmacked. She hadn't meant it, of course, when she'd said there was no need for thanks. 'Fine,' she said, through gritted teeth. 'Fine. Finefinefine. I'll redecorate. Why should you pick up a paint-brush after all? You already pay a whopping fifty per cent of what the rent should be. Don't worry. Leave it all to me. I'll gold-leaf the dado rail while I'm at it. G'night.'

Evie stomped back to her nest on the sofa.

It was impossible to concentrate on the telly. Damn Caroline. Damn her ingratitude, damn her surliness, damn her . . . loneliness. Above all, damn her for bringing out the very worst in me and making me feel unbelievably guilty. Evie pounded on Caroline's door.

'Yeah?'

'I think the whole flat needs redecorating.'

'OK.'

Evie backed away. There would be no whoops of delight from this tenant. 'Good. Right. That's settled, then. See you.'

As Evie reached the bottom stair Caroline's voice drifted down to her. 'Oi! I don't want gold leaf on my whatsit rail.'

Sacha believed that Evie's audition had gone well because earlier she'd cast the runes at Calmer Karma and they'd prophesied it would be a good day for creativity. Evie knew that her audition had gone well because she'd been given well-written material to read and a sensitive, inspiring director to guide her. Hugh James was a small, round, bearded bear who showed lots of teeth when he giggled, which was often. He had spent plenty of time with her, so that by the time she performed, the lines felt like a comfortable cardigan. Hugh's reaction made her dare to hope that he'd liked her.

Bing was impressed that she'd got as far as an audition with Hugh James, and insisted on calling her Judi Dench for the rest of the day. 'Oh, your mum rang while you were out, Judi.'

'What did she want?'

'She was keen to know how things had gone with Dan on Saturday.'

'Noooooooooo.' Bridgie's I-told-you-sos could take off the top layer of skin.

'Don't worry. I didn't tell her the awful truth. I bought you a bit of time by saying that it went brilliantly and you were very happy.'

'Thanks. You're a hero.'

'She said, "Don't forget Saturday", whatever that means.'

'Knickers.' Then Evie corrected herself: '*Giant* knickers. She's expecting me to bring my lovely new boyfriend to her barbecue. Bing, what shall I do?'

Bing picked up the phone and held it out to her. 'Call her now. Get it over with. Say you've found out he's a serial killer. Or he likes marzipan. Whatever. Come on, Judi! They didn't make you a dame for nothing.'

Evie took the phone grimly and dialled. 'Mum, it's me.'

'I've heard all about him! Bing sang his praises.' There was only one topic Bridgie was interested in.

'Not quite all.' Evie took a deep breath.

It was a mistake to take a breath around Bridgie. She leapt in, like the SAS. 'I was just saying to Daddy, I'm so proud of you, getting your life together and finding a decent young man. We can't wait to meet him at the barbie. We're going to . . .'

Evie had stopped listening after 'I'm so proud of you'. She had never heard those words from her mother's mouth before. She felt taller: her mother was proud of her. Evie wanted to prolong the feeling.

Bridgie was approaching a natural break. 'So, do you think he likes potato salad? Will I do a big bowl?'

Bridgie's potato salad somehow incorporated curry powder and liquorice in its ingredients, but Evie was feeling indulgent. 'I'm sure he'll love it. He's looking forward to meeting you,' she added recklessly.

As she hung up she said anxiously to Bing, 'Find me a man by Saturday.'

'Darling, I could find you a hundred but not one of them would be suitable for your mother's barbecue.'

Evie had been about to pick up the receiver to call Sacha in the hope that she fancied making a night of it, when the phone rang.

'Yikes!' she squeaked.

'Yikes? Am I through to the Famous Five?' asked Aden.

'Aden! Hello! This is a surprise.'

'I wanted to know how things went with Dan.'

'Ah.'

'Actually, I'm fibbing. I *know* how things went. I just wanted to hear your side of it.'

'It was poo,' sighed Evie. 'He's a . . . Sorry, Aden, I don't really know you well enough to swear in front of you.'

Aden took a sharp breath.

'Don't tell me you're going to defend him?' said Evie, with spirit. 'He hadn't been to Spain at all! Imagine how I felt when I found that out.'

'I knew. I should have told you, but I reckoned I'd interfered enough by then.'

'I wouldn't have listened. I just didn't want to see the truth about him,' admitted Evie, in a small voice. 'I've made a right twat of myself.'

'Dan's an expert,' Aden said. 'He's done this before and he knew which buttons to push. He's never had a victim who reacted quite like you, though. He rang me just after you took off. Women don't walk out on Dan, it's always the other way round. He was in a right state. So maybe you're not quite the twat you think you are.'

'Maybe.' Evie couldn't help feeling pleased.

'Enough Dan-talk,' said Aden decisively. 'How are *you*? Got another job yet?'

'Nah. Had a *fantastic* audition, though, for a dream job.'

'Do you think you got it?'

'Er, dunno.' Evie was distracted by a flash of inspiration. Experience had not taught her that it was safest to ignore these flashes. 'Aden, do you fancy being my boyfriend next Saturday?'

There was a short silence. 'You're going to have to explain that.'

Evie hated explaining herself so she trotted through the salient points rapidly. 'My mother mad. She think me have boyfriend. She invite boyfriend to barbecue Saturday. Me need fake presentable boyfriend for barbecue. Yes or no?'

'So I'm presentable. That's something.'

'Please, Aden, there'll be free sausages and you can play with my dog. You'd be getting me out of a huge hole. My mother will just go on and on and on and on and on.'

'I don't think I could pull it off.'

'And on and on and on and on and on—'

'OK, OK. I'll be your boyfriend on Saturday.'

Phew. Good old Aden. Evie always liked a man she could manipulate.

'Magnolia is cheaper than off-white,' Evie had argued, in one of the endless aisles of B&Q.

Bing had been adamant. 'You can't do Caroline's flat in magnolia. It's too drab. It's too . . . rented accommodation.'

Which was how Evie had come to be dipping her brush into off-white bright and early on Saturday morning. She did not like decorating. She would rather move house than retouch a cornice.

Bing came up with a tray of coffee. 'More Bernard news!' he said gleefully. 'He was spotted going into a hairdresser's on the high street.'

'No!' Evie almost dropped her mug. This was very good news. They were really making progress with Bernard. Perhaps it was time to try to make headway with another project.

'When was the last time you had a really good night out?' Evie asked Caroline, who was halfway up a ladder.

'Can't remember. I told you, there's nobody to look after Milly. I can't dole out money to baby sitters.'

'My offer still stands. Bing and I will look after Milly. You need to have some fun. Why don't you let us have her one night next week?'

'Maybe.'

Evie put down her brush and stood at the foot of the ladder. 'Not good enough. Name a night. Go on.'

Caroline stared down at her. Evie stared back. Eventually Caroline muttered, 'Friday.'

'Brilliant. I know. Go out with Bernard. Don't look at me like that. He's got a new wardrobe and he's gone to the hairdresser's for a groovy new look. He's intelligent, he's kind, he's good with children.' Evie had no evidence to support that last virtue, but Caroline's look of mingled horror and anger was making her gabble. 'If I'm going to look after Milly for a whole evening the least you can do is give Bernard a chance.'

The horror disappeared, leaving pure anger on Caroline's face. She climbed down the ladder and stood nose to nose with Evie. 'Strings attached, eh? Who do you think you are?'

Just then Evie thought she was a very frightened woman. 'I'm only asking that you give him a whirl. It can't hurt.'

'Ladies!' Bing thrust open the door. Both girls swivelled towards him. 'I present to you Mr Bernard Briggs, modelling his new haircut.'

Bernard shuffled in shyly.

There was no way to describe Bernard's hair: it would have been impossible to do it justice. Suffice to say it had a fringe, a very short one, and most of the back was sticking up. It wasn't a look Evie had seen before, and it wasn't one that was likely to be copied. She broke out in a torrent of praise. If she kept talking she reckoned she'd stave off the hysterical laughter that was threatening to overwhelm her.

'Thank you. I'm not sure about it, actually,' Bernard said faintly.

'No, no, no, no, no, no, it's gorgeous,' gushed Evie.

'Come along, Bernard, stop distracting the ladies.' Bing shepherded him out, raising a telling eyebrow behind his back.

As the footsteps receded down the stairs Evie took Caroline's hands in her own and said earnestly, 'I am truly, truly sorry.'

'Why were you so surprised that I have a car?' asked Aden, as they hurtled Surbitonwards.

'I wasn't. I was surprised you have such a *funky* car.'

Evie was enjoying the drive, her conker-coloured hair swirling crazily as they bombed along in the little red open-top.

'Is it funky?' queried Aden innocently. 'It offers excellent fuel consumption and air bags come as standard.'

'Aden, don't spoil it. Next on the left. That's the house, with the roses.'

'Who's that woman jumping up and down on the pavement?'

'That's my mother.' Evie's heart sank. 'She doesn't normally hop from foot to foot like that but I don't normally bring boyfriends over.'

'Oh, God,' said Aden as he parked and Bridgie Crump broke into a run towards them. 'How did we meet? How long have we been seeing each other? Is it serious? We should have gone through all this.'

'Your name is Dan,' said Evie, as her mother reached her side of the car.

'He knows his own name!' Bridgie leaned rudely over her daughter and shook Aden's hand. 'You can call me Bridgie. Or Mum!' She laughed loudly.

'Hello, Mummy,' said Aden, with the boyish smile that came in so handy at times like this.

Bridgie whispered, 'Thank God he talks nicely,' in her daughter's ear as Evie got out of the car.

'What did you expect?'

'He might be one of those DJ fellas, all rap and what-have-you.'

Evie shook her head. Her mother's take on popular culture, based on information gleaned from *This Morning, Bella* and the woman next door, was always baffling.

'In you come, you two!' Bridgie slipped her arms through Evie's and Aden's and propelled them up to the front door.

Evie realised with horror that there was a crowd on the doorstep. She felt insulted: was it really so unusual and interesting for her to bring a man home?

'Hello!' they all chorused, raising glasses of Buck's Fizz as if they were welcoming sailors home from a war.

'Hello,' muttered Evie.

'Hello, everyone,' said Aden brightly, with a wink in Evie's direction.

'Come on into the back garden, everyone!' trilled Bridgie, in the sing-song voice that was only heard when the Crumps had company.

There were more people in the garden, some of whom Evie didn't recognise. Bridgie steered them towards the new barbecue. 'It's built-in!' She beamed.

'It's the most magnificent built-in barbecue I've seen!' Aden proclaimed.

Evie was impressed. Maybe Aden was good at this sort of thing. She edged away, as her mother guided Aden animatedly through the salads.

There was a tap on her shoulder and Beth's voice in her ear: 'He's cute.'

'I know.' And Aden did look cute, listening patiently to the litany of 'potato salad, bean salad . . .'

'Is he as nice as he looks, or is he a bastard like the rest of his gender?' asked Beth evenly.

'There you go again. Behaving in an unBethlike way.'

'I *am* Beth, so I can't behave in an unBethlike way.'

Evie pulled a face, to admit defeat, and changed the subject. 'Where's the booze?'

'I got you one.'

'Mmm. Buck's Fizz.'

Evie looked around at the sausage-waving throng. 'I wasn't expecting so many people. Nice to see Auntie Bea, though.' A fixture of their childhood, Bea had moved to Scotland and wasn't around much any more. She had always been the sort of woman who was described as 'larger than life'. Always laughing, usually sporting a boa, she'd let Evie smoke in her house and provided a respectable alibi when she'd been snogging sixth-formers in the park.

'I think she looks great,' said Beth fondly.

'So do I. She hasn't changed. I hadn't realised how much I miss her.'

Beth lowered her voice. 'Can I leave the twins with you again this week?'

'Sure.' Evie toyed with her drink. 'How are things?'

Beth's eyes were troubled. 'Things are awful, Evie.'

Evie decided to plunge in. 'You've seen a solicitor about a divorce, haven't you?'

Beth crumpled slightly. 'Yes,' she said wearily. 'It's not what I planned, but I don't have any choice.'

Evie dragged Beth to the side of the shed. 'It's adultery, isn't it?'

Beth was startled. 'How much do you know?'

'I knew something was going on. There's another woman, right?'

'Yes. Yes.' Beth drained the glass. 'Are you shocked?'

'I'm furious!'

'Please don't be angry. Some people just shouldn't get married.'

'That's hardly an excuse,' said Evie pompously. 'Honestly, it makes me *sick*.'

'Keep your voice down,' said Beth urgently. 'She's here!'

Who? The other woman? Evie started to splutter but Beth shushed her, looking about in a hunted manner. 'For God's sake, Evie, we don't want a scene. Oh!' Beth gasped. 'Here comes Marcus and his . . . girl.'

Evie wheeled round. Marcus, in one of his endless supply of suits, was heading their way with a slim, dazzlingly pretty girl at his side.

Beth gripped her arm. 'Just act normally. I won't have my dirty washing aired in public. *Evie*.'

Marcus was upon them, smiling broadly. 'Greetings, sibling-in-law,' he burbled.

As a reply Evie stared at him insolently.

Marcus was either too dense to notice, or too pleased with himself for managing to flaunt his mistress in public. 'This is Tamsin, my dental nurse.'

'Hello, there!' Tamsin was as bright as a button, fresh as a daisy.

'Hello there, yourself.' Evie spoke—she hoped—witheringly.

Tamsin did not appear in the least withered. 'Gosh, I'm so thrilled to meet you. You're an actress, aren't you? How exciting!' The accent was pure Sloane. Evidently Marcus was returning to his roots.

'Yes, I am. But surely things can get pretty hot in the surgery too.'

Tamsin was blind to any subtext. 'Ooh, yes. Specially with Marcus around.' She shot him a glance of collusion.

Evie's instinct was to punch Marcus first, then Tamsin. No, Tamsin first, then Marcus. Whatever. She had to get away from the gruesome pair before the urge got the better of her. 'I'm just going to find my boyfriend,' she muttered, and slid away.

Aden was still firmly under Bridgie's wing. She was introducing him to her 'lovely girlfriends' and Aden was smiling and nodding. Judging by the gales of post-menopausal hilarity he was going down a storm.

'Mum, are you trying to steal my bloke?' Evie was relishing the fiction she'd started. She took Aden's other arm in a lock every bit as strong as her mother's. 'I want to introduce A—er, Dan to Dad.'

'He hasn't put his lips to a sausage yet.' Bridgie did not give in easily.

'There's plenty of time for that. I want him to meet Dad.'

Reluctantly Bridgie relinquished her prize.

John was standing a little aloof from the crowd, one foot in a flower-bed and a bemused look on his face. 'Wasn't this meant to be a family do?' he asked Evie. 'I should have known something was afoot when Mum forced me into my good shorts.'

'And damn fine shorts they are too, Dad.' Evie stretched to kiss his whiskery cheek. 'This is Dan.' Suddenly she felt uncomfortable. She didn't like pulling the wool over her father's eyes.

'Ah!' John stuck out his hand. 'How are you, son? You're very welcome.'

'I'm glad to be here.' Aden sounded so sincere that Evie was impressed.

'What do you do?' John asked, then added, 'Don't worry, I'm not asking about your prospects. I'm just interested.'

'Right now I'm an assistant director on commercials and TV drama, but I've just directed my first independent film and one day I hope to direct full-time.'

'Good for you. Yes. Good for you.' John was obviously unable to conjure up a pertinent question to ask, perhaps because Aden's career was so far removed from his own life at the bank. 'Got any hobbies?' he asked lamely.

Evie smiled. She eyed Aden with interest. He'd done so well up to now. Could he come up with a hobby to chat to her dad about?

'Just birdwatching.'

John and Evie both gasped, John because birdwatching was one of his main reasons for living, Evie because, unless Aden was a better actor than she was, it was *true*.

'Where do you twitch?' asked John breathlessly.

'Suffolk. Best birds in the British Isles. Saw a hoopoe last week.'

'No!' John seemed amazed.

Evie was amazed too. Amazed that she'd introduced a closet bird-watcher to her family as her boyfriend. 'What the hell is a hoopoe?'

It was, she discovered, as Aden and her father fell over themselves trying to describe it, a large black and white bird that visits our shores each summer and sounds like this—*hoopoooo, hoopoooo*.

That was plenty of information—in fact, far too much. Evie spotted Auntie Bea draped over the garden bench and left the men to their feathery impressions.

'Evie, Evie, Evie!' boomed Auntie Bea fondly.

'Auntie Bea, Auntie Bea, Auntie Bea!' Evie hugged her. 'It's been years! How come you're back from Scotland?'

'Fancied a change. You know me, I like to be where the action is.'

'So how come you're here?'

'Now, now, madam. Your mother's gone to a lot of trouble.'

'I know.' Evie looked sheepish. Auntie Bea had always been able to get through to her. Many times during her childhood Evie had blasphemously wished that Auntie Bea was her real mother. 'When did I start calling you Auntie?' asked Evie, in the mood to be nostalgic.

'You didn't. It was Beth. She was only toddling and because I lived a few doors away and was always in and out of your house she must have presumed I was an auntie. I loved it.' She tilted her head. 'Who'd have thought . . .' She turned to Evie with a grin. 'Remember when you came sobbing to me convinced you were pregnant? How old were you?'

'Twelve. How was I to know you couldn't get pregnant from holding a boy's hand during Irish-dancing class?'

'Quite. Perfectly feasible. You came to me again a few years later.'

Evie grimaced. 'That scare was real, though. I was so frightened. You were the only adult I could dream of telling.' She looked into Bea's wide, lined face, framed by pure white hair. 'Thank God you were there. Sex was a hanging offence in our house.'

'It only took a quick trip to Boots and a pregnancy test to sort you out, thank God.'

'And a good ticking-off! I remember you giving me a good ten minutes on how sex is a beautiful thing to be enjoyed by two mature people who had real feelings for each other. My mother never mentioned sex and if anyone else did she had the house fumigated.'

Auntie Bea swerved the conversation. 'Beth tells me you're aware of the changes in her life,' she said.

'Oh.' Evie was surprised that Auntie Bea should already be up to speed but, then, Beth had also relied heavily on her for advice when they were younger. It made sense that she should turn to her now. 'Yes. She has. I've been trying to keep out of it but it's not easy.'

'No.'

'I'm not happy about it. Obviously.'

Bea studied Evie's face. 'Do you remember what I said when we were worried that you might be pregnant?'

'Which bit? There was an awful lot of it.'

'I said that whatever happened you'd have to make the decision on your own, for yourself, based on your own feelings and reasoning. That the only way to be content is to be true to yourself. That you shouldn't waste time worrying what others think of you.'

'I remember now.' Evie frowned. 'Why are you bringing that up?'

'I'm just suggesting that when you look at Beth's situation remember that people, however much you love them, won't always behave the way you want them to. Everyone must follow their own guiding light.'

'I know that,' said Evie earnestly. 'Don't get me wrong. I think she's dead right to leave him.'

'Good for you!' Bea enfolded Evie in another hug that smelt of vanilla and musk.

Suddenly, Evie's ears were assailed by a burst of Latin-American music. 'Oh my God! Mum's starting the salsa!'

A horde of whooping ladies swarmed onto the patio, dragging men ruthlessly after them. One of the men, Evie noted, was Aden.

'Your young man isn't *entirely* at home,' said Bea, with a twinkle.

Poor Aden was almost invisible in the sea of flailing limbs. Bridgie was twirling him like a top.

'I'd better rescue him.' Evie strode over and purposefully grabbed Aden's hand and spirited him away while her mother was engrossed in a complicated manoeuvre involving some maracas. 'Trust me. You'll be safe here.' She bundled him into the garden shed and banged the door behind them. 'Sorry, I should have rescued you sooner.'

'That was scary.' Aden was trembling. 'One minute they were chatting about gardening, the next they were leaping about like a voodoo cult.'

Evie laughed. 'Sit down and make yourself comfortable. When you've recovered we can plan our escape.'

'Blimey. An armchair.' Aden sank into it.

'This is where Dad escapes the long arm of my mother. It's his refuge.'

'I like your mum.' He said it as if it was the most reasonable thing in the world. 'I do!' he insisted, in answer to Evie's disbelieving look. 'She's lively. She's got spirit. She's being very nice to me.'

'Only 'cos she thinks you're my boyfriend. Don't get used to it. You're living a lie,' she ended dramatically, perching on the arm of the chair.

'It's not so funny now we're here, is it?'

Evie sighed. 'I know. Dad really likes you.'

'We could always confess.'

Evie was horrified. 'I'd never live it down. No, you and I can have a huge row next week and vow never to speak to each other again.'

Aden looked distinctly uncomfortable. He shook his head. 'This isn't a made-for-TV movie. No, we'll just have to split up 'cos . . . pressure of work keeps us apart.'

'It'll have to be pressure of *your* work. *I* don't have any. Your career takes off and we never get to see each other so our relationship just dwindles and dies.'

There was silence.

'It feels quite sad,' Aden said. 'I want you to know that of all the fake relationships I've ever had this has been the best. And now that our fake love affair is over, let's be fake friends for ever.'

Evie laughed. 'For ever.'

Aden smiled ruefully. 'Let's be real friends, Evie. This joke's giving me the creeps. We *are* friends, aren't we?'

'Of course we are.' Evie was brisk. She hadn't expected sincere emotion here in the shed. 'What's that pong?'

'Smells like dog to me.'

'Henry!' Evie kissed the black snout sticking out from under the workbench. 'Out you come, boy!'

With a great deal of waddling, straining, huffing and puffing, Henry emerged and a flurry of licks and tail-wagging commenced. 'Ooooh, I love you, Henry.'

'Hello, Henry.' Aden offered a hand, which was politely slobbered over. 'Lovely boy. What a beauty.'

'He likes you too.' Evie was like a stage mother about Henry, absurdly pleased when somebody took to him. 'Sorry about the smell, though.'

'Who minds doggy smells?' said Aden, playing with Henry's ears.

Suddenly there was a loud crash. The salsa music stopped abruptly and was replaced by muted screams. Aden and Evie looked at each other, then raced out of the door.

There was chaos on the patio. Several Surbiton bodies wiggled among the upturned garden furniture. The survivors were staggering to their knees and dusting themselves off. The yelps and shrieks were fading.

Bridgie, hair askew, yelled at Evie, 'Don't just stand there! *Help!*'

Evie righted some chairs, while Aden coaxed a rotund lady to her feet.

'Where's John? Where does that man get to when I need him?' shrieked Bridgie, her hysteria rising a notch.

Evie could see her father: he was lurking on the far side of the shed, his shoulders shaking with mirth.

Beth put an arm round her mother and led her into the house. A moment or two later she emerged. 'Mum's gone for a little lie-down. Why don't we all have a good stiff drink?'

Evie was impressed by her sister's presence of mind. So impressed that she actually helped to hand robust gin-and-tonics to the flushed ladies. I'm proud of her, thought Evie. She knew that inside Beth was in turmoil, but it didn't show. That's where we're different, she mused, as she spied Tamsin giggling animatedly at Marcus's side.

Aden saw the glint in her eye. 'Er, what are you planning?' he asked.

'It's time I sorted out some garden pests.' Evie strode towards the two.

'All right, are we?' The chilling sarcasm was lost on Marcus and Tamsin.

'Yes, thank you very much,' chirped Tamsin brightly.

Ignoring her, Evie asked Marcus, 'Do you have anything to say for yourself, Marcus?'

Marcus looked wary. 'On what subject?'

Aden came up behind Evie and laid a hand on her arm.

'Gerroff.' She turned to Tamsin. 'I know all about you, love. I know your sordid little secret. How can you show your face here, of all places, with him?' She jabbed a finger hard in Marcus's direction.

'Now look here—' began Marcus. He was silenced by the wail that arose from Tamsin.

'She knows! She knows! I'm so humiliated.' Tamsin's perfect face was scrunched up. She darted, sobbing, into the house and through it.

The slam of the front door galvanised Marcus into action. His bland features contorted with anger and he hissed, 'You always have to interfere, don't you?' into Evie's face. Then he raced after Tamsin.

Evie was shocked by the effect of her words. On the far side of the silent, staring guests, she caught Beth's eye. Her sister was standing with an empty tray. Bea approached her to place a comforting arm round her, and Beth turned away from Evie's gaze.

But the look of pain and panic in her eyes etched itself in Evie's mind. 'Aden, we have to go,' she muttered, her throat dry.

With no farewells they went out to his car and drove away.

Eight

THE OPEN-TOP was parked by the river, surrounded by ducks squawking in their daft insistent way.

'They're hoping for a chip,' remarked Evie.

'They'll be lucky.' Aden was making strange shapes with his mouth to cool the fat, hot, delicious chip he'd just popped into it. There was a pause, punctured by the quacking of waterfowl and the mastication of fried potato.

'Thank you for today,' said Evie.

'I had a great time.'

'You mean you enjoyed being squeezed half to death by my mother, talking about birdwatching, witnessing a mass salsa collapse and being part of a family disaster?'

'Yes,' Aden said patiently. 'I enjoyed being squeezed. She meant well. Yes, I enjoyed talking about birdwatching. I enjoyed the salsa incident.

Very few people are privileged to see such a thing. And I don't think that it was a family disaster.'

'Beth was devastated.'

'You're exaggerating.' Aden had a way of saying stuff like this in a non-confrontational way that didn't make Evie flare up. 'You did it for the right reasons, even if it was a bit . . . reckless.'

'I did it because I can't keep my nose out of other people's business,' confessed Evie, in a rare moment of candour. 'Beth made it clear she just wanted to get through the day without any trouble. But I had to go in like Annie Oakley.'

'Beth's your sister. She'll understand. Just talk to her about it.'

'That's what we don't do.' Evie sighed. 'Crumps don't talk.'

'It's time you started, then. You talk to everybody else.'

Evie popped a chip miserably into her mouth. 'I'm sorry to drag you through all this shit, Aden. It's not your problem.'

'Haven't you been listening? I enjoyed myself. My family don't get together much.'

'Why not?'

'Oh, Dad lives in Florida and Mum married again. My stepfather isn't such a great guy. My brother's kind of difficult. Works in the City. There aren't many dos—nobody bothers to arrange them.'

Evie was moved. Who would have imagined that organised, sensible Aden was so lonely at heart?

'So that's why you liked being at my parents'. Well, you're welcome to take my place at all future birthdays and Christmases,' smiled Evie, 'and divorces.' She gulped.

'Let's get you home.' The revving of the engine sent the ducks, much affronted, skedaddling back to the water.

'You promised,' insisted Evie. She didn't relish baby-sitting on her own.

'I didn't,' Bing insisted right back. 'I have plans. I'm busy tonight. You're the big mouth who offered, not me. I don't do kids.'

So Evie went upstairs to flat B on her own. Caroline's door was open. 'Hello?' Evie edged inside. She could hear Milly crying—maybe Caroline was having trouble settling her. She tiptoed towards the kitchen and the sound of the sobs.

When she put her head round the door she saw Caroline at the table. There was a crumpled piece of paper in her fist.

'Caroline, what's wrong?' Evie moved round to face her.

'It's nothing,' said Caroline, throwing the paper across the room. She sniffled and wiped her eyes with a tissue. 'I'm fine,' she said, in a clear, strong voice. 'Milly's asleep. I won't be long.' She stood up.

'You look lovely,' said Evie admiringly. 'Where are you going?' She trotted behind Caroline like a little dog greedy for titbits.

'Cinema. I'm going on my own. That's what you really want to know.'

Evie shrugged unconvincingly. 'No, it's not. You go and enjoy yourself.'

She settled herself on the sagging couch while Caroline checked on Milly and then left.

Barely a minute later Evie was off the sofa like a greyhound and into the kitchen. 'Damn!' The screwed-up letter was gone. Caroline was a fine judge of character. Hating herself, Evie placed a toe on the pedal of the bin. Nothing.

She settled down again in the newly painted sitting room to watch the news, but her gaze was soon drifting round the room. Framed photos of Milly stood on every surface. No pictures of her family, noticed Evie, and felt sorry for her.

The wacky item at the end of the news was about a cat who could answer the phone, but Evie barely noticed it. She was too busy thinking of what might have brought tears to Caroline's eyes. Money, she guessed. Debt. There wasn't much Evie could do about that.

'Darling,' rasped Meredith, 'Hugh James has got back to me about that little audition you did for him.'

Evie crossed her fingers, her legs, her eyes. 'And?'

'You've got the job, darling.'

Evie was stunned. She had prepared herself assiduously for disappointment but she wasn't sure how to cope with success.

Meredith was typically vague with the nitty-gritty. Shooting would start in a few weeks. A script would arrive in a few days. The fee was in negotiation. What Meredith *could* confirm was that the series was called *The Setting of the Sun* and Evie's character was called Hepsibah.

'Hepsibah!' cooed Evie, waltzing round her bedroom. 'What a lovely name!' She stopped when she caught sight of herself in the mirror. She traced her features with her fingers, trembling with emotion. 'Oh, Belle,' she whispered. 'I'm on my way. I'm a real actress at last!'

There was nobody around to share her news. Bing had left for his evening performance. Sacha was having a two-for-one massage evening at Calmer Karma. Evie didn't dare call her mother or her sister after the scenes in Surbiton. Aden! He'd asked her to let him know.

'I got it! I got it! I got it!'

'Great! Calm down!' laughed Aden who, right on cue, suggested a drink to celebrate.

'Good idea! Let's go somewhere special.'

The Hand and Flower was a pub, nothing more, nothing less. There were beer slops on the tables, crisps trodden into the carpet.

'I don't go to special places much. Will this do?' Aden was apologetic.

'This is perfect.' Evie was so elated she would have been happy in an abattoir. She was bouncing in her seat like Tigger when Aden brought their drinks to the table.

'Here's to you.' Aden raised his lager with ceremony.

'Here's to Hepsibah!' Evie raised her vodka and tonic. 'Do you mind if I burble on for a bit? Maybe quite a long bit?'

'Be my guest.' Aden sat back, a little smile on his face.

'I don't have all the details yet but I do know it's a series based on a Victorian novel called *The Setting of the Sun*. I *think* it's six episodes. It's the story of a young woman who is married against her will to this grumpy older guy. He obligingly dies, and leaves her alone with two young children. Victorian society expects her to be all wimpish and faint all over the place but we watch her blossom into a mature independent woman. It's quite weepy, apparently.' Evie leaned back with a sigh. 'It sounds so good I'd watch it if I wasn't in it.' She jumped forward again, elbows in the slick of beer that adorned their table. 'I'm her maid, Hepsibah. I'm very loyal and our friendship grows as we struggle together. Oh, Aden, all that and I get paid too!'

'I should hope so.'

'I'm a real proper actress! A proper one! A real, real one!'

'Yes. You are.'

'Right. That's enough burbling. What have you done today, Aden?'

'Let's see. I spent time looking at pictures of locations for my next job, then I got back to the editing suite to put the final touches to my film.'

'Sorry, Aden, there's too much burbling still in me. It has to come out or I might need to be hospitalised.'

'Go on. It's quite relaxing, actually. You don't seem to need any input.'

Evie opened a packet of crisps. 'I wonder if there'll be any famous names in it.' She sat bolt upright. 'I never thought of that. Ralph Fiennes might be in it. Or Ewan McGregor!'

Aden put his head to one side. 'And if he is?'

'He might fall madly in love with me!' said Evie, through a mouthful of crisps.

'Thought you were off actors,' said Aden, finding something of interest deep in his glass.

'I'm off unknown actors,' confirmed Evie. 'Nobody in their right mind is off famous actors.'

'A famous actor is the same as an unknown actor except he's more . . . well, famous,' persevered Aden.

'I could get my wedding in *Hello!*.'

Aden winced. 'There's a man with odd hair gesticulating at you,' he informed her.

'That'll be Bernard.'

And it was. He was at the bar in one of his less successful new outfits. He wasn't designed to wear leather trousers, particularly not cheap ones. Aden beckoned him over.

'Hello, there,' said Bernard, head bobbing in self-deprecation. 'OK to join you?' He looked liked a puppy fearing a kick.

'Of course. Lovely to see you. Sit down.'

Bernard pulled up a stool, which lifted him much higher than Evie and Aden. Looking down at them from his perch, he said quietly, 'I'll find a chair—oh, and I'll get a round in.' He pronounced the last bit in inverted commas, evidently proud to be talking like one of the lads now that he was in a public house.

After he'd creaked away, Aden whispered. 'I didn't recognise him. What happened to his hair? Was he attacked?'

'No. I'm afraid it's a haircut. Poor thing. He's doing his best—and he's come a long way. He's wearing new clothes and eating properly.' She stared at Bernard's back. 'And the hair will grow,' she added wistfully.

Bernard inserted himself between them at a more comfortable height. 'I ordered myself a Guinness,' he confided.

'Right,' said Aden. 'Good.'

Bernard lowered his voice. 'It's my first ever beer. I feel terribly guilty. Mother abhorred beer.'

'Sip it and see what you think!' encouraged Evie.

With trepidation Bernard brought the glass to his lips. He took a sip. He swallowed. He smiled.

Four Guinnesses later Bernard was talkative. 'Of course I want a relationship,' he said, far more loudly than was his habit. 'I want a relationship more than anything in the world. But I can never have one.'

Aden was slumped, chin on chest.

Unlike Evie, who was electrified and alert. 'Why can't you have one? You're as good as the next man,' she urged. 'You can fall in love and be happy ever after. You deserve it. *If that's what you want.*'

'It is! It is what I want!'

'Then you and I are going out tomorrow night and I'm going to coach you while you approach girls and chat them up.'

All the Guinness left Bernard's system instantaneously and he said timorously, 'Oh, I couldn't.'

'So you want to be alone for ever?'

'Evie, don't be too hard on him,' Aden muttered.

'It's a fair question.' Evie was adamant. 'Bernard, do you want to die alone or do you want to come out with me and possibly meet someone special?'

Bernard hung his head. He didn't have the weapons to fight Evie in this mood. 'I want to come out with you and possibly meet someone special,' he said, his voice very small.

Last orders were called and Aden stood up. 'I'd better get off. Bernard will see you home.'

'There's time for one more,' cajoled Evie, as Bernard disappeared off to the loo.

'Nah. Don't fancy it.'

'At least wait until Bernard gets back.'

'I'll go now. I feel a bit uncomfortable around Bernard, to be honest.'

'Why? He's harmless.' Evie defended her *protégé*.

'That's true. Actually, it's you who makes me feel uncomfortable. You're picking up where his dragon of a mother left off.'

Evie was stung. 'I'm trying to *help* him.'

'Really? Or are you enjoying the power you have over him to make him do what you think is best for him?'

Evie repeated herself. 'I'm trying to help.'

'Why do you treat him like Henry, then?' He shrugged. 'Look, ignore me. It's not my business. I always seem to spoil your fun, don't I?' And, with that, he stood up and left.

Evie and Bernard strolled home together, sunk in their own thoughts.

'There's that car again,' commented Bernard, as they turned into Kemp Street.

'What car?'

'The white one across the road. It's been there on and off for a week. Whoever it is inside, they seem to be watching our house.'

'Come on, let's get inside.' Evie picked up the pace. The knowledge that the stranger's eyes were on her made her fumble with her keys.

'Allow me,' said Bernard gallantly. He took her keys and dropped them. 'Oh dear. A little too much Guinness.'

He had managed to drop the keys over the side of the steps, deep into the holly bush. 'Oh, Bernard!' Evie was exasperated and frightened. What if the figure in the white car decided to step across the road and introduce themselves? With a knife. 'Use *your* keys. *Quickly!*'

'Ah. Yes. Now.' Bernard patted his pockets elaborately.

Footsteps sounded on the path, and Evie yelped as a figure walked purposefully into the circle of porch light. 'Bing! Thank God!'

'That's better than your usual "oh-it's-you". What's going on?'

'He's full of Guinness, he's dropped my keys and there's a stalker watching us, so *open the door!*'

'You're not staying in here,' said Bing firmly. Evie was at the end of his bed, cradling a mug of hot chocolate. 'You'll get me a bad reputation.'

'I'm worried about the stalker.'

'Give me strength,' Bing beseeched the ceiling. 'Why have you decided it's a stalker? At the moment it's just someone sitting in a car. We've only got Bernard's word for it that they were here before.'

'It was only a theory,' Evie said huffily.

'How's this for a theory? *You're deranged.* Now get off my bed. If the stalker jumps you just scream and I'll write to the police straight away. Good night.'

'Good night,' said Evie, but she didn't move.

Bing burrowed under the covers in an effort to evict Evie.

'Aden's not very happy with me,' said Evie abruptly.

'Oh?' Bing stopped burrowing. 'How come?'

'He had a right go at me. Some rubbish about the way I treat Bernard, saying I only try to help him 'cos I'm power-crazed.' She cast a sideways glance in Bing's direction to gauge his reaction. 'That's not fair, is it?'

'No comment, doll.'

'It's *not* fair. I'm not horrible.' Evie yawned. 'Can't I sleep with you?'

'*Never* say that again.' Bing shuddered. 'How do you feel about Aden having a go at you?'

The question was unexpected. 'I feel . . . If I'm honest I feel a bit—a *little* bit—upset because Aden's opinion of me has gone down and he's such a nice, decent person.' Evie nodded. 'Yup, that's how I feel. Aden's a bit of a Goody-two-shoes but I like him. And now he thinks I'm a bitch.' Evie did one of her sudden about-turns. 'Sod him.'

'If I tell you something that will surprise you about Aden will you go to bed like a good girl?'

'No.'

'Then you'll never know.' Bing nestled under the covers again.

'Fine by me.' Evie slurped the last of the chocolate, then said tetchily, 'All right, I promise.'

Bing sat up, plumped his pillows and began. 'This revelation is in two parts,' he began, thoroughly enjoying himself. 'The first part is, Aden put you up for *The Setting of the Sun.*'

Evie puckered her brow. 'No, he didn't.'

'Ho ho, yes, he did. One of the chorus in *Joseph* works part-time in Hugh James's office. Apparently Hugh James always employs Aden for his projects. Aden came in one day and suggested you as Hepsibah. Said you were a star in the making.'

Evie was knocked out. 'Why didn't he tell me?' Vague feelings of guilt swirled in her. 'I went on and on about it. Why did he keep it a secret?'

'Because, and this is the second part of my revelation, *he's mad about you.*'

Now, Evie was as vain as the next girl, and occasionally had fits of self-delusion worthy of Sacha, but she laughed at this. 'No, he isn't! You're crazy!'

'I've always known it. It's in the way he looks at you. I'm telling you, doll. Aden is nuts about you.'

Evie had plenty of evidence to shore up her case for the defence. 'But he encouraged me to go out with Dan. He even covered up for him about going to Spain. And if he fancied me surely he'd have made sure I knew that he suggested me for Hepsibah.'

'How come you spend so much time talking about men and yet understand them only a *little* better than you understand quantum physics? Let me explain. Aden is a decent, modest guy. You have never given him the tiniest scrap of encouragement so he doesn't think he has a hope in hell with you. He's one of those rare things: a genuinely nice guy.'

Evie stared at Bing. Had she really been so blind?

'I like you like this,' said Bing. 'So, the sixty-four-million-dollar question is: how do you feel about Aden now?'

'Why should this change anything?' said Evie, with a hint of her old defiance. 'He's still dull and pompous and a killjoy.'

'Oh, grow up,' said Bing vehemently. 'I have a low boredom threshold and I don't find him dull. He's thoughtful, intelligent and makes you laugh. He doesn't bury you under a mountain of compliments, but that doesn't mean he's boring. As for being a killjoy—wasn't he dead right when he warned you about Dan? If you're frank with yourself, isn't he dead right about the way you treat Bernard?'

There was no answer from the end of the bed.

The next morning the car was there again. Sacha was coming over and Evie phoned her to warn her. Sacha had given the driver a surreptitious once-over as she arrived. 'It's definitely a person. It's wearing dark glasses so I couldn't tell whether it was a man or a woman.'

'I hope it's not some ex-lover with a grudge,' said Bing anxiously.

'Please God it's nothing to do with me,' said Sacha, looking distressed.

Bing closed his eyes and said, with strained patience, 'And why, pray, would *your* stalker be watching *our* house?'

'Who can tell what goes on in their crazy minds?' mused Sacha.

'Whoever it is, it just has to be *bad*, doesn't it?' reasoned Evie. 'I mean, nobody sits outside your house wearing dark glasses for days on end to give you good news, do they?' She slipped into her bedroom to retrieve her flip-flops from under the bed.

Suddenly a dusty smell, sweet yet old, swamped Evie's senses. She closed her eyes and inhaled deeply. It was a nostalgic scent, provoking a vague memory just round the corner of her mind . . . She opened her eyes wide. It was the smell of Belle's big black leather handbag that Evie had played with as a child.

The aroma was fading, ebbing like a wave sliding down the shore. Evie strained after it, but it dissolved.

Oh, Belle, she thought, thank you. Everything was going to be OK. This was Belle's house and Belle was still watching over them all.

Rehearsals would start on September 1, Meredith informed Evie. Shooting would take eight weeks. The stars were Anna Friel and Toby Stephens. The fee was, well, wonderful.

After hopping about, screaming and burping for some time after this call, Evie realised she'd be able to get the front of the house painted.

'Beth!' Evie hadn't expected to see her sister on the doorstep. 'Get inside. Quickly!' She tugged her sister over the threshold and slammed the front door. 'We've got a stalker.'

'You really are the girl with everything.'

When she was sitting beside Beth on the sofa, Evie said in a rush, 'I'm sorry. I'm so sorry. And I'm sorry I didn't ring to say sorry. I shouldn't have made a scene at Mum's.'

'It's all right.' Beth smiled sadly. 'And that is the least of my troubles. I've come to see if you can help me.'

'I hope I can.' Evie was aware that she didn't have much to offer someone as mature and organised as her sister.

'The you-know-what has really hit the fan in Henley,' said Beth. Her interlocked fingers writhed in her lap. 'I've told Marcus I want a divorce. He's rather . . . unhappy about it.'

'Serves him right.'

'*Please* don't talk like that. He won't get out of the house so I have to. Is there any chance of a flat here for me and the twins?'

Evie shook her head. 'I can't help. The flats are occupied.'

Beth nodded. 'I just . . . well, it was worth a try.'

'But you can stay with Bing and me,' exclaimed Evie. 'The twins are small, we can tuck them in on the sofa. You and I can share my bed.'

Beth was laughing and shaking her head. 'That's so sweet,' she said, 'but I have to give the twins some stability. That means beds of their own in a room of their own. Thanks for the offer, though.' She sat back and wiped her eyes. 'I'd better get out there and start flat-hunting. Bea's helping me. She can work miracles when she puts her mind to it.'

'When did Bea lose the "auntie"?' asked Evie.

'I can't call her "auntie" now, can I?' said Beth, and laughed.

'I'll always call her Auntie Bea,' said Evie stubbornly.

'That's different,' smiled Beth. 'I'm planning to live in London, so as soon as I'm settled you must bring the delicious Dan round. You can baby-sit and snog on the sofa all night."

'Eh? Oh. Yes!' Evie remembered, with a start, that Beth thought Aden was Dan. She also thought he was Evie's boyfriend. And, apparently, she thought he was delicious.

Taking Bernard out and showing him to the lay-deez was a two-woman job and Sacha was glad to help out. She felt it would be instrumental in helping him to get over his feelings for her.

Evie tapped her slingbacks in the hall, waiting impatiently for Bernard to appear. *'Bernard, come on!'*

A few minutes later, suitably trousered in dark denim, Bernard followed his guides out into the warm evening. 'Where are you taking me?' he asked, evidently terrified of the reply.

'To Manhattan Dreams,' Evie informed him.

'*Manhattan* Dreams? In Camden?' queried Bernard.

'Yup. Don't worry. It's better than it sounds.' Evie flicked some fluff off his collar. 'We're here to look after you. It'll be *fun*.'

'Yes.' Bernard smiled unconvincingly.

Sacha kissed his cheek. 'Forget me,' she whispered huskily. 'There are plenty of other fish in the nightclub.'

So, puzzled as well as scared witless, Bernard stumbled into the world of Manhattan Dreams.

Untouched since it sprang to life in the eighties, the club had a flickering, multicoloured lightshow and a tiny dance floor lit from beneath. The glossy bar was manned by boys resplendent in red waistcoats and silver bow ties. Palms sprouted from dark corners, bending over the heads of girls dressed to the nines. Now punters were outnumbered by the prowling bouncers, but by midnight the place would be packed.

'What a dump,' said Sacha, under her breath.

'It's perfect.' Evie adored nightclubs. For her, the kitscher the better. 'This is going to be a scream.'

They found a red banquette and ordered cocktails, which arrived bristling with tiny umbrellas.

Bernard picked up a glass. 'I spoke to Mother every day but, really, you two are my only female friends. I'm not sure I could engage another lady in deep conversation.'

'Aaah, Bernard.' Evie squeezed his arm, but gently so she didn't alarm him. 'It's so nice to know that you think of us as friends. You don't have to find a girlfriend tonight, think of it as dipping your toe in the water.'

'Yes.' Bernard rocked backwards and forwards. 'All right.'

The club was filling up and the DJ had turned up the volume.

Evie noticed a dark-haired guy staring at them. She dropped her eyes, then cast a surreptitious glance his way. His eyes were still on them.

'Look around you, Bernard,' Evie focused on him. 'See anybody nice?'

'I think I need another drink.'

'Good idea.' Sacha leapt up. 'I'll get us three more cocktails. Different ones this time.'

Evie studied Bernard. She'd seen that look before: Henry on Bonfire Night. Aden's accusations, buried in the excitement, clamoured to be heard again. She whispered to Bernard, 'If you want to go home, just say the word.'

Bernard looked at her as if he couldn't believe his ears. 'Really?'

'Of course!' She laughed.

His shoulders sank again. 'No. You're right to make me do this. I've got to start somewhere. I'm staying.'

'Attaboy.'

It was eleven o'clock. Sprawled on the banquette in a posture of hopelessness, Evie was saying, with synthetic calm, 'There must be *somebody* you like the look of, Bernard.'

Sacha, who had more energy than Evie and had downed several strange blue concoctions, pointed at a girl gyrating on the dance floor in a fringed skirt. 'Her. What about her?'

'She's too . . . thoughtful.' Bernard had almost exhausted the wealth of adjectives the dictionary had to offer. The girl with a blonde crop was 'too careless'. The one in the sparkly slash neck was 'too cunning' . . . Anyone would have thought that Bernard was trying to wriggle out of the whole thing.

The dark-haired guy was still looking over. He and his gaggle of mates had migrated nearer. They were two banquettes away, growing braver with each pint.

Evie decided to take matters into her own hands. 'Bernard, look, *she* is perfect.'

A girl was sitting alone, awkwardly, on a low pouffe a few feet away, scanning the dance floor shyly. She seemed a little removed from the action, which was what made her 'perfect' for Bernard's first foray into the realm of chatting up.

Bernard surveyed her with trepidation. She was pretty but with none of the sparkly make-up favoured by the other girls. He took a deep breath.

'How shall I begin?' he murmured.

'Introduce yourself and ask if you can sit down,' instructed Evie.

'Right. Right.' Bernard nodded. He stood up, smoothed back the various lengths of his hair, and walked over to the girl on the pouffe.

Evie and Sacha propelled themselves to the end of their banquette and leaned in to eavesdrop on Bernard's endeavours.

The dark-haired guy and one of his mates broke away from their gang to alight on the far end of Evie's banquette. She noticed this out of the corner of her eye and smirked inwardly.

Bernard bent over the pouffe girl, who jolted backwards. 'Hello, I'm Bernard Briggs,' he shouted, sticking out his hand.

'I'm Cathy.' The girl went pink as she shook it.

A voice from behind Evie interrupted her surveillance: 'All right, ladies? Mind if we join you?'

Evie turned and looked into the really rather brown eyes of the dark-haired bloke. 'It's a free country,' she said sassily.

'Ssssh!' Sacha pulled at Evie to get her back to watching Bernard.

Evie rolled her eyes at the dark-haired guy, and turned to see the girl looking uncertainly at Bernard, who was saying, 'May I sit down?'

'I'm Gareth, by the way.' The boy had shuffled closer to Evie. He cocked his head on one side. 'Do I get to know your name?'

'Guess,' said Evie, feeling coquettish.

'Liz, as in Hurley? Pamela, as in Anderson?'

'Look, look! Shit!' Sacha was murmuring urgently.

Evie dragged her attention back to Bernard. Cathy, who was apparently as shy and awkward as he was, had agreed to let him sit down. Bernard, alarmed by his own success, was attempting to make Cathy budge up so that he could join her on the pouffe, which had definitely been made for one.

'Marilyn, as in Monroe?' persisted Gareth.

The only way to fit two bums on the pouffe was to sit back to back. Folded up like a stick insect, Bernard was shouting over his shoulder, 'What's your favourite food?'

'I can go if you'd rather,' said Gareth good-humouredly. 'It's not much fun talking to the back of someone's head.'

'Sorry.' Evie smiled her best, widest smile. She wanted Gareth to stay. It was a long time since she had been eyed up in a nightclub. 'I'm Evie and this is Sacha.'

At the mention of her name Sacha swivelled round and yapped, 'Where did you spring from?'

Gareth's friend, evidently earmarked for her in some secret guy-arrangement, asked, 'You girls fancy a bevvy?'

They did, of course, and while Gareth and his friend battled to the bar, Evie said, 'We've got to put Cathy and Bernard out of their misery.'

She stalked over to them and said brightly, 'There you are, Bernard! Come back and join us, you naughty boy!' She grasped him by the hand, yanked him up and mouthed, 'Sorry!' at Cathy, who looked relieved.

'Hmm. Not too good, was it?' Bernard mopped his sweating brow.

'It was a start,' Evie encouraged him. 'Next time just try to make sure you're facing the girl you're talking to.'

'Courage, Bernard!' Sacha gripped him by the shoulders. 'There's a sexy piece on her own over there with a whole free seat beside her. Go!'

Bernard set off like a shaky Exocet.

'Way to go, Sash,' said Evie admiringly.

'I have to help him.' Sacha's face clouded. 'I'll never forgive myself if he pines for me for the rest of his life.'

Evie was tipsy enough to put her right on this, but Gareth and his mate swooped in with luminous cocktails.

'Cheers!' All four clinked glasses, but as Evie and Sacha knocked theirs back they were watching the seat opposite.

'She's chattering to him!' Sacha said softly. 'Bingo!' They high-fived each other.

'Why aren't you two dancing?' asked Gareth. His arm was arranged casually along the back of the banquette.

'Not in the mood. We're just . . . chilling out.' The flirtatious eye contact was doing Evie the world of good.

Sacha wasn't too good at flirting. She preferred the more direct approach. 'You needn't think you're going to get a snog,' she informed Gareth's mate. 'We're here on a mission.'

'Didn't want a snog,' mumbled Gareth's mate, affronted.

'I do,' said Gareth, close to Evie's ear.

'Like I said, we're chilling out.' Evie smiled, hopefully in a way that was encouraging but not *too* encouraging.

Opposite, Bernard was gazing intently at the pretty brunette while she nattered happily, gesticulating freely.

'He's not saying much.' Sacha frowned.

'He's fascinated by her!' Evie was delighted. 'He's pulled!'

Gareth's mate muttered, 'Lucky bastard.' He was now facing away from Sacha, staring moodily at the dance floor.

The brunette opposite jumped up, gesturing at Bernard to stay put, then tripped off in the direction of the Ladies.

Evie and Sacha beckoned to Bernard excitedly.

'Well?' said Evie.

'Well?' said Sacha.

Bernard seemed afraid to speak. Eventually he said, 'I can't understand a word she's saying. She's foreign.'

Evie groaned. 'Why are you sitting there if you can't understand her? Cut your losses. She left you to go to the loo. Don't be there when she gets back. Be *there*.' She pointed at a red-haired girl standing by a pillar.

'She's got nice hair,' conceded Bernard.

'Off you go.'

And off he went. Henry-like, thought Evie ruefully.

The girl seemed grateful for the distraction. And as far as Evie and Sacha could ascertain, she was speaking English.

Evie sat back. 'What's a nice boy like you doing in a place like this?' she asked Gareth.

'Hoping to meet a nice girl like you.'

'She's not nice, mate,' said a voice close behind them.

'Bing!' He was kneeling behind them, his perfect teeth gleaming.

'Sorry, mate. Sorry.' Gareth removed his arm at warp speed and scooted off down the cushions.

'Oh, get yourself back here,' said Bing impatiently. 'I'm her lodger, not her boyfriend.'

Gareth scurried back, but not as close as before.

Bing appraised Manhattan Dreams. 'Nothing much here for me,' he said. 'It's a temple to heterosexuality. I feel like an alcoholic in a dairy.'

Behind him, the brunette had returned from the Ladies and had bought two drinks from the bar. She was looking around her, puzzled, then spotted Bernard. He had not guessed that she was Spanish, but he might have done if she'd been pawing the ground and huffing angrily as she was now. She downed her drink in one gulp, before shooting Bernard a murderous look and knocking back the drink she'd bought for him. Then she put the glasses down, hurtled towards Bernard and, in front of five shocked faces on the banquette, slapped him hard across his face.

They all held their breath.

Bernard slapped her back.

All hell broke loose. Security men lumbered in from all directions and drunken guys were circling Bernard menacingly, while he spluttered, 'I'm sorry, I'm so sorry.'

Bing was on his feet. 'Look after the bird,' he ordered. 'I have to get Bernard out of here or he'll be torn to pieces.'

Evie rushed over to put her arms round the sobbing Spanish girl and lead her back to their table. She watched Bing, tall and commanding, stride into the middle of what looked like a mob. She couldn't hear what he said but the crowd parted and he escorted Bernard to the exit.

This is all my fault, was the one thought buzzing in Evie's head.

As soon as they had deposited Sacha at the door of Calmer Karma, Gareth took Evie's hand. 'Let's get you home.' He smiled.

His hand wasn't welcome. Evie would have preferred to be alone.

Gareth was growing braver. As they strolled along, he relinquished his hand to snake an arm round Evie's waist.

That felt OK. Or did it? Evie focused on Gareth. 'What do you do?'

'Maths, chemistry, history.'

'You're a teacher?' Evie was impressed.

'No.' He gave a puzzled laugh. They stopped under a streetlight. In the fuzzy glow Evie discerned a couple of spots on Gareth's chin.

Gareth said, 'I'm doing my—'

'*Don't say it!*'

Evie had spent all night flirting with someone who should have been at home revising for his A-levels. She was being held round the waist by a schoolboy. 'I'm old enough to be your . . . big sister.'

'I love older women.' His teenage grasp tightened.

'Older women? I'm twenty-sodding-seven!' Evie struggled.

'Almost thirty! Wow!'

'Surely this is illegal. Does your mother know you're out? Stop that!' Evie tussled with her underage suitor. He was very strong. 'What do they put in school dinners these days?'

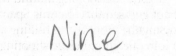

'AND HOW IS THE SEDUCTRESS of *Grange Hill* this morning?' asked Bing, as Evie shuffled, scowling, into the kitchen.

'That's not funny.'

'Oh, but it is.' Bing was warming up for his run. 'It's very funny.'

'You're forgotten to put your shorts on.' Evie sat heavily at the table. 'Oh, no. They *are* on.'

Bing's running shorts were a supremely economically cut item of clothing. 'They are a bit brief, aren't they?' he said. 'I'll get changed.'

'What?' Evie was flabbergasted. Soon Bing returned in a proper pair of full-sized running shorts. She hadn't known he owned such a thing.

While he stretched and warmed his muscles Evie asked about Bernard. 'How was he?'

'It took a while to calm him down.' Bing was touching his toes with elastic ease. 'He couldn't believe he'd struck a woman. You know what a gent he is.'

'How did you manage to get him out of Manhattan Dreams?'

'I said he was on medication and shouldn't be drinking. If you say anything loudly and confidently enough, people believe you.'

'You were very brave,' said Evie, almost shyly. 'Thank God you were there.'

'The difficult bit was getting him to stop crying.'

Evie looked stricken. 'Bernard was crying? That's awful.' Evie laid her head on the table. It was cool, but it did nothing to help.

Bing kissed the back of her bed hair. 'Don't worry. For some strange reason I still love you, and I'm sure Bernard does too.' He bounded away for his run.

'Postie has something for you!' yelled Bing, from the front door.

Oh, thought Evie dully. She dragged herself up the stairs.

On the mat, holding a large envelope, stood Aden.

'You're not Postie.' Evie sucked in her tummy and put a hand up to the matted fright wig that was her hair. She wished she'd bothered to check herself in the mirror.

'That's true. I did meet him on the steps, though, and he had this for you.' He handed over the envelope. 'Looks like your script.'

'Ooh.' Despite the recent memory of tussling with a minor and being the worst landlady ever, a spark of excitement ignited inside her. 'Brilliant.' She paused. 'Do you want to come downstairs and have some coffee while I tidy myself up?'

'Can't. Don't have time. Really, you know, just popped round.'

'Oh.' So he wanted to get away. But why, Evie asked herself, had he come round if he wanted to get away? 'Are we friends again?' she asked.

Aden's face crinkled. 'Of course we are.'

'I might as well tell you that the whole Bernard night out ended in disaster. You were right.'

'I don't need to hear that,' said Aden. 'Let's forget it. I was too hard on you anyway.'

'No, you weren't hard enough on me.'

'It doesn't matter. Friends again.'

They grinned at each other.

'I know you got me the part,' Evie plunged in.

Aden peered down at the floor. 'Ah.'

'So . . . thank you.'

'You're welcome.' Aden met her eye sheepishly.

'Why didn't you tell me?'

'I felt awkward.' Aden shrugged. 'I just wanted you to get it.'

'It's the nicest thing anybody's ever done for me,' said Evie simply.

Aden smiled, then turned away.

''Bye,' said Evie, in a soft voice she didn't often use.

Reverently Evie slipped the script out of the envelope and placed it on her knee. She laid her hands on it and shut her eyes. Shivering, she savoured the feel of it. Her first television script. She raised her cup of tea. 'Here's to you, Belle. You know how special this is for me.'

As she opened the first page, she took a deep yogic breath through her nose, then exhaled deeply through her mouth. She almost jumped out of her skin when her mobile rang.

'Yes?'

'Evie, my heart is broken.'

'Hello, Mum.' Evie was accustomed to melodramatic openers from her mother, but this promised to be a biggie. 'What's happened?'

'Your sister has gone berserk.'

Aha. 'I know about this, Mum. Try to stay calm.'

'You knew?' Bridgie took a moment off from being heartbroken to be affronted. 'I'm the last to know? Isn't that nice?'

Evie didn't bother to defend herself. 'She does have her reasons.'

'Oh, does she?' spat Bridgie venomously. 'Is it because of her beautiful home? Or her two adorable children? Or her devoted husband?'

So Bridgie didn't know everything.

'Does she know she's breaking poor Marcus's heart? He's wretched, absolutely wretched at losing his marriage.'

'Perhaps if he'd valued it more he might not have lost it.'

'So it's his fault now?' Bridgie screeched.

She was not taking the traditionally partisan approach of the average mother-in-law. She seemed to be entirely on Marcus's side. Evie reckoned she understood why. 'I know you think it's sinful even to consider divorce, Mum, but Beth has to do what's right for her.'

'I'm so *ashamed*.' Bridgie's voice trembled. 'We all saw her get married in church. What am I going to tell the family?'

'Don't tell them anything. It's nobody's business.'

'Do you know how she explained the whole thing to me?' Bridgie's pendulum swung back to fury. 'She said she has to find herself. *Find herself!* She'll find herself in the gutter if she's not careful.'

Evie found her mother unbearable in wrathful-suburban-matron mode. She stayed schtum while a lot more ordure poured over her, until her mother amazed her by saying, 'Thank God we have you. You're doing so well. You're going to be in a nice thing on the telly and you've found yourself a presentable young man. I always knew you'd make something of yourself.'

This was too much. Since Evie had been old enough to decipher language she had listened to Bridgie prophesy various bad ends for her. It was even worse hearing her heap unmerited praise on her head. 'Look, Mum, I have to tell you I'm not seeing Dan any more.'

'Holy Mother of Jesus, this family is cursed. Why not?'

'Pressure of work.'

'And what does that mean?'

'It means work, and its, er, pressures. It's complicated. I really have to go now, Mum.'

'Hold on!' ordered Bridgie. 'Your father wants a word.'

'Hello, sweetheart.'

'Dad.'

'This is a sad business, kid. A very sad business.' He sounded tired. 'I didn't see it coming.'

'That's 'cos Beth was so careful to hide it, Dad. None of us realised. Don't be hard on yourself. She has to do this on her own.'

'I have to reproach myself. All I want is for you girls to be happy . . .' John seemed to pick himself up. 'I asked her to come here but she was having none of it. Such an independent lady, our Beth. And so are you.'

'S'pose I am.' Evie had never thought about it before.

'You see what you want and you go for it. I admire that, pet. The only trouble is, life offers so many choices these days. It's working out what you want that's the real problem.'

'You've just hit so many nails right on their heads, Dad.'

John raised his voice: 'What's that you say, Evie? A nude scene in *The Setting of the Sun*?'

Amid the screams and wails this provoked, Evie giggled. 'See you, Dad,' she said, and put the phone down.

Too many choices. How true. Evie was trying to dissect her new feelings about Aden. Standing in the hall he had seemed changed, transformed, supercharged. His fair hair was silky, inviting her touch. His green eyes weren't pale any more: they sparkled.

I fancy Aden. Evie wasn't confused any more. *Not because I've been told he fancies me, but because I've realised he's a damn fine man*.

Most importantly, he was not a Bad Boy. *That* cycle was broken.

'How about a Chinese?'

'Are we talking food? Or your next sexual conquest?' queried Evie. 'Just so I know.'

'Food. My treat, as long as you come with me to get it.'

'Bing, *my script*.' Evie waggled the sheaf of papers at him. She had crept, maggot-like, to the other end of the sofa. Only her head and one arm were out from under the duvet. It was Sunday evening. Outside the sky cast a pall of gloom over London.

'Don't come that with me. You're not reading it. You haven't got past the title page. You've been rolling it into a tube and dropping Revels into your mouth through it.'

'We all have our own ways of getting acquainted with the text.'

'Come on. Think spring rolls. Think sweet and sour.'

'Actually, that sounds brilliant.' Evie bolted off to change her fun-fur slippers for something more pavement-friendly. 'Hey,' she shouted from her room, 'how come you're in tonight? Sunday's normally a big one for you, isn't it?'

'Didn't fancy it.'

But Bing *always* fancied it. Nonplussed, Evie followed him out into the night. The sky was brooding, pregnant with the promise of a storm. Evie shivered, then stopped dead at the gate.

'What is it?' Bing scuttled to her side.

'The car's back.'

It seemed that their days were ruled by that car. 'It's there!' one of them would shout first thing. Or: 'No car today!'

Wednesday was a no-car day. This was a good start. Evie was sorting the post—or, rather, the selection of unsolicited and unwanted special offers—when Bernard let himself in through the front door.

The sun, which was back to its ebullient former self, streamed in behind him, lighting up his worrying haircut like a forest fire. 'Good morning!' he said, with the brightness of a children's TV presenter.

'Bernard. I'm glad we bumped into each other.' Evie hung her head. 'I'm really sorry about the other night.'

'Oh, you have nothing to apologise for. That night opened my eyes.'

'Do you mean that?' Evie was taken aback.

'Gosh, yes. Changed my life.' He grinned maniacally at her.

'We must do it again, then!' Evie was bowled over by the unsuspected success of her plotting.

Bernard laughed in a new, unselfconscious way. 'I'd rather not. I don't need you any more, if you know what I mean.'

Crushed, Evie said, 'Good. That's good. If I've given you confidence then that's my reward.'

The old Bernard emerged to take Evie's hand, shake it earnestly and say, 'I can never thank you enough,' before the new one bounded upstairs like a kangaroo.

Stacking shelves at Calmer Karma, Evie couldn't resist crowing about her triumph. 'He has a real spring in his step. Raring to go.'

'I don't get it.' Sacha handed up curly-toed slippers to Evie high on a ladder. 'It's not as if the evening was a success. He was almost lynched.'

'Oh, be fair. He was getting on like a house on fire with the red-headed girl and the Spanish bird hit him 'cos she was jealous. That's success compared to sitting at home thinking about your dead mother.'

'When you put it like that . . .'

A workshop had claimed Sacha that afternoon, so Evie had agreed to look after the shop. It would give her an opportunity to read her script. She had it open in front of her, but she was thinking about Aden. Specifically, she was thinking about ringing him.

Evie hadn't told Sacha. She didn't want it discussed endlessly. Her feelings for Aden were private, and she hugged them to her.

Evie stared at the big red fifties phone on the counter. I couldn't bear it if he said no . . . She was immobilised by terror.

The bell over the shop door clanged, jolting Evie out of her reverie, and a hundred screaming children stormed in. No, it was only two. And she knew them.

'Charles! Julius!' Evie looked past them to the harassed figure trailing after them. 'So, you must be Beth.'

'I'm what's left of Beth.' She sank into a chair. 'The baby sitter let me down so I had to drag this pair with me.' Beth looked at Evie with an expression of weariness. 'Imagine dealing with them *and* an estate agent.'

Evie did the decent thing. 'Let me have them.'

'Oh, you're an angel.' Beth's shoulders drooped with relief. 'When I went to your house Bing told me you were here. I would have asked him to mind them but he was just off to the Palladium. I know it's an awful cheek, but I didn't know what else to do.'

'Don't worry about it. Things have changed. We all have to rally around. The quicker you get a flat the quicker we can get you away from that *Adulterer*.' Evie whispered it to save the twins' innocent ears.

Beth was studying her sister's face. 'What do you mean, Evie?'

'What do I mean?' Evie laughed, then mouthed, 'Marcus,' while pointing elaborately at the children. 'He's an A-D, etcetera.'

'Marcus isn't the adulterer,' said Beth simply. 'I am. I've found someone else. I thought you knew.'

Quicksand squelched beneath Evie's feet. 'You said you couldn't live with him any more!'

'Not because he was unfaithful. Marcus would never do anything so interesting.' Beth exhaled slowly. 'I had everything a woman is presumed to want, but I've been going quietly bonkers because Marcus and

I have never had a real conversation. Then I met someone I can't stop talking to. It was as if I'd been shut in a tomb for years, then suddenly exposed to sunlight. The decision to end the marriage made itself. It wasn't brought on by Marcus being an adulterer.'

'I thought he'd been unfaithful,' said Evie quietly.

'No.' Beth seemed suddenly fearful. 'It was me. Sis, if you don't want to get involved I'll understand.'

'Oh, shut up!' Not for the first time Evie wished that Crumps hugged. Then she put her hand to her mouth. 'Tamsin!' she said, reddening. 'I made her cry. I told her I knew all about her.'

'That's beyond me.' Beth heaved herself up. 'I haven't got time to dwell on Tamsin now. I've got to find a roof to put over these boys' heads. Can you keep them until about seven?'

'Sure. We'll be at home by then.'

Beth went off to look at flats, leaving Evie with the uneasy knowledge that, once again, she hadn't known what was going on under her nose.

A string of worry beads round his podgy neck, Julius was playing his own symphony on the wind chimes. Charles was munching his way through a carton of organic raisin candy bars.

Not one customer had arrived to perturb Evie, and she had long ago put her script into her bag to protect it from grubby little fingers. Her sole occupation was thinking about Aden.

One minute she was just thinking, the next she was *doing*. Speedily, with no time for scaredy-cat second thoughts, she dialled his number.

'Hello.'

Eek. It was him. Evie reminded herself she was twenty-seven. 'Hi, Aden, it's me.'

'Evie?'

Bad start. If he was mad about her, surely he would know her voice straight away. 'Yes.'

'Sorry, it's a shit line.'

She leaned perilously to her right. 'Is this better?'

'Much. Have you been reading your script?'

'Oooh, yes, I gobbled it up.'

'So you've read episode three?'

'Hmm.' Evie didn't like the way this was going. Specific knowledge might be called for.

'Are you pleased? I don't think you knew about that, did you?'

'No, I didn't and I'm . . . pleased,' said Evie slowly. She had to change the subject. 'Look, Aden, it's like this. Will you go out with me on Saturday?' It came out rather aggressively.

'Er, yeah. Sure. What do you have in mind?'

'Oh.' She wasn't certain that he had understood. 'No, Aden, you're not getting it. I mean *come out with me* as in'—she gulped—'a date.'

Just then the wind chimes fell on Julius. Charles, startled by the noise, ran to his brother's aid and vomited candy bars over him.

'Oh, my God!' wailed Evie. Still clamping the receiver to her ear she bent down and tried to extricate Julius from the tangle of wind chimes and sick.

'What's happening?' pleaded Aden. 'Have aliens landed?'

'It's complicated,' puffed Evie, dragging the screaming Charles towards her. 'Aden, this is a both-hands job. I have to go,' she gabbled. 'Do you want to come on a date with me on Saturday or not?'

'I do.'

'Good. Goodbye.'

Evie screamed even louder than the twins, when Sacha walked through the door. Sacha was tired and she vowed there and then never to ask Evie to watch the shop again.

A small hand in each of hers, Evie turned into Kemp Street. She stopped stock still, yanking two tiny arms almost out of their sockets.

The car was back.

Evie's heart started to pound. She held the children's hands even tighter. If the watcher in the car was dangerous he might turn his aggression on the twins.

Anger simmered beneath the fear. She was walking down her own street and she felt threatened. It was intolerable that she couldn't guarantee her nephews' safety.

Like the cavalry, Bernard hove into view. He spotted Evie, statue-like at the corner, waved cheerfully, and walked towards her.

'Bernard, I'm so pleased to see you. Take these.' Evie transferred Charles and Julius to his charge. 'Don't ask questions. Get them indoors as quickly as you can. There's someone I need to talk to.'

Evie was incensed and had almost forgotten to be afraid. As she marched up to the white car she could see that their mysterious watcher was a plump woman of, maybe, sixty.

Evie tapped sharply on the window. 'I want to talk to you!'

The window rolled down. The woman's face was creased with anxiety and there was a tartan flask in her lap. 'Hello.' It was said in the style of a comfortable aunt, not at all like a lunatic stalker.

'What do you think you're playing at?' Evie eyeballed her tormentor.

'Oh dear.' Once again the stranger had strayed from the accepted behaviour of deranged perverts.

'Oh dear?' mimicked Evie. 'Aren't you going to explain yourself? You're frightening us all to death, just sitting and staring at our house. Who are you?'

The woman fingered the flask awkwardly. 'I'm Caroline's mum.'

'But Caroline's mum is dead,' Bing insisted, a twin on each arm.

'She's not dead. She's on our sofa, crying,' whispered Evie, shutting the kitchen door.

'Caroline thinks she's dead.'

'Does she fu-lip.' Evie modified her language out of respect for the malodorous, snivelling boys. 'Caroline has more family than the von Trapps. She's got a mum, a dad, brothers, nanas and grandpas coming out of her ears. She refuses point blank to see them.'

'This is good,' said Bing approvingly. 'Look, can you wash this one?' He thrust Charles in her direction.

'You'll have to do it.' Evie dodged the proffered child. 'I'm making a pot of tea for Mrs Millbank. Her flask has a crack in it and she's only had a bap since she left Bury this morning.'

'Why don't you bake her a cake? Have you forgotten that this woman's been terrorising us?'

'When you've spoken to her you'll understand.'

Bing did understand. He kept Mrs Millbank ('Call me Deirdre') supplied with tissues as, tearfully, she told them her story.

The children had been gone over with a damp flannel and were watching *The Tweenies* with the sound down in the corner. Charles had been decanted into a 'Take That!' T-shirt of Bing's.

'Another bite, Deirdre?' Evie waved a plate of lumpen oversized sandwiches under their visitor's nose.

'Thank you, no.' Deirdre had struggled with the first. 'I'm so sorry I scared you all.' She began to cry again.

'Now, now, stop saying sorry.' Bing patted her on her arm and proffered the tissues again. 'No harm's been done.'

'You're very kind.'

'We just want to help,' said Evie.

'There's nothing anyone can do.' Deirdre shook her head sorrowfully. 'Caroline has cut herself off from us completely.' This detonated some energetic nose-blowing.

When it had subsided Bing prompted her gently: 'Take us back to the beginning. How did things get to this?'

Deirdre sighed. She seemed embarrassed to be laying bare her troubles to two young people she'd only just met. 'Well, now, let's see.

Caroline was always rebellious when she was growing up. All those black clothes and make-up—what is it? Gothic? She'd be late home. Her dad is strict, you see. He didn't approve of her make-up and her staying out late. One night he smelt alcohol on her breath and hit the roof. It's not that I think my husband's wrong, it's just that he can be very *hard*.

'Caroline started to live her own life. She didn't speak to us much. I didn't like that but at least there were fewer rows. Then one day I found a note on her pillow. It didn't say much, just that she was leaving and wouldn't be coming back.'

'How long ago was that?' asked Evie tenderly.

'Nearly two years.' Deirdre almost wailed. 'We've been out of our minds. Then about a month ago an old friend of hers came to see me. She'd heard how distraught we all were and she gave me an address. I wrote to Caroline. It was hard to know what to say.'

Caroline had wept over the letter, Evie knew. It was the paper she'd crumpled up when Evie had gone in to baby-sit.

'There was no reply,' Deirdre continued. 'Something in me snapped. I jumped into the car and drove and drove until I was at her door.' She paused self-consciously. 'I don't know what I thought I was doing. I had no plan, nothing. I just needed to see her with my own eyes.'

A twin burped and was ignored.

'That was when I got the biggest shock of all.' Deirdre's eyes widened at the memory. 'The little girl.'

'You mean Milly?' asked Evie.

'Is that her name?' Deirdre asked. 'So sweet.'

'You mean you didn't know about Milly?' Evie was amazed.

'I had no idea. Now it all makes sense. Caroline ran away because she was expecting. She was too scared to come to us.'

'Have you told your husband?' Bing wanted to know.

'Yes. He was shocked at first but now he wants to see his granddaughter more than anything else.'

A hasty pow-wow was held in Evie's room under the pretext of preparing more tea for Deirdre.

'Can you believe Caroline?' hissed Evie. 'Fancy doing that to her poor mother.'

'Whoa! Consider how bad her life must have been for her to skedaddle to London on her own when she was pregnant. "Hard" was the word Deirdre used to describe Caroline's dad. Something tells me that's mild.'

'S'pose,' Evie agreed. 'What will we do with Deirdre?'

'I don't want to interfere.' Bing was adamant.

'So, what do you suggest? We send her back out to the car and wave at her every now and then?'

Bing looked uneasy. Then he punched the mattress. 'Dammit, you're going to interfere, aren't you?'

'No, *we* are,' Evie corrected him. 'We'll have a chat with Caroline. Try to persuade her to see her mum, just for a few moments, yeah?'

'All right. We have to do something, I suppose.'

Evie sniffed vigorously, then beamed. 'It's Belle's handbag! She approves. Everything's going to be all right.'

Thunderous. That was the best way to describe Caroline's expression as she barred their way into her flat. 'My family is dead,' she repeated.

'Caroline, why don't you give your mother a break?' Bing could be persuasive when he tried. 'She's come all this way.'

'I never invited her.'

'It can't hurt,' said Evie.

'Oh, can't it?' snapped Caroline. 'What would you know?'

'Well,' said Evie, carefully, 'I can see that your mother's in a lot of pain and perhaps deserves a hearing.'

'You don't know what me dad used to say to me.' Caroline was looking over their heads. 'The words he used. He thinks single mothers are whores. He wouldn't spit on me if I was on fire. I don't ever want to hear him call Milly a bastard.' Her gaze clicked back to meet Evie's eyes. 'And he would, you know. He's . . .'

'Hard,' finished Evie.

'Tell her to sod off and leave me alone.'

Evie didn't put it in quite those words. 'She's adamant, Deirdre. She won't see you.'

'We're so sorry.' Bing sat down beside Mrs Millbank and laid a hand on hers.

The expected tears didn't come. Deirdre was passively accepting. 'She's a stubborn girl. I wish with all my heart I could change her mind, but I know her better than I know myself.'

Evie had to add, 'She seems frightened of her dad's reaction to Milly.'

Deirdre pursed her lips. 'I dare say. My husband always had a lot to say about *unmarried mothers*, as he calls them. I think he was trying to scare Caroline. He didn't want her to get into trouble. The sad thing is he's dying to see his granddaughter. Once he'd got over the shock and we talked it over he got used to the idea. Milly'—Deirdre stumbled over the unfamiliar name—'is his flesh and blood. All we wanted to do was give them a home and make up for lost time. I've dreamt about bringing them both back with me.' She patted Bing's hand affectionately and stood up, brushing crumbs off her lap. 'It wasn't to be.' She stopped, transfixed by the figures coming down the stairs. Caroline, with Milly on one hip. Milly held out her arms and babbled a strange baby word.

'Mum,' said Caroline, chewing the word as if it was a mouthful of iron filings, 'do you want to come upstairs for a minute?'

Deirdre nodded mutely and followed her daughter.

Bing and Evie were stunned. Bing's eyes glistened. A tear travelled down Evie's cheek. They hugged each other.

'It's boring here,' said Julius loudly, from behind the sofa.

'I am in *so* much trouble.' Bing was tugging on a clean pair of jeans. 'I'm going to miss the first number. They'll shoot me.'

'I'll ring and say you've been injured in a freak snogging accident.'

'Please don't bother.'

'Did you see Beth's face when she was stuffing the twins into the car and I told her I'd have a flat for her, after all?'

'Yes.' Bing was curt. He was packing his keys into his pockets.

'Although I'll miss Caroline . . .' Evie said.

'Shit.' Bing held up his denim jacket. A large chocolate splodge disfigured the back.

'Ah.' Evie looked chastened. 'Yes. Perhaps I shouldn't have given Julius that jar of Nutella.'

Bing was too late to waste time criticising Evie's childcare skills. 'Can I borrow your baggy white cotton jumper?'

'Course.' Evie followed Bing to her room and watched him rifle her wardrobe. 'What have you got planned for after the show?' she asked.

'I'll be straight home,' he muttered distractedly.

'Again? Are you feeling all right, Bing? You've been home every night this week. You're not ill, are you?'

'I am as fit as the proverbial flea,' Bing informed her. 'I can't see that jumper. Your cupboards are like a jumble sale in Hell. *Where is it?*'

'Try under the bed.'

Bing tutted eloquently and dived beneath it.

'Why are you living the life of a monk all of a sudden?'

'Monks do not perform nightly at the Palladium.'

'I don't like it,' complained Evie. 'It makes me uneasy when you're not disgustingly promiscuous.'

'Found it.' Triumphant, Bing emerged with the jumper. 'Want to know what else I found?'

'Yeah.'

'You're not going to like it.'

Evie flattened herself against the wall in an untypically swift movement. 'Is it alive?'

'No, nothing like that. I'm shattering one of your illusions.' Bing plonked a heavy old-fashioned black leather handbag on the dishevelled duvet. 'The smell wasn't ghostly encouragement. Belle's handbag was open under your bed.'

'Oh.' Evie bit her lip and Belle took a step back into misty shadow.

Ten

IT HAD BEEN PLANNED as a celebration. 'Meet me in Black's and I'll buy you a very big glass of champagne,' Beth had said, bubbling like Moët herself. 'I'm *so* excited at the thought of moving into Kemp Street.'

'Where's Black's? *What's* Black's?' Evie had asked. 'The only Black's I know of is a snazzy drinking club in Soho.'

'That's the one. I've just become a member.'

'Bloody hell! You don't hang about. You've only been single for an afternoon and you're already joining fancy members-only gaffs.' Evie was impressed.

Right now, as Evie paced the platform at Mornington Crescent she was also preoccupied. She was about to let Beth down. She rehearsed her speech furiously as the platform filled up around her. 'It's like this,' she improvised. 'Unforeseen circumstances have compelled me to retract my previous offer.' Too formal. 'You can't have the flat.' Too abrupt.

The tunnel growled and a train thundered in. Evie wasn't too distracted to nab a seat. She winced as she recalled that morning's conversation. Caroline had been humming as she bumped Milly down the steps in the pushchair.

'Hiya. Somebody sounds cheerful,' Evie had smiled, giving her a hand down the last couple of steps. 'I saw your mum leave quite late. She looked a different woman.'

'Yeah. Well.' Some smiles can't be suppressed, although Caroline did her damnedest.

'I'm so pleased for you.' Evie was sincere though she itched to add, *Even though you've been lying your head off for months.*

'Thanks,' muttered Caroline. 'I . . . I'm sorry about the lies and that.'

Evie nodded and left a space in the hope that Caroline might fill it. She wasn't disappointed.

'There was so much, well, hurt, I suppose,' said Caroline awkwardly. 'Everything that happened at home, with me dad, was so painful I didn't want to think, never mind talk, about it. The easiest thing was just to say the whole past was dead.'

'You wanted to wipe it out and start again?'

'Exactly.' Caroline nodded earnestly. 'As far as I was concerned it was just me and Milly against the world.'

'Not any more, though. You've got a family again.'

'Yea.' Caroline looked pensive. 'It was fantastic seeing my mum, seeing her hold Milly.' Caroline shook her head as if to shrug off the debilitating soppiness. 'But we'll take it slow. Some of the wounds are still raw.'

'God, you're so sensible,' Evie said admiringly. 'I'll be sorry to see you go, even though it's for such happy reasons.'

'Go? Where am I going?' Caroline said sharply, with a flash of the old sourness.

'Home. Aren't you? I presumed . . .'

'I'm not ready for that.' A shudder ran through Caroline. 'Is that a problem?' There was fear in her question.

'No, no no no no,' replied Evie, much too hastily. 'Not at all.'

Caroline studied her face. 'You sure?'

'That flat is yours for as long as you want it.' Evie was emphatic. Caroline was one of Belle's tenants, after all.

'Good, 'cos I don't know what I would have done without this place. Thanks . . .' Caroline faltered, 'thanks for putting up with me.'

That really was the moment for a hug, but Caroline hadn't changed quite that much and ran over Evie's toes with the pushchair instead.

The steps down to Black's basement entrance were slick with rain.

'I'm here to meet Beth Lawrenson. She's a member,' Evie announced to the statuesque Valkyrie on the door.

'OK.' The goddess barely looked up but drew in her airstrip-length legs for Evie to get by.

The interior was not the sleek vision of elegance Evie had expected. The wooden floors and the rough grey walls looked as if they hadn't been touched since the Georgian house was built. A fire roared in a massive grate, and all around private drinkers lounged on wooden benches. If it wasn't for the diamanté tummy rings and combat pants of the clientèle, Evie might have imagined herself back in the days of Hogarth.

'Forgotten to pay the electricity bill?' she quipped, to the sullen-faced supermodel looming behind the bar.

'Eh?'

'I mean, all the candles everywhere, it's so dark, as if you'd forgotten to . . . Oh, forget it. A white wine, please.'

Glass in hand, Evie delved into the gloom. Narrow but cavernous, the club was a warren of small candlelit rooms full of battered baroque furniture. Where was Beth? Evie scowled in the darkness.

'Lost?' asked an unfeasibly handsome boy from a tattered banquette. 'Try the Divan Room. There's always something going on in there.'

'Thank you,' simpered Evie, stumbling off in the direction he pointed. She came to a heavy, tasselled curtain and poked her nose round it. 'Beth!' she squealed, relieved.

The Divan Room was almost all divan. A wall-to-wall mattress was piled with opulent velvet cushions. Beth was lounging among the decadent haphazardness. She was laughing, her hair tousled as she stretched full length. She looked ten years younger and a thousand times happier.

'This place is amazing!' Evie squealed, leaping onto the divan and drenching them both in wine.

A voice came from the depth of the cushions. 'I like my wine in me, not on me.'

Evie drew back on her knees, startled. Beth was not alone in this Arabian Nights fantasy.

A plumpish figure righted itself and knocked a bolster into shape.

'Auntie Bea.' That was a statement. 'Auntie Bea?' That was a question. Evie saw her sister's pale hand snake across the velvet and take Bea's. 'Auntie Bea . . .' That was realisation. Beth and Bea were in love.

The two women, pink-cheeked and shiny eyed, stared intently at Evie, trying to read her. She looked from one to the other, took a deep gulp of the wine left in her glass and said, 'Now I get it.'

'And?' prompted Beth nervously.

'Ssssh,' said Bea quietly, soothingly. 'Let it sink in. The poor girl's only just arrived.' Bea lobbed a cushion at Evie. 'Get comfortable, lovey.'

Automatically Evie did as she was told. *My sister the lesbian*, she thought. It sounded like a porn film.

'Champagne?' Bea had evidently decided to take charge now. 'Chuck that hideous wine in the yucca plant and take this.'

Evie complied and gazed meditatively at the champagne flute.

Bea leaned forward conspiratorially. 'The idea is that you drink it. Apparently the bubbles help you cope with shock.'

Evie managed a giggle, then downed the whole glass in one. This startled them all into laughter, which intensified with the impressive, rolling burp that escaped her. 'You're . . . together!' she yelped. 'You're a couple! She's *your* girlfriend and she's *your* girlfriend!'

Beth was nodding furiously.

'But you're my auntie Bea—'

'She's a woman too,' Beth butted in.

Bea laid an appeasing arm on Beth's arm. 'I'm still your Auntie Bea.'

Evie smiled a small gormless smile.

'It is all right, isn't it?' Beth asked timidly.

Evie looked at her sister. Really looked at her. She had never seen Beth tipsy before and it suited her. Being in love suited her.

'Of course it's all right. It's wonderful!' Evie bounced up and down creating ripples that almost shipwrecked Bea and Beth.

There was no champagne left. Bea clambered off the bed and scurried away to find more. Now Beth could shoot over to Evie's side.

'Bea has a saying: "Love is where it falls." That's beautiful, isn't it?' said Beth. 'We don't choose who we fall for. I mean, on paper Marcus was my ideal partner, but Bea . . . She just amazes me every day and shows me such kindness and understanding and *respect*. Love is where it falls, and it fell on an old family friend.'

'Of the same sex,' Evie couldn't resist saying. She even added, 'And thirty years older.'

'Yes, the same sex and thirty years older. Love is where it falls.'

Evie nudged Beth. They smiled. They understood each other. 'Does Marcus know?' she asked.

A long, expressive sigh. 'Oh, yes, he knows. He said he'd rather I'd become a prostitute. I've never seen him so angry. He's threatened to fight me for custody. Said he'd rather have a nanny looking after the twins than me.'

'He wouldn't win, would he?'

'Those boys stay with me. I've looked after them since I conceived them and I'm not going to give them up now.'

Evie sighed. 'If he makes you go to court you can bring up his adultery.'

'Keep up, Evie. He didn't commit adultery, remember? *I* did.'

'Oh, yes. Sorry. Champagne always makes me stupid.'

'Here's some more stupidity for you, then.' Bea was back with a shapely and expensive bottle. She struggled over the cushions like a spaniel, snuggling one foot cosily under Beth's thigh.

Evie hurriedly knocked back some champagne. That kind of thing was going to take some getting used to. 'What I don't understand is—why did Tamsin burst into tears and run off at the barbecue?'

'Ah. Yes. We got to the bottom of that,' said Bea.

'If you remember,' explained Beth, 'you told her you knew all about her. Poor Tamsin presumed you knew her deep dark secret.'

'Tamsin has a deep dark secret?' Evie was incredulous.

'Of sorts. She'd faked her dental assistant CV.'

Disappointed, Evie said, 'I'd hardly call that a terrible secret.'

'In the cut-throat world of dental assisting it is,' explained Beth.

The mystery was solved. The women clinked glasses and shouted, 'To Tamsin!' Bea added, 'May her starched uniform never crease!'

A question occurred to Evie. 'Have you two told Mum?'

The lovebirds exchanged a look. 'What do you think?' asked Bea.

'I think you haven't.'

Tipsily, Evie got off the tube at the wrong stop. She was pleased that Beth had understood about the flat. As she traipsed through the darkened streets she marvelled at how easily Bea had extracted a confession from her about the Great Dan/Aden Deception.

After Beth's scandalised exclamations had died away, Bea had commented shrewdly that it would be ironic indeed if Evie was to fall for Aden after all that.

'Hmm. I suppose it would,' Evie had replied evasively.

'If Aden really, really likes you,' said Beth, leaning back on a cushion, 'you mustn't go out with him unless you really like him too. It wouldn't be fair.'

'Fair schmair,' Evie had replied blithely.

It was food for thought as she took another wrong turning off Camden High Street. She *did* really like Aden, and these feelings had crept up on her unexpectedly. All the relationships that littered the highways of Evie's heart had been with Bad Boys.

Aden wasn't remotely Bad. In fact, he was Good. Good is fine, thought the girl who had previously considered only card-carrying bastards as snog-fodder. Good might be fun for a change. After all, love is where it falls.

A drunk person has an unerring nose for the next drink. Evie drifted up the stairs, following the sounds of inane chatter and giggling to Caroline's door.

A glass of something acrid and cheap was thrust into her hands by Bing, who was wearing deely-boppers. This was hardly unusual, but it was a surprise to see Bernard sporting a pair too.

Evie sniggered and a morsel of quiche went down the wrong way. After a minute's coughing, during which the others gathered around her, the offending crumb reappeared.

'Thank God,' said Bernard gravely. 'I could never live with myself if my quiche choked you to death.'

Bing turned the Pet Shop Boys up so Evie had to shout, 'What do you mean *your* quiche? You didn't make it, did you?'

Bernard nodded.

'That's wonderful!' Evie felt like a proud headmistress on Speech Day.

'Gosh.' Bernard was watching Bing dance. 'He's awfully, er, groovy, isn't he?'

'Oh, yes.' Evie laughed. 'And double-jointed.'

Bing's dancing wore out the onlookers long before it slowed him down. Wedged on to the small sofa, Caroline, Evie, Bernard and Milly all slumped in silence, watching him swerve and leap about. He was dancing very fast but still had the breath to say, 'I've had an idea.'

'What is it?' Evie felt approximately eighty years old as she watched Bing's thighs, mesmerised.

'Bernard's flat needs decorating. It's the flat of a very old lady, not a young gun. I'm going to decorate it. Funk it up a bit. The sexy new Bernard needs a sexy new pad.'

From where Evie was sitting the new Bernard needed a stiff drink, but she nodded. If he succeeded in pulling a gorgeous, pouting member of the opposite sex he couldn't bring her home to a sitting room that had been frozen in the mid-seventies and a bedroom that boasted a display of stuffed voles. 'One of your better ideas,' she congratulated Bing. 'I'll let you off a month's rent.'

'No need.' Bing wiggled his arse. 'It'll be fun.'

It was imperative to keep Sacha away from the house on the day of the date with Aden. Sacha would analyse, hypothesise and ultimately scupper the whole thing.

A picnic was the chosen activity. Lots of food and drink in the park. Evie had the flat to herself. Bing had disappeared upstairs long ago in his decorating garb of pink towelling hot pants and a medallion. Several large tins of white paint and a stack of hardwood flooring went with him.

Hair washed and dried, armpits shaved and sprayed, lacy thong and matching bra on, fake tan applied to milky legs, Evie took a deep breath and opened her wardrobe door.

What do you wear to get to know a man? What does it mean vis-à-vis cleavage? In Evie's cupboards there seemed to be no sartorial middle ground between lying-on-the-sofa-watching-*EastEnders* and here-I-am-boys-come-and-get-me.

What was that sky-blue fabric peeking out at one end of the wardrobe? Evie pushed the crowded hangers out of the way and extracted a dress she didn't recognise. It was pale blue cotton with a neat, fitted bodice and a knee-length straight skirt. The thin straps were gingham. It was both sexy and wholesome, and she had no recollection of buying it. It had to have been Belle's.

Excitedly she pulled it on, praying it would fit. The zip whispered up her backbone like a kiss. They certainly knew how to make dresses in those days, thought Evie, as she rotated happily in front of the mirror. Her bosom, though mostly concealed, was perked up no end. The seams on the bodice carved inches off her midriff. The tulip shape of the skirt transformed her child-bearing hips into hour-glass ones. She felt light and bright and ready to skip. It brought out her inner Doris Day.

Unfortunately for Aden's stomach, nothing could bring out Evie's inner Delia Smith. The beautiful wicker picnic basket (picked up at a car-boot sale for a quid) was not filled with homemade delicacies to tempt the palate. Evie had dashed madly around the supermarket, swooping on Scotch eggs, pork pies, just-on-the-sell-by-date sandwiches, ham pinwheels and two bottles of own-brand champagne. A litre of the finest chocolate milk completed the sophisticated menu.

Evie crammed it all in and lifted the basket. Blimey, it was heavy. As she hoisted it inelegantly onto her arm, she saw that it had been sitting on her script. Despite its ragged appearance—the script had travelled everywhere with her, from bus to bath to bed and back again—it was still unread. 'Two weeks is plenty of time,' she consoled herself. She would read it from cover to cover when she got home.

Packed buses and picnic baskets don't mix. As Evie sweated and battled to push her way off the bus her inner Doris Day receded. 'Excuse *me*,' she snarled, in serial-killer tones to a little boy before she stepped off.

She tottered through the gate to the park. She loved the feeling she got when she entered. It was as if an invisible curtain had fallen between her and the swarming London streets only a footstep behind her.

Having reached the designated tree, she spread a sheet on the grass. Carefully, in the manner of a serving suggestion, she arranged the cut-price goodies. She rotated a plate of pork pies and stirred the coleslaw in its tub. 'Stop it,' she whispered to herself. 'It's only Aden. *It's only Aden.*'

'What was that?' It was only Aden, standing over her, blocking out the sun.

'Oh!' Evie was on her feet as if the grass had electrocuted her behind. 'You!'

'Yes. Me!' Aden made a wry face. 'Your date.'

Unable to control herself, Evie found she was pulling a wry face.

'It is a date, isn't it? Have I got this wrong?'

'No! You didn't! You're right! It's a date!' Evie's volume switch had careered out of control. 'Sit!'

Obediently Aden sank down onto the sheet. 'Wow. Look at all this grub. I *love* pork pies!'

Concentrating on taking nice deep breaths, Evie endeavoured to conquer her nerves. The champagne bottle lolled suggestively in the basket. 'Here. Open this.' She handed it to Aden as she sat down beside him.

'The perfect accompaniment to cocktail sausages.' Aden took the bottle. A minute later the sheet was doused with fizz. 'I did manage to get some into the plastic cups.' Apologetically, Aden leaned across and handed one to Evie.

Gratefully she gulped down some champagne. It warmed the pit of her empty stomach and sent tingling waves of energy to her extremities.

She popped a Scotch egg with practised ease.

'I like the way you handle a snack item,' said Aden admiringly. 'You didn't drop a crumb.' He helped himself from a plate of food.

It's hard to stay upright on grass. It seems to beckon the body downwards. Soon they were on their sides. Evie was relaxing nerve by nerve, cell by cell. 'I feel we need to ask some date questions,' she said.

'Shoot.' Aden lay back, his arms behind his head. 'I'm an open book.'

'Most recent relationship?'

'Tamara Denskowitz. Complicated name for a complicated girl. She was a scientist.'

'Oh.' This wasn't what Evie wanted to hear.

'Very beautiful.'

'Right.'

Evidently Aden had caught her tone. 'Wore too much make-up, though. And her bum looked big in everything.'

Evie scowled at him. 'Honesty only, please. Why did you break up?'

'Because it wasn't going anywhere. We'd said everything we had to say to each other. Does that sound harsh?'

'It sounds very grown-up compared to the reasons I break up with guys.'

'For example?'

'If we don't count Dan . . .'

'Let's never count Dan again.'

'OK. Well, the bloke before him . . . we split up because he wouldn't stop talking about Liz Hurley so I threw his Simpsons mug at him and it broke.'

'Perfectly understandable.'

'And the one before *him*, we split up because he thought it was funny when my skirt fell off on Oxford Street.'

'But surely it *was* funny?' queried Aden.

'I'll ignore that.'

'OK. My go. Have you ever kissed a girl?'

That was a tricky one. To buy herself time Evie slowly masticated a mini quiche. The truth was she *had* kissed a girl. But was it wise to admit it? 'Well . . .'

'That sounds like a yes.'

'Yes. I have.' Evie raced through the story. 'I was at a party at drama school. I was as drunk as a monkey and this older girl dared me and I can never say no to a dare. So I kissed her.'

'Did you enjoy it?'

She shut her eyes. 'Yes.' She opened her eyes to check his reaction.

Funnily enough, Aden seemed to be relishing her discomfort.

'But,' she concluded truthfully, 'I've never wanted to do it again. I missed the stubble.' Evie started to pack up the picnic. 'Fancy a walk?' That was the kind of romantic thing couples did in films.

'Sure. Let me take that.' Aden stood and reached out for the laden basket. He staggered as he picked it up. 'Whoooah! Is it made of lead?'

'Sorry!'

They ambled off across the grass. Aden was rendered lopsided by his wicker burden.

'Great dress, by the way.' Aden said it abruptly, without looking at her. 'Suits you,' he added curtly, with a brief nod in her direction.

Evie smiled. 'I think I should put my arm through yours,' she declared, in a schoolmarmy way.

Aden looked surprised.

'That's what people do on dates.' Evie slipped her hand through the crook of Aden's elbow. She felt him tense, then draw in his arm, trapping hers.

'How are your plans to matchmake your tenants going?' asked Aden.

'You mean Bernard and Caroline? They'll never get together, but they're both a lot happier. Caroline has patched up a feud with her family and Bernard has been seen wearing clothes from this century. He's on the lookout for a woman and his flat's being redecorated.'

'When you interfere you really go for it, don't you?'

There was a smile in Aden's delivery but Evie found it necessary to get huffy. 'I don't mean to *interfere*. You make me sound bossy and I'm not.' She glimpsed the shimmering lake. 'We *must* go on a boat! That is *the* perfect date thing to do!' She speeded up, dragging Aden in her wake.

'Bossy? *Bossy?* Of course not,' he muttered, as Evie rifled his pockets for loose change to give the attendant.

It was peaceful in the middle of the lake. 'We could be a million miles away from London,' said Evie dreamily. She slipped a fine white cardigan over her shoulders and tipped her head back, enjoying the warmth of the sun on her face.

'Alone at last.' Aden rested the oars. Their knees met.

Evie gazed into Aden's greeny-grey eyes. 'Hey, you,' she said quietly. 'I think it's time we held hands. Get over here.'

'Yes, miss.' Aden got to his feet unsteadily and stumbled to her side. He plonked himself down on the plank seat and the tiny boat rocked alarmingly.

Evie gripped the side. 'It's like *Titanic!*'

'A very low-budget *Titanic*,' corrected Aden, offering his palm.

Evie slid hers into it.

'How's it feel?' asked Aden.

'Good.'

'Good.' He grinned at her. Those crinkly bits at the side of his eyes were sexy close up.

'Now it's definitely time we kissed.' Evie's voice was so quiet it was almost under her breath.

'No.' Aden pulled away.

'No?' Evie dropped his hand. 'What do you mean? I thought—'

Aden put a finger to his lips. When she was quiet he said evenly, 'Don't mistake easy-going for easy to manipulate, Evie. I'll kiss you when I'm ready.' He stood up and sat down heavily on the opposite seat.

Evie was silent but her expression was eloquent.

Aden sighed. Once more he got up and parked himself beside Evie. 'I'm ready,' he said, and took her chin in his hand. His lips pressed down on hers. No rockets went off and no celestial choir warbled. But she wanted him never to let go of her.

Eventually they pulled apart, but only a little. Eye to eye, nose to nose, they grinned manically. There were those sexy crinkles again.

When they handed the boat back to the attendant they owed him double the fee and Evie's cardi was buttoned up wrongly.

Despite the weight of the basket neither of them wanted to go home. The sun was sinking as they strolled hand in hand through the streets. The day was special and they were loath to let it go. Their embrace in the boat had transformed it, as if a black and white film had suddenly blazed into colour. Their date was now a glistening, delicate thing and they were afraid to break it.

'Fancy a pizza?' Aden nodded at the window of a Pizza Express they were snailing past.

'Mmm, yeah!' Evie realised she was ravenous.

'I always have a Four Seasons,' said Aden, as they sat at a minuscule marble table.

'And I always have an American Hot.' Evie smiled. This relationship was moving forward in leaps and bounds: only a few hours in and they knew each other's pizza of choice. Surely there could be no secrets between them now.

'So, you like the script?' asked Aden.

Damn. A secret already. Evie was obliged to perpetuate the pretence she'd started. 'Umm. Hmm.'

'You're perfect casting for Hepsibah. You'll steal the show.'

'Oh, shush,' said Evie awkwardly, praying he'd go on.

'Hepsibah was just a background character in the original draft. The shooting script is much better. She's really fleshed out and believable.'

'You saw the original draft?' Evie hadn't realised that Aden was *that* friendly with Hugh James.

'Yeah. We discussed it before. Blimey, Crump, don't you ever listen?'

The question was playful but if Evie had answered it honestly she would have said, 'Not if you're talking about work, no, not really.' It was more tactful just to advise him to tell her important things in triplicate.

'Fair enough. I'll do that from now on.' Aden squeezed her knee.

So, they were already planning how they'd do things 'from now on'. She laid a hand over Aden's on the marble as the waiter hove into view. She felt comfortable and ever so slightly floaty sitting beside him.

'I keep wanting to kiss you.' Aden looked grave.

'Is that wrong?'

'It is very not wrong.'

They kissed for so long that when they stopped the garlic bread had arrived and was sitting accusingly between them.

'I just can't wait to get to LA.' Aden tore off a lump of bread.

It had just begun to rain on Evie's parade. Rather hard. When, why and for how long was her new boyfriend (for that was surely what he was) going to L bloody A?

'I went once before,' Aden enlarged, oblivious to the thunder cloud hanging over his new girlfriend (for that was surely what she was). 'It was just a flying visit. This time I'll be able to have a good look round, really get a feel of the place. Eight weeks is practically living there!'

The pizzas arrived. As Aden thanked the waiter and endured the performance with the giant pepper mill, Evie's mind raced. Eight weeks! How could he be so jaunty at the prospect of not seeing her for eight weeks when they'd only just got together? She glared at him as he carefully cut his Four Seasons into quarters.

'Obviously,' he continued, waving a forkful of dough and anchovy, 'the best bit is that you'll be there.'

'I'll be there?' This made no sense. 'I'm just about to shoot a TV series. Or had you forgotten?' Evie said angrily.

Aden was staring at her as if she was mad. God knows, she was used to that but it was unwelcome from him.

'Yes,' he agreed, in a voice he had used only once before when trying to dissuade his doo-lally grandma from singing in John Lewis. 'You're shooting a TV series. In LA. With me.'

Evie frowned. 'You mean *The Setting of the Sun* is being shot in LA and you're working on it?'

Aden was doing his utmost not to laugh. 'You really do need it loud and in triplicate, don't you? Yes, darling, I'm second AD on the show and we're going off to La La Land for eight whole weeks together. Doesn't that agent of yours ever read the contract?'

With Aden's arms wrapped round her Evie felt the thunder cloud evaporate. She was off to one of the most glam places on earth, getting paid for it, with her lovely, sweet, kind, funny, fantastic kisser of a new boyfriend. And he had called her 'darling'.

You can't stroll indefinitely, even when you're in lurve. Midnight found Aden and Evie attempting to open the front door while kissing each other as if it was what they had been born to do.

As they stumbled in, Bing was lugging a ladder down to the basement. His hair, arms and legs were streaked with off-white. Miraculously his tiny pink hot pants were unscathed. 'How was the date?' he asked archly, when they were all assembled in the kitchen and the kettle was on.

'Oh, well. A date's a date.' Evie's expression didn't match her words.

'The pizza was all right,' offered Aden.

'The boat ride was OK.'

'The picnic was quite tasty, I suppose.' Aden smiled.

'How was the *snogging*?' bellowed Bing.

'It was like this.' Aden yanked Evie to him and kissed her hard. 'Well, you asked,' he said, and nipped off to the loo.

'I thought you said he was shy,' Bing whispered.

'He's *quiet*. And they're the ones you have to watch,' said Evie contentedly. She went into her room to ease off her shoes, followed by Bing, who was wearing a dazed look.

'This feels really weird,' he was saying. 'I mean, there's no problem is there? No deep, dark secret? I know it's early days yet but you look . . .' He studied her. 'You look happy, doll.'

'I think I am.' Evie prodded herself all over. 'I bloody am!'

'About time.' Bing bear-hugged her, almost cracking her spine. 'Don't screw it up.'

'Such touching faith in me.' Evie froze, sucking in a giant breath through her nose. 'Can you smell that? Belle's handbag! If this was a couple of days ago,' she giggled, 'I'd be claiming that Belle was signalling her approval of Aden from beyond the grave.' She slapped Bing's hot pants as she passed him on her way out. 'I know better now.'

Sitting very close, Evie and Aden ignored their tea and explored each other's bumpy bits instead.

The sitting-room door creaked open and Bing, freshly showered and with a tiny towel doing its best to cover his own bumpy bits, poked his head in and said, 'I know I'm not welcome but I just have to share something with you 'cos I'm so spooked. Evie, I threw Belle's handbag out yesterday. That's all. Good night.' Bing withdrew.

'What does he mean?' asked Aden.

Evie, who wasn't at all spooked, said, 'He means you've been approved by the top brass.'

Eleven

THERE WERE CERTAIN THINGS Bridgie was useful for, baby-sitting, advice on matters Catholic, narrow-minded abuse and suitcases among them. Evie had got to the age of twenty-seven without buying a proper suitcase. On the rare occasions that she left the country she always made a pilgrimage to Surbiton first to filch one from her mother's collection.

At Evie's side, supplying moral support and parent-pleasing manners, was Sacha. Bridgie approved of Sacha, who always wore good shoes and was posh. These particular assets guaranteed Bridgie's high opinion. In her universe, posh people were wise, brave, talented, witty and probably related to the Royal Family.

On this occasion the three women were seated round Bridgie's clinically sterile kitchen table.

'Where is it you're going again?' Bridgie's question carried a whiff of exasperation, as if it was somehow Evie's fault that she had been unable to retain this information, despite being told a dozen times.

'LA, Mum. It stands for Los Angeles. Hollywood.'

'Hollywood!' squawked Bridgie. 'You didn't let on it was Hollywood before, young lady.' She was puce, a colour that had never suited her.

'But Hollywood is in Los Angeles, I presumed you'd know that.' Evie was bemused by her mother's tone, both of voice and skin.

'How am I supposed to know where Hollywood is?' snapped Bridgie. A reasonable enough question from a woman who rarely ventured past Waitrose. 'Promise me, Evie, that you won't take your top off.'

'What are you on about, Mum? It's a British co-production of a quality TV series. It's not a porn film and they're not remotely interested in my chest. Besides, I'll have my boyfriend there to protect me.'

'Dan? I thought that was all over. Pressure of work, you told me,' said Bridgie, proving irritatingly that she did listen sometimes. Her colour was mellowing.

'I did tell you that, didn't I?' Evie was thinking on her feet. 'I was practising acting. If you believed me it would prove I was a good actress,' she finished lamely.

'Then you *are* a good actress. Too good. I was only saying to Daddy last night we'll be too infirm to attend your wedding at this rate, and all along you were still with that lovely Dan.'

'There's one other little thing,' said Evie brightly, hoping to play down the absurdity of what she was about to say. 'Dan's changing his name. From now on he wants us all to call him Aden.'

'Whatever for?' Bridgie was high-pitched and seriously puzzled now. 'Dan suits him. It was the name he was given by his parents.' Bridgie was impatient with her daughter's generation and their self-indulgent ways. 'You should stick with the names you're christened with. If we all picked names we thought *suited* us where would it end?' Bridgie stood up and began to clear the table. 'Get out from under my feet, girls. This kitchen has to be shipshape for three o'clock. I'm hosting this week's meeting of Surbiton Mothers Against Comedians Who Swear.' Bridgie ushered them out to the back garden with the promise of smoothies.

Prone on a lounger, Evie squinted up into the sun. 'Not as hot as it was,' she commented. 'The season's starting to turn. Can you feel it, Sash?'

'Yes. Everything's changing. For *you* anyway.'

'How do you mean?' Evie shielded her eyes with her arm and looked over at her friend, prostrate on the adjacent lounger.

'Oh, you know,' said Sacha reluctantly, as she lay with her eyes tight shut and the straps of her top rolled down. 'A new job. A new boyfriend. And here I am, going in and out of Calmer Karma every day, just like always.'

'I haven't had a worthwhile job or a worthwhile boyfriend for ages. Aren't you pleased for me?' Evie asked.

'Of course I am,' said Sacha passionately. 'You know I am. I just feel a bit . . . Oh, I don't know. Forget I spoke.'

'Do you want to come in for a bit?'

Sacha wrinkled her nose. 'Nah. I'd better get back to the shop.'

The two girls were at the corner of Kemp Street, a monolithic tweed-effect suitcase on wheels standing between them. 'OK. Why don't you come over later? Bring a video,' suggested Evie.

'Oh, right,' Sacha said, brightening up. 'I thought Aden would be around.'

'Well, he is. Or he might be,' faltered Evie. 'Does that matter?'

'No. No, no.' It obviously did. 'I'll see what I'm doing.'

This was difficult. Evie knew Sacha well enough to intuit that she was feeling marginalised, left behind. She wanted to shout, *You're my best friend, you wazzock. I'm never going to leave you behind, you're too important to me.* But instead she just nudged her and wheedled, 'Aw, c'mon. We can get a blanket out and sit under it if you like.'

'Won't Aden mind?'

'Why should he? He'll be getting two gorgeous gals instead of one.'

'OK. About eight.' Sacha started to walk away, then turned with a minxy look on her face. 'Perhaps I'll give Bernard a go, after all.'

Mercifully unaware of this development, Bernard was just leaving the house as Evie reached home. Gallant as ever, he took the suitcase from her and insisted on carrying it to her bedroom.

'How's the redecorating going?'

'It's all finished. Bing has been marvellous.'

'Can I see it?' Vaguely aware that the flat was, after all, her property, Evie was motivated more by idle curiosity than anything else. She wondered if Bernard had managed to tone down the imprint of his mother's presence. Mrs Briggs had smothered him with chintz, lace, ornaments, antimacassars and standard lamps.

Upstairs, Bernard threw open the door to flat C and said, 'Tadaah!'

'Bloody hell.' Evie stepped over the threshold, gawking unashamedly. 'It's beautiful!' Every wall was smooth and neutral and varnished boards ran the length of the flat. More importantly, every knick-knack had been eradicated. The large sitting room was bare, except for a long, cream sofa of modern design and a sheepskin rug. Bernard's books lined one wall. 'It's so clean and fresh and *trendy!*' Evie was envious. If the rest of the flat lived up to this room, she'd have to put his rent up.

'Wasn't this your mother's room?' asked Evie, as she stood in a bright Japanese-inspired one, straight from the pages of an interiors magazine.

Bernard nodded. 'I thought it was time I had a double bed.'

'Absolutely.' Evie smiled down at the futon covered with a crisp white cotton duvet. 'But where's all your mum's stuff?'

'It was time to move on.' This was a subject Bernard evidently found hard to discuss. 'I gave most of it to a charity shop.' He squared his shoulders and said, 'I'm a bachelor now. This is *my* home.'

'Hello, Meredith. May I take your . . .' Was it a wrap? A cape? A pashmina? Meredith was swathed in her customary expensive layers. 'Mmmwah.' She kissed the air eight inches from Evie's cheek. 'Put on a few pounds, have we, darling?' She was wearing every bangle she owned, clanging like a one-man band as she picked her way out to the garden on stilt heels.

'Quaint,' she decreed damningly, looking about her.

In Evie's opinion the garden looked delightful. The grass was mown. The ubiquitous fairy lights were scattered through the trees. A table draped in a floral cloth offered platters of mostly edible food. Chairs were placed in friendly groups.

'Let me get you a drink, Meredith. Gin, isn't it? What do you take with it?'

'More gin,' rasped Meredith.

Bing was barman. He had set up the bottles, glasses and ice bucket in the conservatory. 'I'm just trying to talk Bernard into a Sex on the Beach,' he said equably.

'It's a cocktail,' interjected Bernard nervously.

'Yes. That too.'

'Don't get him overheated,' ordered Evie. 'May I have one gin for my insane agent, please?'

All together, like a herd of cows, Beth, Bea, Caroline, Milly, Deirdre, Julius and Charles arrived. There was an outburst of introductions, hellos and you-look-lovelys as Bing speedily plonked a glass of something in everybody's hand.

A creaking voice, unmistakably Meredith's, was heard to comment misanthropically, 'Nobody said there'd be children here.'

'Is that a witch?' asked Julius innocently, peering out through a dusty window pane.

'Yes,' answered Bing simply, sending a shudder of excitement through the twins.

'Let's take Milly to see the witch!' Charles, who had fallen in love with the little girl at first sight, grasped her hand.

'Oooh, I'm not sure. Better ask Milly's mummy first.' Beth shot a questioning glance at Caroline.

'They can't come to any harm,' said the new, improved, not-quite-so-grumpy Caroline.

Bing said, 'Obviously you've never met Meredith before.'

As the newcomers drifted out into the pinkish twilight Bernard sidled over to Evie. 'I've got to go, I'm afraid.'

'No!' Evie's deep-seated fear of throwing crap parties surfaced violently. 'It's only just started! You can't go! *No!*'

'Have you ever considered a career as a diplomat?' enquired Bing, detaching Evie's fingernails from Bernard's shoulders. 'He'll be back.'

'Yes, I'll be back.' Bernard took a pace backwards, clearly rattled. 'Honestly. There's something I have to do.'

'Of course.'

The devoted but clumsy attentions of the twins were too much for Milly. She burst into tears and was scooped up by Bea. In those capacious arms she was soon giggling again. From the other side of a gnarled apple tree Caroline's mother approached Bea and pleaded, 'Could I have her? She needs her granny.'

Bea was ignorant of Deirdre's recent history but she was an expert reader of faces. 'She certainly does,' she said kindly, handing over the infant.

'Doggie!'

It was a new and sophisticated word for Milly. 'There are no doggies here, darling,' said Evie erroneously, for Henry had just emerged into the garden, attended by her parents.

'What are you doing here, Bea?' Bridgie was surprised but pleased to encounter her old friend. 'I'm sure I don't know what you see in the company of these young people.'

'Oh, some of them are old souls, Bridgie.' Bea's sly wink at Beth made her choke on her drink.

The whirlwind of bangles that was Meredith swept past, headed for the bar at optimum speed. Her glass was empty.

'Oh, Meredith,' Bridgie waved, 'how are you? We're Evie's parents—do you remember us?'

'Of course. Howdyoudo. You must be very proud, et cetera, et cetera.' Meredith didn't break step. She slammed her glass on the bar. 'Fill that up with the same rot I had before,' she ordered, and added, 'Please,' as Bing was handsome.

'Shame for me,' requested Sacha, who had been caught up in Meredith's tailwind and was now draped over the bar, swaying slightly.

'My pleasure, ladies.' Bing eyed Sacha and then poured her a lemonade with a teardrop of vodka in it. 'Get that down you.'

Out of the conservatory, glass with cocktail umbrella in hand, stepped Aden. He looked all clean and new. But, as Evie noted approvingly, sexy, gorgeous and eminently fanciable too.

'Now you can stop watching the door,' Beth whispered in her ear.

'I wasn't!' Evie defended herself.

Beth rolled her eyes. 'Just go and get him.'

Was I watching the door? Evie wondered, as she sidestepped Deirdre, who was jiggling Milly at a dangerous level for a child full of chicken nuggets.

'Hello.'

'Hello, yourself.'

Aden kissed her and his mouth was like a warm feather bed on a frosty morning: she never wanted to leave it.

Bernard was back. Evie noticed him out of the corner of her eye while Aden still had her close. She turned, incredulous. 'Bernard? Your hair!'

'Is it OK?' Bernard grimaced.

'OK? It's amazing. You look completely different.' And completely handsome. The alarming layers and sticky-out bits had all disappeared. A simple short cut with a few spikes on top brought out the lean angles of Bernard's pale face.

'Bing gave me strict instructions for the barber. I hope I got it right.'

'You did. The ladies are going to be flying at you from all directions.' Bernard had such blue eyes, she noticed for the first time. And such a well-defined torso. 'Have you been working out?' she asked.

'I'm afraid so.' Bernard chewed his lip.

'That's wonderful!' Evie laughed and slapped her newly attractive tenant on the back.

The haircut was the talk of the party. A tidal wave of compliments washed over the cringing Bernard, and the change in Bernard's appearance even pierced Sacha's squiffiness. 'He'sh good enough for me now!' she informed Bing.

Bing remained Sphinx-like, saying nothing as he watched Sacha trot unsteadily Bernardwards, then fall into a bush. Bernard manhandled her to nearby deck chair and folded her into it.

'Oh Bernard,' she sighed. 'Don't leave me!' she pleaded, dramatically.

Aden and Henry were looking for Evie and discovered her in the kitchen. 'This old fella needs a drink,' Aden pointed at Henry, 'and this one needs a kiss.' He didn't have time to point at himself before he was engulfed by his lady love.

'Let's send everyone home,' Evie suggested, close to his ear, 'and snog recklessly until the sun comes up.'

They kissed again, bodies entwined like ivy on a column. A loud whine from the kitchen floor reminded them that they were not alone.

'Henreeeee!' Evie smothered his grizzled old snout with kisses then gave him a bowl of water.

'Hey.' Aden pulled her to her feet. He looked serious, holding her by the shoulders at arm's length. 'Just so you know, I'm not like Henry.'

'Of course you're not. Your ears aren't floppy.' Evie tried to put her arms round him again, but Aden held her away.

'What I mean is, you're not going to get away with treating me like Henry. You're not going to get away with your usual tricks, the games, the scheming. This is what intimacy is—two people just being together, being honest, being a partnership.' Aden shook her slightly to stop her squirming. 'Got that? No agony-aunt theorising. Just you and me. Neither of us is the boss. OK?'

'OK.'

'Oh, and another thing,' Aden said gravely, 'it'll be fun.' He surrounded her with his arms and squeezed her with life-threatening intensity.

John Crump was at the kitchen door. 'Come on, you lovebirds. Young Bing's rounding everyone up for a speech.' The woody aroma of his pipe chased away the delicate floral notes.

Out in the garden the slightest of breezes tickled bare shoulders. Summer was saying goodbye.

Evie unfurled herself from Aden to look up at the back of number 18. She'd overseen a lot of alterations to the distinguished but elderly building since Belle had passed it on to her. A lot of paint, paper and elbow grease had been applied. And not only the fabric of the house had changed: Evie looked at Bernard with his new haircut and confidence, she watched Caroline tut at the way her mother had combed Milly's hair. She reached out and took Aden's hand. So much had changed, so much had stayed the same. 'Belle approves of what I've done,' she whispered to herself. '*I know it.*'

Bing tapped his glass for hush, and stepped up onto a crate. 'We're here today to say au revoir, not goodbye, to someone who is very special to all of us. We'll miss her. Well, *I* won't but some of you might.' Bing glanced over at his victim, who stuck her tongue out at him. 'Well, all right, I admit it. She's like the sister I never had.'

'You've got four,' Evie corrected him.

'Who's making this speech?' Bing hissed at her, before resuming. 'This is a big step for Evie's career. She's going to be brilliant in *The Setting of the Sun* and I have a hunch she's going to be a famous actress one day soon. We'd better make the most of her 'cos she certainly won't call us when she's made it.'

The partygoers laughed, confident this wasn't true.

'She's been a good friend to me,' Bing said, with feeling, 'so it's wonderful to know that not only is her career looking up but she's found herself a decent bloke.' He gestured at Aden. 'It's a tough job, mate, but somebody's got to do it.' While the guests giggled and Aden circled Evie's waist with one arm, Bing raised his glass. 'To Evie,' he said. 'Have a fantastic eight weeks away but don't forget to come back.'

'To Evie!'

Hearing her name on the lips of the mismatched crowd was unexpectedly moving. Evie found she had little voice to squeak, 'To you!' in reply. Embarrassed, she wiped her eyes as Aden cuddled her.

Still up on his crate Bing appeared unwilling to step down. After everyone had raised their glasses and sipped, he carried on. His voice was so unusually charged with emotion that Evie found herself staring hard at her flatmate. 'Every so often, folks, Evie says something memorable to me and I can't take the mickey out of her. She was the one who told me that love is where it falls. I think we all know that's true. *To love!*' he shouted.

Evie didn't echo, 'To love!' and raise her glass with the others. She watched Bing's line of sight. She followed it to Bernard.

Who winked at him.

Evie stood with her mouth open as Bing stepped down and made his way towards Bernard. Hand in hand they pushed through the throng to stand in front of her.

'Why didn't you tell me?'

'Some things you can't share. Not until the time is right.' Bing put his head on one side. 'Maybe you can understand that these days, doll.'

'Well, of course I can, you idiot.' Evie stood on tiptoe to throw her arms round Bing's neck. 'Of course I can.' She pulled away. 'Bernard, you sly old dog.'

'Oh, gosh, hardly,' Bernard stammered.

'When did all this start? Hang on, I know.' Evie narrowed her eyes, sleuth-style. 'It was the night of the Manhattan Dreams fiasco, wasn't it?'

Bernard and Bing nodded manically. Bing said, 'Poor B was in a bad way. I sat with him until he calmed down. I was on the lookout for fun, but then we talked. Hours went by in a flash and I discovered that he was fascinating and deep and caring and . . .'

'Do shush.' Bernard was writhing.

Evie was marvelling that Bing was describing a man without reference to his arse.

'And he has a *fantastic* arse.'

Reassured, Evie said, 'So that's why you've been coming straight home from the show. I thought you were ill when you were just faithful.'

'Yup. That's a new one for me and I like it. Every time you closed your bedroom door I was off up the stairs like a guided missile.'

'I still can't get my head round this.' Evie stared at the pair, hip to hip and shoulder to shoulder. 'I mean, Bernard, if you knew you were gay why did you let us drag you into that terrible nightclub?'

'I didn't know what I was.' Bernard struggled to express himself. 'I was just . . . me until Bing came along. When we sat and talked I thought, Ah, here you are at last. I can't describe it any better than that.'

'You don't have to.' Evie pulled Aden to her. There *he* was at last.

'There's one more thing and you're not to shout,' Bing said. 'I'm moving in upstairs with Bernard.'

'Oh.' Evie felt as if the ground was shifting beneath her flip-flops. 'But you'll still come down for *The Antiques Roadshow*?'

'Yes.'

'And you'll still laugh in my face and make sarcastic remarks?'

'Trust me, that will never change.'

'Then you can go.'

'Thanks, ma'am.'

Aden pointed out that if Bing was leaving, the flat would be empty for eight weeks.

'And?' asked Evie stupidly.

'Maybe Beth could use it.'

'Beth! Beth!' Evie waved her sister over. 'Have you found somewhere to live yet?'

Beth hadn't and was thrilled with the offer of the basement for eight weeks. 'It'll get me away from Henley and give me some breathing space,' she said excitedly. 'Thank you, sis.'

'Shucks. It's nothing. Hey,' said Evie, 'now that Bernard's turned this into a coming-out party maybe you and Bea should follow his lead?'

They both turned to seek their mother's face. She was lecturing Deirdre on the peril posed to modern society by allowing *Blue Peter* presenters to drink alcohol.

'Perhaps not,' they concluded in unison.

Then Aden pulled Evie back into their own private bubble. 'All change for Evie, eh? You OK?'

Evie assured him that she was. *And I am*, she told herself firmly, unwilling to accept that she was slightly overcome. She felt a sharp pang of empathy for what Sacha had been experiencing. 'Where's Sacha?'

The deck chair was empty. The shrub had proved irresistible. Sacha was once more in its leafy embrace, only her feet visible to the observer. Aden and Bing hauled her back to her deck chair. As Evie tucked a blanket round the snoring figure, she experienced a rush of tenderness.

'She'll be fine,' said Bing airily. 'Tough as old boots.'

'She won't be pleased when she wakes up and hears about you and Bernard.' Evie stroked a tendril of hair back from Sacha's forehead. 'Can't you leave any men for us heterosexual women? All around me people are turning out to be gay.' Evie frowned.

'Or maybe everybody in the world is gay except you,' suggested Bing.

'I'm not.' Aden was at the conservatory door.

'That sounds like a challenge.' Bing loved a dare.

'Oi! You're monogamous now. And, besides, he's mine,' warned Evie.

'Oh, yeah.' Bing sighed. 'I forgot.'

'There's something else we forgot.' Evie scrambled over to the crate and clambered up on to it. 'Ladies and gentlemen. And Bing,' she said loudly. Expectant faces turned towards her in the purplish night. 'There's one more toast. To Belle!'

'To Belle.' They all drank to the absent old lady while the trees whispered to one another above their heads. And then the giggling began, ripening into hearty laughter. Somewhere in the mix, along with Bing's guffaw, Meredith's phlegmy cackle and Evie's freeform yelping, was the wry, delicate, knowing laugh of Belle O'Brien.

BERNADETTE STRACHAN

As I jumped on a train to Piccadilly, where I had arranged to meet Bernadette Strachan for lunch, there was one question uppermost in my mind: would I discover that she had once been an actress? Anyone who could so vividly portray the highs and lows of Evie Crump, the struggling young actress in *The Reluctant Landlady*, must have first-hand knowledge of the profession. 'No, I wasn't an actress,' Bernadette told me, 'but I did work in a theatrical agency and then ran my own voiceover agency, where I employed lots of actors and actresses. I got to know a number of them really well—it was like being a nanny to them, looking after them, keeping them happy. That side of me is definitely part of Evie Crump—I like trying to help people sort their lives out. Actors can drive you mad, but I really admire them. Their lives can be so hard, and sometimes the smallest thing can make them lose their confidence.'

Bernadette hasn't always had things easy herself. She decided to make a career in radio and worked her way to programme producer, before starting to write short stories in her spare time. When various women's magazines began to snap up her stories, she decided to give up her job to write—only to find that she was soon struggling to survive. She took a variety of part-time work to keep herself afloat, and then a good friend, who was working for a theatrical agency, came to her rescue by asking her to step in for her while she took a two-week holiday. 'I don't think she wanted me to do the job very well, though,' Bernadette says ruefully, 'because she showed me where the kettle was and that was it! But I had the most amazing two weeks and decided that

I'd give anything to have a job like that. As you can imagine, I could hardly believe it when my friend came back and said that she had found God and was going to develop her life through the church! So the job became mine!' Eventually, Bernadette left to set up her own agency, but was then beset by business problems and finally decided that she'd had enough.

At this point, her husband, Matthew, swept her off to what he described as 'an idyllic cottage in Provence'. But it was far from idyllic. 'There was just one bar nearby, full of toothless old men, and nothing much to do! So Matthew said, "Well, you're always saying you're going to write a book. Why don't you do it now?" And so I sat down to write and the words just poured out of me.'

The Reluctant Landlady was the successful outcome, and Bernadette has just completed her second novel, undeterred by the distracting arrival of her baby daughter, Niamh. 'I'm working on the third book now but it's not so easy when I just can't stop looking at Niamh,' she says. 'And Matthew's just as besotted with her as I am and wants to be equally involved with her as she grows up,' she adds happily. The family live in Twickenham, where Matthew, a composer, works from home in an attic studio. His burgeoning song-writing career has also led the couple to spend time in Nashville, Tennessee, where they now have a flat.

As we part company, Bernadette is off to have a look round the shops, before meeting up with Matthew for a special evening out. 'It's all thanks to my wonderful mother-in-law, who's looking after Niamh,' she tells me excitedly. 'It's such a treat. We don't often get the chance just to be together.'

Anne Jenkins

Printed and bound by Maury Imprimeur SA, Malesherbes, France

601-030-1